Set Me Free

Set Me Free

a novel by
Estie Florans

FELDHEIM PUBLISHERS
JERUSALEM · NEW YORK

Copyright © 2008 by Esther Florans

ISBN 978-1-59826-269-8

All rights reserved.

No part of this publication may be translated, reproduced, stored in a retrieval system or transmitted, in any form or by any means, electronic or otherwise, even for personal use, without written permission from the publisher.

FELDHEIM PUBLISHERS
POB 43163 / Jerusalem, Israel

208 Airport Executive Park
Nanuet, NY 10954

www.feldheim.com

10 9 8 7 6 5 4 3 2 1

Printed in Israel

This book is dedicated
le'zecher nishmas our dear uncle,

Harav Shimon Dovid Eider zt"l
Shimon Dovid ben Yaakov Yosef

His drive to carry out the Will of Hashem,

His energy in getting the "job" done,

His many accomplishments throughout his life,

Was only a prologue to his last six years;

When he was driven to carry out Hashem's will despite his illness,

When even in his weakened state he used every ounce of energy in his avodah,

Where his many accomplishments were just "stepping stones" to reach higher,

Because instead of allowing his disease to shackle him,

He steadfastly focused on the Divine Author,

*Setting an example for the rest of **us**,*

Of how to
    *Remain forever **free**…*

Acknowledgments

WHEN ONE EMBARKS on the journey of writing a book, there's the author, the computer's blank screen, and *Hashem*. It was clear to me from page one and on—who the real Author is. I thank *Hashem* for giving me the ability and opportunity to write this book and for those He sent along the way to help me...

My family: my parents, Reb Moshe Mordechai *ben* Chaim Tzvi Stavsky *z"l, ule'hibadel l'chaim* Mrs. Chana Stavsky; my parents-in-law, Rabbi and Mrs. Aaron and Freida Florans, and all my siblings and siblings-in-law. You are *all* great role models and excellent sources of support, and I am very grateful that I have all of you!

Each one of my wonderful children whose encouragement, computer expertise, halachic information, patience, input, ideas, piano background, iced coffee, and everything else that you all did, contributed, and put up with while the book was being written...Thanks! You know I couldn't have done it without you! An additional special thanks to my oldest daughter, Chavie (Weinberg), who read, reread, and kept rereading the manuscript. Who edited it, reedited it, and kept reediting it, and who didn't stop encouraging, advising, and listening. Thanks, thanks, and thanks! It would've been quite lonely if I hadn't had you along.

Infinite gratitude goes to Rebbetzin Feigy Schorr for sharing this journey with me. Thank you for your time that you gave so generously, constant encouragement, invaluable advice, skilled editing, unlimited gracious help, and of course, for the clarity I always get after speaking with you. And thank you for introducing me to Mrs. Pearl Altschuler and Mrs. Leah Lederman, whose wise counsel was most helpful.

Faigy Borchardt, what can I say? Despite your incredibly demanding schedule, you still managed to review the manuscript from cover to cover, you reviewed the script, and you reviewed anything else I asked you to review, as always – in your magnificently "lagniappe" style, with a warm smile and giving spirit. Not only are you a professional writer, but you're also a professional at being a great friend. Thanks, Faigy!

To my dear friend, Elky Gruman, thank you for all your encouragement, listening ear, and for always being there for me. Rochel Diskind, I am extremely grateful for your useful input, and Esther Raizy Horowitz, you've been a terrifically helpful and empathetic sounding board (and everything else in between!) A big thank-you to my sister, Penina Feigenbaum, for the Israel information and to Leahla (Mittelman) Green for sharing your computer expertise (and office) with me. Another huge thanks to my good friend, Miriam Travitsky for the terrific information you supplied me with. Thanks to my niece, Naomi Stavsky for your input and to T.S. for sharing your Aliyah experience with me. Of course, thank you to my friend, Janet Klein, and my sister-in-law and friend, Chana Perel Florans, for those vigorous morning walks, energizing me to sit down and write! Thank you, Esther Heller of *Soferet*, for your editing expertise and thank you, Rabbi Dovid Schulman, manager of Eichler's, for being so generous with your time and advice.

I would like to express my admiration and appreciation to all of you at Feldheim Publishers and especially to Rabbi David Kahn, general editor, for believing in this book and its important message, and for all you did to pave the way. The Editorial Department worked hard on my book, which I certainly appreciate. Finally, thank you, Rabbi Yitzchak Feldheim for your confidence in *Set Me Free*, your useful advice, and for doing whatever you could to make this "voyage" as smooth as possible.

And last but not least. I never would've attempted to begin this journey if not for my husband, Shmuel Dovid, and I definitely wouldn't have continued if he hadn't encouraged me till the very end. "Thank you" is just not enough. May the *Kiddush Hashem* and *chizuk* that I hope will be conveyed through this book's message, be a *zechus* for us, our family, and all those involved in bringing this work to fruition.

Estie Florans
Sivan 5468

Set Me Free

הוֹצִיאָה מִמַּסְגֵּר נַפְשִׁי לְהוֹדוֹת אֶת שְׁמֶךָ...

"Release my soul from its prison to acknowledge Your Name..."

(TEHILLIM 142:8)

Prologue

A DOOR.

Of course, I knew that it was just an ordinary door, *that is*, my brain knew…yet, my heart felt something else.

A door?

Sure, I have gone in and out of doors every day of my life and it never had an effect on me. But, this time was different. This was *her* door, and when I saw it, the old, familiar feelings began to creep up on me.

Standing partially opened at that time—as it should be, allowing entry to all those wishing to proceed—I stood there, staring at the door, immobile, afraid to cross its threshold.

I could turn around…

I stole a sidelong glance at my friend. She gazed ahead steadily, a look of steely determination in her eyes.

We went forward.

Entering through a narrow hallway, we emerged into the main room of the apartment. And then I felt it.

Like a strong gust of wind on a stormy winter night unexpectedly striking the innocent person leaving the warm shelter of his home, the overpowering sadness engulfed me, reminding me that it was true, it was real, and that it had actually happened.

I shivered. *Why am I leaving the comfort of the present to face the storms of the past?*

The room was thick with grief.

Some people were crying overtly and unashamedly, others expressed themselves in a more subdued manner. Their sorrow too was evident.

Yes…it felt almost tangible, this mourning. I could almost touch it.

But, do I want to?

I knew I should, and yet I also knew how much easier it would be to pretend this had not happened.

Slowly, we edged our way through the crowded living room. There were no available seats. Feeling awkward, we mumbled, "excuse me" and "slichah" numerous times until we finally managed to squeeze ourselves into an unoccupied spot in the rear. I sighed with relief. Gratefully leaning my tired back against the wall, I found myself focusing toward the front of the room, my eyes searching out the purpose of my visit.

I could see two young children, a boy and a girl, about eight and six years old. They were showing a sort of candy someone must have given them—I guess to somehow try to cheer them up—to an elderly woman sitting on a low cushioned chair. *She must be the grandmother*, I thought. She was nodding with a halfhearted smile to the two children, while clasping the hand of the teenage girl sitting beside her.

Oh my goodness, I gasped as I gazed at the girl who sat there unaware of the jolt that just went through me, *it's her! It's really her!* And then reality struck. Cold fingers grabbed my heart. *Of course it's not her. It can't be. But, the resemblance is so strong!*

I knew that unusual hair color. Although tied back in a neat ponytail, I could tell it was wavy and bouncy—just as I remembered. I knew her pointy chin and the way it would become more pronounced when she spoke. And I knew the color of her eyes even from where I stood.

Had she not been sitting on that low stool, clothed in a dark brown sweater opened to reveal a white blouse ripped with the "mourner's tear," the object of so much compassion undoubtedly, I still would have known her.

Oh the pain…that strangling sensation. It was growing stronger with each passing second.

I tried pushing it away. *I must push it away.*

Okay, you're here now, I told myself. *You'll stay a short while, do your duty and then be on your way. Don't think. Don't remember…*

But, memories are not like that.

Sometimes, the harder you try to suppress them, the more stubborn they are and the more fervently they fight to rise to the surface. At least, that is the way it has always been with me.

Memories…emotions. But, I'm so much older now than I was then. I let out a deep sigh. *Will I ever be able to dismiss them at will?*

Believe me…I wanted to. I tried.

You see, although I was a mature adult and no longer the eighteen-year-old that I once was, certain things cannot so easily change with the passage of time.

And so, as I stood there, willing it *not* to happen…it did.

Yes…the wind's forcefulness had swung the door open and its powerful strength did not allow it to close. I had no choice. It swept me along, drawing me away from the comfort of the present, compelling me to face the storms of the past.

And as I felt myself drifting toward the recollections of what once was, I remember thinking…nothing, no nothing, would ever be the same.

Part One

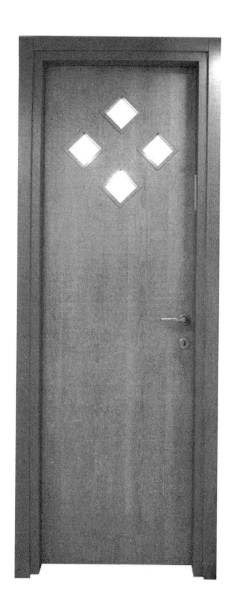

1

THERE I WAS in the middle. Again.

I would have preferred the privacy of a window seat or the comfort of one near the aisle, but, of course, the middle seat had been assigned to me.

Seated to my right was a woman, who appeared to be in her early thirties and was trying rather unsuccessfully to calm the crying baby in her lap. The aisle seat on my left was vacant, and occupying the two rows in front of me were some of the other girls in my group.

One of them, a short-haired, round-faced, amicable girl turned around, and leaning over the back of her seat introduced herself as Chani Frankel from Montiferry.

"And what's your name?" she asked breezily. "Where are you from?"

"Sara," I answered shyly, "Sara Hirsch. I'm from Rolland Heights."

"Oh, so you must be Shuli Hirsch's sister." Her smile widened. "That's terrific! My sister, Blimi, and your sister were together last year at M.B.L.L. You've probably met."

Blimi? Blimi Frankel. The name did sound familiar. She had called Shuli a few times during the summer. Vaguely, I remembered a couple of weeks after her return from Israel, a group of Shuli's friends dropped by the house to pick her up for a weekend in the mountains at Camp Brachah. I thought I remembered Blimi. On the short side and fairly plump, with the same rosy cheeks as her sister, she seemed friendly. Then again, Shuli always had new as well as all her old friends coming and going in and out of our house all the time.

"Yes, I think I know who she is," I said in a polite voice.

"They were *great* friends," she informed me cheerfully with a friendly wink. Is she hinting that the two of us will turn out to be great friends too?

I could not think of anything to say, and not wanting to appear unsociable, I pretended to be busy looking for something in my pocketbook, all the while telling myself that she probably expects me to be just like Shuli.

"Who are you talking to, Chan?"

I looked up. The girl sitting next to Chani had twisted around to face me too. She was a very pretty girl with long chestnut hair pulled back softly with a black headband and an elastic tie.

"Oh, Rochel Leah, this is Sara Hirsch," Chani introduced us. "She's from Rolland Heights. Her sister and Blimi were together last year. And Sara, this is Rochel Leah Wolf from Miami Beach."

"Nice to meet you," I heard my voice emerging stiff and stilted, although I willed it to come out warm and friendly.

Rochel Leah's hazel eyes met mine. "Is this your first time in Eretz Yisrael?"

"Yes."

"Oh, not mine," she waved one hand nonchalantly in the air and grasped the cushioned headrest with the other. "I've been there twice before. The first time, the Pesach of my brother's bar mitzvah and two summers ago I attended Machane Bnot Yaakov in Ashdod. How about you," she questioned, "which camp do you go to?"

"I-I don't go to camp."

Her eyebrows shot up, "Really? Never?"

I shook my head.

"I can't imagine not going to camp. So-o-o, what *do* you do summers?"

"Um, I uh, I go to a day camp—by us, in Rolland Heights. I'm a counselor," I offered.

"Oh…how exciting," she said dryly. "No wonder you don't look familiar. From all my years in camp, I feel as if I know the world! You know, one camp visits the next one, mutual friends, etc. etc. etc…"

She turned to Chani and said something—I do not remember what—and Chani laughed. Then they turned to me, remembering my presence.

There was an awkward silence.

"Do you know each other from before?" I asked, not knowing what else to say.

"Oh, we've been together in camp for years," Rochel Leah said, throwing a conspiratorial sidelong glance in Chani's direction.

"And I can't seem to get rid of her," Chani added affectionately while Rochel Leah laughed, I thought, a bit too loudly.

"So-o-o...did you come here with anybody?" Rochel Leah asked me. "I mean, do you know anyone going to M.B.L.L.?"

"Uh...I...not really, I mean, no," I bit my lower lip while slowly shaking my head. "A good friend of mine was supposed to come, but then at the last minute had to back out." *Why am I sounding so apologetic?*

"Oh well," Rochel Leah's pretty eyes flew over me indifferently.

"I guess you'll just have to make new friends," Chani said with an affable smile. "Blimi says that she and Shuli became great pals practically as soon as they met in the airport."

"I-I'm sure, if everyone's as friendly as you two—"

"Well, there'll be plenty of girls here," Rochel Leah said rather tersely.

Feeling envious and left out listening to their easy banter, I sat silently as the two of them continued talking. They were still hanging over the back of their seats and chatting amiably while facing me. Chani tried to include me in their conversation and I wished—oh how I wished—I could respond in a breezy, friendly manner, but all I could do was answer her questions with dull mechanical responses.

"Probably those empty seats are for the girls from New York." Chani pointed over my shoulder.

I turned around. Although most of the seats across the aisle were rapidly filling up, the few rows directly behind us were still unoccupied.

"I hope they're not going to be a bunch of cliquey New Yorkers."

"C'mon, Rochel Leah."

"Well, Chani, if they're all coming together—"

"But, Rochel Leah, New York's a big place. They don't all necessarily come from the same school and they don't all necessarily know each other either."

"Well, at least I have you, Chani," she swung her chestnut ponytail over her shoulder, and then, thumbing in the direction of the girl sitting near the window on the other side of Chani, added, "and of course, Zehava."

"And," Chani smiled at me cordially, "Shuli Hirsch."

I stiffened.

"I mean *Sara* Hirsch," she quickly corrected herself. "Sorry."

I felt myself blushing and did not know how to respond. And so, I said nothing. Of course. And, of course by then Rochel Leah must have been unequivocally convinced that I was a total bore with no potential for a blossoming friendship.

She turned to Zehava, who had just finished settling herself and was removing her yearbook from her carry-on bag. "I can't believe they didn't send you your yearbook till yesterday, Zehava, and that I didn't get a chance to see it yet. You know how busy I was—running around shopping and everything. I'm just dying to see what you Woodlakers can do!"

"Well, you've been buying out everything in every store in Woodlake since you came back from camp, Rochel Leah," Zehava laughed. "Even if my yearbook would've been in the house the whole week, you never would've had a chance to look at it."

Giggling, they leaned their heads together over Chani's seat and, less than a minute later, with a quick apology, Chani joined the other two.

I swallowed hard, attempting to make the lump in my throat disappear. I was not supposed to be on this plane...alone. Chavie should have been with me.

So, what in the world am I doing here?

Feeling that familiar stinging in my eyes, I blinked a few times, not wanting to succumb to tears.

I tried to distract myself by studying my surroundings. The last few passengers were taking their seats. There were still a number of vacant ones available besides those behind me, and once again I eyed the one on my left, hoping it would remain empty for the duration of the trip. I would move over and give my seat to the woman next to me for her crying baby, and then, perhaps, he would feel more comfortable and would quiet down.

I let out a deep sigh. *If only Chavie were here this would be so much fun. We could be looking at this as some sort of adventure...*

But she was not. And for the hundredth time since entering this airplane I fantasized about exiting before take off and running into the loving arms of my wonderful family.

My wonderful family.

I unzipped the outer pocket of my carry-on bag and slowly reached for the picture enclosed in a shiny brass frame. Taken this past July on a family vacation in Toronto, my parents, siblings, and I posed on the steps of the Ontario Science Center. Lovingly, I studied each of the smiling faces.

Moshe, almost a year past his bar mitzvah, his impish grin spread across his face, had forgotten to wipe the chocolate off his chin. There was more evidence of the chocolate bar he had just swallowed on his camp T-shirt, and as he leaned on our oldest brother, Yisrael,—you could tell that Sruly, as we call him, was trying to prevent any of the chocolate from reaching him. Already quite tall, he stood next to my father, who in his white shirt and dark beard looked very distinguished amid the colorful garb of the passersby. My mother, almost a head shorter than my father, looked small and delicate next to him. I felt a deep longing as I gazed at her radiant face with its warm smile. Her arm encircled Yocheved, better known as Chevy, who seemed older than Moshe, her twin. Chevy, with her easy-going manner, smiled happily at the camera, her dark, wavy hair forming a halo around her face.

I stood between her and our older sister, Shulamis. Compared to Shuli, who I thought was the prettiest girl around and whose effervescent personality charmed all who knew her, I felt plain and boring. Boring, medium-length brown hair, plain round brown eyes on a simple oval face. I was not short and cute like Chevy, and neither was I tall and graceful as was Shuli. Sure enough, there I was in the middle, looking inconspicuous and oh...so ordinary!

How I wished I could be cheery and bubbly like Shuli! When she was leaving for M.B.L.L. the previous year, she was so full of excitement—so exuberant.

And me? I was trying plenty hard to subdue the butterflies dancing nonstop in the pit of my stomach—exuberance was the last thing anyone could expect from me. To me each new step always felt like it was a major challenge. For Shuli, on the other hand, everything just seemed to flow. She was so much stronger than I could ever hope to be!

Just last night, even before my friend, Chava Esther Hershkowitz, came over to tell me her startling news, I was already a bundle of nerves.

Wrapped in my mother's white terry robe—mine was already packed—I had just shut the top flap of my vinyl suitcase and was holding it down for Shuli to zip, when she enthusiastically declared that I was going to have the most amazingly, fantabulous time imaginable, and fervently wished she could return to M.B.L.L. for a second year.

I told her to be my guest and go instead of me.

She and Chevy exchanged benignly exasperated looks.

"Come on, Sara, cheer up!" Shuli began struggling with the zipper, "You'll see, M.B.L.L. is the greatest!"

Chevy took a seat on top of my suitcase to keep the vinyl flap from bulging, so we could finally fasten the buckles. "It might be the greatest," she folded her arms across her chest, her dark eyes twinkled playfully, "but this packing business sure is tough stuff."

"Thanks, Chev, for all your hard work." I applied more pressure to the bulkier corner of the suitcase so Shuli could finish closing the zipper, "But don't worry, we'll help you too, when you go to Sem!"

"I'm not so sure about that, Sara," Chevy stood up, frowning. "By the time I go, you'll be a bunch of old married ladies and I'll have to do all the packing by myself."

Shuli chuckled as she buckled the last strap. "Come on, Chev, you know we'll never abandon you."

"But look, Sara's abandoning me now," she turned to me, her two hands clasped theatrically over her heart.

"Stop being so dramatic, Chevy. You're making Sara even more nervous than she already—"

"I'm not nervous!"

Chapter 1

"I'm the one who's nervous. Shuli, first you left me for a whole year and now Sara and Chavie are leaving," Chevy turned to my friend Chavie, who had just entered my room.

My stomach did a somersault. *What in the world was she doing here now?*

A sudden eruption of noisy giggles from the row of seats in front of me disrupted my thoughts. I could see them still huddled together over the pages of Zehava's yearbook, their bursts of sporadic laughter jabbing into my heart, keenly reminding me of my loneliness.

Gently, I slid the picture back into my carry-on bag.

That's all right…let them laugh now, I tried telling myself as I stood up and shoved the bag into the overhead compartment. *In June, when I'll be called up to the stage as the winner of the Goldstone Award, they'll be able to tell everyone about sitting next to me on the airplane on the way to Sem. They'll say, "Sara Hirsch? We were great friends with her right from the start."*

Oh…me and my dreams!

I am not sure if it was because of that place in the middle I had been born into—sandwiched in between Shuli and Chevy—or if it was due to my feelings of just being a "prop," a person who sits along the sidelines—a necessary part of the stage, but not especially important. Or maybe it had to do with my overactive imagination that stemmed from my analytical nature and my being a voracious reader. I read adventure novels—you know, the ones where the poor little victim turns into the heroine and lives happily ever after. I also devoured pages and pages of biographies, my heart lifting in awe as I perused the histories of those who had valiantly risked their lives to save others or who had died *al Kiddush Hashem* with the words of *Shema Yisrael* on their lips. Probably due to a combination of all of this, deep within me there was a longing to be something special, to do something great and make my mark in the world.

I did not want to be plain, average, ordinary Sara Hirsch for the rest of my life…and I knew…I just knew M.B.L.L. with the Goldstone Award was my answer. *Yes,* I thought dreamily, *the Goldstone Award. It'll be that stepping-stone, my giant leap into world re—*

The loud shrieks of the baby next to me jolted me out of my reverie and for the first time I noticed his mother's discomfiture. She was trying unsuccessfully to calm him down. He must have sensed her tension, which was exacerbated by the disapproving looks the other passengers directed her way.

I saw her reach for a bottle jutting from a large, corduroy diaper bag. She was a petite woman with black frizzy hair framing a dark, small face. I watched as she wrestled with the cap that had apparently been screwed on very tightly, while rocking her baby at the same time.

"Can I help you?" I offered.

She turned to me, a confused expression on her face. "I do not speak good English," she said with a heavy Israeli accent, while trying to shift the baby to a more comfortable position.

"Can - I - help - you - with - your - baby?" I pronounced my words slowly and deliberately while simultaneously reaching for the child. Although I was right next to her, I had to speak loudly to be heard over the baby's cries. "Maybe I can hold him while you prepare the bottle," I motioned toward her bag. And then, just to make sure she understood, I added, "*Ha-tinok? At rotzah letet li es—*I mean—*et ha-tinok?*"

Her expression softened as comprehension dawned. She smiled gratefully, displaying a set of perfect white teeth. Apologizing profusely, she handed me the screaming baby, "I hope it not bother. Many, many thanks to you."

I held the baby and began to rock him gently back and forth. His shrieks barely subsided until his mother put the bottle to his lips. Then, all at once, his cries abated. He sucked vigorously and contentedly, completely oblivious to the bedlam he had caused.

With this quiet respite, we were able to talk. Despite her heavy accent and her claims to the contrary, she did know English quite well. And, although my grammar was not one hundred percent flawless, I spoke Hebrew pretty fluently.

Surprisingly, we spoke with ease. Her name was Gila, and as we conversed, my usual shyness dissipated. I guess when faced with someone even shyer and more vulnerable than myself, I tended to unbend and become more relaxed and natural.

I told her that I would be attending a teachers' seminary and I found out that she had been married for a few years. She was a nurse in a clinic in Be'er Sheva, where she lived. It was not terribly far from where our seminary was situated.

She had traveled with a group of other nurses to America for a three-month course at the world-renowned Rolland Heights University's Teaching Hospital. The group she had been traveling with had returned the previous week. Unfortunately, her baby had developed a serious ear infection, and she delayed her return until it was safe for him to travel. She could not wait to get back home.

"My Yossi…he not very good at housekeeping," she chuckled, a light tingling laugh that reminded me of chiming bells. I could not help but smile back. "He and our little Batti together staying by my brother and sister-in-law's home in Tel Aviv. It closer to the Tzihov Institute, where he work." She closed her eyes for a moment and sighed, "It will be very good to be in home."

The pilot's announcement interrupted us just then. His voice resonated throughout the plane, informing the passengers of their imminent departure and a renewed sense of apprehension gripped me.

The plane had been moving steadily down the runway as we spoke, its speed gradually increasing after the pilot's announcement. We could see the stewardess in the front of our section demonstrating the correct usage of the various devices in the event of an emergency.

I felt the sharpness of my fingernails digging deeply into the skin of my sweaty palms. A high-pitched tone resounded. The "fasten seat belt" lights went on simultaneously. Obediently, I buckled my seat belt. I reached for my pocketbook and unzipping the zipper, found my *Tehillim*.

The plane rounded a bend and then accelerated. It sped down the runway, while the roar of the motor intensified with each passing second.

Stop, I wanted to cry out, *let me out of here!* I swallowed hard, trying to hold back my tears. *Why am I doing this to myself, what am I doing on this plane?* The unspoken questions reverberated in sequence with the pounding of my heart. *What if something happens to me and I never see my family again?*

I seized the armrest with one hand and gripped my *Tehillim* tightly with the other.

The girls in front of me were giggling. I glanced over at Gila. She was holding her baby securely against her shoulder as she gazed out the window. He was fast asleep.

As the plane picked up speed, racing toward the end of the runway, there was a sudden loud noise and I knew we were no longer touching the ground. We were in the air!

And suddenly the grinding sensation in the pit of my stomach left me and my excitement was intense. I was flying! For the first time in my life, I was actually flying. As we continued our ascent, I could see the land slanting sharply beneath us. The large airport could no longer be seen. The houses, buildings, streets, highways, and cars became smaller, and within seconds, they too disappeared, replaced with that giant sparkling blanket of blue glitter, the famous Lake Alberta. Its waters scintillated flashes of the shining sun above, and I could see the shadow of our plane moving slowly over the glinting waves.

I caught my breath in wonder. I was going…I was really going. And I was going to be the winner of the Goldstone Award.

I tried to tell myself that it was *just a piece of paper*, attempting to quell the fervor growing inside me. Yet, I knew it was something much more. It was the key—the key to opening up doors of opportunity for me—the key that would free me from this prison of being just a prop for the rest of my life.

And as the plane soared higher and higher into the clouds, taking me away from the past and hurtling me somewhere into the unknown future, I knew I would do everything I could to get that key.

But, I had no way of knowing then what it was going to do to me.

2

I WAS FASCINATED by the view. The sun was shining brilliantly, and as I peered out, I noticed we were no longer flying over water. I watched the winding streams and rolling hills beneath us turn into masses of wavy pine trees resembling a green, swirling blanket, and I wondered which state we had just flown over.

I finally managed to tear away my eyes when Gila's baby started stretching uncomfortably. Not wanting him to awaken prematurely, Gila attempted to ease him into a more comfortable position.

Luckily, just then a blonde-haired stewardess came by. She was tall with high, prominent cheekbones that were emphasized by the way she pursed her lips when she spoke. Noticing Gila with the baby in her arms, she offered to bring a bassinet. She suggested that I move to the aisle seat so she could secure the bassinet in the center seat.

I was glad to comply. The same thought had entered my mind earlier, but with our conversation and the excitement of the subsequent take-off, I guess I must have been distracted. Taking my pocketbook with me, I slipped into the next seat.

We wondered aloud if the seat would remain unoccupied when the plane stopped in New York and additional passengers boarded.

The stewardess quickly returned with the bassinet, an extra blanket, along with a wrapped toy. She eased the bassinet into place. Gila gently put her sleeping baby in while the stewardess, reaching over my chair, placed the folded blanket on top of him. Tenderly, I tucked it around his small, sleeping body.

I leaned back against my seat, still amazed that I was actually on my way to Eretz Yisrael and even more surprised that I was doing it alone and that Chavie was not with me. Why if it had not been for her, I never would have contemplated going in the first place!

Mindy, Chavie's older sister had gone to Machon Beit Leah LeMorot a few years earlier. She had returned with not only the necessary knowledge and training to become the dedicated and successful teacher she was, but she had also acquired friendships and experiences that she claimed would last a lifetime. And so, ever since then, going to M.B.L.L. became Chavie's undisputed plan for the future and, of course, Chavie's plan for me, as well.

And I, of course, told Chavie that she could forget about including me in those wonderful plans. Chavie, though, did not cease in her efforts to persuade me. She would talk about the traveling and adventure, a whole school year away from home and on our own. I would remind her that I am not the adventurous type and that I really am a homebody with no thirst for independence. She would convincingly speak of how we would make many new friends from all over the world and I patiently explained that I would rather deepen existing friendships. She emphasized what fun it would be to dorm together. I agreed, but added, that I did not want to waste my first year out of high school on having "fun" and that gaining experience in the work force was by far the more practical thing to do.

She burst into wild laughter declaring, "There goes my best friend," and then teasingly called me by the nickname she gave me many years earlier, "Practical Sara."

Then she tried waving the "Eretz Yisrael dream" in front of me. Like so many others, I grew up imbued with a love for, and aspirations to go to Eretz Yisrael. I longed to pray at the Kosel and to walk the land our forefathers had trodden. Fortunately for us, my grandmother had purchased savings bonds at the birth of each grandchild. They were to come due on our seventeenth birthdays and her intention was to finance a year of study in Israel.

And then, when I was in twelfth grade, my sister Shuli ebulliently wrote home that not only was she having "the most amazingly fantabulous time," but she emphasized specifically to me all the knowledge and experience she was gaining as a teacher-in-training.

Suddenly, I was listening. Ever since I could remember, it had always been my fervent wish to be a teacher. From the time I was small, I loved playing school with the twins, pretending that I was their "Morah." I even helped them learn how to read. Throughout my high school years I tutored elementary-aged children on Sunday afternoons, as well.

I was usually so shy. Yet, when asked to explain something to a child who had difficulty grasping the lesson…it was as if I suddenly came alive. I would present the seemingly inscrutable lesson with great clarity, stubbornly refusing to give up. And as we sifted through the problem, breaking it down one idea at a time, it gave me great pleasure to see the child's eyes suddenly flicker with comprehension when she discovered that the problem really was conquerable after all.

However, my fears of the unknown and my difficulties in adjusting to new situations far outweighed my ideals and dreams about teaching. And so, despite Shuli's enthusiastic letters and Chavie's persistent entreaties, I still felt uncertain about going.

Gently, my parents continued to encourage me. My mother reminded me that I was always afraid to take that first step, but once I took the plunge, I did fine. She suggested that perhaps I would always regret having forfeited this opportunity. And my father prodded me, wanting me to realize my dream of being the best possible teacher I could be. We both knew how difficult it would be for me to get a teaching job in one of the few Jewish schools in Rolland County, let alone in Rolland Heights. "You know, Sara," my father softly reminded me, "a teacher's certificate from Machon Beit Leah LeMorot practically guarantees a job in any day school or Beis Yaakov across America. So hopefully it'll help wherever you'll eventually end up living."

Machon Beit Leah LeMorot was renowned for its excellent teachers training program. Rabbi Yaakov Yosef Grossman, a former principal from New York, founded the seminary for young teachers-in-training nearly twenty-five years earlier, sharing the facilities of an Israeli girls high school.

The rules for acceptance were stringent. The girls were not only to take their studies seriously, but also had to be extremely committed about becoming teachers. And since it is not that common for a seventeen or eighteen year old to be so certain of her plans for the future, not that many qualified. Besides, Rabbi Grossman and his faculty endeavored to keep the classes small, thereby helping each and every student-teacher develop into the best educator possible. For a serious teacher-in-training, M.B.L.L. was a dream program!

And yet, a seminary in far off Israel? In a different country? No, I certainly could not commit myself to going.

Then, one day my principal announced that the entrance examinations for Machon Beit Leah LeMorot would be taking place the following week. I was still adamant about staying.

Chavie, though, in her exceedingly persuasive manner managed to convince me to go along with her that Sunday morning and "just for the fun of it" take the test. I agreed to pay the fee and take the exam, "just to see what happens." However, I made it unequivocally clear to her that I would definitely *not* be going.

Well…when the results of the exam were sent to my principal and I found out that I had done quite well, I was not unwilling to be interviewed by Rabbi Grossman. To my utter amazement, that afternoon I was entirely at ease speaking to him. It was probably because I was not planning to go to his school anyway. We spoke of our mutual admiration for my sister, Shuli, and I freely told him of my desire to be a teacher. I felt that he understood everything I was telling him and I thought I detected his approval.

That night, lying in bed, my palms cradling the back of my head, I stared into the darkness in wonder. I could not believe it, but for the first time, I was actually contemplating going to M.B.L.L.

Shuli had gone to M.B.L.L. because she wanted to go to seminary in Eretz Yisrael. She chose M.B.L.L. over other seminaries because she figured that as long as she was going, she might as well get the best possible training as a teacher. True, she wanted to teach. However, being a teacher was not *her* dream. It was *my* dream.

I felt a certain spark ignite in me. I was the "teacher." I was the one who tutored in my spare time. I was the one who went to the local library, looking in books on education for creative ideas and motivational techniques. I was the one who dreamily imagined the class that I would one day teach. And now I felt myself drawn to M.B.L.L. for the

Chapter 2

teaching program they offered...and not just because I wanted a seminary year in Eretz Yisrael.

I could learn so much from Rabbi Grossman and his experienced staff! *And how,* I asked myself, *can I give up the opportunity to go to Eretz Yisrael and make friends with Jewish girls from all over the world? Wasn't this my grandmother's wish? Weren't my parents in favor of it?*

When the month of February drew near, I checked our mailbox daily. Secretly I hoped...

And so, when I received a letter in the mail with the return address of Machon Beit Leah LeMorot's New York office, I nervously tore open the envelope, unfolded the letter and quickly devoured its contents: *Dear Sara,* I read. *It gives us great pleasure to inform you that you have been accepted as a student in Machon Beit Leah LeMorot for the school year starting September...*

Before I finished reading, I knew with a certainty that I would be going. I just had no idea that I would end up going alone.

Letting out a deep sigh, I stood up and made my way toward the restrooms. I passed the other girls in our group and noticed the girl I had seen standing in the airport with a tall man. She was looking out of her window and sipping a can of soda through a straw. Her shiny, coal black hair with its bluish highlights hung in a sophisticated blunt cut, barely touching her shoulders and framing her pretty face.

From close up, I could see her pronounced cheekbones and small turned-up nose. She appeared even more attractive than I had initially thought. I was intrigued. She seemed rather melancholy and lonely, staring at the passing clouds. I wondered if she was shy like me and if she too was thinking about the family she left behind.

Suddenly, she turned in my direction. Her eyes met mine and I noticed the intensity of their blueness. Unique combinations of dark and light hues made her eyes distinctive and I could not help but gaze back at her. I had never seen such piercing blue eyes before. Slowly, they swept over me, coldly assessing me.

From the icy look she gave me, I felt as though I had impinged on her privacy. It seemed as if she was saying: *stay away from me, don't try to intrude.*

Why? What does she have against me? Until a few hours earlier in the airport lounge, we had never even met. And I would not exactly call that airport scene a meeting.

The airport lounge…

We had arrived at Lincoln Memorial Airport way too soon…I would have preferred remaining in our station wagon forever. My father and brothers had unloaded my luggage at the departure area and then went to park the car. And suddenly, everything was happening at lightning speed.

I felt as if I were in a dream. This cannot be happening to me, I thought. I am not really leaving my home, my family, and friends for a year. This must be happening to someone else.

Airports had always seemed so dramatic and exciting to me. That is…as an observer. There is that flurry and frenzy of activity with the inevitable emotions: the thrill of greeting long lost relatives at the Arrivals gate or the excitement of those leaving.

And now, I was to be one of those departing passengers, and suddenly I was not finding it so adventurous.

I could see some other girls from the small group that I was to travel with gathered together in the lounge. Mrs. Fixler, one of the seminary's American representatives was standing nearby, taking care of last minute arrangements.

A few of the faces seemed vaguely familiar, but that was as far as it went. I had no idea of the others' names or where exactly they were from. Besides, I was hardly aware of the other people who were there…I could only look intently at my family. Surprisingly, though, I did notice one girl who seemed to stand out.

Perhaps it was because of her black shiny hair, its dark color so striking and unusual. Or possibly it had to do with the cool, detached expression on her face that mystified me. I could tell she was above average in height, although compared to the tall, broad-shouldered man she stood next to, she seemed fairly small. She was leaning against the wall and facing my direction as she spoke with the man. His back was to me. I could not see his face, but the same dark-colored hair as the girl's was visible below his hat. I figured that he must be her father.

The thought briefly passed through my mind of how strange it was that this girl seemed neither nervous nor excited. She continued to speak with the tall man opposite her. I saw him hand her something. She grudgingly took the small package and slipped it quickly into her shoulder bag. She then pointed toward the watch on her wrist and said something. His shoulders rose and then fell slowly. A moment or two later he turned to leave. I caught the resigned look in his eyes as he passed us. His long strides took him out of the lounge area within seconds. When I turned back to look at the girl, she was still leaning against the wall, her face expressionless and impassive. I wondered where her family was. And then, I quickly turned back to my own family, totally dismissing all thoughts of anyone else.

We sat together, talking quietly. I took hold of my mother's hand and held it lingeringly.

I heard an accented voice announce over the loud speaker that our flight would be leaving shortly and that all departing passengers must board the plane within the next ten minutes.

The minutes could have been seconds.

I tried to be brave. I kept swallowing hard in my feeble attempt to restrain myself from crying, but my efforts were futile. As Chevy clung to me, declaring passionately that she would not be able to manage the coming year without me, we both dissolved into tears.

My father put his hands on my head and blessed me. Then he handed me some *shaliach mitzvah gelt*. My mother reminded me to write, get plenty of sleep, and take my vitamins. Shuli told me to whom to send regards and make sure to visit, and Moshe, his voice alternating between nonchalance and grudging affection, allowed that even he would miss me. Sruly, his eyes twinkling, wished me success and assured me that all would be well. I reciprocated his words. He too was embarking on a new endeavor, leaving the yeshivah he had attended for many years and entering the huge study hall of the Lakewood Yeshivah. Chevy and I were squeezing each other's hands tightly.

Most of the girls had already left the lounge area and from the corner of my eye I noticed Mrs. Fixler approaching us. It was time for me to make my final farewells.

She drew near and tapped me lightly on my arm, prompting me to take my leave. I felt my mouth go dry. I bent down and lifted the heavy handbag over my shoulder. My mother handed me my pocketbook and her kind eyes met mine. Silently, I held her gaze while at the same time groping for my ticket inside. It was there. I slipped the strap of my shoulder bag over my other shoulder.

I embraced my mother tightly, not wanting to let go. I felt my own tears against her wet cheeks.

Gently, Mrs. Fixler prodded me on. I followed her until the checkpoint and then slowly and deliberately went through the gate.

Despite the warm air, I felt a shiver run through me. *Why in the world am I leaving them all… and why is that girl looking at me so coldly?* I felt myself blushing and turned away embarrassed. *Had I been staring at her this whole time? I should really go over and apologize…*

I quickly took my place in the line for the restrooms. There was another Beis Yaakov-type girl waiting there. She guessed that I was also going to M.B.L.L. and I acknowledged that this was so. She said her name was Rivky Weiss and shyly I told her my name.

She was about my height, with a similar build, and I felt quite comfortable standing next to her. Her light brown hair was cut in a short bob, swinging easily as she spoke in a soft, gentle voice. She wore small, round glasses and had an easy smile. I liked her immediately.

She did not ask me where I was from or if I knew anyone else who was going. I felt relieved. I did not want to admit that I did not have any friends with me. She informed me that she was the only one from her school, Yeshivah of Walnut Lake, attending M.B.L.L., but that a good friend of hers, "a great kid from camp" would be joining us in New York.

I must concede that I was not paying complete attention to her. My eyes kept shifting back to that lone girl with the stunning blue eyes staring out of the window. There was something mysterious about that girl, and for some unknown reason I felt drawn to her.

"I'm thrilled," Rivky's tone became more enthusiastic. "Mimi was not planning to go to Israel at all. In fact, I had no idea that she wanted to teach or that she had even applied to M.B.L.L. Both of her parents are very reputable professors," as she said this she rolled her eyes, "and Mimi always claimed that teaching was the last thing she wanted to do. Then," Rivky laughed happily, "suddenly, late last night she called me."

I couldn't help taking another quick look at that girl by the window.

I guess I'm not the only lonely one on this plane.

"She told me that Rabbi Grossman had spoken to her parents earlier in the day," Rivky went on.

I barely heard what she was saying, but nodded as if I did. Instead, I continued to puzzle over that girl's cold attitude toward me. *What is it about me that she doesn't like*, I pondered. *I hadn't even spoken to her yet!* Warning bells began to ring inside my head. I could almost hear my older sister admonishing me. *Stop analyzing everything, Sara, and stop letting your overactive imagination get the better of you!*

"He had called to inform them," Rivky continued, "that one of the girls who was supposed to be coming with us had suddenly backed out due to a *simchah* or something and—"

"Yes?" my voice was sharp.

"And," she paused, probably taken aback by my abruptness, "and Mimi Rosenberg was offered the opportunity to take her place."

She now had my full attention. I leaned forward and asked her rhetorically, "And this girl...this Mimi Rosenberg decided to take the place of the girl...the one who backed out yesterday?"

"Well...yes," she lifted her eyebrows, surprised to be asked the obvious.

A surge of unreasonable resentment swept through me. I do not remember how much longer our conversation continued or what it was we discussed. I do not even remember returning to my seat...I was so preoccupied with this Mimi Rosenberg and how quickly she had slipped into Chavie's vacant slot.

Her vacant slot. Oh, Chavie, how could you have done this to me?

"*Mazal tov!* That's the greatest news," I had told Chavie when she informed me last night of Mindy's impending engagement. "Now I know why you had to stop packing and run over to tell me. But why *are* you in such a serious mood tonight?"

"Be-because," Chavie hesitated a moment, her fair complexion turning even paler, "you know...there's going to be a wedding."

"Of course, there's going to be a wedding," I laughed. "How else does someone get married?"

"Well, you see, the wedding will probably take place around Chanukah time and..."

"And you'll be going back home for Chanukah," I offered.

So, that was it! Chavie, my best friend, was concerned about having to leave me on my own. She knew that making new friends did not come easily to someone as shy as me.

Chavie looked down at the floor, "Sara, there's something I have—"

"It's okay, Chavie. Of course, I'll miss you Chanukah time, but hopefully by then I'll be settled in. I'm a big girl, you know," I chuckled and then continued, excited for my friend. "So now you'll have the best of both worlds, your year in Eretz Yisrael and you'll get to go home in the middle too."

"No," Chavie shook her head grimly, her blonde curls jiggling as well.

"No?" I repeated, "What do you mean *no*?"

"Don't you understand?" Her eyes suddenly filled. "I can't have both. It's either/or. I can stay for the wedding *or* I can go to Eretz Yisrael for the year."

"I don't understand."

She looked at me despondently. "My parents can't afford to send me for a year of schooling in Eretz Yisrael *and* bring me back for the wedding. So they gave me the choice."

"Well...what did you decide?" I asked slowly.

"At first, I thought maybe I could have both. I'd just go late," she said with a shaky voice. "And I'm still not sure. Maybe that *will* work out. But my father said that it's only right that we should inform Rabbi Grossman immediately." She paused long enough to let out a deep sigh. "He said that it could be that the school won't allow it. After all, I'm not the only one who wants to go to M.B.L.L."

"So what happened?"

"We were back and forth on the telephone—long distance—all day," she went on, her blue eyes brimming. "My father just spoke to Rabbi Grossman around an hour ago. You know it's the middle of the night there."

"And?" I asked anxiously.

"And he said that there is a long waiting list of girls who might still want to come, and if any of them are ready to leave immediately as soon as they're notified, then it wouldn't be right to hold the place for me..."

"But that's not fair!" I protested.

"He explained that although I'd be planning to come later on, it's not enough of an assurance that I really would, and since there are still others who want to go and could benefit from the program, why should they lose out? And," she ran on, "you know the school's reputation in keeping the classes small."

"And one more person makes such a difference?"

"I don't know the exact number. Maybe it's thirty girls, maybe forty. It doesn't matter," she shook her head, "they won't budge. They're very strict about this."

"I don't understand. It's not right!"

"I also felt that way. But the truth is...my father explained if they give in to one person, then they have to make exceptions for another. And before long...their small classes won't be so small anymore."

"Still!"

"Rabbi Grossman said that sometimes things come up and girls have to go home in the middle of the term and don't end up staying the full year," her words tumbled out agitatedly. "So when the wedding is over, if there is an open slot, I'll have first grab at it. But," her voice dropped in anguish, "he said there are no guarantees. And now..." I watched helplessly as the tears began to trickle down her cheeks, "my parents left the decision up to me."

"And?"

"And what?"

"What are you going to do?" The words rushed out desperately, echoing the wild beating of my heart.

"Sara...Mindy's the first one in my family to be getting married," she looked at me through pleading eyes. "There's the l'chaim, the vort, an aufruf, Shabbos Kallah...," her voice was hardly audible as she continued, "...the wedding, Sheva Berachos...and even if we could afford to send me back and forth, I'd still be missing out on so much and..." She stopped suddenly, unable to go on.

"So you've decided to stay?"

Slowly, she nodded.

Then and there in my seat I decided that there was no way I would ever like this girl who had slipped exceedingly quickly into Chavie's spot. *Mimi Rosenberg.* I did not care what Rivky Weiss—or anyone else for that matter—thought of her. I would have nothing to do with that girl, no matter what.

Completely wrapped up in those antipathetic feelings, I had not realized that our plane was gradually making its descent toward the JFK Airport. Suddenly we landed in New York and the new passengers began filling the unoccupied seats.

The three girls in front of me were too busy chatting with each other to pay any attention to the new arrivals. I, though, bored and lonely, watched a group of girls approach the blonde stewardess, who had helped Gila settle her baby. Glancing at their boarding passes, she pointed them to the vacant seats behind us.

The girls headed toward us, with the helpful stewardess leading the way. Several seemed to cling in twos or threes; some appeared hesitant and some more confident. One petite, red-haired girl carrying a large guitar case walked jauntily down the aisle, clapped another girl who had been walking with her cheerily on the shoulder, waved her boarding pass at the stewardess, and then smilingly followed her. They came toward my seat.

The stewardess's short blonde hair brushed her cheekbones as she leaned over me and spoke to Gila. Apologetically, she asked her to pick up the baby, enabling me to move over and make room for the newcomer. Gila complied and I immediately took the middle seat.

From the corner of my eye, I inquisitively watched the girl. Wavy hair bounced around her as she tossed her shoulder bag onto the seat and nonchalantly handed her guitar to the stewardess. "Oh, great! You'll put that away for me somewhere until after takeoff," was more of a statement than a request. "Thanks a ton!"

I saw her stuff the remainder of her things into the overhead compartment with an ease that surprised me. She slid into her seat, her green eyes dancing merrily. Two deep dimples flashed as she introduced herself.

It was Mimi Rosenberg.

3

THE NORMAL ME would have turned and, hiding the quivering feeling deep inside, smiled and returned her greeting. But the normal me was probably still in Rolland Heights. Instead, I looked at her condescendingly, and in as icy a voice as I could muster, I told her my name.

"I'm very tired and trying to get some rest," I added, turning away from her and pretending to close my eyes. It was unusual for me to dislike someone with such vehemence, especially when that someone happened to be a person I did not even know. Yet, I felt an impetuous rush of bitterness toward this girl. *She* had taken Chavie's place.

Besides, despite her dancing eyes and friendly manner, I found her high-spirited demeanor overbearing. She had only been sitting there a few seconds when she lowered her food tray, announcing that she was starved, chatting with everyone around her, and not the least bit offended by my frosty manner.

I guess if I had really been honest with myself, I would have had to admit that this type of personality generally attracted me. However, just then I could only think resentfully that had this girl not grabbed my best friend's vacant slot as quickly as she did, I would be looking forward to Chavie joining me in a few months' time and I would not be feeling as lonely as I was.

I tried to ignore the girl on my left. Yet, something in me was pushing itself to the surface and I could not help muttering, "I'd really like to get some sleep. C-can't you keep your voice down?"

"Oh, sure, sorry," her eyes, much to my dismay, were still dancing. "You know, I just LOVE to play guitar. I can't bear to be without it! Do you play any instruments?"

"J-just a little piano. If you don't mind, l-like I said before, I'm tired and I'd really—"

I never did get to finish my sentence. Rivky Weiss suddenly came running down the aisle, her light brown bob swinging as she ran. Mimi quickly unbuckled her seat belt and rushed into Rivky's arms.

They hugged and both of them exclaimed, "I can't believe YOU'RE going!"

"I was so busy schmoozing with one of the girls sitting next to me, I didn't realize you people were boarding already, Mimi," Rivky apologized. "Oh my goodness, I can't believe I wasn't here to greet you the second you came on the plane!"

"You're quite forgiven, Rivky. I was just getting to know my new neighbor," she cocked her head toward me.

I felt myself blushing.

"Oh, great. Mimi, I'm so glad…"

Their enthusiasm caught the attention of all the nearby passengers.

Chani Frankel leaned over, her dark brown eyes widened in surprise. "I don't believe it, Mimi Rosenberg, is it really *you*? Remember *me*?"

Mimi's green eyes darted to the girl sitting in front of me. "Hey, Chani Frank? Wow! You're going too?"

"Yes, I didn't know you were going! I'm so excited."

"I didn't know either," she laughed heartily. Her laughter had a strong vibrating sound that seemed to erupt from deep within her. It surprised me…such a powerful voice issuing from someone so small. Turning to Rivky she said excitedly. "This is Chani Frank. We met at the Beis Yaakov convention last year. Chani, this is a terrific friend of mine, Rivky Weiss, from camp. Did you meet each other yet?"

"Yes," Rivky smiled fondly at Mimi. "And, her name is Chani Frankel. You and your wonderful memory…"

"Oh, sorry," she grinned sheepishly.

"Quite all right, you're forgiven," Chani said, her voice full of cheer. "Meet my friends, Rochel Leah Wolf and Zehava Gross," she nodded toward the girls on either side of her.

"Hi," Mimi grinned. "Glad to meet you, Rochel Leah Gross and Zehava Wolf."

"That was Rochel Leah Wolf and Zehava Gross," Rivky corrected her friend with affection. "Still the same Mimi."

The ever-present dimples deepened.

"And, what's your name, again?" she asked, turning to me.

I felt my face turning crimson. By now, I was feeling quite ashamed of my initial coldness to Mimi Rosenberg. She seemed so warm and friendly. I knew all eyes were on me waiting for a reply and I felt especially uncomfortable under Rochel Leah's scrutiny. I was trying to think of a sharp and witty response, but the stewardess, who just then made her way down the aisle toward the two girls standing there, fortunately saved me.

"Ladies, you must take your seats and fasten your seat belts. Takeoff is about to begin."

Immersed in the fervor of the conversation, I had failed to notice the plane making its way along the runway. Now I surrendered myself fully to the momentum of its accelerating speed. I found the second takeoff as exhilarating as the first, and as we lifted off and ascended through the clouds, I was oblivious to anything and everything save that invigorating sensation of flying.

When the pilot announced that our next stop was Israel and flying time was approximately eleven hours, everyone cheered. I felt my heart lift and my spirit soar. I was really going to Eretz Yisrael! This was it—I was really going!

"Hey, you look a lot more cheerful now."

Turning toward Mimi, I felt myself flushing.

"It's just that I've never been to Eretz Yisrael before," I explained self-consciously, flustered for not hiding my feelings.

"Hey, don't apologize to me. It's my first time too and I'm so excited, I feel as if I'm going to burst!"

"It's also my first time flying," I admitted, not knowing why I felt the need to confess this fact.

"Not mine," she said unassumingly, tucking a strand of wavy red hair behind her ear. "But that's because I live in Barclay and, since most of our relatives live in Chicago, I've flown to family *semachos* and such. But that's nothing compared to this! How about you?" she turned to Gila.

She had warmly introduced herself to Gila when she had taken her seat, but until this moment, Gila had been preoccupied with her baby. Now that Uri was once again sleeping peacefully, Mimi kindly drew her into the conversation.

"Like I told Sara before, until this time I come, I never fly before."

Within the next few seconds, Mimi easily managed to find out all about Gila, her job, her children, and her husband. Also, his job as a research scientist in the Tzihov Institute, what kind of apartment they live in, and almost everything else there was to know. Mimi was inquisitive, but even I had to admit—it was done in a friendly kind of way. People clearly fascinated her and she did not hold herself back from asking that which she was curious to know. Gila, enjoying Mimi's questions and intentness, gladly obliged.

I could not help but feel a mixture of admiration and envy for this girl. I had always been interested in people, but was never comfortable questioning them in such an open and friendly manner. Grudgingly, I had to admit that there was something special about Mimi, although I was, of course, still resentful of her for having slid so easily and speedily into Chavie's opened slot.

Before long, the "fasten seat belt" lights turned off and Rivky Weiss came and perched halfway on Mimi's arm rest and halfway in the aisle, generously sharing a box of Mimi's peanut chews with all of us. Rochel Leah, Chani, and Zehava were hanging over the backs of their seats, passing bags of popcorn and corn chips around, and Gila and I swiveled to face Mimi engrossed in her animated description of the major play in camp.

With Rivky Weiss's occasional interruption, correcting the accuracy of what Mimi was telling us, she had us all completely enraptured. Even Rochel Leah seemed drawn to her.

I studied her face, attempting to understand her magnetism. *What was it about this girl,* I wondered. Feature by feature, she was not especially pretty, although she certainly was not bad looking, either. Her small face was too angular, her chin too pointy, and her nose, with its sprinkling of freckles, was rather long and wide. But, those dancing green eyes and perpetually deepening dimples undoubtedly made up for any imperfections.

"Ooooh, Mimi, how about playing some guitar?" Rivky asked excitedly. "Do the theme song from color war."

"Oh, I don't know if I should," Mimi looked down smiling, with what I assumed was feigned coyness. I could tell that she really wanted to play and that her hesitancy was due only to her enjoyment at being cajoled.

"Yes, do!" Chani urged.

Not wanting to appear to be entirely antisocial, feeling foolish and slightly mendacious, I said with a voice I did not feel was my own, "Yes...please play."

"Well...if you all insist," Mimi laughed with unconcealed delight, clearly relishing center stage. She bounced over to the closet where the stewardess had stowed her guitar and was back in an instant with it. Unbuckling the case and ceremoniously lifting out her guitar, Rivky stood up to make more room as Mimi placed the guitar across her lap, her left hand on the armrest.

She began strumming. Considerate of the other passengers, she did not sing along nor play too loudly, but the tune was clearly audible. I found myself wanting to hum along as I watched her.

She was staring dreamily upward at nothing in particular, a sparkle still lingering in her green eyes. Her head was tilted sideways, with her red ponytail tumbling loosely past her right shoulder and her lips still curved into a smile. Performing came naturally to her, and I could not help but admire her spiritedness and easy confidence.

I looked up suddenly as a stewardess that I had not seen before came toward us. Her sleek dark brown hair was pulled severely into a tight knot at the back of her neck, and as she drew near, her dark eyes narrowed. I could see that she was not smiling.

"You will have to save your singing for when you reach the privacy of your own destinations," her words came out tautly with just a slight trace of an Israeli accent. "There are those who are trying to rest and you are disturbing them," she looked accusingly at Mimi and then at the rest of us before abruptly turning away.

I looked around at the passengers nearby. No one seemed disturbed by Mimi's performance. Actually, some people shook their heads disapprovingly in the stewardess's direction. Yet, I could not help feeling uncomfortable. The other girls began muttering their disappointment under their breath.

Mimi simply shrugged and put her guitar back in its case. "Okay, girls," she announced, "now that we have to *wait till we reach the privacy of our own destinations,*" she easily mimicked the stewardess's accent much to the delight of her friends, "what should we do?"

"Ummmmm," Chani pretended to be deep in thought, "let's eat!"

Everyone laughed. Even I. Chani was by no means heavy, but she certainly was not thin either, and ever since our trip began, she had been busily devouring the contents of a large bag of corn chips.

"Oh look," Zehava exclaimed, pointing in the direction of one of the kitchens, "they're *really* serving dinner now."

"Ah...what a relief," Chani said in an overly dramatic tone that made the rest of us chuckle.

"They're taking care of the first class section first, of course," Rochel Leah noted, her tone disdainful. "And then they'll probably serve business class next. Who knows how long it'll take till they get to us."

"That gives me an idea..."

"Uh oh," Rivky rolled her eyes in Mimi's direction. "I'm afraid to find out what her 'idea' is."

"Oh, it's no big deal," Mimi's eyes lit up and she winked conspiratorially as she delivered another one of her delicious, infectious laughs. "I was just thinking about how nice it would be to take a walk and visit..."

Somehow, Mimi managed to get our little group to ascend the spiral staircase that led up to the first class cabin. Surprisingly (to me, that is), she even got me to join her "tour," but the same critical stewardess interrupted our "little visit" and disapprovingly sent us, like recalcitrant school children, back to our seats.

I was mortified. I self-consciously headed back to my seat, feeling my face reddening with each step I took. Gila looked up at me inquisitively, probably wondering what had occurred. I felt too uncomfortable to say anything and proceeded to study my nails uneasily as soon as I slid back into my place.

The other girls reached us shortly, and with sheepish giggles took their places. Mimi, on the other hand did not seem disconcerted in the least.

"Oh well," she said as she flung herself into her seat, "you win some, you lose some."

I looked up, surprised at her lack of remorse.

"Boy… and I was thinking, 'what a killjoy,'" Rochel Leah declared disappointedly, nodding her head in the direction we had just come from.

"True, it wasn't like we were making noise or anything," Chani protested.

She's also not ashamed?

"I don't understand. Why the big fuss? We weren't disturbing anybody."

"I know. All we were doing was looking. What right did that stewardess have to stop us, anyway?"

I turned abruptly, astonished that these girls could see no wrong in what we had just done. I do not know what came over me. Maybe it was due to my lack of sleep or could be blamed on that strange combination of emotions I was experiencing, but my words tumbled out before I could stop them.

"How can you say that?" I heard myself say hoarsely. "Those people paid extra to be in first class and we had no right to go into their section. The stewardess was right to—"

I stopped suddenly, aware that my outburst had astounded not only me, but those around me, as well.

"Wow, what a straight arrow we have here. I hope you aren't going to be so virtuous every time we want to have a little fun."

"Rochel Leah!" Chani snapped, turning sharply to her friend.

"Sara's right," Rivky came to my defense. "We really didn't have a right to be there."

"You too?" Rochel Leah's voice was heavy with sarcasm.

"Hey, everybody, look what's coming," Mimi pointed to the nearby carts being wheeled in our direction by two stewardesses.

"Oh, good," Chani took Mimi's cue to change the subject. "Finally!"

Her tone was excessively emphatic as she eyed the food cart drawing closer.

Before long, everyone was busily exploring the contents of their glatt kosher meals. I do not remember what I ate, nor if I ate, but I drank the whole can of soda the stewardess had provided. I gnawed nervously on the plastic straw, wondering how soon after we arrived I would be able to get a return flight back to the States.

Mimi chatted as she ate as though nothing out of the ordinary had occurred. She also did not seem to recall the unfriendliness with which I had initially greeted her. Instead, she amiably told me about herself.

She had lived in Barclay her whole life. There were three children in her family. Her parents were both educators. Her father was a professor in a local college and her mother, a physician with a private practice, taught medicine at New York University. Her married sister was the director of a speech clinic in Manhattan, where she lived with her husband and three children, and her brother, who had just gotten married earlier the past summer, had joined the kollel in Australia.

I felt my mood perking up somewhat and it was easier to be myself.

I could see why people liked her so much. She knew how to reach past my reserve and shyness. Slowly, I found myself telling her about my family, and specifically about my sister Shuli, who had been to Machon Beit Leah LeMorot the year before.

Proudly I spoke of Shuli being one of the honorable mention recipients of the Goldstone Outstanding Student Teacher Award. I could tell that she was definitely impressed. She suggested jovially that perhaps I would be the main winner of it the coming year.

I did not find that to be very humorous, and feeling the heat rise to my face, hoped that my blushing did not reveal my innermost thoughts and dreams.

We continued to talk until the stewardess cleared off our trays and Rivky Weiss once again joined us. I wondered if they both hoped I would switch seats with Rivky so that the two of them could sit together. Still, I could not help noticing how kind they were, benevolently including me in their conversation.

Somehow, I did not feel left out and realized that these two genuinely enjoyed making new friends. They did not need to bond with only those with whom they were familiar. *Could it be, I supposed, that some people refrain from making new friends and instead stick to the people they know because of their own insecurities? Funny,* I told myself, *I had never thought of that before.* I knew, though, that had Chavie been with me, we would—of course—have stuck together, but at the same time we certainly would have been affable and forthcoming to all.

As Mimi made another joke, getting, me, Gila, and Rivky to join in her contagious laughter, the latter, once again that day, exclaimed affectionately, "Oh, Mimi, I'm so happy you decided to come. I still can't believe it!"

"Neither can I, but like I told you, they just BEGGED me to come!"

Rivky grinned, knowing full well that Rabbi Grossman did not have to beg any one to come to M.B.L.L., but nevertheless, fully enjoyed her friend's entertaining frivolity.

And then she said something I found to be rather troubling.

"I thought, Mim, you couldn't stand doing schoolwork, especially in a seminary where the emphasis is so much on teaching. I assumed you would just look for a job in an office or something. Isn't that what you kept telling us all summer?"

For just a fleeting moment, I noticed a shadow steal across Mimi's face. It passed so swiftly that I thought I must have imagined it. Then, all at once, her face lit up with a wonderful smile. "See, it's never too late to change," she said with a lilt in her voice.

We continued talking, our voices receding to whispers as the main lights were turned off in order that those interested in sleeping could do so more comfortably. Eventually, Rivky returned to her seat. I almost offered to exchange places with her, but just then, Gila asked me to hold her baby so that she could refill his bottle.

As I spoke with Mimi, I found myself thinking of Chavie. They were quite similar in their outgoingness, although Chavie would never have gotten herself into the mischief that Mimi had found herself. Chavie too, was not afraid to perform, but she did not revel in attention the way Mimi did, and Chavie...well, Chavie was my best friend.

Again, I felt that nagging resentment enveloping me, and yet I could not help being drawn to Mimi. She was kindhearted and high-spirited.

She did not seem to care whether she was seated next to the most popular girl in the group or next to an extremely shy, reserved one like me.

She excused herself to go to the restrooms and "see what's going on" and asked me if I wanted to join her.

I shook my head, insisting that this time I really was going to sleep.

I watched her go, her red hair bouncing as she walked, and I felt my lips twitching into a smile. Still grinning, I turned to Gila to ask her if she needed anything before I went to sleep, but discovered that she had already dozed off with Uri snuggled closely to her.

Reclining my seat, I leaned back against the cushion positioned near my head. I unfolded the blanket that had been stored behind the seat in front of me and closed my eyes, attempting too to get some sleep.

I was feeling more relaxed now that I had spoken with Mimi Rosenberg and Rivky Weiss. They were nice girls and I felt sure that we would be good friends. In fact, almost everyone I had met so far seemed warm and friendly. That is, everyone except for two girls: Rochel Leah and that strange girl sitting up ahead. The girl with those interesting blue eyes.

I wrapped the blanket more tightly around myself, wondering if perhaps Mimi was introducing herself to the girl right now. If anyone could break through her reserve, I knew it had to be Mimi.

Yes, I was glad to have met Mimi Rosenberg, and thankful that if Chavie was not there for me, at least a nice and friendly girl, as the vivacious Mimi seemed to be, was sitting next to me.

She truly was like sunshine, with that halo of red hair surrounding her face and cheerful radiance emanating from her. Like the dancing snowflakes reflecting the colorful prisms of the shining sun on a bright winter day, she appeared to be free of all troubles and worries. *Probably*, I thought with a mingling of admiration and envy, *she never had a care in the world.*

Never a care in the world? Eventually, I would discover how dreadfully mistaken I had been. Life is not always as it seems.

4

"You're too late. I was here first!" Her hands rested challengingly on her hips. Sneering at my friend, her pointy chin appeared sharper than usual.

"That doesn't mean anything. You know I was the one who was supposed to go in the first place!"

"Well, I guess you're just a little bit too late," her voice was calm as she tucked a strand of wavy red hair behind her ear, the defiant smile still on her face. "It's as simple as this: I'm not budging." She folded her arms across her chest, her green eyes narrowing daringly, reminding me of a snarling cat.

"What...what do you mean you're not budging? That's *my* bed, that's *my* suitcase, that's *my* best friend..." My friend's blue eyes widened angrily, looking even bluer against the paleness of her fair skin. She turned them to me, silently pleading for help.

"Boy, you sound like the baby bear from "The Three Bears." That's *my* bed, that's *my* suitcase, that's *my* best friend. Ha, ha, ha," Mimi mercilessly mimicked my dear friend, Chavie, while everyone else surrounding us roared with laughter.

"So-o-o I know what we'll do," said Rochel Leah, who had been brushing her long chestnut hair while looking in the mirror hanging above the dresser. Still clutching her brush, she suddenly turned around, overcome with loud, boisterous laughter. Grasping hold of her sides in an exaggerated gesture of irrepressible amusement and with tears running uncontrollably down her cheeks, she turned her hazel eyes to me, their lashes wet.

I felt myself squirming uneasily under her mirthful gaze as everyone else looked at me, unable to restrain their snickers. I knew I was about to be the focus of one of her jokes.

I held my breath.

Much to my relief, she was laughing so hysterically that it was difficult to discern her words. "Let's...ha, ha, ha...let's..." And then suddenly, to my utter horror, she stopped laughing and distinctly announced, "Let's get rid of *her*, instead!"

My pulse began to race as I saw her lift the brush and throw it in my direction. I screamed, "OUCH!"

"Hey, I'm sorry."

"Huh?" I blinked.

"Yep, I'm really sorry. I accidentally dropped my brush on you, sleepyhead."

Pushing the blanket aside, I sat up groggily, wiping the drowsiness away from my eyes and saw that Mimi was smiling down at me. *Mimi.* I had only been dreaming. She was still that nice, friendly girl she had been all along.

"Boy, Sara, you sure know how to sleep. The pilot just announced that we're landing in less than an hour."

"What?"

"That's right. You've been sleeping forever. We're landing soon!"

I smiled faintly, trying to quiet my pounding heart and shake off that horrible nightmare. *It was just a nightmare,* I tried reassuring myself, *and there isn't even a trace of truth in it!*

I looked at my watch and gasped. I could not believe how much time had elapsed since I had dozed off. I had hardly slept the night before after hearing Chavie's news, and I guess all the tension and excitement must have all caught up with me.

Gila had been gathering her things, and I realized she could certainly use some help with Uri. She thanked me as I reached for him, enabling her to go to the restroom and prepare for landing.

"So-o-o Mimi, we're going to wash up. Want to join us?" Rochel Leah and Zehava were standing in the aisle alongside our seats.

"That's a great idea," Mimi stood up. "How about you, Sara?"

"We'd better hurry," Zehava warned. "The line is growing."

"No way am I going to wait an extra second," Rochel Leah pouted, "and risk getting off the plane looking like this." She spun around dramatically and then headed in the direction of the lavatories. Zehava hurried after her.

"So, Sara, are you coming?" Mimi turned toward me. "Oh, you can't. You're holding Gila's baby." Then, facing the row of seats in front of us, "How about you, Chani?"

"No thanks, Mimi. I went earlier, before the crowd, thank goodness. Have fun waiting in line!"

"Oh, I will," Mimi laughed, "See you all soon!" She sauntered down the aisle, her red hair bouncing.

I chuckled. If anyone could have fun waiting in line, it would have to be Mimi.

"Isn't she just terrific?" Chani was leaning over the back of her seat facing me. "Wherever Mimi Rosenberg goes she's the absolute life of the party."

"Yes. She's a lot of fun. And...and also very nice."

"And it's very nice of you, Sara, to be helping the Israeli lady so much."

"Oh, it's no big deal," I felt myself blush. "He's an adorable baby and she's...well, she's all alone."

"Uh huh. It must be very lonely for her traveling by herself."

"Yes. It must be."

"Actually, I feel so lucky that I know so many people on this plane."

"You *are* very fortunate."

"Yes, I know. No way *I* could've managed coming on my own."

"You—you wouldn't have come by yourself?"

"Who knows? I'm sure glad I didn't have to make a decision like that. There's no way I'd want to miss the M.B.L.L. experience!"

"So you're lucky that you get both—to go to M.B.L.L. *and* have friends going along with you."

"I know. I really am lucky. Rochel Leah and I have been in camp together for years; I feel like we've known each other forever. And I know Zehava for a long time too, through Rochel Leah. They're friends from way back when."

"Really? I thought Rochel Leah lives in Miami and Zehava's from Woodlake."

"Yup. But, their mothers have been best friends from way before any of us were born. In fact, Rochel Leah went straight from camp to Woodlake to stay with Zehava's family instead of going back to Florida."

"Oh?"

"And, of course, I know Mimi from convention. And Mimi you don't forget. And, I feel like I know you too, Sara, because of Shuli and Blimi. And I was schmoozing before with some of the girls from New—"

"Oh, Sara, I am very sorry I take very long time," Gila suddenly appeared. She held out her arms for her baby. "The lines be very, very long. I owe you big apology..."

I did my best to reassure her that she did not cause me any inconvenience, while returning the baby to her outstretched arms. Then, taking my handbag, I made my way as quickly as possible to the restrooms. On my way, I brushed past Mimi and some of the other girls from our group who were bantering and laughing together. Mimi made sure to wish me a hearty "good-luck," while warning me about the lengthy wait.

Two long lines awaited me. Fortunately, Rivky Weiss was at the back of one of the lines and waved for me to join her. She was standing next to that mysterious girl with the deep blue eyes.

I felt completely disheveled as I came up to them. *My face must look all ruddy and full of sleep creases*. I knew my barrette had snapped off while I slept, causing my hair to be tousled and tangled.

"Hi, Sara. Mimi told me you've been sleeping like a log! You must feel great now. Me?" she laughed, "I didn't sleep a wink. I'm absolutely and totally zonked!"

I returned her smile warmly. "I *am* feeling much better now. Just a little bit of a mess," I tucked a few escaped strands of hair behind my ears and tried futilely to smooth out the creases in my skirt.

Uneasily, my gaze shifted to the girl standing alongside Rivky. She was wearing a pleated black and white checked skirt, with a white matching cotton knit sweater, trimmed with the same black and white checked material. Her dark hair was neatly tucked behind her ears, curving perfectly at the bottom. A delicate gold chain with a heart-shaped locket hung from her neck.

Next to her, Rivky, just a couple of inches shorter, looked small and undersized, and seemed an indistinct figure in the crowd queuing up. The girl, on the other hand, despite her unsmiling countenance, with her chin raised proudly, stood out, looking tall and graceful among the others.

"Oh, let me introduce you two, after all, we are all going to be together for a whole year in M.B.L.L.," Rivky said. "Adina, this is Sara Hirsh. She's from Rolland Heights. And, Sara," she turned to me, "this is Adina Stern. Adina lives in Ballington, but is originally from England."

That's interesting. Ballington was in Rolland County and not far from Rolland Heights. I knew most of the girls from Beis Yaakov of Ballington, as our schools often got together for trips and other activities. *So why doesn't Adina Stern look familiar to me?* I wondered. I could have asked if she knew some of the girls that I was friendly with. That would have been a great way to make conversation, but, of course, all I could mumble was a shy, "Hi."

She stared at me icily.

"Um…er…Is this the first time you're going to Eretz Yisrael?"

"No." The word was spoken with a distinctively British accent.

"Oh, so you've been there before."

"Obviously."

"Huh?" My eyes widened in surprise at her abruptness.

"If it's not the first time I'm going there, then I must have been there before."

"Oh!" I could not hide the astonishment in my voice.

Dumbstruck, I turned toward Rivky, but, she was already chatting with another girl and apparently had not heard my attempt at conversation and Adina's frosty response.

Thinking of how Mimi had ignored my initial coldness and how lonely I had been until she and Rivky had befriended me, I decided to try again.

"Uh…did you enjoy the flight?"

"Not especially." She said this while looking past me, or through me, as though I was not there.

Neither of us spoke as we slowly moved ahead and the line gradually shortened. I wished she would say something to me. Here we were waiting in the same line, going to the same destination, and we could not seem to get any sort of conversation started. *And it wasn't as though I hadn't tried!*

Observing Adina Stern from the corner of my eye, I was certain that there was something much deeper than the unexplainable magnetism that she possessed. On the one hand, she seemed so self-assured and secure, and on the other hand, I sensed a certain vulnerability about her. Yes, there was something mysterious about her lurking deep below the surface and I found myself intensely curious to discover what it was.

I shifted my feet uncomfortably. I felt I *had* to break the silence.

"Do you know who you'll be rooming with?"

"No one does," she replied indifferently.

"You're right," I said forcing a grin. "We're supposed to find out when we get there."

Silence.

"I wonder how they'll do it."

Again, no comment.

I should have taken the hint, but I was not one to give up so easily, and besides, there was that compelling force about her that made me want to get her to like me.

I tried thinking of something interesting to say. *What could I ask her that would be halfway intelligent and not seem intrusive? Oh, I know what,* I thought. *I'll ask her if she knows Henny Shapiro from Ballington...*

Then, abruptly, it was her turn for the restroom. I must admit, I breathed a sigh of relief. I had felt a discernible tension in the air that evaporated as soon as she closed the folding door.

When Adina emerged, it was my turn. As we passed each other, I nodded and tried giving her what I imagined to be a warm smile. She did not even acknowledge my presence.

That's it, I'm not going to think about that girl...that Adina Stern!

I washed my hands and splashed the cold water on my face, studying my reflection in the mirror. There were only a few sleep creases on my left cheek. I rubbed them, hoping to make them disappear.

I removed my cosmetic bag and took out my toothbrush and toothpaste and began to brush my teeth. *She really is a strange girl*, I thought, recalling Adina's blue eyes as I peered at my own brown ones. *She certainly has some sort of chip on her shoulder, but what in the world does she have against me?*

Turning off the faucet, I grabbed my hairbrush, and bending my head toward the floor, removed the barrette and let my hair tumble loosely downward. I began to brush my hair vigorously. *She is probably like this to everybody and not just to me.* As my mother always told us, "If you do everything you can to be kind to someone and treat them well, and yet they still do not seem to get along with you, then you should assume that they are this way to everyone."

Oh, Mommy, I miss you so!

Feeling the tears welling up, I flipped my hair back and began to sweep it into a ponytail. I forced my lips to smile as widely as they could go at my reflection until my cheeks hurt. Satisfied that I did not look utterly homesick, I closed my barrette.

Still, my thoughts wandered back to Adina. *She obviously spoke to Rivky...and I was certainly trying to be friendly. What did I do to antagonize her?*

Someone was pounding on the door and telling me that they did not have all day and would I kindly hurry up. I quickly gathered my things, stuffed them into my pocketbook, swung open the door, and muttering a quick and embarrassed apology, hurried down the aisle.

Approaching my seat, I saw Mimi laughing together with the three girls who sat in front of us and two of the girls from the seats behind ours. As I came closer, Mimi looked up and waved a hearty welcome. Some of the others waved as well. I felt a warmth enveloping me and I returned their greeting, lingering a few minutes in the aisle to join in their conversation.

It was not as if my shyness had left me. It was just that because I was seated next to Mimi—she had sort of taken me under her wing. As I was learning, Mimi could charm anyone, me included. She had not allowed my reticent personality to get in the way. And, since I really did want to make friends, I allowed myself to be led in her direction.

The "no smoking" and "fasten seatbelt" signs lit up as the pilot announced we would be landing shortly. The stewardess ushered us into our seats.

Sitting down, I felt refreshed and invigorated. I looked at Gila, who was peering expectantly out of the window. She was returning home to the welcoming arms of her family. For a fleeting moment, I envied her. Then I caught Mimi's eye. Again, that same dark look I had seen a few hours earlier stole across her face. As swiftly as it had appeared, it vanished, almost as if it had never been there. Once more, I thought I must have imagined it. We smiled at each other with mutual anticipation knowing that "our year" was about to begin.

Everything is going to turn out all right, I told myself. *I just know it. It has to!*

The plane had begun its gradual decent, yet all at once it seemed to take a sudden, steep plunge toward earth.

I peered out of Gila's window with Mimi looking over my shoulder.

The sparkling blue Mediterranean Sea lay slanted below us, turning quickly into sand. We watched as the landscape became a dirty white. Gila explained that it was the metropolis of Tel Aviv. It then speedily turned a verdant green. And then, all of a sudden, Ben Gurion Airport was in full view.

As we approached the runway, I could see the modest terminal surrounded by date palms and lush greenery. It certainly was different from the JFK Airport where we had most recently landed and even from the unassuming Abraham Lincoln Memorial Airport of Rolland County.

The singing of "*Heveinu Shalom Aleichem*" was heard through the loudspeakers with some of the passengers joining in. I felt as if I would burst. Mimi was squeezing my wrist. I glanced at her and saw that she too was overcome with anticipation. We had arrived!

At last, the plane came to a full stop.

I do not remember gathering my things together nor if I had said goodbye to Gila and Uri. I do recall, however, emerging onto the metal staircase, leading to the buses that would drive us to the terminal.

I felt a gust of warm, Mediterranean air lift up my hair. I looked around at the palm trees and the clear, blue morning sky. *We're in Israel*, I told myself, *Eretz Yisrael, our home!*

I took a deep breath. *But*, I wondered, *is this home? Am I really…home?*

5

Bs"d
5 Tishrei

Dear All, *a"mush*

Hi! How are you? Thanks a million for all your letters. I'm sorry that all my other letters to you were so short, and I apologize for writing to all of you together instead of individually, but I've been so busy and it's much easier to write one big letter than a bunch of separate ones. Besides, I know you guys. As soon as you finish reading one letter, you'll all be switching with each other and sharing whatever I wrote. At least, that's what we did last year, Shuli, with the letters you sent us.

Anyway, I can't believe that almost one whole month passed and I'm actually still here! It's true that I was extremely homesick in the beginning. Ma, when I unpacked my suitcase and found your letter to me at the bottom, I couldn't help it. I burst into tears!

I'm sure my roommate thought I was foolish, but right then, I didn't care. (And just then Mimi—that's the girl I told you about, remember, the one who was very nice to me on the airplane—just then, she burst into our room through the "*netilas yadayim* closet" to borrow something. That's our nickname for the tiny little room—it's really the size of a closet!—which we share with the girls from the room next door. It has a sink for washing up and brushing teeth, and shelves for our toothbrushes and things. I guess they built the dorm this way in order to avoid having to put a sink in each room. I'm sure glad they did because most of the time we leave our doors to this little wash-up closet unlocked and use it as a shortcut to go to the adjoining room. It's more fun this way since then it feels like we have one big room, instead of two smaller ones—Shuli will explain.

She saw me and put her arm around my shoulder. I really felt connected to her then. I can't believe that at the beginning I resented her so much for taking Chavie's place. I'm really so happy to have her next door. Of course, I would much rather have Chavie, but I realize that what I can't change, I can't change. But, who knows? Maybe, someone from here will leave and then hopefully Chavie will be able to come after *Sheva Berachos* are over... Okay, I know, wishful thinking on my part. But, can you blame me? Besides, it REALLY is possible that someone will leave for some reason or another and Chavie will be able to come... right?)

Out of the four of us (the two of us that room together and the two girls in the adjoining room), unbelievably, I'm probably the closest to my Israeli roommate, Mazal Cohen. Even though we grew up in totally different countries, and she is of Yemenite descent (both her parents were very young children and came during Operation Magic Carpet), we get along quite well. Mazal is not shy and quiet like me, but she is not especially talkative, either. She is a very nice girl. It took a little while for us to get used to each other, her being Israeli (typical "sabra" type, if you know what I mean) and me American. But you know, when you get to really know someone, you realize you're all really very much the same. Anyway, she has much more experience than I do with dorm life (especially since I never went to sleepaway camp, either). So, *b"h* I'm really happy with my roommate. We do a lot of studying together. (TONS!) She understands and speaks English perfectly, well ALMOST perfectly. Of course, she still has an accent. She begged me to correct her whenever she makes a mistake while speaking English. So, I made a deal with her. I'll correct her English if she corrects my Hebrew. I'm hoping that this way I'll really become an expert in speaking Ivrit and that it'll help me when I *iy"h* become a Limudei Kodesh teacher.

Shuli, you might remember Mazal from last year. Dark kinky hair, dark face, on the short side and skinny. She was on a

> different floor than you and she was not part of Rabbi Grossman's Sem program then, but was in the high school of Beit Yaakov HaNegbah and roomed with the other Israelis who dormed. Well anyway, she sure remembers you! (As if it's possible not to!)

Mazal is not the only one who remembers you, Shuli, I smiled to myself.

I was sitting cross-legged on my bed, my back supported comfortably against my plump pillow, which was propped up against the headboard. Engaged in one of my favorite activities, letter writing, I was using the hard back of one of my loose-leafs to support my stationery. Sharing my recent experiences with my family helped me feel as though they were not so far away.

Not so far away?

Well, if I survived the first month, I told myself, then surely I could survive another nine. *Surely.*

I let out a long sigh. Yes, those first few days had been especially challenging for me.

Closing my eyes, I leaned back against my pillow, remembering the day we arrived...

I was too bewildered to focus on details, and despite the excitement, I must have dozed off for a short while after we left the airport. When I opened my eyes I knew we were nearing our destination, for the landscape was drier and sandier than it had been when we left Lod. I remembered Shuli's description of the M.B.L.L. campus and how there were desert areas nearby. My heart quickened. *We're almost there!*

Suddenly, Chani Frankel screamed out alarmingly, "Arabs!"

Some of the other girls leaned toward her window. I craned my neck in that direction too.

"It's only Bedouins," Rochel Leah told her knowingly.

"Ooh, look. Camels and sheep!"

"Wow! It looks like in the time of Avraham *Avinu!*"

"Hey, I didn't know you were around then," Mimi joked. Everyone laughed.

All at once, the mini-bus made a sharp turn, unexpectedly hurling those of us who had been peering out of Chani's window to the other side of the vehicle. We quickly resettled ourselves, giggling nervously. Only a minute or two passed when there was another sharp turn, this time flinging us in the opposite direction. I grasped the top of the seat in front of me tightly.

"Yikes!" Rivky yelped.

"He-e-elp!" I heard myself screech together with the others.

"Hold on for dear life!" Mimi sang out, clearly delighted, as we bounced up and down and the bus swerved unpredictably.

More laughter and jokes followed. It was remarkable that in so short a time a camaraderie of sorts had developed. It must have been the shared feeling of expectancy.

The surrounding desert mountains dotted with grazing sheep, tents, and camels seemed to fly by as our bus wended its way along the rough highway. Despite the sharp turns and bumpy roads, the atmosphere was thick with anticipation. And then, suddenly, we were there.

The minibus came to a halt in front of two huge gates, above which hung a large arched *Beruchim Ha-Ba'im LeBeit Yaakov HaNegbah* sign. Our driver exited the bus and was greeted by a smiling elderly man wearing a uniform. After they exchanged a few words, our driver returned to the bus and the guard unlocked the gates, allowing us to proceed. We were driven over a gravel road shaded by palm trees directly to the courtyard of what I was soon to find out was the main school building. I could hear the tires crunching as they rolled over the pebbles. I could also hear (and hoped no one else heard) the loud rhythmic beating of my heart.

From the window, I saw a large crowd of girls gathered in front of the building. As the bus approached, they turned to one another excitedly, pointing in our direction. I noticed some girls run inside the building—I assume to announce our arrival to others. More girls soon emerged, joining the first group outside.

I was taken aback seeing a modern building after our ride through the desert. It was a stone building, four stories tall, and seemed to be circular in shape—at least that is how it appeared to me just then.

A petite, dark-skinned woman emerged through the doorway. The hair on her short, but stylish wig was so dark—almost black—and so shiny, that the sunlight reflected off it. The girls respectfully moved aside as she walked down the path and made her way onto the bus. From closer up, I noticed that she was even darker than I thought, with eyes as black as coal. That is why I was astonished to hear her speak to us in flawless English. She seemed to be a *Yemenite* Israeli and I braced myself to understand the heavily accented *Ivrit* I anticipated would emerge from her mouth. And so, when she spoke I was not only pleasantly surprised, but relieved as well. She introduced herself as the *eim ha-bayit,* housemother—Geveret Esther Katz.

We would be eating lunch in the main auditorium instead of the dormitory's dining room because the high school girls wished to welcome the seminary girls, as well as the high school's foreigners and out-of-towners. We were not the only ones arriving that Thursday; the European girls had arrived a few hours earlier. Two girls from Australia and three from South Africa would be arriving a little later in the day. The out-of-town Israelis had come on Wednesday.

Geveret Katz assured us that our luggage would be brought to the dorm and said we should proceed to the main auditorium for lunch.

Exiting the bus, I felt dazed. The air was hot and I was overcome with exhaustion. A wave of homesickness came crashing down upon me. Most of the girls surrounding us were babbling in rapid *Ivrit*—it almost sounded to me like a different language, certainly not like the Hebrew I knew. The hot sun felt strong beating down on our bare heads, but with the air so dry…it seemed so…so unfamiliar.

I blinked away the tears that threatened and tried to stand tall, straightening my back. However, my hand luggage was weighing down heavily on one shoulder and my pocket book was on my other one. Without paying much attention to what I was doing, I kept switching my hand luggage from one shoulder to the other.

Before I knew what was happening, one of the nearby Israeli girls grabbed my heavy hand-luggage and was leading me toward the building. She was smaller than me and thinner too but somehow she easily swung the strap of the heavy carry-on across her shoulder with a swiftness that surprised me. I could hardly keep up with her as she made her way through the entrance and I found myself breathlessly trailing her. I noticed her friends doing the same for the other newcomers. Adina looked slightly uncomfortable, but relieved to have the help as she followed the Israeli girl who had come to her aid. Two girls were helping Rochel Leah carry her bags. I could see Mimi speaking with a mixture of Hebrew, English, and hand motions to a few girls who were at her side. They were laughing at her pantomimes and so was she, as she walked burden-free into the auditorium, her guitar held proudly by one of the Israeli girls.

A delicious smell permeated the room when we entered, so that despite my nervousness, I knew I would have no trouble eating this time. The high school girls, giggling and whispering to each other, served us. There was cooked chicken mixed with eggplant, mashed potatoes wrapped in dough—their version of a potato knish, I guess, loads of vegetable salad—Israeli style, tall pitchers filled with hot tea and bottles of grapefruit juice on the tables. It felt rather strange eating a meat meal during the late morning hours, but I really was famished by then and ate most of what was served.

There was a choir performance by the tenth graders. They sang *"Baruch HaBa BeShem Hashem"* and two or three other renditions that I do not remember.

I sat between Rivky Weiss and a girl from France. We had to speak in Hebrew. I knew a bit of French from school and tried it out, glad that I finally had a use for it, as Madame Pumeter, our French teacher, had promised would happen some day. The girl was soft-spoken, but had a quick smile. I felt excited at the prospect of making friends with someone from so far away.

Her name was Ruti Katzenstein, and she told me that she was in twelfth grade and that it was her second year in Beit Yaakov HaNegbah. I asked her if she knew my sister, Shuli Hirsch, and of course, she enthusiastically said that she did.

"I room ze year before vit Shalva Breiger," she told me in a combination of French, broken English, and Hebrew, "and she *chaveirah tovah* vit Shuli."

I felt frustration creep in. *She'll also be disappointed to find out that I am not like Shuli.* It upset me when everyone expected me to be Shuli.

I loved my sister dearly, but I did not want to be forced to step into her shoes. Her shoes, after all, would never fit someone like me.

Chapter 5

I continued to play with my eggplant. Stabbing it with my fork, I thought hopelessly, *we are so different.*

"You are so different."

I looked up, surprised.

Continuing with her French, Hebrew, and broken English, she explained, "I remember ze last year, Shuli, she come in. She valk around vit her plate of food, talking to everyone." Her smile widened. "She see me by myself. She come over, talk to me…"

My feelings of inadequacy turned to pride. *Yes, that's my sister, Shuli.*

And then she said something that really elevated me.

"You know. You very different, but, bot much kind. You also sit next to me and talk. I like you too."

I smiled at her. She was blunt, but sweet and I too liked her.

Yes, my dear, Shuli. I opened my eyes and reread the last few sentences of my letter. *Everyone sure does remember you. How can they not? Oh, Shuli. I miss you and wish you were with me!*

With a deep sigh that encompassed so many different emotions, I continued to write.

> The two girls in the adjoining room (the rooms are so tiny, it's like one big room) are quite different from us — but, even very different from each other. Mimi, as I told you, is super friendly and super talented, but does not have a studious bone in her body. She just wants to have fun! Mazal thinks she is adorable and is crazy over her. (So is everyone else! Yours truly, included.) The other girl (who I think I mentioned is originally from England), the one I told you I'm trying to become friendly with, prefers to study by herself. She must be a genius though, because every time a teacher asks her a question, she always gets the answer right. I don't know how she does it! I study all day and half the night (Okay, a quarter of the night. Ma, don't worry, I do get to sleep), and *b"h*, I am doing well, but I have to work so hard! And, Adina, that's the other girl, Mimi's roommate, just seems to know it all like a walking encyclopedia.
>
> I don't know how someone as brilliant as she is will be able to teach others. I wonder if someone who grasps everything so

> quickly would have a difficult time understanding that most people are not like that?
>
> Who knows? As Rabbi Grossman told us, even though he hopes we will all be teachers, not everyone who graduates from M.B.L.L. goes into teaching. He stressed that as mothers, *b'ezras Hashem*, we will ALL be teachers to our own children, and that if we don't end up in front of a classroom, we shouldn't be disappointed. The important thing is for us to recognize our strengths. You're right, Shuli, he's absolutely fantabulous! I feel like he (and the other teachers) really, really care about us and that they aren't trying to force us into some kind of mold, even though this is a Sem that concentrates on training us to become teachers. They want to help us each grow in our own particular way to fulfill our individual potential. (More about that in the next letter.)
>
> By the way, Rabbi Grossman hasn't yet mentioned anything about the Goldstone Award or about that huge report that you (Shuli) mentioned. Rumor has it that sometime this week he's going to be introducing us to it. Anyway—it's not like it's the main reason we're all here. The most important thing to me is that I get everything I can out of M.B.L.L. to become the best teacher I can be.

I paused and bit down hard on the top of my pen. *Did I sound too desperate? Did I give myself away?* I reread what I had just written to assure myself that I had not revealed my true feelings regarding the Goldstone Outstanding Student Teacher Award and how much it really meant to me. Satisfied, I continued to write:

> Let's see. I told you a little about dorm life, my roommates, and school, and I still have tons more to write!

I put my pen down for a moment to collect my thoughts. There was so much to tell...so much to share. How much I missed them all! Distractedly, I looked across the room to where Mazal sat by her desk doing her homework. Through the window above the desk, I could see silhouettes of the desert mountains.

I sighed contentedly.

Chapter 5

Bubby, I wish you were still alive and I could thank you for giving me this wonderful experience.

I was happy with my roommate. True, we were not as close as other roommates were. After all, she was Israeli and I, American. But, we got along fine. We liked keeping a neat room, were considerate of each other, and in general gave each other the space we each needed. Of course, it was sometimes lonely without a close friend, but most of the girls in the dorm were friendly and fun. It was never too difficult to find someone with whom to chat. The classes were excellent and I even enjoyed the food. On top of that, the most incredible scenery imaginable surrounded us.

There was so much for which to be grateful!

Nibbling on my pen, while deciding what to write about next, I found myself humming along with the familiar music playing in the background. Familiar, that is, to *me*. For Israelis at that time, tapes produced in America by Jewish recording studios with English lyrics were still somewhat of a novelty. After rooming with Mazal for nearly a month, I knew she took great pleasure in listening to songs composed with religious themes sung by American singers in a mixture of Hebrew and English.

Adjusting my papers, I took my pen in my hand once again and, after rereading my last sentence, continued to write.

> I can't believe I almost forgot to tell you about Rosh Hashanah. Truthfully, I didn't know if I would be able to survive a Yom Tov without you all. But, b"H I did. Can you believe it? I actually survived. I went with Mimi Rosenberg, Rivky Weiss, and Malkie Green to Geveret Spitz. It was phenomenal! She's a super-special person and a fabulous teacher. We only had a few of her classes before Yom Tov and I can't wait till the next class. This is her first year teaching at M.B.L.L. and I think she's here only for this year. Even though she hadn't really settled into her cottage yet, she still had us as guests. We tried to help as much as we could, but she is so organized, there really wasn't that much for us to do.
>
> Oh, by the way, Geveret Spitz is not the only new member of the M.B.L.L. staff this year. Geveret Katz, the *eim habayis* is also here for the first time, but in her case I think she's here to stay, at

least for a while. Her husband learns in the *kollel* at Beit Midrash Amsdorf. Anyway, I must admit that I was so relieved, although quite surprised, to hear her speak English so perfectly. Believe it or not, even though she is a Yemenite Israeli, her family lived in America throughout her elementary and high school years and she went to school somewhere in California.

Okay, back to what I've been doing. This past Shabbos—*Shabbos Shuvah*, we spent in Yerushalayim—in the Old City. We heard an incredible, or to be more precise, AMAZINGLY FANTABULOUS (that was for you, Shuli!) *Shabbos Shuvah* drasha from HaRav Tzvi Chaim David, the *Rosh Yeshivah* of Mayim Chaim. We *davened Minchah* and *Kabbalas Shabbos* by the Kosel. It was fantastic! I put in a special *kvittel* for you, Shuli, that you should find your *chasan* very soon and succeed with your class.

By the way, Shuli, what's this you wrote? I can't believe you're thinking of quitting! Don't do that—even if your class is giving you a hard time. Please don't give up. Try to zone in on the girl who's the main mischief maker. There must be a reason why she keeps making trouble. I think you need to find out why she's clowning around. That may be the way to getting your class under control, but whatever you do, Shuli, please don't quit! I know you're really a great teacher! It's way too early to give up. You only started a few weeks ago. You have to give it a chance!

How are your friends enjoying their first year as part of the real world? I was thrilled to hear about Zeesy becoming a *kallah*. Wow! You were probably in total shock! *Mazal tov* and *im yirtzeh Hashem* by you, Shuli!

THIS NEXT PART IS PRIVATE FOR CHEVY:

Chev, don't be so upset about the way they divided up the classes and that they didn't put you with your friend, Shoshana. I know that sometimes the girls can be cliquey, but, you'll see—those girls are usually the most insecure. You go right ahead and be friendly with the other girls. You know, the quiet ones (like yours truly). They might not be as popular, but if you become their friend, then you'll have your own little group. I know that with your friendly and warm personality, all the other cliques are going to want to join yours and soon your circle of friends will be the most popular. I bet, Chevy, you'll get the whole class into one big happy group!

Keep writing, Chevy, and let me know how everything is progressing. Also, did Miss Weinstein announce tryouts for the production, yet? Did she say what the name of it would be? I think you should try out for choir. They don't usually take "freshies" in acting roles, but then again, you are a terrific actress—and when Shuli was in ninth grade she made it into acting, so you never know. Whatever the case is, don't feel let down if you don't end up with the part you want. I remember when we were in ninth grade and Chavie was desperate to be in dance and didn't get in (they only took two "freshies" from the whole ninth grade), she offered to do anything to be part of the production. Do you know what happened? Miss Weinstein was so impressed with her attitude that when she needed someone to take over one of the main parts because that girl (a junior!) got sick, guess who she gave the part to? That's right, Chava Esther Hershkowitz. And, as you know, she starred in the school plays after that each year and was head of drama in twelfth grade. So, you see, it's the attitude that counts.

Like I once read in a book I used for writing a report on body language, our bodies often "speak" their own language. We don't always have to say things to send people a message. Sometimes, we are speaking just by the way we project ourselves. So, keep smiling your gorgeous smile, Chev, and I'm sure you'll be successful with the clique problem in your class and with tryouts, as well.

OKAY, BACK TO EVERYONE ELSE.

I'm so glad that Sruly is gaining so much from yeshivah. I know that he won't read this letter until he comes home for Succos, so I'll write him separately.

Moshe, I found a great present that I can't wait to send to you for Chanukah. Thanks for your short note in the last letter. It was fun reading a letter written in a maze. I kept turning it around in all directions as I was reading. My friends thought it was hysterical. (Not what you wrote. Of course, I would never ever show that to them. It's the fact that you wrote in the form of a maze that "amazed" them. That's not my joke, it's Mimi's. When she saw me turning the letter in all different directions, she asked me what

> I was doing. When I explained, she said, "Wow, a maze. How amazing!" I thought you would like that one.) Anyway, thanks loads, I really appreciate it. But, next time—please don't write during Mr. Fischel's English class. I wouldn't want you to get into trouble because of me.

With a long, drawn out yawn, I stretched my arms and legs as far as I could reach. Then with my pen clenched between my teeth I flipped over onto my stomach. Leaning on my elbow with my chin cupped in the palm of one hand, I used my free arm to set the loose-leaf down on the bed with the stationery on top of it. My legs were swinging casually in the air, moving in rhythm to the beat of the music. Humming along softly, I adjusted the paper I was writing on and continued with my unfinished letter.

> By the way, before I forget. You asked if I need anything. If you can send more music tapes, my roommate (and I) will be forever grateful. She especially enjoys the ones with the English lyrics.
> Thanks a million, Abba, for that *d'var Torah* you cut out from the newspaper. It was great and it fits perfectly with the report I need to submit next week. Abba, I don't know how you always know exactly what I need.
> Mommy, again thanks for everything. I love reading your long letters. I miss being able to talk to you whenever I need your advice. I know how expensive these phone calls are, and I really appreciate Abba and you agreeing to allow our once a month telephone calls. It was great speaking to you on *Erev Rosh Hashanah*, even if it was for such a short time. I can't wait till *Rosh Chodesh* Cheshvan to speak with you again.
> Please don't worry about me. I'm really glad that I came—I already feel like I'm gaining so much! I have both of you, Abba and Mommy, and of course Bubby to thank for this wonderful opportunity. So thanks again for EVERYTHING!
> Anyway, I can't believe that Yom Kippur is in less than five days, and then before you know it, Succos will be here. Of course, I'm thrilled to be in Eretz Yisrael for the Yamim Tovim, but it

> sure won't be easy being without all of you, the greatest family in the world! I know, though, that Rabbi Grossman has many interesting plans for us, so it—

Just then, there was a firm knock at the door.

Mazal stopped singing and, still sitting at her desk by the window, swung around to see who was there.

I looked up. I still remember the pleasant surprise I felt when Adina entered the room.

That warm feeling quickly dissipated.

Till this day I can recall the exact thoughts that passed through my mind at that time. *The calm before the storm. We must have just experienced the proverbial calm before the storm.*

And I knew, without a doubt, that the storm that was brewing was about to unleash.

6

"OH, I BEG your pardon."

I was still comfortably sprawled out with my letter in hand as I smiled up at her with what I hoped was an easy-going expression of nonchalance. "Oh…h-hi, Adina…" my words tumbled out awkwardly while I shifted into a sitting position. "What's up? Do you need something?"

Her face darkened as she surveyed my bed, its various contents and me. "I assumed," her tone became chillier, "you would be studying. I wanted to ask about the Ramban we learned today. But," she added, glaring at the letter, "I can see you're busy doing *other* things."

"It's okay," I swung my feet onto the floor, setting my pen and papers aside. *Adina Stern wants me, Sara Hirsch, to help her with schoolwork?* I took a step forward. I must have had a silly grin on my face. "I was just writing a letter home. I can continue later."

"*Another* letter home?" Her blue eyes widened incredulously, her voice thick with sarcasm.

"Well…" I opened my mouth to explain to her in order to excuse myself. I knew she often observed me writing letters home in between classes and the disdainful look she had thrown my way had not gone unnoticed.

She looked at me coldly and then abruptly swung around and slammed the door behind her.

What in the world…? For a moment I stood open-mouthed, staring at the closed door, too stunned to move. The tape continued playing in the background, but to me its music had ceased to exist.

Turning quickly, I hoped Mazal had not seen my teary eyes. *Only nine more months to go till the end of the year!*

"Why, Sara?" Mazal had not moved from her desk and was still in a twisted position facing me. "What could be?"

"Huh?"

"What do you do to Adina to make her so full of anger at you?"

"What?" I looked at her, dazed.

"You know, she seem very upset."

"Me? Do something to upset her?" Slowly, I sat down on my bed, puzzled. *Why is Adina so angry with me?*

This was unlike anything I had ever experienced before. It was rare for me to be drawn into conflict. Due to my innate shyness new friendships did not come easily, but this served to protect me from involvement in the inevitable disagreements that those with more passionate natures tended to have.

Lifting my chin, I opened my mouth to say something to Mazal and then closed it.

"Something happen between you two. No?"

Slowly, I shook my head. "N-no. N-nothing happened."

Blinking, pretending to have something caught in my eye, I pulled a tissue from the box on my nightstand and wiped away the tears welling over. My homesickness for my loved ones thousands of miles away was difficult enough to bear. Must that lonely emptiness be compounded by the misery of knowing that Adina felt such aversion toward me? *And now, to top it off, Mazal wants to know what I did wrong?*

What did I do wrong?

The tape continued playing in the background. Its cheerful melody contrasted sharply with the uneasy stillness that lingered threateningly in the air from Adina's abrupt exit.

Mazal, however was not one to dwell on disturbing emotional conflicts. "So," she waved her hand easily through the air, "do not let it bother you."

Do not let it bother you? Right.

I sighed heavily. I could almost hear Shuli's voice warning me not to be so paranoid, imagining things. Chavie would undoubtedly tell me to stop analyzing and just get back to being my practical self. *Maybe, I am dwelling on this too much.*

And yet it was as clear as the blue sky outside of our window...Adina had something against me. *Didn't Mazal say as much a few moments earlier? It definitely wasn't my imagination!*

Again I questioned myself, *what have I done to hurt her?* Am I guilty of being too forthcoming? Admittedly, I wanted to be her friend, but not at the risk of alienating her. True, I was not a leader, but I was no follower either! And besides, I had my pride. I was not going to be so foolish as to pursue someone who had no interest in me. Certainly, I did not intend to go where I was not wanted.

Still...something about Adina continued beckoning to me.

Was it her magnetism, her charisma, or her brains? Sure, she was abundantly blessed with all that and more; nonetheless, I was certain that none of those attributes were causing me to long for a friendship that was one-sided. No, there was something else drawing me to her.

Besides, there had always been that obstinate streak. When faced with a challenge, I would not easily let go.

I looked across the room at Mazal. She must have accepted my silence as a desire to end the discusion, for she had turned back to her desk while I had been lost in my reverie.

I picked up my papers and pen from where I had flung them down on the bed and sat back down. *So why is Mazal blaming me?*

She probably regrets having mentioned anything in the first place. Surely she did not mean to blame me—she was just asking what happened. She probably would rather just let things be.

I, of course, could not *just let things be.*

Mazal didn't just ask me what happened. She said, "What did you do to make Adina so angry?" And that's what I would like to know. What did I do to make Adina so angry at me?

I coughed one or two times and then cleared my throat rather loudly.

Silence. Mazal continued scribbling vigorously, still hunched over her desk.

Again, I coughed, this time even louder than before. Again...no response.

"Mazal..." I said slowly.

She turned to face me. "*Kain?*" she asked in Hebrew. Then, realizing that she had inadvertently spoken to me in Hebrew, corrected herself, "Yes?"

Was the expression on her face impatience? I swallowed hard. "If only…"

She waited silently, an expectant look on her face.

"If only…"

"If only…what?"

"If only, I was able—to not let it bother me."

"So, do not let it," she shrugged her shoulders, as if to say, *so what's the big deal?*

"But, you saw how she walked in…and became upset. J-just like that."

"Maybe she have much else on her mind."

"She's so…so…she seems to get so…angry at me and I have no idea why," I rambled on. "I would have gladly stopped writing my letter to do the homework with her."

"For sure, she did not want bother you. Maybe, *b'emet*, she not upset. It probably just her way."

Right. Her way, especially when it comes to me. I did not express my thoughts aloud, though the piqued expression on my face must have given me away.

"Listen, Sara, you cannot be so—how you say it? So…sensitive. You cannot take everything everyone say so serious."

I looked at her, hurt.

Why is it that people are accused of being—that terrible word "sensitive"—if they try to figure out why people say what they say and then feel upset by it? What am I supposed to do, not care about the way others act? Pretend I have no emotions? Make believe others do not exist? Oh, why must I be this way, I lamented, *probably Mazal's right and I am being too sensitive.*

"I am *not* being sensitive," I asserted, a flicker of pride flaring up.

"Good. So, *ain be'ayah*. No problem, like you say in English." She began to turn back to her desk.

"But, I just wish…"

"Yes?" Mazal once again twisted around to face me, her lips

spreading into a knowing grin.

"I just wish…"

Mazal nodded encouragingly, her eyebrows lifting.

"That she wouldn't be such a ….such a…."

"*Nu?*"

"Such a…" I stopped in mid-sentence, uncertain of how to continue.

What words could I use to describe the way I thought Adina felt about me? Indifferent? Distant? *No,* I shook my head, *that's not exactly it.* At the beginning, she was completely apathetic. It was as though I was talking to an ice cube.

Yet, as time went on, I could sense a slight change. More than once, I would find her studying me with a mingling of mild curiosity and intense determination in her blue eyes. It was almost as if *she* were extending her hand toward me. I knew I could not have been imagining this. Then, as I would return her gaze warmly, her expression turned frigid and I could feel her assessing me, as though she could read my mind. Had I been under some illusion? Did she find it amusing that I would want to be her friend despite her frosty manner? Self-consciously I would turn away. I could feel myself blushing crimson and once again was mortified at how easily my innermost feelings revealed themselves to others. With quiet resolve I would vow to never again be misled into thinking that Adina Stern needed me…wanted me as a friend. I would not allow myself to be hurt anymore.

And then, a day or two later another incident would occur where once again I would feel as though Adina was turning to me, as if she was seeking someone she could open up to. And despite my resolution not to, my resolve would soften and I would reciprocate with sincerity and openness, to once more be met with her icy rejection.

No, it wasn't my imagination! Adina was truly reaching out to me, yet something held her back.

"It's as if she's…"

"She is…what?"

I had not realized that I had spoken my last thoughts aloud. *I really shouldn't be talking about Adina…but she just did it to me again! And besides—I miss my family so much and all this time I've had no one to open up to and Mazal's waiting and…*

"She's such a…"

"*Kain…* Yes?"

I hesitated again, and then before I could stop myself blurted out, "A door!"

"A…what?" She looked at me, incredulous, uncertain if she'd heard correctly.

"Door," I repeated, this time with a calm resolve.

"Door? You mean *delet*?"

I nodded vigorously, thinking that Mazal must wonder if all Americans are this strange. For a long moment her eyes held mine, catching the seriousness reflected in them.

Suddenly and simultaneously, we both burst out laughing.

"What in the world, like you *Americayim* say, are you talking about, Sara?" She was still laughing. "A door?"

It felt so wonderful to laugh. It was as though a huge boulder fell off my shoulder and yet I was hesitant. "I - I don't know if I should say…"

She looked at me with interest. "Yes?"

"I'm afraid you'll think I'm silly or—or as *you* Israelis say, *meshuga'at*."

"*Chalilah!*"

"Or *sensitive*," I remarked quietly, however I stressed *that* abominable word, intentionally failing to conceal the resentment in my voice.

"Oh, Sara." Placing her pen on her desk, her expression softening, Mazal pushed back her chair and came over to me. "I do not mean to make you feel bad. I just think you *Americayim* all take everything so…" she rubbed her fingers together searchingly and then with a pleased grin said, "to heart."

I let out a deep sigh of relief. *So, it's not just me, Sara Hirsch.* All of us Americans are "sensitive" and take things too much "to heart."

"So, nu? Tell me, Sara. What do you mean…a door?"

"Okay. But, remember, this is just between the two of us."

"*Betach*," Mazal assured me, and repeated, "of course."

"You see," I began, while pushing my back against the wall, making more room to accommodate Mazal, "sometimes, even though Adina is sitting right there next to me, it's as if she's in another room and I'm locked outside. It is sort of like...Adina herself is this closed door—with a "do not disturb" sign posted on her." I stopped suddenly, embarrassed. "I know, you think I'm crazy. I shouldn't have said anything."

"No, go on," she waved her hand, reassuringly. "This *is* interesting."

I was annoyed with myself for allowing my thoughts to slip so easily off my tongue. Nevertheless, once I began to verbalize that which I had not even been aware of, it was too late. I could not stop.

"Okay," I swallowed hard. "So, there's this "do not disturb" sign. Obviously, she'd rather stay to herself or maybe she's just not particularly interested in being friends." My pride prevented me from saying to Mazal *friends with me*. "Fine," I continued. "I can accept that. Not everyone hits it off with everyone else." I said that in a pretty self-assured tone, attempting to mask the hurt I felt quite keenly.

"*Nachon*. Right."

"But, then...when I don't expect it to happen, she suddenly seems to...want to open that door. I begin to think that she wants me to enter that room. It's as if she is opening the door ever so slightly, showing me that she wants me, yet, the "do not disturb" sign is still hanging there. Because I sense the door slightly ajar, I don't seem to notice the sign and I try to enter. Then, as my foot reaches just past the threshold, the door suddenly comes slamming closed on me."

Alarmed, I stopped talking. Although I had just written to my family that out of the four of us I was closest to Mazal, I did not quite feel *that* close. I could not believe that I had just revealed such private reflections.

"Wow!" Mazal finally said, her accent accentuating this typically American expression and thus making the word more endearing. "I am so happy you share your thoughts with me."

"You are?"

Mazal nodded her head vigorously, her dark curls bobbing up and down. "I did not know, you are that deep. You should be psycodiatrist."

"A what?"

"You know, a doctor for the head."

"You mean psychiatrist?"

"Yes...that is it. Maybe you should be a psychiatrist."

"Thanks."

"*B'emet*. Or maybe…how do you call it…a social counselor."

I looked at her blankly. "Oh, you mean a social worker?"

"Yes." Again, I saw that pleased grin I was beginning to recognize as Mazal's way of expressing delight at finding the correct English word.

I returned her smile. "Then you don't think I'm off-beat?"

"Off what?"

"Off-beat. That means…unusual, strange."

"No, strange you are not," she shook her head. "But, unusual…"

"You think I'm unusual?" My heart sank.

"*Betach*. Of course." Seeing my face drop, she quickly added, "We are all unusual."

"You mean none of us are the same? Everyone is different?"

"That is what I think," she nodded. "You know, it is not my first year living in the dorm. I can see that everyone is different. Everyone living together, each girl comes with…how you say it in America? With her own briefcase?"

"Baggage," I smiled, correcting her.

"Yes. Everyone comes with her own baggage. Each girl is different. Take it from me, an old handle at it—"

"Old hand at it," I commented, this time laughing aloud.

Thinking of doors, it happily dawned on me that one had just opened up…to a new deepened friendship between Mazal and me.

Putting her homework and my letter writing aside, we talked. I told Mazal about my dear parents, sisters, brothers, Chavie, and my dreams of becoming a teacher. I even hinted at my yearning to be the recipient of the Goldstone Outstanding Student Teacher Award.

"Not me," she waved her hand in the air. "I just dream of getting special Machon Beit Leah LeMorot teaching certificate."

She spoke to me about Kiryat Yosef, the *moshav* up North where she grew up and her wish to return and educate the children there. We turned the music back on, chatting happily while sharing hopes, potato chips (mine) and *biscuitim* (hers).

"And…Sara?" Mazal said while digging cheerfully into the bag of chips.

"Yes, Mazal?"

"I and my family very happy for you come and be our guest."

"And I very happy, I mean, *would be* very happy to visit your *moshav* and meet everybody," I smiled back at her.

I could almost have forgotten the unhappiness I had been experiencing, if it had not been for a slight feeling of foreboding. I tried to shake it off, when there was a sudden knock at the door.

Without waiting for our response, the door swung open. One of the Israeli girls, Tehilla Friedlander rushed in. She ran to Mazal and in rapid Hebrew informed her that she was wanted at once at Geveret Katz's office. Without a word, they both hurried out together.

I waited expectantly for them to return. Mazal came back about twenty minutes later and as I nervously watched her throw a few things into her suitcase, she breathlessly and tearfully explained that there was an emergency at home. Their grandmother who lived with her family had just been rushed to the hospital. Mazal must return immediately to the *moshav* to take care of her younger siblings.

I can still remember how foolish and guilty I felt as the door closed behind her. I had just been speaking about *my* problems and they seemed so minor in comparison to the situation awaiting her at home.

When classes began the next day and I took my seat beside Adina, she hardly glanced in my direction. For some reason, she seemed to resent my writing letters home and consequently I refrained from doing so during the breaks between classes. I told myself that Adina did not dislike *me*, and that *this was just her way*, as Mazal had said. I wanted to show her that I harbored no ill feelings toward her.

Throughout that day and the next, I made what I considered a superhuman effort to overlook Adina's coldness.

My efforts were in vain.

The more I pushed, the greater was her rebuff. Finally, uncharacteristic of my stubborn nature, I gave up, admitting defeat. I do not know if it was because of a lingering headache or the overwhelming feeling of loneliness I had been experiencing. But I do remember thinking that I had given Adina Stern my all and that since my all was apparently insufficient for her, *enough was enough*.

When afternoon classes ended on Tuesday, I turned down Mimi's offer to go to "town" with some of the other girls. "Town" was a fifteen-minute walk into the center of Kfar Amsdorf, where the shopping district was less than a block long. My head still hurt and I wanted to catch up on some work. The thought of spending at least a half-hour walking and another hour of action—with Mimi you always knew there was going to be action—made my aching head hurt even more.

I stopped off at Geveret Katz's office for some Tylenol and then at the dorm's kitchen for a glass of hot tea sweetened with honey before heading upstairs to my room.

For a short while, I sat at my desk attempting to complete my report. Slowly sipping tea, I searched through my *sefarim* for the necessary explanations. I stopped short. One of the questions baffled me. Abruptly, I put down my pen, stumped. *I should ask Mazal. She would understand it.*

Mazal.

Only two days had passed since I had shared my deepest thoughts with Mazal and she had departed so suddenly. I had been anxiously waiting to hear from her.

I pushed my chair back and stood up slowly. *It's no use! I can't concentrate anyway.*

Moving toward my bed, I sat down dejectedly. Using the opposite foot to push off each shoe, I removed one at a time, and slipped under my quilt while reaching for my letter writing material on my nightstand. Switching on the lamp above my bed, I adjusted my papers and settled myself more comfortably against my fluffy pillow leaning on the headboard for support.

As I wrote, I strove to camouflage my true emotions by portraying everything in a cheerful and buoyant manner. However, the more I tried sounding upbeat, the greater the loneliness inside me grew.

Sighing heavily, I sank back against my pillow feeling utterly sorry for myself.

Everyone else here seems to have someone. Rochel Leah and Zehava are together all the time and Chani Frankel doesn't seem to be too far away from them. Mimi and Rivky also have each other. And me? No Chavie to share all this with. No roommate…Adina's coldness…my wonderful family so far away… The tears trickled down my cheeks. *It's so unfair! Why can't things ever work out the right way for me?*

Squeezing my eyes shut tightly I snuggled deeply under my heavy down quilt, wanting to hide from the world—yet—unable to hide from my wandering thoughts. My newfound friend Mazal was not here. Next door, Mimi, although warm and friendly, bewildered me with the combination of her vivaciousness and laid-back manner on one hand, and a certain underlying mysterious quality about her that I could not quite put my finger on. Then there was Adina. Well, Adina certainly confused me. Adina.

Adina, the door.

And then, with a suddenness that I was unprepared for, it was truly as though a great big door to a huge room opened before *me*...and unexpectedly the fogginess surrounding me began to dissipate while everything became much clearer.

I sat up abruptly, and throwing my covers off, swung my feet onto the cold stone floor. I stepped over my warm, fluffy slippers and over my shoes. As I indifferently smoothed out the creases from my skirt, I hurried to the window, pulling the *trisim* open all the way.

The golden light of the late afternoon sun was still surprisingly strong. It would slip behind the surrounding mountains quite soon, I knew, and I held my breath observing it cast its vivid hues of lilac and crimson across the mauve sky.

I have no idea how long I stood there, but as I looked out of my window while day turned into night, a shiver ran through me and I caught my breath in wonder. Watching the setting sun make its grand exit, dipping behind the desert's mountains, I could see the moon rise in greeting, illuminating the now darkened sky.

And all at once, I understood.

Aren't we all like that? Isn't every individual person similar to a door? Secreted behind the façade that we all see, isn't there something else, something deeper concealed from those on the outside?

Why does Adina slowly open her door to me, then slam it closed before I can enter? And Mimi? Mimi appeared to keep her door opened all the time, as if there was a "Welcome, please enter" sign on it. Yet, I sensed it was as if that door was a sham and that the real Mimi was hidden deep behind some secret locked door that stood behind the false one.

And, the keys to these doors, the keys that would open them...where were they? Did I want to find them? Did I really care?

I told myself that it was not my concern, that their lives were their own and that they had nothing to do with me. I knew I was there as a teacher-in-training and to realize my dream to be this year's recipient of the Goldstone Outstanding Student Teacher Award. *There's only slightly more than nine months left until the end of the year. Let their secrets stay locked behind their closed doors. I'm not interested, and besides, their lives really have nothing to do with me!*

No, nothing at all, I reassured myself.

Of course, I could not know it then, but like the ripples that form as soon as one single pebble is tossed into the ocean, spreading to the very depths of the ocean bed, no one can remain unaffected by others.

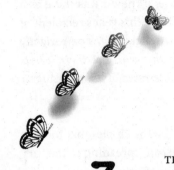

7

THE TRANQUIL SEA spread out before me, its turquoise waters clear. I was lying on a small inflatable raft, drifting along, my legs dangling over its sides, my toes tickled by the coolness of the soothing water. Rocked back and forth by the gentle waves, I felt myself leisurely and rhythmically lifted up and down, up and down while the strong Mediterranean sun warmed me.

"Sa-ra!" A voice called to me from the distance.

With my eyes closed contentedly, I remained in my sprawled position, pretending not to hear anything.

"Sara…" The voice still sounded far away.

Ignoring whoever was calling me, I calmly turned over onto my stomach, feeling the sun's warm rays soothingly massaging my back.

"Sara…Yoo-hoo, Sara, are you there?" The voice was slowly getting louder as the current gradually moved the raft toward shore or rather me—to reality.

I buried my head under my plump pillow.

"He-llo! Sa-ra Hirsch, don't you hear me?"

Go away, voice! I pulled the cover over my pillow. It was so nice and warm under my comfortable feathered quilt. *Ahh…If I could just continue peacefully floating along…*

"Sara," the voice came closer, "do you have an extra white blouse I could borrow? SARA!" This time I heard her loud and clear, she was practically shouting in my ear while simultaneously shaking me, "YOU'RE STILL SLEEPING!"

Chapter 7

Throwing my covers to the side of my bed I stood up abruptly, stretching. Brilliant sunshine streamed into the room.

"Oh my goodness, Mimi, I can't believe it!" Groggily, I peered at the clock on my nightstand and saw it read 7:41 a.m. "Yikes, I'm so late!"

"You sure are late." Smiling broadly, she sang, "Mimi to the rescue!"

I mumbled *Modeh Ani* quickly and ran to the sink to wash my hands. Splashing cold water on my face, I shook my head and reiterated, "I can't believe I overslept!"

"So, could I borrow your white blouse?"

"I probably didn't hear the alarm clock ring. I must've pressed the off button while half asleep without even realizing it."

"Sara...hel-lo?"

I blinked.

Mimi stood with hands on hips, completely dressed minus her white blouse. In its place, she wore the huge rumpled green sweatshirt that she had slept in the night before.

"Oh sorry, Mimi, you want to borrow my blouse...again?"

"It's a good thing I came in to wake you up, Sara. Anyway, I wanted to know if I could use one of your white blouses. I didn't get a chance to do a wash yet."

I hurriedly pulled my skirt on under my nightgown as Mimi spoke, not wanting to waste any more time.

We were required to wear white blouses and navy blue pleated skirts. Most of us brought enough blouses to last for a week. I was sure Mimi brought enough blouses with her. So why was this the third time she was asking to use one of mine?

I looked in my closet and saw that two white blouses remained. I reached for the one I wanted to wear.

"I had been hoping to put off doing laundry until after Yom Kippur, Mimi..."

"Please, Sara, what will I do now?" A shadow stole across Mimi's face, and then a moment later it passed and she was back to her cheerful self. "You know I can't exactly ask Adina. And besides," her green eyes twinkled mischievously, "if I wouldn't have come into your room now and woken you up, Sara, you probably would have slept through all of the morning classes."

"Oh, all right, Mimi," I nervously glanced at the clock as I handed the blouse to her. "Take this one. I'll wear the one that's left. We'd better get going or else we'll—"

"Thanks, Sara, you're a doll!" She grabbed the blouse and ran through the wash-up passageway to her room. "You're a true friend!"

"Really, Mimi," I called back, "you shouldn't put off doing your laundry till the last minute. What if I hadn't been here?" I asked breathlessly while slipping into my shoes.

"But, you were. And you're right, I should've, but I just couldn't. I was so-o-o busy, I just didn't get a chance. Anyway, you're a great friend. I'm almost ready now, how about you? Meet you outside in a minute."

I ran a brush through my hair quickly and gathered it into a ponytail, then rinsed my hands once again. Snatching my pen and loose-leaf, and swinging the strap of my book bag over my shoulder, I rushed out of my room into the hallway. Mimi, her backpack in hand, swung her door closed just as I emerged.

"Adina asked me *to make sure to close the door whenever I exit the room*," she explained, mimicking Adina's British accent.

"You're impossible, Mimi," I shook my head trying to hide my smile.

She laughed aloud with pleasure.

We rushed down the two flights of stairs into the lounge, davened Shacharis and hurriedly made our way into the dining room. There were only three girls remaining. Two of the girls were *bentching* and the third was waiting for them to finish. We mumbled quick good-mornings. Still standing, I made a *shehakol*, gulped down a cup of juice, and stuffed a strawberry leben and a spoon into my book bag to eat later. Mimi smeared a biscuit with chocolate spread .

"Mimi, aren't you going to be hungry?" I asked her.

"Nah, Sara, this is delicious and I have a package of these absolutely terrific caramels to keep me going until lunchtime."

The other girls laughed and I grinned as well; then I reminded Mimi that we had better hurry.

"There goes my practical friend…"

I smiled at her, feeling warm and comfortable inside as we joined the others. Yes, if I could not have Chavie with me, at least I had someone as friendly and fun as Mimi.

I barely managed to slip into my seat next to Adina before Rabbi Grossman entered the classroom. I noticed the surprised look in her eyes when she saw me and knew that I must have appeared disheveled and disorganized rushing in so late.

"I didn't hear my alarm go off," I explained in a breathless whisper while opening my loose-leaf.

Of course, Adina did not respond. And, of course, I told myself that I would not attempt to talk to her again. Ever.

Why in the world did I—Sara Hirsch from Oakland Avenue in Rolland Heights—out of the thirty-something girls in this program have to end up sitting next to Adina Stern? I must have asked myself that question at least a hundred times in the last few weeks, though I knew the answer…

I had entered the classroom feeling very alone that first day, wondering where to sit or rather with whom to sit. *Chavie, oh Chavie, where are you when I need you?* I thought in desperation. There *they* were. *Rochel Leah and her shadow, Zehava.* Together. Naturally, the two of them slipped into seats next to each other. Rochel Leah was calling Chani Frankel to join her too.

Okay, I told myself, *throw back your shoulders, stand tall, take a deep breath, smile a wide smile, and pretend everything is great…just great.*

I smiled a very wide smile and lo and behold, there was Mimi looking at me, grinning and waving warmly with one hand and pointing to the adjacent desk with the other. *Great, this body language idea is really working. All I had to do was project a bit of confidence and Mimi wants me to sit next to her.* I felt flattered that she had singled me out when we had only met forty-eight hours earlier. I was heading in her direction, when all at once, a strange, uneasy feeling came over me.

Mimi's eyes seemed to focus past me over my shoulder.

"Thanks a million, Mimi," I heard Rivky Weiss call from behind. "I knew I could rely on you."

She came around me and put her notebook on the desk next to Mimi. I felt my face turn hot with shame and hoped with all my heart that no one had witnessed my humiliation.

I began to back away.

"Oh hi, Sara," Mimi suddenly noticed me. "Where are you sitting?"

She probably does not realize what happened, I breathed.

"Sara, how're you doing?" Rivky added while turning around and pointing to an empty seat behind her, "Sit behind us."

My stomach tightened. *Maybe they do realize what happened.*

"Um…" I glanced around the room, not wanting to appear desperate. Two seats back I saw Adina sitting by herself. Alone.

Impulsively, I went to where she sat. As shy as I was, when I saw someone who seemed lonelier than me, my own bashfulness would somehow melt away. "Is it okay if I sit here?" I asked Adina.

"Suit yourself."

"What?" I asked, taken aback.

"Yes…Sara?"

I looked up—abruptly returning to the present and away from that horrid first day. My heart skipped a beat. Rabbi Grossman was looking at me with raised eyebrows, "You had a question you wanted to ask me?"

"Oh, no," I shook my head. "I mean I'm sorry…n-no question."

"All right then…as I was saying," Rabbi Grossman continued in his deep voice, "now that the first month of school is over and you have all begun to experience what hard work *really* is…"

There was a soft murmur in the room. A few heads nodded vigorously.

"I would like to introduce a project with which many of you might already be familiar."

My pulse began racing. *He's going to speak about it now!*

"Each year, as a new group of wonderful girls enters Machon Beit Leah LeMorot, I feel humbled and awed by the responsibility of educating these *bnot chayil* to become successful educators. Girls," he paused, slowly looking up and down the rows of desks, studying each one of us individually. There was not a sound in the room and I am sure I was not the only one who felt that he was talking directly to her.

"Girls," he repeated while lifting his hat off the desk and casually fingering its rim, "you are about to embark on a journey, a journey where there will be constant growth taking place. You will be giving to others, but more importantly, you will be giving to yourselves, as well.

I looked around the room. Some girls sat contemplatively, chins resting on the palm of their hands, hanging onto every word he said, one or two nervously chewing the top of their pens, and a few enthusiastically scribbling notes, their gaze never leaving him. I wondered if they too dreamed of being the recipient of the award I so wanted.

"Therefore", Rabbi Grossman went on, "Machon Beit Leah LeMorot has developed a program that we believe will help all of you, and not just during your seminary year. We hope that it will be something for you to take with you into the future, something to serve as a foundation to build upon for the rest of your lives."

He's really going to speak about it now!

"Machon Beit Leah LeMorot has always been a teaching seminary. Every subject that is taught here is taught not only with the *hashkafot* that we hope you will internalize and grow from, but with an emphasis on teaching the subject to others. Presented along with the subject matter are motivational techniques, visual aids, behavior modification systems, and many other methods geared toward helping our students learn *how* to teach. This is the way we have been training our teachers for many years and, *baruch Hashem*, we have been very successful."

He looked around the room before continuing. "Around twenty, twenty-one years ago a very special woman, a relative of mine, in fact, approached me with a unique offer soon after her dear husband, my great-uncle, had left this world. First, though, let me give you some history.

"They had unfortunately never merited having children of their own, however, throughout their working years they were both completely devoted to the teaching profession. Although they remained childless, they felt as though their students were their own children and took incredible responsibility for their students' welfare."

He sighed deeply. I could tell that, although he probably made this same speech every year to each new crop of girls, it did not distance him emotionally from what he was telling us.

"A short time after my uncle's death, my aunt told me that the two of them had no complaints and were grateful for the opportunities they had to help so many children. When my uncle, Reb Zev Goldstone died, he was a content man who had felt fulfilled by completing his life's mission. My aunt, however, wanted to do something special to perpetuate her husband's good name. True, his life's work, the good deeds and *mitzvot* he did, the students he taught were his legacy, yet, it pained my aunt that his family's name would not endure.

"You see, he was the sole survivor of his entire extended family. Everyone else…his parents, siblings, aunt, uncles, and cousins perished in the Holocaust," Rabbi Grossman shook his head sadly, "therefore, she decided to do something about it."

As Rabbi Grossman spoke, he slowly paced up and down the aisles and I could clearly see the tears in his eyes when he passed my seat. I found his words fascinating and when I looked around the classroom, I sensed the others were captivated, as well.

"Throughout their long teaching careers they had always put aside a small percentage of their income and invested it in certain stocks. *Baruch Hashem*, that small percentage multiplied more than tenfold, and blessedly, over the years, it accumulated to quite a sizeable amount."

A low hum spread throughout the room.

"My aunt and uncle," Rabbi Grossman raised his voice an octave, bringing the mumbling to an abrupt halt, "felt that lying dormant within many young people are untapped reservoirs of talent to be outstanding educators," he continued, his tone returning to normal. "They believed that with proper training and strong motivation these dormant seeds of possibility would rise to the surface, flower, and bloom.

"So, my dear great aunt established The Zev Goldstone Outstanding Student Teacher Award, where the winners receive not only the prestige and the job offers that come along with the monetary award. The winner is also the recipient of special vouchers which enable her and the school of her choice to receive teaching equipment, materials, and supplies to supplement her lessons and help her students with their learning."

He allowed a few moments of silence to pass so we could digest everything he had just said. Though I had known most of what he told us, I could have sat fascinated for hours, wanting to hear more. Dreaming…

A hand went up.

"Yes…Devorah?"

Chapter 7

"How *do* you become a winner?"

"I'm glad you asked," he smiled. "I was just going to come to that. Throughout the year you will be giving model lessons, going to classes given by wonderful teachers…"

We heard a few snickers coming from a couple of seats in front of us.

"Yes, *wonderful* teachers," he emphasized, and I noticed him stare in Mimi's direction for a long moment before he went on. "You will participate in Shabbatot and Yamim Tovim with friends in the dorm, as well as in different people's homes. Sometime during the next few weeks Geveret Spitz will start requiring you to keep accurate observation reports that will be graded periodically. There are many other special experiences, assignments, and reports that you will *b'ezras Hashem* become familiar with throughout the year.

"The Goldstone Outstanding Student Teacher Award will be awarded to the girl who best combines all of this—" he indicated by opening one finger at a time, "the different events, the ideas, the trips, the lessons, the speeches, the classes, the student teaching etc.

"She must assemble it all," he lifted both arms in a gathering motion, "and organize everything she has learned. She must analyze and evaluate examples she witnessed in her different experiences. She should also include copies of tests she has taken and reports she has written and submitted throughout the year, along with the grades she received on them. She will be required to write research papers on various subjects, bringing proofs based upon her varied experiences. She will also, whenever possible, back it all up with Torah sources, some of which will be studied throughout the year. We want to see visual aids, innovative behavior modification systems, and other motivational techniques. Anything and everything that gets you, the teacher, to think and create and will help you and your students grow and learn.

"This will be structured into a final, formal exposition called the Goldstone *Proyect*, to be presented to the administration. The more conclusive and innovative, the better. In the past our wonderful students have chosen a specific *pasuk* that embodies the theme of their projects. They demonstrate to us how their various experiences throughout the year have helped them grow as individuals and as future teachers, why they picked their specific *pasuk*, and how they will make a difference in their students' lives. A teacher cannot be successful out there," he pointed his finger in the direction of the window, "without first feeling it in here." He touched his chest meaningfully. "That is why Machon Beit Leah LeMorot has developed a program where we not only learn *how* to 'practice what we preach,' but we first must *feel* what we 'preach' in order that we can 'practice' and become the best teachers possible."

Allowing his words to sink in, he paused briefly before continuing. No one said anything, but I could tell that he had made a deep impression on us all.

"*Baruch Hashem*, we are constantly called from schools all over requesting our graduates as teachers. In the past, there were numerous times when our girls' works were presented at the Torah U'mesorah Conventions in the United States, where many of our graduates were asked to lead workshops," he smiled proudly. "Yes, *baruch Hashem*, we have had our share of *nachat* from our wonderful girls and we are sure that with *siyyata de'Shemaya* it will continue with you." Taking a deep breath he asked, "Any questions?"

"Is there only one winner?"

"Good question, Rochel Leah. Clearly, every single graduate of Machon Beit Leah LeMorot *is* a winner. She is a winner for trying, for learning, and for achieving so much. Girls, these are not just words to placate you. Each recipient of a teaching certificate from here is truly a winner and is fully prepared to enter the classroom. Yet, someone will stand out when she presents her *Proyect* and she will be the main winner, along with two honorable mention winners." He looked around the room and then suddenly his eyes fell on me.

He smiled.

I froze.

"As a matter of fact," he continued, "one of last year's honorable mention winners was Sara Hirsch's sister."

My stomach did a triple somersault.

"Yes, Sara, your sister Shulamit did a remarkable job last year," his voice was warm, "and I'm sure all of you will be terrific this year, as well."

I must have been blushing from head to toe as I felt all eyes upon me. I did not relish being the center of attention, particularly when it was due to my sister's successes and especially when discussing *the* award.

The award! My stomach did another triple somersault. *The award that I must win in order to break free of being plain, simple, boring Sara. The award that will open doors for me, help me make my mark and stop being just a dull, dreary prop. The award that will help me to eventually become…the something special that I've been dreaming of becoming.*

My heart was pounding. I swallowed hard, hoping not to reveal my hidden feelings. Yes, along with the trepidation…I felt a stirring of excitement. *I must be the winner! I will be the winner!*

"Anyone else?" Rabbi Grossman looked around the room to see if there were more questions. "Malkie?"

"What if more than one deserves to be the main winner? What if more than two deserve honorable mention? What if there isn't a main winner at all? What if some—"

"How about you leave the worrying to us, Malkie?"

There were a few soft snickers in the background.

"When exactly does this all take place?" another girl asked.

"You'll be making the *Proyect* presentations for the administration toward the end of the term. The written reports will be submitted one week before graduation and then each of you will meet privately with the faculty committee during that week. We will announce the winners at graduation—without prior notice. The winner will then be asked to give a short impromptu speech summing up what she had presented." There was a slight pause. "Yes, Mimi?"

"Does *everyone* have to do this *Proy*—er—*Proyect*? What I mean is…do we all automatically participate, or is it um—?"

"Optional?" Rabbi Grossman shook his head, "No, Mimi, participation is definitely not optional. Every student must and I emphasize *must* participate. In order to receive her teaching certificate it is absolutely compulsory for each student to submit her *Proyect* in a timely and suitable fashion. Her grades will be recorded in her transcript. The award, the prize, is a bonus. Remember, this is a project that began last month when you stepped off the plane and it continues throughout the year. Building a strong foundation takes months and even years. We do *not* wait until May to start working on it. Understood?"

I could see a few heads nodding.

"Are there any more questions before I go?"

It was quiet in the room and no one else raised her hand.

"All right, girls, that'll be all for now." He glanced at his watch. "Geveret Spitz should be here any minute."

We stood respectfully as he left the room.

When the door closed behind him, we could still feel his presence. The air was charged with emotion. Reactions to Rabbi Grossman's latest disclosure were flying all over the classroom, with girls twisted in different positions expressing diversified opinions. Some students who loved projects and reports (as opposed to tests) were enthusiastic. Some felt it was a waste of time (preferring to just take the tests and get over it) and did not want to deal with what they believed was an unnecessary encumbrance. Most of the girls, however, looked forward to it, although they were wary of the competition.

I turned to Adina, ready to ask her how she felt about the project, but then stopped myself. *No, I will not speak to someone who doesn't want to speak to me.*

Just then, I did hear someone talk to me. My stomach. Its rumbling message reminded me of the strawberry leben waiting in my book bag. I began eating while trying to think of the best way to approach the project. Jotting down some of my thoughts onto a page in my loose-leaf helped me feel that I was taking a first step toward achieving my dream. *I must get myself a separate notebook just for this project,* I told myself determinedly. *I'll take it with me wherever I go—this way, each time I think of an idea, I'll be able to write it down and won't forget it.*

Swallowing another spoonful, I quickly wrote down a few words regarding a certain *midrash* my father had once told me. *It would go great with one of the ideas that just popped into my head,* I thought excitedly.

Suddenly, hearing Rabbi Grossman's voice, I looked up. Only, it wasn't Rabbi Grossman. It was Mimi Rosenberg and she sounded exactly like him. "That's right," I heard her say in his deep voice, "every *wonderful* student at Machon Beit Leah LeMorot MUST and I emphasize MUST participate. Remember, this project began last month when every one of our *wonderful* students stepped off the plane…"

She was standing at the front of the room where Rabbi Grossman had stood only minutes before. She held a book in her hand, pretending that it was a man's hat and gestured with it—fingering around its edges, placing it on her head—as we had seen Rabbi Grossman do a short while earlier.

Explosions of laughter ripped throughout the room eclipsing the tension that was aroused with Rabbi Grossman's exit.

It did not matter if the girls were Israeli, European, American, or from the other side of the world. Everyone was enjoying Mimi's performance. As unbelievable as it might seem, her mimicking was not enacted in a disrespectful manner. She had managed to project the emotional charges that were pulsating around us so that one could not help but laugh with utter abandon.

I too chuckled along with everyone else. Glancing sideways, I noticed that even the ends of Adina's mouth seemed to be twitching.

Then, startled, I saw something that made me take a good second look. Adina's lips curved into the first smile I had ever seen on her. It reminded me of the sun breaking through the clouds after a torrential rainstorm.

And I thought: if Adina Stern can smile, then anything can happen. Anything.

8

"I DON'T THINK Adina is going to smile when she walks into this room," I warned Mimi, waving my hand in the direction of her bed where mounds of clean laundry had been dumped on top of piles of books. "Your stuff is all over the place!"

"Nothing to worry about, Sara dear," Mimi sat on Adina's bed strumming her guitar. In a singsong, she continued with her guitar as the background music, "Not to worry, nothing to *fear*, it's only the schoolwork, I cannot *bear*…"

"Mimi!" I threatened, trying rather unsuccessfully to hide my smile.

"…Yes, oh, yes," she continued singing, "anything you want me to do, I shall *do*, anything oh, anything, anything for *you*! La, la, la…"

"Mimi…"

"La, la, la, *la*…la, la, la, *lee*. What do you do when you have a friend so *sweet*, she cares so much for you to be *neat*?"

Exasperated, I placed my hands firmly on my hips. "Mimi, the day will be gone before you know it! How in the world are we supposed to study?"

"Ah, but you're *right*, it'll soon be *night*. Please don't be so *tight*, better to *light*–en up," she put her guitar down reluctantly. "Of course, my dear, practical friend, you are absolutely *right*." She stood up rigid and straight, her shoulders thrown back like a soldier standing at attention. Placing the side of her right hand against her forehead, she saluted. "Yes sir, sargent, at your service!"

Chapter 8

I shook my head, laughing.

Rabbi Grossman had called me into his office the other day and asked me to help Mimi keep up with her schoolwork. *That's funny,* I had wondered at the time, *what is Mimi doing in seminary if she needs tutoring?* Nevertheless, since Rabbi Grossman had requested my help and I was not the type to question authority, I had quickly agreed. Besides, tutoring had always been my forte. Of course, I liked hanging around with Mimi and I guess I was hoping for some of her carefree nature to rub off on me.

"Okay, Mimi, first thing first," I was determined to do as good a job as possible. Walking over to her bed, I surveyed the jumble of clothing and socks. "In order to get to your books, we'd better get your laundry out of the way."

"Yes sir," she saluted once again. "Let's dump it all into my laundry bag."

"What?"

"Just dump it in," she held the large mesh bag open for me.

"Mimi," I sighed, "we might as well fold it and put it away. Otherwise," I began to sort through her laundry, "you won't have a bed to sleep on tonight."

"I could always sleep in Mazal's bed," she said playfully.

"Sorry, Mimi," I could not contain my excitement. "Mazal might be coming back tonight."

"Really?"

"When we came back from Succos vacation, Geveret Katz told me that Mazal would return one or two days after Shabbos. Today is Monday," I added eagerly, while folding Mimi's sweatshirt, "and I sure hope she will. I miss having a roommate."

"Well, you're lucky to at least have a roommate who talks to you. Adina is hardly ever in the room. She's usually studying in the library, and when she's here, she barely speaks."

"Poor, lonely Mimi," I laughed while rolling two matching socks together into a ball. "Maybe if you didn't have half the dorm hanging around in your room, Adina would keep you company sometime. Here, pair the rest of these socks."

Just then, we heard a couple of familiar voices approaching.

"Mimi, we need a break," Rivky Weiss called from the doorway. "How about going with us for ice cream?" she asked as she and Chani Frankel entered the room. Then, noticing me, she added amiably, "Oh, hi Sara, do you want to join us?"

"Yeah, how about it?" Chani patted her stomach. "I'm starved. I haven't eaten a thing since lunch. Let's go to Pinat HaGlidah."

I looked at Mimi; Mimi looked at me. We both glanced at her bed, which was still a hodge-podge of clothing with the few neat piles I had just folded along the side.

"Hey, I'd love to. But, Sara and I *really* have to study."

"It's good to see you getting a bit studious in your old age, Mimi." Rivky grinned.

"Never too late," she delivered one of her delicious, infectious laughs. "But don't worry, Sara is so good at this, she'll get me done in no time at all. Wow! My laundry never looked so nice, Sara. Thanks a mill—"

"Shalom, everybody…" A petite girl with black kinky hair came through the wash-up room.

"Mazal!"

"How are you, Sara?" For a brief moment she held my eyes in a penetrating gaze and then, turning to Mimi, her mouth curved into a wide smile. "Mimi, it is so good to see you. Sorry, I forget your names," she looked at Chani and Rivky with a blank expression on her face. "It has been a long time."

"Chani Frankel and Rivky Weiss," I reintroduced them to her. "Mazal, I can't believe you're back. It really has been a long time since you left." I stood in front of her awkwardly, feeling tall and clumsy, wanting to hug her, but unsure of her reaction. "How's your grandmother?"

"Yes, how is she, Mazal?" Mimi warmly embraced her. "We all missed you, *especially* Sara," she tilted her head in my direction, green eyes dancing mischievously. "Now, maybe you'll relieve me—I had to be Sara's surrogate roommate all this time. If not for me, she'd sleep through classes, have no one to study with, no one's laundry to do…"

I picked up one of her freshly paired socks and pretended to aim it toward the top of her head. She held up her hands in mock defense and ducked.

Everyone laughed.

Chapter 8

"Oh, Mimi, I sure miss you," Mazal pinched Mimi's cheek affectionately.

"How *is* your grandmother?" Rivky asked gently. "Her name is on the daily *Tehillim* list."

"Well, *baruch Hashem* she is out of the hospital for now and home with us. But," Mazal shook her head sadly, "she is not so well. She has so, so much suffering."

A few moments passed without anyone saying anything. We stood around uneasily until Mimi suggested, "Mazal, Chani and Rivky are going for ice cream right now. Why don't you join them?"

"Yes, come with us," Chani added good-naturedly.

"And you going, Mimi?"

"No. The boss," she pointed her thumb at me, "won't let. She's making me study instead."

"Oh, it is nice to see Sara having much good influence on you, Mimi." She turned toward Chani and Rivky. "I must hang up my clothing so they will not…um…how you say it in English?"

"Crease? I offered.

"Right. Crease. You mind to wait few minutes?"

"No problem," Rivky said cheerfully. "We'll help you."

"Want us to bring anything back for you two?" Chani asked.

"I'll have a triple sundae with one scoop of butter pecan, one scoop chocolate marshmallow, and the third scoop…surprise me. Okay? And make sure they top it with loads of whipped cream and hot fudge," Mimi ordered while rolling her green eyes dreamily. "*Lots* of hot fudge."

"Let's see if I can remember all that, and don't expect the hot fudge to stay hot till we get back to the dorm," Chani laughed, then turned toward me. "How about you, Sara?"

"Um. I don't know. I guess I'll have a vanilla cone."

"That's it? Nothing more adventurous?" Mimi sounded disappointed.

"It sounds perfect to me," Chani said. "It's going to be hard enough remembering your order, Mimi."

Everyone laughed. As they made their exit, Rivky call out, "Happy studying!"

"Thanks," we said in unison.

"And thanks for the ice cream," I added happily. It felt good to belong, to be included as one of the group.

I helped Mimi put the folded piles away in her large closet. Since the only furniture in each room consisted of two beds, two desks, and two night tables, fortunately whoever had designed the dormitory had thought to include a walk-in closet with a light to take care of the girls' clothing storage needs. It also unofficially served as a dressing room, so that while one roommate got dressed in the regular room, the other could use this closet. Floor to ceiling shelves lined one wall and a long rod for hanging clothing had been installed across the other.

It was obvious which shelves were Mimi's and which belonged to Adina—the contrast was so striking. Adina had folded her clothing with faultless precision, lining everything up in perfect formation. I had always been neat and orderly with my clothing and possessions, but compared to Adina, *I* felt disorganized.

I suppose it must have been frustrating for Mimi rooming with someone as efficient as Adina. Then again, it was difficult to imagine anything troubling Mimi.

"All right, Mimi. What would you like to start with: *parashah* or *Chumash*? Or would you rather review Geveret Spitz's assignment first?" I asked as I sat down on her bed.

"Let's just do whichever one is the quickest and then maybe we'll catch the others at Pinat HaGlidah."

"What do you mean, Mimi? Tomorrow is the *parashah* test. We have to review the complete *parashah* with Rashi and we're supposed to look up the answers to all the *Chumash* questions Geveret Greenstein assigned, which, by the way, are also due tomorrow. On top of that, Geveret Spitz said that we have until Wednesday to let her know the type of child we want to work with at Bnot Yisrael. And—"

"And?"

"And she said that the request must be handed in—in writing and with an explanation, but first we must read the thirty-five page booklet she handed out and answer the questionnaire in the back. So, what do you want to do first?"

"Plan the Chanukah *Chagigah*."

"Mimi!"

"Okay, okay, okay—I get the message. Let's do, um…let's do Geveret Spitz's assignment first."

"All right. Did you read the booklet yet?"

"No. Did you?"

"I began reading it right after her class today. I didn't get very far, though, because Rabbi Ossenfeld came in."

"I wish Geveret Spitz would have continued her class straight through, until the end of the day, Sara. She's a lot more interesting than Ossy."

"Mimi!"

"Well, she is."

"But, Mimi…"

"I know, I know. I don't have anything against Ossy, I mean *Rabbi Ossenfeld*—you can stop making that stern looking face, Sara. He's a very nice person. Really. But *dikduk* is just not my cup of tea."

"Okay, granted, but still—"

"Besides, the truth is…I do love Geveret Spitz's class. There's something special about her. She seems to really understand the way different kids learn."

"We *are* lucky to have her this year," I agreed. "Being assigned one specific type of child should really be an interesting experience."

"I wonder who she'll give *me* to work with," Mimi continued, sitting down next to me. Then she added in a voice just above a whisper, "What kind of child could someone like *me* be able to help?"

This last question caught me totally off guard. Thankfully I was able to recover quickly and replied, "Well, I'm sure that whoever the lucky girl is won't be bored for even a second and will have a great time."

"I hope she'll learn something from me," she mumbled dejectedly, "besides having a great time."

"Well then, we'd better get started," I said with forced cheerfulness, trying to quiet the unsettling feeling stirring inside me. I had never heard Mimi speak like this and I found it troubling. "Where's your booklet?" I removed mine from the pile and opened it to the first page.

"I'm not sure where I put it," she started looking through her pile of books, then walked over to her desk to see if it was there. "You know what?" she said when she realized it was nowhere nearby. "I have a great idea." She came back to her bed and plopped down beside me. Propping herself up against her pillow, she continued, "You read and I'll listen."

"What?"

"*You* read and *I'll* listen," she repeated.

"All thirty-five pages?"

"Unless it's too hard for you. I don't want you to get a sore throat or anything."

"No, it's no bother. In fact, I concentrate better when I read aloud. Are you sure *you* don't mind?"

"Nah, it's all right with me," Mimi said generously while leaning back in a comfortable position. "Okay, I'm ready." Feigning an aristocratic British accent, she commanded in an authoritative tone, "You may proceed."

"Yes, your highness," I laughed, glad to see Mimi returning to her cheerful self. Still sitting on Mimi's bed, I kicked off my shoes. Settling myself cozily against the wall, I folded my legs Indian style under me. "All right, let's begin with the letter Geveret Spitz told us about."

"I'm all ears."

"Okay," I cleared my throat, "here it goes." I began to read:

> Dear Students,
>
> You are about to embark on a journey. You have climbed the gangplank and you have boarded the ship. The voyage will soon commence. Once you begin teaching, life will never be the same!
>
> Most of the time, you will experience the feeling that there is absolutely no occupation more thrilling. You will sail across the sea with exuberance, energized and elevated with the lift of each wave. At times, though, it may also be dangerous. The ocean is not always calm and sometimes it is quite stormy. You do what you can to stay the course, knowing that the ship could capsize and you and all aboard could sink.
>
> Remember, the ship is well-equipped with life preservers, a compass, and a map to guide you. I believe that a teacher who is not prepared to work on individual problems and challenges, who is not ready to teach the WHOLE class, is stealing for a living. Just as a parent cannot give up on his or her own child, a teacher cannot give up on a student. Therefore, you must do whatever is necessary to steer the ship in the right direction so that those on

board arrive safely at their destination.

Not every child relates to learning in the same way. Some children grasp information by listening—their auditory receptors are the strongest. Other children learn through concentrated observation, thereby using visual means. Some children learn better through storytelling and others through games with cutout cardboard letters.

There are many examples and different modes that we will study and experiment with throughout the year. The important thing to remember, girls, is what Shlomo HaMelech tells us in *Mishlei* 22:6: "*Chanoch lana'ar al pi darko*—Educate the youth according to his path."

The faculty of M.B.L.L. has invited me to join their staff to help implement a new program. We will be working with students at the elementary and preschool levels from Bnot Yisrael in Kfar Amsdorf and children from the nearby town of Devorah. Although our main station is on the Beit Yaakov HaNegbah campus, we will observe these children in other surroundings, as well. We will visit them in their homes and in general do whatever we are able to do to make it possible for them to succeed in their learning.

Glancing sideways at Mimi while turning a page, I noticed that she had closed her eyes, her forehead creased in concentration. I read on:

After reading through this booklet, you are to complete the questionnaire in the back so that I will have a better idea of with which type of child to pair you.

My dear students, please feel free to approach me with any questions you may have. We will be working together, girls, you and I. We are partners in the hopefully successful implementation of this program. With help and *siyyata de'Shemaya* from our Partner above, and lots of hard work, sincerity, and a true desire to succeed, I believe we will.

I look forward to getting to know you all and learning from each one of you.

Sincerely,
Geveret T. Spitz

I looked up with satisfaction. Mimi opened her eyes and stretched her arms above her head as far as she could reach. "I sure hope the rest of the booklet is as interesting as her letter," she said.

"I'm sure it is." I straightened the pile of papers. "Okay...ready? Here we go!"

"Thirty-three more pages!" She rolled her eyes to the ceiling.

"Thirty-two," I corrected.

"Thirty-two, thirty-three...who cares? It's all the same. I'm starved! I sure hope they come back soon with our ice creams."

"They'll be back before you know it. Let's continue. We still have tons of work to do," I said, anxious to go on.

"Oh, all right. One sec," she stood up and sauntered over to the chair by her desk. Reaching in to her knapsack, she withdrew her hand triumphantly grasping a bag. "Thank goodness I still have some left. Have some Bamba," she offered while I motioned for her to rejoin me on the bed.

"No thanks. Mimi, I really want to finish reading this already. We still have to get to *Chumash* with all the Rambans and *Sifsei Chachamim* to look up, and then we have loads of *parashah* questions to answer—after this is done."

"Oh, okay, Practical Sara." Mimi plopped down beside me.

Again that warm feeling. "Did I ever tell you that my friend Chavie used to call me that?" I asked her.

"Only around three times...So Sara, do I remind you of your friend Chavie?"

"Not really...well, maybe a little bit."

"Which part 'not really' and which part 'maybe a little bit'?"

"Mimi! We have to study!"

"Sara—"

"No, that's it, Mimi," my voice was firm, "I'm reading..."

"Yes, boss. I'm sorry," she said contritely. "Please continue."

"All right. Here it goes," I cleared my throat and looked at page four of the booklet. I read aloud: "The teacher must be aware at all times that her role is comparable to the job of a diamond cutter. She is working with diamonds, each and every one valuable beyond measure.

"At times, a diamond cutter must work with a stone that is difficult to process. Does he discard the diamond, certain that it has no use? A skilled diamond cutter will never dispose of a raw stone. He will work with it, cut it, clean it, polish it, and turn it into the precious gem it truly is.

"The classroom consists of all different types of students. Some are what I refer to as the 'made to order' students—"

"Hey, Sara, that sounds like you. The 'made to order' student."

I looked up. "Thanks, Mimi," I said and then quickly returned to the booklet and continued reading: "...Those are the students that do not present much of a challenge to the teacher and are truly a pleasure to teach. On the other hand, there are students who are similar to the raw stone that is difficult to process—the stone that needs the expertise of the capable and hardworking teacher to bring about its metamorphosis from poor student to radiant diamond.

"Every educator must continuously strive to develop tactics and strategies to penetrate the soul of each student. How can I open the door to this child's soul is a question that every teacher must ask herself. One may never give up. No door is impenetrable—"

Door? So Geveret Spitz also thinks of people sometimes hiding behind closed doors! Maybe my thoughts are not so foolish—

"Hey, Sara, why'd you stop reading? This is really getting interest—"

"Oh, sorry, Mimi," I felt myself blush, "I—I must've been....all right, I-I'll continue now. Now where was I?"

"You were saying that no door is impenetrable—"

"Right. No door is impenetrable, no problem is unsolvable, and no one is a lost cause. Every closed door has a key, you just have to find the right one. It might not open on the first try; sometimes you must try repeatedly. When the first key does not open the door, try another key, a different method. You must never give up. Once, twice, three times, even seven times might not—"

"Seven! That's it, Sara, you just reminded me. I'm thinking of composing a new song about Chanah and her *seven* sons for the Chanukah *Chagigah*. While the few of us do the singing—"

"Mimi, I'm trying to read, in case you haven't noticed."

"Sara, you've got to listen," she was emphatic. "You gave me such a great idea. While some of us sing and do the harmonizing, some other girls will be dressed in authentic costumes like they wore in the time of Chanah and her seven sons, and they'll pantomime the scene."

"Mimi—"

"And we'll use a really sparkling stone to look like Antiochus's diamond ring, you know the one he put on the floor to force Chanah's youngest son to bow down. You gave me the idea when you mentioned diamonds. Thanks a million, Sara. I love you! *You're* a diamond!"

I laughed, but I was not thinking of diamonds...I was thinking of emeralds. Mimi's eyes were shining like two green emeralds opened wide and sparkling with enthusiasm. "Wow, this year's Chanukah *Chagigah* is going to be the greatest," she said.

"I'm sure it will be, Mimi, especially with *you* at the helm. But we're studying right now."

"Done the right way, Sara, it could really be dramatic and effective. I'm so excited! Sara, you're an absolute genius!"

"Can I continue, please?"

"Yes, yes, yes! Sorry," she drew her thumb and forefinger together across her mouth, as if zippering it closed.

I continued reading, reiterating the last sentence, "You must never give up. Once, twice, three times, even seven times might not be enough. Whatever it takes to find the right key to set each child free from that which is hindering—"

"That's it! She *set them free*. Yehudis, that is. Do you think it would be better if we did the story of Yehudis killing the wicked general Elifornus? Yes...that could also be very effective."

Ignoring her, I continued to read from where I left off, my voice rising an octave. "...Hindering his or her growth. The commitment and devotion called for in the field of education goes beyond the level of these same qualities required for success in ordinary careers. In those fields—"

"Sara, it's perfect! *In the fields*...the *battlefields*! It could be *really* dramatic. In the background, we could have the Greeks and *Chashmonaim* at war *in the battlefields*, just as you said. Absolutely, you get the credit. Again, you gave me a great idea, and the—"

I read on. I am sure I was almost shouting, trying to drown out her interruptions. "In those battlefields, I mean *fields*, one must display his or her commitment and devotion to the job only while engaged in it. In education, however—"

"And while the choir is singing and the others pantomiming, some of the girls—"

I was definitely shouting: "IN EDUCATION, HOWEVER, ONE MUST BE ENTIRELY DEDICATED TO THE PROFESSION, EVEN WHEN HE OR SHE IS NOT IN THE CLASSROOM. HE OR SHE MUST—"

"Sara, I can hear you. You don't have to yell," Mimi said sweetly.

"Well, if you wouldn't interrupt me every second, then maybe I WOULDN'T HAVE TO SPEAK SO LOUDLY!" I flung the booklet onto the floor.

"Sorry, Sara, it's just that…"

"YES?" I asked sarcastically. This time I was *really* upset.

"It's just that…forget it," she turned her face away from me, but not before I glimpsed the troubled look in her eyes. "You wouldn't understand anyway."

My heart dropped. *What did I just do to kind, friendly Mimi? Mimi, who reminds me so much of Chavie. Mimi, who is one of my only real friends in this place.*

"I'm sorry, Mimi. I really am," I said worriedly. "I didn't mean to hurt you. Please forgive me."

"Forgive *you*?"

"It's just that we have so much to do and I'm nervous about finishing all the work."

"You want *me* to forgive *you*?"

I nodded, too afraid to speak.

Suddenly, Mimi burst out laughing, the dimples in her cheeks deepening. "Sara Hirsch, you are hysterical. Here you are, giving me your time, trying to help me. Then I don't stop interrupting you, and finally, as great an angel as you are, you finally lose a little bit of your huge amount of patience, and you apologize to *me*? You are *too* funny!"

"You're not upset?"

"Not at *you*."

"But something is bothering you."

"Me? Nah, nothing's bothering me," she said.

"I don't believe you," I insisted.

"Miss Sara Hirsch, could we please go on with our studying?"

"Mimi, I—"

"Tomorrow is the *parashah* test," she mimicked me, grinning. "We must review the complete *parashah* with Rashi. And we're supposed to look up the answers to all the *Chumash* questions Geveret Greenstein assigned us, which by the way is also due tomorrow. And—"

"Mimi—"

"Sara, please! We still have to get to *Chumash* with all the Rambans and *Sifsei Chachamim* to look up…"

"Mimi?" Something gnawed at me.

"And," Mimi continued, ignoring me, "Geveret Spitz said that we have until Wednesday to request the type of child we want to work with at Bnot Yisrael. So, Sara," Mimi's grin widened, "what would you like to start with, *parashah* or *Chumash*?

"Please stop…I know something's bothering you."

"What are you, Sara, a psychologist or something?"

"Very funny, Mimi. I just know. Usually, you're so…so…"

"So *what*?"

"Cheerful."

"And right now I'm not cheerful?"

"Of course, you are, Mimi. I don't know if you know how not to be cheerful. But, right now, it's just not—"

"Not what, Sara?"

"It's not in your…eyes. Sure, you have that big smile of yours. But that's over here, by your lips," I pointed to my mouth. Then, placing my finger beside my eye, I added, "Not here."

"C'mon, Sara," she rolled her eyes.

"Look, I know there's something bothering you. You even started to say something. You said I wouldn't understand."

"Oh boy, Sara. I didn't realize how analytical you are. I'd better be more careful in the future when I'm around you," she joked. "Okay. We ought to continue reading this booklet." She picked it up from the floor where I had flung it a few minutes earlier. "How many pages do we have left now? Thirty-three or thirty-two?"

"Thirty-one. And don't change the subject, Mimi."

"Really, Sara. We'd better continue. Before you know it, they'll be back with our ice creams."

"Okay, Practical Mimi. But, first tell me what you were about to say before and then didn't."

"Wow, you don't let go," her voice was rough, but she was still smiling. She looked down at my booklet in her lap, in concentration, as if reading. I knew, though, that she was thinking about what she had been ready to say to me earlier, deciding whether to share her feelings and open up to me or not. I held my breath, hoping… really hoping that she would.

After a few moments, she looked up decidedly. Tucking the loose tumble of wavy red hair behind her ears, she said, "You know, I really am not so sure you would understand."

"Try me."

"It's just that…"

I waited expectantly.

"It's just that I want this year's Chanukah *Chagigah* to be really special. Better than it ever was."

"Of course you do, Mimi. We all want the Chanukah *Chagigah* to be the best during *our* year."

"No, Sara," she shook her head. "You don't understand. It *has* to be the best ever."

I sat there quietly beside her, the realization slowly creeping upon me. There was something significant, something mysterious that Mimi was hiding. Something that, despite the cheerful façade, lay deep and camouflaged within.

I saw the quiet resolve in Mimi's eyes that I had never seen before, a determination that I found rather troubling.

I was even more puzzled when a few moments later she reiterated, "I don't think you or any one else could understand, but this is very important to me. Very."

9

"Very?"

"Yes, Rochel Leah, it's really very important. We can't be late."

"If it's so-o-o really very important, Zehava, go without me!"

"B-but, Rochel Leah—"

"Look," Rochel Leah sounded irritated, "if you want to wait for me, fine. If you don't, then it's all right with me if you go on ahead."

"I thought," Zehava's voice was shaky, "we'd go together," there was a slight pause, "like we always do."

"Listen, Zehava, I'm truly sorry, but you can't depend on me every time we have to go somewhere. I have other friends too, you know."

"I know...but...I-I thought we were...you know—"

"Look, I like you a lot. And we're really great friends, but, you know, I can't just hang around with you. Chani and I go back a long time too. I told her that we'd wait outside the building before we go to meet the rest of—"

Suddenly, I stepped forward from under the shade of the large awning into the bright sunshine, feeling compelled to make my presence known. "Hi, Zehava. Hi, Rochel Leah," I was deliberately cheerful.

"Oh, Sara." Rochel Leah swung around at the sound of my voice and snapped, "Where'd you come from?"

"I—I...er—"

Her tone was accusatory, "I didn't know you were there."

I noticed Zehava's discomfiture and a fleeting, mean, *it-serves-*

her-right-for-always-sticking-around-with-Rochel-Leah thought passed through my mind. Then, my empathic nature surfaced and I felt truly sorry for Zehava.

"I—I just got here," I told them. "I'm waiting for Mazal. She had to stop at the office to call home."

Standing at the entrance of the Beit Yaakov HaNegbah school building during the morning break, I could see girls milling about the courtyard, some sitting in quiet conversation on benches and some walking in and out of the building. True, it was late October, but the sun in the Upper Negev shone down brilliantly, making it feel as though it was still summer and, clearly, we were glad for this opportunity to be outdoors taking full advantage of the beautiful weather.

We were scheduled to begin observing classes that day at Bnot Yisrael, the girls' elementary school at Kfar Amsdorf, with Geveret Spitz. First, though, we were supposed to attend a preliminary meeting with her which was to be held in the picnic area of the Beit Yaakov HaNegbah campus.

"You're waiting for Mazal?" Rochel Leah repeated what I had just told her.

I did not say anything, but nodded, a growing feeling of discomfort descending upon me.

"I feel so-o-o sorry for you having to room with one of the Israeli girls."

"So...sorry?"

"Yeah. You know, they're so-o-o different and everything. It's so-o-o much harder to be *real* friends."

"Real friends?"

"Yes. But I guess if it doesn't bother you..."

"Bother me?" I shook my head slowly, "I-I'm not sure what you mean." I looked from Rochel Leah to Zehava, and seeing Zehava unhappily biting down on her lower lip, I felt a sting of pity mixed with a sudden charge of adrenaline run through me. Turning back to Rochel Leah I continued purposefully, "I don't think a real friend has anything to do with whether you're Israeli or American. Or," I hesitated for a moment, then looking her directly in the eye, unwaveringly added, "or if you're from Miami Beach or Woodlake."

I saw Rochel Leah's hazel eyes widen in surprise, obviously taken aback by my unexpected jab. She and Zehava exchanged a quick uncomfortable glance with each other, then her eyes narrowed and I noticed a look of anger steal across her face. "Excuse me, Sara Hirsch, but for your information…"

"Hi, everybody! Hope we didn't keep you waiting too long!" Chani Frankel, accompanied by Rivky Weiss, cheerfully greeted us.

"Yeah, sorry we're late. Chani waited for me while I just finished up some notes," Rivky explained.

"Oh hi, Chan," Rochel Leah turned away from me, swinging her ponytail of chestnut hair over her shoulder and smiling widely at the two newcomers. "And Rivky. Of course Zehava and I were glad to wait for you."

"We'd better get going," Zehava reminded them, her voice steadier than it had been a few moments earlier. She glanced at her watch. "It's already five to ten."

"Oh my goodness, I didn't realize how late it was," Rivky exclaimed. "I'm so sorry! You all go ahead," she offered. "I told Mimi I'd wait for her out here in the courtyard. Rabbi Ossenfeld wanted to have a few words with her."

"But Geveret Spitz said we're supposed to meet at the picnic tables in the garden at ten o'clock," Zehava warned. "She'll be prepping us before we leave."

"I know and I don't want to miss it, but what happens if Mimi misses the talk and everyone starts going without her? Then she'll have to walk by herself all the way to Kfar Amsdorf."

"It's not really such a long walk," Rochel Leah commented.

"True, but I know I wouldn't want to walk there by myself," Chani offered.

"Besides," I heard myself say, "Geveret Katz warned us not to go through the woods alone."

"I don't think it's really so-o-o dangerous," Rochel Leah knowingly pursed her lips together. "Personally, I think our *eim bayit* tends to worry a bit too much."

"That's her job," Rivky chuckled softly. "She's the house mother. She's supposed to worry."

Chapter 9

"So what! There's such a thing as overdoing it," Rochel Leah was adamant. "And besides, I think she has far too many rules."

"I think she's a lot more experienced than we are," I said quietly.

"That's not necessarily true, Sara," Rochel Leah laughed rather loudly. "You know it's her first year here. In fact, I believe she's been living in America all these years."

"Well, still…" I opened my mouth to say more and then closed it.

"Besides, there's definitely something peculiar about her—"

"Rochel Leah," Chani warned.

"You know, something just doesn't make sense," Rochel Leah ignored her. "She looks like a typical Yemenite and yet her last name is Katz." Rochel Leah shook her head decisively, "I'm telling you, it's so-o-o strange; something just doesn't add up."

"Excuse me, Rochel Leah," Rivky smiled and then asked in her gentle manner, "who says she can't marry someone whose last name is Katz?"

"I thought of that. But don't you find it odd—a Yemenite woman with an Ashkenazi husband by the name of Katz?"

"Who cares?" Zehava spoke up anxiously. "America, Yemen…if she's experienced or not. It's almost ten o'clock and we're going to miss the meeting!"

"You're right. Everybody, please…go on without me. Geveret Spitz will be upset if so many of us are missing." Rivky looked at her watch worriedly. "I don't know what's taking Mimi so long."

"Do you know what Rabbi Ossenfeld wanted to talk to her about?" Chani asked with concern.

"I have no idea, but you know Mimi," Rivky said affectionately.

"Who knows Mimi?" We heard her buoyantly familiar voice sing out before we saw her.

"Oh, hi Mimi! How'd it go?"

"How'd what go?" she asked innocently. "Oh, you mean with Ossy!" she smiled and then, catching the warning look in my eye, immediately corrected herself. "Uh-oh, I mean *Rabbi* Ossenfeld," she emphasized, giving me a playful wink.

"Tell us all about it while we walk, Mimi," Rivky smiled. "We kept everybody waiting long enough and we're already late for the meeting."

"Okay, folks," Mimi laughed as she breezily swung her book bag over her shoulder. "Let's get going!"

I watched them stroll away, their backs to me. As they sauntered along, everyone focused toward the middle of the group where Mimi was animatedly describing her latest adventure, her hands waving in the air and dancing in all directions as she spoke.

Suddenly, she stood still for a moment and then abruptly swung around. The others also stopped walking and turned with her to see what happened.

I also wondered what brought Mimi to an unexpected standstill.

Only around seven yards separated her from the school's entranceway, still, she had to cup her hand over her forehead to shield her eyes from the bright sun while focusing in its direction. She looked searchingly toward where we had all been conversing just a few moments earlier and I noticed her break into a relieved smile when our eyes locked.

"Hey, Sara," Mimi called out to me, "what happened to you? I just realized you're missing. Aren't you coming with us?"

I felt a rush of warmth wash over me. "I'm waiting for Mazal. I'll catch up soon."

"You're sure?"

"Yes, I'm sure," I waved her on. "Mazal should be here soon. Go, or you'll all be late!"

"Okay, if you insist," she saluted laughingly, and then waved. "See you later!"

I smiled inwardly while watching the small group leave the courtyard and disappear toward the gardens on the other side of the building. *That Mimi*, I sighed, still grinning. *She's really something.*

I leaned against the school's wall, tired from standing so long, looking over the assortment of flowers and plants still flourishing in the garden surrounding the building. Verdant ivy vines climbed up the adjacent stone wall, snaking around the pearl white stones' cracks and crevices.

Shifting my feet impatiently, I placed my book bag on the ground beside them. *What I wouldn't do right now for a tall glass of fresh ice water,* I thought longingly. *I can't believe how hot it is. How long have I been waiting here, anyway?* I speculated nervously. I looked at my watch. *Oh, no! It's already ten minutes after ten. Where in the world is Mazal?*

"Sara…"

"Oh, Mazal." I turned toward her, relieved. "I'm so glad to see you. It's pretty late already and I was getting worried." Then, taking a closer look at her, I asked with concern, "Is everything all right at home?"

"*Hakol b'yedei Shamayim*," she pointed toward the sky.

"You look upset. Is it your grandmother?"

"*Kain*," she sighed deeply. "She take many tests. My mother say they come out not good."

"Oh, I'm so sorry. This is terrible for you."

"She—my Savta never be *meah achuz*. Oh, how you say it in English?"

"*Meah achuz*? You mean a hundred percent?"

"Yes," she nodded. "Savta never be one hundred percent. But she live by us and my Ima, she take very good care of Savta. But, now…"

"Do they know what's wrong?"

"No, Sara. Yes," she shook her head sadly. "Oh, I do not know. They think it something… I cannot say. The doctor think it something so very bad."

"That's awful," I felt my own eyes watering. "I'm really so, so sorry for all of you."

"Thank you, Sara."

"It must be extremely hard on your family. Your grandmother having lived with you all these years. And you're so close to her and everything. I wish I could do something to help."

"How about you come home this Shabbat with me? You see her, you talk with her. My family be so happy to meet you."

"No way, Mazal," I shook my head emphatically. "I can't come when your family is going through such a crisis."

"But I want you to come very much. You care."

"Let's talk as we walk," I suggested, gently prodding her.

We began to make our way to the end of the courtyard when Mazal glanced at her watch, "Oh, I see it very, very late. I so, so sorry, Sara. You wait for me so long."

"That's all right, Mazal. If we hurry, we'll hopefully make it for the tail end of the talk."

"Tale?" Mazal stopped walking, clearly disturbed. "Geveret Spitz speech not...tale. She no telling stories."

I stood opposite her and for a moment wondered what in the world she was talking about, anxious to move on. "Tail?" I scratched my head, puzzled. A few quiet seconds passed, and then suddenly realization dawned. "Oh-h-h," I nodded comprehendingly, "I said *tail end*, not *tale* like in *fairytale*. Tail end means the concluding, the end part of something, *Kimoh zanav*...tail," I explained, using a combination of Hebrew and English while gesticulating with my hands as we continued walking. "I was saying that if we hurry, we'll hopefully get to hear the *zanav*, the *tail end*, the END," I emphasized rather loudly, "of Geveret Spitz's speech."

"Ah," Mazal smiled sheepishly. "*Achshav ani meivina.*"

I gave her a "that's okay" smile, then proceeded to move along a bit more hurriedly.

"Sara, you know, I am thinking..."

"Yes?"

"You be very patient with my many English mistakes. And you wait for me a lot of time. Also you show much care about my family problem," she continued in her blunt manner. Her voice, though, was heavy. "*B'emet*, Sara, you are real friend to me."

"Thank you, Mazal," I swallowed. Happy tears unexpectedly filled my eyes. "You are...a real friend...to me too."

I heard the sounds of chirping birds nearby and, as they hopped from one branch to the next, I was sure they were singing. And I wanted to sing along with them too.

I saw them fly above the treetops, higher and higher toward the puffs of cottony clouds. And as I watched them disappear into the blue sky, I could feel something inside me—bursting forth and soaring upward alongside them.

Real friends! I wanted to sing out, *I have a real friend!*

Smiling, content in each other's company, Mazal and I emerged from the path. I stopped suddenly. I still caught my breath in wonder every time I went this way.

From where we stood, I could see the luxuriant gardens stretched out from one end of the long school building all the way past the other end, until the point where the campus bordered the surrounding desert. In its width, the abundant gardens extended from the rear of the building toward the nearby pocket of woods. Exotic plants, nut and fruit trees, olive and date palms, red, yellow, and white honeysuckle dotted the landscape.

A soft breeze carrying the fragrant scent of coralberry and elder greeted us. Inhaling deeply, I gratefully closed my eyes for a brief second, wanting to savor this utterly peaceful but fleeting moment.

Mazal tapped me lightly on the shoulder, reminding me that time was running out. I quickly opened my eyes and gasped when I looked at my watch. *It's so late!* We hurried on.

We came toward a large clearing and saw the group sitting clustered around Geveret Spitz. Approaching the picnic benches as unobtrusively as possible, we slid onto the closest one alongside a picnic table. I felt my face growing hot, sure that everyone would turn around to look at us. I need not have worried, though. The girls, enthralled by whatever Geveret Spitz was saying, were too preoccupied to pay any attention to us.

Before long, I too was swept along with her talk and felt as though I had been there the whole time. Chewing nonchalantly on the top of the pen, while my ears heard and my head absorbed, my eyes casually roamed around observing the others.

I noticed Rivky, Mimi, Chani and Rochel Leah sitting together on one side of the table directly in front of us, with Zehava squeezing herself on the edge of the bench next to Rochel Leah. *Poor Zehava*, I thought. There was barely enough room for four people on the bench—let alone five. *Why can't she separate herself from Rochel Leah for a few minutes and just go sit on the other side?* There were only three girls sitting there—Naomi, Adina, and Devorah.

Adina. She was paying close attention to Geveret Spitz as she spoke, jotting down notes on her pad every once in a while. I scratched the side of my head with the tip of my pen, puzzled. Adina still mystified me.

"So remember, girls," Geveret Spitz was saying, "not only will we be observing all the grades at Bnot Yisrael, but we will be establishing a resource room for the very first time."

Our perplexed faces must have reflected our confusion.

"Some of you might already know what a resource room is. However," as she studied our puzzled expressions, a warm smile spread over her face, "obviously it is still a foreign word to most of you, but please, don't worry. I'll explain."

"As you know, girls," she continued, and I gripped my pen tightly, preparing to write. "Not everyone is able to learn successfully in the regular classroom. Sometimes, due to a learning disability, or problems at home, or for any number of reasons, a child might have difficulty comprehending what the teacher is successfully conveying to the majority of her students. I believe with all my heart," she pushed back a strand of her light brown wig that the soft breeze had blown out of place, "that every person has potential. In some people, though, it might remain dormant and hidden for a while or *chalilah* forever—if the needed help is not provided. That's why they are not succeeding in the classroom and often throughout their lives, as well. And, that's where the resource room comes in."

She paused for a moment to catch her breath. I looked around and could see the backs of most of my fellow students, each girl hanging onto every single one of our teacher's meaningful words.

They're impatient to hear what she has to tell us—just like me. My eyes swept over to Mimi.

Mimi? What in the world is with Mimi? I could only see her back. And she was sitting as still as a statue. No fidgeting, no whispers to her neighbors, no gesturing of any kind...*What's going on?*

It was strange. I was not used to seeing Mimi sitting so stiffly. Mimi and her bouncing red ponytail were always in perpetual motion. *I hope she's all right*, I thought to myself.

"The resource room," Geveret Spitz continued, breaking through my thoughts, "is a room in the school where individual children leave their regular classroom for a specified period of time each day and participate in an individualized program that was designed especially for them. There is constant communication between the children's mainstream teachers and the resource room and, whenever possible, the home, as well. Each and every one of us has a treasure chest within.

Our job, girls, is to look for the key that will unlock the potential in our students, and set them free from whatever is hindering their growth." She stopped speaking and looked around, "Any questions?"

I felt a flutter of excitement at the thought of working with the children. This is what I loved doing! Focusing on what the problem was, analyzing, and trying to figure out the solution. *Find the key and set them free,* her words reverberated in my mind.

"Who gets to work in the resource room and who works in the school?"

"Thanks for asking, Rochel Leah," Geveret Spitz nodded in her direction. "Each one of you will experience observing and teaching in both the mainstream classroom and in the resource room. However," she explained, "based on the request forms that you completed and handed in this morning, I will have a better idea of whether to place you in the elementary or preschool classroom or if you will do best assisting us in our new resource room. Yes, Malkie?"

"What happens if someone tries working in the resource room, then finds it's not for her? Or, what happens if she's working in a regular classroom and finds she'd be better off with an older grade, or what happens if—"

There was a low murmur of agreement. I heard some soft snickers and some impatient "Sh-sh, let Geveret Spitz speak" comments in the background.

A moment or two later, her soft voice cut through the commotion. "Don't worry, girls," she smiled at us warmly. "Nothing is etched in stone. Obviously, we want you girls to become the best possible teachers you can be and we want to expose you to all different types of students. We want what's best for you *and* what's best for the students. So, please don't worry. If things don't work out, there is always room for changes. We're in this together and with Hashem's help we will do what's best for *everyone.* Any more questions?" she looked around the garden. "Yes, Adina?"

"If Geveret Spitz will only be here for this year," Adina spoke to the teacher respectfully, addressing her in third person, "then what will assure the success of this resource room in the future?"

As usual, Adina's question was asked politely, concisely, and intelligently. Again, there was a low murmur among the girls.

"That's an excellent question, Adina," Geveret Spitz said appreciatively, "and believe me that is indeed a source of concern for me too at times. However, we can only do what we can do." She took a deep breath before continuing. "*Baruch Hashem* we have set up similar programs in a few schools in the United States. We try our utmost to lay a strong foundation, and with a great deal of *siyyata de'Shemaya* they have flourished and grown beyond our wildest dreams. And now, girls," she stepped forward looking at us steadily, her light brown eyes full of determination, "we hope that with Hashem's help and your hard work we will see success here, as well."

It was quiet for a few moments while everyone absorbed what Geveret Spitz was telling us. Her classes were always a pleasure and sitting here on the picnic benches, cooling off under the shade of the date palms and olive trees, with the chirping of birds as the background music, I felt imbued with a sense of "I can do it!"

"All right, girls, do any of you have any more questions?" She looked around. "Yes…Chani?"

"When will we find out if we're in the resource room or the regular classrooms?"

"I'll get to that in a minute, Chani. Zehava, you also had a question."

"How will we know who we're going to be working with?"

"Right. And, what was your question, Malkie?"

"Exactly when do we work with the kids? And what do we do if we like working with the kids but they're not improving, or if they're improving but…" Malkie stopped in mid-sentence as Batsheva elbowed her amiably.

"All right," Geveret Spitz said, clapping her hands together. "I'll try to answer *all* of your questions now." She flicked a small leaf off her shoulder and then went on to explain. "Later on in the day and throughout tomorrow, I will be reviewing your request forms and I hope, *b'ezras Hashem*, to prepare a list with the classes you will be assigned to and the individual names of the children you will each be working with by Friday. I will post the list on the bulletin board in the dorm lounge, hopefully by *Motza'ei Shabbos*. And this Sunday afternoon, *im yirtzeh*

Chapter 9

Hashem, you will begin observing the children. Remember, many of you will be doing additional tutoring with the individual children who have been assigned to you. So," she licked her lips, "have I answered all your questions?"

I found myself nodding and grinning back at her as though she had been speaking just to me. Then, glancing around me, I saw others nodding in agreement too.

"All right, back to what we were speaking about at the beginning of this meeting. The observation books. I know I promised to give you more details and suggestions about how to complete them."

I leaned forward. I had missed the first part of the meeting and knew I should listen closely now.

"Again, I'll reiterate, your observation book is of the utmost importance. It will serve as a journal for you, where you are expected to write down your observations about the child you are working with. You will note the different methods the teacher uses to work with the child and any other student-teacher interaction. You will discover that by writing down your inner thoughts and feelings in your observation book, it will undoubtedly make you more cognizant of each child's progress. So, girls, be conscientious about recording there what you see and hear, and what you think should be done to help the situation. Write down the different pieces of advice you receive. Keep writing. Keep analyzing. Keep working. Write down the action you chose to take and what happened as a result of that action. And if you feel you made a mistake, come talk to me. Then write down what you learned from your mistake.

"You will be handing in quarterly reports based on your observation books. Although these observation reports are a new concept at Machon Beit Leah LeMorot, they will play a big part in the mark you receive toward the *Proyect*, the main report you will be both submitting in writing and presenting orally at the end of the year."

I felt a tremor of excitement run through me. *The Goldstone Proyect!* I was listening closely, hoping not to miss even one word.

"Your first report is due right before Chanukah on 24 Kislev, to be exact."

"But, that's in less than two months!" one of the girls groaned.

"And what about the Chanukah *Chagigah*? The performance?" That was Rochel Leah's voice.

I looked over at Mimi. She was still sitting motionless and had not said a word. *Now, that's peculiar...Mimi sitting still while discussing the Chanukah Chagigah?*

"It's almost eight weeks. If you begin working on it right now, girls, with just a short amount of time invested on a daily basis, you'll see there will be hardly any work at the end. Then it will just be a question of putting it all together. Does anyone have anything else to ask or add?"

No one did. Except for the chirping sounds of the birds and the gentle breeze softly rustling through the branches, all was quiet in the garden.

Geveret Spitz continued, "In a few minutes we will begin our walk to Kfar Amsdorf, but before we go, I would like to tell you about the student body of Bnot Yisrael."

She cleared her throat.

"As you already know, the community of Kfar Amsdorf consists mainly of kollel families with most of the men being *talmidim* of Beit Midrash Amsdorf. You have already met some of their wives, either as your Shabbat hosts in their homes or as your teachers at Machon Beit Leah LeMorot." I felt myself nodding. "You will soon have the opportunity to meet the women who are teachers and mothers at Bnot Yisrael too..."

She continued to tell us more about the children attending the school. We knew that most of the kids were children of the kollel and yeshivah people from Kfar Amsdorf. "Around a quarter of the Bnot Yisrael students," Geveret Spitz informed us, "are bussed in from nearby developments, such as Kiryat Yehudah, Devorah, and there is even a group of children from Be'er Sheva.

"Some of you are aware that most of the families from these places are made up of recent immigrants struggling to make a living. Although not too many of the people are religious, most are from traditional backgrounds, so don't forget when working with these children and their parents the important opportunity you have to conduct yourselves in a way that is a *kiddush Hashem*."

Returning my pen and notebook to my book bag, I felt my heartbeat quicken. *I am really, truly about to embark upon my dream of teaching! It's finally happening…*

"You look happy, Sara."

"I am, Mazal," I smiled while looping the strap of my book bag over my shoulder. "I can't wait to actually begin teaching."

"You will most certainly be a very good teacher," she said decidedly while we fell into step behind the others.

"I sure hope so," I told her. We were almost at the end of the garden, where a stone path led to the patch of woods connecting the Beit Yaakov HaNegbah campus to Kfar Amsdorf. "This is what I've wanted to do ever since I was a little kid."

"Me too. But, by me—maybe my reasons not the best?"

"What do you mean, Mazal? What's wrong with your reasons?"

"Nothing is really wrong," Mazal paused for a moment to take a swat at an annoying mosquito buzzing nearby. "Just, by you it is a very strong dream. By you, Sara, it come from something deep, deep inside you. By me, it come more from outside."

"So, what's wrong with that? And anyway, what do you mean…from the outside?"

"Ah, that a good question." Mazal pursed her lips together, contemplating for a few moments before going on. "*B'emet*, I want to teach because all these years I never stay home. There was no religious school there. For high school, I must go here, to Beit Yaakov HaNegbah. I always travel. I always go back and forth. Now, for the first time, our Kiryat Yosef has a *kitah tet*. All these years, I travel," she shook her head frustrated, then let out a small laugh. "And now…finely?"

"Finally?"

"Ah, yes. Now, finally…could you believe? This year Beit Yaakov begins grade nine."

"That's great!"

"I want to teach," she went on pensively, "to help make high school in Kiryat Yosef good. So, girls in Kiryat Yosef, they not need to travel. Then, *my* girls could stay home with me," she shrugged. "So, see? My reason for teaching is not the same like your reason."

"It doesn't matter, Mazal. You know, there's nothing wrong with wanting to build up a school. It's also a dream and it will do a lot of good for a lot of people."

"Yes, Sara, it is very big dream to have Beit Yaakov school for teenagers in Kiryat Yosef. When you come this Shabbat, I show you."

"Mazal, about Shabbos—"

She waved her hand, quieting my protests, and continued where she left off. "I so happy to show you Kiryat Yosef, the school building. You meet my family, you meet my friends, you—"

"Mazal, I can't!"

"You can't what?"

"I can't come to you for Shabbos."

Mazal suddenly stopped walking, taken aback. A shadow fell across her face and I realized that I must have insulted her.

"No, no, Mazal. It's not that I don't *want* to come," I stood still, opposite her. "It's just…not right. Your grandmother isn't well. Your family has enough on their minds without extra company hanging around…"

"Ach, Sara, you not know what you talking about. We love guests!" She smiled widely and resumed walking. I kept pace alongside her. "Besides, it be good for Savta to meet you. She meet new people, she not be so much in the past."

"But—"

"No *but*," Mazal shook her head determinedly. "You come."

"Okay, okay," I smiled weakly. "I come."

Of course, at that moment I had no way of knowing that what seemed like a simple visit would affect my life in a way I never could have imagined.

10

MAZAL AND I continued walking together in comfortable silence alongside the others as we made our way through the Kfar Amsdorf woods. The crunching sounds of our shoes stepping on pebbles mingled with the girls' voices exchanging ideas and thoughts. Wafting pleasantly through the air was the woodsy scent of bark and greenery, along with the sweet aroma of the fruit trees.

Really, our Beit Yaakov HaNegbah campus was part of the village of Kfar Amsdorf. For us girls, though, it seemed like its own little world, with Kfar Amsdorf being an entirely separate entity.

The school's campus reminded me somewhat of an oversized bungalow colony. With the exception of the contemporary, large school building and the three-story dormitory, there were cottages for some of the teachers, the principals, and the staff members. Although mostly modern on the inside, the stones used to build these small homes were old, giving the cottages a quaint look. It also made me feel as though I was walking in the past and present simultaneously.

Most of what we needed could be found on campus. We ate in the dormitory's dining room. We also enjoyed a well-stocked library in the dorm as well as an even larger one in the school building. Being able to meander along the numerous park-like trails, pathways, and gardens of our campus certainly contributed to the feeling that we were living in a self-contained little town.

If, however, we wanted to do any "shopping," the closest place to go was to Kfar Amsdorf, a five-minute ride when taking the roundabout road at the entrance to the campus. A more direct but longer route was the charming fifteen minute walk through the woods, which we were in the middle of just then.

How I loved this walk!

It was not until we had gone halfway that I realized we had been walking directly behind Malkie, Adina, and Devorah. Adina walked in the middle, as dignified as ever, appearing like a queen accompanied by her two ladies-in-waiting.

I shook my head in wonder. I still could not figure out Adina. I do not think I ever saw her initiating friendships with the others, and yet rarely did I see her walking around by herself. It was obvious that Adina was someone people wanted to befriend, even though she did not seem to make any effort in their direction. I could not deny the fact that she possessed a certain charisma. Girls would approach her to ask questions regarding schoolwork or just to be friendly and I would notice her looking amused at their overtures. She did not lack for Shabbos invitations either, and the teachers apparently held her in high esteem.

What was it about Adina that drew people to her? Maybe it was that genius mind of hers or perhaps the way she carried herself. With her unusual grace, she seemed so sure and confident.

Not like me.

I found it ironic, though, that despite my continuing to feel shy and awkward much of the time, I was slowly but surely beginning to make new friends. Adina, on the other hand, with all her confidence and no lack of admirers, and almost always in the company of others, still seemed terribly alone.

Oh well, I sighed. I certainly had tried to be friendly.

More than three weeks had passed since that uncomfortable time when Adina had done an about-face right after entering my room and I had felt so hurt.

As time went by, Adina stopped being so "biting." She was not exactly warm and friendly or anything like that—she just did not seem to be as stinging as she had been earlier when I had been trying, I presume, too hard.

There I go, letting my mind wander again. I must have been completely preoccupied with my thoughts as I walked alongside Mazal, and so I was surprised to see that we had reached the end of the woods. We emerged onto a path that led straight to the back of the Bnot Yisrael schoolyard. A guard sat in a small booth by the gate and smiled warmly as Geveret Spitz approached him.

After a thorough tour of the school, we were divided into a few groups and assigned seats in different classrooms. It was fascinating to observe the teacher and children from the back of the room, and I was profoundly disappointed when the class ended. I kept thinking, *I can't wait until I become a real teacher. I can't wait until I'm in front of my very own classroom!*

Emerging from the Bnot Yisrael school building into the bright sunshine, I found myself squinting against the powerful midday rays. Shielding my eyes with the palm of my hand, I glanced quickly around the schoolyard and was relieved to discover a comfortable shady spot right under a date tree to lean against while waiting for Mazal to finish asking Geveret Spitz a question.

We were free for the rest of the day. That evening there would be a class on *Chovos HaLevavos* with Rabbanit Abrams, which I was very much looking forward to, but just then, except for lunch and some homework to catch up on—I had no obligation to rush back to the dorm.

I hope nobody notices me standing here by myself. I pressed my back against the tree's bark, wishing I could fade into its shadow while observing clusters of students bantering among themselves as they planned out their afternoon schedules with each other. *If only Chanukah were over! Then, maybe Chavie would be able to come and I wouldn't have to feel so alone!*

Sure, I was beginning to make friends. I really was. Nevertheless, that sense of belonging, of knowing that someone was looking out for me (with the exception of my roommate), continued to evade me. I guess with Chavie, it was kind of automatic that we were always there for each other. It was not something I had to worry or even think about. She was just there and so was I.

Where is Mazal already? I know she told me not to bother waiting and I know I insisted that I wanted to wait for her. I just didn't want to have to latch onto another group in order to have people to walk with on the way back.

Hearing a few familiar voices approaching, I looked up... and swallowed hard. Mimi, Rochel Leah, and a few of the other girls were nearing where I stood.

Lifting my chin and straightening my shoulders, I tried to appear as nonchalant as possible. I casually looked at my watch and then at the school's entrance, then back at my watch while tapping my foot impatiently. I wanted it to seem as though I was completely indifferent to any plans they might be working on.

I heard Chani suggest going to the *makolet* in town to stock up on some goodies. She claimed that too many hours had passed since she last ate and she could not manage the fifteen-minute walk back to the campus on an empty stomach. Mimi agreed wholeheartedly, declaring that she absolutely could not survive without those delicious Israeli caramels and that she hardly had any left. Rivky said it sounded like a great idea, since she was running out of laundry detergent and wanted to restock before she would be forced to borrow. Rochel Leah mentioned that she was low on shampoo and conditioner and fervently hoped the Israeli brands would do justice to her hair because the water was hard and her hair had become "just impossible." Zehava added that she had nothing special to do and was happy to go along.

I would have liked to go too. I especially wanted to stop at the post office next door to the *makolet* and purchase airmail stationery. Of course I would never dream of asking to join them and I would feel mortified if they invited me along out of pity.

I found myself pressing my back harder against the tree trunk, praying that they would not notice me.

"Hey, Sara, is that you? Why are you hiding? How about coming with us to town?" Mimi called out good-naturedly.

No, that doesn't sound like pity.

"Oh...I-I don't know," I hesitated, feeling the blood rushing to my face. "I-I'm waiting for Mazal."

"Okay," Mimi said, "so we'll wait too."

"Um, Mimi, have you checked your watch recently? I don't exactly want to miss lunch," Rochel Leah said impatiently. "I was only going to stop at the *makolet* for a few minutes. I'm like so-o starved."

Chapter 10

"I don't want to hold anyone back," I said hurriedly.

"No problem, Sara," Mimi said. "Rivky and I can wait with you for Mazal. Right, Rivky? And the rest of you can go on ahead. Okay, everybody?"

"I'm not in a major rush," Chani said. "I'm only planning on buying some nosh and stuff. And anyway, lunch today is going to be sandwiches and other *milchig* cold stuff that we can eat anytime we get there."

"Oh, you're right, Chani. I almost forgot. We're having *fleishig* for supper tonight because of *Rosh Chodesh*."

Rosh Chodesh, my heart lifted. *I get to speak with my family early tomorrow morning.*

"This is absolutely terrific!" Mimi delivered one of her delicious, infectious laughs. "Today, I can eat those *milchig* caramels all day long!"

I chuckled along with the others, swept up as usual with Mimi's good humor. That lonely mood I had just been experiencing melted away in the glow of Mimi's warmth.

"So-o-o, is anyone coming with me?" Rochel Leah asked.

"I will," Zehava volunteered.

"Thanks, Zehava." Rochel Leah turned toward Chani. "Anyone else care to join us?" She said those words aloud, but I was certain they were directed at Chani.

I was startled by the contradiction in the demanding tone of Rochel Leah's voice on the one hand and the silent pleading message emanating from her hazel eyes on the other.

Chani shot a quick look at Rivky and then, in a way I thought was overly buoyant, said, "Sure. I'll go with the two of you."

Waving cheerfully, we watched Chani, Rochel Leah, and Zehava exit the schoolyard gates. I turned to Mimi and Rivky. "Thanks, both of you. I'm sorry to keep you waiting. I hope no one's inconvenienced—"

"Hey, c'mon. What's the big deal?" Mimi shrugged. "It's not like you never wait for me, Sara."

It was true. Ever since I started helping Mimi with her schoolwork, I had been kept waiting much of the time. *Waiting for her to show up, waiting for her to get her stuff together, and waiting for her to stop talking and get down to business.*

Squinting at the bright sunlight, I saw a group of girls I had subconsciously been watching approach the corner and I let out a frustrated sigh. *Why do I let Mimi take advantage of me?* No, I shook my head shamefully, *I mustn't think like that.* Once again, as I had lately become accustomed to doing, I tried pushing those uncomfortable feelings away. *She's not taking advantage*, I tried telling myself again, just as I had told myself the same thing yesterday and the day before, *she just can't help it. She's so full of fun and she doesn't mean anything.*

And then again those slightly resentful thoughts would rise to the surface. And I would wonder, *why do I let her do this to me? Maybe I should tell Rabbi Grossman that I can't tutor her anymore! Yes, I must...*

Luckily, before those thoughts had a chance to ferment into anything worse, other emotions would immediately replace them.

It was true that my relationship with Mazal was growing and I was getting friendlier with some of her other friends, as well. And I did feel secure in knowing that I had a roommate who cared about me.

Still.

Mazal was Israeli and even though I considered her a "real" friend, she went home often. Her primary language was different. I wanted...I needed to feel like I belonged with the American M.B.L.L. girls too.

Somehow, when I was with Mimi, I could not feel left out even if I had wanted to. She knew how to draw me into the crowd and strip away the coat of shyness I often wore. I felt enveloped by her warmth, clothed with that sense of belonging that she wrapped around me and everyone else. Tutoring Mimi sort of evened out this friendship. It helped me feel that I was not just a recipient of her kindness, some pitiful case for her to befriend. After all, *I* was also helping *her*.

Surely, I could not remain offended by Mimi's lackadaisical and irresponsible attitude toward our study sessions. *So what if she keeps me waiting a bit!* It was a small price to pay for the wonderful friendship she shared with me.

Of course, there was also that innate stubbornness of mine that prevented me from giving up on her. *No, Sara Hirsch is no quitter!* I knew I would not and could not end our study sessions.

Besides, there really was something else that drove me to continue working with her despite the obstacles she threw in our path. I sensed this magnetic pull, some sort of compelling force that had nothing to do with her captivating personality or my feeling of owing her something for the friendship she gave me. And it had nothing to do with that naturally persistent personality of mine, either.

No. Although each of these reasons alone might have served as a strong enough motivation for me to continue our study sessions together, it had nothing to do with any of this. There truly was something else preventing me from quitting tutoring her.

It was something that had gradually dawned on me. At first I thought, *No, I must be mistaken. It can't be.* Then, slowly these thoughts niggled their way back in, eventually taking hold and not letting go.

And I knew it was true. I knew that I *had* to be there for Mimi, *must* be there for her. I was not mistaken. *Mimi needed me.* Behind that façade of easygoingness and confidence, behind that "door" with the "welcome, please enter" sign she always wore, there lurked, I was sure, a different Mimi. A Mimi who was hiding something…

That troubled look that would sometimes appear, then disappear as fast as a fleeting shadow, could not have been my imagination.

"Sara, aren't you coming?" Rivky's voice broke through my reverie.

I had been so deeply lost in thought that I was surprised to find myself still staring at the empty corner, where, just a short while earlier my eyes had followed the receding backs of the last group of girls leaving the school grounds.

"See, I told you it was no big deal," Mimi said. "Look, Mazal's already here."

I turned. Mazal was approaching and Rivky and Mimi were already swinging their book bags over their shoulders and had taken a few steps in Mazal's direction. *I really must have been daydreaming.* I grabbed my book bag and hurriedly caught up with them.

Mazal was happy to detour through town with us before going back to the dorm. "Town" was actually Rechov Amsdorf, a short block made up of four small buildings.

The first building on the block was the largest. The *makolet*, or supermarket, sold everything from "soup to nuts," as they say; it even had a small pharmacy in the back.

We went in, relieved to be greeted by the cool rush of air from the *mazgan*. We waved to some of the other girls from our seminary milling about, some purchasing items and some just standing about, enjoying the respite from the hot air outside.

Rivky found a bag of Tip detergent, which I suppose was the Israeli version of Tide. Mimi gathered at least five bags of caramels and Mazal searched determinedly through the candy and cookie aisle, all the while muttering that she had to find this Israeli treat for us and that we must not leave before she did.

We browsed around awhile until finally, on one of the upper shelves, Mazal discovered what she had been looking for. Stepping onto the bottom shelf and raising herself on tiptoe, she gripped another shelf tightly with her left hand while reaching for the prized treat with her right hand.

"Ah, these cookies...*hachi tov*! They the best!" she declared emphatically when she grasped hold of the small package. Still on tiptoe, she swung around waving them triumphantly in the air. "Tonight, I give you all special *Rosh Chodesh* treat!"

Elated, she hopped off the shelf she had been standing on. We excitedly gathered around her, curious to see what she was holding. I looked down at the package and then back at the others, my surprise mirrored in their faces. The package contained run-of-the-mill chocolate sandwich cookies. However, we all smiled enthusiastically, not wanting to dampen her fervor.

"Aren't you getting anything, Sara?" Rivky asked me a few minutes later when we stood in line to pay.

"I don't really need anything," I replied, "just some stuff from the post office."

"You're not going to treat yourself to *anything*?" Mimi asked incredulously. "C'mon, Sara...have some fun!"

"I really don't need anything," I repeated, shaking my head and smiling at the same time. "Besides, Mimi. If I'm really hungry, I can always sneak some of your caramels."

"Like I always say, Practical Sara," she replied. "Now, if any of my caramels are missing, I'll know who the guilty party is."

"Right, Mimi," Rivky laughed. "Like those caramels will be around long enough for anyone else to take any. I don't think Sara stands a chance."

Chapter 10

"*Banot, nu! Ein li et kol ha-yom. Mi mishalemet?*

Embarrassed, I realized that while we were busy bantering, our turn had come and the storekeeper was waiting impatiently for us to pay for our purchases. We finished with him and then made our way out of the store and into the sweltering street.

The post office was next door. It was just a miniature-sized version of a typical American post office. The others waited outside while I made my purchase.

I stood behind the only other customer for what seemed to be an unusually long time. He had been signing some papers when I entered and he continued to hunch over them still. I glanced at my watch uneasily, realizing that I had been waiting for over five minutes already. *They're outside waiting for me.* I could hear the hum of the *m'avrer* while it spun the musty hot air around the room and noticed the dust balls clinging to its blades. I shifted my legs worriedly. *How much longer is this going to take?*

Finally, the clerk told the other customer to move aside and finish filling out his form at the other end of the counter so that he could help me. With my accented Hebrew, he immediately realized that I was not Israeli. He asked me if I was from the seminary, and when I responded in the affirmative, he handed me a pile of mail and said I should take it back with me.

I stepped outside, appreciatively taking a deep breath of fresh air. True, it was hot and sunny outside—but the air was clear and pure, unlike the stuffy post office's interior.

Rochel Leah, Chani, and Zehava had joined the others, and I was grateful that they were all chatting animatedly and did not seem to be waiting impatiently for me. When they saw the large pile of mail I was carrying, they insisted we go through it right away to see if any of it was for us.

"Okay," Mimi said, dropping her book bag on the ground. "You start reading the names on the envelopes. As you read, hand them over to me."

"All right, but wouldn't you rather do this indoors somewhere?" I asked.

"There goes Practical Sara!" Mimi declared.

"I don't really see what the big deal is," Rochel Leah said.

"Sara's right," Chani commented. "It's too sunny and messy to do it out here. How about satisfying my very unhappy and empty stomach, Sara's practicality, and your curiosity, Mimi, at the same time? Let's sort the mail at Pinat HaGlidah."

"Sounds good to me," Rivky said.

"Me too!" Mimi patted her stomach and rolled her eyes simultaneously.

"Oh, Mimi," Mazal pinched her cheek. "You turn into ice cream or caramel. I am not sure which."

"I think she'll turn into caramel-flavored ice cream," Rivky joked good-naturedly. "Anyway, I'm all for going. We can eat our ice creams while checking the mail. By the time we get back to the dorm—"

"We'll be ready to eat again," Chani finished her sentence and we all laughed.

"And do not forget my special *Rosh Chodesh* treat!"

"Hey, what treat, Mazal?" Chani asked. "Which delicious food am I missing out on?"

"No, you not missing. You are invited to our room tonight for special cookies I buy for *Rosh Chodesh*."

"All of you are invited," I added, smiling shyly.

"Anyway, what's happening?" Rochel Leah asked. "Are we going or what? It's so-o-o hot standing out here in the sun."

"Yes," Zehava agreed, "I'm broiling. Let's go into Pinat HaGlidah so we can cool off."

We were a happy group walking along that Wednesday afternoon. My book bag hung over my shoulder, freeing my arms to carry the tall pile of envelopes, the top one tucked just beneath my chin. I knew that I would undoubtedly have to stuff them in my book bag for the walk through the woods and back to the dorm, but, for this short while down Rechov Amsdorf, I could manage.

We passed a small shop that was divided into three sections: for a shoemaker, cleaners, and tailor, and then made our way to the last store on the block, the ice cream store on the corner.

After ordering our ice creams, we began sorting through the mail. Rivky had one letter, and while I continued to look through the pile, she finished reading it. There was a letter for me from Chevy. I put it aside as I continued sorting. Rochel Leah had one letter and Zehava had two. Another letter for me was from Chavie. I noticed that Adina had a letter addressed from England and handed it to Mimi to give to her roommate upon our return. Rivky had three more letters and Chani had two. I discovered one more letter to me from Shuli. There was nothing for Mazal, but fortunately, she did not seem too disillusioned. I guess she had not been expecting anything anyway. Mimi was disappointed that there was no mail for her and let us all know it.

"It's okay, Mim," Rivky teased, "you know we all love you."

"So, why don't *you* write me?" she challenged, her eyes twinkling.

Listening to their easy banter with half an ear, I fingered the edges of the envelopes impatiently, anxious to get back to school where I could read my letters in privacy. Something was gnawing at me.

Chevy and Shuli had both written to me. Separately. Usually my sisters stuck their letters in the same envelope, but not this time. That was strange. What did they each have to say that was so private, that neither of them wanted the other to know what she was writing?

What indeed?

11

FOR THE SECOND time that day Mazal and I stood outside the front door of her medium-sized gray-colored stone house, this time though, having just returned from the local *makolet*. Wafting out of the open windows a delicious spicy aroma filled the air, sending inviting messages to my now empty stomach.

I had not really been hungry when we had arrived at Mazal's house about two hours earlier. We had done plenty of noshing during the long bus ride and, besides, I was far too wound up when we finally got there. I was anxious to meet Mazal's family and see a bit of the Kiryat Yosef about which I had heard so much.

After hanging my Shabbos outfit in the closet of the girls' room, we had some soda water mixed with petel to drink. I offered to help with Shabbos preparations, however Mazal's mother urged me to eat something first. She tried to get me to sample her fried pancakes, sprinkled with raisins and drizzled with honey. It really looked tempting, but I guess the combination of my shyness and my desire to look around and meet everybody outweighed any feelings of hunger. Her mother would not give up so easily, though, insisting that after so long a trip it could not be possible for me not to be hungry. I am sure she would have persisted, but just then we heard a cry coming from one of the rooms off the kitchen.

"Ho-da-ya...Hodaya, come back!"

It was odd.

It sounded like the cry of a toddler, but it was the voice of an adult.

Chapter 11

Mazal's mother rushed off into the room the voice was coming from. We could hear her speaking softly over the cries. "Ima, it's me, it's Tzionah."

Mazal's grandmother...crying?

"Bin-ya-min, Ze-chariah..."

"Don't worry, Ima. Sh-sh. I'm here. I'm taking care of you."

"Eli-ya-hu, Tzi-o-nah, Hoda-ya." Then suddenly, I heard a heart-stopping sob, "HODAYA!"

"*I'm* here, Ima, Tzionah is here."

"Tzionah? Who's Tzionah? I want Hodaya." The pitiful moaning persisted, "Where's Hodaya?"

"Sh-sh, *Imaleh*," she soothed, "It's okay. Everything will be all right."

I don't belong here, I remember thinking, *why in the world did I agree to come?*

"But where's Hodaya?" Pause. "Who are you?"

"It's me, Ima, it's your daughter...Tzionah."

"Oh, Tzionah. Tzionah, my dear oldest daughter. I'm sorry, Tzionah," the weeping was growing fainter. "I want to feed Hodaya. We need to find Hodaya."

"Yes, darling Ima," the voice was still soft. "Here, take this, it will make you feel much better. Oh, one minute, there's no more water in the pitcher. Mazal...Mazal!"

Mazal, who had been sitting opposite me at the table, eyes squeezed tightly closed while all this was taking place, jumped up and hurried to her mother. She emerged a second later holding a glass pitcher, refilled it, and then rushed back.

Until this day, I do not understand what made me do it. It really was not my business and I had no right to pry. I should have stayed seated at the table, waiting patiently for Mazal to return. I was a new guest, visiting for the very first time. A stranger, really.

But I did not stay seated. I followed Mazal back into the room. And that is when I met her grandmother. I saw those eyes, those lifeless eyes, blank and devoid of emotion. For a brief moment her eyes held mine...and it was then—during those few seconds—that I saw a flicker of something pass through them, as though searching for something...or could it be...someone?

I was remembering that troubling scene from a few hours earlier when Mazal suddenly asked, "Sara, maybe you could open the front door?" jolting me out of my reverie and back to the present.

She was hauling two large overflowing baskets full of groceries. I was carrying the third basket. "Yes...of course, Mazal."

Timidly, I reached out my free arm and was beginning to push it open, when suddenly the door swung back and I stumbled forward, the basket tumbling to the ground.

"Yichya and Miryam, look what you just did to our guest!" Mazal shouted in rapid Hebrew at the boy and girl scampering out of the house. "Get back right now! Apologize and help pick up the groceries!"

"Help!" the girl shouted while clutching a red ball and running around Mazal. "Yichya's gonna catch me!"

"Yichya, stop it this minute!" Mazal turned to her brother.

"Nope! Miryam took my ball," he continued circling Mazal while chasing his little sister, "she's always taking my ball!"

"Miryam, give him back his ball!" Mazal forcefully placed the two baskets on the ground on either side of her. "Now!"

"Let's go, Yichya!" said another boy standing in the doorway who looked exactly like Yichya except that he was an inch taller. "Yay, Yichya!" He waved animatedly and ran to join the circle.

"You too, Yigal?" Mazal's hands were on her hips. Her head kept turning, watching her siblings running in circles around her. "What's going on here?"

"Salma...catch!" Miryam stopped and threw the ball to another little girl, the smallest of the group (actually an almost identical but tiny version of Mazal), who just emerged panting from the house. The ball flew through the air, landing directly in front of Salma. She snatched it off the grass and ran as though her life depended on it, her sister and brothers at her heel.

"Salmi too?" Mazal sighed helplessly, rolling her eyes upward.

Salma was small, but fast. With long black braids waving behind her, she dashed with the ball through the grass, scampered over a tiny graveled path and disappeared into a narrow space between a metal

Chapter 11

shed and the stone house. Miryam, Yichya, and Yigal ran up to the spot where she had just been.

Yigal tried to slip into the space, but could barely fit his foot in. Yichya likewise made an effort, but was no more successful. Then when Miryam's attempts failed and she too could not squeeze in, she turned around to face her brothers with hands folded across her chest and a wide grin spreading triumphantly across her face. She was the winner, after all. The ball was safe!

In the meantime, I managed to regain my balance and pick up the few things that had scattered on the floor. I then followed behind Mazal as she approached her siblings. I could see her face turning redder with each step she took.

"What's happening here?" she admonished her siblings. Gesturing in my direction she added, "Don't you see we have a guest?" Her voice dropped a couple of octaves, "I am very embarrassed, Sara."

"Oh, Mazal, there's nothing to be emba—"

"Ah! Is this your roommate, Mazal?" Yigal noticed me for the first time. He took a few steps toward me, "*You're* American?"

"The *Americayit*!" The two other children exclaimed excitedly, the pursuit of the ball completely forgotten. "Let's go tell Ima she's here!"

"For your information, Ima already met her. And by the way, you could say hello to me too. You didn't see *me* since Monday."

"Shalom, Mazal," they said in unison.

"We came when you were all in school," Mazal continued. "And if you weren't so busy chasing each other you'd have noticed that we just came home from shopping for Shabbat. Now would you be so kind as to take Sara's basket, Yigal?"

"Sure, I'd love to help out the *Americayit*," he smiled up at me.

"Now, what are we going to do about Salmi?" Mazal stepped toward the narrow space, squinting. "That's all Ima needs right now, for Salmi to be stuck in there!"

"I'm not stuck. I'm right over here!"

We swung around. There, standing at the entrance of the house where we had all been a few moments earlier was Salma playing catch with herself, throwing the ball up in the air and laughing.

"Salmi, how did you—oh, never mind."

"Quick, Yichya. Get your ball!"

"Forget the ball, Yigal. I want to talk to the American lady too."

"I am so sorry, Sara." The flush on Mazal's face was still there. "*B'emet*, I do not understand what happened to my brothers' and sisters' manners."

"Mazal, please don't be sorry," I was laughing, "This is so much fun. They're so cute!"

"Hey, Mazal, don't talk to her in English. We want to understand too!"

"Well, Yichya, maybe I want to tell my friend something private."

"Could you talk to me in private too, Mazal?"

"No, Miryam. That wouldn't be nice."

"So why's it nice to talk in private to *her*? *I'm* your sister," she said indignantly, her mouth forming a pout. "And *she's* just your roommate."

"She think because she is the next girl after me I need to tell her all my secrets," Mazal whispered in English. Then turning back to Miryam, "Sara is our guest. *And* my friend, not *just* my roommate. By the way, watch what you say. She knows Ivrit perfectly."

"Well not exactly," I tried protesting.

No one seemed to hear me.

"She does?" Miryam's eyes widened.

"Really?" Yigal was doubtful.

"Let me hear her speak!" Yichya challenged.

"Yes, Miryam. Really, Yigal," Mazal turned from one sibling to the next, responding to each of them respectively. "And, Yichya, you'll have all Shabbat to speak with her and hear her talk. Now," Mazal bent to pick up one of the shopping baskets, "if we're to be ready on time for Shabbat, would you all help us with these packages and get into your baths quickly. Ima has her hands full enough. Let's go!"

Yigal and Yichya each gallantly took hold of a handle on my shopping basket, while Miryam and Salma helped Mazal with one of hers. I looked at them all, optimism stirring inside me. *I really am excited about this Shabbos!* Mazal was especially hospitable and her energetic siblings so adorably rambunctious that the awkwardness I had felt earlier began to dissipate as we made our way into the house together.

I inhaled appreciatively. The tantalizing aroma I had noticed a few minutes earlier was getting stronger and even more irresistible as we neared the kitchen.

Mazal's mother was bent over the stovetop, stirring the contents of a large pot bubbling on the range with a long wooden spoon. We could hear the sizzling sounds of something frying over another flame, and a fragrant blend of sweet and pungent smells ascended from the oven. The large wooden kitchen table was laden with fruit, crackers, and different kinds of dips and jams. A large bowl of spiced couscous sat on a towel, cooling off on a side counter. Braided challah dough was rising on a baking tray nearby, waiting to be coated with egg mixture.

Everything looked so warm and welcoming. I took another grateful sniff.

Covering Geveret Cohen's head was a tightly wrapped sequined kerchief, its tiny shiny threads catching the late afternoon sunlight. As soon as we entered, she turned around with a wide smile to greet us.

"Thank you so much, Mazal and Sara," she said in Hebrew, speaking slowly and deliberately—I believe out of consideration for me. "And children, thank *you* for helping Mazal and Sara carry everything."

Yigal and Yichya proudly placed their basket on a chair and the girls put their basket on the kitchen floor. Under Mazal's direction, we all began unpacking the groceries as her mother continued thanking us. "It helps me so much that you did the shopping. I was able to cook while Reilya napped."

"That's all right, Ima, it's our pleasure." Mazal opened the refrigerator to put the milk inside. "How's Savta feeling?"

"*Baruch Hashem*, I think much better. I gave her a pill to help her relax so she's sleeping now." She continued to stir the contents of the pot slowly. "Poor Savta."

"It seems worse than last week, Ima," Mazal sighed while placing grapefruits in a bowl in the center of the table. Then, eyeing her siblings cautiously, she asked in English, "Does she do it much, Ima? Does she?"

I looked at the children playing on the floor. They probably would not have heard anything anyway. Yigal and Yichya were preoccupied with the tower they were making out of the lebens they were supposed to unpack. Miryam had abandoned the fruits she had been carrying and was helping herself to some crackers at the table and Salma... *where is Salma?* I wondered.

"Well, unfortunately, it's happening more now."

"Why, Ima?"

"I think it has to do with the new medication the doctor gave her when she left the hospital. That's the way it affects her," Geveret Cohen lifted the wooden spoon from the pot with a helpless shrug. "What can you do? You give one thing to help one problem and then other problems take their place."

"Ima, maybe I should stay home and stop going to school."

"Enough, Mazal. We've discussed this before. We're managing just fine. Anyway," she looked over at me kindly, "this is no way to treat a guest. Mazal, please take care of Sara." She gestured toward the table. "Give her some crackers with jelly or hilbeh, whichever she prefers."

"Oh no, please don't bother with me, Geveret Cohen. I'm fine. What can I do to help?"

"First eat," she said in English, "then we talk."

I took my seat docilely, smiling back at her. "This kitchen smells heavenly."

"Of course. It's *Erev Shabbat*," Yichya said matter-of-factly and began to sing. "*MeEin Olam HaBa, Yom Shabbat menuchah...*"

"It always smells like this on *Erev Shabbat*," Yigal informed me while adding another container of leben to his tower.

"You're very lucky," I told the boys.

"Why are we lucky?"

"To have such a special Shabbos."

"We love Shabbat," Salma said from under the table. "Right, Mazali?"

"Right, Salmi."

"Ima makes the best foods for Shabbat," Miryam said proudly. "Did you ever taste such food?"

"I-I'm not sure," I replied, referring to Yemenite cuisine.

"Never, Sara? You never had Shabbat?" Miryam asked me, her eyes wide.

"Of course I have," I felt myself blushing.

"Of course she has," Mazal came to my rescue. "And please stop being impolite and asking so many questions."

"I'm not impolite!"

"It's really not a problem, Mazal."

"She shouldn't ask. I'm really sorry, Sara. Miryam, you don't ask people such questions. It's—"

"*Shalom, shalom!*"

"Abba!"

"Mazal!"

"Amram, Yehudah!"

"*Shalom aleichem.*" Then turning to me, "*Beruchah ha-ba'ah*, welcome to our home."

Shyly I mumbled in Hebrew, "Thanks for having me."

"Abba, Rebbi gave me a special prize today."

"Wonderful, Yigal."

"I also got a prize today from Morah!"

"That's terrific, Miryam."

"Me too, me too," Salma chirped.

I sat quietly, watching them all interacting, exchanging stories, bantering, and sharing. Laughter came easily, and the comfortable feeling of love and friendliness ricocheted around the room. Of course, it made me miss and long for my own loving family, but the enthusiasm and affection in this Yemenite home washed over me, enveloping me with its warmth.

Late that night while we were lying in bed snuggled under our quilts, Mazal asked me in a quiet whisper, "Are you happy you come, Sara?" We had to be careful not to wake her sisters who were sleeping in the same bedroom, so we kept our voices as low as possible.

"I sure am," I whispered back softly, staring up at the darkness. I could see the shadows of the trees filtered by the moon's light playing across the ceiling. "You have a fantabulous family."

"Fan-tab-u-lous?"

"Yes. That's Shuli's word. It means fantastic and fabulous." I rolled over onto my side to face her in order that we could converse more freely. Resting my head in my hand with my elbow digging into the pillow, I could easily discern her features illuminated by the glow of the silvery moonlight. "You know Shuli."

"Yes, *betach*. How I could forget?"

"No," I shook my head. "It's definitely not easy to forget Shuli."

"She very special."

"I know."

For a few moments, no one said anything. Slowly, I returned to my original supine position. Cradling the back of my head in the palms of my hands, I looked up at the dark ceiling, watching the dancing shadows' graceful movements. We could hear the buzzing sounds of crickets coming from the nearby woods.

"You very special too, Sara."

"Thanks, Mazal."

"*B'emet*, Sara," Mazal flipped over to face me, her expression serious. "Shuli special, she stand out. You special…you *really* special. Inside," she thumped her chest. "As a matter of factual—"

"You mean…as a matter of fact?"

"*Kain…nachon*, as-a-mat-ter-of-fact," she pronounced each syllable slowly and carefully, "I think you, Sara, not stand out special…"

"Huh?"

"You more than special. You be fantabulous!"

Fantabulous…

I drifted off to sleep that night, with the "fantabulous" feeling lingering. And that "fantabulous" feeling stayed with me all through the next day. Well, *almost* all through the next day.

We were in shul bright and early in the morning. Mazal had given me the option of *davening* with the Ashkenazi *minyan*, but I chose to go with her to the Yemenite shul. I will not go into details, but to sum it up, it was different, it was unique, it was beautiful, and I loved every minute of it. I could not wait to write to my family, sharing that wonderful experience.

Walking home from shul on the path that circled Kiryat Yosef, Mazal pointed out some of the more famous landmarks in the distance. Surrounded by green hills and even greener valleys, Kiryat Yosef was a relatively large development. There was ample space between each of the private homes, with a few apartment buildings on the outskirts. Loads of trees, well-tended gardens, and clean streets filled the neighborhood.

Chapter 11

An *eruv* surrounded the community and, nodding amiably, we wished "Shabbat shalom" to those mothers passing by with babies in carriages. I noticed some people looking at me curiously, but not in an unfriendly manner, and I found myself enjoying the walk immensely. It was a beautiful day. The late morning sun shone down brightly and the carless streets were full of families taking advantage of the glorious weather.

When we reached Mazal's street, Miryam, wheeling two-year-old Reilya in her stroller with Salma holding on to the side, came out to greet us. The joy on their faces when they saw me with Mazal, and the affection they shared so generously, filled me with a comfortable sense of familiarity. I no longer felt like a stranger.

The Shabbos afternoon *seudah* was especially nice and lively. The whole Cohen family was there, with the exception of Mazal's two older brothers, who were in yeshivah for Shabbos. They learned, Mazal told me proudly, in the famous Yeshivat HaAlshich, where her uncle, her mother's oldest brother, the well-known Chacham Eliyahu Yitzchaki was the *Rosh Yeshivah*. Also joining the *seudah* was Mazal's Uncle Binny and his three boys.

The evening before, Mazal had explained that her uncle, Binyamin Yitzchaki had lost his wife the previous year and had only recently taken a small apartment on the other side of Kiryat Yosef. It was apparent to me from his and his sons' mode of dress that they were not as religious as Mazal's family. It was also quite obvious that warmth and love between the two families was not lacking and that their divergent paths had not caused any breach in their relationship.

A commotion of sorts evolved when it was time for us to take our seats.

Miryam and Salma fought to sit next to me, Miryam claiming that it was unfair that the night before Salma sat next to me on one side and Mazal on the other, and that it was only right that she too get a chance to sit next to me. Salma, stubbornly refusing to move, remained where she was. She argued that since Mazal could sit next to me anytime, Miryam and she should have first choice. Finally, to quiet things down and make everyone happy, their father suggested that Mazal move over—that is if *I* did not mind.

Of course, I did not mind and so Mazal switched seats with Miryam—much to everyone's relief. Peace reigned once again in the Cohen household.

Throughout the *seudah*, singing resounded through the house, accompanied by traditional Yemenite cuisine. Along with the challah we were able to smear homemade pitot with a delicious dip of fried chatzilim. Miryam offered me some *zehug*, as well, which was a bit too sharp for my Ashkenazi taste buds. She and Salma burst out laughing when I immediately downed two cups of water to wash away the spicy tang from my tongue. Mazal admonished them for their lack of consideration. I found it completely amusing and joined in their laughter.

They also served fish that did not taste like any I had ever eaten. Mazal explained that it was spiced with hawiaj, a mixture of cumin, cardamom, turmeric, and coriander—spices and herbs we do not add to our gefilte fish. I found it to be surprisingly tasty.

There was a large variety of interesting salads, one of which contained chickpeas and couscous, which I preferred not to experience. Of course, there was plenty of Israeli salad too, which I gladly helped prepare when we returned home from the *Beit Knesset*.

I tasted some of the black bean salsa too. Made of plum tomatoes diced small, along with orange sections, spices, olive oil and lime juice with jalapeno pepper, it had a unique and tantalizing taste.

I could not believe it. *Me, unadventurous Sara Hirsch trying out all these exotic foods!* I suppose I was not as cautious as I thought. I told Mazal that I must get that recipe and send it home to my mother to make. I knew my family would love it. Mazal's mother smiled appreciatively, acknowledging that it was her mother's famous recipe.

Savta. I looked toward the grandmother. She sat in a wheelchair that either Amram or Yehudah must have rolled to the table before the meal began. Her eyes stared ahead, vacant with that same empty look.

With Geveret Cohen's cajoling and help, she ate and drank a little. I thought, *Mazal's mother is such an angel.* Throughout the meal, I noticed how she attended to the grandmother with the utmost respect. She fluttered here and there, attending to everyone's needs, speaking softly and supportively. Amram, sixteen, and Yehudah, fourteen, who Mazal told me were home most Shabbosos, were a big help too. They attended a local yeshivah where Mazal's father was a *maggid shiur* and they only dormed during the week. When they came home on weekends, they would do whatever they could to alleviate their mother's burden.

And so I sat there. The guest. Observing, tasting, listening. There was more singing, more *divrei Torah*, more talking, and more eating. After clearing the table of the main dish, Yehudah, at his father's request, brought out a *sefer* of the Chafetz Chaim.

"Abba learns two *halachot* of *Shemirat HaLashon* with us each week," Miryam whispered to me.

Mazal's father, at the head of the table, regally clad in a shiny, colorful caftan, read from the *sefer*, elucidating and giving examples. His words were said slowly and deliberately. I was not sure if he always spoke this way when giving over a lesson, especially in front of the little children, or if he was doing it to make it easier for me to understand, just as his wife did when conversing with me.

And then he began a melody I had never heard before. The words, though, were familiar. He sang *Mi HaIsh HeChafeitz Chaim* in a beautiful, haunting tune. His eyes were closed, his brows furrowed in deep concentration. Amram and Yehudah joined in, enhancing the song with their harmony. Yigal and Yichya with their childish sopranos sang along as well. Then the cousins and their father with their deep voices began gradually to sing with the others. As the blend of diverse voices lifted in unity, I was sure this song was soaring heavenward. The air felt thick with holiness, I could almost touch it and I was positive that any minute *Mashiach* would knock on the door and take us all off to Yerushalayim.

I looked around the room. The little girls on either side of me were also humming along, Mazal was drumming her finger on the table, baby Reilya sitting on Amram's lap was clapping her hands joyfully. Then my eyes shifted toward their mother. She was finally sitting. It seemed that her eyelids were fighting to stay open, but I could see her lips curling up at the sides contentedly. Next to her sat the grandmother.

I gasped.

Her eyes no longer had that vacant, empty look that reminded me of a closed door. In its stead was something else. I had noticed it briefly the day before, when I had followed Mazal into the room. But I had been there for so short a time and it had passed so quickly that I could not be certain I had really seen it.

Now I was sure.

I knew without a doubt, I *did* see the change take place. Until this day, the scene remains before me with every detail clearly imprinted in my mind. I can still see it happening as though it was unfolding in slow motion.

It was like the bars of the jail cell had been raised and the prisoner freed. In Savta's eyes I could see warmth…emotion…pain.

Life.

And then, just as unexpectedly as it had appeared, it was gone. The bars dropped down again in place and she was back in her prison.

I do not think I shall ever forget that troubled look. *What did it mean? Was she looking for something…searching for someone?* And how quickly it had passed!

Suddenly, the song ended. I felt so disappointed.

Dessert, on the other hand, was no disappointment, but I felt saddened that this meal and this exotic, almost magical Shabbos was soon to be over.

"I hope you'll come again soon," Miryam said while taking a generous bite of baklava.

"I hope so too," I smiled over her head, my eyes meeting Mazal's.

"Well if you would treat her nicely, then maybe—"

"Of course we're treating her nicely, Mazali," Salma licked her fingers while trying to catch the sweet syrup dribbling down her chin. "Right, Sara?"

"Right," I grinned.

"So, could you read us that English book?" she asked, referring to the Jewish *middos tovos* book I had given them as a Shabbos gift when I arrived. Shuli had recommended that I bring a stack of these English Judaic books along with me to give as gifts to Israeli families. She told me that they found them to be "amazing" and that the parents appreciated the practice their children got from reading books on Jewish topics in English.

"I don't see why not."

"When the *seudah* finishes, I was planning to take Sara for a long walk around Kiryat Yosef."

"Could we come, Mazal?"

"Yes, could we?" Yigal asked shyly.

"Me too, Mazali. Pleeease!"

"Me, me, me!" Reilya banged on her highchair. "Me go bye-bye!"

"I also want to go!" Yichya declared vehemently and then quietly added, "Well, that is if everyone else—"

"We'll see," Mazal's eyes twinkled. "Maybe if you *all* do a really great job helping with the clean up…"

And so they did. And I read to them that English book. More than once. Then, they asked me to read them some stories in Hebrew, laughing good-naturedly at my accent.

We kept our voices down. Mazal's mother was taking a well-deserved and necessary rest, and I was happy to help keep the children occupied. I wanted so much to do something to help and at least partially reciprocate for the wonderful Shabbos they shared with me.

Then the children begged Mazal to take out some food for a *mesibat Shabbat*.

"Only if you talk very quietly," she warned.

They promised and we all headed for the kitchen. Napkins and glasses were placed on the table and so was mitz tapuzim and petel with soda water to drink. The cabinets were opened and more snacks were brought out. We sat around the table, enjoying our drinks and some more of that delicious baklavah from the afternoon *seudah*. We also noshed on garinim, Bamba, biscuitim, and homemade cake. We nibbled on halvah and some sort of fruit crumble, left over from Friday night's dessert.

As we snacked, the children amiably and with innocent curiosity asked me all kinds of questions. I tried to answer them as well as I could in my broken Hebrew. They wanted to know all about my own siblings and I was, of course, delighted to talk about them. They wanted to know exactly where Rolland County was, what kind of games I played when I was their age, if I was going to be a teacher when I finished seminary, who I was going to marry, and would I consider marrying someone from Israel, how about Kiryat Yosef, how about someone they know…

That was when Mazal grabbed me away from them and told them

to stop asking me so many questions as she dragged me out of the door. I was laughing so hard when we left the house that Mazal, whose face had been completely serious a few minutes earlier, also burst out laughing.

I felt a delightful breeze lift my hair and I wrapped my arms around my chest to keep warm. The afternoon sun still shone brightly, but the Northern air was much cooler than at the Beit Yaakov HaNegbah campus.

I looked around. Shading my eyes with my hand, I could see in the far off distance the snow-covered Har Chermon surrounded by rolling hills and mountains. I took a deep satisfying breath, attempting to capture it all, wishing I could lock this wonderful feeling inside me.

"You like it here. No?" Mazal asked me in English.

"*Betach*," I replied in Hebrew.

We smiled at each other contentedly.

"Sara, Mazali, wait for me!" Salma came bounding out of the house.

"Don't forget about us!" Miryam called from the doorway and then, coming closer, dolefully added, "When you go back tonight, I won't see you again for a long time."

"Isn't Mazali coming back for Shabbat?"

"Sorry, Salmi," Mazal patted her little sister's head, "but *im yirtzeh Hashem*, next Shabbat I have *toranut*."

"Let someone else do it!"

"That wouldn't be fair. I've got to take my turn too. Besides," there was a gleam in her eye, "I'm really looking forward to it. Nu, stop looking so sad, Miryam."

"You'd rather do *toranut* than be home?"

"Of course I'd rather be with all of you, but it's only right that I do *toranut*. And I have to admit, it's bound to be loads of fun."

"Fun?" Miryam persisted.

"Yes! I'm supposed to do it with Mimi Rosenberg. Remember the fun-loving girl in my class I told you about?"

"The *gingi*?"

"Right, Salmi," she nodded at her little sister. "With Mimi, even *toranut* is going to be fun. Am I correct, Sara?"

"Absolutely, Mazal."

"And I almost forgot. Besides having *toranut*, next Shabbat anyway is a Shabbat *chovah*—"

"I also forgot," I said. "Everyone will be staying next Shabbos."

"Sara," Miryam turned to me, "who do you have *toranut* with?"

"I don't know yet. The list is posted every *Rosh Chodesh* and this month I wasn't on it."

"Maybe you and Mazal will be together next month," she sounded hopeful.

"I highly doubt that," I said slowly, trying to make my *Ivrit* as flawless as possible. "From what I heard, at the beginning they don't put roommates together for *toranut* because they want to give all the girls a chance to get to know each other."

"Besides, I've already got it this month. Next month others will have it," Mazal explained. "Anyway, enough *toranut* talk. We'd better get moving. It will be dark soon and I want to show Sara around," Mazal said, cheerfully heading back to the house. "Girls, get your sweaters just in case it gets cold. I'm going in to get Reilya."

"Abba said we could come too," Yichya emerged from the house before Mazal had a chance to enter.

"As long as we return in time for *Minchah*," Yigal, who was directly behind his brother, added.

"Okay, okay," Mazal said good-naturedly. "You can *all* come. Let me get Reilya, already. Yigal, Yichya…please get the stroller from the shed. Girls, don't forget your sweaters. Sara, I'm bringing out a sweater for you too."

I stood there alone for a few moments, waiting for everyone to return and wondering if there was anything I could possibly do to help. Then, realizing that the baby would probably want something to eat while outdoors, I headed for the kitchen to find something we could bring along for her.

Amram and Yehudah were sitting by the kitchen table and learning. Then my gaze moved along the back wall, stopping when I saw the grandmother.

She was sitting in her wheelchair by the large kitchen window. The *tris* was opened all the way and the bright afternoon sun was pouring in, caressing her in its warmth. I could see an intricately patterned, colorful shawl spread across her lap and was sure that it had been handmade. Her chin rested on her chest and her eyes were closed. *She must be sleeping*, I thought to myself. She seemed so at peace. Perhaps she was simply enjoying listening to her two grandsons' melodious voices filling the room with their learning. I noticed that the table still held leftovers from the Shabbos party. *We really should clean it all up before going on our walk.*

I tiptoed over to the table, so as not to disturb the boys or wake their grandmother. Opening a folded napkin and laying it out on the table, I was about to place some biscuitim on it, when suddenly a piercing cry rang out.

"Hodaya!"

I froze.

"Hodaya, is that you?"

My mouth turned dry.

Within seconds, both boys were at her side.

"Savta, it's all right," Yehudah comforted. "Let's let Ima sleep."

"We'll take care of you, Savta," Amram said, rubbing his hand lightly on her shoulder, trying to calm her.

She was crying and shaking. Her eyes were no longer vacant. They were wild, hysterical. "Hodaya, come back!" she screamed.

"Amram, quickly, get Savta's pills from her room before Ima wakes up."

Amram dashed out of the room.

A shudder ran through me and I felt my heartbeat quicken. Swallowing hard, I commanded myself to remain calm.

What could I do to help?

Glancing around the room, I noticed a glass by the side of the sink. I hurried over and rinsed if off. Then, opening the refrigerator, I removed the pitcher of water and shakily poured some into the glass, filling it more than halfway. I motioned to Yehudah, pointing to the glass of water now resting on the table. And then, forgetting the biscuitim and the reason I had entered the kitchen in the first place, I fled.

But there was no escaping. I would remain a captive, chained to this woman's story, shackled by her past. Because once the truth became known to me, I would not... *could* not let go.

Part Two

12

THE BUS SPED through the darkness along the winding highway, with the passing tiny lights swiftly disappearing into the night's blackness. The simultaneous rocking motion of the vehicle together with the steady drone of the motor succeeded in putting most of the passengers to sleep, including Mazal.

I too should have been sleeping, but my racing thoughts would not let me…

I wonder what exactly is wrong with their Savta. Mazal told me that her grandmother is only in her early sixties. I was sure she was at least eighty. Oh, I don't know. And wow! How wonderful Mazal's family is! That Salma is so adorable. How in the world do they keep up with her? And Miryam, such a precocious child. No, nothing could be put past her…Mazal's brothers, all of them seem so sweet and caring…Oh, and her mother. She is really special, a true angel…I don't think I'll ever again be able to hear the words "Mi ha-ish he'chafaitz chaim…" without thinking about the way Mazal's father sang it and how beautiful and extraordinary this Shabbos was.

The bus continued rushing through the night without pause. The food was so interesting. I guess I really am becoming more adventurous in my old age. Kiryat Yosef…It was a wonderful change! I can't believe it. Who would ever have expected me to become such great friends with Mazal…Great friends…

Great friends…Chavie…How I wish Chavie could be sharing this all with me…Oh, no, I almost forgot about her letter. I've been so busy, I still didn't write back to her. Or Shuli. Or Chevy. No, this is definitely not like me… not to answer a letter immediately. I owe so many letters! I can't believe I've allowed them to accumulate. I'm usually so practical.

This time, my rushing thoughts came to an abrupt stop. Suddenly, I sat upright. *What's going on?*

Something was niggling at the back of my mind.

Did it concern Adina? No, I'm not going to allow myself to even think about Adina Stern. I have totally and unequivocally given up trying to become friends with her. So, what was it? Mimi? No, not Mimi. Definitely not Mimi, I shook my head decisively. We had been busy studying together on practically a daily basis as per Rabbi Grossman's instructions, and nothing unusual had happened between us.

So, what in the world is suddenly making me feel so worried?

Mazal's grandmother? No…right now something else is bothering me.

What is it?

All right, Sara, backtrack! Review everything that went through your mind in the last few minutes.

You were thinking about Shabbos at the Cohen's. The father, the mother, the kids. No, there was nothing strange there. The grandmother. Of course, something isn't right about her. And of course, it's not just about her being old and sick. That I know already. I sat up rigidly, my body tensing. *So, what is it, then, that's giving me this uneasy feeling?*

Okay…you were feeling terrific about your new friendship with Mazal. Then you started thinking about Chavie. And that you owe her a letter. And Chevy and Shuli.

That's it! Chevy and Shuli. Ever since you received their separate letters, read them, and reread them, something has been troubling you.

I leaned back against the vinyl of my seat, tightly gripping the ends of the armrests. Squeezing my eyes shut, I let out a deep troubled sigh. *What's going on?*

"You have problem, Sara?"

My eyes flipped wide open. "Oh, no, everything is great, Mazal. I'm sorry, I hope I didn't wake you."

"Sara, you say sorry too many times. How could you wake me? I am not sleeping."

"I thought you were. Your eyes were closed, you sounded like you were snoring…"

"No, I just, how you say it? I was night dreaming—"

"Day dreaming."

"Night dreaming, day dreaming. Who care? I was dreaming of the list from Geveret Spitz waiting on the *luach*."

"I can't believe it," I said eagerly. "I almost forgot."

"I really want to know where *Geveret* Spitz put me."

"And I'm anxious to know what kind of child she'll put me with. Will I work well with her? Will she like me?"

"Sure she like you, Sara. Everyone like you."

I blushed. "No, really, Mazal. I so much want to do a great job. I want to succeed—"

"Sara, you be…um…fan-tab-u-lous."

"Thanks, Mazal," I answered softly.

I turned away from her toward the window. Cupping my chin in the palm of my hand with my elbow leaning on the armrest, I stared hard at my image mirrored in the window. *Sara, I told my reflection, my pulse beginning to quicken…you'd better be more than fantabulous. You've got to take that child and completely turn her around. Make a real impact. Show that you're not just a regular teacher like everyone else, but something more.*

Resting my forehead against the cool glass, I closed my eyes, picturing it. *The dimmed lights of the auditorium, Rabbi Grossman standing at the microphone in the center of the stage. The room thick with tension as Rabbi Grossman clears his throat. Everyone waiting with trepidation. My heart beating wildly, and I am sure, happily sure, that everyone can hear its loud thumping as I make my way up to the stage after he announces my name as the winner of the Goldstone Outstanding Student Teacher Award.*

"Something funny, Sara?"

"What?" I turned around to face Mazal.

"I see you in the window. You have a big smile. So, tell me your joke or maybe you just happy?"

"Sorry, Mazal, no joke. I'm thinking about what a wonderful Shabbos I had with you and your family. I'm also anxious to get back to the dorm and find out who we will be working with. I'm so excited to get started."

Mazal looked at her watch and then twisted her wrist for me to see the time. "*B'emet*, it not be much longer."

"It's so late already," I nodded while trying to stifle a wide yawn. "I sure hope the girls will still be up when we get there."

"Not much longer" turned out to be quite a while. There was some unexpected "after hours" road construction. Then, the driver hired by Rabbi Grossman to meet us at the bus station went home when our bus had not showed up as scheduled and we had to wait for him to return. By the time we finally arrived at the Beit Yaakov HaNegbah campus and made our way into the dormitory, it was indeed very late. All was quiet on the main floor.

We dropped our bags in the front hallway and headed straight to the lounge where the large bulletin board posting all the latest announcements hung. Although on *Motza'ei Shabbos* the *eim ha-bayit* was not particularly strict about curfew and "lights out," there was a timer that automatically switched off most of the lights in the building every night, and that included the large lounge. Light from the hallway shone into the room, but that hardly helped us decipher the words on the notices that were posted there.

"I know what we can do, Mazal. I have a flashlight in our room. Let's go get it. Then we can come back down and see what's here."

"Okay," Mazal yawned. "But our trip took so long that I am hungry again. I want to go take something to eat."

"No, problem, Mazal. I'm also a little hungry myself. Let's see if there's anything left from the *Melaveh Malkah*."

We went into the dining room where the main lights had also gone off. Fortunately, though, there were a few small round fluorescent light fixtures spaced across the walls of the large room that were not connected to the timer. With the help of their soft glow, I could see an open box of biscuitim on one of the tables with a jar of chocolate spread next to it. There was also a crate of oranges on a nearby chair. We were not about to be fussy at so late an hour.

We took a few oranges, and then, smearing the crackers with the chocolate, we placed them on plates and, picking up our bags from the main hallway, made our way up the stairs.

We went up the two flights talking in whispers, trying to keep the sounds of our footsteps from echoing down the long stairwell. We need not have been so careful. As we approached our floor, we could hear the hum of familiar music coming from one of the rooms, mingled with friendly voices and outbursts of sudden laughter. Coming closer to our room, we were startled to discover that the noise we heard was coming from there.

We stood in front of our door, the lively vibrating sounds from inside pulsating out to us.

I looked at Mazal. Mazal looked at me.

Then, opening our mouths at once, we both said one two-syllable word simultaneously… "Mimi."

Slowly, Mazal pushed open the door.

My jaw dropped.

The first thing I noticed was that the music was coming from *my* tape recorder which was playing one of *my* tapes. The second thing I noticed was Mimi, wearing her blue and red striped robe sitting cross-legged on *my* bed. She was strumming her guitar along with the music and singing with complete abandon. The third thing I noticed was that no one had noticed our entry.

Rivky, her pink nightgown peeking out of her matching pink robe, and Chani, in a huge sweatshirt, were dancing in the middle of the room. It looked like Rivky, her small round glasses perched on the tip of her nose, was trying to teach Chani a new dance step, but that Chani, with her two left feet, was not catching on. Rivky's glasses kept slipping forward with each step she took. Finally, she handed them to Malkie.

Malkie and Devorah lay sprawled on Mazal's bed, robes wrapped around their sleepwear. Malkie passed the glasses to Devorah, who handed them over to Rochel Leah, indicating that she should place them on the desk behind her. Rochel Leah, her face smeared with some white beauty concoction, and Zehava, her blonde layers twisted and clipped in pin curls, were sitting on the two desk chairs which had been turned around and faced the middle of the room. Rochel Leah nonchalantly took the glasses and put them on the desk. Then she turned back to continue watching the "show." All four were laughing jovially.

We stood motionlessly, staring and with mouths agape.

While the music reverberated throughout our room, Mimi continued singing and vigorously strumming the strings of her guitar. Chani twirled under Rivky's outstretched arm, and Malkie and Devorah, followed by Rochel Leah and Zehava, stood up and joined in the dancing, swinging in step to the melody, accompanied by more cheerful laughter.

No one noticed us.

The music swelled to a climax and then began its descent, slowing as it came closer to its dramatic ending. The girls, eyes sparkling, cheeks red, and panting breathlessly, gradually slowed down in keeping with the beat, their movements slackening somewhat with their steps paced further apart. As the song finished with its final theatrical notes, they sank to the floor in a circle, giggling uproariously, while Mimi, putting her guitar down on my bed, pirouetted into the center of the group. With a flourish, she took two deep bows first to the right and then to the left, to the applause and cheers of the others.

Everyone was laughing.

Everyone but me.

"Hurray, hurray!" Mazal clapped along with the others. "*Azeh harkadah yaffah!*"

"Oh my goodness!" Rivky jumped up. Someone had finally noticed our presence. She took a few hurried steps toward us, wisps of thin brown hair wet against her forehead. "We didn't even see you come in."

The others turned in our direction.

"Hey, look who's back! Sara…Mazal…when did you get here?"

"We stand here maybe five minutes watching your show, Mimi," Mazal chuckled.

"So how did you like it?" Chani asked, standing up and slowly spinning around. "Think I'm ready to dance solo?"

"So low?"

"Mazal, she didn't mean *so low*," I said softly, suddenly finding my voice. "Solo means by yourself. Chani's asking if she's good enough to dance by herself."

"So, can I get a solo dancing part at the Chanukah performance, Mimi?"

"Um…" For once, Mimi was tongue-tied.

"Just kidding, Mimi. Don't worry, I definitely don't want to ruin your performance. Maybe instead you'll give me a speaking part, or better yet, an eating part."

"Hey, speaking about food…what've you two got for us to eat?" Mimi asked, eyeing the plates of chocolate-smeared biscuitim we were still holding.

"Yup! All this singing and dancing has definitely made me hungry," Chani patted her stomach.

"Me too," Rochel Leah said while rising and dusting off her robe.

"Me, three," Zehava added, also standing up.

Malkie and Devorah shook their heads as they lifted themselves off the floor.

"I don't know if it's such a good idea to eat right now while we're so heated up," Malkie said worriedly, perspiration dotting her upper lip. "It's really boiling in here." She headed toward the window.

"Nothing for me, thank you," Devorah flopped onto the chair. "I'm way too tired to eat."

"I'm *never* too tired to eat," Chani retorted.

"Me neither. So, did you bring us back any goodies from Kiryat Yosef?" Mimi rolled her eyes dramatically, "I'm absolutely famished!"

"Don't you think we should give them a chance to come into their own room before bombarding them?" Rivky suggested in her good-natured manner.

"Hey, no one's bombarding anybody. We're just giving them a friendly welcome." Mimi smirked, then turning to us, she stretched out her hand exaggeratedly, "Welcome to your room."

"Thanks," I mumbled and then ducked past her to the closet to hang up my Shabbos outfit.

"So now, Rivky, can I ask Mazal if she brought us back any leftovers to eat?"

"Be my guest, Mimi."

I turned from the closet, carrying the rest of my stuff to my bed.

"Do not worry, Mimi," Mazal smiled, putting her bags on her bed and removing a heavily wrapped package from one. Then, unwinding the paper ceremoniously, she unveiled three containers as the others gathered around her. "We bring back some baklava and halvah for you and also some zehug."

"Zehug?" Rochel Leah scrunched up her nose. "What's that?"

"I never heard of that before," Zehava shook her head.

"Me neither," Devorah commented.

"What do you do with it?" Malkie asked. "Do you use it as a dip or do you eat it just—"

"It sounds like some sort of Sephardi concoction," Rochel Leah cut her off. "I don't know how you Yemenites eat this stuff."

Why does she always have to sound so patronizing? Concerned, I looked at Mazal.

"Ask Sara," Mazal winked at me, not seeming at all offended.

"So-o-o," Rochel Leah turned to me, "what *is* that stuff?"

"Um," I hesitated for a moment, wondering if Mazal had noticed Rochel Leah's disdainful tone. Suddenly this wicked, mischievous something came over me. I looked at Rochel Leah, her round hazel eyes staring back at me almost demandingly. "It's this really deliciously sweet dip, Rochel Leah. Here, take one of my biscuitim and smear some on it…"

"I'll have some too," Zehava said, reaching for a cracker.

"You know me," Chani commented. "I'm always willing to try something new."

"Me too," Mimi licked her lips.

"Not me," Malkie said. "What if I don't react well to it? Especially so late at night."

"Count me out," Devorah yawned. "At this hour, I can't even think of eating any—"

"Uch!" Rochel Leah screeched, spitting out the little she had tasted. "What are you trying to do, poison me?" Her eyes were dark and tearing, the white paste on her face cracking. "Help! Get me water!"

Zehava ran to the sink, filled my plastic cup with water, and brought it back as quickly as she could to Rochel Leah.

"Hey, what's the matter, Rochel Leah?" Mimi asked, "I think this *hugi* is great."

"Zehug, Mimi," Chani corrected, "and it *is* kind of sharp. But tasty," she smiled at Mazal. "I'll also have some of that water…"

Chapter 12

By the time everyone finally piled out of our room and I finished unpacking, preparing my books for the next morning, tidying up and doing whatever else I had the strength left to do, I crawled under my thick quilt, grateful to be able to go to sleep at last.

I closed my eyes. Sleep, though, would not come.

I tossed and turned a few times, first lying on my left side and then flipping over onto my right, then back onto my left. *Why can't I fall asleep?* I tried lying in a prone position, face down on the pillow with my hands tucked underneath. That did not work either. I was still wide-awake.

Finally, I gave in to the inevitable. Slowly, I once again turned over, this time my back resting flat against the mattress. I lay there, staring at the ceiling, no longer trying to reign in my wandering thoughts.

Mazal and I had not returned downstairs to the lounge with my flashlight to check the posted list, after all. Following the incident with the zehug, Rochel Leah had made a quick exit with Zehava (of course). Malkie and Devorah also left a few minutes later, Malkie desperately wanting to jump into the shower and Devorah desperately wanting to jump into bed. Chani, Mimi, and Rivky hung around a while longer. They managed to talk us out of going back to the lounge, insisting that they could fill us in on the latest announcements posted there.

Rivky said that it did not pay to bother checking the names of the children we would be working with, since we would be meeting them the next day anyway and most of the names were unfamiliar to us. Mimi informed me that I would be doing most of my student teaching in the resource room (she also was assigned there) and Chani noted that she and Mazal were both placed in Bnot Yisrael's eighth grade classroom.

Mazal and I were both relieved. Mazal had hoped to be assigned to an upper elementary grade since this would be good training for her to eventually work in high school. I was thrilled to be placed in the resource room. Ever since Geveret Spitz began talking to us about it, I felt my heart pulling me there. Somehow, I knew that it would be there, in the resource room, where my dreams would come true.

In the resource room, I could make a real difference! In the resource room, working in close proximity to Geveret Spitz with children who truly needed me on a one-to-one basis, I could actually analyze and zero in on their problems. I would have the opportunity to help each child, to free them from whatever was preventing them from learning properly. I would have the chance to prove who I really was, the kind of teacher I could be…to finally make my mark.

Yes… my most fervent hopes would be realized. I would do whatever was necessary to be the winner of the Goldstone Outstanding Student Teacher Award, and it would be there, in Geveret Spitz's resource room, where I was sure it would happen.

I sat up staring into the darkness, once again overcome by that compelling feeling. *Something special is going to happen to me. I am not going to remain "plain, simple Sara" forever…*

We had continued discussing Geveret Spitz's list for a few minutes, then Rivky excitedly told Mazal and me about the *tiyul* planned for next Sunday. My mind, of course, was still preoccupied with the resource room and my secret hopes and dreams. However, Rivky's enthusiasm was contagious and somehow managed to draw my attention to the trip.

"It's only one week from tomorrow," I hugged my knees closely against my chest, remembering the eagerness in her voice.

"What do you mean, *tomorrow*," Chani laughed. "Tomorrow's already *today*. It's Sunday now."

"You're right," Rivky said, glancing at her watch. "Oh my goodness, I don't believe it! It's almost two forty-five in the morning!"

"Time flies when you're having fun," Mimi sang out.

"Tell me about the *tiyul*," Mazal said. "Ach, I so tired."

"Sorry, Mazal. I didn't realize how late it is. We're suppose to leave early next Sunday morning. We'll be davening *Shacharis* at the Kosel—"

"*Kotel.*"

"Sorry again, Mazal. We'll be davening *Shacharit* at the *Kotel*."

Mazal grinned.

"And then," Chani continued, "there will be a walking tour around Yerushalayim. We'll be eating lunch in Geulah. Then we'll be getting together with the other seminaries for a *kinus* for Rochel Imeinu's *yahrtzeit* at the large Binyanei HaUmah—"

"I'm absolutely so excited. I'll get to see all my friends from the other schools," Mimi's green eyes sparkled.

"I don't know how much of a chance you'll have to schmooze, Mimi. There are going to be loads of speeches. After all, the next day is the *yahrtzeit*—"

"I'll still find a way to schmooze."

"She'll still find a way to schmooze," Rivky playfully tapped Mimi on the shoulder.

"Then, that night we're going back to the Kosel."

"You mean *Kotel*," I said, winking at Mazal.

"I mean *Kotel*," Chani corrected herself, "where there's going to be a *hachnasas Sefer Torah*."

"You sound like a tour guide," Mimi commented.

"Thanks," Chani continued. "After that we're scheduled for an exclusive tour of the *Klei Kodesh* Museum—"

"Chani, you forgot to say where we'll be eating."

"I'm getting to it, Mimi. Give me a chance."

"We come back to the dormitory much late?"

"No way, Mazal," Mimi tucked a strand of red hair behind her ear and then dramatically announced, "The trip continues the next day too."

"We'll be sleeping in Yerushalayim?"

"That's right, Sara," Rivky nodded. "We'll be staying that night at the B.R.Y. dorm."

"B.R.Y.?"

"Yes, Mazal. You never heard of it?"

"B.R.Y.? B.Y.R.? B.Y.Y.? B.J.J.? B.Y.A.?" she lifted her hands in exasperation. "Oh, there are so many!"

"Well this one is B.R.Y. It's been around for years," Rivky explained. "It's right on the outskirts of Sanhedria."

"And that's where we'll be eating supper," Chani said, "with the girls from B.R.Y. See, Mimi, I didn't forget."

"Of course you didn't forget. I'm just so excited about sleeping that night with the B.R.Y.ers. I know a bunch of girls that are there." She turned to Rivky, "Isn't that the seminary where Chaya Sara Brisk and Simi Applebaum are?"

"I think so."

"Great! They're a real fun bunch. We're going to have an absolute blast."

"Well, as long as you're with us, Mimi," Rivky ran her finger through her light brown hair, "of course we'll have a blast."

"The next morning," Chani continued, still sounding like a tour guide, "we'll be going to Kever Rochel in Beis Lechem and then on to Me'aras HaMachpelah."

"*Me'arat* HaMachpelah," Mazal corrected, emphasizing the Israeli pronunciation.

"*Me'arat* HaMachpelah," Chani echoed. "And then we're supposed to…"

Kever Rochel and Me'aras HaMachpelah, the names reverberated repeatedly in my mind, making me oblivious to the conversation going on around me and anything else that was happening in our room. *None of the others could possibly know how significant these places are to me.*

Ever since I was little and first heard the story about Rochel and Leah, I felt a special closeness to them. To me they were not just characters in the *Chumash*. They meant so much more.

Rochel and Leah…sisters and their relationships. Was it because of my strong connection to my own sisters and our interactions? I remember as a child feeling so sorry for Leah, the one with the swollen eyes, the one who was doomed to marry the wicked Esav. Did she feel inferior to Rochel? Did she feel less wanted, less special? I could almost sense her pain. But I also felt sorry for Rochel and her tragic ending. Rochel, who so selflessly gave up so much! Could I ever do anything like that? Could I give up something that meant so much to me for someone that I love?

Sacrifice. *Isn't that what makes someone into a hero or heroine? Sacrificing something you treasure for someone else?*

And then another thought came into my mind. *Is it right for me to picture our Imahos, our matriarchs, the great spiritual and righteous figures that they were, in such down-to-earth terms? Am I even permitted to think like this?*

I was not sure.

Of one thing, though, I was sure. I was not going to go down in history as a great heroine like Rochel *Imeinu* or Leah *Imeinu*. I would not be given their special challenges.

Not that I wanted their tests or expected to be like them. But I did want to be something more than just plain Sara Hirsch from Rolland County. And life had not awarded me those kinds of grand opportunities yet…

But who knows?

Okay, Sara, enough!

I looked over at my digital alarm clock on my nightstand, its numbers illuminating the darkness. It was already past four in the morning. It would soon be light outside. *I must get to sleep already. How in the world will I ever concentrate on any schoolwork tomorrow? I mean today.* Reaching over, I checked the switch on my alarm clock, confirming that it was set to "on." *Maybe if I say HaMapil I'll be able to still get in a few hours of sleep. Maybe.*

Laying myself down once again, I buried my head into my soft pillow and pulled the heavy quilt over me, snuggling under its cushiony bulk. I closed my eyes tightly, resolutely turning onto my left side.

Come on, Sara, I commanded, *fall asleep! Now!*

I took slow, deep breaths, inhaling and exhaling steadily, hoping and waiting for sleep to finally overtake me…expecting at any moment to sink into blissful oblivion.

Then suddenly, I remembered the letters.

13

"GUESS WHAT, EVERYBODY!"

Groggily, I looked up from my plate, where I was absentmindedly pushing some vegetables around with my fork. *How in the world is Mimi able to be so alive with such little sleep?* I could barely keep my bleary eyes open.

Michal Weinman, sitting directly opposite me, was about to bite into her *lachmania*. "What should we guess, Mimi?"

"If only you knew," Mimi pursed her lips together firmly while reaching for a chocolate leben in the middle of the table.

"Vat? Vat is ze news, Miemie?" Ruti Katzenstein also helped herself to a leben.

Rivky lifted her eyebrows. "Knew what, Mimi?"

"You mean, you don't know?" Mimi's green eyes danced mischievously as she alternated looking at each of us.

Maybe some of the caffeine in the hot cocoa will wake me up.

I had finally fallen into a restless sleep around an hour before my alarm clock rang and, when it did, my hand slammed down on the "on" button to quiet its persistent ringing sound. However, the rest of my body remained inert, wanting to linger as long as possible under the heavy comforter. Then, when there was not an extra second to spare, I jumped up and headed down the hall toward the shower room. All the doors, though, were locked, with the sounds of rushing water coming from the other side.

Oh well, others beat me to it. I'll just have to wait till later on, I thought…then. But, now, as I sat in the dining room staring hazily through tired eyes, I wished that I had gotten myself into that shower earlier. I was too tired to have much of an appetite anyway and a shower probably would have helped wake me.

I just don't know how I'm going to function today. "Chani," I called, "could you, please, pass the hot cocoa?"

"Sure, Sara," Chani replied, passing the pitcher in my direction. "What, Mimi, don't we know?"

The pitcher went from hand to hand until it reached Michal. "Yes, Mimi," she stretched her arm across the table, handing the pitcher to me, "what's this big secret that you're making us all so curious about?"

"Thanks, Michal," I said, taking it from her and pouring the dark liquid into my cup.

"Well," Mimi's voice grew mysterious as she slowly stirred the creamy contents of her container, "something very special is going to take place in sixty-six days."

"Sixty-six days?" Malkie asked.

"What's happening in sixty-six days?" Rochel Leah, balancing her tray with a bowl of cereal on top approached our table. Pulling out a seat, she looked questioningly at those of us sitting near her, "What's going on?"

I lifted my cup slowly, watching the steam make twirling circles in the air. Everything seemed so foggy. *Am I dreaming or is this real?* I tried unsuccessfully to stifle a wide yawn.

"Mimi is about to tell us about some major event," Rivky said.

I took a cautious sip of my drink. It was quite sweet and a trifle too hot.

"*Na l'ha'avir et ha-chalav,*" one of the Israeli girls sitting further down the table requested.

"Nu, Mimi, are you going to tell us already or what?" Devorah asked, passing the milk.

I blew into the cup before taking another sip. The rising hot vapor felt good against my face. I took another sip and then kept the cup near my mouth, enjoying its soothing steam.

Mimi dug her spoon into the leben. "Guess!"

Slowly, I placed my drink on the table.

Rochel Leah put down her spoon and held out her closed hand.

"Sixty-six days? Hmmm...that's like in two months. And right now we're nearing the end of October. So-o-o," she opened one finger at a time, "November, then comes December..."

"Well, it's actually at the beginning of January. *Yud Alef Teves*, to be exact."

Rivky stood up. "Tell us already!" Then she glanced at her watch. "Oh my goodness, it's already a quarter to eight!"

I'd better finish this fast! I picked up my cup again and swallowed a mouthful.

"You'd better hurry, Mimi," someone said, "we only have about ten minutes to get to class."

"And if we're late for Rabbanit Greenstein..."

Mimi was certainly making us all curious...but not curious enough to come late to Rabbanit Greenstein's class.

I placed my cup down on the table, said a *berachah acharonah*, and started gathering my things together. I noticed that the others were doing the same.

"Okay everybody," said Mimi, not about to lose her audience. "Here goes. Eighteen years ago," she lowered her voice to a dramatic whisper, "something very significant happened."

We huddled closer to hear.

"On that day, someone came into this world."

"So?" a few of us asked.

"So, guess what? It's going to be my birthday!"

"Mimi!" we all screeched.

Rivky shaped her napkin into a ball and aimed it at Mimi's head. Grinning, Mimi ducked. Then tucking her ponytail of wavy red hair under her sweater, she grabbed her knapsack, swung it over her shoulder, waved goodbye, and headed out of the dining room, leaving us standing there, baffled expressions on all our faces.

Adina's face did not have a baffled expression on it when, a short while later, I slid into the seat beside her in class. In fact, she was not showing any facial expression at all.

Why is Adina always so cold? I wondered for the hundredth time while I then stood up respectfully along with the others when Rabbanit Greenstein entered the room. *Why does she always seem to have this huge chip on her shoulder?*

Sara, you are not supposed to think about Adina Stern, I reminded myself while sitting back down. *Concentrate on the wonderful Chumash lesson Rabbanit Greenstein is about to deliver.*

Opening my *Chumash* and loose-leaf, I stole a sidelong glance at Adina. She was busy conscientiously writing down whatever the Rabbanit was saying. I tried to look away, but somehow found myself continuing to watch her. *Why is it that when it comes to schoolwork she seems so impassioned, and yet the rest of the time she's totally blasé and unemotional?*

Unexpectedly, Adina looked up from her notebook, and before I had a chance to turn away, our eyes met. I felt the blood rushing to my face. *So much for my resolve not to pay attention to Adina! Why, oh why do I have to think so much, analyzing and trying to figure out why things are the way they are? Why do I have to be this way? Why is Adina the way she is?*

I took a deep breath, determined to pay attention to the lesson at hand. Rabbanit Greenstein was speaking. Her classes were always fascinating and, before long I too was swept along with what she was telling us.

When the class was over and Rabbanit Greenstein had left the room, there was a small break between classes. I hoped I would have enough time to tend to the letters that I had still not answered.

I took out Chavie's letter first, keeping my eyes focused on what she had written, willing myself not to look in Adina's direction.

> Dear Sara,
> I just received your last letter. Thanks for always being such a great "keeper in toucher" and not making me wait too long for a response. That's my friend…reliable and practical Sara, who I know I can always count on.
> By the time you receive this letter, it will be almost two months since you left. I still can't believe that I didn't go with you, but I'm glad that it was for a good reason and that you still got to go.
> Things obviously are not the same without you. True, there are still loads of girls who did not go to Eretz Yisrael and we get

together on Shabbos afternoons, but I'm used to always having you with me. With the others I can schmooze and have fun, but no one quite understands me the way you do, Sara.

My job as an assistant is okay. Mrs. Brody tries to include me in the teaching part of the job somewhat, but let's face it—the other assistant worked there last year, so when it comes to the monotonous menial tasks, who do you think gets the honor of doing them? You're lucky, Sara, because next year you won't end up being an assistant's assistant. Who knows, maybe if you get a really high score on the *Proyect* (that's what it's called, right?) and do well with your student teaching, you'll be able to get a job as a regular teacher (and not have to be an assistant at all).

Carpooling isn't that bad. Ballington is not that far away, but by the time everyone in the car pool gets picked up, we have to pray hard that there won't be any traffic on the road. Usually, because of rush hour, there is a lot of traffic. The ride is fun, though, even though I'm younger than everyone else in the car. I like listening to everyone talk about their jobs, their degrees, and sometimes even their (guess what?) *shidduchim*!!! (Of course, they never mention names, but you should hear their stories!)

Anyway, between my job, night seminary, and preparing for the wedding, I'm so busy. And, it's definitely thrilling having a sister getting married. I hope that *iy*"H you'll also experience that soon. But you're really so, so, so lucky to be in Eretz Yisrael. I hope I'm not coming off sounding like I'm complaining, but I just wish I could be in two places at the same time.

Remember, I want to hear about everything! Tell me about the girls, the classes, the trips. Have you made any close friends? Where do you go for Shabbosos? Are the classes really as fabulous as everyone says? Do you ever see girls from other seminaries? How many times have you gone to the Kosel? I promise not to be jealous, but Sara, if I can't be there, at least share it all with me. Don't leave out a single detail! REALLY!!!

It's absolutely so terrific that you're going to be able to come back so thoroughly trained to be a teacher. They say that a year at M.B.L.L. is like a year of teaching and the best seminary combined. I so, so, so, so much hope I'll be able to join you Chanukah time! You'll have to help me catch up on everything I missed, of course, but I'm not worried. We all know how good you are at that.

By the way, what's this I hear about your sister? Shuli, that is. I hear that she's planning on leaving her job and that she's just waiting for them to find a replacement. I can't believe it. Is it really true? I always pictured Shuli being the greatest teacher. What a pity!

Mindy *b"h* has a job waiting for her in Lakewood. There are tons of newlyweds there already, and so many of them are looking for teaching jobs, and yet they're holding the job for Mindy. Isn't that unbelievable? One of the ninth grade *Chumash* teachers, who has been there for a long time, is having a baby around Chanukah time. She wasn't really planning on coming back to teach this year at all, but when Mindy applied for a job, the principal, who heard what a great teacher Mindy is (I guess he received a lot of feedback from people in Rolland Heights), figured that this would be a perfect arrangement. The teacher was happy to work for the last few months before giving birth and Mindy is thrilled to have a job waiting for her.

Sara, I'm still really, really hoping that things work out for me after the wedding. I want so much to come to M.B.L.L. (You know that more than anybody.) You know how I saved up money all those years from camp and babysitting jobs. Who knows more than you, Sara, how hard it was for me to reach my goal? Remember last year when my parents surprised me by offering to pay the balance? Remember how we waited and waited for the acceptance to come? Keep praying for me for that open slot Chanukah time. I know that Rabbi Grossman will keep his word. All I need is one open slot...

I finished reading her letter quickly. I practically knew it by heart already; I had read it so many times. I wrote back, trying to fill her in on all the details without making her feel as though she was missing something. I wrote about Shabbos at Mazal's home and about Kiryat Yosef. I told her about the upcoming trip I was so looking forward to, about the student observations and the resource room. I scribbled feverishly, anxious to finish the letter before the next teacher entered the classroom. Finally, I closed by fervently wishing she really would be able to join us at the end of December. *If only a slot would open up for her,* I dreamed. *How perfect everything would be if Chavie were here with me…*

My dreaming ended abruptly. Just then I heard Rabbi Ossenfeld's heavy footsteps and deep voice as he made his way into the classroom. I quickly folded the letter and put it in the pocket at the back of my loose-leaf.

I felt someone's eyes on me.

Glimpsing sideways, I found Adina looking at me. I could see an expression of longing pass over her face, but then our eyes locked, and like a fleeting shadow, that look disappeared. It was as though it had never been there in the first place. Instead, her eyes slowly swept over me, resentment spilling out of them. A moment later, she coldly turned away.

Now what did I do wrong?

Fortunately, there was no time or opportunity to agonize over the latest "Adina incident." In Rabbi Ossenfeld's class, one did not think or worry about anything except *dikduk*. So, for the next forty-five minutes my mind enjoyed a reprieve from all worldly and not so worldly matters, and instead was fully engaged in the intricacies of root words, prefixes, suffixes, syntax, and syllabification.

A longer break was supposed to take place between Rabbi Ossenfeld's class and Rabbanit Abrams' class. From the corner of my eye, I noticed Adina take out a snack from her bag and make her way to the front of the room. Devorah and Malkie immediately appeared at her side. It looked like Malkie was asking Adina a question about the *dikduk* lesson. I saw her showing something to Adina in her notebook and then Adina, tucking a strand of hair behind her ear, confidently pointed inside while explaining whatever it was. They stood there talking for a few minutes. Gradually, a few others joined their group.

Adina stood out from the rest. She was the tallest one there, but instead of seeming awkward, she managed to carry herself with unusual grace. I still found it intriguing. She did nothing to encourage closeness with the others, and yet everyone seemed so drawn to her. *Maybe it's because everything about her is just so perfect,* I thought.

Everything, that is, except her smile.

I watched Mimi and Rivky approach the girls clustered around

Adina. They talked for a minute or so. Then Mimi said something and I saw Adina throw back her head, a wide smile on her face. *I take that back. Even her smile is perfect. When she smiles.*

I could see the others also laughing. Rivky cheerfully thumped Mimi on the shoulder.

How in the world does Mimi manage to do it? Why is she able to get Adina to smile and even laugh, when I can't even get a short conversation going with her? I shook my head, puzzled. *I wish Chavie were with me!*

I reached into my book bag for a bag of pretzels. Tearing it open, I said a *mezonos*, and while helping myself to a few, I unfolded Chevy's letter.

The minute I saw her letter was separate from Shuli's, I thought something was odd. After reading both their letters, I knew for sure.

And I could not get that troubled feeling to leave me.

Leaning my elbow on the desk with my chin resting comfortably on the palm of my hand, I began to read.

> To my dearest (second to oldest) sister in the world,
> Sara, a"mush
>
> Hi! How are you? *Baruch Hashem* I'm fine, the family is fine, and everything is fine. Well, sort of.
>
> Actually, I hate school.
>
> There's tons and tons of work. That would be okay if I knew what was going on, but with fifteen teachers, by the time I find the books I need for that class, I've already missed the beginning of the lesson. The teachers just talk and talk as if I'm supposed to know what they're talking about. (*Chumash* is much different than in elementary school. So many *meforshim*—it's so hard! Every Friday there's a *parashah* quiz, and math this year…forget it! Then, of course, there's French. Why do I have to know French and why does Madame Pumeter make such a big deal out of it?) Of course, the teachers are willing to answer any questions we might have at the end of the class. But:
>
> (a.) If I knew what to ask, I probably wouldn't have any questions.
>
> (b.) I'm embarrassed to ask questions in front of everybody. (Before, I was one of the smartest in the class. Now suddenly…)
>
> I think that it's possible that the only reason I was one of the

smartest in the class in elementary school was because I had this really terrific in-house tutor who was always available to patiently explain things to me. Sara, I'm admitting something. I didn't realize it at the time, but you really saved me all those years. Now that I think of it, there were plenty of times that I didn't know what was going on and you sat down with me, taking me step-by-step through the lesson, explaining everything to me as if you had all the time in the world. You also understood what each teacher wanted us to get out of the class and so you knew exactly which points to stress. No wonder I was at the top of the class! And now, there you are, off in Eretz Yisrael, and here I am, struggling along helplessly without you.

Please don't feel bad or anything like that, Sara. I'm happy for you that you're there. As Shuli keeps saying, you're probably having the most amazingly fantabulous time. I guess this is just my way of saying thank you for all those nights you stayed up late with me. And once you get back here, there's always hope for next year!

I just wish it wasn't so hard! Especially when the teachers look at me and wonder how it's possible that I'm your sister. I know they're thinking that it can't be—that someone as dumb as me could have the same genes as you.

Speaking about sisters, more than once, one of the seniors said to me, "You're Shuli Hirsch's sister? I can't believe it!" How's that for a compliment? They look at me and just can't believe that someone as pretty and talented and popular as Shuli has me for a sister. I didn't even make it into the production!

Maybe in a way it's my own fault. I didn't listen to your advice. You warned me that freshies don't usually get chosen for the acting roles, but I figured that since Shuli did when she was in ninth grade and since she was always in the play, I'd get a part too. I didn't even bother trying out for the choir. So guess what? Now I don't have an acting part and I'm not in the choir. I'm not in anything!

Shuli said I should just go over to Miss Weinstein and ask her to put me into the choir, since everyone gets into it, but I can't do that! After all, why should I go over to her? She didn't think I was good enough for the play and if I go to her now, it'll look like I'm desperate.

I'm still upset that Shoshana was put in the other class. At the beginning, she was also very angry about our being separated. But now she made a bunch of new friends from the other class. She still gets together with me, but it's really not the same anymore. I wish they would put me in the other class, but they said that right now there's nothing to discuss. We have to first try being with the classes we were originally assigned to for a few months.

I don't know if I'll be able to bear it! Our class is extremely cliquey! I don't mean to be speaking lashon hara, but it's just so hard! Your "body language" idea is simply not working with me. The truth is, I'm not exactly walking around with a big smile. How can I, when I'm feeling so down?

I wish you were here so I could talk to you. I know I have Shuli, but it just isn't the same with her. She's always so busy and everything. Besides, things were always so easy for Shuli, she just wouldn't understand. You have this way of listening, really listening when someone has a problem. You totally hear what I'm saying and you really work at finding a solution. That's what I love about you, Sara. You genuinely care.

I don't want to bother Mommy and Abba about my problems. Lately they seem to have other things on their minds. Lots of times I hear them talking in low voices and then, when I come into the room, they suddenly stop their conversation. Maybe it has to do with Shuli and shidduchim or maybe her job. I know that she's not very happy about her teaching, but things always turn out great for her.

Anyway, I'm not giving Shuli this letter to put in her envelope like I usually do. Even though I know she wouldn't read something that I told her not to, I don't even want her to know that I wrote something so private to you. Then she might ask me questions…and she just wouldn't be able to understand how I feel.

All right, I've got to go now. Please don't be worried about me. I miss you tons!!!

Love, your best youngest sister,
Chevy

P.S. Write back soon. This time I really will try to follow your advice!

I looked at my watch. Thankfully, we still had another ten minutes of free time left. I tore out a sheet of paper from my loose-leaf and began to write.

> To my **C**ute, **H**elpful, **E**xciting, **V**ery wonderful, **Y**oungest sister, CHEVY, *a"mush*
>
> Hi! How are you? I'm so sorry for not answering you sooner, but I received your letter this past Wednesday. Wednesday night we had a special *shiur* in *Chovos HaLevavos* and an informal *Rosh Chodesh* party in our room that ran kind of late. I am sorry that I didn't get to speak to you when I called early Thursday morning (my time), but it was still Wednesday night by you (quite late) and you were already sleeping. Maybe next *Rosh Chodesh* we'll get to speak. (Hopefully!) Thursday was packed with tons and tons of schoolwork and on Friday I left school early with my roommate to go to her family up in the Galil for Shabbos, so unfortunately, I didn't get even an extra minute to write to you before Shabbos. We came back very late last night, and so now, finally, in between classes I have a chance to write back to you.
>
> Chevy, please don't think that my not writing back to you right away is because I'm very busy and that I don't care or am not very concerned. I do care and I am very concerned. It's just that I didn't want to scribble some quick reply to your letter. I wanted to think about the different issues you raised and try to figure out a solution with you. It's a little hard, though, to do that when we can't just sit and talk and we are so far away from each other. But that too is for the best. So let's begin.
>
> Firstly, you write that you hate school. I've been thinking, Chevy. It sounds like you think that you're the only one having a rough freshman year, but a lot of girls have trouble adjusting. Everything's different from what they were used to. So while you think it's the school you hate, it's really the change that's bothering you.
>
> In a way, Chev, you and I are in the same boat. We're both trying to adjust to a whole new situation. The difference between you and me is that I was never really the popular type and so I knew that it wouldn't be easy. (And I never was very fond of change.) You were always the leader in your class, so now it's

harder for you to get used to making new friends and being just one in a group. Believe me, Chevy, you have a wonderfully outgoing, friendly personality. People love being with you. Just stop walking around moping. Really! You have a gorgeous smile and loads of personality. Try the body language idea and I truly think it will work. (You know it's not just a matter of body language. I remember learning once that *"ha-adam nifal ke'fi peulasav,"* meaning that a person develops according to his actions. Even when your heart is not really into doing something, just by doing it, by practicing it, it becomes a part of you.) So, Chev, please give it a try!

The schoolwork in ninth grade is always a challenge. It's not just you. I really wish I was there and that I could help you, but remember, Chevy, I wasn't the one taking your tests for you in elementary school and getting the excellent marks that you got. You did that by yourself!!! All I did was help you prepare. But it was you, Yocheved Hirsch, who got the terrific grades. You get the credit and no one else!

Chev, please don't be embarrassed to ask questions in class. If you don't want to ask in front of everybody, go up to the teachers at the end of class. They'll gladly explain to you anything you don't understand.

Also, if you need to get a little extra help, I know that there's a program of twelfth and eleventh graders tutoring the freshies and sophies, headed by Mrs. Brownstein. There's nothing to be embarrassed about. You know that when I was a junior and senior, I was one of the tutors and I worked with some of the greatest kids and it didn't hurt their popularity one bit! Actually, it probably helped them become more popular because they were even more successful in class than before. So, Chevy, I'm begging you: PLEASE GET A TUTOR. It will be a wonderful help to you and it is definitely nothing to be ashamed of!!! You're a very smart girl, but sometimes we all need more individualized help to fill in the missing pieces of what we don't understand.

Also, as far as *Chumash* is concerned: True, you're learning many more *meforshim*, but before you know it you'll start to really appreciate these lessons. You won't look at them as just another class, with more details to memorize and more stuff to

> study. You'll start to really identify with the beautiful lessons we learn from the *Chumash* and you'll find yourself...wanting to delve deeper and deeper into it. It really starts to become part of you. That goes for *parashah* too. Just think, by studying it each week, by the time all four years of high school are over—you'll have a really good grasp of the *Chamishah Chumshei Torah*. Now, *lehavdil*, concerning math and French, a tutor could really help you with math. The problem is that when you don't understand Step One, Step Two becomes impossible. With a tutor, you could begin again with Step One and build from there. I have no doubt that you can do it. With French, believe it or not, I really feel like writing a letter to Madame Pumeter and thanking her! I've become quite friendly with one of the French girls in the Israeli program of Beit Yaakov HaNegbah and guess which languages we speak.
>
> No way, Chevy, is anyone looking down at you for not being more like me. You have tons more personality and talent than I have and I'm certainly no genius. But I will confess a small secret to you. I sometimes feel that way about Shuli. Sometimes—

I stopped writing and thought, *no, I won't tell her about that. I can't share with her that feeling of inferiority, of never being able to be as special as Shuli.*

I crossed out the last few sentences, making sure they were illegible, and continued writing.

> About the play, Chevy. Don't cut off your nose to spite your face. Just because you didn't make it into one part of the play doesn't mean you shouldn't try to be in a different part. It's still fun to be in the production, even if you don't have an acting part. You could still be part of the action by being in the choir. Swallow your pride. Go over to Miss Weinstein. I have no doubt that you'll get into the choir and that you'll have a great time. Maybe you'll even get a solo!
>
> Now, as far as Shoshana is concerned. It's true that she's been your best friend for the last two years, but before Shoshana, you had Ruti, and before Ruti you were best friends with Gitty, and

before Gitty, you had Huvi. So come on, Chev, smile and give things a chance. Don't get stuck on having it only your way. Try to be open. Things can't always go the way you want and it's probably better for them not to. It helps prepare you for real life. When things always go exactly the way you want without any hurdles, then later in life it's harder to adjust to the things you can't control. Does that make sense?

Mommy and Abba are the best people in the world to talk to. Appreciate the fact that you have them nearby. (I wish I could just walk into the next room and talk to them.) You're getting me a bit worried, though. Hopefully, the only thing concerning them right now is which of the boys on their long list is the right one for Shuli.

Anyway, I've got to run right now. My teacher is at the door, about to enter the classroom.

Love,
Your secret admirer and favorite, second to oldest sister

P.S. Write back right away. I want to hear how wonderful everything is turning out!

P.P.S. Regards to everyone!!

P.P.S.S. I love you tons!!!

I did not get a chance to reread what I wrote. There was barely enough time to fold the letter and put it alongside Chavie's letter before Adina slid into her seat beside me and Rabbanit Abrams entered the room.

Two down, one more to go, I thought optimistically. Yet, the anxious feeling tugging at me would not leave. I *had* to write back to Shuli as soon as possible. *I must find a way to help her before it's too late,* I thought with urgency. *Soon. Soon I'll get to it. I must...*

However, that was not to be. Immediately following Rabbanit Abrams' class was "Methods in Teaching" with Geveret Spitz.

As always, her lesson was inspiring, thorough, and thought provoking. It also ran longer than usual. It was imperative that we be properly prepared to work with the children we would be meeting that afternoon.

It felt good to once again hear my name listed with those who would be working with the resource room children. It surprised me, though, when I heard Adina's name announced with the group observing the preschoolers. As Geveret Spitz read her name off the list, I watched her reaction. She nodded slightly with obvious approval. *Adina requested this?* I would have thought that if Adina *really* wanted to teach, it would be to high school girls, not preschoolers. I could not picture Adina having the patience and warmth needed to work with such young children nor could I understand her even wanting to. With her brilliant mind and magnetism, I could see her being a success with a much older age group. *Well, you never know...*

While the first group sat around Geveret Spitz's desk receiving instructions, the rest of us had the opportunity to work on our reports until it would be our chance to meet with Geveret Spitz to discuss our individual situations.

I took out my "special" notebook.

Although it was less than four weeks since Rabbi Grossman had first officially spoken to us regarding the Goldstone *Proyect*, I had been studiously collecting information, vigorously writing notes, and structuring my research as though time was running out. I already had thirty and a half pages filled.

How I loved working on it! When writing, my insecurities would melt away and the words just seemed to flow. I was able to combine my teaching abilities, my past experiences, and my analytical thinking, merging them together to create pages and pages of what I was hoping would eventually turn out into the kind of report Rabbi Grossman was seeking.

I would begin writing and then something almost magical would happen. All my cares, all my fears, and any feelings of inferiority would recede into the background. I was no longer "Sara the prop." I was...I was...

Oh, Sara! Stop this dreaming and get back to work.

I gripped my pen tightly and turned to the thirty-first page of my notebook.

It was interesting. Instead of running out of things to write, the more I wrote, the more I had to say. I had been writing assiduously, rapidly filling another two and a half pages, oblivious to anything else.

Chapter 13

Then unexpectedly the next group was called, disrupting my train of thought. I looked up, stretching and yawning simultaneously, wondering when it would be our turn. *Our resource room group will probably be last,* I yawned again. *That's great,* my eyes shifted around the room, *I'd rather do my writing now, without interruption.*

With my pen clenched between my teeth, I stretched my back while placing both hands behind my tired neck. I looked around at the others hunched over their desks, working diligently.

Suddenly, my heart began to quicken in that familiar way...the way it always did when I thought of the Goldstone Outstanding Student Teacher Award.

Do the others want to win as badly as I do? They're all working so hard, but...do they actually need it in the same way I need it?

I quickly turned to the top of the next page. For a quiet moment I stared at the blank sheet in front of me and then all at once words began to pour through my pen, flowing onto the paper...

Stuck in her world, as plain as can be,
Simple, average, oh so ordinary;
How much she wishes she could break free,
Finally be something special, extraordinary...
Free as a bird and able to soar,
Not just a prop, something much more;
Find the key that opens the door,
"Set me free from my prison" she—

Hmmm, I wondered, biting down on the tip of my pen. *Now, what rhymes with door? Bore...core...for...yes! That's it! For. Let's see,* I looked back down at my paper and read to myself. *Find the key that opens the door, "set me free from my prison," she looked for... she looked for,* I repeated. *No,* I shook my head disappointedly, *that's not going to do it.* I read it again.

And again.

And then, just like that, it hit me!

Implore. That makes sense. I read over the last two lines, nodding with satisfaction and then added the next couple of words to what I had already written.

I reread the whole poem. I crossed out a few words, made a change or two and then suddenly stopped. *Why did I just write this? I can't use this for the Proyect!*

I was about to rip the page out of my notebook when Geveret Spitz said that she was ready for my group.

I quickly shut my notebook and made my way to the front of the room, completely forgetting about the poem on page thirty-four.

And that is where it remained. For a while.

14

WE MADE OUR way through the wooded area connecting the Beit Yaakov HaNegbah campus to Kfar Amsdorf. It was not as hot as the week before, but it did not feel like the autumn weather I was used to at that time of year.

The flowers were still blooming, the birds continued chirping, and the woodsy scent of bark and greenery permeated the air. However, we could not walk at the same leisurely pace, enjoying our surroundings, as we had the previous Wednesday. We had to make our way as quickly as possible to Bnot Yisrael. There were less than two hours until their dismissal.

During our meeting with Geveret Spitz, each of us was paired with someone from our own group. Geveret Spitz explained that since we would be going to Kfar Amsdorf practically every day to work with "our students," she preferred that we not go alone. By providing each of us with a partner, we would avoid the prolonged wait that is inevitable while waiting for a group to assemble. She mentioned, though, that she had another important motive as well. She hoped that by collaborating with another person, we would get some important feedback and advice .

"Remember, girls," she told us, "you're never alone. We're all in this together. There's no such thing as individual successes. If we care, truly care, we will do all we can to help each child, those we're personally responsible for and those that our friend is responsible for. After all, we're all part of the same family, with the same Father, who cares and loves each and every one of us…"

I do not know if it was because we would both be working with first graders who would also be attending the resource room, or if it had anything to do with Rabbi Grossman's "tutoring arrangement," but Mimi and I were chosen to work together as partners.

I had mixed feelings.

I loved being with Mimi. She was so much fun, so easygoing and unpretentious. When I was with Mimi, I stopped thinking about my own problems. She did not seem to care whether she was with someone popular or plain. Mimi simply loved people and life, and you could not help but catch that enthusiasm when being with her.

On the other hand, that same easygoing manner prevented us from getting our work finished. Her interruptions and unreliability could be quite frustrating. And now, I would be working with her even more often and more intensively than before.

Of course, I did not voice any opposition. *For now*, I told myself, *let's see what happens. Besides…who says Mimi wants to be with me?*

After all our meetings with Geveret Spitz were over, we went to the dormitory's dining room for the main meal of the day, finishing as fast as we could. We were in a rush to get to Kfar Amsdorf. We would first be observing the individual children assigned to us in their classroom before joining them the next day in the resource room. Geveret Spitz had explained that once the children met us, it would be more difficult to anonymously observe them in a classroom setting. "And," she continued, "the importance of gaining insight into the way they behave in class before working with them individually can not be overemphasized."

Mimi and I were the only two from the resource room group who were to work with first grade children. We stood hesitantly outside their classroom.

I looked at the number written on the door and then at the index card Geveret Spitz had given me. I held my card up in the air for Mimi to see and then read it to her, "*Sara Hirsch, Ronit K., Grade 1, from Devorah. Hatzlachah, T. Spitz.*"

"Yes, *b'hatzlachah*," Mimi grinned and then held up her card for me to see. "Continue please."

"Oh okay." I peered at Mimi's card and read aloud, "*Mimi Rosenberg, Riki D., Grade 1, from Devorah. Hatzlachah, T. Spitz.*" I paused. "*Hatzlachah* to you too, Mimi."

"Thanks, I'll need it," she mumbled before turning toward the door.

I waited for her to knock.

Nothing.

I waited a little longer.

Still nothing.

"Um, Mimi, we're definitely at the right place."

Pause. Silence.

"I guess we should go in already, Mimi."

She shrugged indifferently. "I guess so."

"They're both from Devorah."

No response.

What's with Mimi? I took a deep breath. "I wonder if they're friends."

She looked through the small window in the top of the door. "I wonder how long this is going to take."

"Boy, Mimi, you sound *really* enthusiastic."

"And you, Sara, sound pretty sarcastic," she turned to me, her brows arched. "I didn't know you had it in you."

"Sorry, Mimi. It's just that you seem to want to be over with this whole thing already."

"And you don't?"

"Of course not. I've been looking forward to this ever since we got here."

"Really?"

"Actually, it's always been my dream—" I hesitated, embarrassed to reveal my inner thoughts. "I mean—"

"It's okay, Sara, you don't need to excuse yourself. You're entitled to your—"

"I'm not excusing myself," I suddenly felt myself getting angry. Angry at being partnered with Mimi, angry at her lackadaisical attitude toward seminary and toward teaching in particular, and angry at myself for revealing my private feelings, and even more angry for being embarrassed about them. "This *is* a teaching seminary, you know. And if you want to be successful as a teacher, then—"

"Who says I want to teach?"

"Well, you're here, aren't you?"

"And who says I want to be here?"

"Huh?" A puzzled silence. "Then what in the world are you doing at M.B.L.L.?"

"Questions, questions, questions...," Mimi's tone was curt.

And then I saw it. That same troubled look that I had seen before. Only this time it did not pass as quickly as in the past.

She swung around, no longer facing me. I stood there for a moment, tongue tied, staring at her back. Then all at once I stepped in front of her and imploringly whispered, "I'm so sorry, Mimi, I didn't mean—"

"You didn't mean what, Sara?" she closed her eyes for a few long seconds.

I did not know what to do. I had never seen Mimi like this. I was petrified that she would suddenly start crying. I remained silent, my heart pounding rapidly.

Then unexpectedly, her eyes flew open. I could see their greenness sparkling like two twinkling stars against the velvet sky. And I could not believe it! *Smiling eyes.*

"You didn't mean what, Sara?" she repeated, but this time there was a buoyancy to her tone. "To ask me a normal question? Will you stop looking so serious, Sara, and would you be so kind as to do me a favor?"

"Sure," I said, relief washing over me, still shocked at the sudden transformation I had just witnessed. "What do you need?"

"For you to please stop apologizing, Sara," she said, tucking a loose strand of red hair that had escaped from her ponytail behind her ear. "And for us to hurry up and go into this classroom before we miss the whole thing."

My mouth obediently formed as wide a grin as I could muster. My heart, though, knew something was wrong and would not comply so easily. I took a deep breath. There was no time for me to delve into it or analyze whatever it was that I was finding so troubling.

Chapter 14

After Mimi knocked at the door, we made our way as unobtrusively as possible to the two empty seats in the back of the classroom, feeling the children's inquisitive eyes on our backs. We sat down and the teacher continued her lesson.

Placing my observation notebook on top of my crossed knee, I turned to the first empty page, grasping my pen tightly, prepared to take notes. *This is really happening*, I thought excitedly, *I'm finally here.* Glancing sideways, I looked at Mimi, eager to share my enthusiasm with her. She, though, was leaning back in her seat, clicking her pen perfunctorily, a bored expression on her face. Her notebook was lying unopened on her lap.

She really isn't the least bit interested in all this, I shook my head, incredulous.

I looked around the room at the little girls. There were mostly dark-haired ponytails, a few blondes, some short hairdos, a couple of curly-haired kids, and some children with long braids. I wished Geveret Spitz had supplied us with pictures of the children.

Which one is Ronit?

I had wondered how we would recognize which two of the over twenty children in the classroom were the ones assigned to us. Geveret Spitz assured us that we need not be concerned and that before the day was over we would find out.

Within the first few minutes of our sitting there, however, it became quite apparent which child was Mimi's Riki D.

As would be expected when two strangers enter a classroom, the children kept turning around to see us and the teacher kept reminding the children where the front of the room was. After the first few minutes, the children, enthralled with the teacher's dynamic lesson, seemed to forget our presence and refrained from turning around. I too forgot about Ronit K., for I found myself completely absorbed by the lesson.

"Riki, please sit down," the teacher told a blonde-haired girl who was standing near her desk. "Now as I was saying, when Eliezer reached the well—"

"Ooh, Morah, ooh Morah—"

"Riki, please sit down. So when Eliezer reached the—Riki, you'll get a chance to tell us soon…"

The teacher continued talking and Riki continued disturbing. I looked over at Mimi. Her brows furrowed in deep concentration, she was staring intently at Riki, completely mesmerized.

Is this the same Mimi who appeared so disinterested just a few minutes ago?

"Mimi," I leaned over, whispering as softly as I could, "I wonder which of the girls is Ronit."

No answer.

"Mimi, it looks like that's your Riki. Which one do you think is Ronit?"

Pause.

"Mimi!"

A few of the children sitting closest to the back of the room twisted around to see where the whispering was coming from. I looked down at my fingernails, embarrassed.

"Okay, who can tell us what Rivka answered Eliezer?" the teacher looked around the room. "Yoninah?"

I heard a little voice say, "I'll give you to drink and also your camels."

"Very good, Yoninah. And when Eliezer heard Rivka's answer, Eliezer realized...what? Who can tell me what Eliezer realized?"

I could hear the "ooohs" and "ahhs" of the many children vying for their Morah's attention, desiring to display their knowledge.

"Now let's see. Who's sitting nicely and not making any noise? Okay, Ronit?"

My head shot up.

"Ronit," the teacher repeated, "could you please tell us what Eliezer realized when Rivka so kindly offered to give the camels to drink?

Silence.

"Ronit, please come up to my desk and hold the Rivka puppet."

"Oh, Morah, can I?"

"It's not fair, Morah. You always call Ronit to do all the fun things."

"Ronit?" she walked to the girl sitting in the front of the second row. "Please come to the front of the room."

The teacher kindly reached over to a thin little girl with dark hair pulled into a messy ponytail. She appeared listless as her teacher led her to the front of the room and handed over a female puppet. Even from so far away and despite the long bangs that partially blocked them, I could tell that her dark eyes were huge. She clutched the puppet with her fingers, but did not bother to slip her hand inside as one does when using a puppet. I watched as her teacher took her limp hand and pushed it inside the opening at the bottom, lifting her arm so the other children could see the puppet. She allowed herself to be propelled into position, but remained inexpressive and passive, completely apathetic to the others' enthusiasm.

While the teacher called some of the other children to the front of the room, handing them the camel and Eliezer puppets and continuing with her lesson, my mind could absorb only one thought.

Ronit K…whatever your last name is, get ready for changes! You will no longer ignore the teacher and the lessons. When I'm finished with you…you will learn to love to learn, because I promise never to give up on you…never!

I felt energetic and excited as I made my way back to the campus with Mimi. There was a bounce to my step, an unusual buoyancy to my movements. I talked more than usual, eagerly sharing my ideas with Mimi. I did not realize it then, so absorbed as I was with my plans for Ronit, but anyone observing us would surely have noticed the irony of our role reversals. We were now bubbly Sara and subdued Mimi. I guess I was too excited to think about anything else but Ronit. My dream was finally coming true. This was the beginning.

That feeling remained with me all through the long evening. After *Minchah* and a quick supper, I went to my room, planning to use the time to catch up on homework and plan strategies for working with Ronit. I had brought a book from America titled *How to Motivate the Unmotivated Child*. I remember debating whether to buy it at the flea market one Sunday a couple of years back. I had leafed through it and discovered that it was full of ideas and games. It was the only remaining volume of a larger set. The seller, with a truckload of used books, offered the thick book to me at a price I could not resist. Although bulky, it was soft-covered and therefore not too heavy, and so I packed it, hoping that it would be useful.

Now, sitting cross-legged on my bed and turning its pages, I was glad I had brought it along. *This will be great*, I thought happily. *There are tons and tons of ideas in here.*

I could hear a few voices coming from the hallway. I looked at the clock on my nightstand. It was still early.

Mazal probably had not yet left the dining room. In my eagerness, I had rushed upstairs anxious to begin, disinterested in the supper being served. My eyes returned to the book on my lap, impatiently wanting to continue scanning its pages. But then my practical side stopped me, reminding me to take advantage of the still vacant shower stalls down the hallway before everyone was due to return upstairs. *Ah…a nice warm shower with plenty of hot water and nobody banging on the door for me to hurry.* I pictured myself clean, refreshed, and all cozy in my soft flannel nightgown with the whole night ahead to take care of everything I needed to do. *Then, when I'm too tired to work, I will simply drop off to sleep*, I thought contentedly.

Allowing my eyes to linger a bit longer on one particular page, I imagined myself using the game form pictured there with *my* student, Ronit. *There she is, smiling up at me with those huge dark eyes, excited to learn, enthusiastic about the game we are playing. And there I am, encouraging and motivating her.* My fantasy continued a bit longer. *In walks her teacher, surprised that Ronit is participating wholeheartedly in the lesson and definitely impressed with my accomplishments. She is so overwhelmed by my success, she rushes to inform Geveret Spitz and Rabbi Grossman, who decide that more students should be assigned to me. This eventually results in my being the obvious winner of the Goldstone Outstanding Student Teacher Award.*

Yes, this book is going to be a real help for me, I thought happily as I let my practical side persevere and reluctantly flipped the book closed. *Maybe, I'll even get Mimi's Riki motivated to sit still and pay attention.* I stood up and poked my head through the door and scanned the hallway. No one was around.

This really is an ideal time for me to take that longed for shower.

Humming softly to myself, I went over to the closet, removed my terry cloth robe from the hook, grabbed one of my neatly folded towels, and headed out to the shower room. I was still humming ten minutes later when I bent my head forward, wrapped my towel into a turban around my hair, made my way down the hallway, and opened the door to my room. I only stopped humming after another few seconds passed, when I suddenly noticed Mazal sitting on her bed clapping.

"No, do not stop," she said when I looked at her with a jolt. "You have nice voice."

"Thanks, Mazal," I caught my reflection in the long mirror hanging on the wall, once again wishing I had some control over my tendency to blush. Still watching myself, I removed the twirled towel from my head and rubbed my wet hair hard with it.

"You look...um...different tonight, Sara."

"What do you mean?" I rubbed harder.

"Like...something very good will be."

I took out my comb and ran it down my scalp, parting my hair at the side. "Yes?" I looked questioningly at Mazal's reflection in the mirror while continuing to comb my hair. "And what do you think it is?"

"I think maybe you not tell me. I do not know. We together a whole Shabbat."

"What do you think I'm not telling you?" I turned around to face her, still holding the comb in my hand. "Tell me, Mazal."

"Maybe you going to be *kallah*."

"What?" I started laughing. "You've got to be kidding!" Then, seeing the serious expression on her face, I walked over to her bed and sat down next to her. "First of all, I'm not even eighteen years old. Second of all, I have an older sister. Third of all, my parents are in America and I'm here and I'm not doing anything without them. And Mazal, if anything like that ever happened to me, which it hasn't, of course, don't you think you, my dear roommate, would be the first to know?"

Now it was Mazal's turn to blush. "I am sorry, Sara. We have good friendship and—"

"And thank you, Mazal."

"Thank you? *Me?*"

"Yes. Thank you for caring..."

We talked some more. I explained my good mood, sharing my plans for Ronit. I even hinted about my hopes for this to eventually evolve into the ultimate reward...the success of my Goldstone *Proyect*.

After showing Mazal the book, she glanced at her watch and then, with a start, told me that Rivky was waiting for her in the library. She had promised to help her with the *Chumash* lesson from earlier that day and hurried out of the room.

I took out my blow dryer and plugged it into the outlet near the mirror. Then, looking at my reflection, I burst out laughing. *Me, getting engaged?* I shook my head, turned on the switch, and felt the hot air blowing against me. *I'm glad I don't have to think about such things, yet. Lucky for me, I have Shuli paving the path before me.*

Shuli.

Her letter.

No, I did not get to that book on my bed that night, after all. Shuli's letter and my response thrust all other thoughts out of my mind.

15

"HAVE A CARAMEL, Sara."

"No thanks, Mimi. I'm still *fleishig* from lunch. Didn't you eat?"

"Nope. These Israeli caramel candies are too delicious. You can't get them in America and since they're made from milk, they're extra scrumptious."

"So you didn't eat lunch?" I asked incredulously.

"Well, it was either lunch or the caramels. If I eat the chicken, then I won't be able to eat *milchigs* for the rest of day." She shook her head emphatically, her red hair bouncing. "No way am I giving up these terrific caramels!"

"Mimi, Geveret Mendlowitz is really a great cook. The chicken and *chatzilim* dish was quite tasty."

"Not as tasty as these caramels!"

"Oh, all right, don't eat lunch. Eat caramels instead. Now let's get back to work."

"Yes, ma'am!"

We occupied the two seats at the desk in Mimi's room, our *sefarim* opened in front of us. Adina was sitting on her bed, folding laundry. A tape was playing softly from the tape recorder on her nightstand.

"Okay. So as we were saying," my tone was businesslike, "if you look at the *Sifsei Chachamim* in *pasuk hey*, you'll see—"

"Hey!"

"Yes. *Pasuk hey*, that's what I said—"

"No," Mimi chuckled in her usual bubbly manner, "I said 'hey' because I just thought of this great idea—"

"Mimi—"

"No, Sara, you've got to hear," her eyes danced. "You know how the choir starts singing about…"

Oh no, here she goes again.

She continued talking, but I was hardly paying attention. I leaned back on my chair, my eyes shifting away from Mimi and glancing briefly around the room. Exasperated, a long sigh involuntarily escaped me. Adina looked up from her laundry folding and our eyes met for a moment. Her lips twitched slightly in mutual understanding.

I smiled back.

"So do you think it'll work?"

A new and warm sensation was settling on me.

"Sara, you didn't hear a word I said. Did you?"

"Huh?"

"I just spent the last five minutes telling you this wonderful idea and you haven't—"

"Mimi," Adina lifted one of her perfectly folded piles and stood up, "Sara has been trying for the last fifteen minutes to explain something to *you*."

"Oh," Mimi said with a sheepish smile, "sorry, Sara."

"N-no problem, Mimi." I turned toward Adina, my eyes sparkling with gratitude, but she had already disappeared into the walk-in closet with her laundry.

When she emerged a few seconds later, she was holding the handles of an empty laundry basket in her hand. "If anyone comes for me, Mimi, please tell them I went down to the laundry room and I'll meet them in the library as soon as I finish."

"No prob!" Mimi sang out as the door closed behind Adina. Then turning back to me, she mimicked my more serious *let's-get-our-work-done* tone, "Sara, we're wasting too much time. As we were saying…"

I laughed. Mimi smiled impishly. Companionably, we proceeded with the lesson.

I spoke and Mimi paid close attention…for about five minutes.

"Did you see how perfectly she folds her laundry?" Mimi said admiringly.

"Yes, Mimi, I did notice. Now, if *you'll* notice, the Radak in *pasuk vav* is telling us—"

"Everything she does is absolutely perfect."

"Well, Mimi, it's *perfectly* clear that this Radak is explaining the reason the—"

"Her shelves, her desk…even her toothpaste tube—"

"MIMI!"

"Sh-sh, Sara, you don't have to yell."

"I'm not yelling!"

"You are."

"I'm not!"

"Your face is all red."

"It is not!"

"It is."

"For your information I'm trying to get some work done. And you don't stop interrupting."

"I know. I'm sorry, Sara. I'm just not as studious as you."

"Can't we just do the work without talking about the production and without speaking about other people? Why can't you just concentrate on the lesson and then be finished with it?"

"I don't know. I guess I'm hopeless," she grinned.

"You're definitely not hopeless, Mimi. When you want to do something, you're…you're—"

"Yes?"

"You're unbelievably determined."

"That's a nice compliment…I guess."

"It sure is. Look at the production…for that you have no problem concentrating. And when I think of what happened today in the resource room—"

"Oh that? It was no big deal."

"No big deal for you, maybe. For me, now that's another story."

Earlier that afternoon those of us assigned to the resource room met with "our" students for about forty-five minutes. Of course, I was there working with Ronit. *Trying* to work with Ronit, that is. It's rather difficult to work with someone when that person will not utter a word, look at you, or offer any sign of communication.

Enviously, I looked around at the others. Everyone seemed busy. Some were sitting with "their" children in front of opened books and a few were utilizing the materials and games from the shelves. I had crayons and colorful markers, large pieces of construction paper, scissors and glue. I was attempting to get Ronit to cut out a picture of a ball and paste it next to the number one that I drew onto the construction paper. But, she would not even lift the scissors.

From the corner of my eye I saw Mimi working with Riki. Riki was giggling at what Mimi was telling her. I could see *they* were having no trouble communicating.

I clasped Ronit's hand in mine. With my other hand, I held a few of our supplies and headed toward the table where Mimi and Riki sat. *Maybe, if she watches them, she'll be motivated*, I thought desperately.

I placed the supplies on the table and then pulled over two low chairs. Docilely, Ronit sat down on the seat next to me.

At first, she had that same listless expression on her face. Then, as the minutes passed and Mimi and Riki continued their session with obvious enthusiasm, I could see Ronit's eyes shifting with interest toward them.

Again, I tried handing the scissors to Ronit.

And again she squeezed her fingers shut, her nails digging into the skin of her palm, refusing to take the scissors.

What should I do? I was ready to teach, ready to motivate with games, ready to do almost anything, but this apathy was completely unexpected. *How in the world will I ever be the recipient of the Goldstone Outstanding Student Teacher Award if I can't even get my student to cut out a picture of a ball?*

Then Mimi, with that brilliant, magical smile, suddenly looked up at us and, grasping the situation, immediately came to the rescue, "Riki, I just love the way you are cutting out that apple. Let's show Ronit how to do it."

Riki, gratified with the compliment, proud to finally be doing something she was supposed to be doing, happily agreed.

"Okay," Mimi said. "Step one. Show Ronit how to put her fingers through the holes of the scissors."

Riki spoke to Ronit while demonstrating how to hold the scissors.

I held my breath. It worked! Ronit put her fingers through the scissors' holes.

"*Mitzuyan!*" Mimi exclaimed. "Riki, you are a wonderful *morah* and Ronit, you're the best *talmidah!*"

Riki's face was glowing and there was a slight smile forming on Ronit's face.

I was afraid to say a word.

"Okay, Riki," Mimi continued. "We're up to the next step. Show Ronit how to open and close the scissors so she'll understand how to cut."

"It's so easy," Riki laughed while snapping the scissors open and closed in the air. "Try it, Ronit."

Ronit opened and closed her scissors a few times, her smile getting wider and wider. In no time Mimi had Ronit cutting and laughing along with Riki.

Now, sitting at the desk in Mimi's room and remembering how she had come to the rescue, I had to express my thanks.

"No, Mimi," I shook my head, smiling at her, "maybe for you it wasn't a big deal, but I've got to admit I was feeling kind of hopeless with Ronit."

"Really, Sara, I don't mind the compliment, but the truth is, it was the natural, obvious thing to do."

"Not for me. She seemed to be in a totally different world!"

"Sometimes, Sara, you've got to step into that world," Mimi said quietly.

"I guess you're right," I pondered aloud. "You know, Mimi, I never thought of it like that." A few moments passed without either of us saying anything, then suddenly I said wholeheartedly, "For your information, I think you would make an excellent teacher after all."

"Thank you, but do you by any chance think my name is Riki D?"

"No," I shook my head, "but seriously, it's obvious that you have a strong intuition about kids."

"Just from one incident?"

"No. I keep seeing it all the time. You somehow seem to understand people. You're able to remove barriers and to…open closed doors."

"Come on," she laughed.

"Really, Mimi. I'm serious!"

"Well, I for sure never thought of myself as a teacher. If my parents—"

There was a quick knock at the door before it swung open. Rochel Leah and Zehava were looking for Adina. They said that she had promised to study with them. We repeated Adina's message to them and they left.

I thought Mimi seemed a bit more pensive. I was gratified, though, that there were no other interruptions and that we were able to accomplish more than usual.

One of the *meforshim* we were learning referred to a specific *tefillah*. Mimi opened the drawer to her nightstand to get her *siddur*. It was not there.

"I'm sure I left it there," she stood in middle of the room, scratching her head pensively. "On the other hand, it's possible that I left it in the lounge when I davened this morning. But then again—"

"I'll just go get mine." I stood up and headed toward the wash-up closet to take the "shortcut" to my room. The door was locked. "That's funny. I thought Mazal was studying with Rivky and Chani in my room. I wonder why I can't open—"

"Never mind, here's Adina's *siddur*."

"It's all right, Mimi, I'll just go around and get mine," I started walking toward the door that led to the hallway.

"Don't bother, Sara. It'll take you more time to go to your room and come back than for us to…hey, look!"

I already had my hand on the doorknob. I turned around to see what Mimi was referring to. "What?"

"Come here. Look what it says," she motioned for me to come look inside Adina's *siddur*.

Mimi…so interested in her schoolwork all of a sudden. She was still looking inside while slowly sitting down on her bed. I sat down next to her.

The small softbound *siddur* was opened—not to the *tefillah* as I had assumed, but to the inside of the cover. I should have stopped right then. I should have stood up and insisted on getting my own *siddur* from my room. I should *not* have remained there, slowing reading aloud the inscription that was written inside.

> To my dearest Adinaleh,
> Although I will not be with you physically when you read this, always remember that I am with you in spirit for all time and my tefillos will be forever with you. Don't forget, my darling Adinaleh, your Heavenly Father, our Partner in Shamayim Whose ear is always open, waiting and listening and wanting to hear from you. He will never leave you.
> My love for you, my darling, lives on forever,
> Mummy

I looked at Mimi and Mimi looked at me.

"Wow!" I broke the silence. "Her mother sounds so special."

Mimi shook her head sadly, "*Sounded* special."

"Huh? You mean…"

Mimi nodded silently.

I took the *siddur* from her hands and reread the inscription. Now the words took on a deeper and more sorrowful meaning.

"I can't believe it. Her mother…is…" I remembered the scene at the airport vividly…only the father was there to say goodbye.

"I didn't know you didn't know."

"I had no idea." I looked up from the *siddur*, shaken. "When did it happen?"

"I heard when she was around four or five years old."

"Really? That's terrible. I *really* had no idea," I shook my head, my eyes filling. "So young…how horrible!"

"I guess her mother must have known she was dying," Mimi pointed to the *siddur*. "From what it says here—"

"From what it says where?"

Startled, I looked toward the doorway. Cold fingers grabbed my heart. *How long had Adina been standing there?*

"Adinaleh," Mimi jumped. "I mean Adina—"

She rushed over to us. Her lips were white. A vein running along her neck was pulsating with rage.

"Sorry," Mimi said as she grabbed the *siddur* away from me and quickly handed it to Adina, "we were doing the homework. We needed a *siddur*—"

"Get out of here!" she screamed, her face crimson, "Both of you get out!"

"Please, Adina!" I stood up and tried to put my hand on her shoulder, "Please, let me explain—"

"Just leave me alone!" She pushed my hand off and pointed to the door. "Get out!"

I stood in the middle of the room, helplessly watching Adina fling herself down on her bed.

"Come, let's go," Mimi whispered in my ear.

Ignoring her, I ran over to Adina, pleading, "We're sorry, Adina, really, really sorry! Please forgive us—"

"I don't need your apologies. Just go away and leave me alone," she said angrily, her voice muffled in her pillow, the *siddur* still clutched tightly in one hand.

I did not know what to do. I felt the wetness of my tears against my cheeks and I was too weak to stop them. I was sure my heart was breaking into billions and billions of pieces.

"Now's not the time," Mimi again whispered. "Let's go."

No, I shook my head without saying anything. *I can't leave her like this.*

Mimi shrugged.

Leaning over Adina's bed, I implored, "Please forgive us, Adina. I know we were wrong. It was private. We understand—"

She turned to me suddenly, lifting her head off the pillow and all at once raising herself to a sitting position. No, there were no tears…no tears at all.

Anger filled her face so completely that there was not room for even a trace of any other emotion.

I took a step back.

"*You*…understand?" she said slowly, her voice heavy with sarcasm. "What do *you* understand, Sara?

"I—I'm—"

"No, you don't understand a thing. None of you do, especially, someone like you, Sara. *You* for sure can't understand."

Me, for sure?

I cannot recall exactly what happened after that. Mimi said something to Adina—I have no recollection what—and then she spoke to me. I do not remember leaving one room and going to the other, but within a short time, we were both standing in my room.

No one else was there. Not Mazal, not Rivky, nor Chani. They were not on my mind, though, just then. All I could think of were those words. *Someone like you, Sara. You for sure can't understand. Someone like you…someone like you…* the words reverberated and entered the inner chambers of my heart.

"You haven't paid attention to a thing I just said, Sara."

"I don't understand, Mimi, what does she have against me?"

"I keep telling you not to worry. She'll get over it."

"But why did she say to me, 'especially you, Sara'? What did I ever do to her?"

"You haven't heard a word. I just told you that she's just upset—"

"But more so at me!"

"Nah, she didn't mean anything against you in particular. She's just as mad at me."

"No, Mimi. She distinctly said that I for sure can't understand. What does she have against me? Why me?"

"Sara, you're just imagining it. Believe me, everyone knows you wouldn't even harm a fly ."

"She's been angry at me from the beginning—"

"You have a terrific imagination."

"Stop saying that, Mimi. She really does have something against me."

"Come on. Let's finish our work."

"I'm not in the mood, Mimi."

"I can't believe it. Sara Hirsch is not in the mood to do schoolwork!"

"Mimi!"

"Please, I beg of you. I desperately need you to teach me that Radak. We have to check out what it says in the *siddur*—"

"Don't remind me."

"Okay. Let's do something else. Let's work on…"

Mimi succeeded in getting me to continue, but she could not take my mind off Adina. I felt guilty…I *was* guilty. I should not have been reading something that was so private. Adina had a right to be angry with us.

Us. Not just me. Contrary to what Mimi said, I knew Adina's anger was focused mainly on me. Why? Was it because the *siddur* was in my hand? Did she think it had been my idea to use something that was not mine, to read something I had no business reading?

Did she blame me? Well, I was not the one to blame.

I was getting angry. Very angry. At Mimi.

Why did Mimi have to take Adina's *siddur*? I would have gladly gone to my room to bring my own. What right did Mimi have to open it up to the inscription and show it to me?

If only Chavie were here instead of Mimi, nothing like this would have happened.

I was glad when Mazal came into the room, surprised to see us still sitting there, and reminded us that it was time for supper. I had had my fill of Mimi for one day.

Throughout the rest of the evening, all I could think about was Adina. Things had not been the greatest between us before this happened, and now I was afraid that it would get even worse.

I had eaten my supper in a hurry, not very interested in the food being served and avoiding conversation with the others. I certainly was in no mood for socializing.

Mimi, on the other hand, seemed anything but ill at ease. She was laughing and joking naturally with everyone around her. I noticed when Adina entered the dining room, she too acted like her usual self. As dignified as ever, her chin tilted proudly upward, there was not a trace of the scene from a few hours earlier when she slipped into the seat between Malkie and Devorah.

I kept glancing nervously in her direction, but not once did her eyes even shift toward me. *Fine. So she's not interested in me and Mimi is busy chatting away. But it's so unfair! Why can they so easily close the door to their emotions? Why can't I?*

Chapter 15

What's wrong with me?

The sugar in my tea did nothing to sweeten the bitter taste in my mouth and the usually appetizing and spicy Israeli salad tasted bland and rubbery. I made a quick exit and returned to the quiet of my room.

Only seven and a half months left till I return home, I tried telling myself. *Only seven and a half months…*

Earlier that day, when we had been in Kfar Amsdorf, I stopped at the post office to mail my letters to Chavie, Shuli, and Chevy. There had been a letter there for me from my brother Yisrael.

I was not going to push off answering his letter. Besides, I was not in the mood to do anything else that evening and I certainly did not plan on writing him in between classes the next day, when I would be sitting next to Adina. *No, I definitely can't do that.*

I slipped into my long, oversized sweatshirt and curled up under my covers. *That's right*, I told myself, removing my pen and airmail paper from the top drawer of my nightstand. *I still have my loving, close family. If Adina wants to be so unforgiving, I can't help it. I know that I never did—until today, that is—anything for her to hold against me. Anyway, today really wasn't my fault. It was Mimi's. She should've let me bring my siddur instead of insisting that we use Adina's. If Adina wants to hold it against me for the rest of her life… it's really not my problem.*

I slammed the drawer shut.

That's right, it's her problem!

I drew the quilt closer around me, and then unfolded Sruly's letter and began to reread it, letting his comforting words of encouragement wash over me. He was so warm and sympathetic, expressing how much he understands that it's hard for me to be far from home and having to adjust to so many new things and new people. He empathized with me, confiding that he too did not have an easy time leaving the familiarity of the small out-of-town yeshivah he had attended all these years and entering the huge study halls of Lakewood.

His letter had come at a perfect time. Reading and rereading it was therapeutic. When I had finished writing to him (and with Sruly I could be completely open) I really did feel much better.

Closing my eyes, I leaned back against my pillow, rehashing the events of the day. I remembered my conversation with Mimi. She had said something that I had not given much thought to at the time, but now could not help but take more seriously. I had been telling her how hopeless I felt trying to work with Ronit.

Ronit seems to be in a totally different world, I had said. And Mimi had answered me with uncharacteristic seriousness, *Sometimes, Sara, you've got to step into that world.*

I let out a heavy sigh. Mimi was right. Sometimes you've got to step into the other person's world.

I sat up, aligning my back with the wall. *What was it like to be in Adina's world? No mother since she was a little child. Did her father ever remarry?* I thought of my own mother and how much she meant to me. *Did Adina have siblings? Was she the oldest, the youngest?*

What was it like in Ronit's world? Why didn't she communicate in a normal manner? What was Mimi's world really like? So much of the time she seemed so frivolous and yet, on the other hand, she could also be unusually intuitive and perceptive.

And my sisters? All these years I thought I knew them so well. But now it seemed their worlds were turning out to be a lot different from what I had always assumed...than what I had always expected.

Shuli, I sighed, thinking once again of her letter. I leaned over, reaching toward the opened top drawer of my nightstand. *I don't know why I am bothering to read her letter again.* I fumbled inside the drawer, pushing papers, stationery, and pens aside until I found it. *I know Shuli's letter practically by heart already, I've reread it so many times. And what's the use? I already sent her my response earlier this afternoon when I was in Kfar Amsdorf.*

I sat still for a moment, unmoving. *Go through the book you wanted to read so badly last night, but didn't because you were too busy writing your response to Shuli*, I tried telling myself. *Maybe you'll hit upon some terrific techniques for handling Ronit.*

I unfolded her letter as another voice squeezed its way to the surface. *Read the letter again*, it told me. *Try to understand Shuli better. Sometimes you've got to step into her world...*

And so, although my reply to her was already beginning its long journey to America, I sat back and read:

Dearest Sara,

Hi! How are you? I'm sure I don't even have to ask that question, because no doubt you are doing great and having the most fantabulous time of your life. Enjoy it...every single solitary minute of it, because you will never again have such an amazing experience. Believe me, I wish I could go back a year and relive it all over again.

I guess I really miss my school days. Being out in the big world sure isn't the same. I used to think that life as an "adult" was going to be so exciting and fun. All that freedom—being able to decide how I want to conduct my day instead of it all being planned for me. I really was looking forward to teaching, to being part of the school's staff. But now I think it was a lot better being on the other side of the desk. I'm not sure if this side of the desk is really for me.

I work very hard preparing my lessons and writing up my sheets. I try to make them as interesting as possible. In fact, they really are impressive. Everyone says so. But somehow, when I get up in front of the class, it just doesn't go. First of all, these little fourth graders stare at me—giving me the complete look over. If I'm not dressed perfectly, forget it. How's that for confidence? Then, when I start to talk, I worry whether maybe I mispronounced something, because their smirking and snickering don't make me feel very secure.

I tried your idea of bribing them with a Chanukah play. At first, they were very excited, but then the politics about who gets which part, the complaints, and the whining began. It's just not worth the major effort I've got to invest in it in order to keep them happy and motivated. They're only interested if it works out the way they want it.

I also tried prizes. That doesn't work either. Yes, Sara, you're right. There is a reason why the class mischief maker is so mischievous. I'm exhausted already from trying to get to her.

Sara, this just isn't for me. I'm not the analyzing type. I can't sit and wait and wait for her talk to me about all her problems. She totally clams up when I try. Maybe I'm not approaching her the right way, but I'm not a psychiatrist! I just want to teach.

I thought if I followed all the rules, did all the things I was trained to do, prepared for the inevitable problems that would arise—I'd be able to handle things. Sara, it's just not working out that way for me. I spoke to Rabbi Epstein, I spoke with Rebbitzen Fogelman, and I sat in Mrs. Liechtenstein's class. Mindy Hershkowitz spoke with me and so did Perel Schreiber. Nothing has helped! It's just too hard and so not worth it.

They all said that I'm doing a good job and that the first year of teaching is never easy. They promised me that it will get better. They said that it takes at least three years until you begin to get it right. Three years??? Tell me, how can anyone have the patience to wait three years? I just don't know. Maybe it will eventually get better and maybe it won't. And maybe I'm just not used to dealing with challenges.

Who knows? It could be that I've been a little bit spoiled in the past. Things always were pretty easy for me, and I guess I expected them to continue that way. But it's just not happening and I'm starting to get these huge headaches every day. My voice is hoarse from trying to talk through the noise and it's only getting worse. I probably sound like a quacking duck. When I was president of the student council, I never had this problem. Then, when I'd get up to speak, everyone was quiet and cooperative.

Sara, I know you don't want me to do it, but I really think I'm going to quit. It's true that the principals want me to stick it out and are very encouraging. But I feel like I can't take it any longer. It's so-o-o-o hard for me!!! Maybe I'll get an office job uptown. Then I won't have to do all this preparation, only to feel such disappointment. I'm tired of feeling like a failure.

Now, on to the next topic. Abba and Mommy have been getting calls about *shidduchim* for me. I wish you were here, Sara. There are certain things I'd rather discuss with you than with my friends and *shidduchim* is one of them. I don't know. I just don't feel ready yet to take the plunge. I always thought I'd be so excited to start, but now I'm not so sure. How do I know what type of boy is for me? Yes, of course I want someone with excellent *middos* and I'm hoping the boy will be a *masmid* and a *talmid chacham*. But do I want a more *leibedik* type or a more quiet type? I used to think a more lively boy for sure, but you know what I'm like. Do you think two lively people in one house is too much? Do you think a really quiet boy and I could be a match?

On top of that, most of the boys being suggested are learning in Lakewood. That means that I would have to go to New York or New Jersey to meet them. I don't want to do that. I don't mind going there to visit my friends, but for a *shidduch*??? Over here everyone knows me; over there I'm nobody. And even though we have family and friends there who wouldn't mind our meeting in their homes, I'd feel so weird being dependent on them. Oh, Sara, life is getting so complicated. It really was much easier in school!

By the way, I got a haircut last Tuesday. Don't be upset. I know you always told me that I should grow it long and then cut it in layers, but now it's this really short, stylish hairdo. Yikes…I wish I would have listened to you. Now I have to wait at least a year for it to grow in. Everyone says that it looks so chic, but it's just not me!!! You should've seen the faces those little fourth graders made when they saw me. I just don't get it. In the past I never ever would have felt even a bit self-conscious, and here I am now, a supposed adult, and I felt so embarrassed in front of those kids.

In fact, I have to admit, I feel like a little kid myself. I thought I wanted to teach, I really did. Now I'm finding out that it's not as fantabulous as I thought. Who knows? Maybe I really didn't want to teach and it was just the thing to do. I don't know. I feel so confused and mixed up. You're so lucky, Sara. You think out things so much more than I do. You seem to know so much better what you want.

Anyway, sorry to keep going on and on about all this. How are things by you? I was so happy to hear that you went to…

I stopped reading and folded her airmail letter along the creases, stuffing it back into the drawer in frustration. *How could Shuli do this to herself?*

Her world, I told myself. *Enter her world…*

Hers was a world where everything always went smoothly—a world where the biggest challenge was choosing which outfit to wear, or which project the G.O. would present, or which theme song would be best. Hers was a world where tests were effortless, relationships uncomplicated, and friendships came easily.

So what was happening to my breezy, talented, good-hearted sister, whose world was always perfect, whose world overflowed with enthusiasm, life, and joy, and whose charm so easily captivated everyone who knew her? What was happening to this sister of mine, who when things were not flowing in the perfectly smoothe manner she was accustomed to, had absolutely no idea of how to cope?

I shook my head apprehensively, overcome by a feeling of foreboding.

Shuli, don't quit! I had written to her. *Please don't quit!* But, my words, I am sure, came too late. Years too late.

You see, my sense of foreboding was about much more than this teaching job she was about to leave. I hoped I was wrong. But, as I entered her world more and more, I felt convinced that she was sliding into a deep, dark abyss from which it would be almost impossible to free her.

16

"SHOCKER OF SHOCKER of shocks!"

"What's so shocking, Mimi?" *Will I ever get used to her sudden interruptions in the middle of our study sessions?*

"I absolutely L-O-V-E those classes!" she said emphatically, her green eyes wide.

"Which ones—the ones from Geveret Spitz?" I pointed to the booklet we were reading.

"You bet!"

"So, why's that so shocking, Mimi?"

"Because, dear Sara, unlike you—the made to order student—I have never loved a class in my life."

"Come on, Mimi. I can't believe that," I shook my head puzzled. I still could not understand why Mimi chose to go to seminary if she had such little interest in school. "In twelve years, you never had a class you loved?"

"Well, I can't say *never*. There were art classes, music classes, discussion classes—"

"Oh, come on," I laughed, "you know what I mean."

"Listen, Sara. Not everyone was created to sit in class after class—like you, my friend."

"Excuse me," I said defensively, pointing to the others occupying various spots in the school's garden, "but I'm not the only one who likes learning around here."

For a brief moment, her gaze followed mine. From where we sat on a blanket spread out on the grass, we could see our fellow students—M.B.L.L.ers as well as Beit Yaakov HaNegbah girls—relaxing in the garden, *sefarim* and school books opened in front of them. Several sat on benches alongside picnic tables, some parked themselves comfortably on the grass, and there were a few strolling along, in deep discussion. It was a glorious first day of November, unseasonably warm—even for this part of the world.

"Hey, Sara," Mimi turned her eyes back to me, "don't get insulted; I meant it as a compliment."

"Well thanks…and I'm not insulted!"

"Okay, great! I mean it's not my fault that I'm surrounded by all these geniuses."

"I'm no genius, Mimi."

"Could've fool me."

"Really. I work hard to get good grades. *Very* hard."

"So what. At least, you get good grades in the end," Mimi mumbled. Then, returning quickly to her animated self, she said, "By the way, I disagree with you. I think you are a kind of genius. You got me to sit and study and take notes this week. And my roommate also loves to study. Maybe some of it will rub off on me and I'll become a genius too."

"What's this about geniuses?"

We looked up. I cupped my hand over my forehead, squinting against the bright sunlight. Chani and Rivky were smiling down at us.

"So, do you two geniuses want to join us?" Chani asked.

Mimi's eyebrow lifted. "Where're you going?"

"We're on our way to town," Rivky replied.

"The stores are only going to be open for another hour, I think," Chani said. "I want to pick up some nosh for Shabbos. It'll make being in the dorm more fun."

"I'd love to," Mimi's eyes caught mine, "but right now we're studying."

"No breaks?" Chani asked.

"Mimi, we really could stop now," I closed my notebook. "We're going to have to stop soon anyway."

"Decide one way or the other," Chani said. "It takes fifteen minutes each way and we still have to take showers and everything else before Shabbos."

Chapter 16

"Just pray that with everyone in the dorm this Shabbos," Rivky spread out her hand emphatically, "there'll be enough hot water left for the rest of us!"

Mimi stood up, dusting herself off from some fallen leaves. "So, Sara, let's go," she said while glancing at her watch. "There's still plenty of time."

"I don't know about me." I slowly rose and then bent over, gathering the ends of the blanket together. "I've got to do some ironing and I didn't take my shower yet. But, Mimi, you could go—"

"No, Mimi, you go no place." Looking up, I was surprised to see Mazal. I had not noticed her approaching us. She must have hurried over to us, since her words came out in a breathless rush, "You forget, Mimi, you have *toranut*? We must go to the dining hall to set up. I look in your room, I look in library, I look in lounge, I look in kitchen, I look all over for you—"

"I'm so sorry, Mazal," Mimi smacked her forehead. "I can't believe I forgot."

"*Az rutzi!* Geveret Katz and Geveret Mendlowitz not very happy with you now!"

"Okay, okay...take it easy, Mazal. I'm hurrying." Then Mimi turned to me and asked sweetly, "Will you do me a favor, Sara? Will you take my stuff upstairs for me. I'm in a huge rush..."

"Sure, Mimi, no problem..."

"She's already gone," Rivky laughed softly. "Need help?"

"No, it's fine. I'll manage." I stacked the blanket, *sefarim*, and notebooks in my arms and attempted to prevent my load from toppling over by pressing my chin into the top of the pile. "You two should go already before the stores close."

"You're sure you don't want to come, Sara?" Rivky asked. "You could leave the stuff on the bench. No one will touch it."

"No thanks, it's really all right," my voice must have come out muffled, with my chin bearing down hard on the precariously balanced pile. "I'd better get going."

"So should we," Chani said, grabbing Rivky's arm and steering her toward the path leading into the woods. "I mean, how would I ever manage a whole Shabbos without all those goodies?"

I heard Rivky's easy chuckle. "Want us to get you anything, Sara?" she turned her head while continuing to walk.

"That's all right, thanks anyway." I took a few steps in the direction of the dormitory. Suddenly, I stopped walking and, turning slowly, called out, "Rivky…Chani…"

"Yes?" they spun around simultaneously.

"Um…if you don't mind. You know those cookies Mazal likes?"

"The sandwich ones? The kind with the cream in middle?"

"Yes. Could you pick up a package for her? I'll pay you later."

"Sure, Sara," Rivky said, "No problem."

"Thanks. She'll be so happy we thought of her. And…um…one more thing, if it's all right with you?"

"Yes?"

"For Mimi. A package of her caramels. We should be *milchig* by the time it's *Shalosh Seudos*. She'd enjoy it. Okay?"

"Okay, Sara," Chani said to me. Turning to Rivky, she added good-humoredly, "We better get out of here fast. Before you know it, Sara will have us buying something for each girl in the dorm."

"You're right," Rivky winked at me. "Take care, Sara, we'll see you later."

"Bye and thanks a ton!" I was about to wave, but could not extricate my hand from the bottom of the pile without risking having the complete load topple to the ground.

I continued on my way, humming to myself. Despite the towering stack in my arms, I felt light and happy as I carefully picked my way along the twisted path leading toward the dormitory. *Life is really good!*

That week Shabbos in the dorm promised to be especially wonderful since it was a Shabbat *chovah*. On the rare occasion that everyone in the dorm *had* to stay, the program was richer and more exciting than usual. There would be fascinating speakers, interesting workshops, singing, and a choir performance. And, now that my friendships with some of the girls had deepened and we were no longer strangers, I was really looking forward to spending Shabbos with everyone.

A soft breeze carrying the scent of coralberry and elder lifted my hair. I smiled at a multicolored bird hopping from one nearby branch to the next. It kept me company all along the shaded path leading toward the dormitory. As I approached the building, the aroma of Shabbos foods cooking and baking drifted toward me. Inhaling deeply, I reveled in the pleasant fragrances.

I was beginning, with Mimi's help, to make a slight dent in communicating with Ronit, Mazal and I were getting even closer, and I was finally starting to get somewhere in my learning with Mimi. It was true, I was still unhappy about my relationship with Adina. I continued to puzzle over what it was she had against me, especially after the *siddur* incident. Just thinking about how she caught me holding the *siddur* in my hand while reading the inscription caused me to flush. I had tried at least three times this past week to apologize to her—but, well...*I'm not going to think about that now.*

No, I shook my head, watching the multicolored bird fly off into the blue sky, *I will definitely NOT think upsetting thoughts right now. I have so much to be grateful for.*

Fortunately, I had caught up on all my correspondence, and although my sisters' letters caused me much concern, I was hopeful that they would find my responses helpful. Shabbos was going to be great, I was sure, and to top it all off, I was very much looking forward to the two-day *tiyul* that was to begin Sunday morning. Monday's itinerary with the trip to Me'aras HaMachpelah and Kever Rochel was especially meaningful to me and I anticipated that part of the trip the most. *Baruch Hashem*, I sighed contentedly, *things are really turning out great!*

I stood motionless for a few quiet seconds in front of the closed door, attempting to take it all in. I could hear the cheerful voices of the girls going about their Shabbos preparations emanating through the open windows, mingling with the sweet sounds of birds chirping nearby. I could look up and see the stunningly blue cloudless sky and then gaze at the garden surrounding the building, feasting my eyes on the dazzling palette of multihued flowers with their bursts of color vibrant against the verdant green shrubbery. I stood there feeling my heart lifting higher and higher, knowing I was in the holiest country in the world and that even though things were not perfect for me, I would soon have the opportunity to visit the graves of our *Imahos*. There, I felt sure, I would be able to pour out all my feelings...all those doubts and insecurities. *Leah...the sister who had been the less favored wife...Rochel...who gave up that which could've been hers.* And somehow it would help me in fulfilling one of my greatest dreams.

Thank you, Mommy and Abba. Thank you, Bubby. And of course, thank you, Hashem. At that moment, I wished the seven-and-a-half months left until I had to return to America would stretch on forever. *If only I could stay here and have my family join me too.*

My eyes flew open because, just then, the door to the building swung open. Two girls conversing in rapid Hebrew emerged. Noticing that I was struggling with the stack of notebooks, *sefarim*, blanket and other paraphernalia, one of them held the door open for me while the other offered to give me a hand. I shook my head, thanked them, and told them I could manage.

I entered the large hallway and took another whiff of the delicious Shabbos aroma. I smiled. I could almost taste what was being prepared.

Passing the lounge, I glanced inside. Girls were sitting around chatting, reading books, and writing letters. I climbed the steps to the third floor.

Here and there, girls passed me, either running up the steps ahead or making their way downstairs. Someone with a towel twisted like a turban around her head held a blow-dryer, its wire dangling and banging against the steps, in one hand and with the other, she clutched a large round brush. Saying a quick hello, she apologized and wriggled in front of me, taking two steps at a time.

Be careful, I wanted to call out to her, *you might trip on the wire.* However, by the time I opened my mouth to speak, she had already disappeared from view.

Malkie Green, holding an iron in one hand and the tops of two hangers over her shoulder with the other hand, her blouses fluttering in the air behind her, muttered a quick "Is that you, Sara? Hi!" as she dashed down the steps past me.

"Hi, Malkie," I replied. However, I do not think she heard me. She was already out of earshot.

Two other girls who were heading in opposite directions, stopped on the steps when they saw each other. One showed the other the letter she was holding, resulting in shrieking and kissing, jumping and calls of *mazal tov*. Heaving my load carefully, I finally reached the step they were standing on. Trying to squeeze through, I breathlessly and politely wished them *mazal tov*. One of the girls grabbed me in a huge bear hug and started kissing me, resulting in the inevitable. *Sefarim*, pens, the blanket, and notebooks tumbled down the steps.

Apologizing profusely, she immediately ran down the steps, picked up the *sefarim*, kissed them, and handed them to me. The other girl helped me with the blanket and notebooks. I found the pen and loose papers and then, gathering all the stuff together, hurried as quickly as I could to my room to get ready for Shabbos before any other mishap could take place.

My preparations did not take long; I had the room and the sink in the wash-up closet to myself. Mazal and Mimi were still downstairs busy with their *toranut* and Adina…well, Adina was preoccupied.

I had knocked on her door to borrow some shampoo. (Someone—*and I'm not saying who*—had taken mine and not yet returned it.) When I opened the door, I saw a bespectacled, gray-haired woman sitting on a chair opposite Adina, with some photographs spread across the desk. Adina quickly stood up and with a few graceful steps in my direction, handed me a somewhat empty bottle and informed me that this was all she had left. Before I could change my mind, she stiffly asked me to please close the door. As soon as I did, I heard her hook the latch closed.

Oh well, at least she gave me shampoo.

I grabbed my towel and robe, hurried down the hallway, and was in and out of the shower as quickly as possible. There was still plenty of hot water and I hoped there would be some left for the others.

I slipped a cassette into my tape recorder and pressed the "play" button, allowing the lively, cheerful music to fill the room. Then, still wrapped in my terry cloth robe, I plugged my blow-dryer into the wall socket and turned it on. While drying my hair, I cheerfully sang along with the music. *Everything is absolutely great…I'm just not going to let Adina's behavior get me down.*

When my hair was done, I chose a solid pale-pink ruffled blouse with a tiered floral-patterned matching skirt. By the time I was passing my belt through the loops in my skirt, Mazal rushed into the room, laughing and breathless.

"Wow, Mazal," I looked at her flushed cheeks and shiny eyes, "you look like you're having fun."

"Oh, I am. You know, with Mimi—it always very, very fun."

"Hey, Mazal!" we heard Mimi calling from the hallway. "I'll race you!"

"Very nice, Mimi," Mazal laughed while poking her head through the opened door. "You win. You already almost there!"

I smiled. Life with Mimi certainly was not dull.

While Mazal went about her own preparations, running around the room, breathless and rushing, I continued with mine. I ironed my outfit for the next day and then, after offering to do Mazal's dress, carefully pressed it, as well. I made sure my alarm clock was not set to ring in the morning, dusted our desk with the *sefarim*, restacking them neatly when I finished, and did a quick *sponja* on our floor. Then sitting on my bed, I said *Shir HaShirim*.

When we heard Geveret Katz's voice over the *ramkol* announcing that Shabbos was in twenty-five minutes, Mazal and I, clean and refreshed, made our way along with the others downstairs and into the dining room.

The tables were pushed together in the center of the room to form the outline of a square, with white starched tablecloths spread across them. Each place setting included a ceramic plate, an artistically folded napkin in its center, with shiny stainless steel cutlery placed on the sides. Small vases containing pink, white, and red geraniums picked from the campus's garden were spaced evenly along the tables.

I looked on admiringly, complimenting Mazal on a job well done.

"Not only me," Mazal said modestly, "all the girls do much helping."

"I love the way those napkins are folded. How did you do it?"

"I am not sure. Ask Mimi. She think way to make the napkin like flower."

"Really?"

"Yes. We see her fold and fold. We think she do one of her funny games."

"I can imagine—"

"She fold napkin into hat and put it on her head—"

"And everyone laughed, of course." I tried to keep the cynicism out of my voice.

"Yes. Then she make napkin look like *arnav*—"

"*Arnav*?"

"*Nachon*," Mazal said. Then seeing my eyebrows lift uncomprehendingly, she placed both of her hands lengthwise beside her ears and flapped them back and forth. "*Eich omrim b'Anglit?* Eh-eh-"

"Do you mean," I watched her wagging hands pantomiming long, floppy ears, "rabbit? As in bunny rabbit?"

"Bunny rabbit? Where's the bunny rabbit?" Mimi suddenly appeared with Rivky.

"I just tell Sara you do a lot of art with napkins. You make hat, you make *arnav*, you do pretty flowers on the table—"

"They're gorgeous, Mimi," I complimented, "really gorgeous."

"Yes, Mimi, they are," Rivky added her approval.

Grinning, Mimi curtsied. "Thank you, thank you and thank—"

"Mimi, Mazal! I've been looking for you," Hindy Mandel approached our small group. "We've got to go to the kitchen."

"I hope there no problem," Mazal looked worried.

"No problems," Hindy said. "We've just got to help Geveret Mendlowitz with a few of the last minute preparations."

The three of them went off together, leaving Rivky and me alone. As we continued chatting about the room's décor, we drifted toward the corner, where a crowd of girls had gathered. They were looking at one table that had been pushed against the wall.

There were slices of potato kugel, bowls of *cholent*, and bottles of soda water and *petel* laid out. I had not realized how hungry I was until I finished eating a portion of potato kugel and forced myself to resist a second. Instead, I helped myself to a bowl of *cholent* and washed it down with a cup of soda water mixed with *petel*.

After completing the *berachos acharonos*, Rivky and I strolled over to the kitchen to see what was happening with Mimi and Mazal. Mimi, Mazal, and Hindy were rolling aluminum foil over the bronze-colored *platah* under Geveret Mendlowitz's watchful eye. Then, two other girls lifted first one huge pot and then another, carefully placing them side-by-side on the large hot plate.

Just then, we heard Geveret Katz's voice coming from the dining room. It was candle lighting time. As Geveret Katz lit the candles, the flickering of the flames reflecting against her dark wig, caused its shiny spots to appear like twinkling stars and I felt wrapped in that familiar aura of holiness that envelops us when we usher in the Sabbath Queen.

The girls stood around her solemnly. *Are their thoughts similar to mine?* My mind wandered over the Mediterranean Sea, through Europe, past the Atlantic Ocean—all the way to Rolland Heights, to my own mother, and I suddenly felt a compelling tug in my heart. *How I miss you, Mommy!* My gaze shifted toward Adina—*Adina, who doesn't have a mother waiting for her on the other side of the world.*

I shook my head, taken aback.

Unlike the somber, serious expressions reflected on most of our faces, the sides of Adina's mouth curled upward. *She's actually enjoying this*, I thought, momentarily taken aback. Then my analytical antennas went up. *Who knows,* I told myself, *it's true, the rest of us might feel kind of homesick at a time like this, even though we're grateful to be here. I guess, for Adina, it must be different. I wonder if she can even remember her own mother bentching licht...*

We gathered in the lounge to *daven Kabbalas Shabbos* and it was then that I heard Adina singing for the first time. She had a stunning voice, and I guess I should not have been so surprised. Whatever Adina Stern did was perfect!

The beautiful singing and harmonizing during *davening* and the inspiring words of *emunah* and *bitachon* by Rabbanit Abrams would have been enough to satisfy us. Yet, there was more...

The *seudah*, with its delicious and tastefully served food, the stirring melodies sung by the choir, and the rousing speech delivered by Rabbi Grossman continued to move us.

When we all finished *bentching* and helped put the dining room in order, everyone began to disperse. Some girls went to their rooms, some headed toward the library and lounge to learn, read, or just relax, and some girls went outside to take a stroll through the garden.

I was in the kitchen helping Mazal and the rest of the girls that had *toranut* finish up. Rivky and Chani were also there, hoping their assistance would move things along so that Mimi would soon be free to join them.

I was standing near Mazal, handing her one clean glass at a time while she lined them up on trays ready for placing on the tables the next morning. Although we were a bit further away from the others, I could still hear Geveret Katz briskly dispensing a few last-minute instructions. While she spoke, she walked around, pointing out where the different items went.

I looked on in fascination. I had not yet had *toranut* for a Shabbos, and I found the running of this huge kitchen amazing. I guess I was not the only one, because just then Rivky expressed her admiration to Geveret Katz.

"Yes," Geveret Katz agreed, "this kitchen has to be large and organized to serve so many people. In fact, in the last place where I was the house mother—"

Mimi stopped sweeping. "You were *eim ha-bayit* someplace else?"

"Oh, yes. I've done this for quite a few years."

"Another seminary?"

"Well, not exactly a seminary," she shook her head. "It was more like a home for girls who can't live in their own homes."

"How sad," I heard myself say, while handing Mazal another glass.

"Yes, it is sad, but believe it or not, the girls were happy there."

"How could they be happy if they didn't have a home to go back to?" Hindy asked as she hung her towel over the rack.

"That's a good question. I guess they sort of looked at it like it was camp."

"Camp?" Rivky wondered aloud. "But that's still not home."

"True," Geveret Katz continued, "but what they can't change they can't change. Most of them will never be able to move back home: their home life was just too dysfunctional. However, when these girls come to accept their circumstances—knowing that their situation is not going to change no matter what they do—they learn how to make the best of it."

"I don't understand," Mimi rested her chin on top of the broomstick she was holding, her eyes turned skeptically toward Geveret Katz. "How can they make the best of not really having a home?"

Mazal and I finished stacking the glasses on the trays and came closer to where Geveret Katz stood.

"Well, firstly, they think of each other as sisters. Picture having thirty sisters."

"I don't think I'd want that," Hindy said. "My one and only sister and I fight like cats and dogs!"

"Remember, because these girls come from troubled homes, they need to make each other their family. They have to create their own stability and find people who will love them and be there for them. They take care of each other emotionally. You can only imagine what their weddings are like."

I softly said, "The girls must also become very attached to their *eim ha-bayit*."

"And I to them," she smiled sadly.

"So why did you leave—" Mimi caught herself. "I mean, I shouldn't have, I mean I'm sorry I asked—"

"That's all right, Mimi." She paused for a few moments. We stood there quietly, not knowing what to say, listening to the gentle bubbling sounds of the *cholent* pot simmering on the *platah*. "Actually, we moved back here to be near my elderly father. And my husband was also very excited to be part of the Kfar Amsdorf *kollel*."

"It's so...um...nice that you do this sort of thing. I mean—*eim ha-bayis*-ing."

We burst out laughing at Mimi's off-handed compliment and her wording. So did Geveret Katz.

"I guess," Geveret Katz smiled at her, "it must be in my blood."

"What do you mean?" a few of us asked simultaneously.

"Well, many years ago, when I was still a baby—and don't ask me how many years ago..."

We laughed again.

"My father was also in charge of a camp."

"Really?"

"Which one?"

"Was he the head counselor?"

"They had sleep away camps then?"

"No, no, girls," she shook her head smiling, "I suppose I'm not making myself very clear. It wasn't a regular camp—"

"What kind was it?"

"Sh-sh, let Geveret Katz finish!"

"It was a camp for the Yemenite Jews who had just arrived in the newly founded State."

"Oh, no wonder. We thought you looked Yemenite."

Geveret Katz looked embarrassed. "Actually, both of my parents are Ashkenazim from Warsaw." Then, clearing her throat, she announced briskly, "Okay, girls, the kitchen looks spic-and-span. You're free to go."

"Great!" Mimi said, putting away the broom in the closet. "What do you want to do?"

"Let's all go for a walk," Rivky suggested.

"It's a beautiful evening," Hindy commented, "and I heard this weather is definitely not going to last."

"Before you all run away," Geveret Katz said, "I need one of you to be in charge of unlocking the kitchen in the morning and a few of you to slice up the *kakosh* cake and put it out with the milk, cups, and cutlery."

"I'll be glad to help you out with the *kakosh* cake," Chani offered. "Geveret Mendlowitz makes the best *kakosh* cake around."

"Thank you, Chani," Geveret Katz said. "How about some help from those of you on *toranut*?"

"I'll do the milk," Hindy said, "and help with the set-up."

"I'll be there too."

"And I can be in charge," Mimi grinned generously.

"That's very thoughtful of you, Mimi," Geveret Katz led the way out of the kitchen. We followed closely behind her, watching her close the door firmly when there was no one left inside. "Remember girls," we stood around her, in front of the closed door, "the grape juice is in the main refrigerator. You can use the same table that the *kugel* and *cholent* were served on, but make sure to use the *milchig* tablecloth. You'll find it in the *milchig* pantry. Oh, I almost forgot," she turned to Mimi. "Here, Mimi. You offered to be in charge. Here's the key. Remember, you're responsible to be there bright and early to open up—"

"Um, Geveret Katz, it's really okay," Mimi covered her yawning mouth with one hand and with the other held the key as far away from her face as possible, as though there was something wrong with it. "I don't really need to be in charge. I was only—"

"That's all right, Mimi," Geveret Katz smiled. "I think you'll do an excellent job…"

Mimi frowned, took another look at the key, shrugged her shoulders, and then slipped it nonchalantly into her pocket.

I tried to stifle a smile.

However, I was not smiling a couple of hours later when I was getting ready for bed and heard someone pounding on our door.

"Mazal…Sara…open up!" Mimi's voice came through the wash-up closet in a loud whisper.

"Yes, yes, Mimi, I am coming," Mazal was sitting on her bed, taking off her shoes. "One minute."

I came from the walk-in closet, where I had just changed into my nightgown. Although there were no lights on, my eyes had adjusted fairly well to the darkness and, with the *trisim* still open, the moonlight illuminated the room, making it even easier to see.

What was going on?

Mimi was standing in middle of the room, a robe wrapped around her long nightshirt, her feet encased in fluffy pink slippers.

I could not hide the fear in my voice. "Is everything all right, Mimi?"

"I guess so."

"So what's wrong?"

"Yes, Mimi, what is the problem?"

"The problem is," she paused dramatically, "I'm starved!"

"Oh, Mimi," Mazal laughed, "you scared me."

I did not think it was so funny. "That's why you came in…now?" I tried to make out the time and turned my watch toward the window in order to see the dial more clearly. "Mimi, it's almost half-past midnight. What in the world?"

"Well, I was thinking that since I am *in charge*…" she said the words *in charge* in the brisk voice that was undoubtedly that of our *eim ha-bayit*. Again Mazal laughed, this time at Mimi's perfect imitation of Geveret Katz.

I just stood there, my hands on my hips. "Yes?"

"And since I'm the one in charge," her green eyes reflecting the outside light were twinkling mischievously as she waved the key in front of us, "and I'm hungry and I happen to know that there is a delicious *cholent* bubbling away on the *platah* in the kitchen—"

I shook my head emphatically, "No, Mimi—"

"Just waiting to be eaten—"

"Mimi, *zeh lo b'seder*—"

"And it smelled heavenly the last time I was near it—"

"Mimi, we can't—"

"And there is so much of it, that after tomorrow's *seudah* it might end up getting wasted..."

Please, do not ask me why I went along or how Mimi induced Rivky, Chani, Rochel Leah, Zehava, and Mazal to join us. Wrapped in our robes, we tiptoed down to the kitchen. The stairway and hallways remained lit, but most of the other rooms were already swathed in a cloak of darkness, lending an extra air of tension to our creeping nighttime adventure.

Giggling nervously, we stood at the kitchen door while Mimi fumbled with the key. Chani held the door to the dining room wide open so that Mimi could use the light coming in from the hallway. But it did not help much because the kitchen was pretty far from the hallway. The only light in the dining room came from those few round fluorescent light fixtures, their soft glow lending an eerie appearance to our faces.

"Nu, Mimi?"

"I need more light!"

"Do you need help? Let someone else try!"

"This better be worth it, Mimi."

"Hurry up! It's taking too long."

"I'm trying, I'm trying—"

"Sh-sh..."

"Mimi, *b'emet*—"

"One minute. Here we go...see?" She swung the door open triumphantly. "I got it!"

Suddenly, light cut through the darkness. A small overhead light was on in the kitchen. Chani closed the dining room door and ran over to join us. We piled inside the kitchen and someone quietly closed that door.

Inside, the huge pot of *cholent* was softly bubbling away, completely oblivious to the excitement it had caused. It really did smell delicious. After having been in the darkness for so long, the kitchen's small light dissipated all of our apprehensions about this nighttime escapade. We gathered around the stove excitedly, most of the tension gone. Someone placed a towel on the *fleishig* counter and someone else ran to the pantry to get out the cutlery and bowls. Mimi and Rochel Leah went over to the *platah* and lifted the heavy pot.

This was going to be fun!

There was a sense of camaraderie mingling with laughter as our cheerful banter filled the room. We were no longer afraid. We were just a group of girls engaging in harmless enjoyment. Mimi's enthusiasm was infectious. I was thrilled to be part of the crowd.

"Okay," Mimi held the ladle in her hand and began dishing out the *cholent* into bowls, "who's next?"

"Yum, this is really excellent *cholent*."

"My turn, Mimi."

"It's so-o-o good!"

"Next—"

"Thanks for convincing us to do this."

"I'm having a blast!"

"Mimi, let me know when you're ready to give out seconds—"

"No, prob, Chani," Mimi sang out while delivering one of her deep, throaty laughs. "Sara, you still didn't—"

"MIMI!" I suddenly yelled, my shaking finger pointing at the *cholent* pot on the counter.

"What's wrong, Sara?"

"Yes, why are you getting so hysterical?" Rochel Leah asked me while taking another fork full of *cholent*. "What's—"

"OH NO!"

"What's with you, Rivky?" Rochel Leah turned from me to Rivky.

Suddenly, one by one everyone's mouths dropped open as realization dawned. Mazal's dark complexion turned pale and Mimi's already pale one turned even whiter. Her freckles appeared to be jumping off her face.

Rochel Leah's big eyes grew larger and rounder as they moved from one face to the next. Following my still shaking finger to where I was pointing, she finally comprehended the gravity of the situation. "Oh no!" she raised the back of her hand to her mouth. "We're in big trouble!"

Trouble. That was an understatement.

We had let go of the *cholent* pot on the counter without thinking, and now we could not return it to the hot plate. The food would be spoiled by the next morning.

"What a huge waste!"

"Forget about the waste, Chani," Zehava cried out despondently, "what's Geveret Katz going to say?"

"What will all the girls say when there no food for *Se'udat Shabbat*?" Mazal turned to Mimi. "Mimi, what we going to do?"

"W-what—we going to…" Mimi stared at the *cholent* pot, unable to meet our eyes. She scratched her head thoughtfully, her lower lip caught between her teeth. "Um…um…what we…" All at once she looked up, the corners of her mouth curving into a charming smile. "*I know what we're going to do…*"

I was not sure what Mimi's ultimate plan was, but she managed to convince us to make room for the huge pot in the refrigerator before we returned to our bedrooms to sleep.

She was all smiles the next morning, when she made *Kiddush* and served the *kakosh* cake and milk. She was still smiling when she returned from Geveret Katz's cottage, where she had confessed our exploit of the previous night and had taken full responsibility for the episode. And she continued to smile when she served the cold *cholent* with a dollop of mayonnaise in the center.

Her smile grew wider and her dimples deeper when the Israeli girls complimented her on a delicious dish and wanted to know if this was the way Americans ate *cholent*. She laughed heartily, accepting their praise—but, assured them, that this would probably be the last time they would ever have this type of *cholent*.

There she is…again the center of attention!

I was disappointed in Mimi, but I could not stay angry with her. No one could. She refused to divulge to anyone which of the girls participated in the nocturnal adventure. And although many of the girls wanted to know, Geveret Katz actually did not seem interested. She made it clear to Mimi that since the key was given to her and she had been in charge, it was *she* who was solely responsible for any harm caused.

Mimi knew that there would be consequences. She also knew that she would have to wait until Shabbos was over to find out what they would be. And yet (don't ask me how she did it), she was all smiles throughout the day, laughing, joking, and continuing to charm everyone.

In the end, the punishment she received was thankfully not too severe. I waited outside Geveret Katz's cottage while Mimi went in to talk with her. We had been planning to do some schoolwork together before the *Melaveh Malkah* and I offered to walk Mimi over to speak to Geveret Katz, in order to put an end to our suspense and finally hear the verdict.

Standing outside in the moonlight, I shivered. The light sweater I had thrown on right before we left was not enough to warm me. Or, perhaps my nervousness was really the culprit that was causing me to feel so cold.

I knew Mimi deserved to be punished. Her constant seeking of attention and fun was no excuse for such impulsiveness and mischief. But, still…

I paced back and forth on the little path leading up to Geveret Katz's cottage, my thoughts whirling around in my head. Finally, the door opened and I rushed to Mimi to hear the decision.

We started walking slowly toward the dorm while she spoke. Mimi would not be allowed to join us for the Sunday segment of our *tiyul*, but she would be permitted to be with us on Monday. She was fine with that part, accepting it like a brave soldier. The only thing that caused her disappointment was the fact that she would not be able to be with us Sunday night at the B.R.Y. dorm.

I empathized with her. "Oh, you must be so upset, Mimi. You were really looking forward to getting together with all your friends—"

"Sara, will you kindly stop feeling sorry for me," she quickened her pace.

I hurried, trying to keep up with her, "But I know how much—"

"I'll manage," she pasted a wide smile on her face.

"Mimi, how do you do it? When I'm upset about something, I...I—"

"You, what?" she stopped walking and looked at me.

"I guess...I have such a hard time hiding it. And you—"

"Yes?"

"You're always so cheerful and smiley."

"Maybe that's really the way I feel," she said. "Maybe I'm not hiding anything."

"Mimi," I looked into her eyes searchingly, "that's not true. Sometimes...sometimes I see that tiny bit of sadness and—"

"Sara, I hate to disappoint you," she turned away from me, walking on, "but that imagination of yours—"

"No, Mimi," I caught up to her and put my hand on her shoulder. "I know I'm not imagining it."

"Sara...will you—"

She stopped talking. She stopped walking. She turned her back to me, staring into the darkness.

"Mimi...what?" I stood directly behind her.

She did not say anything. We could hear the crickets' chirping in the background, and sounds of music and girls' voices coming from the dormitory. I did not move. Slowly, Mimi turned around. I could see the moonlight reflected in eyes glistening with unshed tears. And this time she did not try to hide them.

"Sara..."

"What is it? I'll stay here with you—"

"No," she shook her head, smiling. But this time it was a real smile, not one of those fake, charming, pasted on ones. "That's not it."

"So what's wrong, Mimi. Please tell me..."

"It's what you said. You were right—"

"What did I say? I'm sorry, forgive-"

"Will you stop it already, Sara? First, you go on and on...as stubborn as ever. And then, when I admit that you're right, you start apologizing—"

"What am I right about?"

Mimi laughed as a large tear made its way down her cheek. "I never had a friend like you. You're so funny. You really, really care…"

I stood still, rooted to the spot.

"And you stick with it…you say it like it is," she wiped the tear with her finger, "and then suddenly you haven't a clue—"

"A clue?" I felt helpless.

"Well, you're right, Sara. I am hiding something. And I'll let you in on a little secret. Probably the whole world is. Are we all supposed to go around telling everyone our problems?"

"Friends…"

"Sorry about that. I personally would rather go around smiling. You know the good old saying: Smile and the world smiles with you, cry and you cry alone…"

"You're not alone, Mimi."

"No thanks, Sara. I like you and I even trust you. But from now on, do me a favor. Please stop asking me questions…and just leave me ALONE."

I stood rooted where I was, astounded by her words and unable to move, watching Mimi's receding back as she went inside the dormitory.

17

THE CRY, AT first, was so low, I could not be certain I had actually heard it.

In fact, I was unsure that I had heard anything at all. *Maybe I'm still dreaming*, I thought while turning over and trying to find a comfortable position.

And then, I heard it again. *A faint cry.*

I opened one eye and then the other. Slowly, I lifted my head, raising my chest upward while leaning sideways on my elbow. I tried looking around the dark room.

Nothing.

Everyone seemed to be sleeping. Enviously, I listened to their rhythmic breathing, wishing that I too could be sound asleep. *What's with me?*

I plopped my head back down on my pillow, squeezing my eyes shut. *I should be exhausted!* We had risen early that morning when it was still dark outside, and that had been after going to sleep late the night before, after the *Melaveh Malkah* had finally ended. The day was packed with wonderful, non-stop action, culminating in a late supper and sleepover in the B.R.Y. dormitory.

Mimi's absence was especially noticeable when we arrived at B.R.Y. A few girls, mutual camp friends of Rivky and Mimi, were sorely disappointed when they heard that Mimi had not come with them. Rivky tried her best not to reveal what had transpired over Shabbos. I think they assumed that she was just not feeling well.

I had never been to sleep-away camp, so our getting together that evening was not the reunion for me that it was for many of the others. Nevertheless, the B.R.Y. girls were warm and welcoming to us all and I did not suffer from my usual shyness. Rivky, of course, went out of her way to introduce us to some of her friends. They gave us a tour of their dorm and classrooms. Afterwards, there was a choir performance, followed by a hilarious comedy act about some American seminary girls lost in Israel and the way they misconstrued the directions given to them along the way. Everyone was hysterical with laughter, tears streaming uncontrollably down our cheeks. One of the actresses, apparently a born comic, had us all in stitches when she jumped off the stage, running awkwardly through the aisles. *Mimi would love this!* I felt a sudden sinking in my stomach when I thought of her. *I wonder how she's doing…*

While we sat around the tables eating supper, I again thought of her. How could I not? *The way the napkins are folded…Someone telling a funny joke…A girl with red hair passing by…*

"I'm sure Mimi is giving those Beit Yaakov HaNegbah girls a grand old time," Rivky unexpectedly said, as though reading my mind.

"What a pity she didn't come," Simi Applebaum, Rivky's B.R.Y. friend, said. "When we heard that you guys were coming to us after the *Kinus*, I was so looking forward to seeing her. And—"

"Me too. I remember how shocked I was when I heard she was in Eretz Yisrael," Chaya Sara Brisk, another B.R.Y. friend related. "It was so sneaky of Mimi. She didn't say a word during the whole eight weeks of camp!"

"Well, she surprised me too," Rivky told them.

"Really? Come on, Rivky, *you* didn't know anything?"

"Absolutely, Simi. I was as shocked as you when Mimi called me the night before we left."

"Really? Wow!" Simi exclaimed. "Well, you know Mimi—"

"I really was hoping to see her—"

"You will, Chaya Sara. First of all, if we get permission, you can come to our dorm for a Shabbos. We'll have a blast. You know, Mimi's in charge of a fabulous Chanukah production. She'll be absolutely thrilled if you surprise her and come to it…"

Since when was Mimi chosen as head of the Chanukah production?

Chapter 17

And why DID Mimi decide to come to M.B.L.L. at the last minute? Mimi Rosenberg. She was such a mystery to me.

Why does Mimi always think up these crazy, mischievous ideas? I thought back to the previous evening, *and what is this "thing" she's hiding?*

I tried to tell myself, *what's the difference? Why in the world do I care? First she opens the door a little, confiding in me that there IS something…that I'm NOT wrong. And then she turns around and slams the door in my face!*

Well, who cares? What—

Again, that crying sound, but this time it was louder. My eyes flew open and I sat up at once.

Where did that cry come from?

I squinted into the darkness, trying to look around the B.R.Y. dining room. After we helped the B.R.Y.ers clean up from supper, all the tables and chairs were pushed against the walls, and mattresses and sleeping bags were spread out on the dining room floor for us.

I know that I had no trouble falling asleep despite my sleeping bag being spread on the hard floor and the loud whispers of those around me. I was thoroughly and indisputably exhausted by the time my head touched my pillow. I had hardly slept the night before.

How could I sleep after having that talk with Mimi?

During the *Melaveh Malkah*, Mimi smiled and acted like our conversation had never taken place, yet her words continued reverberating in my mind that whole evening and throughout the night. Yes, maybe *she* could walk around smiling and get the whole world to smile along with her, but I could not surrender to sleep that night, not after what Mimi had said to me. This was not some mystery one reads about in a novel. This was real! Mimi was real and she was really hiding something…

And now, after having slept deeply for a couple of hours, something woke me. Sleep, I was sure, would not come again to me very easily that night.

My eyes began to adjust to the darkness. I looked around— everyone seemed to be sleeping soundly. I knew, though, that I had not been imagining anything. I had definitely heard someone cry out…and it was not in my dreams!

I looked at Mazal. She was in the same sleeping position I was used to seeing. Rivky also seemed to be in dreamland, her toes sticking out of her blanket. Rochel Leah, eyes closed and face surrounded by her chestnut hair spread out around her on her pillow, looked so young and vulnerable. I felt so sorry for Zehava, lying on the mattress next to her. It must be so difficult to be completely dependent on another person. *Big shot, Sara,* I smiled to myself, *until a short while ago you couldn't imagine being here without Chavie.* My gaze moved along to Chani. She also appeared contentedly asleep, her arm dangling over her sleeping bag. By now, my eyes had grown completely accustomed to the darkness and shifted easily around the room. Malkie. Even when sleeping, she looked worried. *I wonder how I look when I sleep.* Devorah, next to her was also fast asleep. Adina…

What was that?

Adina was rolling back and forth, first to one side, then to the other. *That crying sound!* I watched unbelievingly.

She flipped over once again, her back hard against the mattress. She was gripping her right cheek with both hands. Her eyes were closed, but she was grimacing in pain.

I was at her side in seconds.

"Adina, what's wrong? Are you okay?"

Her eyes opened. They were dry, but obviously pain-filled. "Not exactly," she groaned.

"What is it?" I whispered.

"Sh-sh!" someone near us mumbled.

"I don't know," she squeezed her eyes shut. "I think I'm dying."

"Come, Adina. Can you get up?" I put my arm behind her back. "Let's go to where there's some light."

"I—I…ow-w! Help…this pain is—"

"It's all right," I panted. "You stay here. I'm going to go try to get help."

"Will you be quiet already? I'm trying to get some sleep!" someone grunted. I did not look to see who it was.

"No, don't leave…oh-h-h!" Her face was crimson. "I can't take this—"

Chapter 17

"Adina, it's probably a terrible toothache. I'm going to try to get you something for the pain. I'll be back as quickly as I can—"

"Hurry...just hurry!"

With almost all the floor space occupied by sleeping bodies, it was dicey making my way out of there. When I eventually got to the hallway, I was not sure where to go for help.

The stone floor felt ice cold against my bare feet. I had not put on my slippers before I left...everything had happened so quickly. I wrapped my arms around my chest, trying to warm myself.

The sound of rain cascading down outside, accompanied by thunder and lightning, did not lighten my spirits. The air felt cold and damp and my knees were shaky. I stood at the bottom of the staircase, wavering.

What should I do? I felt so alone. I shook my head wryly, finding it hard to believe that I was in the midst of my second nocturnal adventure within seventy-two hours. This time, though, no one was with me.

A sudden flash of lightning pierced through the window, followed by a tumultuous crack of thunder. I jumped.

Sara, will you stop being so edgy, I tried telling myself. *It's just thunder!*

Slowly, I began to climb the steps.

"Who's there?" a voice shot out from the darkness.

I grabbed hold of the banister, trembling.

"Ah...so you're the one who's sneaking around at night." A large, broad shouldered woman came down the stairs, her flashlight pointed at my face.

I closed my eyes.

"You've been taking things that don't belong to you. I'm glad we caught you before you could do more damage."

I stood on the step, unmoving, my white-knuckled grip on the banister tightening.

"All right, turn around and start walking to Mrs. Braun's office and we will call the police."

"It's a...mis-mistake."

"You bet it's a mistake. I knew I'd catch you. No one gets away with such things when Hilda is in charge."

"I'm not—"

"I know. Now you'll tell me that you're not the one. Let's go. Forward...march!"

"I didn't do anything," I pleaded, my eyes filling.

"Look here, young lady. You can save your tears for someone else. I don't want to have to use my hands. Now, you be a good girl and march to Mrs. Braun's office."

"My friend," I pointed toward the dining room, my voice hardly audible. My tears were on the verge of spilling over.

"Ah...so you're in this together with a friend. I knew it—"

"No," I shook my head emphatically. "I'm not from here. I'm from the other school. I—"

"You're part of the group of girls that—"

"Hilda, what's going on?" Wrapped in a flannel robe, her head covered with a white turban, the woman who I recognized as the B.R.Y. *eim ha-bayit* was slowly making her way down the steps. "I heard such a commotion. Oh," she suddenly saw me, "are you from *Machon Beit Leah*?"

I nodded. Tears were rolling down my cheeks by now.

"I thought she was the one—"

"That's all right, Hilda. You can go back to the entranceway now. Please, Hilda. Don't go up the stairs."

"Yes. Yes. I'm sorry," she said humbly while backing away in the opposite direction. "I thought we finally caught her..."

"Please don't mind her," the *eim ha-bayit* said softly when Hilda left us. "My name is Mrs. Pass. And you're?"

"I'm sorry for causing such a commotion. My name is Sara Hirsch. One of my friends woke up in terrible pain...I came out of the dining room looking for someone who could help...and then—"

"And then you were accosted by Hilda."

I nodded.

"The girls here know her already. She's unfortunately not completely...Well, she thinks...Oh, it doesn't matter. Please tell me, what's wrong with your friend?"

"She's in horrible pain. I think it's a toothache. Yes, it's probably just a toothache. Please…maybe you have something to help her…"

By the time we came into the dining room, most of the girls were up. Adina was sitting on her mattress, with a few of the others surrounding her. Malkie, Devorah, and I went along with Adina and the *eim ha-bayit* to the infirmary, where she was given some extra strength Tylenol, an ice pack, and a bed. With the *eim ha-bayit*'s urging, we returned to the dining room for whatever sleep we could get before it turned completely light outside.

I must have fallen into a deep sleep, because suddenly I heard Mazal's voice coming from some place faraway. "Let her sleep. She was up in the middle of night caring to Adina."

"Yes, but we need to put all the mattresses and sleeping bags away before everyone can eat."

I jumped up. *Oh no, I'd better hurry!* I saw that everyone was already dressed and that my sleeping bag was the only one left on the floor. *I'm so embarrassed!*

By the time we finished davening and eating breakfast with the B.R.Y.ers, Mimi arrived. I looked on in mild bemusement as a large crowd gathered around her, their boisterous voices filled with laughter and easy banter while filling her in on the events of the past day. Mimi, of course, delighted in all the attention. As we loaded our overnight bags onto the bus, Mimi enjoyed a tour of her B.R.Y. friends' rooms and the school building.

Then Rabbanit Greenstein announced that we had twenty minutes until we would be boarding the buses for our trip to Kever Rochel and Me'aras HaMachpelah. I felt a renewed tremor of excitement. *It's finally happening…I'm going to the places where Rochel and Leah are buried.* Every time this past week when I thought of the troubles my sisters were facing and when my own doubts would creep upon me almost threateningly…it was as though I took those uncomfortable feelings and shoved them into a bottle, twisting the cap tightly and locking them inside. *Soon I'll be able to open up the bottle and release all those pent-up emotions.*

Many of the girls instinctively used this time to make their farewells to their old and newly found B.R.Y. friends. Girls could be seen in the hallways, on the staircase, in and out of bedrooms—some hugging tearfully, some laughing, and some vigorously scribbling down names and addresses and autographing yearbooks.

I made my way to the infirmary to see how Adina was doing. There was no way she would be coming with us on the trip that day. Rabbanit Greenstein, with the help of Mrs. Pass, had arranged for Adina to see a dentist and then for a driver to take her back to our dormitory. I felt so sorry for her that she would not be able to join us.

"Um...thank you, Sara," Adina told me in a weak voice when she saw me standing hesitantly in the doorway. Her face looked unexpectedly pale against the stark white pillowcase.

I took a couple of steps forward. "Oh...sure...it was nothing."

"Mrs. Pass told me that it wasn't very pleasant for you."

"It's all right," I felt myself blushing. "I guess things are scarier during the nighttime."

"So...thank you."

"N-no problem. Um...you're welcome." Slowly I turned to leave and then turned back around. "Uh...Adina?"

"Yes?"

"Um...*refuah sheleimah*."

"Thank you, Sara. Sara?"

"Yes, Adina?"

"Uh...have a nice time."

"Thanks, Adina," I faltered, not knowing what to say. *Should I empathize with her or will she get angry with me, thinking I'm pitying her. But I can't just walk off and not say anything.* "D-do you mind not coming? I mean, does it bother you...going to the dentist...alone?"

"Nah, it's no big deal. I've been to the dentist by myself before. It's nothing."

"You sound so brave and independent. I—"

"Listen, Sara, I'm not the dependent type," her voice grew crisp, "I'm used to doing things on my own, not like..." she paused and then said more softly, "I'm all right. Really."

"Oh...okay...Um-so, bye."

"Bye."

Slowly, I made my way down the hallway.

Poor, Adina. Having to go to an Israeli dentist all by herself and missing the trip with everyone else…

I continued walking.

Dentists can be scary…especially in a different country.

I stopped walking.

To be in so much pain and have to face the dentist all by yourself? I let out a deep sigh. *Maybe, I should—*

No, I told myself firmly, *you've been looking forward to this trip—you've been dreaming for so long about our Imahos, Rochel and Leah.*

But, I wavered, *think about poor Adina. You're not leaving Eretz Yisrael yet. You'll have other opportunities to go to these kevarim during the next seven months.*

My eyes narrowed. *Adina is really the independent type. She doesn't want me—especially someone like me. Isn't that what she told me only one week ago? Especially someone like you, Sara. Especially someone like you.*

I took a deep breath.

Sara, don't think about that now. Think about Adina. Right now, she's in pain. She has no one here. Independent or not independent, it's at times like these that you need a real friend. What happened to Malkie and Devorah? Where did her usual group of friends go? Sacrifices, Sara, sacrifices! What if it were you… what if…

I swung around and headed back to the infirmary.

I was sure that despite Adina's nonchalance regarding my insistence that I stay with her, she really was grateful. When a person is in physical pain, her usual ability to hide behind a façade becomes somewhat inhibited. And despite her insistence that she does not need anyone…well, everyone needs someone, at least some of the time.

I suppose, that is why she allowed her figurative "closed door" with the "do not disturb" sign on it to unlock and slowly open. True, it only opened ever so slightly—just a crack, in fact—but open it did.

I could not be sure, though, how long it would stay that way.

18

Bs"d
25 Cheshvan

Dear Home,

Hi! How are all of you doing? I miss you all tons and tons and tons and I'm so happy to finally be writing to you.

Please, please forgive me for not writing in such a long time, but things have been so busy lately.

I'm now sitting at a tiny round table in the corner of the library. Gorgeous floor-to-ceiling, wall-to-wall bookcases line one wall, and the other wall (opposite the entrance to the room) has some huge windows with a stunning view of the desert.

One of the huge windows is also a door which leads out onto the new patio. They used special stones (I think they come from the desert itself) to build the patio—which makes it blend in amazingly with the scenery. There are a few tables there that we can sit at to do our work—weather permitting. If Mazal happens to be studying with someone in our room or if Adina (Mimi's roommate) is studying in their room, then we inevitably end up doing our studying either here (in the library) or in the garden. Lately, though, the weather has been turning colder and colder, and so right now neither the garden nor the patio are options.

Can you believe it, I've been away from home for more than two months...and I'm actually surviving? Anyway, the truth is, I think I'm more than surviving. *B"H* things are really working out great. I'm so glad (I mean it, I'm not just writing it) that I came. I really love it here!

We had the most phenomenal Shabbos this past week in B'nei Brak. All the girls from M.B.L.L. were placed in groups of two or three with different B'nei Brak families for sleeping and the Friday night meals. I stayed in a really gorgeous house. They had four floors with marble stairs and a long winding mahogany banister. I had no idea that houses in Eretz Yisrael could be so stunning. Well, this house was not only stunning in its appearance, the atmosphere in the house was also beautiful. What I mean is, the whole house just radiated with *kedushah*. Right before Shabbos there were people coming and going in and out of the house collecting *tzedakah*. They also have rooms reserved for guests and they were all full! There were also loads and loads of *sefarim*, and you could tell that the father and sons are all big *talmidei chachamim*. Seeing such material and spiritual richness working that beautifully together was so inspiring!

I was placed there with Adina Stern. She's the one who's originally from England, but now lives in Ballington. (Mazal and Mimi were placed together. The school must have decided to mix up the roommates from adjoining rooms.) I'm glad I got to spend Shabbos with Adina. We've been sitting next to each other in class this whole time (since the beginning of Sem), but we haven't actually had much to do with each other. That is—until two weeks ago.

Remember in my last letter to you, when I filled you in on my Shabbos with Mazal's family, that I wrote about how excited I was about our upcoming trip to Yerushalayim, Beis Lechem, and Chevron? Anyway, that night (Sunday) when we were sleeping, poor Adina woke up with the worst toothache imaginable. The next day, when we were supposed to continue onto Kever Rochel and Me'aras HaMachpelah, it was impossible for her to go since she needed emergency dental care. I felt so sorry for her, having to stay back and go to the dentist by herself, so I offered to go with her. It was really no big deal, I can go again a different time. Ever since then, we've been getting a bit friendlier.

Friday night, we ate and slept with a family in B'nei Brak, and on Shabbos we ate together with everyone else in the auditorium of the local Beis Yaakov. Shabbos afternoon, we visited Rabbanit Lerman. She lives in a really small and old apartment. She took in thirteen children throughout her lifetime, one child sicker than the next. Many of the children died. Can you believe such a person? She is such a *tzaddekes*!

For *Minchah* we went to the same shul that Rabbanit Karitsky davens at and afterwards she gave us a berachah. Her voice was low, so I didn't really hear what she was saying, but, of course, I made sure to say amen. I would have liked to ask her for a *berachah* for Shuli, but I couldn't exactly do that in front of everyone. Anyway, I was thinking it and I'm sure that helps. Afterwards, I went over to say "Good Shabbos" and I shook her hand, but it was very quick and everyone was standing around me.

I just stopped writing for a few seconds and looked at my watch. I can't believe it! Twenty minutes passed already since I began writing to you. No wonder my hand is hurting! I can't imagine what's taking Mimi so long. We're supposed to study together and made up to meet here a while ago. Well anyway, I'm glad I took advantage of this time by writing to my fantastic family. I feel so connected to all of you when I write or read your letters, so I guess I am kind of grateful that Mimi didn't show up yet.

Now...to continue:

Last Monday we went on a tiyul to places in and near Be'er Sheva. It was just a one-day *tiyul*, since it is so close to us, but we had tons of fun. First, we went to Avraham's wells. They are not sure they are the real ones, but we went anyway. Then we went to the bottom of a crater. Mountains are connected all around in a circle and on the bottom it's hollow with shorter mountains. You'll understand from the pictures I took. We went to the big rocks. It's really fascinating. If you scrape them with coins, you get colored sand, so we got glass jars and filled them with all different colors of sand. I made a few extras to give away as gifts. Then we did a lot of hiking. We climbed up really steep mountains and then down again. It was scary. If you made one wrong move, you could roll off the mountain, *chas v'shalom*, but it was also tons of fun. One of the girls (I'm not going to say who) kept making believe she was about to step off—and got us all shrieking. I'm disappointed, because right then my camera stopped working (later on I found out it was the battery), so I don't have pictures of that part. I'll get negatives from someone and make them into pictures.

On the way back, we stopped for pizza in Be'er Sheva. It was really nice. The funniest thing happened. I was eating with my friends, when I noticed this familiar-looking woman dressed in white—like a nurse. I couldn't figure out from where I knew her. She was looking at us girls, then when our eyes met, it suddenly hit us both at the same time. This was the woman who sat next to me on the plane. We schmoozed for a bit. Can you believe it? We had really been pretty friendly on the plane, but I never thought I'd see her again. Well, everything is *min HaShamayim*. Anyway, she wrote down her telephone number and address on a napkin and insisted that she wants me to come to visit her with my friends. Actually, she invited us for a Shabbos, but I'm really not sure if we could go. I get the feeling that she's traditional, but I'm not really sure if she's religious. Anyway, I thought it was cute to see her.

I just stopped writing again and went to look and see if Mimi is coming, but no one seems to know where she is. I know that we spoke to each other when classes finished and we made up to meet here. So, now let me tell you a little about what's going on in Sem.

The schoolwork is definitely getting a little less difficult, I guess that's because we're getting used to the teachers and subjects. We have a huge report due next month that is very important. That's what Mimi and I are supposed to be working on right now. I'm kind of nervous about it. Shuli, you didn't have this last year because it's from Geveret Spitz. It's a sort of journal and observation report combined, where we have to analyze, cite from different sources, and bring examples from *Tanach* and include the *mekoros*. It's not at all easy and it's going to impact our *Proyect* marks.

I've been working hard on my *Proyect*. (Shuli, you know what I'm talking about.) I've already written more than forty pages. I'm still not sure what I'm going to choose as my main topic. Rabbi Grossman said that right now we should just put together our different ideas, observations, etc. etc. etc. and not worry about the topic. He said that as the year progresses and we have different experiences, the topic each of us wants to use will hit us and that we'll then hopefully be able to find the appropriate pasuk that goes along with it too. Shuli, I know that your topic was joy. What made you decide to write on that particular topic? It was such a great idea. I wish I could think of something so good. I don't know what I'm going to do yet. Well, Shuli, you did such a great job and became the honorable mention winner. It's not that I expect to win (there are so many brilliant geniuses here this year) and winning is not such a big deal, but I know how important these term papers are and I'd just love to think up some really original idea.

Anyway, this Shabbos I'll probably stay in the dorm for a nice, quiet, restful Shabbos since the last few have been so full of action. It's an optional Shabbos, so most of the Israelis will go home, and a lot of the M.B.L.L.ers will also go away. Next Shabbos, *iy"*H, I'll probably be going back to Kiryat Yosef with Mazal. I'm excited to go. Her family is a lot of fun and very special. It's funny, but in a certain way they remind me a lot of our family.

I've been working with this little six-year-old girl in the resource room. She hardly says a word and it's so hard to teach her anything. You know me, I always thought of teaching—especially tutoring—as something that just comes naturally. It's not as easy as I thought, though, especially when the child is coming with something (some sort of problem or "baggage" as they say) that I have no idea how to handle. But it's fascinating watching Geveret Spitz. She treats each child with the utmost respect. I watch her building their self-esteem. As she explained to us, without self-esteem, the child cannot accomplish anything. In fact, she told us, without it no one can accomplish anything. She's such an amazing person, Geveret Spitz. I wish you could've had her too, Shuli. Well, maybe when Chevy comes, she'll get to have her. (If she stays on, that is. I don't think she plans on staying, though. Her specialty is that she travels around setting up these programs, but who knows? Maybe if she loves it here enough and with her kids getting older, she'll want to put down roots.)

Tomorrow, *iy"*H, Mimi and I are suppose to meet with Geveret Spitz to discuss our progress. I'm both nervous and excited. To have Geveret Spitz to ourselves is fantastic. But I'm also very nervous. I don't feel like I'm accomplishing anything with Ronit (she's the child I'm working with), so how will I be able to discuss my progress? I guess I should really call it "lack of progress."

Anyway, what's doing by you? Shuli—are things getting better with the teaching? Did you start yet with shidduchim since we last wrote to each other? Please let me in on every single detail, and if anything happens, you'd better call me. I don't want any shockers. (That's Mimi's word.) I'll write Sruly separately. Will he be coming home for Shabbos Chanukah? How's school, Moshe? I haven't heard from you lately. No more amazing mazes? Chev, please write back to me already. I'm positive that you've received my long letter by now and I'm anxiously awaiting your response.

Anyway, I'm going to finish this letter. Mimi just showed up. Now she ran upstairs to her room for a minute to get something to nosh on while we work, so I'm going to sign off. We've got to begin working as soon as she comes back down. (We have tons to do!!!)

Again, Abba and Mommy...THANKS FOR EVERYTHING!!! YOU'RE THE BEST!!!

Love & Kisses,
Sara

Bs"d
25 Cheshvan
Dear Chavie,

Hi! How are you doing? I just got your letter yesterday. I can't believe that I'm actually writing back already. I thought that for sure I wouldn't get a chance to write for a while. Things have been so busy lately and I know that I'm going to be extremely busy with tons of schoolwork in the next few weeks. Finals, reports, student teaching etc. etc. etc. Nevertheless, b"h I'm grabbing this chance to write to you while I sit here in the library waiting for my friend to come study.

Thanks so much for writing back to me so quickly. I'm not even sure if your letter to me was a response to my last letter or if

> our letters crossed and your letter was just a new letter. Anyway, it doesn't matter. I'm glad to hear from you either way.
>
> I also miss you and wish you could be here. Your gown sounds stunning! Please, please take loads of pictures. How are you going to wear your hair? I can't wait to—

"Sara, sorry for keeping you waiting all this time—"

"That's okay, Mimi—"

"You are the most patient person I know…"

"Na, it's really all right. I'm catching up on some letter writing."

"Ah-h-h, so I see," Mimi leaned over the table, attempting to read what I'd written. "So, who's that to?"

"My friend, Chavie," I quickly folded the paper and stuck it into the side pocket of my loose-leaf. "Now, Mimi, it's really getting late. Let's get down to work."

"Sure, Sara, you know me. I *love* work," she dug into her bag of caramels. "Are you *fleishig*? Have one—"

"No, thanks, Mimi. I ate lunch. And you should too. It's a lot more healthful than living on caramels every day."

"There goes Practical Sara—"

"Mimi, it's not called *practical* to eat a normal meal. Anyway…enough time's been wasted already today. Let's take out our observation books and get started."

"My observation book?"

"Yes, your observation book. You know the one that we're supposed to be writing in every day in order to prepare our reports," I said while pointing to mine. "Let's go, Mimi, we've got to get started already. It's getting late."

"I'd love to, but…guess what?"

"What?"

"I think I left it in my desk at school."

"What! You left it in school?"

"Sh-sh," Mimi put her finger to her lips while motioning to the others sitting near us, "we're going to disturb everybody. Anyway, what do you think about the *Maccabim*'s costume? Will—"

"Mimi…"

"Will the silver fabric be the right kind or is the—"

"Mimi!"

"Sara, dear...I do hear..." she sang to me in an undertone, "you don't need to shout—"

"Will you stop it already?" I hissed, my eyes flashing impatiently.

"Calm down. You've got to lighten up—"

"I'll lighten up, Mimi, believe me I will—when we finish this work." I let out a long sigh, attempting to control my anger. "Now will you kindly explain to me how in the world you left your observation book in school? You know how important it is—"

"Ah...yes, our wonderful Sara Hirsch," Mimi kept her voice down in order not disturb the other girls working in the library, however the deep and masculine inflection was still quite audible. She stroked her chin in the same manner that Rabbi Grossman stroked his beard while she stood up and began pacing around our small round table, "Our wonderful Sara Hirsch would like to know," she cleared her throat before switching to a higher-pitched feminine tone, "How in the world—"

"That's enough, Mimi!" I said through gnashed teeth.

She smiled sweetly while returning to her seat, "You don't like my imitation of you, Sara?"

"I love your imitation, Mimi, I just love it," I sat rigid on my chair glaring at her while stiffly clapping my hands. "Can't you see how much I love it?"

"Mimi and Sara, please! We're trying to study!"

"Sorry," I mumbled to the girls at the next table, feeling the blood rush to my face as I glared at Mimi. "Can't you see we're disturbing everybody?"

"Yeah...sorry, Goldie. Sorry, Yaffa," Mimi smiled at them, then turned to me. "Why do you have to be so serious all the time?"

"So...serious?"

"Yup," Mimi began imitating Rabbi Ossenfeld, "ve are veery seeerious heeear."

That's it! I had enough. I slammed my loose-leaf shut, and then regretted it a second later when I felt the other girls' eyes upon us. My face by now must have been turning an even darker shade of crimson. Leaning forward, I took a deep breath in an effort to calm down, but was unsuccessful in hiding the mounting frustration from my voice. "Mimi Rosenberg, is that how you want to be known as?"

"Vat do you meeeeean, Sara Heeeeersh?"

"Vat I mean," I stamped my foot, "what I mean, Mimi, is...is that how you want to be known...as Mimi the mimic?"

"Mimi the mimic?"

"Yes. Is that what you want? For no one to take you seriously," I stood up angrily. "Want a laugh? Oh, just go to Mimi Rosenberg!"

"Sara—"

I swung around and, blinded by my frustration and oblivious to all those around me, headed straight toward the new patio. "Is that what you want from life? No responsibility?" I whispered furiously over my shoulder as my hand gripped the doorknob. "Oh, you need something? So sorry, Mimi the Mimic is too busy mimicking everyone—"

"Sara, I'd like to—"

I pushed open the door and stepped outside onto the patio, heedless of the rush of cold air slapping against my face. Mimi followed me outside. "That's right," I repeated while staring mechanically at the mountainous skyline. "Mimi the Mimic is busy mimicking, so why should she bother bringing her observation book to work on something, even if it's due—"

"SARA, I'D LIKE TO SAY SOMETHING!"

I turned around to face her. She was trying to keep the escaped tendrils of red wavy hair behind her ear, but the rough winds thwarted her attempts. Shivering, I wrapped my arms around my chest, suddenly aware of the outside cold weather...and suddenly aware of my unrestrained anger.

"Um...sorry, Mimi. I'm just very upset."

"I can see that...I'm not *that* dumb."

"I never said you're dumb—"

"You said I'm irresponsible.

"Irresponsible is not dumb."

"Irresponsible...dumb...who cares? It's all the same beautiful compliment to me."

"Well, I never said dumb," I could not hide the irritation from my voice. "And please don't put words in my mouth."

Chapter 18

"What in the world do you mean?" she flashed a wide smile at me.

"And stop imitating me—"

"Otherwise you're going to call me, Mimi the Mimic. Right?"

"Okay, I get the point. I'm sorry. I didn't mean to insult you. But really…it's not right to always go around imitating everyone."

"I'm not harming anyone…"

"Still…it's not right."

"Okay, Sara. I'll try to stop…Now, could we pleeeeeease go back inside. I'm freeeeeeezing and I'd love to study."

The sides of my mouth twitched upward. "All right, Mimi. But really…"

We went back into the library. I tried ignoring the curious glances from some of the girls we passed as we headed toward our seats.

Mimi immediately sat down on the edge of her seat, her hands placed primly on the table in front of her. "Okay, Morah Sara. Please tell me what I should do."

I shook my head. *How did Mimi do this to me? One second she had me as angry as ever, and the next she had me cast under her spell.* "Well, first it would be a good idea if you'd show up with your observation book."

"And first, like I told you before, I forgot to bring it. But even if I did bring it," she added matter-of-factly, "it wouldn't make a difference."

"Why wouldn't it make a difference?" I repeated, surprised.

"Because, dear 'made for order' student. I haven't written a single word in my notebook."

"What!"

"Sara and Mimi…please!" Goldie once again tried to quiet us down, "We're trying to concentrate."

Yaffa pointed toward the door. "Why don't you go someplace else if you want to talk to each other?"

"Yaffa's right. The library is for studying, you know," Goldie murmured. "You can schmooze in the lounge."

"Y-you're right. I—I'm sorry," embarrassed, I apologized again—I think it was the third time in the past ten minutes. Then, turning back to Mimi, I asked in a whisper, "What do you mean, you haven't written a thing?"

"Sara…you don't understand…it's just not my cup of tea—all this writing."

"But, Mimi," my voice was low, yet incredulous, "how in the worl—" I quickly stopped myself, "I mean, how do you expect to write the report and pass the course if you don't take notes for the observation report?"

"Sara, dear," her unruffled demeanor was in complete contrast to my flustered one. "Who says I care about the observation report?"

"What?"

"Who says I care about the observation report?" she calmly repeated.

"Well, if you don't do the observation report…then how will you do the *Proyect*? How will you pass the—"

"You don't get it, Sara."

"Get it?" My eyebrows lifted. "Get what?"

"That I don't care," she said simply. "That I don't plan on—"

"You don't plan on what, Mimi?" I leaned forward.

"I don't plan on staying here—"

"WHAT?"

"SH-SH…" This time I barely heard Yaffa's request for quiet. "Come on, Mimi and Sara."

"Forget it," Goldie stood up before I realized what was happening and could apologize. "Don't bother. Let's switch to a table on the other side of the room."

"Mimi," I shook my head slowly, "I don't understand—"

"What's there to understand, Sara? I don't plan to stay in M.B.L.L."

"But, Mimi—"

"Hey, Sara, why are you reacting this way? You, of all people, should be the least surprised."

"Huh?"

"Well, you've been telling me over and over again how I have to buckle down. Right? I know you've been wondering what I'm doing here in the first place, and don't try to deny it. So guess what? That's it. As soon as the Chanukah production is over…I'm out of here."

"Huh?"

"Can you say something else, Sara, besides 'huh'? Like maybe, 'Oh, so sorry to hear that, Mimi. We're all going to miss you.' Or, 'I wonder who's going to take your place, Mimi?' Or, how about, 'Mimi, do you have any plans for what you'll do after you leave?'"

I stared at her dumbly, a million questions bouncing around in my head, a zillion thoughts zooming through my mind. Yet, as I turned to her, willing myself to say something, only one sound emerged from my lips.

"Huh?"

19

Hi again, Chavie. I'm back now.

I didn't get a chance to continue my letter to you Monday night like I thought I would. Something came up and I just couldn't get to writing. Then, Tuesday I met with Geveret Spitz (I'll tell you about that later), and that night and all day today in between classes I've been busy writing up stuff in my observation notebook and filling my folders for the report that's due in a few weeks and of course for the *Proyect*. Tonight, though, I'm giving myself a break from all the schoolwork, and instead, I'm sitting here all "cozied up" in the dorm's lounge, writing to you while I wait for the washing machine to finish.

Anyway, I just reread what I wrote so far and I can't help but repeat here: I can't wait to see the pictures from the wedding! I'm sure you're going to look fantabulous (as Shuli would say).

But, before I continue with anything else, guess what? GREAT NEWS: I heard that one of the girls might be leaving around Chanukah time. Yes, Chavie, you're reading correctly and no, your eyes aren't playing tricks on you. Isn't that the best news ever? It's going to be perfect timing for you. I really hope that you'll be the one who ends up taking her place. Isn't that what Rabbi Grossman said, that if someone ends up leaving, then you're first on the list? I know for a fact that this girl is staying just until the end of Chanukah and that's when you'll be able to come. I can't believe it, Chavie. No one else knows about it yet, but it definitely works out perfectly for us…

Perfectly. So why am I not having that perfectly happy feeling? I looked up from the letter I was writing to Chavie and stared ahead at nothing in particular.

Why do I feel like...well, I should be happy...thrilled...in fact!

I am happy...I am thrilled, I insisted. *Why shouldn't I be?* I had done everything I could to help Mimi. She was a big girl. I was not responsible for her lackadaisical attitude. It was not my fault she continuously wasted time and showed no interest in her schoolwork.

No, I'm not at all guilty. I'm allowed to be happy. That's right, and I am happy. Hopefully, it will all work out as I had dreamed and Chavie will come once Rabbi Grossman notifies her. *My best friend.*

Chavie would take over Mimi's bed. Adina, who was just beginning to exhibit a little more warmth to me, would surely be won over by Chavie's friendliness and sensible nature. Inevitably, I would also become good friends with Chavie's roommate. Yes...Chavie, Adina, and I. And Mazal, of course.

I could just picture it. Chavie and I would go together with Mazal to Kiryat Yosef. Chavie would love it there, just like me. And Mazal would love Chavie. And...so would everyone else in the dorm. I would never again be lonely. Everyone would see that I have a great friend... that I'm someone. Yes, having my best friend with me would be perfect.

I bit down hard on the top of my pen, staring straight ahead. *So why are these feelings of guilt tugging at me?*

Instinctively, my eyes wandered around the room. Some Israeli girls were sitting on overstuffed chairs surrounding the coffee table a few yards away from me, giggling and bantering lightly. *Why do things always seem so complicated to me? Why can't I just "lighten up" and stop being so serious...*

I saw Rochel Leah and Zehava standing by the bulletin board, reading its notices. *There they are together again.* Reflexively, I shook my head. *Why does Zehava always allow herself to be used at Rochel Leah's convenience? At least when Chavie comes, I won't be alone anymore and people like Rochel Leah won't look at me as some lonely case.*

My eyes shifted to another corner of the room where three earnest M.B.L.L.ers appeared to be in the midst of some penetrating debate.

I wonder what they are discussing. They seem to be in another world. Maybe I should get up and join them and find out what's going on. I paused for a moment. *No way!* A smile tugged at the sides of my mouth. *Sara,* my grin deepened at the thought, *a few weeks ago, you wouldn't have even contemplated such an idea! Maybe you're actually starting to come out of that shell of yours.*

Slipping my pencil under the hinged clasp of my clipboard, I leaned back against a plump cushion and looked around the lounge. Whoever designed and decorated this room had achieved a warm, homey feeling. It looked like an oversized living room, with a few separate seating areas, some to encourage friendly conversation and some to enable private relaxation. Until recently, I had spent most of my studying or leisure time out in the beautiful garden. Now, though, with the weather becoming so much cooler, I found myself spending more time in the library (to study) and lounge (to write).

I glanced at the small mahogany bookcase against one of the walls, filled with Judaic reading material in various languages. Across the room on another wall painted in a contrasting color, an assortment of watercolors, oil paintings, and charcoal drawings hung gallery style. The Beit Yaakov HaNegbah girls had skillfully produced these pictures over the last few years.

Yes, this room really has a deliciously inviting, homey feeling, and soon Chavie will be here to share all of this with me.

When Chavie comes—you'll be the one to introduce her around since you've already paved the path for her. Not that she'll need it. Chavie never had a hard time making new friends. But I guess it helps. And now that I'm thinking about it…maybe that's why it worked out this way in the first place. Had Chavie been here with me in the beginning, I possibly, in fact, probably, would've been too dependent on Chavie. See how Hashem makes everything work out? You had the chance to grow and make friends in a way that you never would've had Chavie been here with you…and now that you've settled in and adjusted on your own, Hashem is arranging for you to have your best friend join you.

This all really will have a fairy tale ending.

Clad in a comfortable, oversized bright white cotton sweatshirt and long black skirt, I was sitting cross-legged on one of the more secluded club chairs. Still lying against my knee was the clipboard holding my letter to Chavie, but my eyes and mind were suddenly focused elsewhere—on the room's doorway.

Mimi and Rivky were entering the lounge and heading straight for the piano. They waved and chatted briefly with some of the girls they passed. *I wonder if Rivky knows…*

Mimi took her seat at the bench and began to play an upbeat, merry tune. Rivky slipped in next to her. As the musical notes echoed in the air, I noticed the girls who had been intently discussing something gradually stop talking and slowly make their way to where Mimi and Rivky sat. Then Rochel Leah, turning to the source of the cheerful music, left her place by the bulletin board and slid onto the piano bench on the other side of Mimi, with Zehava following her and standing nearby. Steadily, the Israeli group broke up and one by one they sauntered over to the piano. Within a short time, almost all the girls in the room had shifted to there, exuberantly gathering around Mimi.

By now, she was playing a jazzy, choppy tune and singing in rhymes she must have thought of while taking a shower. (The whole dorm knew that was where she created her more comical jingles.) Everyone was laughing. I could see her red ponytail bobbing up and down, as she bounced from side to side. Although her back was to me, I was certain her green eyes were sparkling and her dimples deepening.

This was Mimi in her element…but for me, she was a puzzlement.

Most of the time, she's the most easygoing person I've ever met. She doesn't seem to have a care in the world and yet she admitted to me that she's hiding something. I wonder if this secret has anything to do with the reason she's planning on leaving M.B.L.L. And…what could this secret be, anyway?

Who cares? I should be perfectly happy about the way things are turning out. But, I know that she's hiding something, something that's causing her to walk around smiling so the world will smile with her. But at the same time, she's concealing something…something, I think, that is causing her much pain. Is that what's bothering me about her leaving and Chavie coming to take her place—that all this cheeriness is just a show that's camouflaging something very painful? Is that why I'm not able to be perfectly happy about Mimi's news?

She was singing the lyrics by herself, cajoling the others to join in the chorus. There were smiles on everyone's faces and a cheerful mood filled the air. Some of the girls tried singing or humming along and some of them were completely off tune. It did not matter. Everyone was having fun. Singing…giggling…joking. Mimi…wherever she went, laughter followed her. Mimi…so popular and well-liked.

So popular and well-liked…

So why do I feel like Mimi Rosenberg, the "life of the dorm," is in desperate need of a real friend? Why do I feel that Mimi Rosenberg, who you'll never find alone, really feels terribly alone?

Stop it, Sara, stop it! I tried telling myself. *You wanted to help her, you cared…you really cared! And you even got her to open up a little. So what happened then? Slam!*

"Don't bother asking me questions," she tells you, "just leave me alone."

Fine…I'll leave her alone. That's right, I'll simply leave her alone.

I stood up abruptly, still grasping my clipboard with my pencil and Chavie's letter. *Let Rivky help her, or maybe Rochel Leah and Zehava, or any of the other tens of girls who are always surrounding her. Let them be her real friends!*

Yes, my real friend is practically on her way here, I squeezed the clipboard holding the letter to Chavie tightly. *And now, I'm going to make my way out of here.*

I left the room huffily and headed for the staircase leading to the basement.

Why should I care? She doesn't want my help anyway! Why should—

"Yikes…Sara!"

"Oh sorry, Devorah! Um, I was—"

"We nearly crashed," Devorah exclaimed breathlessly. "I was just coming to get you. Your machine just finished."

"Thanks, I'm on my way down. Did you notice if any dryers are available?"

"Yes, Malkie is taking her clothes out of one. I'm not sure, though…I think she might have another load. Maybe the other one's available. I'm running upstairs to get my stuff; I'll be back down in a minute. Could you try to save your washing machine for me?"

"Um…if no one is there…I mean…I'll try."

Passing the *miklat*, the maintenance closet, and the storage room, I followed the lemony fragrance of laundry detergent into the laundry room.

"Oh hi, Sara. I'm so relieved to see someone! I don't know what to do! I—"

Alarmed, I asked, "Malkie, what's wrong?"

"I have this huge problem. Maybe you can help me. I put this white shirt by mistake in with my colored load. See? Now it's turned gray. Is it better to put it now in my bleached load—or do you think the gray color will run onto my whites? Or maybe I should wash it again with my colored load - or will it turn even grayer? But maybe that's not such a bad idea. It's kind of a nice gray. What do you think?" she held the white/gray shirt in front of her face. "Do you think this color is becoming on me or should—"

"It's nice, Malkie…I think," I began emptying out my clean, wet laundry from the washing machine and piling it into my laundry basket.

"On the other hand, I do have a gray shirt already," she continued. "But it's a different style and I always wanted to have a gray shirt in this style."

"So maybe you should keep it gray," I shook out one of my pleated skirts that I was planning to hang-dry.

"But, then I'll have one white shirt less, so…what do you think I should do?"

"I think…well…what do you want to do, Malkie?"

"I think I'd like to keep it gray."

"So then you should do that, Malkie. Keep it gray."

"Oh, Sara," she embraced me, "thanks a million. You're the greatest!"

I laughed. "Do you know who's using this dryer?"

"Yes, I think Adina's stuff is in there."

"She's usually on time. Do you think she'll mind if I empty it out?"

"Probably not. That is—if you take the stuff out and fold it neatly so that it doesn't crease."

"Well, if I leave it in here, then for sure it will crease. I'll go see if she's coming...I don't want to hold up the line."

I should just leave with my wet laundry and hang it all up to dry, and not even bother with the dryer. I was going to hang a few of the pieces anyway. But then again—even if I don't use the dryer, if I leave Adina's laundry in there, it's bound to get all creased.

I went up the steps and peeked into the library. I did not see Adina. I checked in the dining room and did not see her there either. Passing the lounge, I could still hear Mimi's cheerful music. I knew Adina was not in there. I asked a few girls lingering in the hallway if they had seen her and they mentioned that she had gone upstairs over an hour ago. I ran up the steps to the third floor and knocked on Adina's door.

No answer.

I knocked again.

Still no answer.

Slowly, I pushed open the door and took a few steps into the room. Adina lay sprawled out on her bed. She appeared to be fast asleep, but I could not be sure. Her eyes were tightly closed and she was clasping a small tape recorder in her right hand. I noticed that she had headphones on. I tiptoed out of the room and closed the door softly behind me.

Back in the laundry room, Devorah was loading her dirty clothes into the washing machine I had just emptied. "Thanks a billion, Sara, for saving the machine for me."

"I didn't exactly save it—"

"Well...thanks anyway."

"No problem." I began emptying Adina's clothing from the dryer and folding each item as carefully as I could. *I wish I could do it as perfectly as—*

"Wow, Sara, you fold so neatly."

"Not really, Devorah. It's not my stuff...it's Adina's and she does it much nicer than I ever could."

"Everything Adina does is perfect."

I piled Adina's folded laundry into my basket, draping my two wet skirts over the sides. I slipped a coin into the dryer that had my wet load and started the machine, glancing at my watch in order to estimate when the machine would finish.

"I guess it'll be finished during supper," I told Devorah. "I'd better hurry. I'm going to bring this stuff upstairs, then I'll come back down to eat, and get the rest of my laundry afterwards. See you later."

"Bye. When you see Adina, please remind her that she promised to help me study for the *Chumash* final tonight."

"Sure, no problem, Devorah. Have fun with your laundry."

"Thanks, you too."

Climbing the basement steps, Mimi's cheerful melody floated toward me, and although the music faded away as I made my way to the third floor, I found myself humming the catchy tune that was still reverberating in my mind.

First, I went to my room to hang up my two wet skirts over the makeshift line Mazal had hung across our window back in September. *Mazal probably went downstairs already*, I decided, while smoothing the skirts' folds so the pleats would look crisp when they dried. *We must've missed each other while I was down in the laundry room.*

Still humming Mimi's latest composition, I carried the basket with Adina's clothing through the wash-up closet and knocked on the door leading to her room.

"Come in."

I opened the door. Adina was sitting on her bed, stretching.

"Hi, Adina. I brought you your laundry. I hope—"

She stood up at once. "You, what?"

"I brought you your laundry. You were sleeping when the dryer fin—"

"Excuse me, Sara Hirsch," her hands were on her hips, "but who gave you permission to touch my stuff? Don't you have any respect for privacy? First—"

"But, Adina—"

"Don't 'but Adina' me. First you intrude on my privacy by taking my *siddur* and reading something that was not meant for—"

"Adina, please—"

"That was not meant for you. Then, you go through my laundry without my permiss—"

"Adina, let me explain. I—"

"I'm not interested in your explanations," her blue eyes flashed angrily. "Just leave the basket here."

Obediently, I placed my laundry basket on a nearby chair and silently watched her empty the laundry onto her bed. *Why did I have to ruin everything? We were just beginning to…*

"Here's your basket. And here," disdainfully, she held my clipboard with the tips of her fingers far away from her body, as though it it was some kind of disgusting insect, "here's another one of your letters." She had accidentally emptied it onto her bed along with her laundry and handed it over to me with a look of utter contempt on her face.

"Please, Adina. I'm really so s-sorry," I was pleading. "I was just—"

"I'm not interested in what you were *just*—"

"Trying to do you a favor."

"I don't need your favors."

"Adina…friends are…"

"I don't need your friendship. I don't want your friendship."

"But in the dorm," desperately, I tried another tactic, "it's like family…"

"Family? Ha! Don't you dare talk to me about family."

"I'm only—"

"Keep your lovely family to yourself and just leave me alone…"

> Hi, Chavie, I'm back again. I still haven't finished my letter to you. It's hard to believe that I began this letter on Monday, continued it on Wednesday, and now it's *Motza'ei Shabbos* already. Wow, it's really taking so long to finish!
>
> Dorm life is so unpredictable. You could think: Okay, now I'm going to write a letter and then someone comes bounding into your room and suddenly the time you planned on using to write is gone. Or you could be busy studying—planning on accomplishing a ton—or you're peacefully doing laundry, and suddenly someone starts a conversation with you unexpectedly and then you can't concentrate on your schoolwork or the laundry is no longer so important.
>
> Oh, Chavie, I wish you were here. Of course, I can't give you any details, but something so unpredictable happened on Wednesday. People can be so complicated. First you think

someone will appreciate it if you do something for her and then you find out that she's angry at you for doing it. It's so confusing. People are confusing.

Mazal tells me that I'm just not used to dorm life and that everyone comes with their own baggage and that's why people react unexpectedly much of the time. Oh, I don't know. It's really so confusing. Sometimes, it seems like someone really wants to open up and then suddenly they slam the door in your face. Chavie, you probably think I'm nuts talking like this about doors and everything, but lately that's how I see people.

I just reread what I wrote and I see I wrote the word 'confusing' three times already. That's probably how this letter sounds to you…confusing. I was thinking of crossing all this out, but then decided that since you don't know what I'm talking about and we're such good friends, you'll be able to just ignore my temporary state of mind.

Anyway, now I'll try to get to more cheerful topics.

Wow, I can't believe I forgot! I'm so sorry, I feel like I'm becoming completely self-centered. Forgive me, forgive me, forgive me. Chavie!!! *Mazal tov* on passing your driving test!!!!! Wow!!!! You must be so excited! *Mazal tov* again and may you always drive safely and to good places, as they say.

Okay, back to M.B.L.L.

This past Tuesday I had a meeting with Geveret Spitz in the resource room. Before our meeting began, I got to watch her in action. Chavie, believe me you never saw anything like it. She has this amazing way of working with the children. Somehow, she figures out how to reach the child and she uses that 'key' to open them up and get them to learn.

For example, there's a girl I'll call Orit. She's extremely slow and has a very difficult time learning. But Geveret Spitz figured out that she loves singing, and after testing her found that she learns better through auditory modes (that is through hearing) as opposed to sight. So in order to teach her the *alef-beis*, Geveret Spitz does it with song and sound, only occasionally flashing the letter cards.

Then, there's someone I'll call Avigail. She's this sweet, darling, friendly girl, but also getting absolutely nowhere in class.

But guess what? She loves drawing. So, Geveret Spitz had the girl who's working with her do the lessons with pictures and artwork.

It's hard to explain everything in a letter, but it's utterly amazing. The thing that's so special about all this is that Geveret Spitz won't ever give up on anybody. She says that everyone has a key and that in some people it's just harder to find. (Maybe that's where I got this 'door' idea from.) I wonder what my key is. (Ha, ha. Just joking!)

Anyway, this child that I'm working with is almost completely silent. It's very hard to work with someone who hardly says a word. Geveret Spitz says we just have to find the key. Mimi, my partner in the resource room, seems to be doing a better job than I am in trying to figure out how to get to this child. Her own student is a mischievous little girl—who Mimi seems to understand completely—because when Mimi works with her, the child behaves beautifully. I think Mimi is arranging some sort of system with her to get her to behave in class, as well. It's really unbelievable. Mimi never really was interested in teaching, yet she's doing a phenomenal job with this child and she's also helping 'my' child. Mimi claims that 'my' child is just lacking confidence and that if she was encouraged more, and if her self-esteem would improve, she would be able to accomplish more. She is one of the children who is not from Kfar Amsdorf, but is bussed in from the nearby town of Devorah. She comes from an extremely poor home with a very sad background. Her father was killed in Lebanon and her mother had a nervous breakdown. She lives with elderly grandparents and it's really so, so sad. I wish I could help her.

I've been working so hard on my reports and *Proyect*. In fact, I already have fifty, yes fifty pages toward it. My folder is definitely bulging and I must get over to Kfar Amsdorf to buy some more folders (since my notebook is just not ample!) as soon as possible.

I hope I'm not making you nervous by telling you all of this. I'll definitely try to help you catch up on everything when you come, and besides, I'm sure you won't be held responsible for stuff you couldn't do when you weren't here.

This past Shabbos (today) was very relaxing for me because

I stayed in the dorm and it was pretty empty. I was too tired to let the quiet atmosphere depress me, and instead,—believe it or not—I really managed to enjoy it. As much as I enjoy going away to different places and experiencing Shabbos at so many different families, it was nice for a change not to have to pack and travel. Besides, I haven't had Shabbos toranut for a while and I'm definitely due to have it soon. So, I let myself enjoy a restful Shabbos in the dorm, being served by others.

As a matter of fact, I'm going to stop writing in a few minutes because I want to go down to the dining room to eat something for *Melaveh Malkah* and also to check the bulletin board in the lounge to see if the new *toranut* list is up yet. It's supposed to be posted on *Rosh Chodesh* (to tell us who has *toranut* that month), and since today was *Rosh Chodesh*, it will probably be put up tonight.

Early in the morning, I'll *iy"H* be calling my parents to wish them a good *Chodesh*. Sometimes I wonder if it really is such a treat that I get to call them. Since we can only speak for a short time, it's a bit of a tease. Even though I'm glad to talk to them (and wouldn't change that for the world), I do leave the office (after speaking to them) definitely more homesick than I was before making the call. (Please DO NOT tell my parents a thing. I'd still rather speak to them than not.)

Mazal will probably come back late tonight. I'm going to try to stay up and wait for her. I want to hear how her grandmother is doing. I'm supposed to go with her next Shabbos to Kiryat Yosef. On the one hand, I loved it there when I went last time. On the other hand, her grandmother is not well and I feel a little bit like I'm intruding. (Not that any of the members of the Cohen family make me feel that way. Actually, they do the opposite—they make me feel extremely wanted and welcomed. *Iy"H*, when you come, you'll see what I mean.) Anyway, we'll have to see what happens. It's very possible that I'll have toranut next Shabbos and then I'll have to put off my visit to Kiryat Yosef for a different time.

That's it—about me—for now. I'm sorry that so much of this letter was about me, but you asked me to fill you in on everything.

By the way, Chav, I hope things are getting better with the

teaching by you, but hopefully, *iy"H*, all that will soon be a thing of the past, since *b'ezras Hashem*, very, very soon (in around a month), you'll be joining me here at M.B.L.L.!!! I absolutely can't wait. It's so hard for me not to say anything to anybody because I'm bursting!!!

Love, your friend, who absolutely can't wait to see you,
Sara

P.S. Write back as soon as you can. I can't wait to hear your reaction to the big news.
P.P.S. Don't leave out any details about your gown, the guests that are coming from out-of-town, the plans, EVERYTHING!!!
All right, that's it, now I'm really running downstairs.
P.P.S.S. I'm back again. I finished eating my *Melaveh Malkah* (delicious lachmaniah spread with techinah, and biscuitim, tea, and halvah) and I just came back upstairs. I'll be able to go to Mazal's next week after all, since next week I don't have *toranut*. (I have *toranut* the week after—meaning in two weeks.) And that's it! I hope to bring this letter tomorrow to the post office in Kfar Amsdorf, and while I'm there, I'll buy that new folder. Reminder: Remember to bring enough notebooks and folders with you from America when you come. You'll need them! (I can't wait to go with you to Kfar Amsdorf. You're going to love the walk there through the woods. I also can't wait to show you the campus...the flowers and plants are stunning! And, I can't wait. Okay, I really better finish this letter.)

I folded my letter to Chavie, this time making sure to seal the edges of the envelope before I could think of something additional to include. *I definitely must go to the post office tomorrow. Otherwise, this letter could go on forever. There's just no end to everything I want to share with Chavie.* Yes. Any more news would have to wait for my next letter.

My next letter to Chavie.

As I licked the seals closed, I had no idea how long it would be until I would once again write her. And I had no idea how different my next letter would be.

20

KIRYAT YOSEF.

Shabbos with the Cohens was once again wonderful. I could not get over how Reilya had grown in the past few weeks. Salma was still adorable and mischievous and Miryam was as precocious as ever. You certainly could not put anything past her! Yigal and Yichya were the same loyal friends and helpful hosts, and Amram and Yehudah's warm and practical natures continued to shine in an exemplary manner. Mazal's two older brothers, Yishai and Dovid again stayed in their yeshivah for Shabbos, and her Uncle Binyamin and his children again joined the family, this time for all the Shabbos meals. Her father led the Shabbos *seudah* in the same beautiful manner and I continued to be impressed with Mazal's mother and her assiduous care of the grandmother.

Yes, the wonderful food, the *zemiros*, the learning, and the warmth enveloped me as it did on my first Shabbos with Mazal's family. I was not disappointed. Everything seemed pretty much the same.

Everything…everyone…but the grandmother.

She still sat silently in the wheelchair and she still appeared as ill as before, or perhaps even worse. What struck me this time, though, was that whereas on my previous visit I had occasionally glimpsed a bit of alertness in her usually vacant stare, now it appeared that even that small flicker of light had been extinguished.

It was so sad.

I knew that behind her stony expression there was a complete person, who once upon a time had been young and lively. Is this what happens when people get old and sick? Must they turn into lifeless creatures whose blood pulsates, but whose brain ceases to function?

Mazal did mention to me that her grandmother was on much stronger medication than she had been on during my last visit, due to the progression of her illness. That could explain the worsening of her mental state. But I do not think I shall ever forget the feeling of sadness that swept over me when I looked at her. To see a live body with a dead mind…

Sitting in this energetic and cheerful household, though, one could not hold on to such depressing thoughts for long. And so, I must admit, throughout the weekend I was not really thinking much about the grandmother. Occasionally, when I would pass her, a similar thought as the one I just described would briefly run through my mind, but it did not linger. I was caught up in the constant action, having so much fun and gaining so much from watching the amazing Cohen family that I did not dwell on the disheartening condition of the grandmother.

Until Shabbos was almost over.

Contentedly, we had been sitting on the porch just off the Cohen kitchen, watching the sun dip behind the hills until it disappeared and exchanged places with the rising and glowing moon. The men and boys were in shul *davening Maariv*, Salma and Miryam were playing hide-and-go-seek nearby with some neighborhood children, and Reilya had been put to bed a short while before.

Mazal's mother, Mazal, and I sat alongside each other, occasionally sharing our thoughts, but mostly enjoying each other's company and the unseasonably warm evening. Mazal's grandmother sat in her wheelchair, wrapped in a large, crocheted sweater and with a light blanket draped across her lap. Every once in a while Geveret Cohen would lean attentively toward her mother, fussing with the blanket—but I do not think it had anything to do with the weather.

Gradually, the pastel-colored sky turned a velvety shade of ebony. First one, then two, then three stars appeared.

"I should really be inside cleaning up from Shabbat," Mazal's mother suddenly said.

I began to rise.

"No, Sara," Geveret Cohen put her hand on my arm to stop me.

Chapter 20

"This night is too beautiful to miss. We can clean later. Besides, I am happy for my mother to get some fresh air. Who knows how many more nice evenings we have left until winter?"

"Ima, you stay outside with Savta. Sara and I can begin cleaning up. We have to leave soon anyway—"

"Abba didn't tell you?"

"Tell me what, Ima?"

"Uncle Zechariah has to be in Be'er Sheva first thing tomorrow morning. He needs to buy supplies for his farm. He's planning on sleeping tonight in Kfar Amsdorf and he offered to give you a ride to the dorm."

"That's terrific, Ima. That saves us so much time."

"I know. I was so glad when I heard. I guess before Shabbat Abba was too busy to tell you about it."

"And, of course, on Shabbat Abba will not speak of something taking place after Shabbat."

"Of course."

"So, that's great. We don't have to hurry."

"Yes. He'll be stopping here for our *Melaveh Malkah* first. He wants to see Savta."

"Great. We get to stay for the *Melaveh Malkah* here and we won't arrive so late at the dorm."

"So let's just relax." Geveret Cohen leaned back, taking a deep breath and looking up at the star-studded sky. "It is so beautiful."

"It looks like black velvet covered with tiny sparkles," I said self-consciously, unsure if they understood how moved I was. "It's almost like I could reach up and pick a star—" I stopped, feeling the blood rushing to my cheeks.

"Yes," Geveret Cohen said, "it reminds me…" She closed her eyes.

"What, Ima, what does it remind you of?"

"Oh…I don't know if I should talk about it. Such memories…"

"Are you worried about Savta?"

Geveret Cohen looked over at her mother and nodded, "Yes."

"Ima, Savta is fast asleep. Tell us!"

"Oh…I don't know."

"Ima, is it about when you came to Eretz Yisrael?"

"Yes. It was just like this, that night when we arrived. It was also around this time of year."

"I know a little bit, but I want to know everything. What happened?"

"Ah," she smiled faintly, "I should really share it with you, Mazal. If we do not tell, then how can the next generation know? Yes, things were so different then..."

I was unsure of what I should do. A mother was finally going to fill her daughter in on their family history. Was it right for me to remain there, listening? Was I impinging on their privacy?

I'll start cleaning up from Shalosh Seudos, I thought as I began to rise. Once again, Geveret Cohen stopped me, insisting that I stay put. She made me feel welcome, almost as though I was part of the family.

At first, I felt uncomfortable. *I really don't belong here!* Before long, though, such thoughts erased themselves quite easily from my mind.

As she spoke, I sat spellbound on the edge of the bench, my eyes and ears transfixed. Although she spoke in Hebrew, I had little difficulty comprehending all she was telling us. Sometimes, when the heart speaks, language differences are no longer a barrier and the listening heart can understand. And so, as a piece of metal is drawn to a magnet, I felt myself pulled into her story, unaware of the powerful impact it would have on my life. I sat glued to the bench, incapable of leaving now, afraid of missing even one word of her narrative. I felt transported back in time...to a place very, very far away.

"I was only a child at the time," Geveret Cohen began, "not more than five years old, when they came and forever changed our lives. I think I can trust my memory. Some things remain vivid despite the passage of time." She stopped for a moment, her eyes lingering on her mother. Reassuring herself that the elderly woman was sleeping peacefully, she continued.

"We lived in a small village on the outskirts of Assada, which was in the Southern part of Yemen. Beautiful is the only way to describe it. The main part, the city, was on the mountain, and that is where most of the non-Jews lived. We Jews lived in the valley.

"It really was so beautiful," she smiled sadly. "The river snaked around the valley. Yes, I think it was called Wadi Bana. I remember my mother's weekly hike to the river. With her long dress and her kerchief tied tightly on top of her hair, she and the servant girl would carry the week's wash from our home to the river. Oftentimes, my siblings and I would accompany them through the winding paths of the village, where we would pass the many different trees and plants. Ah…I recall it grew very green, oh so green. We would meander along until we reached the river. Then, my mother would wash the clothing while we little ones played. It was never very cold. When the weather was very warm and the sun was shining strongly, my mother would allow us to swim. It was such fun!

"Yes, that river was very much the center of our lives. It was a place to wash, play, and bathe. The river was good to us, but it also brought us terror. I will never forget that horrific summer day," she shuddered, "when little cousin Avraham drowned. Oh, how I hated the river that day."

A chill ran through me and I shivered.

"During the week, my brothers went with the rest of the Jewish boys of the village to the *Mori* while we girls stayed home. Our mothers taught us what we needed to know. My father engaged a tutor to teach me how to read *lashon ha-kodesh*. He was very proud of my accomplishments.

"My father was an important and rich man who had to do much traveling for trading and, therefore, he was the only Jew in Assada allowed to own a horse. I guess the non-Jews knew it would benefit their own businesses if my father did not have to rely on a donkey like the other Jews. How proud I was when my father, his long, dark beard flowing, would return *Erev Shabbat*, sitting tall and erect on his horse, along with his sacks of goods.

"The village children would crowd around us, the boys with their curly black *simanim* and the girls with their long black braids. I felt so important, the envy of the other children. Everyone would stand around staring as my father unloaded his packages, with the servants carrying the merchandise into the store."

"Ima, the store was in your house?"

"Yes, Mazal," she replied, "our house was the store."

"So, what did you do on Shabbat?"

"Ah…Shabbat," her smile was radiant, and once again I noticed how white her teeth were in her dark face. "On Shabbat everything was transformed. Our house was no longer the "business." We closed the store. It was our Shabbat home. During the week," she chuckled, "we spoke Yemenite, but on Shabbat," her voice lifted with pride, "we spoke only *lashon ha-kodesh*.

"During the week we ate mialuga, a sort of pita bread. But, on Shabbat we had my mother's wonderful and special *Shabbat* bread.

"I was quite young, then, and so it seemed to me to be an extremely late hour, after the Friday night *seudah*. How I cherish those memories! My father would sit with me on his lap, and with tears flowing down his cheeks, he would say *Tehillim*, praying for the *Mashiach* to come. Yes, although we led a comfortable and safe life, we all yearned and waited anxiously for the end of our *galut*.

"Even when naming my brother and me, my father had Eretz Yisrael in mind. Tzionah is what he called me, with his thoughts always directed toward Tzion, and my oldest brother was called Eliyahu, which was my father's way of expressing his fervent plea for *Mashiach Tzidkeinu*.

"Throughout our history, there had always been individuals and small groups who had made their way up to Eretz Yisrael. Some were idealistic, endeavoring to make their lifelong dream of seeing the Holy Land come true, and some of them were the orphans.

"Although life for us Jews under the Imam was good, there was one major obstacle impeding our path and instilling fear in our hearts. There was a law in Yemen during those days. Any orphaned child, Jewish or Moslem, was "adopted" by the Imam. This meant that the child would not only have the necessary financial and educational help to enable him to grow into a respectable Yemenite citizen, but he was compelled to become a Moslem as well.

"Of course, this was out of the question for us Jews. Unfortunately though, we did not have a choice in the matter. A child whose father was no longer among the living faced a forced conversion, a life devoid of Judaism.

"There was not much the Jewish community could do about it. Yet, desperation leads to creativity. Caring Jews would secretly adopt the child, making him their own. However, this was risky and problematic, especially when the family was large. Therefore, many of the orphans were sent to Aden, a British colony in the South of Yemen. Eventually the child was smuggled for a fee aboard a British boat and brought to Palestine.

"Occasionally we would hear from these individuals, the orphans that had grown up. They were living, working, and loving the land, turning into idealistic young settlers, attempting to persuade others to join them. Yet, most of us knew that we would not be going until the *Mashiach* came to escort us there, *al kanfei nisharim*—on the wings of eagles.

"My father had a friend who had lived in Sana'a and had moved to Eretz Yisrael. They had befriended each other during my father's travels and had remained close. His friend wrote him repeatedly, urging us to come. My father, though, felt it was not yet the right time.

"And then, the *shlichim* began coming. It was 1949 and we were ignorant of world events. With the establishment of the State of Israel, government representatives came to Yemen to invite the Jews to immigrate. At first, we were wary, but after they persisted, we allowed ourselves to believe that what we were hearing was the truth. They told us that Eretz Yisrael was no longer Palestine. It was no longer under the jurisdiction of the British. It was our land…it was Israel.

"We listened with joy, our hearts soaring, our eyes lifted heavenward. Hashem had finally answered our prayers, we thought. Our exile is over, He has sent us *Mashiach*. The *geulah* is here!

"Yes…we would go. With enthusiasm and in retrospect…naiveté. We believed everything that the Jewish Agency told us.

"I will never forget that day. Dressed in our very best Shabbat outfits, my father placed my brother, Binyamin, who was the youngest boy, and me in baskets that hung on each side of the donkey. My two older brothers, father's proud and able assistants, Eliyahu and Zechariah, were busy with the last-minute preparations. Our excitement knew no bounds. I felt insurmountable pride as I saw the other children lingering nearby, watching us enviously, wishing that they too were going. For the past few weeks, I had watched some others making their exodus, and now my family was to be the one to leave.

"Bursting with happiness, I watched the servants load our donkeys. *Oh, when will we be leaving already*, I wondered with a mixture of impatience and joy. Sacks filled with all our belongings were piled high upon the donkeys' backs. Much of what we owned had already been sold and converted to gold. This my father placed carefully in cans and tied them as inconspicuously as possible to the sides of the donkeys. My mother had sewn small pockets into the insides of our clothing and my father placed some of the gold and jewelry in them. All this added to the thrilling sensation already surrounding us.

"Suddenly, amid all the scuttling around, I worriedly turned toward my mother. She looked flushed running about, taking care of all the final details. I wanted to climb out of the basket and help her. Despite my young age at the time, I knew she should be extra cautious in her condition. My heart swelled with joy as I remembered what my father told me. This baby would be very special…it would be the first one in our family to be born in the Holy Land."

For a brief moment, Geveret Cohen stopped talking as she glanced anxiously at her mother.

"Don't worry, Ima," Mazal reassured her, "Savta is still fast asleep."

Gratefully, she smiled at Mazal and then continued.

"Ah, yes," Mazal's mother shared the excited feelings of a five-year-old. "While I watched my mother moving about, I secretly hoped the baby would be a girl. Oh, how I wished for a sister! And to be born in Eretz Yisrael!

"I saw my mother tearfully saying her goodbyes to the others who were not leaving. The remaining Jewish Yemenite families would be joining us, but the gentile friends and servants we had known for years, we knew, we would never see again. Emotionally, we said our farewells as we joined the procession of the other Jews making their departure.

"Our non-Jewish neighbors stood at the sides of the road, some weeping and waving sadly, as we joined the caravan of travelers slowly leaving Assada. We had gotten along well. They would miss us, and we knew they would miss the prosperity we had brought them. We had contributed to the trading market, and among the villagers it was the Jewish people who could read and write. We had lived together in peace all our years, and if not for the burning passion glowing within us, drawing us with great fervency to the Holy Land, we would have had no reason to leave.

"Within two months, Assada was completely empty of Jews.

"We passed through many villages as we made our way toward the city of Aden, the procession of donkeys, carts, and people growing as other Jews from other villages joined us. In the evenings, we set up tents, encamping overnight alongside the roads and early in the morning, we continued on our journey. As we passed through the villages and traveled through the outskirts of cities, people would stare at us. Some elderly people shook their heads, wondering why we would bother to give up so much to go to an unknown land. The more youthful gaped at us enviously, as we would be experiencing adventure and making so major a change in our lives. We just continued on with our hearts full of yearning."

Geveret Cohen stopped speaking, letting out a deep sigh. I feared that she would not continue with her narrative, so long did this silent interlude last. I did not say anything and neither did Mazal. I guess Mazal understood her mother's need for a few quiet moments before she could go on.

We sat there, silently listening to the chirping of the crickets accompanied by the playful sounds of children's voices in the background. I desperately hoped she would continue before the men and children would appear.

"Yes," Geveret Cohen finally broke the silence. I sat up straighter, hoping not to miss out on a single word. "I was drunk with the innocence of childhood, captivated with the adventure of travel, unaware of the dangers we were spared.

"That is...until one night."

I saw her take a long look at her mother before continuing. "That night I had fallen asleep early, dreaming my usual dream about the *Mashiach* greeting us upon our arrival in Eretz Yisrael. As I lay underneath my covers picturing the new *Beit Hamikdash*, imagining the gold and splendor, the silks and majesty, I continued dreaming...

"Suddenly...suddenly I felt something sharp and cold against my neck. I froze. This was not a dream...this was a real live nightmare. 'Your money or your life,' they said. Although it was dark, I could see my mother's white face.

"No…it was not turning into an exciting adventure. I tasted real fear. But, that was only the beginning.

"Finally—I do not remember how long it took, since I was, after all, only a child and time seemed to stretch on forever—but, yes, we finally reached Aden. There was a building, large and modern, unlike anything I had ever seen before. There was also a very long line of people. The *shlichim* were there and insisted on immunizing all of us. Children were crying, screaming, and wailing. Yet, the *shlichim* or government officials kept telling us that we had nothing to fear. It was very important that we receive these shots, they said. This way we would not catch diseases. We must get the shots before we could enter the land.

"And then, at last, I saw it. It was the biggest bird I had ever seen in my life. It was like seeing a giant. And I heard my father and the others whisper in awe "*al kanfei nesharim.*" And I knew, this was the eagle that Yeshaya had spoken about in his *nevuah*.

"The *shlichim* informed us that it would take hard work, but that Israel was our land and that we could return it to its original beauty. They also said that we would benefit from the new, modern way of life Israel had to offer. We were to be part of a group that would be leaving the next morning.

"That night, a few of the Israelis who were part of the group of *shlichim* came to talk to us. Quietly, I heard them advise my father to put aside some of his heavier belongings. Perhaps he had some hidden jewelry or gold? They explained that the airplanes could only hold so much and that the weight of our belongings might prevent the plane from being able to take off. They were not telling him what to do with his things, they assured him, but as friends, they were offering him advice. After all, they said, they were not going to be flying on the plane with him that day, and they would not suffer if the plane fell down from the sky because it was too heavy. They were just, again they stressed—as friends—making a suggestion. They informed him that they would be happy to hold his heavier possessions there for him, and later on, when these men returned to Israel, they could bring them along. But, for now, with so many people going, they strongly suggested that he not take anything except the clothes on his and his family's backs.

Chapter 20

"Much later we were to find out that we were not the only ones such warnings were whispered to, but just then, trusting souls that we Yemenite people were, we thanked those men profusely for their advice. My father gave them half the gold and jewelry that remained after the robbery, not quite ready to part with it all. At the same time, he felt guilty that he had not given it *all* to them and worried that we would be the ones to cause the plane to fall from the sky.

"How sparkling the giant eagle looked as we climbed into it early the next morning and how insurmountable our excitement was as the airplane took off! The tears flowed down my father's cheeks as he said *Tehillim*. It reminded me of all those Friday nights that my father rocked back and forth until very late, chanting the holy words…praying for this day. Only now Dovid HaMelech's prophecy was coming true. We were on our way to Eretz Yisrael.

"I know now that it should have taken us only a short time to travel by air the distance from Yemen to Israel. Nevertheless, because we could not fly over Saudi Arabia and were compelled to go around it, we did not arrive in Eretz Yisrael until late that night.

"Yes, it was a night similar to tonight. A night just like you described it, Sara, where I felt I could reach out and touch the stars."

I looked up at the sky. It was covered with shiny, twinkling stars. I turned back to Geveret Cohen. I so much wished she would continue.

"So what happened next, Ima? Your family settled and—"

"I wish it had been so simple. No," she shook her head, "the comfortable life we had known in Yemen became a thing of the past. We were placed in a refugee camp. It was called Rosh HaBe'er. Originally, it had been a British army camp. There were rows of stone houses with a round metal roofs on top that had at one time housed soldiers. Of course, I had never seen anything like this before. There were at least three families assigned to each barrack.

"I will never forget how upset I was that first day at Rosh HaBe'er. They made us take showers, and if that was not bad enough for a little girl who had never seen a shower before, I was forced to give them the dress I wore. I cried. It was my best dress and I loved it. And now they were taking it away from me. It would be burned!

"The young girl, Yael, who was my group's leader, promised me that they had something else beautiful for me to wear. They were only taking my dress away from me because they had to burn out any germs it might have. It was for my own good, she claimed. 'And,' she said reassuringly, 'you will love your new outfit.'

"I did not. I wanted my own Shabbat outfit back.

"At first, I was inconsolable, but then as Yael helped me get dressed and braided my long hair, I allowed myself to be comforted. She promised me that I would get many new outfits and that I must be a brave big girl in my new land. Taking my hand, she led me back to my parents, into the big dining hall.

"We ate in a central dining hall, the children separately from the adults. I remember how strange some of the foods were. I had never eaten olives before, and there was an abundance of them, served at all meals. We had eaten cheese in Yemen, but the cheese in Israel tasted different and the milk was served to us in large, shiny metal pitchers.

"My father encouraged my mother to drink much of the milk. 'We want our Eretz Yisrael baby to be strong and healthy,' he cheerfully reminded her. I was so excited. My new baby brother or sister was to be born in less than three months and I did not know how I would be able to wait until—"

"The baby! The baby!" Mazal's grandmother suddenly shrieked, "Where is my baby? Where is Hodaya? My baby!"

Within seconds, Geveret Cohen was beside her mother. "Ima, it's all right. I'm here."

"Hodaya! Hodaya!" The screams were frightening, especially coming from someone so weak and feeble. "You must find my baby!"

Mazal jumped up. "I'll go bring Savta some water."

"And get her pill, Mazal, quickly! She's trembling!" There were tears in Geveret Cohen's eyes. "It's my fault. I should not have spoken."

I stood awkwardly. "Can I do anything?"

"I cannot believe it. I did not think she was aware of what I was saying. Lately she has not seemed aware of anything. Oh," she shook her head from side to side while trying to soothe her mother, "she remembers. She remembers. We must not talk about this anymore."

And we did not. That is, for the rest of the evening. Yet, there would come a time when the remainder of this story would be told.

21

SHOCKER OF SHOCKERS *of shocks…I cannot not believe what happened just a few minutes ago.*

I had been sitting cross-legged on my bed that Tuesday afternoon, innocently doing my homework. Mazal was downstairs in the library working with one of her Israeli friends and I was enjoying the freedom of doing my work alone while listening to one of my tapes and not having to concern myself with Mimi.

Mimi.

You see, ever since that day over two weeks ago when Mimi had informed me that she would be leaving, I had refrained from planning any study sessions with her. At first I felt rather guilty; after all, Rabbi Grossman had asked me to work with her. But then I reminded myself that I was not officially her tutor and that even Rabbi Grossman could not fault me for not running after her. She was a big girl—supposedly mature enough to make her own decisions—and I had no obligation to chase after her and try to change her mind. After all, I could not be held accountable for the fact that she found all this studying, as she said, not her "cup of tea."

No, it was definitely *not* my problem.

Naturally, I had to repeat this to myself several times. I was far too sensitive to ignore those other feelings…the ones that sympathized with Mimi, the ones that worried about her. *How could Mimi do this to herself and her future? What will people think if she simply drops out of seminary in the middle of the year?*

Then, not surprisingly, my emotions would swing back toward Chavie and my dream of our being together for the remainder of the year. *If Mimi leaves, then Chavie comes.* With that in mind, my doubts would quickly vanish—temporarily.

And so, for the past two weeks, the pendulum swung back and forth.

Of course, Mimi had no idea that I was experiencing such an emotional storm on her account. She might not have even noticed that I had decided not to study with her. She was far too busy with the Chanukah production, which was less than three weeks away, and her interest in academic achievement—which was never of much concern to her in the first place—was now almost nil. She held absolutely nothing against me. Her breezy personality never allowed her to feel offended by anyone anyway. Mimi walked around as though everything was status quo, enjoying being the center of attention as usual. I was sure that no one had any suspicion that Mimi would be leaving.

Right then, however, as I sat cross-legged on my bed enjoying the music and my work, I was not thinking of Mimi. My mind was overflowing with ideas and I was attempting to write down my thoughts fast enough in order that nothing would be lost. After all, if I was to become the recipient of the Goldstone Award, I had to take advantage of those times when my imagination was most fertile and my creative energy just seemed to flow. Gripping my pen tightly, I was scribbling vigorously. I already had seventy completed pages in my special notebook. Some of this would be rewritten and used for Geveret Spitz's report and some would go directly into my *Proyect* folder.

I stopped writing for a moment, sighing contentedly as I gazed at the next page. Its lines were empty, the paper fresh and unused, waiting invitingly to be filled with my many ideas. *Yes*, I thought dreamily, *I can't believe it...I'm about to begin writing on page seventy-one of my notebook.* I tightened my grasp on my pen and began.

Suddenly, a knock on the door interrupted my writing. I looked up.

Adina entered my room.

Phew. At least I'm not writing any letters. That was my first thought.

My second thought was, *Uh oh, what did I do now,* followed by, *This time, I'm just not going to let whatever she's going to confront me with upset me.*

And then, I experienced the first "shocker."

"Um…uh…Sara, I hope I'm not disturbing you…"

Adina hesitant? Adina shifting back and forth on her feet uncomfortably? What's going on?

I was afraid to say anything.

"Sara, I…um…came to…er…well…"

She came to…what? Apologize? How many times in the last thirteen days had I attempted to apologize to her? And apologize for what? For trying to help her out with her laundry? For emptying her clothing out of the dryer, for putting forth my complete effort to fold it precisely the way she likes it, for carrying it up three flights of steps and delivering it straight to her room? And then for saying the "wrong" thing to her when she flew into a rage at me for doing her the favor?

It was not hard to remember how hurt I felt when she slammed the invisible door shut in my face, rejecting all my overtures. I could not easily forget the way I dejectedly, head down, walked out of her room toward my own, closing the door softly behind me.

Yes, that *other* door, the invisible one, the one I had thought was beginning to open, had been slammed closed with such a piercing bang that it continued echoing deafeningly in my mind throughout the coming days. Of course I tried to approach her again. A few times. Yet, it was as if that tiny crack of an opening had never really been there. She had remained as closed, cold, and impenetrable as ever.

And now, she expects me—

"Sara, I'm…er…trying to—"

I stood up. "It's all right, Adina. You don't need—"

She came closer. "I do need to, Sara. I was wrong. I've been behaving intolerably."

"It's all right, Adina. Sometimes—" I was about to say something about friends, but then stopped myself. "Sometimes people do things that they think will be helpful, but then—"

"No, Sara. You did nothing wrong. I should have been down there in the laundry room earlier. I was listening to something…a tape…that, well…it doesn't matter. I must have gotten carried away and not realized what time it was. And then suddenly you appeared in my room—"

"I tried coming to you earlier…to ask you what to do. But I thought that you were sleeping. I didn't want your laundry to crease."

"It was wrong the way I reacted to you. I—I should explain—"

"Adina, really. You don't owe me—"

"Yes, I do owe you an explanation. You've gone out of your way for me more than once. I—I guess I'm just not used to it," she waved her hand in the air.

"It?"

"Yes…dormitory life. I—I'm an only child, you know…"

"No," I shook my head.

"And I'm just not accustomed—"

"I really didn't mean to invade your privacy, Adina. I was just trying to help…"

"I know," she nodded, "and I also know, Sara, that you're not the type to read something that wasn't meant for you."

"I'm really, really sorry about that, Adina."

"Well, anyway, I assume that it must have been Mimi's idea—"

"No," I shook my head, "it wasn't like that, Adina. It wasn't intentional. It—"

"Please, Sara. Don't try to defend Mimi. I room with her. I know what she's like. Anyway, I didn't come to discuss her. I just wanted to tell you that I know I was wrong in the way I treated you and I apologize."

And, that was it. She apologized and went out, leaving me utterly baffled.

It proved difficult for me to get back to work. I was still in the midst of getting over this "shocker." I sat on my bed, willing my creative juices to start flowing again. Well…it was to no avail. I just could not concentrate. I kept replaying over and over again that brief conversation with Adina.

I tried hard to focus on my work. I really did. I sat. I squirmed. I stood. I sat back down. And, page seventy-one was still empty.

Oh, well, I thought. *Adina's interruption was worth it. Anyway, in a short while it'll be time for supper and so my momentum would've been lost either way.*

Chapter 21

I must have skipped down the steps to the dining room. I was feeling lighter than I had felt in days. Adina was not angry with me anymore. True, I had no great expectations. I had already experienced way too many disappointments in that area. *Doors swinging open and then slamming closed,* I mused philosophically. However, the burden of having been the focus of Adina's anger had been lifted. I was free!

Smiling, I took my seat. *When Chavie comes, she'll be Adina's roommate and if anyone can help Adina open up, Chavie's the one!* Chavie had the perfect balance of outgoingness and respect for others' privacy.

I sighed contentedly. Things were really starting to work themselves out. Adina had apologized! Chavie would be here sometime soon. I was making terrific progress with my report and *Proyect*. Mazal and I were developing a really special friendship, the kind that would last despite distances and differences. Yes, a real, real friend...

I did not pay too much attention to the conversation going on around me. *Wow! I still can't believe it,* I thought excitedly, *only about three more weeks until Chavie comes...* Not that I had heard from her since my last letter, but I had no doubt that the planning was under way.

Somewhere in the background, I heard the Chanukah production being discussed. Mimi's name kept cropping up, of course. I sprinkled some salt on my salad and asked Naomi, who was sitting next to me, to pass the *chatzilim*. Someone else spoke about the recent final exams. Another girl nervously mentioned Geveret Spitz's report due in less than two weeks.

Eating rather hurriedly, I hazily listened to the discussion going on around me. I was anxious to get back to my room to continue working on my report. The initial giddiness of having Adina Stern actually apologize to me had worn off and I was coming back down to earth. Yes, I was all geared up to begin page seventy-one and almost ready to transfer the information to my special folder for the Geveret Spitz report. I was hoping to have my report completed a week before it was due. *After all, you never know what can happen at the last minute...*

I reached for the pitcher of tea. I poured the light brown liquid into my glass and then mixed two teaspoons of sugar into it. *Something sweet and warm to help me wash down my supper.*

The girls around me began talking about the coming Shabbos. Yehudis asked Hadassah what she was doing. When she mentioned that she would be going to a relative and she found out that Yehudis did not have any plans, she asked Yehudis to join her. Yehudis gratefully accepted.

I sipped my tea. *Ah, this really hits the spot.*

"Chaya, do you have any plans?"

"I'm not really sure, Ahuvah. Why, do you have any good ideas?"

"Well, I was thinking of inviting myself over to some distant relatives in the Old City," Ahuvah replied. "Want to come with me? I'm way too embarrassed to go by myself."

"You think they'll mind? *You're* related. Me? I'm a complete stranger."

"Chaya, they're known to have an open house…anyone can come."

"How about you, Mimi? What are you doing this coming Shabbos?" Rochel Leah asked.

"Oh…I don't know yet. I still didn't decide. Right now, the only thing on my mind is the Chanukah production."

"We noticed," the words were out of my mouth before I could stop them.

Mimi and the others laughed good-naturedly, assuming I had meant it as an affable joke.

"*Nu*, Mimi," Mazal said, "maybe you want to have vacation from the work. Come home with me to Kiryat Yosef for Shabbat."

"I was about to ask you to come with me to my mother's friend in Kiryat Sanz, Mimi," Rochel Leah interjected.

"But, Rochel Leah, I thought—" Zehava stopped in mid-sentence, her pale face turning a dark shade of pink.

"Mimi, I was going to ask you to come with me to the Shlomitzky's. We had such a great time last time," Chani laughed. "I guess with so many invitations you'll just have to decide."

Mimi's green eyes twinkled merrily, her smile spreading from ear to ear. "Well, since Mazal asked me first and I was never in Kiryat Yosef before, if it's okay, Mazal, I'd love to go to you for Shabbos."

"Oh yes, it be very okay," Mazal sang out happily. "My family very much enjoy your company."

I gulped. *Mimi is going with Mazal?* The tea was suddenly tasteless.

"That should be an interesting Shabbos for you, Mimi," Rochel Leah said. I could hear that trace of sarcasm in her voice. "All that Yemenite food—"

"It's wonderful," I unexpectedly found myself saying, despite that strange, unfamiliar feeling that had come over me a few seconds earlier. "Mimi, you're going to have the best time. Mazal's family is the greatest, and by the way, Mazal, don't forget to bring back some zehug for Rochel Leah. Remember how much she loved it last time?"

Those around me, familiar with the latest zehug experience, laughed. I had not meant to be cruel to Rochel Leah, but I could not sit by idly while she offended Mazal.

"Hey, Sara, how about you coming too?" Mimi asked.

I looked at Mazal, embarrassed. *The invitation should come from her, not Mimi.*

"Yes, Sara. That be wonderful idea. Please also come."

"Um…I—I don't want…Oh," I suddenly remembered, "I almost forgot. I can't come this Shabbos. I have *toranut*."

"That is true. Yes. I too forget."

"I also have *toranut* this Shabbos," Malkie said to me. "So does Devorah."

"Adina does too," I heard myself say.

"So-o-o, Chan, how about coming with *me* for Shabbos?" Rochel Leah offered.

"I really wanted to go to the Shlomitzky's this Shabbos. Thanks anyway."

"No problem. I'll just go with you there."

I saw Zehava squirming uncomfortably. She appeared to be elbowing Rochel Leah, but Rochel Leah was either ignoring her deliberately or too busy with her own arrangements to notice anything else.

Poor Zehava…

I said my *berachah acharonah*, waved to those still at the table, cleared off my plate, and headed toward the library. I wanted to check something out in one of the *sefarim* there before returning to my room.

Passing the opened doors of the lounge on the way to the library, I could see one of the Israeli girls from Beit Yaakov HaNegbah sitting at the piano and playing a familiar tune. Its melody echoed through the hallway and resonated softly within the library's walls. I hummed along as I reached for the *sefer* and brought it to a nearby table. Skimming through a few of the pages, first turning them forward and then backward, suddenly I stopped. *Aha*, I thought happily while pointing to the part I had been looking for, *I found it!*

I looked up, wondering if anyone had an extra piece of paper and a pen that I could use to write down the information I had just discovered. Most of the girls were still in the dining room eating supper. *I don't know why I didn't I bring my clipboard down—*

And then, suddenly I saw her. Shoulders slumped and sitting forlornly at one of the corner tables near the windows was Zehava Gross.

I went over to her immediately. "Zehava, are you all right?"

She looked up. Her eyes were brimming with unshed tears. "Yes, I'm fine. I—I just have a headache."

"Can I get you something? Some tea? An aspirin?"

"No thanks," she smiled weakly, "But thanks for asking."

"Zehava," I hesitated for a moment before taking the seat next to her, "you look upset about something."

"No…no. I'm really okay," a large tear trickled down her cheek.

"Please…I'm sorry. I didn't mean to—" I ran to the large bookcase where one of the shelves held a box of tissues and brought a few back to her. "I'm sorry, Zehava."

"It's all right. Don't look at me," she said as she took a tissue to wipe her eyes. "I hope no one sees me. I'm so embarrassed."

"Don't be embarrassed. There's nothing wrong with you. Everyone feels horrible once in a while."

She blew her nose. "I think I'm okay."

"Do…do you feel like talking?"

"No," she shook her head slowly. "It's not going to help."

"Can I get you anything?"

"No thanks. These tissues are all I need now," she blew her nose again. "Do me a favor, Sara. Just block me for a few minutes, so no one can see me."

She twisted her head in the direction of the windows. I heard a few sniffles and tried to hide Zehava from the view of anyone entering the room. A minute or two passed before she turned back.

"I'm all right now." She faced me, showing me a half-hearted smile. "See? I guess I was just in a yucky mood. I'm really all right now." She stood up. "And thanks, Sara. Thanks...for...for helping me."

She began walking away.

"Zehava?"

"Yes?" she turned around to face me.

"A bunch of us will be in the dorm this Shabbos. It's probably going to be lots of fun."

She shrugged.

"I hope you'll join us."

"I'll see," she mumbled.

I stood staring at her back while she headed for the door. When she reached it, she unexpectedly twisted around. "Sara?"

"Yes?"

"Thanks again."

And again, I thought...*poor Zehava. I wish I could help her. Anyway,* I sighed, *the kind of help she needs, she won't want.*

This time *I* shrugged my shoulders and then, remembering the *sefer* that was waiting for me and noticing that no one in the library had pens or paper, I figured it would just be quicker to get my own. I dashed up the steps to my room.

By the time I returned to the library, many of the chairs and tables were filled with girls studying. When I went to retrieve the *sefer* I had been using, it was not where I had left it. I went back to the bookcase, but it was not there either, so feeling slightly foolish, I went from table to table trying to find it. Finally, after around fifteen minutes of searching, I found two M.B.L.L.ers, heads together, busily reading from it.

I sat down and patiently waited for what seemed like forever until the *sefer* was finally available.

"Here, Sara," Nina brought it to me. "Pardon our taking so long."

"Thanks. I hope you finished what you needed to do and didn't rush because of me."

"That's gorgeous of you, Sara." (Nina was from England.)

I immediately found the correct page and vigorously began to scribble onto my paper. Again, the ideas started to flow. I was writing unhesitatingly with one thought leading to the next. Then, I jumped up and went to the bookcase to find a *Tehillim*. *Yes,* I thought excitedly, *that's the perfect pasuk to emphasize this idea.* I turned to the back of the *Tehillim* and then flipped through the last few pages until I came to the right *perek*.

There was the *pasuk*!

I bit down on the top of my pen. *This will absolutely tie my ideas together. That's it, Sara. You've found yourself your topic for the Proyect,* my pulse started rushing. *Now, start writing!*

Licking my lips, I gripped my pen eagerly and began to write. Suddenly, a shadow fell across my paper. Before I had a chance to look up and see who it was, I heard her breathless voice and knew.

"Hey, Sara, I've been looking all over for you."

I barely lifted my eyes to her. "I'm working on something, Mimi. Not now—"

"Sara—"

"Sh-sh, Mimi, everyone here is trying to work. Quiet down."

"But I've got to talk to you," she sat down in the seat next to me.

"Mimi, I don't know what color is the right one for the *Maccabim*'s costume, and I really couldn't tell you if each of Chana's sons should sing their own solo, and in case you didn't notice, I'm trying to get some work done. So, please—"

"I need to—"

"And I really don't know if the soldiers should harmonize when they sing or whether the audience will want to hear the—"

"Please, Sara!"

There was an uncharacteristic urgency in her voice, and so finally, I lifted my eyes from my paper and gasped. Her eyes were puffy, her nose was red. "Mimi, what's wrong?"

"I need to talk to you, Sara."

I looked around the room. "Here?"

"No, not here," she shook her head. "Someplace private."

"Okay, I'll meet you in my room in five minutes." I was afraid that others would see her looking upset and I did not want her to have to wait for me in the library. "I just have to put these *sefarim* back and then

I'll come right up."

"Thanks, Sara," she said and disappeared quickly from the room.

I was upstairs on the third floor in less than five minutes. Mimi was standing at my door.

"What's wrong, Mimi? Why don't you go inside?"

"I can't, Sara. Mazal is in there studying with a few girls."

"Oh," I started walking next door, toward her room.

She took three steps sideways while keeping her back to the wall and then stood in front of *her* door, blocking my entry.

"Mimi? What in the world—"

"No," she shook her head. "We can't go in there either. Adina is studying with Devorah and Malkie."

"So where should we go?"

"We can't go outside—"

"I know—"

"It's pouring."

"Right…how about the lounge, Mimi?"

"It's too crowded."

"Um…let's go to the basement."

"That's a great idea, Sara," Mimi's eyes lit up. "If anyone's in the laundry room, we could use the *miklat* or even the storage room."

And that is where we ended up until way past midnight that Tuesday night.

Talking. There, in the storage room, among the broken furniture, musty mattresses, and extra night tables is where I experienced my second, but by far more serious "shocker" of the day.

Then again, perhaps it really was not so shocking after all.

22

"I still don't understand."

"What's there to understand, Sara? I'm asking, I'm *begging* you—"

"Please, Mimi—"

"Sara, you're my only hope."

"Mimi," I shook my head, "I don't get it. And please stop being so dramatic…"

"But, Sara—"

"The whole time I was trying to help you. I kept waiting for you, Mimi, reminding you. I felt like such a nag."

"No…you're definitely not a nag."

"Well, you sure made me feel like one." Sitting in that musty room, this unexpected conversation was turning more bewildering with every passing second. "And how about that night in the library when you told me in no uncertain terms that you were planning on leaving M.B.L.L.?"

"Oh that." She waved her hand dismissively.

"Oh that," I imitated her. "Well, what's that suppose to mean?"

"I'm not sure."

"What do you mean *you're not sure*? Are you leaving or aren't you? She lifted her shoulders and sighed. "Who knows?"

"Who knows?" I repeated, incredulous at her indifference. "Do you have any idea how much you upset me? I wanted to help you but then you just…" I shook my head again, more baffled than ever. "And now you're asking me to help you do your report?

"*Begging* you," she corrected. There was a mischievous gleam in her eyes. No longer did they look swollen and her nose too had lost its redness.

I was sitting on a large overturned drawer adjacent to one of the walls and Mimi sat opposite me on top of an old night table. Swinging her legs back and forth, she appeared to have returned to her usual, cheerful self.

Well, *almost*. There was an uncharacteristic sense of urgency about her that I found puzzling. *Why is the report suddenly so important if she's planning on leaving? Or isn't she planning on leaving?*

I sighed, leaning back against the wall. "Didn't you say that these reports…all this studying…is just not your cup of tea…?"

She suddenly laughed. "Well, maybe if we put a little sugar in it."

I did not laugh. I shook my head, perplexed. "I don't get it. I just don't get it."

"Sara, for the last half-hour you've been shaking your head back and forth like one of those wind-up toys. There's nothing to get. Just…just, will you do it?"

I let out another deep sigh—ready to acquiesce, ready to say, *well, do I have a choice?* Then suddenly I remembered…Chavie.

"Mimi, you can't just go around manipulating."

"Manipulating?"

"First you tell me you're leaving…definitely leaving. I'm sitting there, concerned for you, but you're too busy to even notice, because the only thing on Mimi Rosenberg's mind is the—"

"Chanukah production."

"Chanukah production, thank you."

My legs were beginning to cramp. I stood up, shaking my legs one at a time. "Two weeks…it's been two weeks I've been concerned about your leaving. I've been wondering this whole time if I should run after you and force you to do your work."

"Sara, you are absolutely so caring."

"And you absolutely didn't seem to care. Suddenly you come to me tonight. I *think* what you're telling me now is that you plan on staying, that you haven't done a thing on your report, and that you want my help with it," I said coldly. "I thought this whole seminary thing wasn't for you. I thought you *wanted* to leave."

"You almost sound like *you* want me to leave," Mimi countered.

I did not answer.

Mimi did not seem to notice. She jumped off the night table that she was sitting on and came toward me. "So, will you do it, Sara? Will you help me?"

She's so sure I'll say yes. "I don't know, Mimi. We tried before and it didn't go so great. Besides, it's due in less than two weeks."

"Well, we could start right now," she said hopefully and then started to sing, "The night is still young…"

"Maybe for you," I stood up and headed for the door, "but I'm really tired."

"Please, Sara!" she said beseechingly.

Something in her voice stopped me. I turned around to face her, my heart beginning to melt. This did not sound like the Mimi I knew. Then I saw her grinning, that same charming, dimpled smile making her pointy chin even more angular. My heart hardened. "All those interruptions when we were studying…"

"I promise, Sara. This time, I won't interrupt. Puleeeeze…"

I bit my lower lip, turning away from her, trying to think. An old, slightly cracked mirror leaned carelessly against the wall. I noticed its splintered frame and the black spots at the edges of the silver glass and wondered for a moment why they did not just get rid of it. *Maybe they think there's something left to salvage. After all, you don't throw good things away.* Suddenly I held my breath. *Sara,* I told myself, *listen to yourself. There's a lot of good in Mimi. You can't just walk away from her.*

And then, I saw her expression reflected in the mirror. *That mischievous grin! Here I am all concerned about her, ready to use my time to help her out, and she's still got that same silly, irresponsible smile on her face,* I thought, infuriated. *She probably thinks I'll do whatever she wants. She always gets people to do what she wants. And besides, what about Chavie?*

I was still staring into the mirror, my thoughts racing. All at once, I became aware of my reflection. My eyes were flashing angrily and I could see that the rest of me looked odd as well. There was a thin crack running crookedly down the center of the mirror, making me appear as though I was split in half. *That's how I feel. Split into two. One part of me can't refuse Mimi, and the other part...*

"So, will you do it?" Mimi's eyes met mine in the mirror.

"The production, Mimi," I said, flustered. "It's on your mind twenty-four seven."

"Not when we'll be working together, Sara. Really. I won't even allow myself to *think* about it."

"Right," I swung around, facing her directly. "And the waiting. Do you have any idea how much time I've wasted waiting for you?"

"I'm sorry, Sara. I really, truly am. Give me another chance. You'll see, this time I'll be the one waiting for you."

She has all the answers. I was feeling utterly drained. Bending my knee, I propped my foot against the wall. *What should I do?* I sighed. "And what about my own report, Mimi? When am I supposed to write mine?"

"C'mon, Miss Made to Order Student," her eyes danced playfully, "I'm sure you're almost done with yours."

"It just happens that I'm not done. And by the way, while you were busy running to Pinat HaGlidah or working on your production or entertaining everyone at the piano, I was hard at work."

"Like I said, the made to order stu—"

I dropped my foot down to the floor with a loud bang. "Stop that, already!"

"What?" she asked innocently.

"Just...don't do it anymore, okay?" my tone was curt. "I can't stand it when you call me that name and you act cute and take advantage. You do whatever you want to do and then—"

"And then I come to someone I *think* is a friend and I ask for help."

"Right. I'm a friend when it's convenient for you. You leave everything for the last minute because you're sure you can come to me and—"

"Okay, forget it," she turned away from me. "Forget I ever asked."

I'm doing the right thing, I reassured myself while I watched her walk to the door. *I know I am. Maybe now she'll start taking some responsibility.*

When she reached the door, she suddenly turned around to face me. I was surprised to see tears in her eyes, but even more surprised by the sincerely remorseful tone of her voice. "I just want you to know, Sara, I never intended to take advantage of you. And, I'm truly sorry if you think I did. I really didn't plan on doing the report and I thought I'd get away with it, but…"

"But what?"

"Forget it. It doesn't make a difference anyway."

I was at the door in seconds. "What was the *but*, Mimi? Did something happen?"

"Excuse me, Sara. I'd like to leave."

My foot was blocking the door and preventing her from opening it. "Tell me," I insisted.

For a long moment she looked at me and I looked back at her. Neither of us said a word.

And then I saw it. That same troubled look. But this time it did not pass.

Mimi did not break out in her usual throaty laugh, pretending she did not have a care in the world. Instead, she did something I never expected. She released her grip on the doorknob, walked to a stack of mattresses, sat down on the top one, and with her elbows on her knees and face in her palms began to sob.

What in the world?

I stood motionless, my foot frozen in place—still blocking the door, listening to the terrible sounds of Mimi crying.

What's wrong with me? How could I be so cruel?

I wanted to run over to her, I wanted to beg…to plead with her. Anything so stop the crying. But I could not move.

Suddenly the sobs stopped and Mimi looked up. Her face was red and blotchy. "Sara, why are you still standing there like that?" she sniffled.

"I—I…I'm horrible, Mimi," I moved away from the door and took a few steps toward her. "Of course, I'll help you."

She shook her head and then burst out laughing through her tears. "No, Sara. That's not what I meant."

I sat down next to her, the old, dusty mattresses creaking under my weight. "I'll help you. We'll start tonight. We'll figure out exactly what to do...we'll make a schedule for the next twelve days."

"No, Sara," she shook her head again. "Forget it."

"Please forgive me. I want to help—"

"Sara, stop it already. You've got to stop apologizing."

"But I was wrong."

"You were a hundred percent right, Sara. You're a good friend."

"I'm a horrible friend," I shook my head in disgust, "horrible!"

"You're wrong, Sara. You're the first *real* friend I ever had."

"Huh?" I looked at her, shocked.

"Yes," she nodded. "You're the only one who takes me seriously. You're honest. You care."

I nodded. "I do care, Mimi."

"I know."

"So what's the problem? I'm going to help you with your report. Just tell me...when can we start?"

"Sara, this time I want to be a real friend to you. I'll...I'll manage. I don't want to bother you."

"I've almost finished my report. I really can help you."

"No, Sara. You were absolutely right. I've been taking advantage of you...but really, I never meant to. I guess I just didn't realize. But I was wrong and I'm glad that you pointed it out to me."

"It really wasn't so bad. I must be a little overtired. I didn't really mean—"

"Sara, don't ruin things by taking back what you said when you were finally being honest with me." She looked me straight in the eye. "You weren't speaking out of tiredness or anger. You were saying what was bottled up inside you for a while."

"Now you sound like the psychiatrist, Mimi."

"It must be your influence, Sara."

"Well, if I'm so influential, then listen to me and let me help you do the report."

"This is really almost funny. Now *you're* almost begging *me* to let you help me."

"It's not funny, Mimi. I feel bad about giving you a hard time. I *want* to help you."

"No, Sara," she shook her head determinedly, "and I'm not trying to manipulate you this time by playing 'hard to get.' Now that I realize how much I took advantage of you—no, Sara, let me finish, don't interrupt—now that I've been made aware, I refuse to do it anymore. I'll just go to Rabbi Grossman, admit the truth, and hope—"

"Hope for what, Mimi?"

"And hope..." her voice trailed off.

"Mimi...hope for what? What were you going to say?"

"Hope?" she made an effort to sound jovial. "Did I say hope?"

She's hiding something and I'm not going to let her get away with it this time!

"Mimi...please! Real friends aren't afraid to..." I stopped. "Unless you didn't really mean it...about me being your first real friend."

"Of course I meant it, but...well," Mimi bit her lip. "Oh, all right, Sara. Right after supper tonight I got a message that Rabbi Grossman wanted to speak to me. I thought that maybe he was upset about something that happened that day with Ossy, I mean, Rabbi Ossenfeld, but no. That wasn't what he called me in about."

"So what was it?"

"Well, it's a long story, but, well...I was accepted here on a trial basis only."

"What?"

"Why are you so surprised? I know you've been wondering what I was doing in M.B.L.L. in the first place. *I'm* not exactly the made-to-order student."

I did not say anything.

"As you know, I first found out that I was coming here the day before we left...when someone who was supposed to go suddenly backed out."

"I...I heard about that."

"But then we got the phone call."

"The phone call about the vacant spot?"

"Yes. You see, Sara. I never even thought of going to M.B.L.L., but someone else did."

"Someone else?"

"Yup. My parents."

"They wanted you to go?"

Chapter 22

"And how!" she nodded. "You know, I'm very different from the rest of my family."

"So?"

"So, that difference has made me who I am. You see, they're all, well…"

My eyebrows lifted. "They're all…what?"

"Brilliant!"

"So what? Who cares? That makes you different?"

"I'm not just talking smart, Sara, or *very* smart either. We're talking…exceptionally brilliant."

I did not say anything.

"Okay, I'll start with my sister. She's the director of the Crane Clinic. Prestigious, no?"

I squirmed. "Yes…um…you could say that."

"And my mother. She's a physician with a private practice in Manhattan *and* she teaches at N.Y.U. So are you beginning to get the idea?"

I nodded.

"Now, on to my father. Besides having written three *sefarim* on his own, he edited the recent Greenfeld Judaic Encyclopedia series and—"

"Really?" I blurted out. "I had no idea."

"And besides all the writing and editing my father does, he's also a well-known professor."

I swallowed hard. There was this lump in my throat that kept growing as Mimi spoke.

She went on. "And my brother who's studying in kollel, was asked…no, *begged* to join them. They almost *never* take in newlyweds. Everyone says that he's a future *Rosh Yeshivah*. So, you know, we're not exactly talking average here. And then," she gave out one of her deep, throaty laughs, "there's me, Mimi the Mimic or Mimi the Clown. You choose."

My eyes were filling. I could not say anything.

"I see you're getting the picture. So, now you understand. My parents couldn't have me…their child…stay home from seminary and take some low-level job."

"You could get a teaching position, Mimi. I've seen how you interact with the kids in the resource room."

"Please, Sara. Don't ruin our friendship now by giving me a false compliment."

"It's not false…You do a great job there!"

"Well even if we pretend that you're being honest, Sara, we both know that the resource room is not *really* teaching, it's not a real classroom. It's just…"

"Just, what, Mimi?"

"You see…in the resource room…I feel so…so…"

"Yes?"

"I feel…well…at home."

"What do you mean?"

She looked at me long and hard. "Sara, I trust you. So I'm going to tell you something I never ever in my whole life told anyone."

I was afraid to move.

"All my years in school—ever since I was a little kid—I never felt that I belonged. I always felt like an outsider."

"You, an outsider?" I whispered.

"Yes. Oh, I know I pretended…I made it look like I belonged. I learned how to do it from a very young age. And you know what? I became really good at it." Then suddenly she started laughing, a strange hollow laugh. "Ha, ha. An expert at faking! See, there's something I excel at."

"You're wrong," I shook my head slowly, my eyes welling. "You're good at a lot of things."

"Mimicking, clowning…"

"Being warm and friendly. Helping people feel like *they* belong."

"Taking advantage of people, manipulating…" her eyes were brimming.

"No, Mimi," I shook my head slowly, my tears falling onto my cheeks.

"Sara, I'm sorry. I didn't mean to make you cry."

"Don't worry about me, Mimi. I cry very easily. Especially when the person next to me is crying."

"I'll try to stop," she sniffed, "so now, you've got to."

"Okay," I reached into my pocket and, taking out two clean tissues, handed one to Mimi. "Here."

She took it and blew her nose. I blew mine.

All at once, we started laughing.

Mimi let out a sudden deep sigh. "Sara, thank you. This feels so good."

"What does?"

"This cry. For once I was able to just…let go."

"I'm glad."

"It's not easy always pretending…always putting on an act."

"I can imagine."

"Talking like this made me feel so natural. So free…"

"There were times, Mimi, when we were talking, that I'd see something in your face—that something was bothering you…"

"Oh, no! And I thought I was such a good actress. I hope no one else—"

"You know no one else noticed anything, Mimi. You *are* good at it. So good, that at first I thought I was imagining it. But really, just because you're not like your family—that doesn't make you an outsider. It doesn't mean you won't be able to get a decent job."

"Sara, you still don't understand."

"Understand what?"

Mimi blushed and looked at the floor. "It's not just that I'm not like my family."

"What do you mean?"

"Sara, I…I have problems learning. From the beginning it's been very hard for me."

"But…"

"I used to wonder…What's wrong with me? Why can't I read and write like everyone else?

"Mimi…I'm so sorry," my tears were starting again.

"Pre1A. The others were learning the *alef-beis* and I couldn't identify all the letters until I reached third grade. And even then I would mix up the letters all the time. Even now, lots of times I confuse the *shin*s and *sin*s, the *gimmel*s and *zayin*s. And the English alphabet wasn't much better."

"Oh…Mimi."

"And the teachers. Sara, don't ask. Some were young and didn't know better; but some of the more experienced ones realized that I had a problem. Now, remember, back then there was no such thing as a resource room. Only the dumb kids had tutors. My parents refused to hear that their precious daughter could possibly have a learning problem. Denial. Yep, they were definitely in denial.."

"But, Mimi, maybe—"

"Now, Sara, don't get the wrong impression. My parents are good people. They're loving in their own way. But, sometimes brilliance just makes you...out of touch. They never had me tested or diagnosed, you know—all that stuff that Geveret Spitz has been teaching us about. Then again, I'm not sure those kinds of tests even existed ten years ago. Anyway, it doesn't matter. They wouldn't have allowed me to be tested, even if the tests were readily available." She paused. "Actually, my mother and father would have had access to such tests. But, no," Mimi shook her head.

I shook *my* head.

"There's no way that their child could be stupid. Lazy?" Mimi nodded firmly. "Yes. Overtired? Yes. Not making an effort? Sure. But, not brilliant? No! You know, Sara, despite or maybe *because* of their brilliance, they really had no clue."

I just looked at her, my vision blurred by my tears. *What could I say?*

"But, I knew," she continued, "I knew...I was dumb."

"Stop saying that, Mimi."

"I'm just telling you the truth."

"Mimi...if you were...so dumb...then you wouldn't be so successful at so much."

"You mean the production?"

"Yes," I nodded vigorously, "and all those instruments that you play so easily. And your sense of humor and your perceptive abilities. No, Mimi, stop laughing. It's true. Somehow, you know how to get to people. That's an important skill."

"Don't you see? I *had* to do those things. When my classmates would laugh at my mistakes, I...I wouldn't let myself get hurt. Instead, I found different ways to compensate. Either I would turn my mistake into some kind of joke or I would be the class clown in other ways. So, my wonderful sense of humor isn't really so wonderful.

"The mimicking helped me a lot too. I'd get the kids to read to me by promising them that if they did, I'd impersonate them to a T. I'd make a whole show out of closing my eyes to concentrate on their voices. And it really helped me remember what they read. Oh, they loved it when I mimicked them! I'd do the imitations with different accents just to make it a bit more fun, and this way it would appear spontaneous. No one had a clue."

"Mimi, don't you see?" I tried again. "That also takes a certain kind of brilliance."

It was as though I had not spoken. I think that once Mimi was finally beginning to unburden herself, she could not absorb anything else.

"I'm the baby in my family. I felt that if I couldn't get my parents' approval by bringing home excellent report cards like my older siblings, I'd have to win them over in other ways.

"Yes…despite my poor academic achievements, they loved my play acting. They'd sit through my performances, my puppet shows, the plays I directed. Sara, they really were a great audience."

I nodded.

"When my parents saw how music came so easily to me, they encouraged me. And so I went from one grade to the next, living for the summers…desperate for camp, where schoolwork didn't matter and where my musical accomplishments and acting abilities were appreciated. *Really* appreciated!"

Again, I nodded, afraid to talk.

"And I quickly learned how to joke my way out of difficult situations and to win approval in ways that, well…I know you don't approve of."

"Please, Mimi."

"So now, Sara, the big question after all this is: How did I end up here?"

I looked at her. It was awful to see Mimi like this…to hear about all she had been through. Mimi, who always managed to break down others' barriers, had erected one around herself…hiding inside and trying to find protection.

"Anyway, as I was saying," finally Mimi *wanted* to talk and I, of course, wanted, no, *needed* to listen.

"I wasn't supposed to come. I begged my parents not to pressure me about it and they begged me to try it.

"My father had been a very close *talmid* of Rabbi Goldstone a long time ago. Later on, he became good friends with Rabbi Grossman, Rabbi Goldstone's relative. They kept in touch over the years. My father helped Rabbi Grossman with various projects, enabling him to get certain grants from America for his school. He had also helped him over the years with other things.

"Anyway, every once in a while Rabbi Grossman takes into his *very difficult to get into seminary* a girl to be his "personal challenge," and he turns her into a success story. Did you know that, Sara?"

"No," I shook my head. "I had no idea."

"Of course, my father wanted it to be *me* this year. And, of course, when Rabbi Grossman checked me out, he didn't think it would work. My father must have tried everything at his disposal to convince Rabbi Grossman to change his mind, but he kept turning my father down."

I looked at Mimi with admiration. There was not a trace of self-pity or bitterness in her voice.

"Believe me," she said, "I was relieved. I didn't want to go. I was really glad that Rabbi Grossman didn't want me. But then we got that phone call."

"The phone call saying that you *could* come."

She nodded. "Yep, but it wasn't so simple. You see, the funny thing is, Rabbi Grossman must have been feeling stressed at the time. He really meant to call a girl who had been on the waiting list from the previous year. A girl by the last name of Rosenblum.

"Anyway, my father picked up the phone and was already a few minutes into the conversation with Rabbi Grossman when the mistake was discovered."

"Wow," I said.

"And, you should know, not only is my father brilliant, but he's persistent. I don't know whether he said it first or whether Rabbi Grossman said it first, but one of them said it and the other one agreed that perhaps this mistake was *bashert* and I was meant to come after all."

"So, Mimi, you see—"

"Well, I sure didn't agree about it being *bashert*. I absolutely wouldn't hear of it. My father, my mother, my sister, and even my brother all the way from Australia did whatever they could to convince me that I couldn't let an opportunity like this pass me by.

"They waved the idea of the *tiyulim* in front of me. They spoke about the yearly Chanukah production...Well, to make a long story short, I'm here."

"I'm glad about that, Mimi. I really am."

"But Rabbi Grossman made it very clear to me that I'm on trial until Chanukah. So, I figured, *great*. I'll work on the performance. I'll make it so good, they'll be begging me to stay." She winked. "Well, not exactly begging me, but I did think...I hoped I'd be able to get away with things."

"You were used to that."

"True. And maybe I was relying on you more than I should have. I was so used to getting people to help me with the schoolwork. So, I really thought I'd manage." She regarded me approvingly, "Sara, you're really great at what you do."

"Thanks," I said weakly.

"But then the studying was getting to be too much. I felt like I couldn't take it anymore and I decided I wanted to leave. No more reports or other schoolwork. And I became even more involved in the production, shutting everything else out of my mind."

"I know."

"That is...until tonight," she continued. "Suddenly, out of the blue, Rabbi Grossman called me into his office. He asked me how everything was going. He wanted to know how my report was coming along. Of course, there was no way I could tell him the truth."

"Of course not."

"He mentioned that he heard I was very busy with the Chanukah production. He wanted to know how often you and I get together to study. Then he mentioned that he had received a telephone call earlier today from the father of one of the girls on the waiting list."

My stomach took a sudden dip.

"This girl, even though she was accepted into M.B.L.L. for this year, had to back out at the last minute because of a *simchah* in the family. This girl's father..."

Did she mean Chavie's father?

"...was calling to remind Rabbi Grossman that his daughter would be available to come right after Chanukah, since that *simchah* would be over then. It seems that the father *expected* a specific slot to open up after Chanukah. He thought that one of the girls here was leaving—for some reason or another."

That dip in my stomach was fast turning into a grinding sensation.

"Anyway, I don't know if he was talking about *me* or someone else. Do you think someone else is planning on leaving?" she mused aloud.

"I-I have no idea," I replied hesitantly.

"Well, one thing's for sure. *I'm* not leaving because of a *simchah*, no way," she laughed. "Besides, how could they possibly know about my situation and that I'd been thinking of leaving? Sara, you're the only one I told."

I'm the only one she told...

"All I can say is that while I was talking with Rabbi Grossman, I felt like he was saying something to me...without actually saying it. It was almost as though he was reminding me that my trial period was almost over and that nothing, no production or anything else, should stand in the way of my report or other work. Maybe by telling me about this other girl, he was showing me that he had no problem at all filling my spot here."

With Chavie? I shouldn't have written to Chavie. But I need her...

"Hello...Sara...are you with me?"

"What?"

"I was asking you, do you think that's the reason Rabbi Grossman asked how often we get together to study? Do you think he was reminding me of my trial period? Do you think he's warning me that I shouldn't be putting all my energy into the Chanukah production and that I need to hand in the report on time?"

"Yes...probably."

"Sara, the weird thing about this whole thing is...now that I feel like it might be taken away from me...I don't want to leave anymore. I want to stay. I can't do this to my parents. If I leave or if I'm forced to leave, they'll be devastated. Can you imagine how embarrassed they'll be in front of all our neighbors in Barclay if I should suddenly turn up in the middle of the year? Anyway, I really do want them to be proud of me."

"I'm sure that they're proud of you already."

"No," she shook her head emphatically. "Proud of *me*...not of my performances. I want them to be really proud of me. I know it seems crazy, but I have this dream. And every time I think of it, I feel like my heart is flying. I mean, I know it's impossible...but, I wish...I wish that even the possibility could be true. Please, don't laugh!"

"I'm not laughing," I said. I was almost crying.

"I want to be the winner of the Goldstone Award. I know it's nuts...absolutely nuts. But...can you imagine how proud my family would finally be of me?"

I swallowed hard, nodding.

"I'm picturing it, Sara," she continued earnestly.

I felt some kind of agony deep within me pushing its way to the surface. And it had nothing to do with feelings of competition or fears of Mimi being the winner. Shivering, I wrapped my arms around my chest and all I could think was...*poor Mimi.*

Through blurry eyes, I saw her stand up and lift her chin determinedly. She was facing me, but she was gazing elsewhere...seeing something that only she could see.

"Yep, there I am," she said dramatically, but in a tone that was more serious than I had ever heard her use, "at the Arrivals gate in Kennedy Airport. I'm walking toward my parents, the precious paper in my hand. And then, I pass it over to my father and he can't believe his eyes. His hands are shaking from excitement. He's holding the award named after his beloved teacher and my name, Miriam Mina Rosenberg, has been filled in as the recipient of the award." She turned to me, the tears rolling unabatedly down her cheeks, "Can you imagine that, Sara? Can't you just picture it?"

23

"IS THERE A problem, Sara? You have much difficulty with the report?" Mazal twisted around to face me.

"N-no, Mazal," I looked up from the paper on which I was writing. "I'm practically finished, *baruch Hashem*. I just have a little more to wrap up."

"Wrap?" her dark eyes widened in surprise. "You make the report into *matanah*?"

"No," I shook my head, poised to write, "Wrap up. It means to end off…summarize."

"Summer? Rise?"

"No, no, Mazal," I let out an exasperated sigh, still clutching my pen. "It means the end…*sof*!"

"Oh…I am sorry." I glimpsed the hurt look on her face before she turned back to her desk. "I bother you. I say a lot mistakes in English."

"No, Mazal, please. It's not your fault." I put my pen down and went to her. "I'm sorry. I love helping you with your English." I sat down in the other chair at the desk. "I'm just very frustrated with something."

"I do not understand," she looked into my eyes, "You say you wrap-up report and you ready for the *sof*. Then what is the problem?"

"I'm not sure, Mazal. I can't really talk about it."

"When the weight of a problem is heavy, it is lighter when two people carry it."

I stood up and tried to smile. "That's true, Mazal, my mother always tells me that…but…this time I—I can't."

"Okay," she turned back to what she was doing. "I continue my work."

"It's not just about me, Mazal," I found myself suddenly saying. "Otherwise, I would tell you."

"Okay," she said, still hunched over her books. "*Ain ba'ayah.*"

Stuffing my pillow behind my back, I leaned my head against the wall, letting out another deep sigh. *What should I do?*

I looked at the last sheet of paper I had intended to write the closing paragraphs of my report on and saw that it was full of doodling, scribbled notes, and thoughts which had nothing to do with my report for Geveret Spitz. My eyes quickly scanned over what I wrote.

> If I don't help Mimi, then Mimi might be sent home. Then Chavie could come. But how can I do this to Mimi? She really needs me. But, Chavie's my best friend. I need her and she needs to come. Am I being disloyal to Chavie if I help Mimi? It could be it's just a waste of time with Mimi. But, shouldn't I try? She's so desperate…but then Chavie wants to come so desperately…and I desperately want her to come. I'm learning to manage without Chavie…but if it wasn't for Chavie, I never would've come here in the first place. Chavie wants to be here so badly. But can Mimi face her family if she's sent home? But if we do manage to finish the report on time…then what? She stays and Chavie can't come? I can't do that to Chavie.
>
> Poor Chavie!
> Poor Mimi!!
> Poor, poor me!!!

What am *I supposed to do? Oh, this is just impossible!* Maddeningly, I took the paper I had just read, crumpled it up into a tiny ball, and threw it into the pile on my bed of other balls of crushed paper.

I took a deep breath. *I've got to do the right thing. Yes, I need to know what to do. I wish there were someone I could talk to…to ask. But I can't do that without betraying Mimi. So, what should I do?*

If I don't help Mimi, then probably Chavie will get to come. If I help Mimi and she stays, then Chavie can't come.

Sara, you always wanted to be this great heroine, and now, when someone is drowning, you're just going to let her sink?

And what about Mimi's wanting to win the Goldstone Outstanding Student Teacher Award? How does that affect me?

It doesn't affect you, Sara, not at all. And you know that more than anyone else does.

It was so sad, so pathetic. My heart went out to her and I only hoped that, for her sake, she was not serious about wanting to be the winner.

Just then, there was a quick knock at the door and Mimi *(is there really such a thing as mental telepathy?)* sauntered into the room. "Hey, Sara," her face was flushed and she sounded out of breath, "here you are. I've—"

"Oh my gosh," I jumped off the bed, suddenly remembering that Mimi and I had planned to meet at a quarter to five to study. "I completely forgot. What time is it already?"

"It's five-fifteen, Miss On Time Hirsch. I waited and waited for you in the library and then decided to check if maybe you fell asleep or something."

"Mimi, Sara been working very hard. She sure not sleeping," Mazal informed her.

"Sara, working hard? Impossible!"

"Mimi, I'll be ready in a minute. That is, as soon as I clear up this mess." I gathered all the crumpled balls of paper from my bed and headed toward the wastebasket near the desk.

"So where do you want to study, Sara?" Mimi followed me to the desk, while I quickly disposed of the papers that held the secrets of my dilemma. "I really don't think the library is the best place, after all. You know me, with all the girls hanging around there, I'll probably get distracted." She glanced doubtfully in Mazal's direction, where she was hunched over working diligently. "How about your room?"

"Not a good idea." I shook my head then added in a hurried whisper, "A few girls asked Mazal to help them with *Chumash*."

"Oh," Mimi pressed her lips together. "Um...let's see. The lounge won't work either. It's even busier than the library, especially with that gorgeous piano just waiting to be played. How about the storage room?"

I bent down to retrieve a couple of squashed pieces of paper I had dropped on the floor. "Did you say the storage room?"

"Yep, but maybe that's not such a great idea. It's really so musty down there. Um…"

"I guess your room is out. Adina is probably studying there."

"Actually, I was just about to suggest it. Adina was studying there earlier, but when I was coming up the steps to find you, I saw her walking down. So, maybe I'll get to use it for a change."

"Okay," I nodded. "That's probably the best place, then. If you think it'll be all right with Adina, that is."

"It's my room too, you know."

"Fine. I'll be there in a few seconds. Let me just put my room back in order and get all my stuff together. And, I'm sorry I kept you waiting so long."

"No prob! As long as we get my report done on time," Mimi sang out, while exiting the room through the wash-up closet. "It'll be all right. Sara's so bright. My report we'll complete, in a beat, that's no easy feat, it'll be really neat…"

I could still hear her voice singing away in her room as I went about gathering my things. Mazal and I looked at each other.

"That Mimi," Mazal smiled at me before resuming her work, "she is all the time happy. No problems for her to wrap up."

Right, I kicked my slippers under my bed and stepped into my shoes, *no problems for her*. I lifted my blanket and shook it forcefully in the air. *If only that were true*, I thought, while punching my pillow hard before placing it against the headboard. Recalling that talk I had with Mazal about baggage, I thought about Mimi and how she was carrying one of the heaviest pieces of baggage around.

No, Mimi could no longer hide behind that cheery mask with me…but then again, had she really ever been completely successful in camouflaging it when we were together? *Hadn't I almost from the beginning suspected that Mimi was not really as she appeared to be?* Still, now I knew for sure. And I was certain that once she had let me in, our relationship would never—could never—be the same.

I felt a mingling of compassion and admiration for Mimi. She had suffered for so long, never sharing her pain with her own parents. That alone was horrifying. Yet, while shouldering this burden by herself, she somehow managed to remain so cheerful and warm. *How does she do it?* I knew that I could never be that way. My feelings would never readily submit to being hidden away in some secret part of me.

And as expected, when a few minutes later I joined her in her room, her problems were not at all evident. Had I not had that late night conversation with Mimi, I too would have thought she had "no problems to wrap up." Mimi was practicing her "smile and the world smiles with you" philosophy unabatedly, with her demeanor as jolly as ever. She sat at her desk humming cheerfully, her dazzling smile brightening the space around her. The only difference between the old Mimi and the new one was that she was actually sitting at her desk and her notebook and *sefer* were opened to the right place.

I was genuinely surprised. *She really is taking this seriously. She wasn't kidding.*

We wasted no time. First, we reviewed the homework that was due for the next day. Next, we reviewed some *meforshim* that we needed to know for the *Chumash* midterm. Then we decided to tackle her report. Leafing through the papers she showed me, I was awed by the amount of material she had managed to gather in two days.

Actually, for the last two days—ever since our Tuesday night talk—the new Mimi had not ceased to amaze me. Sure, she was the same in terms of her jovial disposition, warm nature, and breezy personality. But I saw a difference. Suddenly from her there were no comments, no disturbances, no interruptions. She sat diligently, writing and trying to pay attention. This certainly was not the same Mimi.

And when we worked together, again her conscientiousness surprised me. She was always on time, had all her supplies with her, and did not interrupt…even once.

I wondered, though, how long this would last. I knew that, right now, getting the report completed on time was uppermost in her mind. I could only speculate as to what would happen afterward.

"So what do you think?" she asked anxiously, as I turned the pages of her scribbled report. "Is my idea any good? Do you think I'll be able to finish everything before next Monday?"

"I didn't read what you have yet, Mimi. I'm just glancing through it. It looks good. Yes…and it's really interesting. Wow…that's an original idea," I said as I flipped to one of the pages and read the title on top, "what made you think of doing an interview?"

"Well, when I was working with Riki yesterday, I figured that the best way to get to her probably was by doing this interview. You think it was a good idea?"

"I think it's fantastic. It's so original…so creative!"

"Really?"

"Absolutely," I replied, and I meant it. I continued perusing the pages, though it was not easy. Her handwriting was atrocious and her spelling was not much better, but as an experienced tutor I probably was able to decipher this sort of writing better than most people. "And this, Mimi. What is this about? The keys to the different child? Is this Ronit?"

"Yep. I hope you don't mind, Sara. I know that Ronit is really your student…but…Geveret Spitz did say that we should also think about our partner's student, and I wanted to show how the same key that works with Riki isn't going to help Ronit…"

Mimi and I continued working, our heads bent together over her desk.

I had to admit. Her ideas were atypical, but they made sense. I was not sure, though, if these original channels of thinking would be accepted by the standard educational system. *It's really not bad*, I thought as I turned the pages. It was, actually, quite…inspiring. I just hoped that the *Hanhallah* would agree with us.

With us.

Yes, I was in this with Mimi…all the way. Once I made up my mind to help her, I would do all that I could. I would be that heroine tossing out the life preserver and pulling her safely to shore. I could not allow myself to think of Chavie.

As I continued reading, the beauty of Mimi's message came through to me even louder and clearer. It really was excellent, and I had no doubt that Geveret Spitz would think so too. And if Geveret Spitz approved, then the other faculty members would hopefully approve as well.

However, before this report could be submitted, we had our work cut out for us. Mimi had written the report in English and we needed to translate it into Hebrew. Also, it was written in a rather unsystematic and disorganized manner. That too would have to be rectified.

It was Thursday night. The next day, Friday, Mimi would be traveling with Mazal for Shabbos up North to Kiryat Yosef and they would not be returning until late Motza'ei Shabbos. That meant we had only one week left to finish everything. We were definitely cutting things close.

But, we would do it!

We continued working. We heard the girls bustling in the hallways, heading downstairs for supper. We continued working. We heard the girls returning to their rooms. We continued working. We heard someone knocking at the door. We continued working. The knocking persisted.

We looked up.

Mazal entered the room, pushing the door open with her shoulder. She was carrying a tray from downstairs filled with food.

"Mazal!" I stood up and ran to help her.

"Thank you, thank you, thank you," Mimi eyed the food and rubbed her stomach simultaneously. "The boss wouldn't let me stop."

"You have boss who is good friend who does much work with you, Mimi." Mazal placed the tray on the desk. "I think you two professors need to eat."

"Thanks so much, Mazal," I eagerly looked over the contents of the tray. "It must have been hard for you lugging all of this up to the third floor."

"No prob!" Mazal winked at Mimi. "It my pleasure."

There were fresh lachmaniyot, a few slices of halvah, two glasses of hot tea, two chocolate lebens, babaganush, and a dollop of techinah spooned onto the center of one of the plates.

My stomach rumbled. I had not realized how hungry I was. Within a few minutes, we were eating heartily and chatting with Mazal, who was sitting on Mimi's bed, munching on chocolate sandwich cookies.

I do not remember the babaganush ever tasting so flavorsome nor do I recall lachmaniyot being so soft and scrumptious as they were right then. The sweet (a bit sweeter than I was used to) tea went down smoothly and I enjoyed nibbling on the halvah along with it.

I was feeling rather content and pleased with myself. I had conquered the urge to do what was good for *me*. I could have ignored Mimi and hoped that Chavie would come and take her place. Instead, I did what seemed to be the right thing. And, everything was working out nicely.

Mimi and I would have a friendship unlike anything I had ever imagined. Until then, I thought I had needed her to help me manage with the loneliness of Sem life. I had hoped that her happy-go-lucky attitude and cheerful disposition would rub off on me and help me become a part of things…hopefully leading me to feel that I belonged. I now knew better. I was making friends on my own, slowly but steadily. I enjoyed being with Mimi, because who would not like being with someone with her sunny temperament, but I did not *need* her in the way I had thought. I knew, though, that Mimi needed *me*. And, I had to admit, something about that newly discovered knowledge made me feel good.

"Hel-lo, Sara!" Mimi's voice cut through my reverie. "No, Mazal, she hasn't heard a word you or I said. She's in her own dreamy world."

"What?" I blinked. "Did one of you just ask me something?"

"We try," Mazal smiled, "but as Mimi did say, you in your own world."

"I—I'm sorry. What was it?" I looked from one to the other.

"I was asking Mazal about Kiryat Yosef and I wanted to know when you'll let me start packing, boss. I can't wait to get there and—"

"Pardon me."

We looked toward the doorway. Adina was standing at the threshold, her blue eyes flashing angrily.

"Oh hi, Adina," Mimi said nonchalantly, while reaching into Mazal's box of cookies. "Welcome. Have some—"

"I do not care to participate in your parties," she surveyed the mess on her side of the desk. "I'd appreciate it if—"

"C'mon, Adina. Calm down and stop being so—"

"I'm sorry, Adina," I cut in, quickly rising, "I thought—"

"I don't care what you thought, Sara," she hissed, causing me to freeze in place. "I would have thought that you had some semblance of respect for someone else's privacy by now."

"Please, Adina, we didn't mean—"

"I'm not interested in what you meant!"

"Come. Let us take the food to the next room," Mazal said calmly, while piling the food on the tray. "We very sorry, Adina."

"Uh huh, believe it or not, we were just trying to study and eat at the same time," Mimi informed her, while lifting her cup of tea. "Sorry, Adinaleh."

Adinaleh?

"Don't you dare call me that!" Adina rasped through clenched teeth.

Mimi flinched. "I was only trying to lighten things up a little. Seriously, Adina, calm down."

"Who do you think you are to tell me to calm down?" Adina's face suddenly crumpled, losing its frosty expression. "Get out! All of you get out of here."

"I—I," Mimi shrugged her shoulders helplessly, her eyes widening in shock. For once, she did not have anything to say.

Adina flung herself down on her bed, burying her face in her pillow. *Is she crying?* It did not seem so. She was lying there stiff and unmoving—which, in a way, was even more frightening than if she had been sobbing.

Mimi looked frightened. Lifting her eyebrows and shoulders questioningly, she turned to Mazal and me, unsure of what to do. Mazal gently placed a hand on her back, guiding her out of the room while carrying the tray strewn with the leftover food.

I remained where I was, rooted to the same spot I had been standing in. "Adina," I attempted. My voice was hardly audible.

No response.

"Adina," I tried again.

Again, there was no response.

I took a step toward her and whispered, "Adina, I'm really sorry."

"Just get out and leave me alone," her voice was muffled in her pillow.

"Adina, please—"

"Please?' she slowly lifted her head off the pillow and turned to me. *No, not a tear on her face…just anger. Cold, frigid anger.* "Please, what? Please forgive you again for infringing on my privacy? For breaking the rules and bringing supper upstairs, for—"

"I know we're really not supposed to," I explained hoarsely, "but, you know this is one of the rules that they're really not so strict about—"

"That's no excuse. This is *my* room—not some public domain for you to come into and do as you please," her tone was icy. "And I thought you learned your lesson—"

"I did, Adina, please don't be angry—"

"Just get out of here already. I'm sick of you and everyone else in this place."

"I—"

"No, don't start feeling sorry now. You should've thought about that before…before you and your pals decided to party in my room. Just get out and leave me alone. I wish I could go home and never have to see you or anyone else here again!"

I left.

And I wondered. Does she mean it? Will she really go home? And if she does, could it be…is there a possibility that Chavie could come and take her place?

24

WHEN I SMILINGLY waved goodbye to Mazal and Mimi the next day, I felt a wave of emotions I had never really experienced before. True, that lump in my throat was not unfamiliar and the uneasy feeling that comes with not having close ones near me was not foreign either. But something else must have been disturbing me—because it was not loneliness I was feeling.

So what was it? What was tugging at me and making me feel so…

No! It can't be! Sara, you're not the jealous type.

But is that what I'm feeling? Am I feeling sorry for myself because I'm not with Mazal and Mimi is going instead?

No, I tried telling myself, *you're not allowed to be like that. Just because you've become so close to Mazal, it doesn't mean you have exclusive rights to Kiryat Yosef and the Cohen family or to your friendship with Mazal.*

Or Mimi.

After all, aren't both of them your friends? Real friends?

Each of them—separately—had told you that you're a real friend. And they had both spoken spontaneously…

"B'emet, Sara, you are real friend to me," Mazal had said. And that had been before my trip to Kiryat Yosef, when I had drawn so close to her and her family. And then, this past Tuesday night, Mimi told me, "You're the first real friend I ever had…"

So why in the world am I suddenly feeling so threatened?

"Sara…"

Are you afraid, that if the two of them become real friends with each other, then you'll no longer be in the picture?

"Uh...Sara..."

Are you so insecure in your relationship with Mazal and Mimi that your friendship with each of them can't...

"Sara?"

...Can't be shared?

"He-llo, Sara...are you okay?"

"Huh?" I swung around. "Oh, Zehava, I didn't see you."

We were standing in the dormitory's lobby. My eyes quickly swept around the large entranceway and I could see girls milling about, many with overnight bags slung over their shoulders, making their farewells.

"I know. You didn't seem to see me or anyone else," Zehava laughed lightly. "I've been trying to get your attention for the last...whatever."

"S-sorry. I was just...I—"

"You seemed so preoccupied."

"I did? Oh...I-I guess it's because I'm so zonked. I was up almost half the night."

"Studying? Schmoozing?"

"Both."

We began making our way toward the lounge.

"With?"

"With?" I repeated, unsure of what she wanted.

"With...oh, I'm sorry. I'm being nosy. I meant with whom? With whom were you studying and schmoozing? But that's all right," she sat down on the edge of the large, overstuffed couch leaning against the wall, while I sat down on the chair opposite her, "I really shouldn't have asked."

"Na...it's okay, it's no big deal. I was studying with Mimi."

"You and Mimi do lots of studying together. That's r-really nice."

"Well...I guess we enjoy each other's company...and...and..." I cleared my throat while fumbling for an explanation regarding our studying arrangement, not wanting to reveal anything about Rabbi Grossman's involvement or Mimi's learning problems, "and our studying habits... They...um...well...sort of complement each other, if you know what I mean."

"Yes...I think I know what you mean."

For a few moments neither of us said anything, then Zehava suddenly asked, "Did you know each other from before?"

"Who...me and Mimi?" I shook my head. "No, not at all."

"You became friends from just being here at M.B.L.L.?"

A warm feeling suddenly wrapped itself around me. "Well...yes, Zehava...from these last few months."

"That's really nice."

"I know."

A group of Israeli girls from Beit Yaakov HaNegbah came into the lounge. We watched them stroll over to the piano while bantering in rapid Hebrew. Two of the girls began to play the keyboard together, with one harmonizing the other. *They play so beautifully,* I thought as their music filled the air, *if Mimi would get together with them, then—*

"And...Sara?"

"What, Zehava?"

"How about you and Mazal? The two of you seem really close."

"W-we are. *Baruch Hashem.*"

"That...that's also...very nice."

"Yes...it is."

"It's really something..."

"What?"

"That she's Israeli and you're American. You don't exactly speak the same language, and yet you're able to—"

"Become such good friends?"

"Yes, that's just what I was going to say. And she's so different and everything—"

"Well...I guess...if...if someone... really has things in common with you ... you know, on the *inside*..."

"Then the Sephardi/Ashkenazi thing doesn't really matter?"

My back went rigid. "I'm not so sure what your're asking, Zehava. Mazal and I have more in common with each other than not. Maybe even more than people who come from the same background," I added indignantly.

Zehava did not seem to notice my sarcastic tone or my insinuation.

"So then, you must be happy that you and Mazal were put together in the same room."

I softened. These prejudices were probably not really her fault. "Maybe if we wouldn't have been put together as roommates we wouldn't have ended up being friends...but I'm sure glad we got to know each other."

"You know, Sara...my roommate and I are both American. Tova is really nice and everything...but well...we aren't exactly the same."

"*Exactly?*"

"Well...you know..."

"To be friends with someone, Zehava, you don't have to be exactly the same."

"But...well..."

"What?"

"Well, Sara...even you said that you and Mazal have a lot in common."

"That's true...but," I suddenly thought of Mimi and how it was our dissimilarities that brought us together. "But, you know, sometimes it can be even the opposite. Sometimes the differences between two people can complement each other."

"You mean like with you and Mimi?"

Even though *I* knew how different Mimi and I were—and that the others probably wondered why someone as popular as Mimi was hanging around with someone as simple as me—I was taken aback by her bluntness. "I guess so." *Everyone probably thinks we aren't really friends and that Mimi is just being nice to me.*

"Is that why you're such good friends...because you're so different?"

So people do think of Mimi and me as such good friends! I felt that warm glow enveloping me once again.

"I don't know, Zehava. I—"

"Maybe I haven't given Tova enough of a chance. I guess, I sort of...you know...me and Rochel Leah," her bottom lip caught between her teeth contemplatively for a few seconds, "But what you're saying has given me something to think about. Really."

"Thanks, Zehava. I never really gave it much thought before, myself."

Mimi and Mazal...did our friendship develop only because we were put together by circumstance? Mazal as my roommate and Mimi with our study sessions? Would we have become friends if we had not been put together? Something about this disturbed me. *Well, Hashem put us together for a reason,* I tried reassuring myself. *But what would happen if Mimi suddenly didn't need you or ...*

"I hope you don't mind me asking you all these questions, Sara, but...well... on Tuesday, you seemed to pick up on what I was feeling and I sort of was wondering," she hesitated, "I—I need to talk to someone."

"Of course, Zehava." I felt my heart opening, my own troubling thoughts gone.

"You know, I came here with Rochel Leah. I don't think I would have been able to come on my own like you did. I guess I sort of envy you, Sara."

"Envy me?" *Was I hearing correctly?*

"Yes. You shouldn't be so surprised. Most people wouldn't come on their own."

I should set her straight. "I was really very nervous, Zehava. Don't think I was so brave."

"Right...but, you did it."

"I guess I really must've wanted to come." *The Goldstone Award!*

"I wish I could be that way."

"Huh?"

"Look...you've made new friends. And me? Oh, I don't know what's with me today. I'm so embarrassed for talking like this."

"I—I'm...I'm flattered, Zehava that you're being so open."

"I get kind of worried that people will look down on me if I tell them how I really feel," Zehava's face was turning red. "You know what I mean?"

I sure do. I nodded, but did not say anything.

"I feel so foolish talking this way," Zehava continued.

"Don't. You don't have to pretend with me," I insisted.

"I believe you, Sara, I really do," she said. "It's just that not everyone is so...

"Zehava," I said quietly, "if someone is your *real* friend, then you should be able to trust and feel safe with her."

"*If* someone's a real friend…that's a big *if*—"

"Sara, Zehava," Tzila Green's sudden appearance brought an abrupt halt to our conversation. "Geveret Katz said that if anyone still wants to eat lunch, they should do it now. They're going to be washing the floors soon."

We thanked her for telling us and made our way into the dining room for a quick bite. Just a few girls were still lingering there.

Due to M.B.L.L.'s location in the upper Negev, classes finished early on Fridays so the girls would have plenty of time to travel to where they needed to go for Shabbos. Therefore, those who stayed behind usually found the dormitory to be unusually quiet by early Friday afternoon.

Too quiet.

At least that is how I felt about the dorm as I made my way up the stairs. *I wonder where their bus is now. Is Mimi finding the scenery as fascinating as I did? Is it possible that she's opened up to Mazal—and revealed the real Mimi? And what about Mazal? Does she think of Mimi as a good friend, the way she thinks of me?*

Come on, Sara. You've got to stop it! You can't keep thinking about them…

Then the other part of me came to my defense. *I can't help it if I'm suddenly feeling so lonely. I don't have any good friend here with me this Shabbos. I'm all alone. True, Zehava has opened up somewhat to me…but, Zehava's room isn't even on my floor.*

So who's left? Adina? Adina, who yelled at me the night before and who completely ignored me when I sat next to her this morning. *The night before…*

Does she mean it? Is she really going to leave?

Well, everything is in Hashem's hands, I tried reassuring myself. *And see, now Hashem is rewarding you for your sacrifice and making it all work out for you, Sara. You'll have done the right thing for Mimi and you'll have Chavie join you too—if Adina leaves. And, you won't have to deal with Adina's moodiness any longer.*

"Oops…sorry, Sara."

"Oh, hi, Malkie. *I'm* sorry. I wasn't watching where I was going."

"Anyway, I'm so glad to see you. This whole place is so empty! Do you know when we're supposed to go downstairs to set up?"

"Yes. Geveret Katz said that we have to be downstairs at two o'clock sharp."

"You think that'll leave enough time? I still have to take a shower afterwards or maybe I should take it before. And right now it's," she glanced at her watch, "Oh no! Have you seen Devorah or Adina anywhere?"

"Not recently."

"I don't believe it! They went to Kfar Amsdorf a while ago. They should've been back already!"

"Maybe they are."

"I was just in Devorah's room and she wasn't there. I'll walk you up to the third floor and I'll check on Adina," she said as we continued climbing the stairs. "They left so long ago and they're still not back?"

"Don't worry, Malkie. I'm sure everything's fine. I'm going into my room now, and you can check next door by Adina. If you still can't find them, let me know."

"Thanks, you're a doll, Sara. See you later."

I walked into my quiet and empty room. *Poor Malkie. She's always worried about something.*

"Sara," Malkie poked her head through the wash-up closet. "Just wanted you to know that Devorah and Adina are next door studying and everything's fine. See, there was nothing to worry about."

"I wasn't worried…" I stopped speaking. Malkie was no longer there.

I heard the sounds of studying and an occasional burst of laughter coming from the other room. *How come Adina manages to laugh with them?*

The lonely cloud surrounding me grew even thicker.

It was one-twenty. *I could take my shower now, but then again, what's the rush? Setting up downstairs shouldn't take more than a half-hour. There isn't too much competition for the showers on this floor (there's only Adina, me, and a couple of others), and knowing Adina I can safely assume that she's already taken hers and is probably completely prepared for Shabbos. I don't exactly have to worry about hot water either, because with so few girls staying for Shabbos there should be plenty. Maybe I'll*

Chapter 24

continue working on the Proyect. My report for Geveret Spitz was finished and Mimi and I were completely updated on our other work as well.

Mimi.

I sat down on my bed heavily.

What exactly is Mimi's problem, I pondered. *When I work with her she's able to grasp the lessons pretty easily. But that's probably because the majority of the time I'm the one doing the reading.*

Poor Mimi had erected a huge fence around herself since she began school many years ago, and I wondered if this fence—this fence that had been built with so much energy and for so many years—had really protected her or had it imprisoned her? Would she ever be able to set herself free?

Mimi had trained herself throughout the years to record everything that was being read to her, as though she were a tape recorder—to listen and absorb it all auditorily and then play it back whenever she needed. And the way she could figure out music and direct plays! Even choreography came easily to her. She certainly was very talented.

I thought of her relationship with her family. By making herself the center of attention and getting laughs from them all, she was able to win their approval and love despite being so unlike them. Yes, she could cover up her intellectual inferiority to them by playing up her special gifts…yet she could not escape the feeling that she was a disappointment to them.

How does she do it? I asked myself. *How can she carry around this huge burden and still act so cheerful all the time? I could never do it! I could never hide anything so major from my family—and I would never want to. Even with strangers—I would not be able to walk around smiling, as though everything was perfect. No, I was never a very good actress.*

Except about one thing.

That special secret of mine…my dream! This was something no one could possibly understand, this deep yearning in me, this need to be the winner. No, it was not a simple case of just wanting to be the winner. I *needed* to win because I needed something that would break me out of *my* prison.

Yes…I knew that I had the greatest and the most wonderful family in the world, and yes, I knew that their love for me was unconditional, and I would never want to trade them in for another family.

But, *me*? Now that was a different story!

True, my family's love for me was unconditional, but *my* love for me?

No, I admitted, I can't really say I love myself the way I am.

I leaned back against the wall and let out a deep sigh.

If I could trade myself in for someone else, I pondered, *I would, first of all, definitely not have been born in the middle of the family. I would still have a sister like Shuli, but I would be a lot more like her. I wouldn't be the ordinary girl that I am. I'd be much more fun and certainly not just a prop on the side. I would have loads of friends, I would dress just right, be graceful and pretty. Always know the right thing to say. Yes…people would all know me, but in a good way. I'd be a role model, a sought-after speaker, the principal of the school—the one who'd never give up on a child. All the organizations would come to me to help them and I'd never turn anyone down. I'd help children and their families, and my own children—besides being perfect in their own right—would join me in my many endeavors as well. Yes, we'd be the perfect team and I'd be at the helm…a true heroine in Klal Yisrael.*

Well, Sara, I shook my head, *you can't exactly trade yourself in for someone else.*

But, I knew there was something I could do…to *almost* become someone else. Something I could do to set me free from this prison of being plain old Sara Hirsch for the rest of my life. If I won the Zev Goldstone Outstanding Student Teacher Award then… then everyone in Rolland Heights would know about me. In fact, word would spread to the day schools and Beis Yaakov schools all across Rolland County. Teaching offers would come rolling in. I would be able to choose whichever position I wanted. *I'd…I'd…*

Sara, stop all this fantasizing right now, the practical part of me abruptly yanked me out of my reverie. *You want to win? Instead of sitting here daydreaming…get up! Get to work!*

I stood up. *The Proyect!* Yes. I must keep working on it. I'll take my shower after I finish setting up in the kitchen. Now, how much time do I have left before I have to be downstairs, I asked myself as I looked at the clock on my nightstand. *Oh, no! Where'd all the time go?*

I glanced at the door that led to the next room. *No wonder why it suddenly got so quiet in there; they must've gone down already. It's ten after two and I'm still here in my own little dream world. I'm so embarrassed! Everyone's downstairs working and I'm probably the only one who's not there yet.*

I flew down the steps within seconds. There was not much left to be done by the time I reached the dining room. There was only a small group staying for Shabbos, so we only needed to set up two tables, which were pushed together to form one long one. The napkins were folded rather typically, and I wistfully thought of Mimi and the artistic flair she added to the Shabbos table when she had *toranut*.

I missed her. She had become so much a part of my life lately and, for a brief moment, I again worried about whether our friendship would continue once her report was completed.

I avoided contact with Adina. I was embarrassed in front of "perfect Adina" for coming late and did not want to deal with her resentment. Besides, I had come to a final decision regarding her, and this time I meant it! I was no longer going to be the victim of her anger. I had tried so many times to be her friend, but she always turned on me. Enough was enough! I had Mazal, I had Mimi, and I was quite friendly with Rivky and Chani and some of the others. No, I certainly did not need Adina Stern and I was no longer interested in dealing with her. *Really!*

And maybe, maybe, maybe, I dared to hope, *she really will leave and Chavie will take her place.*

I took a shower, ironed my skirt, swept and did *sponja* in my room, and was finished with my preparations for Shabbos with a half-hour to spare.

I was pleasantly surprised when Zehava came by my room to pick me up before candle lighting, and I continued to be pleasantly surprised when I found myself enjoying both my *toranut* job as well as the Shabbos *seudah*. I only thought about Mazal and Mimi once that whole time—picturing Mimi sitting at the table with the Cohen family and little Salma and precocious Miryam fighting over her. I wondered if Mazal's Uncle Binyamin was there, along with his boys, and if any other company had joined them. I hoped I would be going there again soon.

That is, I thought worriedly, *if Mazal wants to take me. Maybe after having Mimi there for a Shabbos, she's not going to be so interested in boring me coming anymore.*

Zehava hung around with me after the *seudah*. I did not allow myself to think about this new friendship too deeply. *Wait and see what happens when Rochel Leah comes back,* I told myself wisely.

We sat around with some of the others in the lounge, schmoozing while munching on sweet oranges and *garinim*. There were many more Israelis from Beit Yaakov HaNegbah in the dormitory for Shabbos than there were M.B.L.L.ers, and it was fun spending time with them and getting to know them better. I could see that Zehava was enjoying herself immensely. We found ourselves giggling and bantering pleasantly until our eyelids started feeling heavy and closing.

On the way upstairs, as we came to the second floor, I turned to Zehava to wish her goodnight before making my way up to the third.

"Good Shabbos, Zehava," I covered my mouth to stifle a yawn.

"Good Shabbos, Sara."

I had already climbed a few more steps. "Um…Sara."

I stopped and turned in Zehava's direction. "Yes?"

"Um…I just wanted to thank you. If it wasn't for you, I don't know what I would've done for Shabbos. When you told me that a bunch of you would be staying in the dorm and that it probably would be a lot of fun, I…I just couldn't believe it. I couldn't believe that you were inviting me—me who never said a word to you."

"Please, Zehava. What I did wasn't anything special…Anyone would've…"

"I…I never would've noticed that someone else had no plans."

"Maybe because you've never experienced loneliness before."

"I…I…I'm sorry, Sara. I didn't realize—I just…you know, me and Rochel Leah…we've always been so…our mothers—"

"You don't have to explain, Zehava."

"But I see now that all this time I've been so busy doing everything with Rochel Leah I've been missing out on making new friends the way you have—"

I laughed a little. "I guess something good comes out of being lonely."

Chapter 24

She smiled. "I guess so." She was silent for a few pensive moments. "Um...Sara?"

"Yes?"

"I'm really glad in a way...you know...that I ended up being upset Tuesday night."

"You are?"

She nodded. "I see that it gave me this chance to get to know you."

As I made my way up the stairs, I felt my heart lifting higher and higher. I remember thinking: *Sara, this is real! Zehava really does like you, and she's not just using you the way Rochel Leah uses her—when it's convenient and when she needs you. She really means it.*

Yes, I thought happily as I pushed open the door to my room, *Zehava really does want to become friends.*

Entering the room, I softly closed the door behind me and was surprised to find that I could not see a thing. The room was pitch-black. *That's strange*, I thought, *didn't I leave the small light on in my closet? Oh well, I guess I must've closed the closet door when I left the room right before Shabbos.* I groped my way toward the closet, blindly touching first the wall...then the door... when I suddenly heard a rustling sound coming from further inside the room.

I froze.

I could barely make out the form sitting on my bed through the darkness.

"I've been wondering when you'd get up here already," I heard the unmistakable inflection of her British accent. "I've been waiting all night to talk to you."

25

MY HEART WAS pounding and my voice was shaking, but I did not care. Maybe it was because of my new resolve after the previous night not to fall victim to Adina's moodiness anymore, or perhaps it had something to do with my conversation with Zehava that had filled me with a confidence I did not know I had. It could be that I really was fed up with all my efforts toward reconciliation with Adina and now I was hoping Adina would finally leave so that I would no longer have to put up with her. Chavie could take her place instead of Mimi's. I was also overtired—I had gone to bed very late the night before and I had not recovered from the shock of finding someone so unexpectedly in my room.

I am not trying to make excuses, but at that moment I certainly was not myself.

"Who do you think you are? And...and what right do you have coming into my room like that—without permission, scaring me? What ever—"

"Sara, I didn't—"

"What ever happened to respect for other people's privacy? Only *you* count? Only *you* have—"

"I didn't mean to frighten—"

"Only *you* have the right to privacy? Only her highness Adina Stern counts? And now Queen Adina decides—"

"Please, Sara—"

"To pay a visit to her lowly subject and I'm supposed to bow down with appreciation to her highness for taking the time to acknowledge my existence. Well, that's it. I'm not taking anything from you anymore. That's it. No more apologies from me. Enough! I've had enough! Do you hear me? I've had enough of you!"

"Sara, please—"

"Don't *Sara please* me. Just get out of here. Leave!" I pointed a trembling finger toward the door.

The room was still shrouded in darkness; I had not yet opened the closet door. My eyes, though, must have adjusted to the dark because I could clearly make out her huddled form. She seemed to shrink at my words, but she did not stand up.

"Sara, I'm trying to—"

"Apologize?"

"Yes…and—"

"Why? So you can blow up at me again tomorrow?"

"I'm—"

"Well, I'm not going to take it anymore, Adina. I've had enough." I did not care what Adina Stern thought of me any longer. "You've hurt me too many times already!"

"I'm sorry. I—"

"*You're* sorry? Until the next time…?"

"I don't mean to—"

"So why do you do it?"

"I—I…"

"You…what?"

"I don't know."

"You don't know…what?"

"Why I do it." She suddenly stood up and came toward me. "Sara, I really don't know why I do it."

I stood opposite her. The pounding of my heart was slowing down. There was something in her voice that caught my attention…stopped me. There was this bewilderment…this innocence…this vulnerability that stripped away my anger at once. "You don't?" I asked in disbelief. "*Really?*"

"Please believe me," Adina's voice was unsteady. "I know how nice you are and I don't want to hurt you. I really don't know why I keep doing it. I know I don't *want* to be mean..."

"Huh?" I was utterly baffled.

"I..." she sat back down on my bed, "I must be crazy or something. I go around hurting the person I really want to be friends with—"

"Friends?"

"Yes. I know what a warm person you are, Sara. You're also loyal. I know you'd be a real friend...Oh, I just don't understand myself. I've tried a few times. I get a little close to you and then suddenly I get upset—I don't understand..."

I sat down on my bed next to her. "Is it *me*, Adina...is there something about me that...that you don't like?"

"I don't think so...of course not. How could that be? You've got a heart of gold."

"How about," I took a deep breath, "when I'm writing my letters? You seem so resentful."

"I do?" she paused. "Maybe you're right. Yes...there's definitely something I feel when I see you writing. I—I think..."

"Yes?"

"I think I feel kind of...jealous."

"Jealous?"

"Yes. You're always busy writing to your family and..."

"So why can't you write to your father? And don't you have relatives and friends to write to?"

She did not answer and I felt her stiffen. *All right, Sara, get ready. Adina's about to stand up, say something nasty, and slam out of the room. But this time...I'll beat her to it.*

"Okay, Adina, so you don't like my question and you're about to yell at me that I should stay out of your life. Go ahead...I'm waiting."

I sat there rigidly listening to the silence, expecting the blow to come at any moment.

"I do write to my father...once in a while. And I dutifully write to my grandparents in England once a month, as well," she said softly. "But...friends? Sara, I don't have any friends to write to."

"Huh?"

"I—I...don't have friends."

"H-how could that be? Everyone over here wants to...I don't

under…Oh, now I understand. You moved to Ballington only recently, right? So you haven't had a chance to make new friends yet. But, your friends from England…I'm sure you're still in touch—"

"You don't understand, Sara."

"What?"

"I never had friends in England either," she said matter-of-factly.

"Huh? I don't understand. How could that be? And…and what is it that you have against *me*?"

"I don't have anything against you, Sara," Adina looked genuinely surprised.

"So why do you keep saying *someone like you* to me?"

"I suppose…I suppose…because someone like you can't understand what it's like to be me. Really, we're worlds apart."

"What do you mean?" my voice trembled. "I think I'm an understanding person. I try to get along with others. W-What did I do wrong?"

"Nothing. Oh Sara, you must forgive me! I'm saying this all wrong. You see, at the airport… I saw you—"

"And I remember seeing you too."

"You were standing there with your family—"

"And you were with your father—"

"I'm surprised that you noticed me, Sara."

"Well, Adina, you're not exactly the unnoticeable type."

"You were completely absorbed with your family."

"I know…I didn't know how I'd leave them."

"There was so much…so much…love."

"We were crying."

"You could see how your mother didn't want to let go…but knew she was doing the right thing."

"*I* didn't want to let go."

"And your father…"

"He's very warm and compassionate and at the same time very strong."

"And those were your sisters?"

"Yes…Shuli and Chevy."

"The younger one was clinging to you."

"We're very close."

"And the other one...she seemed so happy and excited for you."

"Shuli...Shulamis is her real name, is *always* enthusiastic about something."

"She's the one Rabbi Grossman mentioned? The one who was the honorable..."

"...Mention winner of the Goldstone Award? Yes."

"And your brothers, they also seem to be very attached to you."

"We are...we're all very close. That's why," I explained, "I'm always writing to them."

"And that's why," Adina's tone was blunt, "I said you couldn't understand."

"I...I don't understand."

"See? I told you."

"No, I mean...what does my family have to do with-" I suddenly stopped in mid-sentence as comprehension dawned. "You mean...you mean, Adina...what you're trying to say...Are you telling me that because—"

"You have this very close relationship with your family...you can't understand what it is like...to be...me...Adina Stern."

"Oh..."

"Now you understand?"

I nodded, but it was dark and I hoped she did not see me because I did not want her to know that I agreed with her, that I was admitting I could not understand Adina Stern. I did not want it to be that way. I *wanted* to understand her. It was obvious that she needed understanding, that she needed a friend—and *I* wanted to be that friend...even if she felt that we were worlds apart.

Sometimes, Sara...sometimes you have to step into that world.

That is what Mimi had told me. Mimi...who despite her problems, or maybe *because* of her problems knew how to find the key, unlock the door and step into another person's world.

Sara...step into Adina's world...

Even though it was dark in the room I leaned back against the wall and closed my eyes to think.

Adina's world.

No mother since she was a little girl...an only child with just her father for company...a move to a new country...seminary...

"Adina," I suddenly heard myself say. "Why did you come to M.B.L.L.?"

"What?"

Step into her world.

"Adina, you just recently moved to Ballington...you...you don't seem to like dorm life. You're extremely smart and capable...I-I'm sure that if you wanted to get a job teaching you'd be successful even without an M.B.L.L. certificate...so why did you come?"

"Well...why did *you* come, Sara?"

"I asked you first."

"All right...I came because I really do want the M.B.L.L. certificate...and..."

"And...what?"

"And nothing."

"Adina, look. We're trying to figure out why you have these...um...outbursts when you really don't want to. So, we've got to examine all the—"

"You sound like a psychologist, Sara."

"Well, I'm not and I'm not trying to be," I said indignantly. "I-I'm just trying to be a...friend."

"Well, I'm not a..." she stood up angrily.

"Go ahead!" I snarled. "Go ahead and run out of here and yell at me that you don't need any friends, especially someone like me. Run away from your emotions like you always do. Like you probably did back in England and that's why you don't have any friends from there. Go ahead—"

"Sara—"

"Yell something at me and leave!"

She stood where she was, unmoving, and I could hear her breaths coming heavily and in short intervals.

"Sara," her voice finally emerged in a hoarse whisper.

"What?" I replied crisply.

"Y-you're right. I'm sorry." She sat back down next to me on my bed.

My tone softened. "Adina, you said more than once that I can't understand you. You're blaming it on my family?"

"No...no...I'm not blaming you or your family. It's just that...we're so different."

"Why...just because I have a family...and you..."

"Sara, it's so normal by you...so nice and ordinary."

"Ordinary? You also think of me as ordinary?"

"I mean it as a compliment. Normal...ordinary...I wish..."

"What do you wish?"

"Never mind. It doesn't matter. It's just that we're so...different."

"And..."

"And when I try to get closer... something stops me."

Enter her world, Sara.

"And when you see me writing letters, you..."

"Wish I could be doing the same. Wish that I had people close to me. Wish that I could be close to you."

Adina wishes she could be close to me?

"So what's stopping you? What's holding you back?"

"Oh...I don't know. I...I—"

"What, Adina? Think! What suddenly stops you each time?"

"I...I...I'm scared, Sara. It's crazy right? I think I get afraid."

"Afraid of what?" I pressed.

"I don't know!"

"Okay, I'm sorry. Don't get upset."

"I'm not upset, Sara. It feels...good."

"Good?"

"Yes... I need to understand this."

"All right. Something stops you...it's a fear. Right?"

"Right."

"You're about to take a step. You want to become friendly with someone, you open the door and then—"

"I slam the door shut!"

"Because?"

"Because I'm afraid. I'm afraid I'll lose them. I'm afraid we'll get close...and then they'll leave."

"Leave?"

"Yes…just like my mother…"

"Adina, do you realize what you just said? Do you think that if you become close with someone, it'll be like it was when your mother…?" I could not finish the sentence.

"I—I don't believe I just said that to you. I don't think I've ever said that to anyone."

"Adina…" the tears were trickling down my cheeks.

"What?"

"I'm so sorry."

"No…Sara," she said sharply, "don't feel sorry for me. I don't want pity," her voice turned cold and hard, "I don't want to be *poor Adina*."

Her anger sobered me. "Is that why…is that why you put on this tough *don't touch me* exterior?"

"What do you mean?"

"Is that why you turn into a porcupine?"

"Excuse me, Sara," she stood up indignantly, "I don't have to—"

"Take this from me? So you're running away again?"

"I'm beginning to regret having said anything."

"Please, Adina, will you stop it already? I-I'm just—"

"Just calling me names?" She took a few steps toward the door. "If this is what friendship with Sara Hirsch is all about, then I'd better choose more wisely."

"Stop it already." I ran toward the door to block her from leaving and a feeling of déjà vu came over me. *Didn't I just do something like this recently?*

"Kindly stop blocking the door and move out of my way."

"No."

She swung around. "Then I'm leaving through the *netilat yadayim* closet."

"No!" I raced over to block the other door. "You're not leaving until we have this out. Every time someone says something you don't like, every time you feel vulnerable, you run away. We're finally getting somewhere and we're going to finish this."

"Stop it, Sara!"

"So you slam the door shut before anyone can get too close to you, right? Or you turn into a porcupine with its stiff needles sticking out.

Don't touch me, I'm Adina Stern!"

"Get out of my way!"

"No," I said stubbornly. "I'm not getting out of the way and I'm not giving up on you either. You're not getting rid of me so quickly."

I heard her sharp intake of breath, but she did not say anything. She just stood in place, unmoving.

My heart was pounding so hard I felt as though it would burst out of my chest. *Hashem,* I prayed silently, *You know I don't want to hurt her. She's been through so much pain already. Please...please Hashem take my words...words that are coming so sincerely from my heart...and make them enter Adina's heart. Let her realize that I...*

"I think you really do care about me," she whispered hoarsely.

"Yes, Adina, yes," I whispered back, sniffling.

"You're crying, Sara, and it's not even your problem."

"Adina, a friend's problem becomes *her* friend's problem too."

"I was never able to speak about this before..."

"When you take away the *do not disturb* sign and open up...you're taking a chance. But if you don't, then you lose out on so much."

"I don't know, Sara. I honestly think it's too late for me. I don't know how to do this open door thing. I think..."

"What?"

"That I should leave Sem...go back to England...to my grandparents."

If she leaves, then maybe Chavie will come. The thought flitted briefly through my mind and I quickly dismissed it. "Why England? I thought you live in Ballington?"

"I do. Well, my father does—I don't really. I guess England is my home. Oh, I don't know, but not Ballington—"

"I don't understand. Isn't home the place where your father lives?"

"Uh, Sara," she let out a heavy sigh. "Can we sit down? It's kind of a long story..."

Once Adina opened up to me, she spoke in a way I never would have imagined. We sat side by side on my bed that Friday night and we watched night turn into morning while we continued talking...talking as neither of us had ever done before.

She told me all kinds of things. And then she shared with me the diary...and the letters. At first I told her not to—that opening up did not mean she should share with me things that were so private. But then she almost seemed hurt. She insisted. She said that if we were to be true friends, and if I was to help her come out of her shell, I needed to hear her story...the whole story.

I admit I did not fight her too hard on that point. I had been wondering ever since I met her what it was she was hiding behind that closed door of hers, and I did not want to miss this opportunity. But to be honest, there was something else I was feeling...something that was far greater than my curiosity or even my stubbornness.

You see, despite her vulnerabilities, Adina still had that dignified aura about her, that unusual and rare combination of defenselessness and stateliness that drew people to her. That magnetism that made people want to be her friend, even when their reaching out was not reciprocated. Now that she had chosen to confide in me, I was ready and willing to do anything...anything to help Adina Stern break free from her self-imposed isolation.

And so, as the dawn's light shone through my window, casting its morning glow upon us, we sat and we read her mother's diary.

26

Dear Diary,

I can't believe I'm actually keeping a diary. But I can't help it! I'm just so excited that I feel like I **have** to write my feelings down.

Who knows—maybe one day I'll show it to my baby. My baby! I still can't believe it. Me, a mother, an Ima? Or maybe, I'll be a Mummy, as the English say. No, definitely not a Mummy…I don't want to think of my baby as English. Well, maybe that's not so fair to Rafael. He's such an Englishman, how could I do that to him?

After someone from Dr. Schneider's office called me with the news, I tried calling the future Abba in yeshivah, but I kept getting a busy signal. I am simply bursting. I can't call my Ima and Abba yet, because I can't tell them anything until I speak with Rafael. And, of course, I'm not very comfortable calling Rafael's parents. What would they say anyway? "Oh, we're so happy for you, Aviva. Now we can finally welcome you to the family."

Nope, I can't call anyone until I speak to Rafael. And so, my dear diary, I grabbed my notebook from my night table drawer and decided that if I can't talk to my dear husband, then I'll pour these wonderful feelings into my notebook.

Thank You, Hashem, thank you with all my heart for this baby. Thank You, thank You, and thank You!!!

Okay diary, I'm going to try Rafael again in yeshivah and I'm going to say Tehillim!

Love,
Aviva

Dear Diary,

I had an appointment with Doctor Schneider today and b"H he said that we (me and the baby) are doing great! He gave me a prescription for vitamins and instructions about what to do and what not to do. I know that I do get loads of sunshine and fresh air on my walks to and from work—so that's one instruction I won't have a hard time abiding by. But sleep? Ha, ha! Me get plenty of sleep? That's going to be a difficult thing for me to do.

You see, there's always just so much to do! I'm simply not the type to waste time sleeping. I've got so many preparations to complete for my teaching job. Not that I'm complaining! Not at all! I just love teaching so much, I'm sure it's part of me...in my genes, in my blood. I sometimes wonder...if my baby is a boy, will he grow up to be a rebbi, or if she's a girl, will she be a teacher like me. Will she also love teaching these adorable preschoolers the way I do? There I go again, jumping ahead...dreaming. I'm like that...always dreaming of things way ahead.

Rafael is much more practical than I am. Well, like

I always tell him, if I didn't dream, I'd be missing out on so much of the fun in life. He says it's all right to dream, just don't let those dreams carry you away too far, because if you keep flying higher and higher with your dreams—then if they don't work out the way you hoped, pop goes the balloon and you can crash down into the ground with all that disappointment.

Anyway, I've got to go now. I want to make this wonderful new dish for my wonderful Rafael for when he comes home from yeshivah. It's our engagement anniversary (last year at this time we became chasan and kallah) and I want to surprise him with a really fancy meal.

Love,
Me

Dear Diary,

Rafael loved the surprise meal I made him yesterday, but my baby sure didn't! After I finished eating, I felt so sick. In fact, I was sick all night. Rafael looked really worried. He told me that I'm working too hard and that I'd better take it easy. He didn't want to let me go to work today, but I told him that I'm much better and that if I don't go, then those poor little girls won't learn anything all day long. I'm glad I went. We had a great day at school today.

When I finished teaching, I stopped at Leibovitz's Fabric Store. They always have such beautiful materials that I'm dreaming of using to decorate our apartment, but unfortunately they're very expensive. We're on such a tight budget these days, I'm sure those fabrics are way

Chapter 26

out of our reach. Well, it doesn't hurt to look. Right? So today on the way home from work I found myself staring longingly at the fabrics, just as I do everyday.

Only today, something different happened. Geveret Leibovitz saw me (probably for the hundredth time) staring at her merchandise, but this time she actually invited me into the store. Of course, I apologized to her immediately and told her that I'm just looking and dreaming and not really buying because I can't manage the prices, even though it's all so gorgeous. She laughed and told me she also used to be that way, and offered me a few rolls of fabric for free. I told her my husband would never let me take something for free. But then she said that it's a gift, not just for free. I asked her, "Isn't that the same?" She said, "Not really. For free would be if I felt sorry for you. A gift is more something you give to someone because you want them to have it." I thought that was interesting, but I still said no thank you and insisted on paying her. (I thought Rafael would be upset if I accepted such a gift.) She explained that these were really seconds and she wouldn't be selling them anyway. I'd need to cut away the damaged parts of the fabrics first and that I would really be doing her a favor by taking them. A favor? I love doing favors for people.

So, anyway...guess what? I took them. I'm so excited! I'm planning on sewing a weekday tablecloth and a Shabbos tablecloth, curtains for the bedroom and kitchen, and I have so many other ideas and projects I want to do. I was even thinking that if everything comes out well (it will, I'm sure), I'll invite Geveret Leibovitz over to see everything. Then maybe she'll offer me a part-time job giving sewing lessons. I'd really love doing that, teaching and sewing—two of my favorite activities and we could sure use the money. (There I go again...dreaming! But it really could happen.)

I'm going to try surprising Rafael with my new sewing projects. He'll probably say it's not necessary, after all we do have trisim. But curtains add such a beautiful touch. They're warm and colorful—oh, I'm quite sure it'll add so much to the apartment. And tablecloths! I know one of his aunts gave us a tablecloth, but it's really way too elegant for our simple apartment and it's also too large for our tiny table. And so I'm very excited. I can't wait to lug out my sewing machine and get started on my new projects. (Now I'm picturing teaching my baby to sew...if she's a girl, that is.)

Love,
Aviva

Dear Dairy,

Wow! Today I heard my baby's heartbeat! It was the most wonderful sound in the world. The most gorgeous music! Rafael said that now it's definitely the time to tell our parents about the baby. I know how happy my parents will be to hear the news. They so much deserve to hear good news after all they've been through. It will be so good for them to experience that feeling of continuity that they so much deserve after suffering the losses of their entire families during the Holocaust. I'm glad that even though I've disappointed them to a certain extent, I'll also be the one to bring them this happiness that they so much deserve.

Well now, we'll also have to tell my in-laws. I'm hoping, really hoping that now they'll begin to accept me. After all, I'm their grandchild's mother. It's not that they were ever mean to me...no, nothing like that. But, I know that they still haven't been able to really accept me and I know that even though they try to hide it, they're disappointed that things didn't work out as originally planned. Oh well, I'm still hoping...

Anyway, I've got to go now.

Love,
Me

To My Dairy,

Guess what? I just got off the telephone with England. First Rafael spoke to his parents and then they wanted to speak to me. So his father got on the telephone and told me how happy he is to hear the news. He really did sound happy. And then his mother asked to speak to me. She actually told me to take care of myself and also expressed her happiness. I'm so thrilled!!!

I think they're starting to like me. It's not that they were ever nasty or anything of that sort. No, they were always polite and respectful to me. But, well, something else has always been missing. I guess it's because of the disappointment and everything. And I'm definitely not imagining it. Polite and respectful, yes. They're too fine not to be polite and respectful. But, accepting...now that's another story. They really can't accept me. Worse, though, is the feeling that they're ashamed of me. I really can't blame them, being the important people that they are. My background is not exactly their cup of tea. And of course, Rafael is the apple of their eye. And I certainly can't blame them for that either, because Rafael would be the apple of anyone's eye. There truly are few men like him. He's so perfect!

I still can't believe how lucky I am. In fact, the whole way our shidduch came about was an absolute miracle. Of course every shidduch is a miracle, but this one surely must've surprised everyone. I know it was a major shock to his parents, and if it wouldn't have been for the da'as Torah that was involved, I don't know if I could've gone through with it.

Well, Rafael is very wise. He told me that it was obviously bashert and to just give his parents a chance—they just needed time to get used to the idea. He told me that since we have da'as Torah behind us, and we didn't do anything wrong, I should stop being so afraid. But, well, that's me. I like everything to be rosy and happy. And during the short time I spent at their home in London, it was everything <u>but</u> rosy and happy. I know it made Rafael very sad to see me being treated like a visitor they were hoping never to see again, but he was sure that they weren't acting like that intentionally.

Well, just now when I spoke to them they really did sound a bit warmer. So, now I'm starting to think that, yes...maybe things will start to get better. And I'm also hoping that maybe Rafael will stop being so adamant about not accepting the help that they're offering us. Wow, it's really great to put my feelings on paper.

Love,
Aviva

P.S. Maybe for Rafael's sake, I will be Mummy. Maybe he'll be Daddy.

※

Dear Diary,

Guess what! I decided to celebrate our half anniversary with a party. That's right, we'll be an old married couple of six months in less than a week. And I decided to make us a surprise party. I've got to go soon, so that I can pore over all my cookbooks and find the most gourmet recipes imaginable. I'm also about to start a new sewing project that I'm hoping to finish on time for the party.

I've almost finished the kitchen curtains and now I have something else up my sleeve. I found a couch the other day on the street that someone was throwing out and I managed to convince (I begged!) Rafael to take it into the house. He was completely against taking someone else's garbage. But I told him that by the time I'm finished with it, he'll never recognize it, and that if he still doesn't like it and thinks it's a piece of garbage, then he could throw it out. He threw back his head and laughed. "That's my Aviva," he said happily. Well, I'm really going to make that couch gorgeous! You see, Rafael comes from a very, very wealthy home. But he was willing to give up everything...the fancy house, the prestigious job as manager of his father's factory...the comfortable lifestyle, so that he could continue learning here, in Yerushalayim Ir Hakodesh undisturbed and without distractions. So, can you blame me for wanting to do whatever I can to make our home into our own palace?

I don't want Rafael to ever regret his decision to marry

me (no dowry, no support, and no important family) and I want him to devote his life to learning Torah. I want everything to always be beautiful for him...perfect...because he's so perfect! So, I'll be so busy with all this baking and cooking and sewing and teaching and preparing my lessons, that I don't know when I'll have time to write to you, dear diary. I'll just have to remind myself that writing to you is good practice for when I'll have to stop everything in order to take care of my baby.

Anyway, once our half-anniversary party is over, I'll have more time.

Love,
Aviva

Dearest Diary,

It came out gorgeous! Everything came out gorgeous! The party was a real hit. Rafael walked into the apartment on the day of our half-anniversary. I had hung balloons everywhere. I had baked a three-tier strawberry shortcake (that's his favorite) and then cut the whole cake into two. Half for now and I put the other half in the freezer. I told Rafael that I'm saving the second half for our first anniversary. I hung up this huge sign across our tiny kitchen. The new tablecloth was on the table and looked really stunning with the fringes I sewed around its edges. All the food came out delicious. Rafael was so surprised. But the biggest surprise was when I led him into the parlor. I opened the door and I said, "Surprise!" He looked at the couch sitting against the wall and said, "Aviva, where did you get this couch? Did my parents send it without my knowledge?" My heart dropped. I didn't want him to be upset. I know he still doesn't want to accept any luxury items from them. (Even though I feel like, why not? Just because they're not so happy with the life he chose and with the wife he chose, that doesn't mean you shouldn't accept a gift that they want to give you.) But, anyway, this wasn't the case. This was <u>my</u> gift to him. It was the couch that I had reupholstered, sewing new cushion covers to hide the old fabric, and covered with coordinating throw pillows in all different shapes and sizes. And (even if I say so myself) it came out stunning! It was beautiful, warm, and welcoming. Rafael couldn't believe it. I had to bend down and show him the old fabric underneath to prove to him that it really was the old couch and not a new one. He said, "Aviva, it's beautiful! I can't believe you did it. And you sewed and sewed while I was busy in yeshivah learning. How did you manage with your teaching and everything?"

Then he looked sad. I quickly asked him what was wrong. I really thought he liked it. He reassured me that yes, he did think it looked wonderful, but that he was worried about me working so hard. See, I'm the luckiest woman in the world! Then he said, "Aviva, like your name, you really are like the spring. So warm and sunny—I'm the luckiest husband in the world to have such a special wife like you."

So now...tell me...is there something wrong with dreaming? Baruch Hashem, my dreams are all coming true! (And I hope my baby's do too!)

Love,
Me

Dear Diary,

I am the proudest, happiest wife in the world! Rafael just surprised me with the nicest present imaginable. He said that he was going to wait until our anniversary, but since I didn't, he's going to give it to me now — and because it's only half-done, it'll make a fitting half-anniversary present. I couldn't believe it. I had no idea that this is what Rafael had been doing early every morning.

After davening Shacharis at the vasikin minyan, Rafael would go to the beis midrash. And before his morning chavruta would show up for the first seder, he would spend the time putting together chiddushim that he has been writing ever since he was a child. He wants to put out a sefer...and it is already half done!

My husband is just so brilliant! I still can't believe how fortunate I am that I ended up marrying him. Sometimes, if I allow myself to really think about it, I get kind of scared. How could it be that someone like me ended up with someone as great as Rafael Stern? Not that there's anything wrong with me — I'm just a regular, average person. But my background being what it was, I never could have imagined getting someone like him for a husband. Yes...I dreamed...I prayed...and I guess Hashem, in His great understanding and kindness, answered my tefillot. I just hope that His kindness to me continues.

I'm so happy that it's scary.

Love,
Aviva

Dear Diary,

My parents came to visit today. They kept looking at me and grinning from ear to ear, then they couldn't stop telling me to take it easy. Oh, they're so happy. I think that by now they've completely forgiven me for not following exactly in their footsteps. Not that we ever didn't have a close and warm relationship. No, despite our religious differences, they were always warm and loving and as helpful as possible to me. They are really such wonderful, good, giving people and they certainly never meant to do any wrong. Life just led them in a certain direction and now I see life leading them along in what I'm hoping will turn out to be a more Torah-directed path.

Rafael says that it's never too late. He is so wonderful to them. He really tries to be for them the son they never had. Despite his heavy learning schedule, he finds time each week to go over to them and help them with their shopping and other needs. Oh, my husband is really a tzaddik. A perfect tzaddik!

Anyway, when they left, I again thanked Rafael for being so wonderful to them. "What's the big deal, Aviva, they are very good people and haven't they given me the most wonderful, beautiful, loving, supportive wife a man could ask for?"

Oh...I must be the happiest person in the world! I don't think it's possible for anyone to be happier!!!

Love,
Aviva

Dear Diary,

Guess what? Rafael's parents called this morning. His father has to take a business trip and needs to meet some people in Tel-Aviv next week, and his mother decided to accompany him so that they could spend some time with us. Oh my goodness! I don't think I'll get a chance to write to you for a while. I suddenly feel this new surge of energy that I've been lacking lately. I have to clean up the apartment until It's spotless, stock the pantry, cook and bake and load up the freezer. My in-laws are coming! Help!

Rafael doesn't want me to work so hard. He said that they're anyway going to stay in a hotel and that they'll probably invite us out to eat dinner with them, but still...

I don't want them to see their son living in anything but a palace. I want to serve them homemade cake on my beautiful fringe-edged tablecloth. I want the little furniture we have to be polished to a shimmering shine, the curtains to appear rich and elegant, and there not to be a streak of dust anywhere. I want them to see how happy we are and how light and warm our apartment is. I want them to see how perfect everything is. I want them to be happy that their son married me.

Love,
Aviva

Dear Diary,

Well...they're on their way here. Almost, that is. They won't be arriving until early in the morning. I'm so nervous. Rafael is getting upset with me. He says I should be taking care of myself (and my precious baby) rather than worrying about what his parents think, and I should stop working so hard...but I can't help it. Anyway, he's in bed sleeping right now. I couldn't sleep. So, I got out of bed and came into the kitchen. I'm writing to you (it's funny that I think of you as a person now) while drinking a cup of warm milk mixed with honey.

I'm sure I'm not the first daughter-in-law experiencing insomnia the night before her in-laws' first visit. I did a really thorough cleaning of the apartment throughout the whole week. Rafael did a sponja after we had supper, but then when he went to Ma'ariv I did another one. I want everything to look perfect! I frosted the chocolate cake already and it's sitting so elegantly on the platter in the refrigerator. Rafael says that the cake looks delicious and that there's no way he'll be able to wait until his parents come, but I made him promise he won't touch it until we all sit down for tea together. (I don't want them to think they're getting leftovers.) The vases are filled with flowers I collected from the garden and the large glass bowl in the center of the table is full of fresh fruit. I really want them to see what a good wife I'm being to their Rafael, and how happy and complete our lives are. Hopefully, they'll express satisfaction, and then maybe...maybe they'll accept me and our way of life.

From the beginning, they were completely against our marrying. They probably think it's my fault that Rafael doesn't want to go into the family business and instead is learning in kollel. They don't realize that even if Rafael had married someone else, his heart would still be leaning in this direction. They feel like the business is suffering from lack of his brilliance at the helm. I know that he would have suffered greatly if he hadn't been given the opportunity to grow in Torah. And obviously this is what Hashem wanted for him...for us. Otherwise, the whole way our shidduch came about never would have happened. One day I hope to tell my baby the whole story. It really is kind of comical...

Anyway...uh oh, I'm feeling it again. Let me check my watch. Yes. They are definitely coming. Guess what? I think it's going to happen soon. Yes...I think it's really going to happen.

Love,
Me

Dearest Adinaleh,

A beautiful girl was born and she has a beautiful name.

Ever since I found out I was expecting you, I've been keeping a diary. I was never the type of person to do that, but once I knew that I was going to become a mother, I suddenly felt the need to express myself on paper.

But now that you have finally arrived, I decided that rather than writing in a diary, I will write to you. I don't know if I'll ever end up showing the letters to you or how much longer I'll continue doing this. Only time will tell. Talk about time—it's been a long time since I've written in my diary. So much has happened since then.

As I write this letter, you are sleeping peacefully in your bassinet. I can't stop looking at you. Oh...you are

Chapter 26

the most beautiful baby I have ever seen in my whole life. Five fingers on each hand and five little toes on each foot, I keep kissing them over and over again. Your hair is black, really black, and your eyes behind those closed lids are blue. A lot of people tell me that your dark hair may fall out and lighter colored hair will grow in, and that your blue eyes may darken and lose their blueness. But no, Adinaleh, I don't think that's going to happen to you. Your Daddy (that's what he wants to be called because that's what he calls his father) has very dark hair and the bluest eyes in the world. I think you're going to look like him. (I'm hoping you'll look like him!) I'm blond with light brown eyes — I don't think your coloring will change to mine.

Well, it really doesn't matter. The important thing is that you be healthy and inherit your father's beautiful character. I pray to Hashem that you grow up to be as beautiful on the inside as you are on the outside.

You just stirred and I jumped. Daddy says I'm going to spoil you by picking you up the second you move. But it's hard for me not to.

Love and kisses,
Mummy

(Yes, I decided that if Daddy is going to be Daddy like his father, then I'll be Mummy like his mother.)

My Darling Adinaleh,

I can't believe it but my three months home with my darling baby are almost over and I will be going back to teach. I do love teaching those preschoolers—teaching them all about Hashem and the Torah. I feel like I'm giving them their first real taste of learning and I absolutely love it! But I just don't know how I'll be able to leave my darling, darling Adinaleh.

Anyway, I'm going to be meeting a lady tomorrow who is looking for a babysitting job. She's a friend of Rabbanit Gartenhaus (the Rosh Yeshivah's wife, who was very involved in our shidduch) and has been babysitting for years.

I want to make sure that she'll hug you and kiss you and give you all the love in the world!!! You know, Adinaleh, as much as I love teaching, if we didn't need the parnasah I'd gladly give it up to stay home with you, but your Daddy no doubt is a talmid chacham who belongs in yeshivah right now. So, this is what we've got to do...even though my heart is heavy at the thought of leaving you.

Love,
Mummy

Dearest Adinaleh,

It was so hard to leave you...but I did it. The truth is that Hinda Klein, or rather Savta Hinda, as she prefers to be called, is a darling lady who fell in love with you the moment she saw you. (I'm not surprised!) I feel you are in wonderfully safe hands, and as hard as it was to separate myself from you, I actually managed to do it. I must've called home at least a dozen times, but that's because I couldn't stop thinking of my darling daughter all through the day. Anyway, I'm sure I'll get used to these separations...I'd better!

Love,
Mummy

Dearest Adinaleh,

I'm not getting used to being separated from you. I miss you so much when I leave you, but I tell myself over and over again that it's for a worthy purpose. Sometimes I really wish I hadn't gotten married during seminary year, but instead waited until I had a teaching certificate. Then my salary would be higher and I wouldn't have to be away from you so many hours, especially if I had won the award.

You see, the seminary that I went to, Machon Beit Leah LeMorot, is one of the best teaching seminaries in the world. And everyone knows that a certificate from there upon graduation is practically a guaranteed job.

B"H I got this teaching job anyway—even though I didn't finish seminary—thanks to Rabbanit Gartenhaus, who pulled some strings. (Her sister is the principal of the school where I teach.) Originally I was hired to just be an assistant, but then when the main teacher had to go on bed rest, Geveret Finkel (Rabbanit Gartenhaus's sister) decided to hire me to take her place. But, being that I don't have the certificate, I'm only being paid an assistant's salary.

I had plans last year, that is before I met my wonderful chasan, to not only end up with a teaching certificate from Machon Beit Leah, but I was also hoping to win the Goldstone Award. Two years ago someone donated money—some sort of prize or something—for the girl who accomplishes special things in this seminary. When I heard about it, I had my heart set on being the winner. I wanted to marry a boy who was serious about learning, and I thought that money would help with expenses and the prestigious award would help me get a better paying job.

Maybe I should go back to seminary. I need to discuss it first with Daddy, of course. But, I'm beginning to think that that's the only way we'll be able to increase my teaching salary—with the proper certification. My friend, Yedida Adler, says that it's a pity for someone with my teaching abilities not to have this coveted certificate, and she really thinks I'm capable of winning the award. I really must discuss this with Daddy as soon as possible if I want to apply to become part of the program when it begins again this Elul. On the other hand, I'm not really sure it's such a great idea. The schooling costs money (even with a scholarship), and it would mean relocating to the upper Negev (that's where the school is), and Daddy is learning so well in his kollel in Yerushalayim. I'll suggest it to Daddy and see what he thinks, but I'm sure I'll have to think up another more practical idea.

I was just thinking, Adinaleh...wouldn't it be cute if you ended up going to Machon Beit Leah LeMorot? Maybe you'll win the Goldstone Award and I'll be the proud mother shepping nachas... (There I go again...jumping so far ahead. But I can't help it! It's so much fun!)

Love,
Mummy

Chapter 26

Dear Adinaleh,

Today you got your first tooth. I made you a tooth party. Daddy says I make parties for everything. But he laughed when he said it and I know my parties make him very happy.

Now that you're almost seven months old, I feel like I'm ready to take on more work. I spoke to Geveret Leibovitz and asked her what she thought of the idea of my giving sewing lessons in the back of her store a few evenings a week. She was very enthusiastic and said that she would discuss it with her husband. I'm waiting to tell Daddy about it, when I know for sure.

I'm really thrilled that we found Savta Hinda Klein. She is the best babysitter in the world! She never married and absolutely loves kids. We've become really close to her. She often comes to us for meals on Shabbat and she's so much fun. When I leave you with her, I feel like I'm really leaving you with a Savta and not a babysitter, so that helps me feel less guilty.

Only the best for our Adinaleh!

Love,
Mummy

Dear Adinaleh,

Guess what! Surprise!!! We're going on a trip (or as the English say "on a holiday"). Yes, during Bein HaZmanim we will be going to England to visit your grandparents. They met you as soon as you were born, in fact they got to see you even before they saw me when they came that last time. But now they'll meet an adorable eight-month-old. I'm sure they will fall in love with you just like everyone else does.

Love,
Mummy

Dearest Adinaleh,

Oh, I'm the happiest person in the world. Yes, everyone in England fell in love with you, just as I knew they would. That's not the surprise. Guess what? My mother-in-law, your Grandma, took us out for the day. We went shopping in all the fancy stores. She insisted on buying me a new dress for the Yamim Tovim in Harrods. It was so expensive, I nearly fainted. But she told me that it was very becoming on me and I shouldn't concern myself with the price. Can you imagine? And you behaved like a little angel all day long.

Then we took you for a stroll in Hyde Park and sat down on a bench together to have sandwiches. It was one of the most beautiful days in my whole life! Grandma was pushing your pram/carriage, and then suddenly turned to me and said, "Aviva, we see that Rafael is very happy. We've only wanted what's best for him and we did not think he would be happy learning all day long. But we're very happy that he's happy."

Well, I felt great when she said that. When I told it over to Rafael, he just shrugged, but I'm really glad she said that.

Anyway, before we left back to Eretz Yisrael, your Daddy told me he had something to give me and he held out this cute little box. I said, "What? A present?" He

Chapter 26

said that he would love to give me something larger, but that was all he could afford right now, and he wanted it to be from his money and not his parents'.

I told him that being married to him was the biggest gift of all and that the cherry on top was that Hashem had blessed us with Adinaleh. He blinked. I think he had tears in his eyes. Now, that was really a surprise, because he's not like me. I cry all the time, but he never cries. Anyway, he told me to open it.

I slowly tore away the wrapping paper and opened the little white box. Lying in a cloud of cotton was the most beautiful, white gold heart-shaped locket I had ever seen in my whole life. He told me to open it. In it, written in Hebrew, was folded a small little poem with my engagement picture pressed against the back of the locket. I couldn't believe it. This was so unlike him! He's not the type to write poems or prepare surprises. He told me that he'll be forever grateful to Hashem for making me his wife.

I'm floating...

Love,
Mummy

27

"IS THAT THE locket?"

Adina had not realized she was fingering it with her right hand. "What? Oh, you mean...this?" she clasped the necklace tighter while turning it upward to see more easily. "Yes, Sara, this is it."

"Is...is your mother's picture...um, you know..."

"Is my mother's picture still in it? Is that what you're asking me?"

"I-I guess so."

"Come, take a look," she said while removing the chain from around her neck. I glanced sideways at Adina. She seemed so much more composed than before. I watched her twist the tiny latch and then open the small case of the locket. She turned the palm of her hand toward me so I could see inside.

There was no folded paper with a poem in it, but the portrait was still there. I held my breath. "Adina...she's beautiful!"

"*Was* beautiful."

"I—I'm s-sorry. She was so beautiful."

"I know."

I sat there staring at the picture in wonder. Golden-blonde curly hair framed a clear bright complexion, laughing light-brown eyes, and a warm sunny smile. "She's, I mean...she wasn't just beautiful, Adina, she...she..."

"Yes...?"

"Her whole aura...her whole being seems...I mean was...so full of life."

Chapter 27

Adina just shrugged.

I continued studying the picture. "She really looks like spring...*Chodesh HaAviv*...she has—"

"*Had—*"

"All right...*had* this optimistic look about her. And from the diary and letters you can tell she is...I mean was...so happy, so warm and friendly, so—"

"So unlike me."

I turned away from the picture and looked quizzically at Adina. Her blue eyes looked right back at me, challengingly. *All right, Adina is testing me...daring me. I'm not afraid and I'm going to ask her straight out.* "So why, Adina? What happened? Both your father and mother seemed so...so warm and happy. What happened when your mother died?"

"She died."

"And you?"

"I wasn't even four years old."

"Really...? I thought—"

"You thought I was four or five years old."

She's thinking about the incident with the siddur. I felt the blood rushing to my face.

"So you were really very young."

"You could say that."

"D-do you remember her?"

"Hardly...I mean how much can a three-and-a-half year old remember?"

"Um...that's true. It must have been very hard for your father. I mean he and your mother...they really seemed so perfect for each other."

"They were. My father died too."

"But I thought...your father...huh?"

"You mean the man you saw at the airport?"

I nodded. I was too afraid to speak.

"Well...yes. That man *is* my father."

I was speechless. I had no idea Adina had lost both parents. *Did Mimi know? I was growing more and more upset. If Mimi knew, why didn't she tell me...warn me? And what's Adina talking about—this man* at the airport? Was that man her adopted or foster father? But how could that be...they looked so alike? This was really so—

"Strange, no?" Adina's voice cut into my thoughts. "See, I told you, Sara. We're very different. You grew up so normal, such a nice simple ordinary life and me—"

"Will you stop saying that? And stop being so mysterious. Just tell me...did he adopt you or foster parent you?"

"Pardon?"

"Well, if you're going to attempt to...you know...open up to me and we're sharing all this..." I pointed to the pile of letters strewn across my bed, "Then you'll have to be more clear. I'm not good at guessing things, Adina. So when were you adopted by that man in the airport?"

Adina's blue eyes opened wider than usual. She looked at me strangely and then suddenly did something I never would have expected.

She started laughing.

I gulped. *What's going on?*

She tried to stop, but then her eyes locked on mine and she continued laughing even harder. Tears were rolling down her cheeks.

"Adina—"

"Oh..oh..." she was still laughing.

And then suddenly so was I. I do not understand what made me laugh...it must have been from all the solemnness and tension, coupled with our tiredness. Emotions can be like that...tossing you unexpectedly from one extreme to the next. For a few minutes we giggled uncontrollably, until finally I managed to squeak out, "Adina, what in the world is so funny?"

She wiped her eyes. "I never said that I'm adopted. I didn't mean to laugh at you...but you looked so shocked and then suddenly it hit me—how I must've upset you with what I said, and then I couldn't stop."

"So you're not—"

"No, Sara, he's not my foster father or my adopted father. He's my real father...whatever that means. You know, the one from..." She pointed to the pile of papers on my bed.

"You mean the Rafael Stern from the diary?" I asked, sobering.

"Yes," she nodded.

"Then...then why did you say," I was completely serious again, "that he died."

"Be-because, Sara, the Rafael Stern from the diary, or as I should really say, my father...you see, my father died when my mother died, that is the person he was...he became someone else."

"Oh..."

"When my mother died, my father felt at first that he had nothing to live for. His queen was no longer there. His palace was gone. All the sunshine, all the hopes and warmth had gone out of his life."

"Your mother was really special."

"Yes...and my father forgot he had a baby."

"Poor Adina."

"No! Don't ever say that."

"Why not?"

"Because I don't want to be some pitiful case! And if you're—"

"What? If I do it again, you'll stomp out of here? Quit it already, Adina. Maybe it's time to face the truth—that yes, poor Adina suffered plenty—and that you're really entitled to feel sad. Then we can start to figure out how to deal with all of this in a good way!"

For a moment she did not say anything. I also could not utter a sound. I was shocked at what had come out of my mouth...but I was happy too. Yes...I was happy I had said what needed to be said. Adina really needed to feel all she had suffered so she could begin to heal. I just hoped I was capable of helping her.

"You're right, Sara," she said, quietly looking back down at the locket. "And my father...my father..."

"Yes...?"

"Now he really wishes that he could make all those lost years up to me...all that suffering. That's why he gave me those letters and the tape."

"The tape?"

"Yes...I'll tell you about that later."

"So what happened?"

"He gave me the tape and the diary with the letters at the airport...He's been writing me, begging me to read the diary, listen to the tape. And...I've been refusing."

"Why?"

"Now...suddenly he wants me to get to know my mother. All those years...all those years he wouldn't let me ask him anything. Until I heard the tape—I had no idea what my mother's voice even sounded like."

"So you did listen to the tape."

"Yes, remember that day when you came in with my laundry all neat and folded?"

"Oh...Adina, I'm so sorry. No wonder!"

"You don't have to be sorry, Sara. Like I said when I finally apologized later on...I had no right to be upset with you for doing me the favor. I should've been down in the laundry room on time...but once I started listening to the tape—"

"Of course!"

"So you understand? It wasn't you—"

"Please, Adina. I-I'm...it's so clear that none of us have any right to judge anyone else. I had no idea."

"Well, at least something good came out of it."

"What do you mean...something good? It's wonderful that you finally listened to it."

"When my father gave me the package in the airport, I told him I wasn't interested."

"In a way...you probably wanted to punish him—"

"Sara!"

"Isn't that the truth, if you really think about it?"

"I...I don't know. I was so angry when he gave me the package in the airport! I kept feeling that it was way too late for that, and that he gave it to me at the last second, when we wouldn't be able to talk."

"But, Adina...you did listen to the tape and you did read the diary in the end."

"Only because he sent Hinda Klein to speak to me."

"Hinda Klein?"

"You know...the babysitter that we read about in the letter."

"You mean...?"

"Yes. At first I didn't want to speak to her when she called. Then, remember that Shabbos we all stayed in the dorm? She called me that Friday from Kfar Amsdorf. She has friends there. And she said she was there for Shabbos and she'd like to come over and talk to me."

"Wow!"

"Yes…believe it or not my father had been in touch with her all these years. I guess she sort of considered him, in a way, to be like a son. And so, she made sure to keep up their connection. Well…with my coming to Eretz Yisrael this year, my father contacted her. I guess he started thinking it was time to make amends. I think his wife must've—"

"His *wife*?"

"Yes…he got remarried less than a year ago. I think she's the one who must've convinced him to try working on our relationship."

"Wait…I don't understand. Your father remarried?"

"Yes…someone from Ballington."

"Oh…so that's why you moved to Ballington. I know a lot of people from there. It's not far from us." My eyebrows lifted, "Who?"

"Who what?"

"Who did he…um…marry?"

"I don't know if you ever heard of her. She's much too young to be your mother's friend and she's too old to be yours or your sister's," Adina replied nonchalantly. "Her maiden name was Scheinerman…Bina Scheinerman. Her father is—"

"Oscar Scheinerman? Of course I heard what happened. His son-in-law was killed in a terrible car accident around two, three years ago. It was horrible. Everyone all over Rolland Heights was talking about the tragedy. So that's who your father married?"

"I guess so."

"Adina, practically everyone knows Oscar Scheinerman. He's a very well-respected man in the community…in all of Rolland County…in fact…probably in the United States! He's a big *ba'al tzedakah*. I heard he has this huge house with tons of guests all the time and he's very involved with—"

"Yes, something like that. I've met him…he *is* nice, but—"

"But right now you're not really interested."

"Well…how would you feel? For the last almost fourteen years my father hardly acknowledged my existence. True, he bought me loads of gifts each time he came back from one of his business trips…but that man you just read about in those letters…that life…" She shook her head, her eyes narrowing. "I don't need a nice Mr. Scheinerman or anyone else at this point," she continued, through clenched teeth.

"Tell me what happened," I coaxed, trying to quell her anger. What does Mr. Scheinerman have to do with your father?"

"Well, now that my father remarried *Mister* Scheinerman's daughter, they would all like to warmly welcome me into their home in Ballington. But…but…it's too late."

"Why, Adina?"

"I thought you'd understand, Sara. That's exactly what my father keeps asking me, over and over again. Why? Why? That's also the reason he sent Hinda Klein to me. He thought it would help."

"And it didn't?"

"No…it just made me angrier."

I was not sure how to respond. "So, what did Hinda Klein tell you?"

"She came to me that Friday afternoon. Mimi was busy with *toranut* and even when she came into the room, she left right away because believe it or not…Mimi can be quite perceptive when she wants to be…and she understood that I needed my privacy."

"So you were left alone with Hinda Klein…until I came to ask you for shampoo."

"I'm sorry for being so—"

"That's all right, Adina. I understand now."

"Anyway…she came. She brought pictures of me when I was a baby." Adina looked at me, "I really was quite cute, you know."

"I'm not exactly surprised."

"So, she showed me pictures. I felt myself thawing. Then, she started talking to me about my mother. She took out more pictures. You know…it was the first time anyone explained to me who my mother was. I had no idea."

"Really?"

"My father never wanted to speak to me about her, or her family… not a thing."

"It's so unbelievably sad," my eyes filled.

Adina, though, Adina's eyes were flashing angrily. "It was more than sad…it was infuriating. What right did he have to hide it all from me?"

"He sent Hinda Klein to you…to talk to you."

"That's true. But he waited years too long."

"So what did she tell you?"

"First, she told me about my mother's parents. They had both come from Russia…irreligious Communists who fled to Palestine during the war. After years of living on a kibbutz, they became disillusioned with the socialist way of life—that's what she said my mother told her—and left for a community that was mixed, irreligious and religious Israelis living together. Savta Hinda told me that my mother ended up becoming religious at a young age and, being the idealistic person she was, always dreamed of marrying a *talmid chacham*."

"She married your father."

"Right. But you won't believe how that happened."

"What do you mean?"

Adina continued. "My father was learning in a yeshivah in Yerushalayim. His parents were pressuring him to come home and join the family business. He still wanted to learn. They felt that once he got married, he'd return to England, settle down, and take over the business from his father.

"Sara…they're good people. I know them well. They're just not the passionate type…like my mother was and how my father must have been in those days," Adina seemed defensive. "I guess in those days in England, the idea of learning full time was foreign to most people. My grandparents were business people…not *Roshei Yeshivos* or *Rabbanim*. They really meant it for my father's good…and the family's good. At least, that's the way I understand it…and the way Hinda Klein explained it to me."

"It's okay, Adina. I'm sure they're wonderful people."

"Well…there was my father totally immersed in his learning…and there was my mother attending seminary. And there were my father's parents hoping to marry my father off, so that he'd return to England and settle down. A girl who was studying in Beit Yaakov HaNegbah was suggested to my grandparents."

"Do you mean—"

Adina put up her hand, signaling me to be patient. "They checked her out thoroughly. Her background was similar to theirs. She was from Belgium, not England, but had grown up in the same European environment. Her father also had a very successful business and his lineage could be traced back to the great-great grandfather who had attended the same *cheder* as my father's great-great-great grandfather. I don't know what her first name was—it doesn't matter—but her last name was Schawisosky.

"My grandmother was supposed to come meet her, but unfortunately, or maybe it was fortunately, she broke her leg and was unable to make the trip. Nevertheless, once the *shidduch* had gotten underway, she did not want to push it off until she would be able to make the trip to Eretz Yisrael. So, she spoke with Rabbanit Gartenhaus, my father's *Rosh Yeshivah*'s wife and asked her to arrange the match. Rabbanit Gartenhaus was only too glad to help out, since she thought very highly of my father. She wanted to make sure that the girl being suggested was worthy of a man who had such great potential to grow in Torah.

"She called up the seminary, only instead of calling the principal from Beit Yaakov HaNegbah, she figured that the suggested girl was in seminary, not in high school. She thought that when Mrs. Stern from England said Beit Yaakov HaNegbah, she really meant Machon Beit Leah LeMorot—the seminary program sharing Beit Yaakov HaNegbah's campus. So she ended up calling Rabbi Grossman instead."

"Wow! It's hard to believe he was running the place way back then."

Adina did not seem to hear me. She was completely immersed in her parents' story. "Remember, communication in Israel in those days was not the best. So, until everyone got through to everyone else, it was possible for a mistake to be made. Well, in this case, when Rabbi Grossman heard the name Schawisosky, he was sure he heard Sawososky.

"And as Savta Hinda Klein explained…it was perfect, both for my mother and my father. She said that she has never seen a happier couple in her whole life. She claims that when I was born, it was impossible to imagine that they could become even happier. In fact, their happiness rubbed off on anyone that came into contact with them. But then, when my mother died, it was all over."

"Your mother…was so full of life."

"When she died, her father, who had lost the apple of his eye, died too. And then her mother had no reason to go on living…and she also died. And my father…well…his spirit died too. And then it was like everyone who was left simply forgot about me."

"You sound angry, Adina…angry at your mother."

"My mother? No, I don't think I'm angry at her."

"You even sound a little angry at your grandparents for dying."

"Stop that! I'm not angry at any of them…they didn't die on purpose."

"So then, Adina, just who are you angry at? Your father?"

"Well…he went back to England in the end…to his parents. And that's where I grew up…in my grandparents' home. My father was more like…like a brother to me, a very distant sort of brother. My grandparents were always so formal…and my father never discussed my mother. The subject was taboo. In a certain way, my grandparents had grown to love my mother. From what I hear, it was impossible not to. I think that the way they all chose to cope with it was by never ever discussing her. Except for this locket…no one bothered to show me any pictures. Can you imagine…I barely knew what my mother looked like?"

I looked at Adina. *No tears. Still no tears.* I did not say anything.

"At first my father thought he'd stay in Israel. Hinda Klein told me that he tried to continue with his and my mother's dream. Savta Hinda babysat me…but…it just didn't work. With all that pressure he was under, Savta Hinda says, he just lost his ability to concentrate on the learning. He missed my mother so much and his parents kept asking him to come back home. They wanted to take care of him…and the baby."

"You."

Adina did not notice that I'd spoken. Her blue eyes were staring straight ahead…into the past. "So, he left the yeshivah world, went to England with his baby and left her with his parents, traveled all the time on business, trying to get away from his unhappiness and the life that could have been. I'm sure it wasn't easy. I tried to please him…I wanted to make him proud of me. I was an outstanding student. I tried so hard to be perfect! But…he was never around long enough to notice."

"Yes, when he came home from each of those trips, his arms were laden with gifts for me. But I didn't want his presents...I wanted his presence." She suddenly started laughing. "Look at that, I'm getting punny."

I did not laugh.

Adina continued. "At first I used to cry when he left, but eventually I learned not to." There was pride in her voice, "You know, Sara, I never cry."

I winced. "I...I've noticed."

"My father didn't like tears. I think I remember him saying something like, 'Don't cry, Adina. Crying makes you weak and you've got to stay strong.' Anyway, something like that."

"It sounds like he was trying to numb himself."

"I know. Like when there's a wound—and you put ice on it, it becomes so cold that you don't feel anything. Yes, he did that."

"And you got so angry at him, Adina, that there was no way for him to make up with you."

"Sara...it took him years and years. Then finally he tried, and I admit I didn't exactly give him an easy time. At the airport I kept telling him to leave already. He's been begging me this past year to try to understand...but I can't forgive him. All those years in England, all those years, when he'd never speak of my mother. When he'd go off on those long trips."

"It was too hard for him."

"Well, how about me? It wasn't hard for me?"

"His whole life changed, Adina, when your mother died."

"You know, he swore he'd never remarry."

"How do you know that?"

"When I was around eight years old I heard my grandparents talking to him. They were in the library. They thought I was asleep, but I heard them. They were trying to convince him to think about the future. They kept telling him that he's still young and that Adina needs a mother. He said he'd never find anyone like Aviva and that he'd never take a different wife."

"And now he married Bina Scheinerman..."

"Yes. Last year, he was on one of his business trips to the United

States. He had to be there over Shabbos, and was sleeping in the Ballington Hilton. Well, he went to shul and when Mr. Scheinerman saw him, he invited my father to eat all the meals with him. So, my father agreed, and when he came to the house, he met the family. There was a daughter there about thirty years old, who he was surprised to find out was a widow with four little children. Mr. Scheinerman, having no idea that my father was a widower, confessed to him that his daughter didn't want to ever remarry."

"Wow!"

"Well…my father hears that and thinks about his last fourteen lonely years. He claims that he thought of me and the mistake he had made by not providing me with a mother. So, he tells this young woman…Bina…that she's making a grave mistake. Anyway, to make a long story short, he arrived back in England last January sixteenth—"

"January sixteenth? That's my English birthday."

"Really, Sara? That's my birthday too."

"You're also turning eighteen, right?"

"Right."

"So, Adina, then we have the same Hebrew and English birthday."

"That's…interesting."

"Y-yes. It's really something. Maybe…maybe that has something to do with it—our becoming friends, that is."

"Yes, I suppose so. Anyway, my birthday present was my father's news to me that he had found us a family," her voice was crisp.

"It shouldn't have made you so upset, Adina."

"And I thought you were my friend."

"I am. I'm just saying, that now…now you have a family. That's what you wanted."

"You don't understand, Sara. What do I need with a new family NOW?"

"Who says you can't become a real family with them?"

"Sara…it's ridiculous. I'm almost eighteen years old. What is she…twelve…thirteen years older than me? Her oldest kid is all of nine years old. No, my father's found a new family. Not me."

"Please…Adina."

"Well now I've answered all your questions, Sara. Why I'm at

M.B.L.L. and why I can't go back to Ballington."

"I hope you're happy you told me all of this, Adina. Instead of being so angry at your father—"

"I'm not really so upset at my father."

"So, who are you angry at, Adina? You could try denying it from today till tomorrow…but it's obvious you're angry at someone."

"Me, angry? Why should I be angry? Life has been so…so wonderful for me."

"Adina—"

"You asked me earlier if I'm angry at my mother for dying at such a young age and leaving me. No, you can't blame a person for dying. Angry at my grandparents for dying immediately after her? Can't blame them for that either, can I? Angry at my father's parents for not accepting my mother in the beginning? No, that wasn't their fault. They were good to her once they got to know her. Angry at them for being so formal? No…that's not their fault either."

"I'm not say—"

"Angry at my father for remarrying? Well, I'm not exactly thrilled that he suddenly decided to do it without bothering to consult me, and then expected me to be happy about it. No, he's still reasonably young himself, even if it took him so long to wake up…but *angry* at him?" She looked me steadily in the eye and then shrugged, "No, I can't completely blame *him*."

"So then Adina, who are you angry at?"

"I'm not—"

"Yes, you are, Adina," I took a deep breath. "You're very angry and I think I know who you're *really* angry at."

"Who?"

"Could it be…is it possible…Hashem?"

Part Three

Part Three

28

Bs"d
23 Kislev

Dearest Shuli, *amu"sh*

I had dashed to the post office during a break here, and they gave me your letter. I read it right away and now I can't seem to concentrate on anything else. Right now I'm sitting in the back of the seventh grade class in Bnot Yisrael, trying to follow Morah Verner, but it's impossible for me to focus on what she's saying because I can't stop thinking about you and what you wrote.

Why, Shuli, why did you do it? The principal was willing to work with you—it wasn't like they were firing you. Why didn't you stick with it? So, it wasn't turning out perfect. Big deal! What do you expect? It's your first year teaching. How will it look when it comes to jobs in the future? Okay, so right now you have that temporary office job in the city, but you know that's not going to last. And anyway, is that what you REALLY want to do? You have the greatest potential to be the most magnificent teacher...how could you give it up so easily?

Shuli, what really bothers me is that you claim that you feel like such a failure in the classroom. Just because it's not running as smoothly as you hoped...that makes you a failure??? You really didn't give it enough of a chance. You say that if I were in your boat, I'd manage to stick with the job even if I wasn't so success-ful at it. Come on!!! Don't say, "It's just not like me to stay with something that's not working out, like you would, Sara." As if I have more strength than you, Shuli! You're the one with the major talents and personality. You're the one with all the *kochos*! Not me! The only reason why I'd stick with it would be because I had no choice. Yes, you're right, ever since I was a little kid I had this stubborn streak in me. But that comes from the fact that I could never afford to give up on something just because I didn't like it. I think it's because I don't have your adventurous personality or talents. Oh, I don't know! Whatever the case, Shuli, please, please rethink things. Don't say—well this is just the way I am. Don't give up!!!

Oh—by the way—I almost forgot! A big, huge *mazal tov* on Blimi Frankel's engagement! I was deep in dreamland early last Sunday morning. I hadn't slept a wink Friday night (up all night talking with my friend Adina), and then hardly slept on Shabbos (I had toranut), and on *Motzaei Shabbos* I went to sleep extremely late (don't tell Mommy) because Mazal and Mimi came back from Kiryat Yosef and I wanted to hear all about their Shabbos. Anyway, there I was having some interesting dreams when suddenly I heard loud screams. I woke up with my heart pounding away! I couldn't imagine what had happened. Then suddenly Mimi came dancing into our room. I heard Rivky and a bunch of other girls singing "*Od Yishama*" in the hallway. Well, there went my beauty sleep. Right after I washed neigel vasser and joined all the singing and dancing in the hallway and wished Chani a hearty *mazal tov*, it was time to go to school. (It was so funny, though, the way everyone was dancing around Chani. Some of the Israeli girls were sure that SHE was the kallah and we had to inform them that it was her sister in the United States who became engaged.)

Anyway... IM YIRTZEH HASHEM BY YOU, SHULI!

By the way, the teachers here started talking to us about *shidduchim* and we're still in Sem! So what's going on with you, Shuli? You really don't have to wait until I come home to become a *kallah*, you know. Abba and Mommy promised me that if you get engaged before I come home, that either the *chasunah* will wait till I finish Sem or that they'll somehow manage to bring me home for the wedding. Anyway, I'm really only joking about that—I'm sure it's not because of me that you haven't started yet. I just can't understand what you're waiting for! I was sure that as soon as I got here you'd be ready to break the news. Before you know it, I'll be back *iy"*H, so you better get the ball rolling. (Just kidding! I don't think I can even THINK about *shidduchim* until I see you take that first step and walk down the aisle! You know what a scaredy cat I am…)

Anyway, I'm starting to feel guilty. Morah Verner is REALLY into the lesson and I'm hoping she thinks that all my vigorous writing is because I'm taking notes on her teaching methods. I wouldn't want to hurt her feelings or be disrespectful by having her realize that I'm not paying attention to a single word she's saying, because I'm writing a letter. But, it's so hard for me to concentrate on one thing when my mind is on something else! I wish I wasn't this way and could just take my feelings and bottle them up until a more appropriate time. I guess I'll have to work on that.

Okay, Shuli, I can just hear you sighing as you read this—thinking that I'm being too analytical again. But, really, is it so wrong? Doesn't it help us figure out who we are and where we're going, instead of just letting things happen?

Just letting things happen…

Biting down hard on the top of my pen, I thought of Shuli, who simply flowed along with the tide. That is—when things unfolded in the expected way and when life was good to her. Under those conditions, she coasted along smoothly, enjoying the ride, peacefully observing the surrounding scenery. But as soon as the detour signs cropped up or a bump appeared on the roadway, she became helpless.

No… Shuli had no idea how to handle challenges.

Unlike Mimi.

Mimi, who had been walking around all these years with the same hard challenge, laughingly jumping over the potholes in her path. Mimi, who had to follow the road with all its detours, yet somehow managed to climb around the rough spots, joking all the way.

And yet, I pondered, would she be able to reach the end of the road like the rest of us?

Challenges!

My mind wandered to Adina, whose path was full of bumps and cracks, whose life was one huge challenge. Would she ever reach the end, strong and whole? Could she? Was it possible for someone who had gone through so much to be able to live a normal, happy, productive life?

Why…why must it be this way? Why must life's roads be full of potholes, twists, and turns? Why did Hashem do that to Mimi—put her with her learning problems in that brilliant family? And Adina, who was so young at the time, why did Hashem take her mother away from her, leaving her with a father who could not parent her properly?

Wanting to escape these depressing thoughts, I tried focusing on the front of the room. My eyes followed the teacher's animated movements and my ears heard her expressive voice, but my brain absorbed nothing.

I waited impatiently for dismissal.

As soon as the session was over, I hurriedly made my way out of the room, mumbling *todah* to Morah Verner. My eyes, though, would not meet hers. I felt guilty and disappointed in myself for not paying attention, and feared that my feelings were written all over my face. Morah Verner had a phenomenal reputation, and although I had observed her already a couple of times before, I had been eagerly anticipating observing her class again.

Earlier that morning, Geveret Spitz had divided the M.B.L.L.ers into small groups and assigned each group to one of the Bnot Yisrael classrooms, to sit and observe. I was one of the six chosen to sit in with the seventh graders. Everyone raved about Morah Verner, and a few girls had even told me how lucky I was to be able to observe her class. I had wasted a wonderful opportunity because I could think of nothing else but my sister's issues.

We were to meet the rest of the girls and Geveret Spitz in Bnot Yisrael's lobby before heading back to our campus. It was really an oversized hallway strewn with a few vinyl-covered chairs on chrome legs. Geveret Spitz sat on one of them, waiting patiently with the earlier arrivals gathered around her until the rest of the M.B.L.L.ers finally showed up.

To my dismay, she handed us observation forms with instructions to fill out information regarding the classes we just observed. I had no idea how I would complete the form! Luckily, we did not have to submit the paper until the next day and I was fortunate that Mazal had been with me. I would undoubtedly need her help.

Most of the girls started to make their way out of the building once Geveret Spitz dismissed us. I was standing next to Mazal, Mimi, and some of the others, with my notebook in hand, bracing myself for the chilly walk home. I closed my zipper all the way to the top of my jacket until the zipper-pull touched my chin.

"So-o-o, who wants to go to Pinat HaGlidah?" Rochel Leah asked as Mimi was about to push open the door. The question had been posed aloud, but was really directed at Chani.

"Pinat HaGlidah? Not me, Rochel Leah," Chani shook her head. "B-r-r-r, it's so cold outside."

"How about you, Mimi? Are you also afraid of the cold weather?"

"I'm not afraid, Rochel Leah, and it sounds like fun," Mimi said buoyantly before glancing in my direction. "But no way can I go today."

"Why?" Rochel Leah's eyes followed Mimi's gaze. "Oh, you still have work to do with Sara? You still didn't finish?"

I felt the blood rushing to my face, convinced that everyone was staring at me.

"Well, you know the reports for Geveret Spitz are due tomorrow—"

"And you both didn't finish yet? What's taking so-o-o long?"

"Sara finished hers a long time ago," Mimi said, "and I'm going to polish mine off today."

Polish it off? We had been busily working on Mimi's report, in fact we had been occupied with it practically non-stop ever since this past Sunday. Mimi still had a lot more to do than just *polish it off.*

"So you can't spare a half-hour to come with me to Pinat Glidah, Mimi? I'm suddenly so-o-o in the mood for ice cream."

"What about the observation report Geveret Spitz just said we have to fill out for tomorrow?" I figured I had better add in my own two cents before Rochel Leah managed to convince Mimi to join her. "And we're also having a *halachah* quiz tomorrow."

"Oh, my goodness, I forgot all about it!" Rivky exclaimed.

"What's the big deal?" Rochel Leah rolled her eyes. "It's stuff we know about anyway. It's only about Chanukah."

"Hey, Rochel Leah," Mimi thumped her on the shoulder while grinning, "just because you happen to be brilliant, it doesn't mean the rest of us don't have to review."

"And anyway," I heard myself say, "don't forget tomorrow night's Chanukah. It's really important to review the *halachos* even if we didn't have a quiz to study for."

Rochel Leah ignored me. "So come on…Chani? Mimi? None of you want to join me for just a short visit to town?"

"Really, I'd love to," Mimi smiled, "but I've got to be practical."

"Practical, shmactical," Rochel Leah mumbled.

"I'd also love to go. You know I'm always game for something good to eat," Chani said and we all laughed, "but right now the only thing I'm dreaming of is Geveret Mendlowitz's hot potato soup."

"You know what? You all sound like a bunch of old fogies. Rivky, are you also too cold, or too practical, or are you willing to brave the elements and join me?"

"Actually, I'd like to, but I promised Ruti to help her with her English homework and oh no!" she exclaimed after glancing at her watch. "It's much later than I thought and now Sara reminded me of the *halachah* quiz…"

"You're right Rivky, it's really late," Chani said. "Geveret Spitz didn't dismiss us until every single girl showed up. Do you want me to hurry back with you now, Rivky, ahead of the others?"

"Oh, that would be great. Do you mind? I have so much to do and I promised Ruti."

"And I sure won't mind getting one of the first portions of Geveret Mendlowitz's soup…"

We felt a rush of cold air when Rivky opened the door. They hurried off, their voices fading the further away they got.

"So-o-o, no one wants to come with me?" Rochel Leah turned to the rest of us, her face displaying an exaggerated pout.

I saw Zehava take a step forward and open her mouth to speak. Then quickly, she closed it. She glanced at me.

I tried to avert my gaze.

Rochel Leah laughed. "Okay, I guess it's just Zehava and me. Come on, Zehava," Rochel Leah started walking toward the door.

Zehava did not move.

Rochel Leah stopped. "Well, what're you waiting for? Aren't you coming?"

I held my breath.

"Uh…um, Rochel Leah, I-I hope you don't mind, but I'd rather…um…go back to the dorm with everyone else."

Rochel Leah grimaced. "Come on, Zehava. Don't tell me you're also freezing."

"N-no…I'm not so cold, but I'm really not in the mood for ice cream. So…um…maybe some other time?"

Rochel Leah's hazel eyes opened wide in surprise. "What?"

"I…um…er…w-would rather…" Zehava looked helplessly in my direction.

Without thinking, I winked at her.

Suddenly, Zehava's face broke into a broad grin and she winked back. A warm feeling came over me.

And then it happened.

Zehava said with confidence that surprised even me, "I'd rather go back to the campus for some of that delicious potato soup."

So Rochel Leah ended up walking back with us.

The mood turned more jovial as we made our way through the woods to the Beit Yaakov HaNegbah campus. and we were quite a cheerful crowd by the time we reached the dormitory's dining room. It was already time for lunch and we sat around the tables enjoying our hot potato soup with fresh *lachmaniyot*, tasty breaded chicken with fried eggplant, and Israeli salad. Even more pleasant was the warm bantering and I could not help but marvel at the changes that had taken place ever since I had come to M.B.L.L.

I was no longer the lonely outsider and it had not come about because of Chavie or anyone else. Well, maybe that was not entirely true. Mimi had definitely helped me, but then again I had also helped her. It was a special feeling, this friendship of ours.

But, what's going to happen after we hand in our reports? Will Mimi still think of me as her first real friend then—when she doen't need me as much?

The food was suddenly not as tasty as it had been a few minutes earlier.

Sara, stop thinking like that! If your friendship is "real," then of course it will last. Besides, Mimi still has plenty of work to do if she wants to get through this seminary year successfully. She can't afford to simply forget about you.

I put my fork down on the table. Fortunately, there was not much time to mull over these troublesome thoughts. Mimi finished eating, we *bentched*, and headed upstairs to my room in order to get started as soon as possible. We had a full night's work waiting for us. The reports had to be submitted the next day.

"We're really lucky that Mazal could study elsewhere," I told Mimi as I pushed the door to my room open.

"I know. Most of the time Adina uses *my* room for studying," Mimi sighed. "It's a good thing you're right next door."

"Thanks. I'm glad I'm...so useful."

"Sara," Mimi said nonchalantly, "you sure are useful."

I flung my jacket onto my bed. "Thanks."

"Hey, what's wrong?"

"Nothing." I turned to face her. "Who says something's wrong?"

"Oh...I don't know. You just seemed a little...um...upset."

"Upset? Me?"

"Okay, great. I'm going to my room to get my stuff. I'll be right back," she left through the wash-up closet.

I sat down on my bed next to my jacket and put my notebook down beside me.

"Alrighty...I'm back!" Mimi bounced into the room, as cheerful as ever, and plopped down on the bed next to me. "What are we going to do first?"

I swallowed hard. *Sara, stop being so worried all the time. Mimi probably likes you because you're you and not just because you help her so much.* "I think we should leave the report for last, because that's going to probably take the longest. Maybe we should do the other writing homework first."

"Okay, sounds good. So what should we work on?"

"Well, Geveret Spitz gave us those observation reports. The problem is that I wasn't in the same classroom as you were, so I can't really help you with that. How about I review the questions that are on the form with you? Then you'll need to answer the questions yourself."

"All right. I was really paying attention to Morah Leibb. She's fantastic! Did you ever observe her class?"

"Yes…two or three times. She's really something."

"Adina was with me there today. I guess I could ask her for help if worse comes to worst."

"I'm sure Adina will be glad to help you," I said while opening my notebook and removing the folded sheet of paper Geveret Spitz had handed out.

"Hey, Sara, what happened with you two last Shabbos when you had *toranut*?" Mimi's green eyes danced.

"What do you mean?"

"After that scene Thursday night, I was afraid of how Shabbos would go for both of you, but you two seemed okay when I saw you sitting together in class on Sunday."

"We are okay," I unfolded the paper and tried smoothing out its creases, "*very* okay."

"And then you went away with Adina this past Shabbos to Yerushalayim. Uh oh, Sara," she laughed, "I'm afraid you're going to abandon me."

"Very funny, Mimi Rosenberg. I'm sure you're absolutely petrified."

We kept up this light banter for another minute or two and then I reminded Mimi that we'd better get down to work. I did not want to have to stay up all the night finishing her report.

Sitting side by side on my bed, we first went through all the questions on Geveret Spitz's form. Ever since our conversation in the storage room, when I was first made aware of her problem, we had developed certain techniques for working together. I read the questions to Mimi and then slowly translated them into English. Then Mimi read them back to me and explained what she read. If she had any difficulty reading, we would go back to the problematic word and slowly dissect it, reread it, and review it until we felt sure Mimi had conquered it. It took us longer to finish doing it this way, but it was worth it. Mimi was truly accomplishing!

After we felt certain that Mimi could read and translate each of the questions on Geveret Spitz's observation form, she went next door to Adina to find out when she would be available to help her with answering her questions. I did not doubt that Adina realized Mimi had a problem. I was also certain Adina would do what she could to help.

While Mimi was next door, I went over to my desk and tried to fill out my form. I could complete most of it, but I could not fill in the parts regarding the last two subjects. I definitely would need Mazal's help. Although I had been in the seventh grade room during that entire period, because my mind was elsewhere I had not learned a thing.

I should have known, though, that this self-recrimination was useless. There was no way I could have prevented myself from thinking about Shuli.

I looked out the window above my desk and stared at the spectacular desert mountains.

Shuli…

Through my mind's eye, I saw Shuli, who always had everything going for her, who traversed life's paths with ease. That is…until an obstacle crossed her path. Then she quit.

And then a picture of Mimi flashed before me. Sure she was breezy and talented, just like Shuli. But, I now realized that she could not simply skip down life's paths as my sister had. Her road had never been straight and smooth, yet she continued making her way. No, she would not give up! Even now, when she thought she might lose something that she really wanted to hold onto, she worked even harder for it.

Mimi was used to battling. Only, until a few days ago, she had been fighting to hide something, but now that she wanted so badly to succeed, she was using that strength to reach her goal.

I had always thought of Shuli as someone gifted with unusual strengths. But sitting there at my desk, I wondered if that was really true. When the going got rough, she did not have a clue as to how to handle it. Instead of confronting a problem and trying to work through it, she became overwhelmed. Weak…

Unexpectedly, I found myself thinking about Miss Lyn, our gym teacher back at Beis Yaakov of Rolland Heights. "Girls," she would tell us during calisthenics, "you want to strengthen those muscles and make them strong? You have to work them! Let's go...in out! In out!"

We would stand there stretching, groaning, and complaining and she would push us harder and harder, telling us, "If you want strong muscles, you've got to keep 'em moving. If you leave 'em alone, it'll be your undoing."

Maybe that's it, I pondered. Mimi, because of her situation, has been strengthening her muscles constantly, never allowing them to deteriorate. But Shuli? She had in essence been sitting around all this time. Will this inertia be her "undoing"?

And me? Am I like Mimi or Shuli? Have I been working my muscles or have I—

"I'm ba-ack," Mimi called out. "Hey," she leaned over my shoulder and peered down at the observation form lying on my desk, "I thought by now for sure you'd be finished."

"Well...I...I—"

"That's all right. No one's perfect."

"Mimi!"

"I take that back. Some people *are* perfect. My roommate for example—"

"Mimi, stop—"

"I went into my room and asked Adina if she'd have time later to help me with the observation form. She said she'd already finished hers. Can you believe her? She's already finished!"

"So?"

"So she's way ahead of us and she's already busy reviewing the *halachah* questions with a bunch of girls. I don't understand how she does it. Even you, the made to order—"

"Mimi, I asked you to stop calling me that. Anyway, did you do your sheet or not?"

"Well, believe it or not, 'perfect Adina' stopped working with the other girls for a couple of minutes and helped me finish it. And believe it or not, it went pretty quickly because you helped me with the questions and I *really* had paid attention and—"

"Okay, I get the idea," I laughed. "It sounds like *you* did a perfect job on it. Now let's review *halachah* and then we'll *polish off* your report, as you so eloquently told Rochel Leah."

Reviewing the *halachos* took about an hour. First, I read and Mimi closed her eyes and concentrated. Then I tested her orally. Finally, she read the questions I had written down for her slowly and carefully and answered them in writing. By doing this, we felt she would be amply prepared to take the test along with everyone else the next day.

When she finished writing in the last answer, I nodded approvingly. "Great job, Mimi. You're becoming a real pro."

"Why thank you," she tossed her pen down on the desk and let out a big yawn. "You've been a huge help. You're pretty much a pro yourself."

"Thanks, Mimi. Okay," I said quickly, not wanting to lose the momentum, "now we'd better start organizing your report."

Mimi slowly moved her chair backwards and stood up. Stretching her arms as far out as she could, she let out another exaggerated yawn and said, "I can't wait till tomorrow, Sara."

"Why?" I twisted my neck around to face her.

"Cause then I'll be finished with THE report."

I swallowed hard. "And?"

"And then, Sara, you know, then I'll be free!"

"Free?"

"Yes…free from all this work! Free to have fun again!"

"Oh," I felt a dip in my stomach.

"And I'll be able to throw myself into the Chanukah production again. You know I have friends coming from a bunch of the other seminaries to see it and…" Mimi suddenly stopped.

"And what, Mimi?"

"And," she said slowly while sitting down on the edge of Mazal's bed, "and I'm hoping that it'll end up being so perfect, so good, that we'll be asked to perform the production all over the place and then…"

"And then what?" my heartbeat began to quicken.

"Rabbi Grossman will be so happy with me…he won't ask me to leave M.B.L.L."

"Oh, Mimi," I sighed with relief. *So that's what Mimi's worried about. That's what she means when she says she wants to be free. Free of worry. Poor kid, she's really afraid Rabbi Grossman will send her home.* I got up

Chapter 28

from my chair near the desk and went to sit next to her. "Mimi, Rabbi Grossman's not going to ask you to leave if he sees you working hard. You've been doing a great job these last two weeks!"

"Yeah, but I can't keep it up. I'm hoping that if I behave and make a success out of the performance, Rabbi Grossman will go easier on me."

"What're you saying, Mimi? You think he'll let you stop doing homework? Stop writing reports?"

"Well, sort of, Sara. I'm hoping that if I follow the rules and do *some* of the homework...," she pointed to the papers and *sefarim* on the desk, "I won't have to do all this studying."

"But, Mimi, you can't do that!" I cried out weakly. I wanted Mimi to still need me. I knew I needed her. I was clutching helplessly at straws. "What about the Goldstone Award?"

"Sara," Mimi let out a long hollow laugh, "did you actually think I was serious about the Goldstone Award?"

"Yes, of course I thought you were serious, Miriam Mina Rosenberg!"

"Stop yelling, Sara."

"I'm not yelling. I'm just trying to understand..."

"But you can't understand."

Understand...understand...didn't someone else say the same thing to me recently? "Yes, I *can* understand!" I insisted.

Mimi's laugh was rough. "No way. Schoolwork comes easily for you. It doesn't frustrate you. Yes, you work hard, but nothing like me. For every tiny step you take, I have to take a hundred steps."

"So?"

"Again you're telling me *so*? For me, Sara, it's all one big struggle. I know you want to encourage me and all that, and you're a terrific tutor, but you can't possibly understand."

"First of all, I'm not your tutor...I'm...I'm your friend."

"Okay...*friend*. You still can't understand."

"Maybe, Mimi, *you* don't understand."

"Me?"

"Yes...I don't think you understand your own self."

"And *you* do?"

"Yes...I think so. All those years you've been putting on a show for the world—that took strength, major strength."

"I had no choice, Sara," she abruptly grew quiet.

"Oh, but you did have a choice. You could've sat in the back of the classroom, depressed that you couldn't keep up with everyone else. You could've become a very bitter person. But you didn't. You used whatever you had to its fullest—until now."

"Now?"

"Mimi…imagine all that energy. And you can't deny it, Mimi, you have tons and tons of energy. Imagine if instead of using it to hide your problem or using it to be Mimi the Mimic, the funniest girl in M.B.L.L., you use it to…to work on getting that award."

I stood up and walked toward my bed, unable to look Mimi in the face. She did not say a word but I felt her eyes on my back. Fortunately, she could not read my mind, because right then my thoughts were not quite as altruistic as they sounded and I was beginning to feel a little guilty.

I swung around. "And even if you don't win it…the award, that is…imagine how much all this work will do for you. Look," I picked up the batch of papers sitting on my bed that were to be her report for Geveret Spitz, "you've thought of the most innovative ideas here. You're report is excellent, Mimi, excellent. And part of this counts toward your *Proyect*. You're partly there already!"

"But, Sara," Mimi stood up and came over to me, "we've been working so hard till now. I can't keep it up for the rest of the year."

"But Mimi…you've always worked hard, just maybe not on your schoolwork. I'm here. I'm right next door. I'll help you, Mazal will help you, and I'm sure Adina would help you too, if you'd ask."

Mimi had this pleading look in her eyes, "I don't know. I can't—"

"You can!"

"How come you're so sure about it?"

"Because…because…I know you're no quitter. I'm starting to see that the people who always have things easy are the ones who have a hard time handling challenges. They throw up their hands and quit. But the people who don't have things so easy…"

"Yes?"

"Are stronger and keep at it. I was even thinking…"

"What?"

Why didn't I ever think before I spoke? I felt myself blushing, "Forget it."

"No, Sara, tell me. What were you thinking?"

"Well, it's kind of silly."

"Come on. You've made me really curious. What were you going to say?"

"You can't laugh at me, though. It was about…uh, you've heard people say that someone has, you know, baggage?"

"You mean like with me…something that's been troubling them for years?"

"Uh…"

"Sara!"

"Yes, Mimi, that's what I mean," I said feebly.

"Right, so I have baggage. I know that."

"No, that's not what I wanted to say," I swallowed hard.

"Sorry, Sara. Go on."

"All right. So let's say a person has…baggage. Well, instead of dragging it around or…or even trying to hide it or ignore it, what if they took all that energy they'd been using and laid…laid that suitcase down to sort of step on top of it? You know, use it to help them climb higher…"

To this day, I do not know what made me think of that. Yet, once those words came out of my mouth, I suddenly believed them with all my heart. I was not certain of how it would work…how it could be possible, but I was convinced that if Hashem gave someone a challenge, then somehow…some way, that person could take that challenge and use it to his advantage to reach greater heights.

"That's interesting…" Mimi was thoughtful. "So, let *me* ask *you* a question."

I waited silently for her to continue.

"You say that there's the group of strugglers lugging their baggage around and you think they're stronger because of it. Right?"

"Well…yes, Mimi. That's what I think."

"And the other group, the people who have it easier…the ones without the suitcases…"

"Right…they can't be as strong as the first group, the ones with the…um…baggage…"

"So, Sara, I'm wondering," she tucked a loose strand of red hair behind her ear, "which group do you belong to?"

"Huh?"

Are you a struggler with her suitcase or are you one of those who've got it easy?"

29

"HEY, I CAN'T believe it was two weeks ago that I was by you, Mazal. It feels like it was just yesterday!"

"And I am very happy to have you back, Mimi."

"Are you sure that you have room for all of us, Mazal?" I asked for the fifth time since our bus pulled out of the bus station in Be'er Sheva.

"Stop being such a worrier, Sara," Mimi said. "You're going to make us all feel bad for coming."

"No! No! No one should feel bad," Mazal shook her head vigorously, "I and my family very, very happy to have you for guests."

My heart lifted. Mazal was so warm and caring. When she invited me to come for Shabbos and Mimi heard and decided she wanted to come too, I thought it would be a great opportunity to include Adina.

We did not have any school that Friday morning, and decided to get up early and make the six o'clock bus out of Be'er Sheva. We were so tired though, that we were tempted to take the next bus instead. Fortunately we did not. As we were later to find out, had we waited, we probably would not have been able to go at all.

Anyway, we had good reason for being so fatigued. The previous night, after Chanukah lighting, a riveting *shiur* by Rabbanit Greenstein, a long and festive supper, practice for the Chanukah production, and finally showers and packing, we did not get to bed until it was almost time to get up. With so few hours of sleep and the monotonous lull of the rocking bus, it was no wonder that my friends around me eventually dozed off.

Sinking back against the vinyl cushion I too closed my eyes, thinking and listening to the drone of the motor.

This would be Adina's and my third Shabbos in a row together, and I did not take that fact for granted. It was only two weeks since that fateful Shabbos when she had opened up to me. I felt I should be careful. *Very careful.* I did not want to undo the progess we had made.

On *Motzaei Shabbos* two weeks ago, after we had completed our *toranut* chores, Adina had come into my room with her tape recorder in one hand and a tape in the other. *Her mother's tape.* She wanted me to hear it. Adina, who had never opened up to anyone before, had no idea of where to go from there. I think she felt that because I already knew so much about her, she was compelled to share *everything* with me.

I knew it would be wrong for me to listen to the tape. It had been recorded for Adina by her mother when the doctors told her she had only a short time left to live. Emphatically, I told her that the tape was for her…and her alone. Not me.

At first, she seemed offended. Here she was offering to share something precious with me… and I was turning her down. I tried explaining to her that a real friend is there for you when you need her, yet she is able to respect your privacy too.

I am not sure she understood. I noticed that she did withdraw from me somewhat after that. Though I consciously made an effort not to continue speaking about what she had told me, I was sure I detected a trace of resentment from Adina because she had bared so much of herself. Of course, it was nothing like the coldness or hostility of the past, yet I was certain that a different kind of antagonism had developed.

That is why I was surprised when the following Wednesday evening Adina came looking for me in the library and invited me to go away with her for that Shabbos. I was undeniably flattered. She could have asked Malkie, Devorah, or any of the other girls to go.

She took me to Hinda Klein in Yerushalayim for Shabbos and we had a magnificent time there. We did not talk about Adina's family, the diary, the tape, or her situation. Adina seemed a little tense, but Savta Hinda did not notice, or at least she pretended not to. She did not raise the subject of Adina's parents even once.

It was just a pleasant visit with a vibrant elderly woman, whose warmth spread to all those around her. Other girls from different seminaries and neighbors stopped by to visit during the afternoon—girls I had never seen before. She supplied us all with plenty of nosh and we chatted happily together over tea, candies, and pastries. It really was a wonderful Shabbos.

The following week had been a demanding one, handing our reports in on Monday, lighting the Chanukah menorah each night, and writing a few short reports, essays, and research papers. Then Mimi was on top of us, relentlessly driving us all to practice for the production. Yes, Mimi had managed to get me involved at the last minute too. No, I did not have an acting, dancing, or singing part. I think Mimi knew I would never agree to any of that. So, finally she convinced me to do the one job I would be good at.

I was in charge of props.

So, with all the regular schoolwork, refining my *Proyect*, and working in the resource room, gathering together props for the Chanukah production, and participating in the practices, I was able to successfully shove away my worries about how Adina felt about me. More importantly, this hectic schedule helped me ignore those pangs of guilt I was feeling for encouraging Mimi to go after the Goldstone Award when I was certain she had no chance of winning it—something I had done only because I wanted her to still need me.

Lighting the Chanukah menorah without my family was an emotional affair, but I noticed that I was not the only homesick one. Looking around the room, I could see that most of the others were trying to hold back their tears too. The first night of Chanukah Rabbi Grossman gave us a beautiful *shiur*. And each night, as another flame was lit, another moving speech was delivered by one of the faculty members. It was truly an uplifting and enlightening Chanukah.

I do not think I shall ever forget the look on Mimi's face the night Rabbanit Abrams spoke to us.

Throughout the year, one evening a week we had the good fortune to gather around her for a *shiur* in *Chovos HaLevavos*. We had been studying *Sha'ar HaBitachon* in depth. Her lessons were always stirring, speaking directly to the heart. Chanukah was no different. Again, she shared with us the inspiring words of Rabbi Bachya ibn Paquda. And again, we were not disappointed.

That Wednesday evening, though, sitting with the flickering flames of the menorahs around us and with the scent of fried latkes and sufganiyot permeating the air, there was an additional aura enveloping us. Not surprisingly, her talk evolved from *bitachon* to the story of Chanukah. She spoke of different kinds of darkness and how when situations seem especially bleak, it is only because we human beings have not yet been privileged to see the complete picture.

"Girls, when we say *Al HaNissim* in *Shemoneh Esrei* and *Birkas HaMazon*, we say the words '*giborim b'yad chalashim v'rabbim be'yad me'atim*,' it should serve as a reminder to us that salvation is always possible, that nothing is beyond Hashem's abilities. Yes, Hashem 'delivered the strong into the hands of the weak, the many into the hands of the few.' Sometimes a situation seems beyond help, but deliverance is there, just waiting to be sent by Hashem. And this girls," her large dark eyes scanned the room, "is something that affects us all—not just on a national level but on an individual basis as well. When our own problems seem insurmountable, when it feels like there is no light on the horizon, we, as the *Chashmona'im* did, must turn to Hashem in prayer and do our *hishtadlus* to conquer the enemy within us, the *yetzer hara*.

"The Evil Inclination tries to convince us that our difficulties are overwhelming and unfair, when in reality Hashem has given us these challenges to help us grow and reach greater heights. As we just quoted from the *Chovos HaLevavos*, 'He rejoices in whatever the situation is in which he is placed.'"

Whatever the situation is in which he is placed? My eyes darted toward Adina. She stared ahead, her expression impenetrable, her face a stone wall. *How was her situation good for her and what kind of deliverance could she hope for? Is that what she's thinking right now?* I could just hear her asking herself, "Deliverance? Like my mother suddenly appearing and telling me she's really alive and we can go back to being a perfect family?" I shook my head sadly. *No, that isn't exactly a realistic "deliverance."*

"Often, when a problem is so terrible, so painful, the Evil Inclination

Chapter 29

will do whatever he can to crush our hopes for deliverance. He will attempt to convince us of the hopelessness and injustice of it all and thus, G-d forbid, succeed in severing our relationship with Hashem. He will make us think of our problems and our challenges as burdens, instead of the stepping-stones that they are meant to be."

Stepping-stones? Something to make us climb higher? Isn't that what Mimi and I spoke of the other day?

I glanced at Mimi. Her green eyes seemed glued to Rabbanit Abrams. She appeared to be drinking in her words with a thirst I could only imagine how desperately needed to be quenched.

"There is a story told," Rabbanit Abrams went on, "of the bird complaining to Hashem. 'Why is it,' the bird protested, 'all Your other creatures were given hands at their sides, and what do I have? Two heavy things to carry around wherever I go? It's not fair!'

"And girls, do you know what Hashem answered the bird?

"'Little bird, instead of looking at what others have and what you don't have, look closely at those things you are carrying at your sides. True, they are not hands, but do you know what they are? Take them, flap them back and forth, raise them, and they will lift you higher and higher. They are wings. Instead of seeing them as burdens that hold you back, see them for what they really are. They are the very things that will help you soar!'"

And that is when I saw that look on Mimi's face. When we heard Rabbanit Abrams's words, I knew what she was thinking. She was comparing the bird's wings to her challenges—her "baggage."

Suddenly she looked up and our eyes met. I smiled at her, but she did not return it. Her lips were pursed together grittily, her brows furrowed in deep concentration. I could see a look of steely determination in her eyes, unlike any I had seen before. I had seen her looking resolute a few times in the past. But, never like this.

What could Mimi's deliverance be? I pondered. *How does someone take a severe learning problem and turn it into a stepping-stone? And even if Mimi has the ability to do it, does she have the staying power not to give up?*

Could the pain of Adina's past be something upon which she could build? Can our "baggage" really help us to soar to greater heights?

I am not sure when I drifted off to sleep and to dreamland, but all of a sudden I heard someone shout, "*Sheleg!*" Then there were more cries of, "*Sheleg!*" I felt someone shaking me and Mimi's eager voice saying, "Wake up, Sara, we're almost there and it's snowing!"

My eyes flew open, my heart contracting with excitement. *Snow? Snow in Israel?* We had heard rumors that it might snow, but no one really believed them. Enthusiasm vibrated throughout the bus. This was so unusual and so thrilling!

Then the arguments ensued.

One woman scolded everyone for being so happy. "What're you all smiling about?" She complained. "Now we'll never reach our destinations."

"Why not?" the woman sitting next to her innocently asked.

"Why not, you ask. Why not? I'll tell you why not," she spat out bitterly. "In our country, no bus drives in the snow!"

"Hey, lady! Stop making such a fuss! We're almost there. And it's just a few flurries. This is no—"

He was interrupted by another man a few seats in front of him, "What do you mean *stop making a fuss*? In 1969 it snowed much worse and it started with just a few—"

"It wasn't '69," a woman opposite him huffed. "It was in '75. I know because I was at my daughter's and—"

"Who cares—'69 or '75?" the first woman cried out. "The buses aren't going to run anymore. They're afraid of the snow. See, the bus is stopping!"

Indeed, the bus did come to a halt just then, but that was because it had reached the first stop on its route.

As the woman who had been at her daughter's in '75 and the man who could not understand what the fuss was all about got off the bus and collected their suitcases, the others wished them a hearty *Shabbat Shalom* and a happy Chanukah and told them to enjoy the snow. The bus then continued and so did the arguments. Opinions regarding traveling and snow inevitably turned into political debates, with many of the passengers unabashedly expressing their strong views and the remaining ones taking different sides.

It was fortunate that we had made the six o'clock bus, because had we not, the next one out of Be'er Sheva would probably have been cancelled due to the snow. We wondered aloud how many girls would be stuck in the dormitory for Shabbos. We watched the flurries fall to the ground and speculated about whether they would indeed stick. Mimi worried about Sunday's travel schedule. The Chanukah production was slated for that evening. Mazal told her not to be concerned, snow was rare in Israel and it would probably stop soon. By Sunday, the transportation system would surely be back to normal.

The bus chugged along, making various stops at *kibbutzim, moshavim*, and neighborhoods along the way, climbing somewhat higher after each stop.

When we reached Moshav Shoshanim, the lady who had initiated the argument about the snow took her leave. She hugged the woman who had been sitting next to her, blessed everyone on the bus, and then waved a cheerful goodbye as she alighted. The bus started moving again.

Mazal told us that we would be reaching Kiryat Yosef in about fifteen minutes. We were all giddy with expectation.

Emerging from the bus a short while later, we breathed in the crisp mountain air and felt the soft touch of the snow flurries against our faces. Gratefully, I looked around at the surrounding hills and valleys. *It really is great to be here, sun, rain, or snow!*

"Isn't this place gorgeous?" Mimi asked rhetorically while surveying the scenery.

"It's beautiful," Adina's voice was no more than a whisper.

Mazal's brothers and sisters were waiting for us at the bus stop. Mazal threw her small suitcase to the ground and lifted Reilya out of the stroller, wrapping her in a big bear hug. "Oh my sweet little Reilya. I'm so happy to see you!"

"Not me, Mazali? You're not happy to see me?"

"And me?"

"Sure I'm happy to see you, Salmi and Miryam," Mazal smiled at them, her chin resting on the top of Reilya's head. She turned to her brothers, "And Yichya and Yigal too."

Yichya blushed. "Um, Mazal, did you see the snow?"

"Yes, did you see it Mazali? Ima said we could build a snowman."

"Well, I don't think—"

"There isn't going to be enough snow to build a snowman," Yigal informed us. "Ima said that it's probably going to turn into rain."

"Well, either way we'd better get indoors," Mazal said.

"Do you have to leave on *Motzaei Shabbat*?" Miryam asked.

"We just arrived. And you're already talking about leaving," Mazal laughed. "No, Miryam, but we have to leave Sunday morning."

"Why Mazali? Why can't you stay longer?"

"Because we're putting on a special Chanukah production Sunday night and we need to get back early enough to practice, set up the stage, and get into our costumes," Mazal explained. "Anyway, we have all of Shabbat to talk about it. Now, is this any way to treat guests? Leaving them standing out in the cold?"

Embarrassed, everyone turned and headed for the house. I saw Miryam stare at Adina in open admiration, commenting to Mazal that the new guest was extremely pretty. Adina's face turned a deep red. Mazal reminded Miryam that all the guests knew Hebrew quite well and she should be careful of what she said in front of them. This caused Adina to blush even more. Then Salma slipped her hand into Adina's, pulling her quickly along the steep path, and I noticed that Adina could no longer suppress her smile.

"Hey, no one remembers me?" Mimi complained while walking beside me, directly behind Adina, Salma, and Miryam.

"Of course we didn't forget you, Mimi," Miryam turned to face us while maintaining her pace beside Adina and her little sister, "or you, Sara, but you are our old guests. Now we need to get to know the new one."

"Nu, everyone, let's hurry," Mazal warned. "The snow is starting to get heavier!"

"Yay! Yay!" Salmi jumped up and down.

Her joy was contagious. Everyone was grinning happily as we walked up the hill and entered Mazal's house. And we continued smiling throughout the whole Shabbos.

I had never seen Adina as happy as she was throughout that Shabbos or as talkative. She read stories to the children, chatted with the various family members, and joked and laughed with the rest of us.

Chapter 29

It was unusually cold that Shabbos, but with my warm jacket and old gray scarf, I had no problem keeping warm when we went outdoors for a little walk. And the warmth inside Mazal's home was as comfortable as one could wish.

The only sad part about Shabbos was seeing the grandmother in her feeble state. I did not notice any improvement since my last visit, and in fact, she seemed even more sedated than before.

I wondered about the rest of Geveret Cohen's story. I remembered how Mazal and I had sat with her mother outside on the deck, listening to her recollections about leaving Yemen and coming to Israel. And I would never forget the grandmother's cries as she screamed for her daughter.

What had happened? I pondered. I very much wanted to hear the rest of Geveret Cohen's story and wondered if I ever would.

Of course, once I did hear it, there was no turning back.

30

"I REMEMBER. EVERY time it snows, I remember."

"Ima, it doesn't snow that often."

"That is true, Mazal. I suppose it is better that way."

We looked from one to the other uncomfortably. Apparently, there was something about the snow that Geveret Cohen found disturbing. That is why I was surprised when she continued talking.

"Yes…at the time I thought snow was the most wonderful thing on earth. It was to be the happiest day of my life."

We were silent; a gloomy fog enveloped us.

It was late Sunday morning and we were sitting around Mazal's kitchen table, talking with her mother over steaming glasses of hot tea and biscuitim smeared with chocolate spread. We were not really supposed to be there still. We should have been on the bus traveling southward, toward Kfar Amsdorf.

We had awakened about an hour after dawn, expecting to begin our trip back. However, when we looked out the window of the girls' room, we saw a white blanket of snow covering Kiryat Yosef and beyond. The snow was falling heavily and the distant hills and valleys glistened brightly under the early morning sun.

That peaceful scene belied the turmoil that suddenly gripped us.

"What're we going to do?" Mimi cried out. "The production!"

There were countless telephone calls to the central bus station, all with the same result. "No buses are running now, Geveret. Call back in another half-hour."

After numerous conversations between us and Geveret Katz, it was decided that since many of the girls were stranded in various places across Eretz Yisrael where they had spent Shabbos, and an inestimable number of guests would be prevented from coming due to the weather…the Chanukah production would have to be postponed for the time being.

To say that Mimi was disappointed would be an understatement. We were all disappointed! Then Mimi, in keeping with her cheerful, happy-go-lucky personality, informed us that since we had no control over the weather, we should make the most of our stay at Mazal's.

"And maybe," she added, her green eyes twinkling, "we can turn this into wings. You know…the bird's wings that Rabbanit Abrams spoke to us about on Wednesday night."

With that, an indescribably warm feeling came over me.

By the time we finished *davening*, eating breakfast, and straightening up, it had stopped snowing. Mazal's father and the boys went over to the local yeshivah to learn. Reilya was put down for a nap and the two little girls went outside to play in the snow. Geveret Cohen's mother sat dozing in her wheelchair near the window, the sun shining warmly over her.

We called the bus station again. They still did not know when the next bus to Be'er Sheva would be.

Geveret Cohen prepared a pitcher of hot tea and Mazal took out the biscuitim with various spreads. We sat around chatting about the topic of the day: snow.

That was when Geveret Cohen began talking about her memories of when she first arrived in Eretz Yisrael from Yemen. It seemed that during that year of her family's *aliyah*, there had been the unusual occurrence of snow and it had awakened some recollections.

"Oh…I am sorry, girls. I see I am causing you to feel sad. This is not good."

"No, please, Geveret Cohen," Mimi declared passionately. "We'd love to hear you tell us about when you came to Israel. Ouch!"

Mimi threw me a questioning look and I felt myself blushing. I had kicked her under the table, trying to tell to her to be quiet.

"I do not want to make you sad, Mimi or any of you," she looked from each of us to the next.

"Um...don't worry about us, Geveret Cohen. We're all right."

"Thank you, Sara. I see Mazal wants me to talk. Mimi, you look like you are very interested. Adina?"

"Me?" Adina asked while pointing to her chest. "Whatever is good for you, Geveret Cohen."

"Please, Ima. I know so little of that time!"

"I know, Mazal, and last time when we began—"

"Savta wasn't feeling well then, Ima. But now..." She looked toward her grandmother and then at her mother, "I don't think Savta will—"

"You are right, Mazal," Geveret Cohen shook her head sadly. "I do not think Savta will even realize," her voice cracked.

"Ima, if it's too hard for you..."

"I do not know, Mazal," Geveret Cohen sighed. "Difficult for me...not difficult for me..."

I sat silently, not knowing what I should do. Last time when Mazal had implored her mother to speak, I had been their only guest. I felt that my presence during that mother-daughter talk was an intrusion, and had it not been for Geveret Cohen's insistence, I surely would have left them alone. However, this time it was different. I was with Mimi and Adina. And they were both staring at Geveret Cohen, openly expectant.

"Maybe Ima, it is better for you to sit back and relax. You don't need to talk about it."

"Relax, Mazal? No. I cannot relax, not when it is snowing outside. It brings back the memories..."

"But, Ima—"

"You know, Mazal, sometimes even if it is difficult, it is better to talk. The snow... the memories come to me uninvited. Yes, it is better I should not fight the memories..."

We waited for her to go on.

"Girls, you understand my *Ivrit*?"

"Yes."

"Sure."

"Pretty good. Just please speak a little slower."

"Yes, Mimi," Mazal's mother smiled for the first time that morning. "I shall speak slowly, but please tell me if you do not understand what I say and I will try to explain. All right," she continued. "I already told Mazal and Sara a little bit about where we lived when we first arrived in Eretz Yisrael. Not in regular homes, but in a refugee camp called Rosh HaBe'er. This was the camp we Yemenite immigrants were placed in."

"It sounds like the place Geveret Katz was telling us about, the place her father, ouch!"

Mimi eyes met mine. *What did I do this time?* she seemed to ask me. I put my finger to my lips, indicating that she should be quiet and let Geveret Cohen talk.

"So, my group leader's name was Yael. We children were placed in her care. We ate in a central dining hall, children separated from their parents. There was a *shomer* in charge of the camp—"

"Just like Geveret Katz's father..."

I elbowed Mimi.

"The *shomer* would speak to us from a makeshift stage. I'll never forget the first time we heard him. He spoke a strange *lashon ha-kodesh*. *Ivrit*, he called it and said that it was the language we would all be speaking from then on. It was a revision of the old biblical language. 'Yes,' he proudly said, 'A new language for a new land.'

"The children would attend classes and so would the adults. He explained the rules, schedule, and other things about life in the camp. This was to be our home until we were able to manage on our own, familiar with the culture and language of the new land. He spoke to us with warmth, making us all feel wanted.

"Yet, despite that smile, something frightened me.

"I do not know what it was. Perhaps it was because he seemed so large, much taller than my father or any other Yemenite man. Or, maybe it had to do with his tragedy.

"Yael had told us that the *shomer* came from Warsaw, Poland. 'His only child was killed by the Nazis, *yimach shemam*, in front of him and his wife. Now, his wife was ...' Yael had pointed her finger to her head sadly, indicating that she must have gone insane.

"I know how silly this must seem. Here he was a tragic victim of unspeakable horror, and yet I was afraid of him.

"We tried our best to settle down in our barracks that we shared with two other families. We followed the rules to the best of our ability, always with the goal of eventually being allowed to set up our own home—to leave and live as a family once again."

"Did you ever leave the camp, Ima? Like go on trips or something?"

"Trips?" Geveret Cohen shook her head slowly and sadly. "No, we never went on trips. We were not permitted to leave the camp.

"Sometimes I would look at the surrounding fields and mountains, wondering what lay beyond the camp's gates, but I would never dare venture out.

"The days passed, slowly turning into weeks and months. Gradually, changes started taking place among our Yemenite people. Children did not listen to their parents as they always had in the past. They were ashamed of their parents' old-fashioned ways. Some boys cut off their *simanim*. 'Here in the new State you do not need *simanim*,' we were told. 'Here it is not like in Yemen. Here we are all Jews, so you do not need to stand out and look different. We are all the same.'

"One day, while I was playing with the other children, I felt someone's eyes on me. I turned around and found the *shomer* staring at me. A tremor ran through me. There was something disconcerting about the way he was looking at me. I wanted to run away.

"Suddenly, as if sensing my unease, his face broke into a warm smile. He came closer to me. 'Don't be afraid,' he tried to draw me into his big arms. 'You are a beautiful little girl...How old are you?'

"Five and a half, sir," I answered politely, stiffening and trying hard not to cry.

"'I'm sorry if I frightened you,' he looked genuinely apologetic, 'but you remind me of another little girl—a very precious one.' His eyes filled and I felt real pity for him as he slowly said, 'Yes, she would have turned six years old next month. You look so much like her.'

"I must have been quite mature for my age, because I understood that he meant that I reminded him of his dead daughter, and although I felt uncomfortable with that fact, I suddenly was not so frightened of him anymore. Instead, I was filled with pity for the man who had suffered so much.

Chapter 30

"While I still felt uneasy in his presence, I became used to his frequent visits to my classroom and to the barrack my family occupied. He told my parents that he enjoyed watching me play and telling me stories. Although they were not very comfortable with him always looking at me, they did not protest. They also felt truly sorry for this large, but tragic man. And I certainly did not mind the chocolates he always gave me."

Geveret Cohen let out a deep sigh before continuing. "I will never forget the day he found out that I had the chicken pox.

"My parents had kept secret the fact that I was ill and covered with pimples and eruptions all over my body. They kept me in bed, not wanting me separated from them. Anyone ill would immediately be sent to the infirmary. We had been through so many transitions in the previous couple of months, that they knew I could not bear the thought of being sent away from them.

"When two days had passed and the *shomer* realized I was missing from the dining hall and my classes, he came over and found me in bed. Oh, was he mad! He yelled at my parents, telling them that they should have reported my illness—how dangerous it was for a disease to go untreated. He carried on in such a way, you would have thought that *he* was my father. My parents were overwhelmed with guilt for not having done what was in my best interest. From then on, he did not allow a day to go by without a visit, and of course he always brought me chocolate."

Geveret Cohen suddenly stopped talking. None of us said a word. Our eyes were on Mazal's mother and we followed her gaze to the window. We saw that snowflakes were once again falling gently to the ground.

"That winter it snowed," she continued. "We had been sitting in our classroom and looking through the window—just as we are doing now. I could see the white flakes falling from the sky.

"It was not easy for us to sit still in class that day. The teacher stood beside her large *luach* in the front of the room. It was difficult for us children, each holding our own little *luach*, to copy the letters the teacher was writing. We kept looking longingly toward the window.

"After what seemed like forever, she dismissed us. We ran outside—

ignoring the cold, laughing and screeching, making balls out of the frozen white powder and throwing them joyfully in the air.

"What bliss! I had never seen snow before, and now the whole camp and as far as my eyes could see was covered with a white blanket... Yes," she nodded sadly, "something like today."

Geveret Cohen suddenly stopped talking and stood up. She went to her mother who was still sound asleep by the window. Behind her, we could see the snowy hills and fields in the distance. We watched her tuck the blanket around her mother and fuss over the elderly woman for a moment or two. We sat waiting for her to continue.

Finally, she edged her way back to her seat by the table. Her eyes looked moist, but her voice was strong as she continued speaking to us from where she had left off.

"I ran outside with the others and played with the snow gleefully. I did not think it was possible for anyone to be happier than I was at the time.

"Then something even more wonderful happened that day. My brand new baby sister was born! My joy knew no bounds. And on top of all of this, our *shomer* came to visit me while my father was visiting my mother and gave me *two* chocolates. It is unlikely that there was another child happier in the entire world than I.

"My father called the baby Hodaya. He said "*Hodu l'Hashem*," we are grateful to Hashem for allowing us to live in Eretz Yisrael and for granting us the privilege of bringing another child into the world in this holy land.

"The only thing marring my joy was that my mother could not bring my new sister home to me. I wanted so badly to see her, to play with her, and dress her. I pictured her as a live doll. How I yearned to be with her!

"One of the rules in the camp was that the newborn babies had to stay in the *beit tinokot* building of the hospital until the family could afford to move into their own apartment. Only then were they permitted to take their child out of the hospital and into their new home. This, it was explained to us, was for the safety of the baby. With so many people occupying a relatively small space, the infant would be at risk of greater exposure to germs, they claimed.

"My mother would go daily to feed her, while the rest of the family was only allowed to visit on weekends, when we were always separated from her by a glass window.

"The snow and cold continued throughout the winter, but my father could not stay put. He was anxious to get an apartment and begin a normal independent life and was frustrated with life in the camp. He was a proud man and he wanted us to be a family again.

"Meanwhile, I was busy going to school each day, visiting my baby sister on weekends, and playing with the other children in the camp. I was young enough to keep myself occupied with the various activities in the camp, yet adequately mature to realize how confined my parents felt there. I too waited for the day when we would be able to leave the camp and live as a family in our own home.

"Finally, the weather changed and it grew warmer. Our future, also, began to look brighter. My father's friend, who had left Yemen around a year before us, had already settled into the new land. He helped secure a job for my father and arranged for us to move into an apartment. We had great expectations and we prepared to move.

"However, the authorities in the camp told us that we were not ready.

"I could not understand. My father had a job and we had an apartment. We were a family. Why could we not leave?

"We would have to be patient, we were told.

"What choice did we have? We had to obey.

"Almost immediately afterwards a strange and frightful incident occurred.

"I was outside hanging out the wet wash to dry. I wanted to help my mother. She had been so busy these months running back and forth to the *beit tinokot*, and although I was quite young, I understood how important it was to assist her. She was still indoors when two men suddenly came into view. I glanced at them shyly and they beamed wide smiles at me.

"I looked away and, standing on tiptoes, tried to reach the top of the line. From the corner of my eye, I noticed the two men coming closer. I did not know what to do. My heart was beating fast and I was overwhelmed with a feeling of foreboding. There was something sinister when they smiled at me, something alarming. I tried not to pay any attention to them. I did not want to run away and seem like a fearful little child. What should I do?

"All at once, an older girl, a neighbor of ours, appeared. She grabbed me by the arm and pulled me away from those men and into the barrack where my mother was.

"The next day, we were told that we would have to relocate to a new camp site. Aggravated, my father headed to the hospital to retrieve his daughter. A nurse met him at the front door.

"'May I help you?'

"'Yes, please. I have come to fetch my child.'

"'Her name, sir?'

"'Hodaya. Hodaya Yitzchaki.'

"'Yitzchaki? Is that what you said?'

"'Yes. I said Yitzchaki…I want to take my child, Hodaya Yitzchaki. May I please come in and get her?'

"'Yitzchaki. You are Mr. Yitzchaki?'

"'Yes. Is…is there a problem?'

"'Mr. Yitzchaki, I am sorry, sir, but your child is dead.'

"'No!' he screamed, 'No!'

"He argued with the nurse, claiming that it could not be. She shook her head, insisting that it was indeed true and that there was nothing to be done anymore. Finally, she suggested that he leave at once, otherwise she would have to call someone to forcibly escort him home.

"My father walked back to our barrack in a state of shock. As he came through the door, my mother immediately knew something was wrong. She just did not suspect *how* wrong.

"When my father spoke at last, he was surprised at my mother's reaction. He was certain she would go into mourning, expecting her to grieve and weep, but instead my mother reacted calmly. She told him not to worry, that it was apparently a grave mistake. She explained that it was impossible. They must have confused her with a different child or a different Yitzchaki. Just yesterday, my mother explained, our beautiful seven-month-old child ate and was in perfect health.

"'Go back,' she told him. 'You did not understand. Their Hebrew is different than our *lashon ha-kodesh*. It must be a different child that died.'

"My father went back. The nurse maintained that his child was indeed dead.

"'What did she die from?' My father asked her. 'She was in perfect health the day before.'

"The nurse had no answer.

"'I want to see her,' my father insisted. 'I want to see my baby's body!'

"'That is impossible,' was the nurse's reply.

"'I want to bury my baby,' my father cried out to her. 'I need to bury her!'

"'Mr. Yitzchaki, she has already been buried so please calm down.'

"'Where is she buried? I must go to the grave.'

"'That is impossible. Go home, Mr. Yitzchaki, to your other children. You are fortunate to have other children at home.'

"The weeks and months following this living nightmare were more horrible than any words can describe. Every door my parents tried to open to seek out the truth, to find out what really happened, was immediately slammed shut in their faces.

For a while, my mother was near death and had to be hospitalized. My father too suffered immense health problems afterward.

"Finally, my parents came to terms with the reality and gave up their search for the truth."

The truth.

What was the truth? Did Mazal's aunt really die or had she been kidnapped—as the Yitzchaki family believed—and given to some other family to raise as their own?

Early the next morning on the bus ride home, Mazal told us that until now the subject of her mother's missing sister was taboo. It was only recently, with the progression of her grandmother's illness, that small bits and pieces of what happened so long ago came to light. It seems that the medication her grandmother was taking revived long-buried memories. The children naturally asked questions and Mazal's mother could not escape her recollections of that terrible time.

"It is my wish," Mazal's eyes filled, "to find the truth before…" she stopped speaking mid-sentence.

"Before what?" Mimi's brow lifted.

"Before it is too late."

"What do you mean, Mazal?" I asked. "Too late for what?"

"Sara, you don't understand?" Adina was incredulous.

I felt myself blushing.

"You see my Savta? She very, very sick."

"And she lost her daughter, Sara," Adina said to me.

"I know. I was there too when Geveret Cohen spoke to us."

"And maybe if she didn't really die all those years ago, she's still alive," Adina went on. "You know, it's not easy to lose a daughter."

Or a mother.

Mimi inquired, "Do you really think it's possible that she's still alive?"

"I've read articles about this," Adina said. "There have definitely been a number of cases of kidnapped Yemenite children. Children who had been perfectly fine and then suddenly they were gone, with their parents told they're dead. I remember reading about a case of a Yemenite family that received a draft notice from the Israeli Army for their eighteen-year-old son to come register. The only problem was that this son supposedly died when he was three months old."

"That's so creepy!" Mimi exclaimed.

"It was a lot more than creepy," Adina continued. "When the parents got over the initial shock, the old suspicions once again surfaced. If the child had really died, then why was there no death certificate? If there had been a death certificate, the government never would have sent a draft notice."

"So what happened, Adina?"

"I'm getting to it, Mimi. It seems they weren't the only family who had that happen to them and eventually, as word got out, more and more stories of missing children unfolded. I'm surprised none of you know about this."

"I think I once read a novel about it, that is, about a missing Yemenite child who grew up with another family and almost married his birth sister. But I had no idea that such things *really* happened," I said.

"Well, now you do."

"Okay, Adina, so do you think it's possible that Mazal's aunt really is alive?"

"I don't know, Mimi. I guess it's possible."

"Well if it's possible," I suddenly found myself saying, "then…then I think…"

"What, Sara?" Mimi asked.

"I think… we've got to try to find her."

31

MY NAME WAS not on the list.

But, Mimi's and Adina's were. And so were Zehava's and Rochel Leah's.

For the *same* Shabbos.

"I'm glad I don't have *toranut* this month!" Tova said aloud to the rest of us, while turning her back to the large bulletin board. "I'm scared stiff of all the work we're going to have now that Chanukah is coming to an end."

"I know what you mean," Naomi agreed. "The payback for our Chanukah break most probably will be more work and more work and more work. That's all I need is to be tied up on Shabbos with *toranut*—"

"And don't forget *Erev Shabbos*."

"You're right, *Erev Shabbos* too."

"Thanks, both of you, for all the encouragement," Malkie sighed. "I'm on this week's list and now you're scaring me out of my wits!"

"Sorry, Malkie, I didn't realize that you have *toranut*. But, the truth is, I heard from my friend's older sister, who went to M.B.L.L. a few years ago, that until now all the work we were assigned was a walk down easy street. Once Teves comes, you'll be wishing for things to be as easy as they've been until now!"

"Easy?"

"It's true, Malkie," Chani joined in. "Blimi said that the months after Chanukah till Purim time are extremely difficult—much harder than the work was until now."

"I can't imagine that," Malkie flopped onto the closest chair. "Just thinking about it exhausts me."

Devorah sat down opposite her. "At least we have Adina, Malkie."

"You're right. She's great to study with and she always knows the answers."

"How come the two of you get to have Adina for yourselves?" I turned to see Rochel Leah enter the lounge. She glanced in our direction and then went closer to the bulletin board. "Oh look, Zehava. We have *toranut* together on Shabbos *Parashas Vayechi*."

"Really?"

"And look…Mimi's with us too. And Adina."

"Don't get too excited, Zehava," Tova informed her roommate. "That Shabbos is a Shabbos *chovah*."

"Are you serious?" Rochel Leah drew nearer to us. "There's so much more to do on a Shabbos *chovah*!"

"And not only that," Devorah said. "We're about to be loaded with tons and tons of schoolwork."

"Hey, why's everyone looking so glum? It's still Chanukah!" Mimi bounced into the lounge with Adina walking gracefully beside her.

"We're waiting for you, Mimi, to come cheer us up. Oh, hi Adina."

"Well, Chani, now I'm here. Mimi to the rescue!"

"Mimi, don't be so cheerful. You have *toranut* with me next Shabbos."

"So, what's wrong, Rochel Leah? You're not *that* bad."

Everyone laughed.

"That's not what I meant, Mimi. It's a Shabbos *chovah* and you know what that means."

"The whole dorm is going to be here," Zehava explained.

"So what?" Mimi said. "The more the merrier. We'll have a blast. Remember the last Shabbos *chovah* that I had *toranut*?"

"We sure do, Mimi."

"How could we forget?"

"Mimi, do us a favor. Please don't take the key on Friday night after the *seudah*."

"Yeah, Mimi. Give it to Rochel Leah."

"Good idea. Or someone else."

"Adina," Devorah said, "you also have *toranut* that Shabbos."

"I do?" Adina checked the bulletin board. "Yes, I see I do."

"It's a good thing," Chani laughed. "Hopefully, you'll keep an eye on Mimi and make sure she behaves herself."

"I'll behave. I'll behave. I'm not in the mood of serving cold *cholent* salad for the afternoon *seudah*, despite all the compliments I got last time," Mimi let out her deep, throaty laugh. "Anyway everyone, guess what?"

"It's going to be your birthday one week from Thursday."

"Oh, hi Sara. I didn't see you."

That's because you've been hanging around with your roommate ever since we returned from Kiryat Yosef more than twenty-four hours ago. "Hi," I said back.

"Anyway, like I was saying…guess what?"

"Sara already guessed, Mimi. The famous event is only nine days away."

"Eight and a half. But guess some more," her eyes had that mischievous gleam.

"The Chanukah production, Mimi? Is that it? Wasn't it pushed off until next Sunday?"

"Actually, I'm thinking of calling it the Asarah B'Teves production. Imagine that—a story about Chana and her seven sons in Teves."

"C'mon, Mimi."

"Or maybe we should push it off *two* months. How about making it the Purim production. V'nahafoch hu! The dance of the *Maccabim* in the middle of Adar, with spinning hamentashen instead of spinning *dreidels*."

"I can't believe it. Mimi Rosenberg is starting to sound down!"

"Down? No way," Mimi forced a smile. "Anyway, nobody guessed my news yet."

"Well, we don't know what to guess. We've run out of ideas."

"Hi, everybody! What's going on? You all look so pensive."

"Oh, hi Rivky," Chani greeted her. "We're in middle of one of Mimi's guessing games."

"Really? Then I'm glad I got here on time," Rivky said in her easy manner. "By the way, did you all hear? Geveret Spitz is coming over here soon. She's returning our reports."

"Really?"

"Already?"

"Hey! Excuse me, but that was suppose to be *my* news, Rivky."

"Sorry, Mimi. I had no idea—"

"No prob, Rivky. After supper, I got a message that Rabbi Grossman wanted to speak to me. And guess what? He said my report was excellent. Can you believe it?"

"That's great, Mimi."

"Congrats, Mimi."

"So…" Mimi sang out a drum-roll, "Dump ta da dump…I'm here at M.B.L.L. till the finish line!"

Finish line? The others know about Rabbi Grossman's warning? I can't believe it! I felt my heartbeat quicken. *And I thought I was the only one she confided in. Her first real friend.*

"I'm so happy for you, Mimi," Rivky embraced her warmly.

"I guess all that studying paid off," Rochel Leah said.

Chani wrapped one arm around Mimi's shoulder and with the other tapped her own stomach. "I definitely think this calls for a celebration. Don't you?"

"Absolutely! Let's have a party!" Mimi's eyes sparkled. "All right, everybody, what'll we serve?"

"I've got biscuitim to donate."

"And I have a grapefruit."

"I have around half a box of gum."

"I'll supply the drinks. Water from the tap and I have a quarter of a can of ice tea mix left over."

"And Mimi, I'll contribute my leftover sandwich cookies. You know, the kind Mazal raves about."

"Thanks, Rivky. And thanks everybody. What'll I give? The only thing I have are caramels and they're *milchig*!"

"So are we, Mimi. Lunch was over a long time ago. I guess you'll have to part with your cherished caramels after all," Chani laughed.

"Um…don't we need to meet with Geveret Spitz?" Zehava asked.

"You're right. That's what I came to tell you," Rivky said. "I'm supposed to pass the message along. I'll see you all soon in the dining room. I've got to go tell everyone else…"

"I wonder what I got on my report. I hope I did well. I'm so nervous. I don't think I'll be able to party, Mimi, if I didn't get a good mark."

"Don't worry, Malkie. If *I* did well, I'm sure *you* did well. Anyway, we'll make the party late tonight, like after eleven, so come in your sleeping stuff. Okay, everyone?"

"Sure, Mimi. Where's it going to be?"

"It'll be in *our* room, of course," she grinned at her roommate. "Right, Adina?"

I looked at Adina, hoping she would say no.

"Right, Mimi. All your hard work definitely calls for a celebration."

All her hard work?

I swallowed. The lump in my throat was getting harder with each passing second. *If only I could escape to the privacy of my room!* But instead, I found myself moving along with the others into the dining room, where the rest of the M.B.L.L. girls were gathered to meet with Geveret Spitz. I sat down, oblivious to whoever was sitting next to me, and waited rather impatiently for the papers to be returned. I was hoping Geveret Spitz would hurry and hand me my paper already.

I've got to get out of here!

"Applegrat…Atlas…Berger…Braun…Green…Gross…David… Halb…Horovitz…Hirsch…"

Finally!

I glanced at my mark, folded my papers, and dashed out of the dining room, up the stairs, and into my room.

I was not surprised to have received an *alef* minus. After all, I did not exactly expect an *alef* plus on a first report.

What did surprise me, though, was my apathetic reaction when I saw my mark. *Why did I suddenly not care?*

I am not sure when it began to dawn on me, but some time after we left Kiryat Yosef I came to the realization that Adina and Mimi must have confided in each other. I do not know who started first or how it came about, but it was clear to me that I was no longer the sole guardian of their deepest secrets.

So, why am I letting it bother me? They're allowed to tell each other anything they want.

Chapter 31

Something changed in Adina over our long weekend at Mazal's, and I had no doubt that it had something to do with Mimi. Mimi could be as perceptive as she was playful. Sitting together during that long bus ride home, Mimi must have revealed something of her past to Adina, and undoubtedly, Adina divulged some of her own secrets.

And, I was suddenly feeling utterly left out and alone.

Oh Chavie, I wish you were here!

I shoved my report into the box under my bed that contained all the papers and collections for my *Proyect*. My box was filling up rapidly and I was already on page one hundred sixty-three in my notebook. (Actually, it was my *third* notebook!) I would probably have to get a new box soon to accommodate the growing assortment of papers.

At that moment, though, I could care less.

What time is it now in America? I looked at my watch. *If it's nine-fifteen Israel time, then by Chavie it's two-fifteen in the afternoon.*

I sat down on the edge of my bed. *I wonder what they're doing now?*

I knew the wedding reception was to begin at six-thirty and the *chupah* one hour later. *Chavie must be dressed in her gown already.* I pictured Mindy posing for the photographer.

If I were in America, I would already be at the wedding hall. Chavie would have insisted that I come early.

But, I'm not there...I'm here.

I stood up and went into my closet, changed into my terrycloth robe, and hurried down the hallway toward the shower, all the while thinking that I should have stayed in Rolland Heights and never have come to M.B.L.L. in the first place. *Only six months left until I go home!*

My mood brightening somewhat after the soothing shower, I slipped into my soft flannel nightgown. *Sara, you really should try looking at the bright side of things,* I told my reflection as I brushed my teeth. *If you hadn't come, then it would be impossible for you to win the Goldstone Award. Right? And, if you hadn't come, you'd never have met Mazal and her special family either.*

Well, even that was not destined to last.

Two days later, in middle of one of our morning classes, Mazal was suddenly told to gather her things and go to the office. By the time I returned to our room, she was already gone. The urgency she must have felt when she left was apparent from the disarray in which I found the room. But, that was nothing compared to the feeling of dread that came over me.

I spoke to some of Mazal's Israeli friends, but they did not know more than I did. I went to the *eim ha-bayit* and she did not have much information either. I did not know if I should call Mazal or leave her alone. I certainly did not want to seem like a nuisance or put any more stress on the family.

That evening, after supper, Mimi and Adina finally seemed to be able to tear themselves away from each other and express their concern for Mazal and her grandmother.

"So you don't know *anything*, Sara? What did Geveret Katz say?"

"I told you already, Mimi. She said that the grandmother had to be hospitalized and Mazal was needed at home to take care of the children."

"Then it must really be bad," Adina said sadly. "No way would her parents have allowed her to miss school if the situation wasn't serious."

"That's why I'm so afraid," I said, close to tears.

"Listen, Sara, besides *davening* and saying *Tehillim*, there really isn't much we can do. Come with Adina and me. We're about to go to rehearsal."

"I'm really not in the mood, Mimi."

"Come on, Sara. We hardly practiced this week and—"

"We all know what to do, Mimi. After all, the production was supposed to be on Sunday."

"But it wasn't. And I'm absolutely petrified that everyone will forget their parts if we don't have at least two practices this week."

"I'm just props, Mimi. It's no big deal."

"Sara, even a prop is important. Every detail counts."

"Yes, Sara, Mimi's right. That's why Mimi's productions always come out so gorgeous," Adina gushed. "She's so meticulous about the details."

Suddenly everything Mimi does is gorgeous? What's with Adina?

"I-I don't…really…"

"C'mon, Sara…"

Chapter 31

Of course, I went, and I really have to admit, it was more fun than staying in my room alone like I did two nights earlier, when Mimi made her party. After I had taken a shower and slipped into my deliciously soft flannel nightgown, I cuddled up under my covers, escaping to the comfort of my bed. *My bed.* The most private spot in the dorm, where my pillow proved to be my truest friend and the recipient of the tears and new emotions I could not understand.

Anyway, I really did manage to fall asleep for a short while, dreaming about Chavie at Mindy's wedding, but naturally, with so much noise coming from the room next door once eleven o'clock arrived, I could not stay asleep for long.

I tried burying my head under my pillow to muffle out the sounds, but it was to no avail. I turned over and stared soulfully at the ceiling, listening to the cheerful clamor while telling myself that I should just get up and go join everyone.

Then suddenly, I heard two clear and familiar voices coming from the wash-up closet.

"Maybe we should check."

"I just did, Mimi. She still sleeping. I think she sick."

"You really think so?"

"Yes. When I come into the room I see she sleeping, so I turn off the light and go to the library."

"I don't know. She seemed fine to me, Mazal, when I saw her after supper in the lounge."

"I too do not know. I go to the closet, get into my nightdress, and see she still sleeping."

"Oh, boy, I feel so bad that she's missing the party, but if she's sick it's probably better to let her sleep."

Better for whom, Mimi or me?

I remember thinking that maybe Mimi hoped I would sleep and stay away. Then she could enjoy her party without me. Me...the one reminder that she did not do all that work by herself.

I'm going to stay right here under my covers, where I won't be a burden to Mimi or anyone else. I once again stuffed my head under my pillow, this time pulling the cover on top. *After all, Mimi doesn't need me anymore. Especially, now that she has Adina.*

"So, Sara, aren't you glad you came to practice?" Mimi cheerfully asked as we made our way up the steps as soon as production rehearsal was over.

"I guess so, but I'm still really worried about Mazal's grandmother," I said.

"You know, it might sound strange, but I was wondering…"

Mimi's eyebrows lifted. "What, Adina?"

"Well, remember on the bus when we were talking about the situation of the missing Yemenite children?"

"Of course," Mimi and I both said.

"So, I was wondering about what you said, Sara."

"Me?"

"What did Sara say?" Mimi asked and then suddenly stopped short. "Oh my goodness, I just realized I've got to find Rivky! She's in charge of calling the schools, and since I'll be going to Yerushalayim for Shabbos I'll never get a chance to take care of this tomorrow. I'll see you later," she rushed back down the steps taking at least two at a time.

We never did get to hear what Mimi needed to tell Rivky. She was out of earshot before she finished her sentence.

"What were you saying, Adina?" I asked as we slowly continued ascending the steps toward the third floor.

"Do you remember when you suggested that we try finding the missing daughter?"

"Yes, b-but…"

"I think it's a—"

"Crazy?"

"*Gorgeous* idea."

"G-gorgeous?"

"Yes," Adina stopped walking when we reached her room. "That poor woman has been aching all these years. If we could somehow…before she dies—"

"Dies?"

"Come on, Sara, don't be so naïve," she pushed her door open and I followed her inside. "It's obvious she's dying. If we could help reunite her and her daughter, you can imagine—"

"But, Adina, it's practically impossible."

"Why's it impossible?" she sat down on her bed. "If this baby had really died in the hospital as they said she did, there would be a death certificate. We just need to trace the hospital records. If there's no death certificate, then obviously she didn't die. And if she didn't die—"

"Then what happened to her?"

"Exactly. There would have to be records. People don't just disappear. Even if the adoption wasn't official, there has to be some written proof."

"But, Adina, it sounds impossible. We're two American…I mean one American and one English girl in Israel. How in the world can the two of us—"

"What, Sara?"

"Go after something that's so unrealistic."

"I guess I shouldn't have expected someone like you to understand."

There she goes again, my heart skipped a beat.

She opened her loose-leaf, ignoring me while turning its pages, as I stood there uncomfortably, waiting for her to continue. But she didn't.

"Adina, what did I say that's so bad? What don't I understand?"

"Sara," she looked up from her loose-leaf impatiently, "I really want to review something and then I've got to pack for Shabbos. I don't want to get into it right now."

"B-but, Adina," I swallowed hard. *I mustn't cry!* "I-I thought…I thought we had become closer. I-I thought…"

She must have seen the tears in my eyes because her voice softened. "Sara, it's true that I opened up and shared a lot of my life with you, but there are still certain things you'll never be able to understand."

"Why?"

"Why?" She let out a hoarse laugh. "Because, Sara, your life has been easy in so many ways. And even though you were a big help to me and it was great to finally open up and talk, I can't expect someone like you to understand everything."

"And Mimi?" I whispered, my voice hardly audible. "Can Mimi understand?"

"Mimi?" Adina echoed while she thought. "Well, yes, Sara. Someone like Mimi actually could understand."

I am not sure how we ended the conversation or how I managed to fall asleep that night, but the overwhelming feeling of loneliness I had been experiencing lately grew even worse the next day.

I had heard Mimi mention Shabbos in Yerushalayim, but I had not realized that it was with Adina at Hinda Klein's home. Suddenly, I was no longer part of the picture.

True, they were roommates. True, life had not come easy to either of them and a common thread of suffering and pain tied them together. And unlike me, they both came from families that were not especially supportive. But was that a good enough reason to forget all about my existence?

I knew I would be facing a lonely Shabbos and it felt like weeks—no months—since the past Shabbos, where only one week earlier we had all shared such closeness and warmth in Mazal's home. What a contrast this Shabbos was going to be!

Well, I'd better take advantage of my free time Erev Shabbos, instead of sitting around and moping, I told myself as I made my way down to the library. *At least, I still have my dream.* And suddenly, that same familiar flutter of excitement I always felt when thinking about the Goldstone Award ran through me.

I reached for the *sefer* Tehillim and turned to the *pasuk* on which I was planning to base my *Proyect*. I wanted to find as many *meforshim* as I could to back up my topic. It was an important theme, one I truly believed in.

I was deeply immersed in a Radak when I suddenly heard Zehava's voice. I looked up.

"Oh, hi Sara," she came closer. "I'm about to leave with Rochel Leah. We're going to my second cousin in Ashdod and I just wanted to pick up a *sefer* that I need to use over Shabbos. How about you, what are you doing this Shabbos?"

"I'm...I'm staying in the dorm."

"You are?" she lifted her eyebrow. "If I would've known—"

"No, Zehava, it's really okay."

"I guess you couldn't exactly go to Mazal this Shabbos."

"No..."

"And Mimi?"

"She left this morning to Yerushalayim with Adina. That's all right, Zehava," I quickly said, trying to erase the pitiful look on her face. "I-I could've gone, but I wanted to stay in the dorm for Shabbos. You know, there's so much work to do. And Fridays are our only free day."

"Zehava, what's taking so long?" We heard Rochel Leah's voice before we saw her. "Oh, you're talking. I thought you were just getting something."

"I was, but then I saw Sara."

"You have *toranut* this Shabbos?" Rochel Leah asked me.

"N-no."

"So, where're you going for Shabbos?"

"She's staying. She wants to get a head start on all her work. Maybe I'll do that next week."

"We'll have to see. We'd better leave now or we'll miss the bus."

"Okay, Rochel Leah, I'm coming. Bye, Sara, have a good Shabbos." She then added softly, "Maybe we'll go somewhere together next week."

"We'll see," I forced myself to smile. "Have a great Shabbos!"

As soon as they left the library, I closed my *sefer* and slipped it back onto the shelf. *Well, at least things are getting better for Zehava. I wish I could say the same for me.*

Ever since we spoke together a few weeks earlier, she seemed to have developed much more confidence. She also appeared to handle Rochel Leah in a much healthier manner, and as a result, I had the impression that Rochel Leah was no longer taking Zehava for granted. Of course, that helped Zehava's self-esteem grow even more.

Rochel Leah, though, was getting increasingly possessive. *Why can't she understand,* I thought frustratedly, *that she doesn't own Zehava. If she really thought of her as a true friend, she'd be happy about Zehava's growing friendships with others, instead of being so blatantly jealous.*

I gathered my things together and started to make my way out of the library. *Obviously, Rochel Leah must be very insecure. I'd never act like that with Chavie. If she were here with me and wanted to make new friends, it wouldn't be a problem for me. In fact, it would give me the opportunity to make new friends too. That's how it's always been for us.*

I began climbing the steps to the third floor. *That's how friendships should be,* I determined, *like a candle's flame.* If you light a candle and then use it to light other candles, the original flame is not diminished in any way. This flame can continue to light many other candles, each burning with their own bright flames.

Friendship, like a candle's flame, can be shared among others without it being diminished in any way.

I opened the door to my empty room. *So why in the world can't I get Mimi and Adina out of my mind?*

32

IT WAS DURING *Shalosh Seudos* that the realization hit me. I do not think I shall ever forget the unexpected thrill that ran through me at the time. I was bursting. I needed to speak with Adina immediately.

But, of course, she was not there. She was in Yerushalayim with Mimi.

And suddenly, that did not matter either.

If I could only speak to her, if I could share with her my suspicion—no not suspicion—it was practically fact, then I was sure...absolutely positive...everything would turn out all right. *More* than all right.

I could not wait until they would come back.

When Shabbos was over, I felt like calling Mazal. But I knew I must not. I first needed to talk it over with Adina and Mimi.

I helped the *toraniyot* clean up from Shabbos and then went upstairs to shower. *What if they don't think my idea makes sense*, I asked myself while sliding a comb down my wet hair. *What if they think I'm crazy?*

I gathered my hair into a ponytail, not bothering to blow it dry, and then went back downstairs to eat *Melaveh Malkah*. I peeked into the school's front hallway. *Maybe they got a ride home...a very fast ride.*

Naturally, they still had not returned.

I sat down with the others at the table in the dining room, lightly participating in the conversation around me. Many of the girls were back in the dormitory, having spent Shabbos nearby. We chatted, passed the food around, talked about Shabbos, and of course discussed the production scheduled for the next night.

"Sara, could you pass the babaganush? By the way, where's Mimi?"

"She went to Yerushalayim, Chani. You didn't know?"

"No, I had no idea. I assumed she was staying 'local' because of what happened last week."

"She was supposed to," Devorah offered, "then Adina asked her to go with her to someone she knows in Yerushalayim."

"Really? I can't believe she went so far away two weeks in a row. Especially with the production tomorrow night."

"Well," Devorah said, "*Adina* asked her to go."

"I still don't think she should've gone. What happens if it snows again, or if there's a huge rain storm in Yerushalayim and she can't get back on time," Malkie asked. "What if—"

"What if what?"

"Oh, Mimi. When did you get in?"

"Yeah, Mimi. We heard you were in Yerushalayim. We were worried about the production being pushed off again."

"Well, as you can see, here I am," she grinned, "and the production is definitely not being postponed!"

Unfortunately for me, I did not get a chance to speak to Adina and Mimi that *Motzaei Shabbos*, as I had intended. Girls were bombarding their room all evening, running back and forth preparing for the production, trying on costumes, and reviewing their parts. Our regular school day would begin bright and early the next morning as usual, and everything had to be prepared before we stepped into our first class of the day.

I could not get to Mimi and Adina even if I tried. Their room was overflowing with paraphernalia from the production, with most of the props stationed in my room. Anyway, what I had to tell them needed to be said in private, and privacy would be virtually non-existent until the production was over. So, the news of my discovery would just have to wait until after we were finished with the Chanukah production.

The Chanukah production.

It was finally over, and I am sorry to say did not end up turning out quite as "gorgeous" as we might have hoped. It must have been due to the postponement. Fewer people came than we expected. I guess the general lack of enthusiasm about a Chanukah production a week after Chanukah was responsible.

But that did not deter Mimi. She was already trying to dream up some new idea…another performance for some future date. At least, that is what she told us all while we packed away the props and cleaned off the stage.

Later that night (or rather early Monday morning), after the performance had long ended and the postproduction celebrations had died down, I changed into my cotton nightgown, slid my feet into my slippers while wrapping myself in a robe, and made my way through the wash-up closet into the room next door.

Mimi and Adina were sitting on their respective beds talking softly.

Tentatively, I knocked on the opened door before going inside.

Mimi smiled warmly, welcoming me. "Sara, you've really got to move your bed into our room. It's not right for you to be all alone."

"Thanks for the offer, Mimi, but I hope Mazal will be coming back soon."

"Did you hear from her yet?"

"No, Adina. And I'm not sure if I should call."

"I feel so bad that Mazal missed the production," Mimi said. "It's a good thing that Carmella was able to take over her part."

"Well, I hope everything is all right with her grandmother," I said. "By the way, Mimi, congratulations on a job well done."

"Why thank you. I couldn't have done it without you."

"Thanks. I guess props come in useful."

"That's not what I meant, Sara, even though I certainly appreciate the terrific job you did as props head. By the way, we don't charge. Have a seat," she tapped the spot on the bed next to her.

"Thank you," I sat down on her bed.

"What I meant was, thanks for all your help with the report."

"You already thanked me a few times last week."

"Well, that was because you weren't here when I made my speech at the party thanking you. But right now I'm thanking you again, because if it wasn't for you, I could never have been in charge of the production."

"Come on, Mimi."

"No, really. If I hadn't written the report—and I couldn't have done it without your help, Sara,—then I wouldn't have been allowed to do the production."

My brows lifted and I shifted my eyes skeptically in Adina's direction and then moved them back to Mimi, my question asked in silence.

"Oh, you're wondering if Adina knows about Rabbi Grossman? Yes, I told her all about it, and I also told her how you came through for me even though we had such little time left."

"Yes, Sara. You're a very loyal friend," Adina commented. "Obviously, I saw you and Mimi studying together all the time, but I hadn't realized to what degree you were involved."

"I—I was just being a...I was just helping," I swallowed. "But, now that the production is over, and now that you know all about Mimi's...um...Mimi's desire to do well, I'm sure, Adina, that you'll be happy to—"

"What, Sara?" Mimi laughed, "Are you trying to get rid of me so soon?"

"Stop joking, Mimi."

"I'm really insulted, Sara. I thought you liked helping me."

"Funny, Mimi. When I'm needed I'm glad to help, but now that you have Adina..."

I never finished the sentence. And, I did not get to tell them that night about the discovery that had so excited me on Shabbos and that I had anxiously been waiting to share with them either. Somehow, the conversation had taken a different turn and all at once, I found myself overwhelmed with those other unfamiliar emotions, the ones that were squeezing something strange and peculiar out of me.

Before I would burst out in tears in front of them, I mumbled something and ran out of their room to the safety and privacy of my bed.

When Mimi came in a few moments afterward, she found me sobbing softly onto my pillow.

"Sara, what happened to you? What's wrong?"

"Nothing," I mumbled.

"Obviously, not nothing. Come on, Sara, what's bothering you?"

I stopped crying, but did not say anything. I kept my face pressed hard against my pillow.

I felt the mattress move as she sat down next to me. "Sara, I know something happened, but I haven't a clue what. You know you can tell me."

A few minutes passed. I did not move or say anything. *Should I tell her? Could I tell her?*

"How come, Sara, you get me to talk, but if I ask you what's wrong, you just say—nothing?"

I sat up sniffing. "I'm so embarrassed."

"Don't be. What happened?"

I wish I knew! "Nothing, Mimi. I don't know what's with me. Really, nothing's wrong."

"Really now…"

"Really," I was feeling so utterly foolish. "It's almost four o'clock in the morning and we have to get up in a few hours." I blew my nose. "I'm sorry for being like this."

"Sorry?"

"Yes, this was supposed to be your night. I'm sorry for ruining it for you."

"You didn't ruin it, Sara. You're upset about something, obviously, and I want to help."

"Thanks, Mimi, but I'm okay now."

"You're sure? Because if you're not—then I'm staying."

"Yes," I forced the sides of my mouth upward, "really."

"All right. Then I guess I'll be going," she stood up. "I'm zonked!"

"Thanks again," I watched her walk toward the wash-up closet. "And Mimi?"

"Yes?"

"Could I ask you a question?"

"Sure," she tried stifling a yawn, "shoot."

"Does…does Adina have any idea that I was crying?"

"I don't think so."

"What did…what did she say when I left the room?"

"I don't know. I don't think she said anything. Before you came into the room she was telling me how tired she was and that she didn't think she'd be able to stay up much longer. I think she fell asleep as soon as you left."

"Oh good. Thanks, Mimi."

"No prob!" She left the room through the wash-up closet.

I said *Shema*, put my head on my pillow, and surprisingly fell into an exhausted, short sleep.

In school the next day, neither Adina nor Mimi acted differently to me in any way after the previous night's uncomfortable encounter. I hoped that they had been too sleepy to make much of my foolish behavior, and if anything, blamed my unusual conduct on my overtiredness.

Thankfully, my mind shifted to other things once the day's classes began. We had another phenomenal *Chumash* lesson with Rabbanit Greenstein, followed by one of Rabbi Ossenfeld's intricate *dikduk* lessons. Then there was to be a brief break and a quick walk through the woods to our assigned classes.

I had hoped that I would finally get a chance to talk to Mimi about my discovery. After all, she was still my partner in the resource room and I would have her company during the walk there. True, I really wanted to speak to Adina first, or at least to both of them together, since Adina had seemed so interested in the subject, but she had already left with her partner, Shaindy Applegrat, to Bnot Yisrael's preschool. Besides, this was not something I could discuss in front of Shaindy. *First I'll speak to Mimi and see what she thinks. Then I'll tell Adina about it.*

I just could not wait to get it off my chest already.

I waited impatiently for Mimi. Rabbi Ossenfeld had asked her to stay for a few minutes after class to have a word with her.

I noticed the rest of the girls leaving and felt myself growing more tense with each passing minute. *Why does Rabbi Ossenfeld want to speak to Mimi? What did she do now?* I really did not like walking through the Kfar Amsdorf woods, just the two of us alone, but then again, I was glad to finally have Mimi to myself, even if it was just for the fifteen minute walk. *I've got to tell her what I found out!*

"Oh, hi Sara," Mimi waved, "sorry, but Os—I mean Rabbi Ossenfeld wanted to congratulate me on doing so much better on the *dikduk* test we took before Chanukah."

"Great, Mimi," I zipped up my parka while Mimi pushed opened the door leading outside to the Beit Yaakov HaNegbah courtyard. The air felt clear and crisp, with a strong sun shining down on us. "I'm relieved. I didn't know why he wanted to speak to you."

"You figured I must have done something wrong, right?"

"I didn't say—"

"You didn't say it, but that's what you were thinking."

"I—"

"C'mon, don't deny it."

"But, Mimi—"

"That's it, I'm damaged for life," she frowned exaggeratedly. "Guilty until proven innocent."

"Oh, Mimi," I started laughing. "That's not true."

"Yep," she walked with her usual cheerful gait, her red ponytail bouncing in the sunshine, "that's how everyone's going to always look at me. Mimi the—"

"Not true, Mimi. If you keep going in the direction you're going now—"

"Yes, Sara?"

"Y-your past will be…um…history."

"That sounds nice. If only…."

She suddenly stopped walking. I saw her eyes following a little bird as it flew in the air and then perched itself on a nearby branch.

"If only what, Mimi?"

Mimi continued to stare at the bird. "If only what you were saying was possible."

"Of course, it is. Even Rabbi Ossenfeld complimented you, Mimi. He noticed—"

She swung around to face me. "But that's only because of all your help, Sara. And probably because Rabbi Grossman must've spoken to him. The truth is…"

"What?" I interrupted.

"The truth is that I'm seen as a struggling student. I'm not…I'm not—"

"Not what?"

"I'm not like everyone else."

"You're really exaggerating."

"It's compliment Mimi Rosenberg, the problem child, on a job well done. Because what can we expect from her anyway?"

"That's not true, Mimi. You're so special. You have such unbelievable gifts—"

"So now I'm gifted...gifted with the gift of mimicking. Like you called me a few weeks ago, Mimi the Mimic—"

"I'm sorry, Mi—"

"Don't worry, Sara, you were right. And anyway, I don't want to be known as Mimi the Mimic."

"There are so many things you excel in. Better than the rest of us. Your music, your artwork, the plays—"

"Hey, I don't want to go around directing plays the rest of my life!"

"But if you're good at certain things, Mimi, what's wrong with having a job in those fields?"

"Because then, I'll still be different and I hate being different...I want to be like everyone else, do what everyone else does. You know...be normal!"

We continued walking along slowly and silently. What could I say? I so much wanted to stand out and be special—not a run of the mill person. But would I want to be Mimi?

I would love to have her charm and her sense of humor. I would love to have her friendly and warm disposition, her huge talent. But her brains?

Adina's brains, on the other hand... I certainly would not mind having those! However, if Adina's brains came along with Adina's past, would I still want them?

No way...never!

We were suddenly standing in front of Geveret Spitz's resource room door and I realized that I still did not get to tell Mimi about the discovery I made on Shabbos.

"Mimi! Mimi!" Riki, Ronit, and a few of the other children surrounded us.

Us? No, I do not think they even noticed me.

I still could not figure it out. Mimi had a much more difficult time with the language barrier and yet she seemed to communicate with the children much better than I (or anyone else, for that matter) could. There was a load of professional material in the resource room which I used regularly. Mimi, though, relied on her own creative ideas and they appeared to hold our students' attention much more effectively. She had done much less (if any) research about the children and their learning problems than the rest of us, nevertheless she succeeded in getting them to sit and learn a lot quicker.

Wanting desperately to succeed with the children, I tried employing the many ideas I had so studiously learned from professional textbooks. And yet, where was all this research getting me?

"All right," Mimi spoke to the children in her broken Hebrew. "We will play a game soon. Everyone go back to her own Morah; just Riki and Ronit come with Sara and me to our table."

Riki and Ronit held hands, and with wide smiles, made their way to the small table in the corner of the room where Mimi and I were supposed to work with them.

I took out the *beis* and *veis* flashcards from Ronit's cubby and also happily went to our table. I had a great game planned.

"Okay, Ronit. Let's begin."

But Ronit was not looking at me. Her eyes were focused somewhere else. On Mimi and Riki.

And I looked on, bewildered.

Ronit did not have a problem with being easily distracted or difficulty in sitting still, like Riki did. The problem with Ronit was almost the opposite. She was quiet and unmotivated—with an unusual lack of interest in anything. That is why it was so surprising to see her completely riveted by what Mimi and Riki were doing.

Of course, once I started looking in their direction, I too became absorbed.

Mimi had taken a few small shoeboxes and stapled them together, two on top of two. She placed a sign in the front that read *HaMakolet shel Riki*, with a cut out photograph of a smiling Riki on the front. And indeed, that is what it looked like—a miniature supermarket with its owner welcoming everyone inside. The real Riki was grinning from ear to ear; after all, it was *her* supermarket!

There was a large closet in the back of the room, in which sat a colorful prize box containing an assortment of inexpensive little toys that Geveret Spitz made sure was always well-stocked. These prizes were to help motivate and reward the children. Mimi (with permission from Geveret Spitz) chose about fifteen of them for Riki's *makolet*.

I tried to catch Ronit's attention, but she was completed captivated by what Mimi and Riki were doing. We observed the two of them busily discussing and analyzing the pros and cons of which was the right "room" in which to place each prize.

And I wondered, *Why is Mimi wasting so much time?*

Then, when they finally finished placing the prizes in the "right" box and I finally got Ronit to color the *beis* and *veis* cards, Mimi took out these cute little round tags from her book bag. I could not believe it! Mimi still was not finished!

Ronit put down her crayon, and with those huge dark eyes, stared in awe at what Mimi and Riki were doing. We watched Mimi instruct Riki to copy various numbers onto the tiny tags (*finally, she's doing something educational!*) and then they took the tags and tied (*fine motor skill exercises?*) them onto each of the little prizes, but not before an interminable amount of time passed while they sat discussing the worth of each prize.

I did not want to hurt Mimi's feelings, especially after our discussion on the way to Kfar Amsdorf, but I felt that it was necessary for Geveret Spitz to set her straight. She was squandering away precious resource room time, hours that would be better spent giving the children the individual tutoring they so badly needed, instead of playing a game with the prizes (and distracting the other students.) Yes, it was critical that I speak with Geveret Spitz!

It was not unusual to request a private meeting with her. Geveret Spitz generally arranged for the girl to come to her cottage sometime later the same evening, and so, when I asked her what time would be most convenient, I was not surprised when she told me to come that night at nine o'clock.

We returned to the dorm for lunch with the other girls who worked in the resource room, and once again I was disappointed at missing the opportunity to share my recent discovery with Mimi.

Chapter 32

When will I ever get the chance to tell her and Adina what I found out?

After the school day was finished and there was still a pocket of free time to study before supper, I went down to the library to continue working on my *Proyect*. In the past (before Chanukah, that is), this had been the hour that Mimi and I worked on *parashah* and *dikduk*. Now, that her report had been handed in and she was making a giant effort to pay attention in class, I figured she no longer needed my services. And, even if she decided that she did want help, I had no doubt that Adina would be her first choice.

I took out my notebook and began writing, trying very hard to be practical and not allow my turbulent emotions to dominate my thoughts.

"Hey, there you are, Sara. I should've known I'd find you here."

I looked up. "I didn't know you were looking for me, Mimi. Is everything okay?"

"Sure, everything's super. Except that I had to look all over the place for you."

"Why? What's wrong?"

"What do you mean, what's wrong? What about *parashah* and *dikduk*?"

"Wha—?"

"Yes. Remember them? Those two little subjects that are constantly vying for my attention?"

"What about them, Mimi?"

"He-llo, Sara," she sang out. "Don't we usually study for them at this lovely hour? Did you forget our schedule because of Chanukah? You know, the one that you wrote out so clearly for me?"

"N-no, but I thought…"

"What?"

"I thought…that you wanted to be free from all this work…I thought that once the report was handed in—"

"I'd be free to have fun again?"

"Yes, that's what you said."

"And then you said something about not being a quitter, Sara. Right?"

"Well…yes. B-but—"

"But what? Unless," she sat down in the seat next to me and whispered, "unless you don't want to work with me anymore."

"Not true," I protested a bit too loudly before some girls sitting nearby shushed us. I turned to them to apologize and then, in a low voice, said to Mimi, "I just didn't think *you* wanted to study with me."

"It's not that, Sara. I want so much to be normal...like you...to eventually be able to study on my own, like others—"

"Not everyone studies by themselves," I said and waved my hand in the direction of the girls working with their study partners.

"You know what I mean. They help each other. When we study together, it's just you helping me."

And there are plenty of ways you help me too, Mimi, I thought to myself, but, of course, could not say aloud. Instead, I said, "But, Mimi, why would you want to study with me now that you told Adina about everything?"

"Because Adina can't do it, not the way you can."

"What do you mean?"

"Well, she's just way too brilliant."

"Thanks a lot."

"You know what I mean, Sara. It's not an insult to you...I've always told you what a genius I think you are. But Adina is not the type to tutor. Not the type to slowly and carefully explain—"

"So can you tell me why in the world Adina wants to teach preschool if she can't even teach such a," I gulped, "such a...good friend like you? How will she have the patience for preschoolers?"

"Isn't it obvious?"

"Obvious?"

She was silent for a moment. "Adina told me that she told you everything."

I nodded. "I guess she must've told you everything too."

"Yes. We...finally opened up to each other."

"I—I figured," I mumbled, feeling as though a massive rock was pressing down on my chest.

"It was wonderful," Mimi's eyes sparkled. "Finally...I feel like I've found a kindred spirit. You know what I mean? Someone...just like me."

"Just like you?" I repeated weakly.

Chapter 32

"Well, not exactly like me," she laughed. "But someone who…didn't have an easy time of it. Who is like the way you described me—a person who is carrying…you know…baggage."

"I shouldn't have said that."

"There you go again, Sara. Will you quit trying to take back everything you say? Anyway, thanks to you, Adina and I finally confided in each other."

"Thanks to me?"

"Yep. If it wasn't for you getting us both to talk, I don't know if Adina and I ever would've. But now that we did, we see that it's just what we needed…each other."

"Of…of course."

"Yes, Sara, thanks to you, Adina and I found each other. We'll probably be friends for life."

"I-I'm so happy for you both."

"So now do you understand why, even though she and I are becoming unbelievably close, Adina wouldn't have a clue how to help me with my schoolwork?"

"No, not really," I shook my head. "I still don't get it…If you're both so…so close with one another and she really wants to work with preschoolers—"

"You don't understand why she's chosen that?"

"No," I shook my head again. "Adina would be so much better at teaching high school or even seminary."

"And I thought, Sara, that you were such a terrific psychologist—"

"Would you stop that already, Mimi?"

"Sorry, I meant it as a compliment. Well anyway, *I* thought it was obvious. Adina wants to work with preschoolers because that's what her mother did. But more than that…I think…"

"Yes?"

"I think she's trying to make up for her own sad childhood."

"Wow. I never thought of it that way."

"Well Sara, maybe that's because it's really hard for someone like you."

"Like me?"

"Yes, hard for someone like you to step into *our* world."

33

FINALLY, THE OPPORTUNITY came, but, of course, when I least expected it.

Later that evening, Mimi and I were sitting in my room studying. There was no time left to work on *parashah* and *dikduk* after our talk in the library, and so immediately after supper we went upstairs to my room and got to work.

I *had* to do whatever I could to help Mimi. Although it was obvious to me that I was no longer her sole confidante, and that she viewed me more as a tutor than as a real friend, I knew I would do anything to stay close to Mimi.

Grateful to resume our study sessions, I threw myself into the lesson, completely forgetting about the information I had been so anxious to share with her and Adina. That is, until Adina suddenly entered the room.

"Hello. Pardon the interruption, but have either of you seen my *Tanach*?"

"No," Mimi leaned back in her chair. "I'd love to lend you mine, but I have no idea where I put it."

"You could use mine," I offered. "Oh, I just remembered, I lent it to Miriam the other day."

"And I just remembered that Mazal was studying with Miriam the day before she went back to Kiryat Yosef and I lent her *my* copy," Adina sighed.

"I think they were studying together right here. I'll check the shelf and see if I can find it," I suggested as I began rummaging through the *sefarim.* "I don't know...I don't see it...but anyway, I've been wanting to call Mazal ever since she left...so if you want, I could ask her..." I spun around, "Oh my goodness!"

"What's the matter, Sara?"

"Yeah, what happened?"

"Nothing's wrong, nothing's happened," I exclaimed. "I've just desperately wanted to speak to the two of you ever since *Shalosh Seudos* this past Shabbos, when I found out. I can't believe it! I kept trying to find a time when I could talk to you both privately—and now that you're both here, I almost forgot!"

"What are you talking about?"

I took a deep breath and sat down on the edge of my bed. "You're not going to believe this. It's about Mazal's missing aunt. You know, her Savta's missing daughter."

"But I thought you said—"

I shook my head. "No, Adina, forget what I said when we talked about it last time."

Mimi looked confused. "Talked about what last time?"

"I don't get it, Sara. You said I was being so unrealistic. That it was impossible—"

"Adina, that was before I found out—"

"Found out what?"

"Before I found out that our *eim ha-bayit* is adopted!"

"She is?"

Adina raised an eyebrow. "What does the *eim ha-bayit* have to do with Mazal's aunt?"

"And what are the two of you talking about?" Mimi asked.

"Don't you see," I turned toward Adina, "everything fits. Geveret Katz told us that many years ago, when she was still a baby, her father had been in charge of a camp. A camp for Yemenite Jews."

"I had no idea."

"She wasn't with us that Friday night in the kitchen, Sara, when I had *toranut* and Geveret Katz was talking to us about her *eim ha-bayit* experiences," Mimi said. "But I still don't know what the two of you are talking about."

"You're right about Adina not being in the kitchen that night.

I forgot. Anyway," I explained to Adina, "she told us that her father headed a Yemenite camp when Israel first became a state."

"So? There were lots of people who were in charge of camps."

"But someone, maybe it was you, Mimi," I turned excitedly toward her, "then said to Geveret Katz something about her looking Yemenite."

"I think it was me. I still—"

"And what did she say to that, Mimi? She was a little embarrassed and then said that both of her parents are Ashkenazim and from Warsaw. *Warsaw*," I repeated with emphasis.

"And Warsaw was the place that *shomer* in Geveret Cohen's camp was from."

"That's right," I nodded to Adina.

"Well still, it can't be," Adina continued. "It's way too coincidental."

"Why? Just because it's right under our noses? Just because Mazal's missing aunt might be our *eim ha-bayit*...that makes it impossible?"

"Sara, Adina," Mimi interrupted, "will one of you kindly tell me what's going on?"

"Sorry, Mimi. What's going on, is that Adina suggested the other day that we try finding—"

"*You* were the one who suggested it, Sara—when we were still on the bus."

"Suggested what?" Mimi rolled her eyes exasperatedly. "Will someone please tell me?"

"That we try to find Mazal's missing aunt."

"Come on. That's impossible!"

"That's what I thought at first," I said. "I only suggested it on the bus because I was feeling so terrible about the story and I guess it was really wishful thinking on my part. I didn't really—"

"She didn't really believe it could be done," Adina continued. "I think that if we do things in an organized way, there must be proper channels to appeal to, to research—"

"But now it's not necessary, Adina. I'm sure that our *eim ha-bayit*, Geveret Esther Katz, is really the person we're looking for."

"I just can't believe it," Adina shook her head.

"But her father was a *shomer* in one of those Yemenite camps. And he was from Warsaw, just like Geveret Cohen said, and remember how she described the way the *shomer* used to hang around her family, and then when they said that they were leaving, that they found a place to live, all of a sudden the baby disappears—"

"Died, Sara. They said she died."

"That's what they *said*, Mimi, but—"

"Sara's right, Mimi. Like I've told you, I did a lot of reading about this subject. Just because they said she died doesn't mean that she really did."

"So you think what Sara is saying is really possible, Adina?"

"No, I don't. Geveret Katz grew up in America, so how could—"

"Don't you see," I was adamant, "that's even more of a proof! If the *shomer* really kidnapped the baby and didn't want to be discovered—then what better place to raise her than the United States?"

"Sorry to burst your bubble, Sara," Mimi said in an uncharacteristically serious tone, "but if you remember, when I mentioned to Geveret Katz that she looked Yemenite, she said that both her parents are Ashkenazim."

"Right, Mimi, and I would absolutely agree with you that if that were true, then Geveret Katz can't be the missing Hodaya. But, that was before I found out that she's adopted—and so now we know it doesn't matter what her parents are. Look," I leaned forward, "even the ages make sense."

"How come you're so sure Geveret Katz is adopted?" Adina's eyes narrowed. "I can't imagine that she suddenly announced it to everyone on Shabbos."

"Of course she didn't, Adina," I shook my head. "You know how it is when the dorm's pretty empty on Shabbos. For *Shalosh Seudos*—"

"The teachers and staff divide up the girls and invite them to their homes for the meal," Adina crossed her arms in front of her chest. "So?"

"So, I was on my way to Geveret Katz when Geveret Spitz suddenly—oh no!" I glanced at my watch and jumped up. "It's so late!"

"Sara, what's wrong? It's only a bit past nine."

"I can't believe it!" I grabbed my jacket and ran for the door. "I forgot all about it!"

"Forgot about what?"

"I'll tell you about everything later," I called breathlessly from the doorway. "I'm supposed to meet with Geveret Spitz at nine o'clock."

I raced down the steps. *How in the world did I forget about my meeting?*

By the time I reached her cottage, I was panting and out of breath. I tried apologizing, but she brushed my explanations aside and told me that she had been busy until that very moment, assuring me that the time of my arrival was perfect.

We sat in her kitchen, where she placed a glass of warm tea and a slice of homemade sponge cake on a plate in front of me. After a few minutes of small talk, she asked me what it was that I wanted to discuss.

I began by telling her that I was hardly making any progress with Ronit. She told me that climbing from one step to the next could take time, but that often one must approach the problem from a different angle than one might be accustomed to.

"And, Sara, it might be by using a method that we've never used before."

"Like…with M-Mimi?" I asked hesitantly.

"Well, yes, something like what Mimi is doing with Riki."

"But I don't understand. Isn't she wasting a lot of time with this prize store? Aren't we supposed to really be covering the material?"

"Of course, Sara, the goal is to eventually help the child to learn what she needs to and grow to higher levels. But sometimes, in fact more often than not with these children, one must take the time to find the right behavior modification system for that specific child."

"Something like Riki's *makolet*?"

"Exactly…Riki's *makolet* is a perfect example."

"B-but how did Mimi know?"

"Mimi realized that there is no way she'll be able to get Riki to sit still if she doesn't enter Riki's little world and figure out what makes her tick. She saw that Riki is an extremely 'street smart' little girl who's always busy trading what she has or what she gets from others for something better. Riki's a little businesswoman. So Mimi decided to put Riki in charge of her own store and teach her things in the context of that store. It's just what Riki needs.

"But," I opened my mouth to speak, then closed it.

"What's wrong, Sara? What bothers you about this method?"

"I—I'm not sure. I guess I always thought that…won't things take too long this way? I mean, when will she finally begin to teach her things? It's distracting Ronit."

Geveret Spitz smiled. "Sara, have you ever heard the saying that bigger investments earn greater dividends?"

"Of course," I smiled back.

"So Mimi needs to invest this time in Riki right now…and *b'ezras Hashem* we will see greater dividends from Riki later."

"But how about the distraction it's causing—"

"For Ronit? Yes, Sara, *you* need to think of a behavioral modification system that's right for her. If she's happy with what she has, she's not going to keep looking at Riki and her *makolet*. You have to figure out which key on the key chain will unlock Ronit's door."

"B-but how do I do that?"

"Ask Mimi, Sara. She's your partner and she's obviously very good at this…"

I made my way back to the dorm utterly piqued. *Mimi is suddenly an expert? Isn't Mimi the one with the learning problems, the one who struggled all these years with reading and other schoolwork? Now Geveret Spitz is recommending that I ask her for advice!*

Dragging myself up the steps to the third floor, I was in no mood to speak to anyone. And, for once, I was glad that I had the room to myself.

I swung the door open and flung myself on top of my quilt. My huge book *How to Motivate the Unmotivated Child* was lying unopened near the end of my bed. I stretched out my foot and angrily shoved it onto the floor, causing it to land with a loud thud.

"Oh good, you're back," Mimi burst through the door. "I just heard you coming into the room…Hey, what's wrong?"

"Who says something's wrong?"

"Your face, your voice, your—"

"Thank you. Are you entering *my* world now, Mimi Rosenberg?"

"What?"

"Oh...nothing. Forget it!"

"Sara...what's with you lately?"

I turned toward the wall. "Nothing."

"Okay, Sara Hirsch, I see that with you it's only a one-way street. With you, it's always *nothing*. Sorry to bother you." I heard her take a few steps toward the door.

I sat up abruptly. "Wait, Mimi, don't go!"

"Yes?" She came closer and sat down on my bed. "So what's with you lately, Sara?"

"I—I'm not really sure. I'm just...I don't know."

"Are you homesick?"

I hugged my knees and sighed. "Not nearly as much as I was in the beginning, but I guess it never completely leaves. You know what I mean."

"Well, not really. I mean I love my parents and everything...but I must say there's something about being here that sort of..." She was silent.

"Sort of what, Mimi?"

"*Nothing,*" she smirked.

"Come on, Mimi. Tell me!"

"Only if you tell me what's gotten in to you lately."

"I...I...all right."

"Okay," she continued, "what I'm saying is that being here, it sort of frees me from the pressures I had at home. I guess you could say I'm feeling more relaxed here, even though I'm probably working harder on schoolwork than I ever have before." She rolled her eyes, "Isn't that funny?"

"I guess so." Neither of us said anything for a few moments. "Well, maybe, if you think about it, maybe the fact that you're accomplishing so much is what's making you feel more relaxed."

"Come on, Sara, let's not exaggerate. I'm not accomplishing *so* much."

"Of course, you are, Mimi," I lifted my hand and pointed to one finger at a time. "Your report, the *dikduk* test that you got back today, your consistency with studying, Riki's *makolet*—"

"Riki's *makolet*?"

"Yes. Geveret Spitz thinks you're doing an excellent job and… and…"

"Yes?"

"And she said I should ask you for help in finding the right behavioral modification system for Ronit."

"Ask me?"

"Yes, she really approved of the *makolet* idea that you're doing with Riki. And…um…I could use the help with something to motivate Ronit. That is, if you have the time."

"You're wondering if I have the time for you, Sara?"

"I mean, I know you're so busy and everything. And you keep telling us that you're thinking of ideas for another performance, and—"

"Well now, let me think," she paused. "Sara Hirsch. Who is she again? Oh that girl in the next room who has only given me hours and hours of her time, who—"

"Mimi, please don't think that my tutoring obligates you in any way—

"To give you some time?" she started laughing. "Sara Hirsch, you really are funny. Stop taking everything so seriously. Of course, I'm thrilled to help you…that is…if I can."

"Like I said, Geveret Spitz suggested it."

"Sara, you can't imagine how flattered I am by the whole idea. It's the first time I've ever experienced anything like this. I know she really likes my ideas; she told me so a few times. She even said that I have certain abilities." Mimi bit her lip pensively, "Do you think she really means it, Sara?"

"Of course, Mimi. Geveret Spitz isn't the type to give false compliments."

"Wow! If only my parents knew about this."

"I'm sure—"

"Wait!" she put up her hand. "There I go again, talking on and on about myself. You were supposed to tell me what's going on with you."

"I—I'm so embarrassed."

"Even with me?" Mimi looked hurt.

"Well…"

There was a sudden knock on the door.

"Come in," Mimi sang out.

We both turned toward the door to see Adina gliding into the room. "I figured you were here." She was freshly showered, her flawless complexion scrubbed to a shine, a flannel robe wrapped around her nightgown. "I finished showering and saw you weren't in the room anymore. So I came looking for you, Mimi."

"I was here. Visiting Sara."

"Visiting Sara? And you didn't tell me..."

No, Adina, she didn't tell you. And I did not get to tell Mimi all those things that were bottled up inside me, either.

The days passed and I threw myself into my work, continuing to fill the pages of my notebook as rapidly as possible. Unattainable as it seemed, the *Proyect* and the Goldstone Award still stood before me—at the finish line, a goal that I so badly wanted to reach. I was not going to waste my time fretting about friends and feelings of being left out. I had aspirations that were far more important.

I fasted well on *Asarah B'Teves* and celebrated Mimi's birthday, along with everyone else, the next day. And I tried pasting a big smile on my face the whole time.

In the resource room, I noticed Mimi studying Ronit with an intensity I could only envy. I watched Mimi consult with Geveret Spitz numerous times and saw the respect in Geveret Spitz's eyes when speaking with her. How I wished I too could earn a similar look of approval from our teacher!

Then it was almost Shabbos. Zehava invited me to go along with her to relatives in Tifrach. It was nearby, and I was glad to go along. Still, I worried about what Rochel Leah's reaction would be. I had nothing to fear, though. Rochel Leah invited Mimi to go with her to a family friend in Nachala. Mimi agreed, but asked if there would be room for Adina as well. Rochel Leah was thrilled. She had wanted to spend a Shabbos with Adina for a while and now she had Mimi *and* Adina.

Somehow, my Shabbos with Zehava did not turn out to be as enjoyable as it should have. Not that Zehava did anything wrong. *I* was the one who could not shake these disturbing emotions that kept cropping up. I kept thinking about Adina and Mimi, and wondering what they were doing and what they were talking about.

Chapter 33

When the school week resumed, our workload seemed to double. Whoever said that the weeks between Chanukah and Purim were going to be tough sure knew what she was talking about! As difficult as it was, though, there was a silver lining in all of this for me. The more work there was, the less time I had to think and feel sorry for myself.

There was another unanticipated benefit. Mimi needed me now more than ever.

It was late Thursday afternoon, exactly two weeks since Mazal had unexpectedly returned home, and Mimi and I were diligently studying together in the library. All of a sudden—until this day, I still have no idea what came over me—I told Mimi that I had to call Mazal right away.

"What? In middle of studying?"

"If you don't mind, Mimi. You could work on the *parashah* sheet while I make the call."

"But, Sara, you have to do your sheet too."

"I know. I'll do mine later—after supper."

"Why don't you call Mazal after supper?"

"I—I don't know. I just have this feeling that it has to be now. Besides, after supper I can't get into the *eim ha-bayit*'s office, and it's so much easier to call from there than to use the public telephone."

That sounded reasonable and I left Mimi in the library, hunched over her papers on the table. Purposefully, I walked passed the lounge and went through the long hallway straight into Geveret Katz's office.

When, a short while later, I placed the receiver back on the hook, my hand was shaking. *It was a good thing I called*, I thought to myself as I made my way back to the library. *Now, they've got to listen to me.*

Yes...they had to. Before it was too late.

34

"COULD YOU KINDLY explain why you made me leave the library, find Adina, and come to your room?" Mimi asked. "You know it's almost suppertime."

"Yes, Sara, what happened?" Adina's eyebrows arched in surprise, "I never saw you like this."

I took a deep breath and then looked from Adina to Mimi. "I just spoke to Mazal and now I've got to talk to both of you!"

"Why? Did something happen to her grandmother?" Adina asked.

"Yeah, I've been wondering about her," Mimi turned to me. "How *is* she feeling?"

"Not good," I shook my head, "Not good at all. Mazal said that ever since her grandmother went into the hospital two weeks ago, she's been getting worse and worse each day. That is…*physically*."

"What do you mean—*physically*?"

"She has this rare form of—I'm not exactly sure. Mazal kept mixing in words in *Ivrit*, words I never heard before. But there was one thing I understood—"

"Yes?"

"She said that she's no longer on the medication they were using before, the medicine that had such a strong, sedative effect. They had to take her off it—I think because it can't be used together with these other more aggressive treatments. And now—"

"She's more lucid?"

"Yes, Adina. I'm positive that's what Mazal said…something about her mind now being clear…*tzalul*. And then she said something else."

"What?" they both asked me.

"She said that her grandmother is…is…calling out for one last chance before she dies…to—to see Hodaya."

Mimi shrugged. "And you're convinced that Geveret Katz is Hodaya?"

"Yes," I said. "Yes! And we—"

"And I still say it's impossible, Sara," Adina said. "But I do feel it would be helpful to the Cohens if we could find out some concrete information about what really happened to the baby."

"And I still say, why search all over Israel when it could very well be that our answer is right under this roof," I persisted.

"Adina, it doesn't pay to argue with Sara," Mimi rolled her eyes, "when she makes up her mind about something."

"Thanks a lot, Mimi."

"I meant it as a compliment, Sara. You're very determined."

"Mimi's right, Sara, it *is* a compliment." Adina pushed back her dark, shiny hair. "Let's suppose your theory is correct. We can't exactly go over to the *eim ha-bayit* and say 'oh, hi, Geveret Katz, we've discovered your birth family.' Now can we?"

"Of course, not. What do you think I am?"

"Come on Sara, don't be cross. I didn't mean to offend you. It's not that I'm against the whole idea—it's just that I think this has to be approached properly. We've got to find proof…hospital archives, logs of funerals, adoption papers, copies of passports…something to…"

Adina's sharp mind was working at full speed. I wanted to get up and hug her, but of course, I did not. Instead, I took out a pen and paper, and as Adina made suggestions I began to write.

We decided that our first stop should be the library in Devorah. Geveret Spitz had once mentioned that, although the residents of Devorah were mainly immigrant families, they had an extensive research library there which people traveled from all over the country to use. We would see what information they had on the refugee camp the Yitzchaki family had lived in when they first arrived, the hospital where the baby was kept, and any other records or institutions affiliated with that camp.

Monday was the earliest day we could make the trip. The girls from *Bnot Yisrael* had off from school that day, and so we M.B.L.L.ers were going to be given off the few hours we usually worked with them. It was a mere fifteen-minute bus ride away.

I was excited. I was sure that our research would corroborate my suspicions. *It just had to!*

I felt like a heroine already. I could almost picture the *Seudas Hoda'ah* party that would be given in our school. What a glorious feeling it would be for me. Everyone would know that Sara Hirsch was the catalyst, spurring the search that reunited a long lost daughter with her dying mother.

I would have to stop thinking about the celebration for now, though. As Adina said, first we needed to have the proof to present to our *eim ha-bayit*. I just did not know how I would have the patience to wait until then.

Jauntily, I made my way down to supper alongside Adina and Mimi—in a far better mood than I had been in the past couple of weeks.

I wish it had lasted.

On the Sunday after the Shabbos that Mimi, Adina, and Rochel Leah had *toranut* together and once again I felt lonely and left out of things, Mimi and I were taking that familiar walk back through the woods from the resource room. Mimi was looking uncharacteristically pensive.

"What are you thinking about, Mimi?"

Mimi grinned. "Believe it or not, about you and Ronit."

"Me and Ronit?"

"Yes, you did ask me to help you out, didn't you?"

"Well...yes."

"So, I've been watching the two of you. And you know, Sara," Mimi's tone dropped to a dramatic whisper, forcing us both to stop walking, "I think I have the solution."

"You do?" I was surprised. "So what do you think I should do with her?"

"I think..." she let her voice trail off theatrically.

"Yes?"

Her tone suddenly became serious. "I think that what you've got to do before anything is to watch her closely and find the key."

A moment passed. "Right. And?"

"And...that's it."

"That's it?"

"Yep. You've got to find the key," she repeated.

"But Mimi, that's the whole problem. Ronit's very quiet and doesn't seem to be interested in anything. How in the world am I supposed to find this key?"

"She's got to be interested in something," Mimi insisted.

I shook my head and shrugged. "You see how she just stands by the side watching everyone else all the time? It's impossible for me to get her involved in anything. Even if I did what you did with Riki, that *makolet* idea, it wouldn't help. She'd still be looking at Riki's."

"Maybe, Sara, that's because she sees you looking there."

"Excuse me, Mimi," we stood still, facing each other. "What exactly are you trying to tell me?"

"I'm trying to suggest that instead of looking at us, you should concentrate more on Ronit."

"Thanks for the wonderful advice, Mimi," I turned away and began walking.

Mimi caught up. "Really, Sara. If you would just—"

"I'd love *not* to look at you and Riki," I mumbled while glancing at her before quickening my pace, "but you don't realize how distracting the two of you are."

"Why? If you would just—"

"You're just so much more interesting than I am...so much more colorful, not plain like—"

I stopped mid-sentence.

"Plain like what, Sara?"

"Oh, nothing," I looked ahead as I continued walking.

"There you go again, Sara. Nothing! Nothing...what?"

"Just...nothing."

We made our way back to the Beit Yaakov HaNegbah campus silently. My heart, though, was pounding and the voices inside me were protesting wildly at what Mimi had said.

And Mimi did not try to appease me. She was upset at me for not telling her what was bothering me and I was upset at Mimi for saying what she had.

Well, when you add one upset plus another upset together, you know what you get. I cannot say we accomplished very much studying together that evening.

I lay in bed that night, my heart heavier than usual. *Maybe Mimi's really right,* I stared into the darkness. *Maybe I do tend to look at what's going on around me, instead of concentrating on what I'm really supposed to be doing, that is—helping Ronit.* I punched my pillow hard. *That's it,* I told myself determinedly, *tomorrow I'll focus on her and then we'll see if that's really been the problem.*

More than anything, though, I had to make up with Mimi. *Tomorrow, in the resource room we'll talk…*

But when tomorrow arrived, I remembered that this was the day the *Bnot Yisrael* children had off from school. I would have to wait one more day until we would work together in the resource room. Instead, as planned, we would spend the afternoon with Adina at the Devorah library. *Well, hopefully by then Mimi and I will have patched everything up,* I thought optimistically. This trip to the library was something I certainly was looking forward to.

When school was over for the day, I went to the *eim ha-bayit*'s office in the dormitory to meet Adina and Mimi and officially "sign out." *How ironic,* I reflected, *we're about to do something that will most probably change Geveret Katz's life forever, and she—who has absolutely no idea—is the one granting us permission to leave!*

"Where's Mimi?" I asked Adina after we each wrote down our name, time of departure, and place of destination. "Why isn't she here yet?"

"She decided not to come with us," Adina said. "She didn't think she'd be very useful in the research department."

My heart sank. *Is Mimi still upset with me? Is that the real reason she's not coming? Or, is it because she's avoiding what she suspects will be an uncomfortable reading experience?*

Unfortunately, it turned out to be more than an uncomfortable experience. And, it had nothing to do with reading.

Chapter 34

At first, things went more smoothly than I could have dreamed possible. Adina's command of the Hebrew language was impeccable and her eloquent manner demanded serious and respectful treatment from the librarians.

We explained that we were doing a report for school on the many different immigrants coming to Israel when it first became a state. In a way, this really was the truth. As Rabbi Grossman told us at the beginning of the term, we were to research anything that would be relevant to our individual themes and to eventually submit it as part of the Goldstone *Proyect*. Somehow, we would each find a way to tie this investigation into our reports.

We went from one department to the next, managing to maneuver our way through the many desks and different floors, until we finally ended up in the basement, where information regarding early immigrants was stored.

We had the full attention of the one and only librarian who was down there. She helped us quickly locate the file on the Rosh HaBe'er transit camp. What we read confirmed what Geveret Cohen had told us. It had originally been a British Army Camp. We were surprised, though, at the number of people who had lived there at that time. It was a huge camp that held over twenty thousand immigrants during any given period throughout those years. However, we were unable to find any record of the different *shomrim* that ran the place.

Of course, there were no records of missing children either. There were a few newspaper articles filed in the back of one of the cabinets, referring to an investigative committee set up by the State in 1966 to look into the matter of Yemenite children whose parents were told they had died.

"You see, this is what I was telling you about," Adina said. "Read what it says here," she handed me the article.

I perused the piece and nodded. "Yes, there was definitely a pattern of parents being told that their children had died suddenly in hospitals or in the children's homes."

"And they couldn't even bury their babies."

"It's just like you said, Adina." I looked down at the article and read aloud in a low voice, "*After a number of parents, who had been told that their children died in the camps, received draft induction notices for those children—"*

"That's when the Commission of Inquiry was established."

"But look, Adina, it says here," I continued reading, "that *although the government commission of inquiry received three hundred forty-two complaints from parents who had been told that their children had died, of these the commission concluded that three hundred sixteen had, in fact, died. Twenty-two were not accounted for and four were still alive and living with different families.*" I looked up from the paper. "So there really isn't any absolute proof."

"Read on."

I did. I read interviews with different Yemenite parents who told their stories, stories similar to the one Geveret Cohen had shared with us. There were even a couple of stories with somewhat happy endings, of children who had been missing and later reunited with their parents. But those accounts were few.

"So where do we go from here?" I asked Adina when I finished reading. "It's all so sad. But what should we do to prove who Geveret Katz really is?"

"You mean," Adina corrected me, "what should we do to help find out what happened to Geveret Cohen's missing sister?"

"Same thing."

"No, it's not, Sara," she insisted, "not until you can prove it. And since you can't, I'd appreciate it if you'd cease talking about it as though it were fact. If we do this, we do it sensibly. Otherwise—"

"Okay, Adina, whatever you say." I certainly did not want to get into an argument with her and risk her abandoning this project. "So, what's our next step?"

"I think we need to look for the hospital records."

I followed behind her as she briskly made her way to the desk on the other side of the room where the librarian was sitting. She spoke rapidly with the librarian just like any born Israeli would. (*She is a born Israeli!* I reminded myself.) It was almost impossible for me to grasp the meaning of their conversation. I watched them, tried reading their expressions, and attempted to follow their hurried hand gestures. Yet, I had no real idea of what they were saying to each other. What was obvious to me, though, was that their exchange was not flowing very pleasantly.

Then Adina's tone changed and she said something more. I caught the word 'sick' and then 'fatally sick.' Suddenly, the conversation seemed to take a different turn. The words between them poured out a bit more slowly than before. I heard words like 'file'… 'secret file'… 'security'… 'special key.'

Finally, the librarian pushed back her chair and stood up. She turned around and began heading toward a back room. We followed closely behind her.

The librarian's back was to us and Adina sent me a triumphant grin. A deliciously warm feeling ran through me and I smiled back. *Less than six weeks ago I wouldn't have even dreamed of this!*

And now my dream—my dream about Adina and I becoming good friends—was coming true. And maybe, maybe my dream about finally accomplishing something momentous would soon come about.

The librarian stopped in front of a heavy metal door. We stopped behind her.

I stared at the key she withdrew from her pocket.

Is this the key that will unlock the door to the hidden files, files that hold the secrets of the missing children? Will this be the key to making my dreams of greatness come true?

I guess I would have stood rooted to that spot indefinitely, my head somewhere in dreamland, had Adina not brought me abruptly back down to earth. "Shirley just checked the file on Rosh HaBe'er for us and she found out—"

"That Geveret Katz is really Hodaya Yitzchaki?" I asked excitedly.

Adina's eyes narrowed. "Sara…"

"What?" I blinked innocently.

"I told you not to jump to conclusions."

"But I thought—" I looked on helplessly as Shirley started locking the door to the private file room.

"Well, obviously I also thought it would help. Otherwise, I wouldn't have spent fifteen minutes trying to convince her to open the files," Adina murmured then turned to Shirley and thanked her for both of us.

I added my American-accented *todah*, and smiled to show my gratitude. I am sure, though, that my disappointment must have shown on my face.

I tried not to let my heavy mood prevent me from keeping pace with Adina's brisk steps as we made our way upstairs. We emerged through the library's revolving doors into the brilliant sunshine. Despite the frigidness in the air, the light lifted my spirits.

"It's really a pity that hospital doesn't exist anymore," Adina said as we made our way down the stone steps that led us away from the library's entrance.

"What do you mean?" I asked.

"Well, if that hospital that the Yitzchaki baby was in was still around, we'd be able to go there and start asking questions. Of course, not exactly straight out. We'd have to think of some way to...anyway, like I said, *if* that hospital still existed."

"But what happened to it? Did Shirley say? Was there a fire?"

"No, nothing like that," Adina looked at me strangely. "Sara, you really didn't understand what she was saying?"

"Well, the two of you were speaking kind of quickly, and—"

"I'm sorry."

"No, Adina, it's not your fault. My mind was also wandering," I admitted. "But anyway, it's not important. So what were you saying? What happened in the end to the Rosh HaBe'er hospital?"

"The way I understand, it's now defunct. The whole camp eventually disbanded, with the internees gradually finding homes on the outside."

"And the hospital didn't remain?" I knew the answer, but I guess when you feel so disappointed, helplessness causes you to sort of grasp at anything.

"Without people, Sara, you don't exactly need a hospital."

"Well, not every refugee camp hospital disappeared, Adina."

"I didn't say that every hospital disappeared, but the one from Rosh HaBe'er did, or at least ceased to operate as a hospital. Unlike many of the other camps, Rosh HaBe'er wasn't situated in an area that turned residential, so it became some kind of educational institution...a research campus. Something like that."

Chapter 34

We reached the bottom of the steps.

"So Adina, even if there's no hospital anymore, the original building's still there. I bet all the records were put into some kind of storage room or something."

"Sara, be realistic. Why would some modern research facility save old hospital records?"

"Why would they throw them out?"

"Because they don't need them, obviously."

"But they don't know that they'll never need them. Educators, researchers...they don't just throw things out."

"That's true."

"So you agree?"

"I didn't say that I agree that it's realistic to chase after these records. I just agreed that they probably didn't throw them out, and that yes, they probably put them somewhere."

"So why can't we try to see them, the same as we'd do if the place was still a hospital?"

"Sara, we can't walk into a research facility. We'd have to get special permission from the *Hanhallah* and from the institution's authorities. It's complicated."

"True, but there *has* to be a way."

Adina was silent for a moment. "Mimi was right about you, Sara. You're very determined."

I smiled. I was sure Adina meant it as a compliment. "So, let's go back inside right now and find out exactly what the new place is called and where it is. And then we'll try to figure out what our next step should be."

"It's not necessary to go back inside. I remember exactly what it's called and we can get its precise location from the telephone book in the dorm."

My heart lifted. *So she wasn't giving up!* "What's the name of the place, Adina?"

"Its official name is The Be'er Institute for Applied Research, but it's more popularly known as The Tzihov Institute. Apparently, it got its name because it's near the town of Tzihov."

There was something familiar about that name, but I could not put my finger on it. "Do you have any idea where Tzihov is?"

"I assume it's somewhere up north. Well, not quite as up north as Kiryat Yosef—"

"Everything is up North from here," I laughed.

"That's true," she smiled back.

We bantered lightly, enjoying the fresh crisp air and the pleasantness of each other's company. We decided that after stopping for a snack, we would return to the dorm and fill Mimi in with the details. Then, we would find out the exact address of the Be'er Institute and write them a letter requesting information for our "report." Once we had a copy of their stationery with names of people to approach, we would figure out what our next step would be.

After checking out the freezer in a nearby café for packaged ice cream with a good *hashgachah*, we settled around one of the small tables in the store's garden. It was cool outside and the ice cream did not exactly lessen the cold. But we were feeling accomplished and chatting amiably. And I guess, that sometimes the warmth of a blossoming friendship helps warm you up inside despite the chilly temperature.

"So, I'm really glad, Adina, that you're doing this with me."

"I feel it's the right thing to do. It's a terrible thing for a mother to lose her daughter."

"And for a daughter to lose her mother," I added gently.

"Yes," she looked into my eyes. "It's a terrible thing for a daughter to lose her mother."

I looked down at my ice cream cone, unsure if I should say anything else. It had been quite a while since we had discussed anything intimately, and in the back of my mind, I knew that Adina now had Mimi to talk to. Yet, I so much wanted to draw closer to her and, at the same time, was afraid of pushing her away.

"It's wonderful of you, Adina, to try to help them reunite."

"Well, I want to help. But like I said, I'm only going to do what seems realistic, Sara, and that doesn't mean that we'll be successful in the end."

"Of course we'll be successful," I said fervently. "Hashem will help us."

Chapter 34

Adina laughed tersely. "If Hashem had wanted to help, Sara, He might have prevented the kidnapping—if it really was a kidnapping—in the first place."

"You can't say that, Adina. Hashem knows what He's doing."

"I didn't say He doesn't. But rather than bringing about a happy reunion, I think that not permitting the loss to take place in the first place would have been a lot better."

"Adina, it's not our place to judge the way Hashem chooses to do things," I said quietly. "You know what we always learned. Everything Hashem does is for the best."

Adina did not respond, but started humming the tune of the song "*Gam Zu L'Tovah*—Everything Hashem Does Is for the Best" in a slightly detached, sarcastic manner.

"Come on, Adina," I had to say something. "Everything that happens really is *gam zu l'tovah*. You've got to believe that everything Hashem does is perfect."

"Oh, really, Sara, do I?" her voice suddenly turned icy, causing a chill to run through me, a chill that had nothing to do with the cold weather. "That missing child was either kidnapped or died. And you're telling me that everything Hashem does is perfect. Take a look around. You see that memorial over there?"

I looked where she was pointing.

"That's in memory of a group of school children who were killed when their bus overturned a few years ago."

I shivered. "I know, it's horrible, but we can't question the ways of Hashem."

"Question? Who's questioning? Just don't tell me that everything Hashem does is perfect."

"But it is! We learned that—"

"I don't want to hear about what we learned, Sara. Maybe for you everything's perfect, but for me—"

"I know, but—"

"*You* know? What is it exactly that you know? Have you ever lost someone you loved? Has there ever been any serious hardship in your life?" I felt her angry blue eyes boring into mine. "Yes, Sara, it's easy for you to talk about everything being for the best. But try speaking to other people...people whose lives have not been so perfect. Then go preach about everything being good."

"Adina, please!"

"Oh yes, everything's been just perfect for me. My mother dying when I was so young and leaving me with a father who had no idea how to father all these years. Perfect? Speak to Mimi—oh you did already. How do you think it feels walking around feeling like damaged merchandise? Oh, you want to hear about perfect? How about poor perfect Rochel Leah?"

"Rochel Leah?"

"Yes. Listen to the perfect life Rochel Leah's been living all these years. Flying back and forth from Miami to Woodlake, not knowing if she should live with her father's family in Woodlake or stay with her mother—who is too busy pursuing her career to deal with a daughter or marriage. Perfect, no?"

"I never said anything about everyone having a perfect life, Adina. What I'm trying to say is that Hashem is perfect and whatever He does is perfect."

"Well then, I have a question for you. If Hashem created imperfect lives, then how can everything He does be perfect?"

"Adina, you...you sound like an..."

"An *apikores*?" she looked at me accusingly. "Admit it! Isn't that what you were about to say?"

"I'm sorry, Adina," my voice cracked, "but you sound like you don't believe—"

"I do believe in Hashem, Sara. I just don't understand how He can be perfect when so many people's lives are so miserable—"

"Don't you see, Adina, your anger is making you—"

"My anger?"

"It's blinding you. We learned—"

"Don't tell me what we learned! You think everything is so simple and can be tied up in a nice little package." She stood up, squashing her ice cream wrapper into a ball and aiming it into a nearby wastebasket. "I'm going back to the dormitory now. If you want to join me, you may. Otherwise, I'll go by myself."

No, Adina, I wanted to shout, *don't leave...don't run away! Don't you see how wrong you are! Everything Hashem does is perfect and for the best—even if we don't understand it, even if we're surrounded by so much pain!*

But I said nothing.

Instead, I looked at the unfinished ice cream cone in my hand and trembled. Slowly, I stood up and dropped it into the waste basket. I watched it fall and land, squished and distorted alongside Adina's wrapper. And I wondered, *what in the world made me buy ice cream on such a frigidly cold day anyway?*

35

I KNEW ADINA was upset with me, but I did not realize how much until later that evening.

During supper I tried making small talk with her. She answered my questions with monosyllables. I went back to my room in a miserable mood. Replaying our conversation over and over again in my head, I could not think of one word I should have said differently. So why was I feeling so utterly awful?

When Mimi joined me in my room for our study session, there still remained between us some of that resentment from the day before, although we both tried pretending that everything was fine. But that was nothing compared to what I was feeling when I thought of Adina and that strange conversation we had!

We opened our *sefarim* and took out our notes, but despite all my efforts, I was finding it hard to concentrate. Apparently I was not being the world's best study partner.

"So what happened today with you and Adina?" Mimi asked. "I guess you didn't find out that Geveret Katz is the missing Hodaya."

"No, we didn't. And please don't joke about that, Mimi."

"All right, so what did you find out, Investigator Hirsch?"

"We found out that the hospital where the baby was last seen by her parents was taken over by some research college or," I waved my hand apathetically, "something like that."

"So what's bothering you, Sara? What *really* happened between you and Adina?"

Chapter 35

"Who says something happened?"

"Hmmm, this little birdie came and told me," she teased, trying to lighten the mood. Then suddenly her tone changed, "It's so obvious that something happened. Adina is miserable and so are you."

"Adina's not miserable, she's…oh, never mind!"

"There you go, again. Cutting me off. And you're the one who told me that true friends shouldn't be afraid to open up to each other. Or does that only go one way?"

"I…I want to Mimi, but," I stopped abruptly.

"But, what?" she pressed. "You're afraid of what I'll think?"

How in the world? "Y-yes," I answered quietly, "but also something else."

"What?" she asked and I knew it did not stem from simple curiosity, but from sincere concern.

I swallowed hard. "It's not just about me, but also Adina. And…it might be—"

"*Lashon hara?*"

"Yes. But she's very upset at me about something I tried to tell her. And while on the one hand I can't blame her, on the other hand, I know I wasn't wrong for saying what I did."

"Sometimes a person can say something right," she said softly, "but it comes out wrong."

I thought about that for a moment. "Y-you might be right, Mimi." Unexpectedly, I felt the sides of my mouth turning upward. "You know, Mimi Rosenberg, you really have a lot of common sense."

"Why thank you, Sara Hirsch," she answered lightly. "What a nice compliment." A few seconds passed with neither of us saying anything, then suddenly Mimi's expression turned serious. "So, why did you become so offended yesterday when I made that comment to you about not looking at me and Riki?"

"I didn't—"

"Yes, you did."

I looked away and stared out of the window over my desk. "It…it doesn't feel very good to be told that I should focus more on Ronit when I…you know, Mimi," I turned back to face her, "I've been working so hard with her."

"It's true you're working hard, but maybe that's the problem."

"What do you mean?"

"You're working hard, Sara, but maybe...you're going in the wrong direction. It's like you want to go North but you're traveling South."

"Huh?"

"You're working with Ronit the way you assume she should be learning. The way *you* would want to learn. Even her *morah* thought that by giving her the main part in the play, it would make her happy, make her want to participate."

"And it didn't help one bit."

"That's right. Like I told you yesterday, you've got to find *her* key, you've got to enter *her* world. Think about it, Sara. Her father suddenly dead, her mother dysfunctional...poor, elderly grandparents, a tiny stuffy apartment. Her grandparents probably hover around her day and night and don't let her out of their sight when she's not in school. Imagine what it must be like for her in a world that's been turned upside down. She probably feels so little control in her life. I don't think she wants to be put here and there, told to do this, have fun with that—even if she ends up getting a great prize or the main part."

I sat there listening, trying to absorb what Mimi was saying. "You're probably right, Mimi. I think I understand now what you were trying to tell me yesterday...I just wish I knew how to do it, how to enter Ronit's world the way you do."

"So, I guess I said the right thing to you, Sara, after all—but in the wrong way." There was a gleam of mischief in her eye as she stretched out her hand toward mine, "Forgive me?"

"Forgive you?" I laughed. "You were the one who was right all along. Besides, I don't think anyone could ever stay upset with you, Mimi Rosenberg."

"And I don't think anyone could stay upset with you either, Sara Hirsch."

If only that were true, I thought about Adina.

I felt as though a huge boulder had been lifted off my back. Mimi was not upset or disappointed with me, and she did not assume that whatever it was that happened between Adina and me was my fault either.

I decided I would do what I thought Mimi would do. I would find some way to finish that conversation with Adina—and hopefully, this time I would do it right.

Later that night, I knocked timidly on Adina's door. I had just heard Chani and Rivky leave with Mimi and knew I would find Adina alone.

"Come in."

She was sitting on her bed, her back up against the wall, her loose-leaf opened up on the middle of her lap.

"I—I hope it's not a bad time for you, Adina. I need to talk to you."

"We have nothing to say to each other," she answered coldly.

"Please don't be like that."

She continued writing in her loose-leaf as though I was not there.

"Adina, please," I felt the tears spring to my eyes.

She looked up for a moment and our eyes met. She turned away instantly.

And then suddenly, I felt something stir within me, something I could not hold back making its way to the surface. "Is that how you want to always be, Adina?" I found myself saying, "You want to spend your life angry at Hashem, angry at the world, angry—"

"I am not angry!"

"You are! Look, what did I ever do to you? You resent me because of my family. You resent me because of what you perceive to be my perfect life."

"I don't. I just can't stand to hear you preach about a perfect world when you have no idea of what life can be like."

"Granted, Adina. You went through something horrible and now you're going through something else that's very upsetting. And…and I wish you didn't have to suffer. But look at Mimi, look how she—"

"Mimi's different."

"Why? She also suffered…suffers. But, she's trying…she—" I stopped midsentence. Another person came to mind. "You know, Adina," I continued softly, "I know someone else who always had things easy. You think *I* have things easy? Believe me, this person *really* had things going great for her all the time. Great student, super popular, fantastic family, tons and tons of personality and talent. And then you know what happened to her? The second she had to face a difficulty, she didn't have a clue what to do."

"So?"

"So, suffering helps make a person stronger. It—"

"You can have some of my strength any time you'd like."

"Adina, we don't *ask* for suffering, but if it finds us, instead of looking at it like it's the end of the world, like we are damaged goods because of it—."

"But, I am damaged, Sara. So is Mimi, so is—"

"Stop it, Adina!

She looked at me and did not say a word. I stared back at her, my heart pounding hard. *Please, Hashem, help me say the right thing and help me to say it right!*

I walked over to her bed and sat down. I did not try to stop the tears from rolling down my cheeks. "Adina, please listen to me for one minute without interrupting or getting angry with me. I'm not trying to sound preachy and if *chas v'shalom* I were in your shoes, I don't know what I'd do. But, it can't be. Hashem doesn't make mistakes. There has to be a reason for Mimi's problem, for your suffering, and for any difficulties we face."

"I don't see any reason for someone to be born with something wrong with her brain, or for two people who were filled with joy and goodness to have their lives destroyed, their baby left alone—"

"I don't understand it either and maybe none of us human beings can. But, Adina, you have to believe that Hashem loves us."

"Maybe He loves you, but I sure have trouble feeling it."

"Adina, you're one of the smartest girls in the class. Probably, *the* smartest. And you know it. So, maybe Hashem really loves you more than anybody else. After all, he gave you the brains, he gave you—"

"Very funny, Sara."

"Remember when we learned *Parashas Va'eschanan* in *Chumash* with Rabbanit Greenstein and she reviewed the *Shema* with us? She explained that there's no contradiction in anything that Hashem does and that's one of the reasons we cover our eyes when we say *Shema*—we are proclaiming our *bitachon* in Hashem while blocking out our perception of what we think might not be fair."

"Fine. So everything Hashem does is fair and…well…I guess,

perfect," she admitted grudgingly. "But that doesn't make *me* perfect. Or Mimi. *We're* still damaged goods."

"Why do you keep saying that?"

"Because…because that's the way it is. We're different in certain ways than other people."

Even if we had stayed up all night talking, I do not think I would have been able to convince Adina that she was not damaged. *Adina Stern damaged?* What an oxymoron! For all the months that I had known her, I had only thought of her as someone who was as close to perfection as a person could get.

Brilliant, gorgeous, charismatic…

Then I found myself wondering, *is it possible that she's right? Is she like a beautiful painting with a hole punched in the middle of the canvas? And…is that fair?*

I was feeling guilty for not understanding Adina and I was feeling guilty for questioning Hashem's fairness. I did not want to walk around with such feelings locked inside me.

The next day, instead of returning to the dorm for lunch, I went to the ninth grade classroom, where I knew Rabbanit Abrams could be found. Besides teaching us M.B.L.L.ers *Chovos HaLevavos*, she was Beit Yaakov HaNegbah's ninth grade *mechanechet*. The door was wide open and I was grateful to find the room empty of students.

Rabbanit Abrams was sitting at her desk with an opened *sefer* lying before her and a sliced apple on a piece of aluminum foil on the side. I stood at the doorway, wavering—unsure if I should knock or turn around and forget about the questions I wanted to ask her.

All at once, she looked up and smiled warmly. "Oh, good afternoon, Sara, please come in."

I took a step forward. "I—I hope I'm not disturbing the Rabbanit."

"Not at all. Please, have a seat," she motioned to the student desk opposite her.

At first I was very nervous. I did not want her to consider me heretical, G-d forbid, or to think any less of me for questioning Hashem's ways, but she was quite encouraging, reassuring me that there was nothing wrong with asking questions—as long as I would be open to hearing the answers. She even said it would be wrong *not* to ask, and instead to walk around as though everything were fine while harboring questionable thoughts.

After much hesitation on my part, Rabbanit Abrams' sharp mind deduced that my main question was this: Why would Hashem cause someone to have a handicap, a deficiency, or anything that causes suffering—through no fault of their own—thus preventing them from leading a normal life?

"That's an excellent question, Sara, and it shows that you think about things instead of just going about your *avodah* in a routine manner."

I blushed. Of course I could not tell her that it really was not my question, and had it not been for Adina, I probably never would have thought of it.

"First of all, everything Hashem does is good and is perfect, but we human beings, with our limited vision, might not see it now or we might not *ever* see it or understand it—in *this* world.

"*Chazal* tell us that before we were born, we were shown what our life's circumstances—*material* circumstances, that is—would be. And we agreed to that particular life, because we understood that these circumstances would help us grow in our *avodas Hashem*."

"So...is Rabbanit Abrams saying that a handicapped person agreed to be handicapped?"

"Yes," she nodded.

"But, but why would a person do that? Doesn't it limit her—doesn't it prevent her from being able to serve Hashem properly?"

"In this world, we might see it as a limit. But in the spiritual world, everything is infinite. Once born, we forget what we agreed to before entering this world, because that amnesia allows us to have *bechirah*, the free choice necessary to fulfill our *tafkid*. The ability to make the right decisions and to follow up on them is what helps strengthen us spiritually and grow in our *avodas Hashem*."

"But the person would still serve Hashem better if...if she wasn't handicapped."

"Who says?"

"Well—wouldn't she have more strength?"

"Physically...yes."

"Right. So then by not being handicapped she would have more physical strength to serve Hashem."

"But spiritual strength is what counts, Sara. And before that person was born, she was able to see with complete clarity that for her *neshamah*—her soul—to reach its potential, it needed to be born into a physically impaired body."

"Does that mean that people who are physically handicapped are better off—are on a higher spiritual level than the rest of us? Does that mean that we would all be better off like that *chas v'shalom*?"

"No," she shook her head. "For that person, that was the best thing for him. For another person, being strong and healthy might be what's best for his *neshamah*. We don't know. Life is full of all different kinds of challenges. Of course, in this world we pray to Hashem to ease our way and not to confront us with difficult tests. And we do hope for a life full of worldly blessings.

"Part of our belief is to accept that whatever the circumstances are, those that seem problematic, as well as the ones that are obvious blessings, are what Hashem chose for us. Whether weak or strong, ill or healthy, rich or poor, smart or slow—Hashem has gifted us all, yes *gifted* us with what we need to fulfill our potential."

I imagined myself telling Adina that losing her mother at a young age was a gift. I certainly did not want to imagine what she would tell me I could do with that gift.

"I see something is still disturbing you, Sara."

I swallowed. "What if...what if someone is suffering terribly...um...for example, on the surface everything seems like it is going great for the person, but underneath it all, she...she can't connect to people. She's so angry at certain things that happened to her when she was young...she suffered terrible losses and because of those losses couldn't live a normal life. Isn't that different than the handicapped person?"

"No, not really. And I'm definitely not one to judge which is worse. But an emotional handicap is also a handicap."

I pondered what Rabbanit Abrams said for a few moments. "I guess I never really thought of it like that."

"You see, Sara, even the person who is emotionally handicapped could use her situation to grow in serving Hashem. But it takes work, *hard* work...it's an *avodah*."

"And...and how about someone who has terrible learning problems or someone whose parents are divorced...that's also not her fault."

"Who ever said anything about any of this being someone's fault? People are born into different circumstances and people experience all different things throughout their lives. But, Sara, don't forget, we are not who we are at birth," she paused for a moment. "We are what we make of ourselves."

"But...but it must be so hard—almost impossible—when someone is weighed down by all these problems."

"Do you remember what we spoke about during Chanukah? About the *yetzer hara* doing whatever it can to crush a person's hopes and to view his challenges as burdens instead of the stepping stones they're meant to be?"

"Yes, I do remember. Rabbanit Abrams spoke about the bird and its wings."

"That's right. When used correctly, these so-called handicaps can be used to lift us higher...to enable us to soar."

I thought of Mimi and of her recent growth. And then I pictured Adina and felt my heart sink. "But what if someone can't look at her situation as a gift...as the wings it's meant to be—because she views herself as...as damaged merchandise?"

Her eyebrows lifted, "Damaged merchandise?"

"Yes. She thinks of herself as damaged because for her things were different."

"Different from what?"

"Different from normal..."

"Normal? What's normal?"

"Normal is normal. The way it is by everyone else."

"Sara, I suggest that you tell this person to stop looking at everybody else. That's one of the *yetzer hara's* strongest weapons. When people are busy looking at the way others are living their lives, it prevents them from using their *own* gifts to fulfill their *own* mission. Just like each person who needs, wears prescription eye glasses that are right for him, Hashem provides us with the 'prescriptions' that are right for us to fulfill our individual spiritual needs." She took a deep breath, "Do you understand what I'm saying, Sara?"

"Um...yes...I think so," I slowly nodded.

"So remember, if the bird is busy watching everyone else flap his wings, but he doesn't bother flapping his own—how will he ever be able to fly upward?"

If the bird is busy watching everyone else...

I thought about that later that afternoon as I made my way alongside Mimi and a few of the others to Kfar Amsdorf. Something was bothering me and I knew it had nothing to do with Adina.

It had to do with me.

I had to admit that Adina was not the only one guilty of comparing her life to others'.

Is that why Mimi, despite her handicap, is so successful—because she doesn't look at others and what they have, but does the best she can with what she has?

I resolved to truly try to focus on Ronit that afternoon. I would not look at Mimi or any of the others.

When we entered the resource room, Riki ran happily to Mimi, with Ronit and a few of the other children following quickly behind her. They were certainly in a livelier mood than usual and Geveret Spitz had to use a more authoritative tone of voice on them in order to bring things under control.

It worked immediately. Each child proceeded along with her M.B.L.L. *morah* to her cubby to pick up her worksheet before continuing on to her table. From the corner of my eye I noticed Riki's enthusiastic gait as she walked along with Mimi to their corner of the table.

Ronit trudged slowly beside me.

Oh, how I wish I could find that key already!

I looked down at Ronit's worksheet. Her teacher had written that she was still having trouble discriminating between a *bet* and a *vet* and would I please try to work on that with her. *I would be glad to*, I felt like writing back, *if I could get her to look at me instead of at Mimi and Ronit.*

There they were, with that *makolet*! Riki was gleefully counting her play money from the wallet Mimi kept nearby, and of course, Ronit was looking at them longingly.

Sara, stop it! If the bird is busy watching everyone else...

"Ronit," I said in Hebrew, "you like watching what Riki is doing?"

She nodded slowly.

A makolet for Ronit? No, that's not the solution. She doesn't really want her own makolet and she'd probably still look at Riki's even if I made her one of her own. No, I shook my head, *that's definitely not the key.*

I let out a deep sigh.

Think, Sara, think.

Ronit isn't happy with herself. Right now she's looking at Riki's makolet. I glanced quickly around the room. *But, if it wasn't Riki's makolet, she'd be looking at Nini's ladder chart or Elisheva's sketch pad or Daphne's puppets.*

Poor Ronit. Everything seems to evolve around her—but she's not part of anything. It's all so out of control for her that the only thing she could ever do is look...and watch.

I've got to get Ronit to focus without any distractions on what she has and what she needs. Focus...focus...

"That's it!" I said aloud.

"What's it?" Mimi asked from her corner of the table.

"Oh, nothing. Sorry," I mumbled with a smile, "I'll tell you later."

She winked. "I can't wait."

I turned back to Ronit, my heart beginning to race. "We're going to make something very special, just for you, Ronit," I said excitedly as I took her hand and went to the closet where the crafts supplies were stored.

"A *makolet*?" she asked hopefully.

"No." I saw her disappointment but I kept my voice determinedly cheerful. "Something else. Something special for you."

I rummaged through the closet until I found what I was looking for and then, satisfied that I had what I needed, led the way back to our table.

It did not take long. I cut, stapled, cut some more, made a few colorful *vet* letters and we were ready to begin.

"Okay, Ronit, this is for you." I held my homemade movie camera in front of her.

She took it from my hand hesitatingly. "Me?"

Chapter 35

"Yes, your very own movie camera. Now, don't be afraid. Look inside. Go ahead...do you see the *vet*?"

She nodded.

"Good," I said enthusiastically.

I moved my "film strip" to the next slide. "Now what do you see, Ronit?"

"Another *vet*," she replied.

"Great, Ronit, you're doing great."

I proceeded to ask her what she saw next. She was so busy looking at her private "show," focusing completely on what she was seeing on her "screen," that she did not look at Riki even once.

I cut out another piece of colorful paper, and with a dark marker drew some balls and some *bet* letters and slipped the "film strip" into her "camera."

And that is how we went from *vet* to the little balls and finally to *bet*. She identified each *vet* and each little ball. Then I had her tell me which of the *vet* letters had the little balls and which ones did not. She got them all right.

And then, while she was still viewing her "film," I told her that I had a secret I wanted to tell her. She continued looking inside as I whispered in her ear that the *vet* with the little ball is called a *bet*. I then put in a new "film strip" that had a mixture of both the letters *bet* and *vet*. I held my breath as I asked her to identify each letter as I kept pulling the strip of paper downward.

She did not make one mistake.

I wanted to pick her up and swing her in the air. I felt like dancing with her merrily around the room. I was so happy. But then suddenly my heart sank. *What if she can't do it without her private "show"? What if she can't read the letters on a regular paper?*

Think, Sara, I told myself, *she needs to focus and she needs to feel some sense of control.*

"All right, Ronit," I said encouragingly, "you did a great job! Now, we're almost ready to perform your show for everyone else. But only when you tell me you're ready. First we've got to practice, though. So we're going to move it over to something bigger, so more people can see your show. Wait here, I'll be back in a minute."

I had noticed a flashlight hanging near the entrance to the room the first time we visited the resource room, and I had never given it a second thought. But now I was desperate for it! With a sigh of relief, I saw that it was still hanging there. I asked Geveret Spitz for permission to borrow it, and of course permission was granted immediately.

I then hurried over to the supply closet and found a larger box than the one I originally used. This time I made the inside of the box look like a stage and I hung the same "film strips" on its back wall.

Ronit looked at me skeptically, but—I realized with joy—she was looking at *me* not at Mimi and Riki.

"You see, Ronit," I said as I handed her a scissors and black paper. "This is *your* special stage, *your* theater. In fact, let's put a big sign on the top of it saying *Ronit's Play*. After all, *you're* the director."

"Me?"

"Yes, you, you're the one in charge. Now, Ronit, let's make the backs of all the people sitting in the audience. Here...like this."

We cut and pasted together. For a moment, I felt guilty spending all that time preparing for teaching without actually teaching, but then I remembered, *the bigger the investment, the greater the dividends.* We stuck shiny star stickers all around the sides and then we wrote Ronit's name with a glittery marker. Although, she could not yet read phonetically, she recognized her name and smiled broadly seeing it stand out in its sparkling glory.

There was a dazzling shine in her eyes that I had never seen before. I just hoped it would stay there, because the real test was about to begin.

"All right, Director Ronit," I took a deep breath, "I'm going to be the spotlight person. I'll shine the spotlight on each member of your cast and you can tell me what their names are."

She did not say anything, but I saw a proud smile tugging at the sides of her mouth.

I pointed the flashlight at the ball. "Who's that?"

"That's the *kadur*," she said importantly.

"Good. Now, who's that?"

"That's the *vet*."

"Very good. And...and who's that?"

"That's the *vet* with the *kadur* inside."

My heart quickened. "What's its name?"

Silence.

"Remember that secret I told you before? You know its name, Ronit. Tell me…please, tell me!" I urged.

A few seconds past. *Don't look away, Ronit,* I silently begged, *stay focused!*

Then, suddenly Ronit cleared her throat and in a confident, deep voice declared, "A *vet* with a *kadur*? That's a *bet*, of course. And now, if you don't mind," she reached for the flashlight I held in my hand as I sat there gaping open-mouthed while releasing my grip on it, "I'd like to have the flashlight to point with. After all, *I'm* the director."

36

"Isn't it just fantabulous?"

"It sure is, Sara," Mimi grinned while pointing to the *sefer* sitting opened on my desk. "Now can we continue studying, please?"

"But I just can't believe it, Mimi. All this time I could never get her to pay attention—"

"I know, because she was so busy looking at everyone else. But—"

"But then, when I gave her something to focus on, something that was—"

"Hers," Mimi continued, "she suddenly grasped what for weeks—"

"I was—"

"You were—"

"Trying to teach her," we said together, then burst out laughing.

"Sorry, Mimi." There were tears of joy pricking my eyelids. "I must be boring the daylights out of you. I just can't stop talking about it!"

"I know. Every free second, you've been bubbling over about Ronit," she winked good-naturedly. "But, that's all right, Sara, I'm really glad that you finally found the key."

"The key…you were right, Mimi," my voice suddenly grew serious. "I really needed to concentrate more on what Ronit's needs were, rather than thinking that I had to do something…something like what you were doing with Riki."

"Well, that's what Geveret Spitz has been telling us all along," Mimi said modestly. "It had nothing to do with me."

"Maybe, I just needed to hear it again. From…from a real friend

Chapter 36

like you." I added solemnly, "Thanks again, Mimi."

"You're welcome again, Sara." There was a mischievous gleam in her eye. "Now could we get back down to work?"

We continued working together on *parashah* for a short while without any interruptions. Then, after around five consecutive constructive minutes…

"Mimi?"

"Yes, Sara?"

"You were really right about not looking at anyone else and about focusing on Ronit."

"I know," she rolled her eyes. "I think you told me that already."

"Right. You know, it's like prescription eye glasses. One person's prescription isn't necessarily going to work for the next person."

"That's true."

"That's not my idea. Rabbanit Abrams told me it."

"She's a very smart person."

"So are you, Mimi."

"Right," there was a tinge of sarcasm in her voice despite the smile on her face, "a brilliant genius."

"I didn't call you a genius, Mimi. I just said you're very smart. And I wasn't joking around, either."

"Oh my, Sara, you really do look so serious. Come on, let's get back to work. After all, you're supposed to be the made-to-order student. Not me."

"Mimi, I was thinking. Just like there are different prescription eye glasses, and like Rabbanit Abrams said, Hashem puts people in different situations according to what each person's individual needs are, I think that there are all different kinds of smartness too, and Hashem chooses to give different people different kinds of smartness."

"Okay…so?"

"It's true I always did well in school and…and you might have this… problem with reading…but, look, when it came to figuring out how to work with our kids in the resource room, you found the key a lot faster than I did."

"So?"

"So, there are things that you, Mimi, seem to have sharper antennas for than the rest of us."

"That's a very sweet thing for you to say, Sara."

"I'm not trying to be sweet. I'm saying what I really think is the truth."

"That's nice, but—" Mimi stopped mid-sentence.

"But what?"

"I'm not interested in being the 'key finder' or the '*makolet* builder.' I just want...I just want to have a normal, yes *normal* brain!"

"Mimi, don't be upset—"

"You don't seem to understand, Sara, because with you everything is so normal. I'm—"

"Mimi, what's normal?"

"Normal? You know what's normal."

"Seriously, Mimi. I was just talking to Rabbanit Abrams about all this. No—not about you, just...just sort of in general about how when things are different for some people, we think of them as burdens. Remember we spoke that time about baggage and the muscles we build by carrying them around?"

"Of course."

"So, Mimi, I'm serious. You have a certain kind of smartness. Maybe it comes along with your problem, maybe it's something Hashem gave you as a compensation for your problem, or maybe *it* compensated for your problem."

"Sara, what in the world are you talking about?"

"You know, like a blind person has a stronger sense of hearing."

"So now I'm like a blind person?"

"I didn't say that. I'm just trying to say that we all have different positives and negatives about us. And if for some people there's a bigger negative in one thing, so to balance it out, they might have a bigger positive in another thing." I looked deeply into her eyes. "Do you get what I'm saying?"

"I'm trying to."

"Like with you, Mimi. You had a difficult time in school all these years, but you're able to approach different problems from an angle that let's say I could never think of."

"So are you telling me, Sara Hirsch, that if you had a choice, you'd trade in my shoes for yours?"

"Trade in…huh?"

"Yep, Sara, how about trading brains? I'd give you mine and take yours anytime."

"Mimi…I didn't mean…I'm sorry. I guess I'm saying this all wrong." I looked down at my nails and then back at Mimi. "Maybe you want to do well in school like I did all these years, but I really don't think you'd ever want to…to be me."

This time when Mimi suggested that we get back to work, I agreed to immediately. And this time there were no disruptions.

That is—from me and from Mimi.

Rivky and Chani came in to find out how much longer we would be studying. They were in the mood for a break and wanted to know if we wanted to go with them to Pinat HaGlidah. I told Mimi that if she wanted to go, it would be all right with me, but that I still had a lot of work I wanted to catch up on.

Mimi said she wanted to stay with me. "But don't forget to bring back three scoops of my favorite flavors," she told them as they made their way to the door. "And make sure they pour on a mixture of toppings too. Okay?"

"Sure, Mimi."

"And one vanilla scoop for Sara. Right, Sara?"

"Right, Mimi," I smiled.

"Oh my goodness," Rivky laughed. "We're also picking up ice cream orders for Malkie, Naomi, Ruti, and Devorah. All right, let me see if I can remember everything. Three scoops of Mimi's favorite flavors with a mixture of toppings, one scoop of plain vanilla for Sara, two scoops of butter pecan for Malkie, Naomi wants an ice cream sandwich… See you later," she said as she exited the room.

"I hope they get back soon. I'm absolutely starved," said Mimi.

"That's what happens when we don't have *fleishigs* for lunch. The *milchig* meals are much simpler."

"They served *milchigs* today? I skipped lunch," Mimi said.

"You did? Then you really must be starving. Why didn't you eat?"

"I—I was upstairs…in my room."

"Why?"

"I went to find Adina."

"She also missed lunch?"

Mimi nodded, "Uh huh."

I was not surprised that I had not noticed. My mind had been preoccupied with replays of the scene with Ronit from the day before. I had not been aware of their absence nor of much else going on around me since then. "What was wrong? Why didn't she want to eat?"

"I don't know. When I saw that she wasn't around, I went to the room to try and find her—and there she was."

"She wasn't feeling well?"

"She seemed upset. I asked her what was wrong and she didn't want to talk. I don't understand," Mimi suddenly looked worried. "Ever since that trip to Kiryat Yosef, we've become so unbelievably close. We've been able to open up to each other in a way that...well..."

I swallowed. "Neither of you ever...um...opened up before?"

"I guess...sort of. I mean, I've been really open with you, Sara, and like I told you, if I wouldn't have had that talk with you down in the storage room, I probably wouldn't have had the confidence to open up with Adina. But, you have to understand..."

I felt my heart sinking. "What?"

"Adina and I have both been through a lot. And even though our problems are very different—we sort of—complement each other. Know what I mean?"

I nodded slowly. "I think so."

"So now I don't understand what's bothering her and why she doesn't want to tell me." Mimi bit down on her lower lip pensively, without saying anything for a few seconds. "Do you think...do you think, Sara, that it has anything to do with Monday? Remember you told me something happened?"

"I didn't exactly tell you something happened."

"Okay, but something did. You admitted that you told her something."

"I—I did. But then I tried speaking to her again, and I think I said it the right way the second time around. But she was still—"

"Still what?"

"Still so...so..."

"So—what, Sara?" Mimi sounded impatient. "Will you say already?"

"Mimi," I took a deep breath, "do you believe in Hashem?"

"Of course, what kind of strange question is that?"

"Do you ever feel—I don't even know if it's the right thing to say—but do you ever feel angry at Him?"

"Angry—why should I feel angry?"

"Because…because of your problem."

"Angry?" she shook her head slowly. "No, not angry. Frustrated? Yes. Sad…yes…but not angry at Him *chas v'shalom*."

"So then, you don't look at yourself as damaged either. Right?"

"Damaged? What does damaged have to do with being angry?"

"Just answer me, Mimi. Do you view yourself as damaged?"

Mimi let out an uncomfortable laugh. "Why are you asking *me* these questions? We're discussing Adina and why *she* seems upset lately."

"Because, Mimi, Adina thinks of herself that way."

"So?"

"What do you mean *so*? There's no such thing as a person being damaged merchandise."

"That's easy for you to say, Sara."

"But, Mimi, Hashem doesn't make people damaged! No one's perfect, but that doesn't mean they're damaged!"

"Well, Sara, some people are a lot less perfect than others and that certainly feels damaging to them." She looked me directly in the eye and then quietly added, "I know that this is hard for you to understand."

I was taken aback. "You—you're starting to sound like Adina."

"Thanks," Mimi smirked. "If only I could look like her and take tests like her too."

"But…but you're not really like her," I went on. "She…she's so angry she can't see anything else except for her problem. It's like…it's like Adina is in this cage and the bars are the problems she went through. And because of what happened, she won't let anyone in or out."

"She lets me in."

"Then why isn't she telling you what's bothering her?"

Mimi shook her head pensively. "I don't know."

"Well, I think she's ashamed. Ashamed because she sees herself as damaged and inferior in some major way. And she assumes that if she's damaged, then that means Hashem didn't do a good job with her."

"But all that Hashem does is good."

"I tried to tell her that, Mimi. Then she got mad at me."

"Maybe she's really mad...at Hashem."

"That's what I thought at first, but I don't think so anymore," I shook my head. "I think that deep down Adina's really upset at herself—for thinking that way. And that's why she's slamming the door shut again."

"So then, I think, Sara," Mimi's said unwaveringly, "we've got to help her find the key to open up that door."

I nodded solemnly, but did not say anything. We could easily hear the background hum of dormitory life taking place outside our walls, but the only sound in my room was the sound of silence. A thick weightiness permeated the air, enveloping us in its grasp, engulfing us with a strong sense of purpose. *We have to help Adina! We must!* The steely determination I felt, was mirrored wordlessly on Mimi's face.

I am not sure how long we sat there staring at each other, gazing at our reflections in each other's eyes, but suddenly I noticed Mimi's mouth turning upward while I simultaneously felt the sides of mine involuntarily twitching. All at once, before either of us knew what was happening, the quiet in the room was shattered with our peals of unexpected laughter. Doubled over, we were giggling hysterically, tears streaming down our cheeks. And the harder we tried to stop, the worse it got.

"I think..." Mimi finally managed to say between giggles, "I think we're totally...totally out of...it."

"And...and I think," I squeaked back, "we desperately...need a break."

"And I think," Mimi continued, "that I agree."

I volunteered to go down to the kitchen and bring up a pitcher of juice to help stop our hiccups. Mimi said she would go to her room and search for some caramels and potato chips to accompany our drinks. And we both decided that as soon as we could, we would get back to our studying. We had a lot of schoolwork to finish and wanted to be free after supper to talk with Adina.

Chapter 36

Fifteen minutes later I was hurrying to the third floor with the pitcher of juice. I had also piled some biscuitim onto a plate and, except for a few that were snatched by some of my hungry dorm-mates on the way up, I managed to get upstairs, food and drink intact.

But when I kicked open the door to my room, I nearly dropped the tray I was carrying.

"What in the world—"

"Oh, hi, Sara, back already?"

My mouth dropped open. "What do you think you're doing, Mimi Rosenberg?"

"Doing? I came back in here around five minutes ago and sat down on your bed to wait for you. Want a caramel? How about some olives? Did you know I had an unopened jar of olives sitting on my shelf and I totally forgot about it?"

"Mimi," I said through clenched teeth, "what's that you're reading?"

"Your notebook, of course. Don't you recognize it? It was lying on the bed. So I decided it's as good a time as ever to practice my reading—you know it doesn't come so fluently to me. Here, have an olive, they're delicious!"

"Mimi, that's *my* notebook. You had no right—"

"Okay, okay, I'm sorry. I didn't realize that you'd get so upset. It's just a notebook, not a diary. It's not like I'm planning on taking any of your ideas for my *Proyect*."

"That's not the point."

"Come on, Sara, take it easy. I already said that I'm sorry. It's too late now—I won't do it again, all right?"

"All right. But really, Mimi, remember that time with Adina? I thought we learned our lesson then."

"That wasn't the same thing. I was sitting here waiting for you on your bed. It was just your notebook."

"Don't you understand? What if I would've written something private in there? Then what?"

"I guess...then I wouldn't have read it."

"And how would you even know that it was private—if you didn't read it?" I mumbled. "Oh, forget it." I poured a cup of juice and handed it to her. "Here, have some."

"Thanks...have a caramel."

"Thanks." I poured some juice into my cup, made a *berachah*, and then sat down next to her.

We drank and munched for a few minutes, not saying much. We each seemed preoccupied with our own thoughts, but nevertheless, sat side by side companionably while refueling our bodies and resting our minds before resuming our study session.

Suddenly, Mimi broke the silence. "Sara?"

"Yes, Mimi?"

"Like you said before...how would I know it's private if I didn't read it first?"

"I told you it's okay. I forgive you. I know that you didn't realize...and anyway, there's nothing private in there."

"Good. So you don't mind—"

"I told you already."

"That when I was turning the pages, I guess...I sort of..."

I swallowed hard. "You guess, you sort of—what?"

"I guess, I sort of came across your poem."

"Poem?"

"Yeah. On page thirty-four of notebook number one."

"What in the world are you talking about, Mimi? I didn't write any poem..." my voice suddenly drifted off as my thoughts focused and my cheeks began to burn. "Oh no! You read that poem?"

"Yes, and it was good, really good. But, Sara, how could you accuse Adina of thinking of herself as damaged, when it's so obvious that's how you think of yourself."

"Me?" My cheeks were burning even hotter. "What are you talking about?"

"Look," she waved the notebook at me and pointed. "You think of yourself as plain and ordinary—just a prop. Like you're stuck in a prison. That's what you wrote. Set me free from my prison—"

"Stop!" I jumped up. My hands were covering my ears. I was shaking.

"But why, Sara, I'm just trying to help—"

"Get out of here," I yelled, trying to hold onto my pride and keep in my tears. "Leave me alone!"

"Sara—"

I turned away, not wanting her to see my face. "I said I want to be alone."

"No, Sara, I'm not leaving," she slid in front of me. "You're the one who's always trying to help everyone else. And right now you could use a little advice."

"Please leave," I begged her while pointing my finger at the door. She saw the tears rolling down my cheeks, but I could do nothing to stop them, "I'm so embarrassed."

"Why?"

"That was so private. I didn't even remember that I wrote it. I thought I threw it away..."

"But you meant what you wrote, Sara," Mimi gazed into my eyes. "Right?"

"Please, Mimi."

"Sara, don't you realize that you're doing the exact same thing as Adina? 'Stuck in her world' you write, isn't that what you're accusing Adina of? You feel stuck, Sara? Is that the way to look at the life Hashem has given you?"

"Who are you to talk, Mimi? You have no idea what it's like to be me. You never experienced shyness, sat there tongue-tied, feeling like an utter fool the way I have."

"But, Sara—"

"You weren't sandwiched between a sister who succeeds in everything and a sister who's the most adorable girl around. You don't have to depend on everyone else to get anywhere—to be noticed. No one ignores you, pretending you don't exist when you're sitting right in front of them. You're always the center of everything, not this plain, ordinary prop like me."

"And you think that Hashem would make someone a plain, ordinary prop?"

"He made me."

"Yes, Sara, He made you—a girl with extraordinary depth and sensitivity, who cares, truly cares about others and is ready to give of herself and do anything to help. So what if she's a little shy and not the center of attention. She doesn't *need* to be in the spotlight."

"And you, Mimi...you need—"

"I don't know. But remember what you just said to me, Sara? That sometimes, if we have a bigger negative in one thing, we might have a bigger positive in another to balance it out?"

I nodded.

"So that's like on a stage, where there are people with main parts, minor parts, *and* there's the props."

"Props?"

"Yes, props. The play couldn't be a play without the props. They're also important." She paused, "Sara, don't you realize that by comparing yourself to others, you're viewing Hashem's handiwork as damaged?"

"I...I guess I never thought of it like that."

"And don't you see, on Hashem's stage, each and every actor, each scene, each prop, each act—is special and unique. It's just not possible for everyone to have the same exact part."

I looked down at my nails, studying them pensively and thinking about what she said. *She's right, you know, she's really right. Just like with the prescription eye glasses.* I looked up. I knew my eyes were red and teary and my face blotchy, but suddenly I did not care. Mimi was not looking at me strangely, she was not looking down on me. An involuntary smile tugged at the corners of my mouth. "How do you know all this, Mimi Rosenberg, how come you're so smart?"

"Smart? Me smart?" she laughed. "I guess there are different kinds of smartness out there. At least that's what one of my closest friends told me. Know what I mean, Sara Hirsch?"

"I guess so."

"Besides, as you know, I've been directing plays for a very long time. And not everyone is always satisfied with their assigned parts. So I guess..."

"You sort of figured it out...right?"

"Right," she grinned back. "Sort of."

Part Four

37

Bs"d
28 Shevat

Dear Chavie, *a"mush*

Mazal tov! Mazal tov! Mazal tov!
I just hung up the phone from you (around two hours ago) and I'm still in a state of shock! I was literally crying from happiness! Wow! Wow! And triple wow!!!

You were speaking so quickly and I was so absolutely completely overwhelmed with the news that I'm still not sure what you said. I think you said that your *chasan* (did I just write that?) is Mindy's *chasan's chavrusa* and good friend from way back. Is that true? You must be thrilled! And now you'll probably be moving to Lakewood and living near Mindy. Wow, again! I still just can't believe it!

No wonder you didn't get a chance to answer my last two letters to you. I couldn't understand what was going on. When my roommate Mazal came in the day of Adina's and my double birthday party and broke the news that she was packing up and leaving permanently, I immediately wrote to you to let you know that there was a vacancy and I was hoping you'd be the one to fill it. I was very sad about Mazal leaving, but I was hopeful that you would take her place. Well, *baruch Hashem*, you're already occupied with bigger and better things (and no, I don't have another roommate yet and don't think I will. Since she left more than a month ago, nothing has happened, and now that we're nearing the end of February, it doesn't look like Rabbi Grossman is going to take anyone new in.)

Do you have any idea when the wedding will be? I'm sure glad that you said that you're definitely waiting for me till I get back, because otherwise I don't know what I would do. Chavie, you're the first one from our class to get engaged. Does it feel real or do you still think you're dreaming? I think I'm dreaming! I feel bad about missing your *vort*. (I can't believe I just wrote that—your *vort*. Wow!) Chavie, it just hit me—it's a good thing you didn't come to M.B.L.L. after all. See, while the two of us were upset about the way things were turning out, Hashem was working it all out for the best.

Anyway, I must admit—it was probably for the best that I ended up coming here on my own too. (Not that I wouldn't have been thrilled to have you with me and, at times, I felt really desperate for you!) I think, though, that because you weren't here with me, the situations I found myself in ended up bringing out certain things in me that I didn't know I had. Being on my own brought me out of my shyness to a certain extent and then I wasn't so afraid to open up to others. And by opening up, I am really learning so much more about others and growing myself too. (At least I hope so!)

You know, there are some really special people here, with everyone having so much to offer. Also, living in a dorm has taught me that a lot of the time people are not necessarily the way they appear, but there is so much more below the surface, and so much more to learn from them.

I'm also realizing that I have a lot to be grateful for. There were things that I'm sure I took for granted about my family and even about myself. I feel like this is really turning into a great experience for me. It could be, Chavie that you didn't need this and that's why it didn't work out for you—and look—you've been gaining so much in a different way.

When you get a chance, write to me and fill me in on all the details of everything that's going on (even though I'm sure you're busy with tons of things to do).

Mazal tov again and I sure hope your *chasan* knows what a lucky guy he is!

Love,
Sara

Chapter 37

Bs"d
28 Shevat

Dear Home,

Please, please forgive me for not writing in a while, but we've been so unbelievably busy lately. Thankfully we were just granted a surprise free period and I figured that since I'm planning on dropping by the post office after we go to the resource room (which is next on today's agenda), I'll take this opportunity to write to you (instead of studying).

By now you must have heard the news. Can you believe it, my best friend a kallah? I'm still in a daze about the whole thing. I keep picturing all those times Chavie and I slept over at each other's houses, Chavie heading the dance group, Chavie and I at the mall shopping together—it's so strange and exciting at the same time!

Anyway, when I say things have been extremely hectic lately, it's probably an understatement! We have tons and tons of work to do, reports, homework, tests etc. etc. etc. Besides that, we're all busy with the *Proyect*. And on top of that, there's Mimi's new production (I'll tell you about that later). Also, we've been going back and forth to Be'er Sheva a few times these past two weeks to help out Gila (the lady from the airplane).

It's a long story how that evolved and, hopefully, I'll have the chance now to write to you all about it before we have to leave. Remember that terrible tragedy I wrote to you about Mazal's grandmother and what the family went through when they first came on Aliyah? So we decided to try to find out what really happened to her daughter in that hospital, but unfortunately the hospital doesn't exist anymore. We weren't sure what our next step should be (the hospital is now some sort of research institution located up North). The only way to communicate with them and access the old hospital records was through the mail, and things just weren't moving along.

I was really starting to feel down about it, when one of the most amazing things happened. Mimi, Adina, and I were in Be'er Sheva picking up a few costumes for the new production from someone who knows someone who knows Geveret Spitz, when we ran into Gila. We were walking toward the bus, talking so excitedly about the stunning butterfly costume we borrowed, that I almost didn't even see her and nearly passed her by.

All of a sudden I heard someone call my name. I looked behind me and saw a familiar-looking petite lady in a nurse's uniform. And then it hit me! It's Gila from the plane! My mind started racing and I suddenly remembered. Gila's husband is a research scientist who works in—you guessed it—The Tzihov Institute. For the past few weeks, we had been referring to the place as The Be'er Institute for Applied Research and so I totally forgot that it's referred to unofficially as The Tzihov Institute.

I got so excited I was hardly able to talk. Mimi and Adina couldn't figure out what had gotten into me and Gila was also looking at me kind of strangely. When I finally told them what was making me so excited, Mimi and Adina were also thrilled. Gila, though, was very hesitant about agreeing to help us. She said that her husband was just a struggling research scientist, not in a managerial position, and that gaining access to old records being stored in the Institute's basement was probably impossible. Well, she said "probably"—she didn't say "for sure."

So I begged her to try and help us. I took her telephone number with me and gave her our dorm number. For two days, I waited impatiently for her to call. Finally on the third day, I called her. She apologized for not calling me—her children weren't well and things were kind of chaotic by her, and she hadn't had a chance to discuss it with her husband.

Anyway, to make a long story short, I got permission for Mimi, Adina, and I to go to Gila's house to help her with her kids and she was extremely grateful. We've been going there three times a week for the last two weeks. (They have a bad case of chicken pox, and since all of us already had it, we didn't need to worry.) Her husband, who stays overnight once a week at the Institute, is doing what he can to get permission to go downstairs to the records' room. So we're waiting anxiously and hopefully, and, in the meantime, being kept very busy.

The production is scheduled for the Sunday before Purim, so we have only a week and a half to go! I still can't believe how quickly the whole thing unfolded. It was Mimi's brilliant idea, and after speaking to Geveret Spitz (the resource room kids are part of the production) and getting permission from the *Hanhalah*, she managed to get us all into action. Believe it or not—I helped Mimi write the script. The name of the production is *Metamorphosis*. Uh oh—the free period is ending now and I've got to run, so there's no time for me to give you the details right now.

I'll probably be speaking to you in two days on *Rosh Chodesh* Adar, before you even get this letter. But whenever I speak to you, I forget all the things I wanted to say, so it's a good thing I wrote all this down.

I love you all and miss you!!!

Love always,
Sara

P.S. I just thought of a great idea—I have an extra copy of the script. I'm going to enclose it in the envelope so you can all read it. (Just remember, it's not really a play, but a song-dance production with only two speaking parts. Obviously, the script doesn't include the songs or the choreography.) And by the way, Mimi convinced me to write the theme song. She thinks I'm good at poems. It's at the end of the script. Mimi is fitting the words to a beautiful tune. Enjoy!!!

Metamorphosis
An Original Dramatic Dance & Choir Production by the Students of Machon Beit Leah LeMorot

Act I/Scene 1
(kitchen scenery)

Background sounds: birds chirping

Mother: *(Hums same tune as theme song while stirring pot on stove with long wooden spoon, then glances slightly worriedly at clock hanging on wall)* Riki has been playing outside an awfully long time. I should call her in now for dinner. *(Walks to left side of stage and calls out)* Riki!

Riki: *(from off stage)* Yes, Ima?

Mother: It's almost time for dinner. Come in and wash up.

Riki: *(enters from left side)* But, Ima, look what I found!

Mother: *(glances at Riki's opened palm, makes obvious grimace to audience, then forces a smile at Riki)* How lovely, a caterpillar.

Riki: Yes, Ima, it is lovely! Can I keep it?

Mother: Riki—

Riki: Please, Ima, I'll take such good care of it.

Mother: Well, *(smiles)* I guess it could turn out to be a very good learning experience for you.

Riki: So then I can keep it?

Mother: Yes, Riki, I guess so. *(She lovingly puts her arm around Riki's shoulder.)* You can keep it—up until the time it turns into a butterfly. Then, you've got to set it free.

Riki: The caterpillar is going to turn into a butterfly? How can that be? Butterflies fly and this *(looks at palm)* is just a crawly worm without any wings.

Mother: You'll see, Riki. There's a special cycle that Hashem has created for the caterpillar to go through before it turns into a butterfly. It's known as its metamorphosis. Let's find a jar to put it into *(she bends down and reaches into cabinet and removes large jar)* and then we can watch as it transforms into a graceful and beautiful butterfly.

(Curtains close on kitchen scene as dancers from Caterpillar Dance enter in front of curtains from right side of stage.)

Scene 2
(garden scenery)

(Dance troupe performs Caterpillar Dance.)

Scene 3
(garden scenery)

(Choir sings "Life's Cycles," with slide production in background.)

Scene 4
(garden scenery)

(Mother and daughter sit on garden swing with Riki holding caterpillar jar in her lap.)

Riki: Ima, now that you explained to me all about the four stages the caterpillar must go though until it turns into a butterfly, I'm so excited. I can't wait until it flies with the wind.

Mother: I understand, Riki dear, and I'm sure you can't wait to run along with it in the wind as well, but we must be patient and give it a chance to develop as Hashem intended.

Riki: I'm so glad I gave it all those plants to eat. See how my caterpillar is growing, Ima? It's getting bigger and bigger! And see how it likes climbing on the stick I put inside?

Mother: Yes, Riki dear, you have an active little caterpillar. I'm sure it'll turn into a nice, strong butterfly.

Scene 5
(kitchen scenery)

(Mother putters around the kitchen. Sounds of birds chirping in background.)

Riki: *(runs in breathlessly from left side of stage)* Ima, Ima, something's wrong!

Mother: What happened, Riki?

Riki: My caterpillar is acting very strange, Ima. I'm worried.

Mother: Oh…you had *me (emphasize)* worried there for a moment. *(sighs deeply)* What's strange about your caterpillar, darling?

Riki: *(lifts jar in front of mother)* Look, Ima.

Mother: *(retreats slightly, then sees Riki's sad face)* Um, let me see *(examines jar)*. Oh…Riki, your caterpillar isn't acting strangely…no, it's not acting strangely at all. It's entering its next stage. Its skin is splitting to reveal the pupa or chrysalis. *(her voice lifts excitedly)* Its caterpillar tissues are becoming fluid and it's getting ready to become an adult butterfly.

Riki: *(enthusiastically)* Really, Ima?

Mother: *(nods)* See? That's its cocoon. What you are witnessing, my dear Riki, is the caterpillar's metamorphosis into a butterfly.

(Curtains close.)

Scene 6
(cocoon scenery)

(Dance troupe performs Metamorphosis Dance.)

(Choir sings "My Transformation.")

(Dance troupe and choir perform together Metamorphosis Dance and "My Transformation" song.)

Act II / Scene 1
("In the Jar" scenery)

(Curtains open. Stage is completely dark at first. Then small spotlight

focuses on center of stage, where caterpillar with wings is struggling in its cocoon, which is in "giant jar" prop.)

Music: Theme song (no words)

Riki: *(voice off stage)* Oh, wow! A hole! My caterpillar butterfly just made a hole in the cocoon. It's almost ready to become a real butterfly. But, wait! How sad! My caterpillar butterfly is struggling so hard to come out of its cocoon. It's beating its wings so hard—but the hole is not getting any bigger.

(Choir sings *"Give It a Chance to Build Its Strength."*)

(Dance troupe performs *Wing Dance* around the jar.)

(While dance takes place, caterpillar switches place with butterfly, and when dance is finished, butterfly is in partially opened cocoon inside jar.)

Scene 2
("In the Jar" scenery)

(Stage is dark. Spotlight on Riki.)

Riki: *(standing off to the right side of stage holding jar)* Oh my, you poor, poor butterfly. You are no longer a caterpillar, but there you are, still imprisoned in your cocoon, still struggling to break free.

(Spotlight on "giant jar" in center. Butterfly does solo dance while Choir heads sing "Set Me Free.")

(Curtains close.)

Scene 3

Riki: *(voice off-stage)* I know what you want, my darling little butterfly. You yearn to be free. I will help you! I will get a pair of scissors and cut your cocoon open. You will no longer need to struggle...you will have your dream come true. You will be free!

(Dance troupe does Scissors Dance.)

(Curtains close.)

Act III / Scene 1

(kitchen scenery—appearing exactly as in Act 1 Scene 1)

Background sounds: birds chirping

Mother: *(humming same tune as theme song while stirring pot on stove with long wooden spoon, then glances slightly worriedly at clock hanging on wall)* Riki has been playing outside an awfully long time. I should call her in now for dinner. *(walks to left side of stage and calls)* Riki!

Mother: *(worried tone of voice)* Riki!

(Complete silence.)

Mother: *(hurries off left stage and audience hears her voice cry out)* Oh no, Riki, what happened?

(Curtains close.)

Scene 2

(garden scenery)

(Mother and daughter sit on garden swing with Riki holding butterfly on the palm of her hand. Jar is lying open on the ground. Riki cries and her mother has arm around her shoulder.)

Mother: Riki dear, please don't cry.

Riki: I can't help it, Ima. My butterfly won't fly. It is so small and its wings are shriveled.

Mother: That's because you helped it come out of its cocoon too early, my dear.

Riki: But, I was just trying to help it along. I thought that by cutting a hole in the cocoon, I could help it be free.

Mother: Free? Free for what?

Riki: Free to fly.

Mother: But it needed that extra time in the cocoon to strengthen itself. By moving its wings against the walls of the cocoon, it would get the necessary exercise to make its wings strong.

Riki: And I took away that wall…thinking that I was helping, when really it needed to struggle in order to build its muscles. Oh,

Ima, *(bursts into loud sobs)* now the butterfly will never fly in the wind!

(Curtains close.)

Scene 3
(grand finale)

(First: Mother and Riki in front of curtain.)
(Then: Chorus and choir join.)
(Then: Dance troupe.)

Theme Song

Mother:

> It is true this butterfly will never fly,
> It will never have a chance to ascend up high;
> Never soar among the colorful, vibrant flowers,
> Never achieve its potential and prove its true powers;
> Its struggle was cut short way too soon,
> When it was freed early from its cocoon…

Chorus:

> Yes, its struggle was cut short way too soon,
> When it was freed too early from its cocoon…

Mother:

> Sometimes when it seems life is a long, struggling night,
> When problems are overwhelming, when things don't feel right;
> When we feel trapped and imprisoned—surrounded by an impenetrable wall,
> When we yearn to break free and our weeping becomes a call;
> Crying out "set me free" and "open the doors of this prison!"
> I must remember I was put down here to fulfill a certain mission…

Chorus:
> Oh yes, when I cry out "set me free" from my prison,
> I mustn't forget I'm here to accomplish my mission...

Mother:
> And I could only do that from the perimeters of my unique situation,
> Within the walls of my own cocoon where my wings beat in desperation;
> Where I whine and I cry, where I plead and I strive,
> Where I wish I did not have to try so hard to survive;
> But, alas, if only I would have realized the truth all along,
> Instead of a painful test, it could have been my song...

Chorus:
> Yes, if only I would have known the truth all along,
> My life could have been a long, beautiful song...

Mother with Choir soloists:
> Of strength, of growth, of redemption and of hope,
> Of muscles reinforced like tight knots on a rope;
> Of obstacles on the path collected and assembled together,
> To form stepping stones, used to climb further and better;
> Of a caterpillar turned butterfly and of birds in flight,
> Of their struggles and growth because of their plight;
> They've grown powerful wings, enabling them to fly high,
> With its metamorphosis complete, it'll soar up toward the sky...

Everyone:
> Yes, they've got powerful wings enabling them to fly high,
> And with its metamorphosis complete, it'll surely soar and soar and soar...
> Upward toward the sky!

The End

Chapter 37

"Boy, Sara," Mimi grinned while we waited for the clerk at the post office to weigh my letters, "you sure write long letters."

"I didn't really write so much, Mimi." I eyed the scale while nervously wondering how much it would cost me to mail an overstuffed envelope to the United States. "I sent along an extra copy of the script for my family to read."

"And they like reading your scripts?"

"I...Mimi, it's the first time I was ever involved in writing a script," I felt myself blushing. "To you it might seem silly, but—"

"Sara, you don't have to excuse yourself—"

"But, you sound so...so—"

"So...what?"

"*Geveret*," the post office clerk interrupted, "*I'ma at michakah?*"

After informing me what the postage would cost, I opened my wallet, counted out the exact change, and handed it to him while saying *todah*. We then made our way toward the exit.

"You were saying, Sara," Mimi swung her book bag over her shoulder when we reached the door, "that I sound so—what?"

We stopped for a moment to hold the door open for a woman with a baby carriage, who was trying to maneuver her way inside, and then we continued outside.

"I don't know." I shrugged, while zipping up my hooded sweatshirt. "You sound almost like you think it's strange of me to be sharing this with them. You do these things all the time, but—"

"Strange of you, Sara? No way! I thought you were going to say that I shouldn't sound so jealous."

"Jealous?" I stopped walking.

"Yes...jealous, Sara," Mimi looked me steadily in the eyes. "Jealous that your family is always so interested in everything you're involved in."

"And your family *isn't*?"

"Of course they show an interest." We continued walking. "And I told you already, Sara, they're happy with my performances and stuff. But, I know the truth. They'd be a lot happier and a lot more interested if I could show them success with the school stuff. That's why..." her words trailed off as she stared dreamily ahead.

I was gripped by a sudden sense of foreboding, "That's why...what?"

"That's why," a look of steely determination swept over her face, "I've got to do what you've convinced me to do, Sara. That's why I want to be, no, that's why I *must* be the winner of the Goldstone Award."

38

"Why does this have to happen now of all times? What am I going to do?"

"Are you sure, Mimi? Are you sure she's not going to do it?"

"It's not that she doesn't want to, Sara. She *wants* to," Mimi's shoulders drooped helplessly, "but she can't!"

"It's so upsetting."

"Upsetting? It's *more* than upsetting, and things were going so well."

"What exactly did the doctor say?"

"I told you already. He said that Rochel Leah must, *must* stay in bed."

"And she can't come out just for the performance?"

"Especially not for the performance. She's contagious and Geveret Katz and Doctor Epstein are not interested in having a *tzahevet* epidemic spreading through the Beit Yaakov HaNegbah campus."

"So what are we going to do?"

"That's what *I* want to know. I was counting on this…I really was hoping…" her words drifted off.

Warning bells started ringing in my ears. "Hoping for what, Mimi?"

"Hoping?" She grew silent for a moment, that same dreamy look filling her eyes. "Hoping for the play to come out perfect, of course."

"Oh," I mumbled to Mimi, *but*, I wondered to myself, *does she really mean that she's hoping the production's success will help her to win the Goldstone Award?*

She suddenly jumped up. "I've got it, I've got it, I've got it!"

"Got what, Mimi?"

"I've got the way to convince Adina to do it."

"Forget it, Mimi. She's not going to do it. When you first thought of the idea of turning the story into a production and suggested that Adina play the mother, she said no way. What makes you so sure you'll be able to convince her now?"

"That was different, Sara. It wasn't planned," she sat back down on my bed next to me. "The story with the butterfly just came to me while the three of us were sitting and talking together that night." She pushed some loose strands of hair away from her face. "I suddenly remembered it from way back when I was a little kid."

"But when you told us the story and said that people have problems and struggles in order to strengthen them, Adina got upset with both of us." I let out a heavy sigh. "It's better to leave it alone, Mimi."

"I can't." Her eyes flashed determinedly. "Adina and I were so close for a while…so in tune to what the other was feeling. And now…ever since she had that talk with you—"

"Sorry, Mimi, for ruining things—"

"I'm not blaming you, Sara."

"Right…you're just telling me how wonderful everything was between the two of you, and then because of me she slammed the door on you too."

"No, that conversation you had with her would've eventually come out with me." She shook her head. "No way am I blaming you, Sara. It's just that…I think…to be true friends with Adina we've got to help her."

"Well, I don't think it's going to happen by making her the mother in "Metamorphosis," Mimi. True, she has a stunning voice and is extremely talented, true she'll capture the audience, but—"

"And true, I've got to convince her. She's got to do it for me. Now that Rochel Leah can't do it and we've got less than a week to go, there's absolutely no choice. If this play is going to be the success I'm dreaming of making it, she's going to have to do it!"

"And how, Mimi, do you think you're going to get her to agree?

Chapter 38

Granted, you could convince Geveret Spitz to include the resource room kids and you could convince me to write the theme song, and you could get almost everybody to do anything. But," I crossed my arms in front of my chest, "how in the world are you going to convince Adina Stern to take that part when she'll be forced to say things she absolutely doesn't want to say?"

"Wait and see, Sara Hirsch, wait and see," she rolled her eyes mysteriously.

There was a knock at the door.

"Come in," I called.

The door to my room swung open and Zehava walked in. "Hi, Sara, hi, Mimi," she held out a yellow paper toward me. "Someone called you this afternoon, Sara. Geveret Katz told me to give you this message."

"Someone called *me*?" I glanced down at the note she handed me. "Oh wow, Mimi," I exclaimed. "Gila called! I'm running downstairs right now to call her back."

"But, Sara, what am I going to do about the production?"

I already had one foot out the door. "We'll talk about it later, Mimi." I turned quickly to Zehava, "Thanks a million for the message."

I dashed down the steps, taking two at a time, my heart beating wildly. *Gila's husband got permission to go through the files and now she finally has an answer for me! Is Geveret Katz the missing Hodaya or not? And what if I'm wrong, what if I'm making a mistake? No, I can't be!*

"Whoa, Sara, where're you off to?"

"Oh, sorry, Malkie," Without stopping I breathlessly apologized for having just managed to avoid bumping into her. "I just got a message that someone called, and I'm in a rush to call her back!"

"Another friend from the States became a *kallah*?"

"No," I laughed, calling over my shoulder, "not this time!"

Although Geveret Katz was preoccupied at her desk on the other side of the room, with the receiver of one telephone up to one ear and the receiver of a second one up to the other—and I knew she was way too busy to pay any attention to my telephone conversation—it was still strange making the phone call with her in the same room. *What will I do if Gila tells me her husband found out that the missing Hodaya Yitzchaki is really the present day Geveret Katz? And then I thought with* greater trepidation, *what'll I do if she doesn't?*

"If only Yitzchaki wasn't such a common Yemenite name," I complained morosely to Mimi around ten minutes later, while we sat opposite each other on my bed.

"If only I could have convinced Adina to take that part," the sulkiness in Mimi's voice mirrored mine. "Then this production would top any production I ever did before. But she wouldn't even hear of it, she was so negative!"

"Gila wasn't very optimistic either," I let out a deep sigh. "She said that there were so many Yitzchaki families listed, that her husband's time in the archive room ran out before he could go through the whole list and the guard in charge made him leave."

"I went into my room to try to talk Adina into doing it, but she absolutely refused to even discuss it. When I tried explaining to her how desperate I am, she stood up and left the room."

"*I'm* feeling so desperate, Mimi. I was sure we had the answer. Now, we'll have to wait—who knows how long—until Gila's husband gets permission again to go into the archive room."

"*I'm* the one feeling desperate, Sara. I was sure Adina would agree to do it. Now, I don't know what I'm going to do and the production is in less than a week—"

"I don't know how *I'm* going to wait until then—"

"What do you mean, Sara? Without a mother, there's no production!"

"No production?"

"Yes, no production. How can we have it if—"

"Mimi, you haven't heard a word I said. I was telling you about Gila and her—"

"And I was telling you about the fact that Adina is still refusing to take the part and all you can talk about is the Yitzchaki family!"

"Well, this is real—not some production, Mimi. Don't you care about finding Mazal's missing aunt or is the production the only thing you care about?"

"For your information, Sara, to me the production *is* very real and now I'm afraid it's going to all be for nothing." She glared at me. "I don't know why you're not helping me think of some solution, instead of running after something impossible that took place so many years ago."

"It's not impossible," I insisted, "and, in case you forgot, there's a dying woman who's waiting to see the child who was taken from her. And that child might be right under the same roof as us right now. That's a lot more important than some made-up production."

"It's not some made-up production. It's an extremely important theme that a lot of people can gain a lot from, Adina included. Especially if she takes that part!"

"You don't really care if Adina does it or not—for Adina's sake. You want her to do it because you're stuck and Adina has a fabulous voice and knows how to act, and for some reason the production's success is the only thing on your mind!"

"And how about you, Sara? Why are you so obsessed with finding the missing child? Is it because you *really* feel for Mazal's grandmother or because you're trying to be some kind of heroine?"

"Excuse me," I sprung off my bed, seething, "but I don't have to take this from you."

"And excuse *me*, Sara Hirsch," Mimi stood up angrily opposite me and with arms on hips sputtered, "but I don't have to take this from you either. Accusing me of not caring about Adina. I'm leaving. Some friend you are!"

I hurried after her into the wash-up closet. "I never said you don't care about Adina. Mimi, don't leave…please."

She must have heard the desperation in my voice. Slowly, she turned around. Though the wash-up closet's light had not been switched on, the hurt look in her eyes was clearly visible, and suddenly it was no longer fear I was feeling…but pain. Pain for having hurt Mimi and pain for the hurt she had caused me.

"Even though I'm desperate for the production to be successful, what you said about me is not true," Mimi said quietly. "From the beginning, from when I first started telling Adina the story of the caterpillar, I felt it would be good for her to be a part of the story."

"But she was so upset."

"She was upset because she doesn't want to hear about obstacles causing growth. She doesn't want to sing songs about it and she doesn't want to have anything to do with it. But if Adina would at least act the part, say the words—it could help her and maybe give her the strength she needs to—"

"You're right, Mimi. I…I'm sorry," I swallowed hard trying to keep my tears from rising to the surface. "It was totally wrong of me."

"And then when Adina refused to take the part, I figured we were lucky that Rochel Leah is such a great actress and has such a phenomenal voice."

"I know. Everything was turning out so beautifully."

"It was more than beautiful. The kids from the resource room were all so excited to be a part of this. Rivky and Leilei did a spectacular job with the choreography, the choir was stunning, and you wrote a terrific theme song."

"And the production had so much appeal for both—the kids and us."

"And then Rochel Leah got sick—"

"And all I can talk about are the Yitzchakis," my eyes filled.

"I'm also sorry. I know how important they are to you."

"But right now we really have to find someone who can take Rochel Leah's place."

For a few moments neither of us said anything. My heartbeat gradually returned to normal, with the tension in the air slowly leaving us.

"You know, Sara," Mimi broke the silence, "I'm glad we made up before this turned into some kind of fight between us. I was afraid there for a minute—"

"*You* were afraid?" I suddenly felt the sides of my mouth turn upward. "I was petrified! I really should have been more attuned to what you were going through. You put so much into the production."

"Well, I can't deny that. But, I guess I should've realized that you had just spoken to Gila—"

"But I kept going on and on and you were trying to tell me about what happened with Adina and—"

"I kept going on and on too." Mimi grinned. "So, Sara, it sounds like we both started out saying the right thing—"

"But in the wrong way," I laughed. "Okay, Mimi…I hereby declare that I'm really, really totally sorry."

"And I hereby declare that you're really, really totally forgiven. And I know you forgive me too. Right?"

"Right," I replied, "totally. And now we've got to think of a solution. Someone to take Rochel Leah's place."

"Thanks, Sara," Mimi let out a deep breath. "I feel so much better now that I know I have you around to help me. But could we possibly continue this conversation in your room and get out of this tiny closet that barely has room for a sink—let alone the two of us?"

Laughingly, we returned to my room.

Unfortunately, though, there did not seem to be a solution to our problem. Who could take over for Rochel Leah? Undoubtedly, Adina would have been the best choice, even if we had a large pool of actresses with great voices to choose from. *A large pool?* Our M.B.L.L. group consisted of numerous dancers and many girls who were happy to participate in the choir, but there were very few girls who could act and none who could also sing.

"That's it!" I stood up determinedly. "We've got to get Adina to do it."

"But I've tried," Mimi said.

"Mimi, you know I can be stubborn and I'm not about to give up now."

"But, Sara, we've only got a few days."

"It'll take Adina no more than a half-hour to memorize her part and maybe an hour or two of practicing with Riki. If she comes to two rehearsals, it'll be fine," I said reassuringly.

"You've just got to get her to say yes."

"Ri-ight..." And as the clock continued ticking, I wondered, *how in the world am I going to do that?*

"Did you speak to her yet?" Mimi kept asking me almost every hour.

"No, Mimi, I need to catch her at the right time."

And I really did try to, but it never seemed like the "right time."

"Sara, it's Wednesday already." Mimi finally cornered me two days later. "How much longer do you plan on waiting until you speak with Adina? The advertisements are already hanging all over the place, people bought tickets, mothers reserved babysitters, the resource room kids can't talk about anything else…Sara, we don't have a mother for the play!"

"I know…I know. I'm going to speak to Adina. Like I said, I'm just trying to find the right time."

"Sara, we're desperate!"

"I know—"

"If Adina doesn't do it, I don't know what I'm going to do." Suddenly her eyes flashed mischievously, "Oh, I know what I'll do. I'll make you be the mother, Sara."

That did it. I went to find Adina immediately.

She was not in her room. I went to check if she was in the lounge or the library, but she was not there either. *Where could she be?* I hurried downstairs to the laundry room.

"Did any of you see Adina?"

"No."

"I don't think so."

"I saw her studying in the garden with Malkie and Devorah around an hour ago."

"Thanks." I rushed toward the garden benches, where some of the girls were studying.

I went from one bench to the next, but did not see them.

"Did any of you see Adina, Malkie, and Devorah?" I asked a group of girls huddled together over someone's notes.

"Yes, they were on the next bench until a short while ago," Batsheva Perlowitz said.

"Someone came and gave Adina a letter and then they all drifted apart."

"Did you see where they went?"

"I think Malkie and Devorah went back inside," Michal Weinman said, "but then Adina went down there…I think," she pointed toward the wooded area leading to Kfar Amsdorf.

"By herself?"

Michal shrugged. "I don't know. I think. I was busy studying."

"Okay, thanks, Michal."

Slowly, I made my way toward the path leading into the Kfar Amsdorf woods, the crunching of my footsteps on the forest floor clearly audible. *This is silly of me. It can't be that Adina came here alone,* I thought while walking further in. *No one goes into the Kfar Amsdorf woods by themselves.*

I was about to turn around and return to the dorm. Suddenly I froze. A strange sound was coming from behind the trees.

What is that? My heart pounded. *I must go back!*

And then I heard the sound again.

An animal? Terrorists?

I knew I should run to the safety of the campus, but something held me back. I stood still. A chill ran through me.

This is insane! I shouldn't be here alone.

Tentatively, I took a step forward. Cocking my ear toward where I thought I heard the sound coming from, I tried to identify the noise.

Weeping? Is it a wounded animal or is it some kind of trap?

I took another step.

What in the world?

All at once I saw her.

She was sitting on the ground, her back against the tree. She must have heard my footsteps, because she suddenly turned to see who was there. I stared at her, stunned. Red-rimmed eyes on a blotchy face gazed back at me, with tears rolling down her wet cheeks.

"Is that you, Adina?" I asked.

She must have been as surprised as I was. "What are you doing here, Sara?"

"I came looking for you." I crouched down next to her, my voice full of concern. "What happened?"

She turned her face away. "Leave me alone. I came here to be by myself."

Even when we had that long heart-to-heart talk, even when we read the diary and letters from her mother, and even when I found her listening to her mother's tape, I never saw her cry. "You're...you're crying."

"How observant of you," she said icily. "Could you leave now that you've found me like this?"

"B-but, Adina, I only want to—" My eyes suddenly caught sight of fragments of paper scattered across her lap and on the ground around her. "Adina, what did you rip up?"

She glanced at me uncertainly and then her eyes shifted to the pieces of torn paper strewn around her. "That's none of your business. Now…leave."

My heart sank. "But Adina…"

"I don't want your pity or your company," she snapped. "If I'd wanted someone to talk to, I would have gone to the dorm. Apparently, I want to be alone."

"So that you could cry with no one seeing you?" I felt like *I* was going to cry. "Not even Mimi?"

She stiffened. "I never cry."

"I know that, Adina," I swallowed hard, "but you don't have to be ashamed."

"Crying is a sign of weakness."

"Who says?"

"It doesn't matter. *I* know it's not the proper thing to do. Now, if you'll please leave."

"Why?" An agonizing feeling deep inside me was pushing its way to the surface. "Because you never saw your father cry? Because your grandparents don't cry?"

"Excuse me, Sara, but who are you to—"

"I'm just trying to tell you that you have nothing to be ashamed of." *Hashem, please help me say the right thing in the right way!* "Adina, even your mother cried."

"My mother was weak."

"Adina! How could you say such a thing?"

"It's true. Even my father felt that way!"

"What?"

"Yes, I know. That's why he didn't like tears. My mother was way too emotional and that's what made her sick."

"Adina, what in the world are you talking about?"

"Sara, you're a pretty smart girl. Don't you know? People who are emotional are more vulnerable, so they are more susceptible to illness."

"Your father told you that?"

"Not in those words. But I know that's how he feels."

"How do you know…if he never said it?"

"Sara, first of all, I just know. He *never* cried and he didn't like it if I ever did. And second of all, I read a lot. And I've read numerous articles about the effect emotions have on physical health."

"Adina, just because a person cries it doesn't mean that there's something wrong with her. Lots of people cry…great people. I've heard holy *Rabbanim* crying when they speak and it inspires everyone around them. And I've seen my own parents cry. And believe me, they're emotionally *very* healthy. And you even saw Rabbi Grossman when he was talking about—"

"The Goldstones," Adina sighed. "That's true."

"And we learned…I mean we know," I quickly corrected myself, "that the gates of tears are never closed to Hashem."

"Sara, don't start with me on *that* again."

"I'm not. I'm just trying to say that there's nothing wrong with crying. And maybe if you cried a little, you'd get some of those feelings out of you and you'd feel a lot better."

"What feelings?"

"The ones you keep locked up inside that make you so…angry."

"I'm not angry—"

"Okay, fine, you're not angry. But my mother always says…oh," my hand clamped over my mouth. "Adina, I'm so sorry—" *Why don't I think before I talk? Now, she'll never forgive me!*

"What does your mother always say, Sara?"

I took a deep breath and looked away. That agonizing feeling was rising higher, and with each passing second, tightening its hold around my throat. *Poor Adina, doesn't have a mother and now—*

"What were you about to say, Sara? Sara," I heard her intake of breath, "*you're* crying!"

I touched my wet cheek. "Oh…I'm so ashamed."

"Why? What happened?"

I felt myself blushing. "I cry so easily."

"And what were you about to tell me?"

"She says," I sniffed, while groping in my pocket for a tissue, "she says that tears help wash away the pain."

"And are you feeling better right now…now that you cried?"

Am I?

That choking feeling was gone…definitely gone. I nodded while blowing my nose. "I think so."

I eased my legs into a more comfortable position and leaned back against the peeling bark of a tree. A moment or two passed with neither of us saying a word. *She's not telling me to leave,* I thought hopefully. I stuck the tissue back in my pocket and looked around. Now that the harshest part of the winter was over, the greenery was beginning to push its way to the surface. Birds were hopping from one branch to the next, one following the other, their playful chirping sounds filling the silence. Suddenly the forest did not seem so forbidding anymore. I inhaled the woodsy scent of bark which mingled with the sharp smell of clean, crisp air and then looked over at Adina. Her face, still blotchy and streaked with old tears, was studying mine.

I smiled. And I saw the sides of Adina's mouth reluctantly twitching upward until it too curved into a hesitant grin.

"How about you, Adina? Do you feel better from whatever was bothering you," I pointed to the scraps of paper spread around us, "now that you...cried?"

"From whatever was bothering me?" She shook her head slowly. "Not exactly. I mean, you're right—it felt good to cry, I can't believe *I'm* saying that, but I...I still have this problem."

"Adina, I'm not trying to be nosy, but my mother—" I suddenly stopped. *Here I go again.*

"What about your mother, Sara. What were you going to say?"

"D-do you mind?" I hesitated. "I-I mean, that I keep telling you what my mother said?"

"No," she shook her head, "I don't mind. I mind more that you start and then stop."

"Okay. My mother says that when you share your problem with someone, it helps lighten your burden. But you don't have to tell me, I'm—"

"I don't want to tell you, Sara."

My heart sank.

"But your mother is probably right. So, I guess it might be better if I share this with you. Especially now that you've caught me crying."

I held my breath.

"My father wrote to me," she pointed to the scraps of paper. "He wants me to come home, that is, to *his* home for Pesach."

"And that made you so upset?"

"No. He said he's not forcing me and that if I really want to stay in Eretz Yisrael, he understands, and that Hinda Klein already told him that she's inviting me—and if I want, I can bring along some friends," she sighed heavily.

"So what's wrong?"

"He tells me, he writes," Adina crisply said, "that I should say *Yizkor* this time. He tells me that it's wrong that I haven't been saying it all these years and that now…now I should start."

I was incredulous. "You mean you haven't been saying it?"

"No!" her voice was sharp. "And I don't plan on saying it now either."

I swallowed hard. A new lump was forming in the bottom of my throat. "B-but…why?"

"Because…" Her mouth clamped shut.

I looked at her anxiously, waiting for her to continue, doubtful that she would. But then after a tense few seconds passed, she surprised me.

"Because at the beginning, my father felt I was too young—well I was kind of young. Then one Yom Kippur, I was about seven or eight years old, my father and grandparents decided it was time for me to go to shul and say *Yizkor*."

She leaned back against the tree, gazing into the distance.

"So I went to shul. And I'll never forget what it was like. When it was time for *Yizkor*, I watched everybody, well *almost* everybody, file out of the room. And as they left, children and adults—I felt them staring at me. Do you know what it's like to literally feel your back getting hot because people are staring at you?"

I lifted my shoulders, but said nothing.

"Well, I know what *I* felt like. I wanted to reach over my shoulder and wipe off their stares. One woman who was new in the neighborhood came over to my grandmother and told her that it was time for me to leave. 'They're saying *Yizkor*,' she said. And my grandmother and a few others had to tell her that I belonged there.

"*Belonged there?* I'll never forget the way she sighed and I'll never forget the pitying looks thrown my way as the other people returned to the *Ezras Nashim*. And I'll never forget the way I felt as I swore to my father and grandparents that I would never go back to shul to say *Yizkor* ever again.

"And now...my father thinks that I'll change my mind. J-just because he remarried, just because he's beginning a new life, he thinks I'm suddenly a new person?" She clenched her teeth together. "I'm so...so..."

"Angry at him?"

"More than angry at him!"

"And that's why you won't say *Yizkor* for your mother? Because you're angry at him?"

"No," she shook her head, "I just told you why—"

"But now you're older, Adina. People aren't going to stare at you."

She bit her lip. "Still...I don't want to say *Yizkor*."

"But, Adina, can't you say it at home? Why don't you just say it by yourself?"

"Sara, stop it! I said I don't want to say *Yizkor!*"

"But why?"

"I hardly even knew my mother, I can't remember her. Why should I put myself through the discomfort?"

"But isn't saying *Yizkor* supposed to be that you're *davening* for your mother's *neshamah* to rise higher? It's supposed to be a merit for her soul, I think."

"So?"

"So maybe you should care about *her*? And maybe it's time for you to build a relationship with her."

"What do you mean? She's dead."

I flinched for a moment, but then went on. "Maybe, Adina, you should *daven* that she should be an advocate in *Shamayim* for you. And instead of being angry at her—"

"Who says I'm angry at her?"

"Adina, I don't have to be a genius to see that you're angry at your mother for dying young. You're angry at your father for the mistakes he made—and that he's trying to rectify now, and you're angry at Hashem for putting you in that situation. And now—"

All at once, she stood up, her blue eyes flaring furiously at me.

"Wait Adina, don't leave yet!" I lifted myself off the ground. "And now you're angry at me for saying all this, and soon you're going to be angry with Mimi…"

She did not say anything, but turned her back to me with an abruptness that spoke louder than words and began taking long strides away from me in the direction of the campus.

I stood staring at her receding back for a moment and then quickly hurried after her, calling for her to wait. She ignored me.

When a few seconds later I had almost caught up with her, my words tumbled out breathlessly. "Yes, Adina, you're going to be angry with Mimi too, because she desperately needs you to be the mother, otherwise the whole *Metamorphosis* production will fall apart."

She still ignored me. Her legs were longer than mine and she was faster. I was frantically trying to keep up with her quickened pace, knowing that it was useless to hope she would slow down.

"Adina," I panted, "maybe it's time for you to think about someone else, for the first time in your life…and maybe that'll help you stop being so angry at yourself!"

She suddenly stopped walking and swung around to face me. Her face was a deep red and her blue eyes were steely as they locked onto mine.

I took a deep breath. "And then," I said in a low voice, "maybe you'll stop being angry at everyone else."

For a moment we stood staring at each other, neither of us saying anything. *What more could I say?* I was shocked at my bluntness, but I did not regret what I had said. I had spoken without my usual self-consciousness and need for approval. And I wondered, *did Hashem just help me say the right thing in the right way?*

Then suddenly, Adina spoke, her words clipped. "Is…is this also something your mother told you to do? Tell someone off, put them down? Make them feel like damaged goods?"

"I—I never said you're damaged, Adina. I said you're angry. And that maybe by doing something for someone else, helping *them* when *they're* desperate for help, it'll help take away some of your own anger…and you'll feel happier then."

Her lips were pursed together tightly. "I see," she said in a taut voice.

I knew right then that whatever hope there was for a friendship with Adina Stern was now gone forever. "Um...Adina...I-I just want to clarify something," I said, before turning to leave and before my new rush of tears would begin. "My mother would never hurt anyone...and I...I for sure didn't say what I did to hurt you."

Slowly, I began walking away alone, miserable about Adina and miserable about facing Mimi and her disappointment. *Maybe Mimi could play the part. True, she needs to direct the band and she really isn't a "mother" type, but she's a good actress and no one else will be as good as her. That is...besides Rochel Leah and Adina.*

"Uh...Sara?"

I turned around, "Yes?"

"Um...If you want," Adina face was impenetrable. "You could let Mimi know that I'll do it. I'll think about someone else for once in my life, Sara." She paused. "I'll be the mother in *Metamorphosis*."

39

I GLANCED AGAIN at the playbill and again that wonderfully delicious feeling ran through me. *You aren't just some piece of paper,* I mentally told the playbill in my hand, *you signify so much more.*

And then for maybe the twentieth time, I re-read the English version of it. There were parts, though, that my eyes would linger on a bit longer. Not because I had trouble reading them, of course, but because I wanted to savor those sweet emotions that enveloped me each time I saw those words.

Mother...Adina Stern, was one in which I definitely took a special pride. Adina's performance had surpassed anything we could have dreamed of and now I could only hope that the words she sang so meaningfully would begin to mean something to her too. *Riki Dovidison* was another name my eyes would linger on. She had been adorable and absolutely captivating as the little girl and I was truly happy that Mimi was progressing so well with her. *Lighting...Sara Hirsch and Ronit Kitlovitsky* was especially gratifying. I would reread that line several times, the sides of my mouth tugging upward, thinking of the way Ronit went around with her flashlight telling everyone that she was the "lighting director." I remembered how she gripped my hand tightly and dragged me to meet her grandmother, and I will never forget how her grandmother thanked and blessed me for "bringing light into Ronit's eyes."

Of course, the credits... *Theme Song of Metamorphosis...Lyrics written by Sara Hirsch and music composed by Mimi Rosenberg* caused my stomach to do wonderful flip-flops every time I read it. Mimi and I were a team; we were great friends and partners! Did everyone else realize it too?

Then, there was the *"Special thanks to Sara Hirsch for all her help with writing the script and everything else! Love, M.R."* that Mimi had inserted at the bottom of the playbill without my knowledge.

I thought back to the previous night, *Motzaei Shabbos*…how in the midst of all our busy preparations, I suddenly remembered Rochel Leah lying all alone in the infirmary. I hesitantly stood at the threshold of her room and told her that we would miss her and that I would tape the production for her to listen to the next day. She seemed really appreciative when, after the performance, I brought over my tape recorder with the recorded cassette inside.

I was finding out—people were not necessarily what they seemed. Sometimes their intimidating, overconfident, superior behavior was just a camouflage for their internal insecurities and vulnerabilities.

I think that right then I was ready to forgive anyone about anything. At that moment, stretched out on my bed in the Beit Yaakov HaNegbah dormitory and staring at the beautiful lines on the tiled ceiling, I wanted to hug life, to wrap my arms around it and embrace it with my whole being.

And I wondered *how in the world will I ever fall asleep tonight? I'm so amazingly, fantabulously happy!*

Yes, right then I was feeling on top of the world, more than I had ever felt in my entire life. The production of *Metamorphosis* had metamorphosed me! I had written the theme song and everyone knew it. Many of the faculty members complimented me on a job well done and some of them even wanted to know when Mimi and I would be teaming up again for another special performance. And from the admiring look so many of the girls gave me, I could tell that Mimi must have told them that it was me, Sara Hirsch, who convinced Adina to play the mother. I was no longer this pitiful case, this lonely, unpopular girl who came to M.B.L.L. all by herself. Now everyone knew that Mimi, Adina, and I were a trio.

Approval. I finally had everyone's approval.

And for the first time since coming to M.B.L.L., I was not thinking about the Goldstone Award.

Chapter 39

Nor was I thinking about Mazal's grandmother, Gila and her husband, or Geveret Katz.

I was too busy enjoying the compliments, relishing my new friendships, and basking in everyone's admiration.

I really was on top of the world!

Well, as we all know, the world is round like a ball. And no one can stand on top of a ball forever.

On *Ta'anis Esther*, at the close of morning sessions when everyone returned to the dorm, and after dropping by the lounge to chat a bit, I cheerfully made my way upstairs and went directly into the room next door.

I knocked and then, when I heard a British accented "come in," I pushed the door open.

Adina, with her back against the wall, was sitting on her bed with an open book leaning on her knees. She looked up as I entered the room, her eyebrows lifted.

Mimi did not notice my entry.

She was lying face down on her bed with headphones covering her ears. Her legs were bent at the knee and her ankles were intertwined, waving nonchalantly in the air, while she casually skimmed through the pages of a photo album parked on her pillow.

"Hi," I said rather loudly, approaching Mimi's bed in order to let her know I was there.

"Oh, hi, Sara," Mimi flipped herself over and pushed her headphones down around her neck. "I've been listening to this amazing speech! How long have you been standing here?"

"Just two seconds," I laughed. "Sorry to disturb you."

"That's okay," Mimi sat up, "we're just relaxing a bit before we get busy."

"That's unusual of you, Mimi," I smiled, "relaxing, that is."

"Well, it *is* a fast day today and we can't eat until tonight."

"Did you need something, Sara?" Adina asked, her eyes shifting from me to her book.

"I was thinking that it would be a good idea if the three of us would bring Gila a *Mishloach Manos* package this afternoon, since tomorrow things will be kind of hectic here."

"Sorry, Sara," Mimi said. "We can't."

"Why not? There won't be time to make a special trip to Be'er Sheva on Purim. And with all the help they're giving us, we really should—"

"You're right, Sara, we'll certainly chip in with you," Adina said to me and then turned to Mimi. "We really must participate in a *Mishloach Manos* package for Gila, Mimi. It's only right."

"No prob! How much do you want to spend?"

Adina shrugged. "You tell me."

"I figured we could pick up some packages of nosh and a pineapple and put it in a basket. So when do you want to leave?" I asked.

"Who said anything about leaving?" Mimi laughed. "Sorry, for the misunderstanding, Sara. We'll chip in, but we can't go with you to Be'er Sheva."

"We've got to make the bus for B'nei Brak which is leaving from Mishmar HaNegev at three o'clock," Adina explained.

"B'nei Brak?"

"Yes, we'll be there for tonight and Purim." Adina ran her fingers through her hair. "Then we're going with the Mintz's to Yerushalayim for Shushan Purim."

"Huh?"

"You know the Mintz family Mazal and I stayed by when we had that school Shabbos in B'nei Brak?" Mimi spoke quickly. "So anyway, they invited us to come back for Purim, and since Mazal can't come, I figured I'd ask Adina."

"Oh."

"She *is* my roommate."

"I know."

"I'm sorry, Sara. They didn't tell me that I could bring a third person and they have a tiny apartment, so I didn't think it was right to ask. I hope you don't mind…"

She hopes I don't mind. Right! I'm really sure Adina and Mimi are all worried about whether I mind.

So much for being on top of the world!

I ended up delivering our *Mishloach Manos* basket to Gila by myself. Actually, I went along with Chani and Rivky to Be'er Sheva. They had some baskets they wanted to deliver there, so we took the bus together, but then separated so that I could go to Gila and they could go where they wanted. We made up to meet again at four o'clock at the same spot.

It felt so silly tagging along with them. Of course they were warm and friendly, but knowing that right before Mimi left with Adina, she arranged for me to go with them made me feel like some ridiculous child. She found out that they were also going to Be'er Sheva and decided that I should not go alone. *How sweet of her!*

Well, it did not feel sweet to me. I kept thinking about Mimi and Adina and the fact that they made plans…plans that did not include me. *So that's her appreciation? Their appreciation? That's what I get for saving the production for Mimi, that's what I get for helping and caring so much about Adina?*

If they couldn't have a third person join them at that Mintz family in B'nei Brak, then they shouldn't have gone, I thought miserably, as I climbed the stairs to Gila's apartment. *The last time I was here, they were here together with me. The three of us were a trio.*

Some trio!

My mood was not buoyed by Gila's news either. Her husband still had not found the information we were seeking regarding the Yitzchaki family. And suddenly I could not wait any longer. It was absolutely essential to me that we get back to solving that mystery immediately.

I am sure I was not great company to Chani and Rivky as we detoured to the town of Devorah to deliver some *Mishloach Manos* packages there. And although I really tried, I was not much more cheerful when I brought over a basket to Ronit's grandparents' apartment either. I guess I never was very good at being able to "smile and the world smiles with you."

Unexpectedly, I found myself thinking of Chavie and I felt overcome by emotions that…well…were not the most pleasant. Whereas two weeks earlier I had, at first, felt slightly disconcerted at her news, those feelings had given way to true happiness and excitement for her. Besides, I had been so busy with the *Metamorphosis* production while waiting eagerly for news from Gila concerning Mazal's missing aunt, that I had not really thought that much about Chavie. Nor did I dwell on the inevitable changes that were bound to take place in our relationship as a result of her engagement. But, bumping along the road on our return trip to the Beit Yaakov HaNegbah Campus, I was suddenly overwhelmed by a mixture of all sorts of uncomfortable feelings. Life was suddenly not as smooth as I had thought.

Later that evening, as we sat listening to the *Megillah* reading, I tried not to think about Adina and Mimi, or about Chavie and the unfairness of the way things were turning out for me. I wanted to concentrate on the *Megillah* and the miracle of Purim.

Esther HaMalkah...things must have seemed unfair to her, too. It must have been lonely in the wicked Achashveirosh's palace, surrounded by the evil Haman and his ilk. But in the end, it was through her that Hashem saved the Jewish Nation. Yes, she had not thought of herself. She had risked her life and became a true heroine.

That's what I've always wanted to be. Someone, who does great things...

Obviously, I'm not going to be another Esther HaMalkah. I'm not going to rescue the Jewish People from threatening annihilation. But I could do something else—at least for starters. I could help reunite a lost daughter with her dying mother. Now, that would be major! And the Goldstone Award? Have I forgotten that great ambition, that giant leap into the educational field? If I want to return to Rolland Heights not simply as another seminary graduate, but as the winner of the prestigious award, I had better begin taking bigger steps in that direction too!

There was a new determination in my stride as I made my way into the dining room alongside Zehava and a few of the others. *Okay, so I don't have true, loyal friendships with Mimi and Adina and my dear friend Chavie is abandoning me for Lakewood and her new life. So what! I still have something no one can take away from me. I have my dream!*

I slipped into a seat beside Zehava and poured myself a cup of freshly squeezed orange juice.

And then, with a suddenness I was completely unprepared for, it hit me like the unexpected appearance of the sun on a gloomy, frigid day. *That's it! I'm going to combine it all together! My pasuk, my Proyect theme, and the Yitzchaki search. Why didn't I think of that earlier? No one—absolutely no one—will have a Proyect like that. And I know how I'm going to do it. It'll be unbelievable! I wrote the theme song and now*

Chapter 39

I'm going to write the most amazing Proyect that M.B.L.L. has ever seen! I'm going to—

"Sara, are you planning on fasting another day?"

"Huh?" I looked up abruptly. "Oh, Zehava. What did you say?"

"I asked you whether you're planning on continuing your fast. You haven't eaten a thing."

My eyes shifted to my untouched plate and then to my full glass of juice. I laughed. "You're right. My mind was someplace else." I made a *berachah* and took a sip of juice.

Somehow, I did manage to detach myself from my *Proyect* plans. It must have had something to do with the power of the Purim spirit, its joyfulness washing away any feelings of negativity. Everyone around me was especially friendly and forthcoming, and I found myself chatting cheerfully with the others—the gloominess of the past few hours turning into a distant memory.

The next morning after *Megillah* reading, I went with Zehava to the infirmary to bring Rochel Leah a *Mishloach Manos* package filled with plain crackers, flavored teas, sucking candies, and an assortment of small jars of jelly. We stayed a little while talking pleasantly and then, seeing that Rochel Leah was still weak and wanted to go back to sleep, we left. We stopped off in the dining room to eat something and then, along with a bunch of other girls, stood around a table in the corner of the large room assembling *Mishloach Manos* packages to deliver to the teachers and staff.

It was fun putting together the various fruits, pastries, and candies, and with the lively music from someone's tape recorder blasting upbeat "*MiShe'Nichnas Adar Marbim B'Simchah…*" and "*LaYehudim Haysah Orah…*" melodies, we found ourselves cheerfully singing along. The only chink in my otherwise perfectly happy mood was when someone mentioned what a pity it was that Mimi was not there and how much more fun everything was when she was around. *A pity indeed!*

After all the baskets were ready, we divided ourselves into pairs and then, attuned to the essence of the day, picked "lots" to decide who would deliver which baskets to whom. Zehava and I were lucky. We did not have far to go. Some of the girls had to lug their baskets through the Kfar Amsdorf woods to make their deliveries. We had Geveret Katz's and Geveret Mendlowitz's baskets, and they both resided on campus.

Our first stop was Geveret Mendlowitz's cottage. We wanted to bring her basket to her while she was still home. Soon she would be returning to the kitchen to prepare the next meal, the gala Purim *Seudah*.

Along the way we met different girls, many dressed with funny hats or masks, and laughingly tried to guess who was who. We saw some of the staff's children carrying overstuffed shopping bags and wearing the most adorable and original costumes. And with the staff's cottages open to outside guests, there was an interesting array of characters and sounds in the campus, unlike we had ever seen there in the past. Purim in seminary in Eretz Yisrael sure was different than Purim in Rolland Heights!

I was surprised to be greeted with the aroma of freshly baked challah as we neared Geveret Mendlowitz's cottage. She was truly amazing! Constantly busy cooking in the dormitory kitchen, she still wanted that delicious smell to exude from her own home too.

We stayed by her for a quarter of an hour, munching contentedly on the delicious cinnamon *rugelach* she offered us, while enjoying her children's animated descriptions of the singing and dancing that had taken place the night before in Yeshivat Kfar Amsdorf. After making a *berachah acharonah* and thanking Geveret Mendlowitz, we walked along the gravel path toward Geveret Katz's home. Again we were greeted by a delightful smell, but this time it was fresh *hamentashen* coming straight out of the oven.

Entering the kitchen, we saw three adorable clowns bouncing around the table, waiting impatiently for their mother's permission to sample the warm pastries cooling off on the trays in its center.

"You must have *savlanut*; you don't want to burn your tongues on the hot jelly," we heard her warning them. "Ah, look." She turned to us as we placed the huge basket on the table, a relieved smile spreading across her face—apparently glad to have something that would distract them. "How nice this basket from Zehava and Sara is!"

The children gathered around and peered inside eagerly.

"Oooh, Ima could we have?"

"Yes, could we? Could we?"

"Ima, chocolate! Chocolate!"

"It's not polite, children, to take before we say thank you," she replied and smiled in our direction.

"It's not *just* from us," Zehava quickly set things straight.

"It's from *all* the girls in the dorm," I added.

As Geveret Katz divided some of the treats from the basket among the children, while chatting with us and trying to convince us to sit down and have a cup of tea, my eyes kept shifting to the framed photographs on the wall.

There were pictures of the children: some taken individually and some with the children posed together as a group. In one picture, Geveret Katz and her husband were sitting alongside the children with everyone dressed formally. *It must've been a family simchah*, I thought to myself. We had seen her husband many times before, but looking over at that particular photograph, where he was surrounded by his wife and children, the contrast between his Ashkenazi looks and the Yemenite appearance of the other family members was certainly more defined. The children apparently resembled their mother. One of the kids especially reminded me of Salma Cohen. *Her cousin,* my heart skipped a beat, *they have to be first cousins!*

My eyes eagerly continued combing the walls. *Where is it?* I kept looking…searching, *where's the picture of Geveret Katz's "supposed" father…the shomer?*

"Oh, I see you enjoy looking at family photographs," Geveret Katz's voice suddenly broke through my reverie.

I felt myself blushing. "Um…er…yes. I guess so."

"We have an interesting collection. One Shabbat afternoon, when you have time, you are welcome to come see them."

When I have time? How about right now? If I could, I'd sit here this very minute and look at every single one of those pictures. Then, I'd surely be able to prove my theory! "Th-thank you," was all I managed to say.

"How about you, Zehava? Do you also like looking at photographs?"

Zehava nodded, "Sure."

"So you'll come along with Sara. I have pictures from my early years in Israel, soon after this country became a state. I was a little girl at that time, you know. I was born here. Israel during those years was so backwards. You won't recognize it as the Israel of today," she laughed. "Then, when I was still quite young, we went to live in America. So I have photographs of life in California, as well."

"You don't mind?" I asked eagerly. "That is...if we come and look?"

"Of course not. I always enjoy showing my albums."

"Ima, Ima," one of the clowns called, "Seffy's taking all the chocolates. I also want chocolate."

"Oh—excuse me. I've got to settle this."

"Esther...Esther!" We suddenly heard a voice coming from the back of the cottage.

"Oh," Geveret Katz looked from her kids to the back room and then to us, flustered. "My father just awoke and needs some help. Could you girls keep an eye on Seffy and Raffi? Shimmy, you come with me and help Saba with his walker."

Trancelike, I walked over to the table with Zehava and helped her divide the chocolate between the two remaining clowns. But it was surreal. My hands broke the chocolate into pieces, but my mind was in the back room. *He's here, her father is here! I'm going to meet him. At long last, I'm going to meet the shomer!*

I heard the scraping sounds of his walker before I saw him. And when I tore my eyes away from the chocolate to look at him—I knew with a certainty.

He looked exactly how I had pictured him.

Naturally, he was much older now; his face was wrinkled, his body was bent over. But there was no doubt. He had once been a tall, powerful man who evoked fear in those around him, whose commanding presence compelled one to obey his every word.

And there was his "daughter," so assiduous in her care of him. So similar to Mazal's mother. *Her older sister.*

I was mesmerized. I kept thinking about Mazal's grandmother and the fear she must have had of him. I wondered if it was at all possible that Geveret Katz remembered anything of that time, and then I realized that obviously she could not have. She had been far too young.

Of course, I felt sorry for this large man. He had suffered through the Holocaust, seen his young child killed, and had experienced the horror of a wife gone mad. *But that didn't give him the right to do what he did.* No one, even during those turbulent times, should get away with separating a child from her real family. *And I, Sara Hirsch, will expose the truth.* Not because I want to hurt this elderly man. But because a woman is dying and has the right to see her kidnapped child before she leaves this world. *And how grateful they'll all be to me…Geveret Katz, Geveret Cohen, and Mazal's grandmother…*

"Sara," Zehava hissed while elbowing me.

I looked up.

"As I was saying, Abba, this is Zehava Gross and Sara Hirsch. Zehava and Sara, this is my father."

"Michael Benshalom," he grinned widely, "is my name, Michael Benshalom. How do you do?"

He spoke English with a strange accent—the enunciation of his words a mixture of his European and Israeli backgrounds. But it was not his accent that surprised me.

What did surprise me was that I was not finding myself completely antipathetic toward this man. He was turning out to be a jovial and cheerful character, enjoying meeting "mine daughter's children from de dormitory."

"Dat means you are like my grandchildren," he laughed heartily.

I shuddered at the thought.

"Abba, let me get you something to eat. A piece of herring with a slice of fresh bread or maybe you prefer something else?"

I do not know what he chose to eat or how he spent the rest of the day. Zehava urged me on, realizing that Geveret Katz was busy enough without our company, so reluctantly I left. My mind, though, was left lingering behind. Yes, despite the excitement and activity taking place the rest of that day and the next—when we spent Shushan Purim in Yerushalayim—it was difficult for me to stop thinking of that man and his impact on the Yitzchaki family.

I knew I had to do something; I had to take the next step. I just was not sure what that next step should be. *How could I prove that Michael Benshalom is the shomer who kidnapped Hodaya Yitzchaki?* It was definitely turning out to be a lot more complicated than I had originally thought. *And how could I reunite Geveret Katz with Geveret Cohen and her mother?* my mind raced on. *It would have to be done soon. Who knew how much time Mazal's grandmother had left? Could photographs be used as proof or should I wait and see what Gila's husband can find out for us? How long will that take?*

And who could I discuss all this with? Adina and Mimi? No…no way! They're way too busy with each other and they're not really interested in me.

Well, that's okay, I'll manage without them, I told myself, lifting my chin. *I've succeeded once…I wrote the theme song…and I can succeed again.*

That's right, I threw back my shoulders, *who needs Mimi and Adina?*

When a bunch of us returned from Yerushalayim late Wednesday night, I went straight to bed, managing to avoid Mimi and Adina until the next morning at breakfast.

I tried my best to ignore them.

As I slipped into my seat for Thursday morning's classes, I nodded coolly to Adina and then busied myself with preparing for the next lesson. I did not say a word to her and in between classes wrote a long, detailed letter home.

That Shabbos was not a Shabbat *chovah*, but most of the girls chose to stay in, so the dorm was quite full that weekend. Being that I was one of the girls who had *toranut* that Shabbos, I had my hands full.

I do not think I had ever been as thankful for my *toranut* job as I was that Shabbos. It would keep me way too busy to concern myself with thoughts about Mimi and Adina.

Rochel Leah was still in the infirmary and I knew that, although Zehava was making friends with the other girls, she appreciated my presence. We spent whatever free time I had in between my *toranut* jobs and the *seudos* hanging around together in the lounge or in her room.

I tried not to even glance in Mimi's or Adina's direction.

A couple of times—quite a few, in fact, Mimi came over to me and tried, in her cheerful manner, to joke around and make conversation as though everything was fine between us. Sure it was fine…fine for her and Adina. It was fine to continue pretending that we were friends.

Chapter 39

After all, let's be nice to the pitiful Sara.

But I was not going to fall for that any longer. Mimi does not really need me, except to help her out with her schoolwork. *Well, I don't need her anymore, either. Whenever she forgets about me, I manage fine without her, and I'll manage just fine now too. Just fine.*

I did not go to bed Friday night until late, and I was sure Adina and Mimi were asleep. Then, removing my shoes before opening the door, I slowly tiptoed into my room.

I would avoid them no matter what!

Shabbos morning I awoke bright and early with the sun pouring into my room, got dressed quickly, and hurried downstairs before the two girls in the room next door woke up. After davening, I busied myself with my *toranut* duties while chatting with the other girls who shared my job and tried very hard not to think about Adina and Mimi.

But I had to fill that active imagination of mine with something!

So, as I set the tables and bantered lightly with the others, my mind drifted off into fantasyland. I visualized the reunion between Geveret Katz and the Cohen and Yitzchaki families and my heart fluttered with excitement at the thought. Then, while I placed a shiny fork to the left of each plate, I saw myself being called up to the stage by Rabbi Grossman. A hush falls upon the audience as he announces that not only is Sara Hirsch the winner of the Goldstone Award, but that she accomplished far more than anyone else in M.B.L.L. ever did. "Sara Hirsch," I pictured him saying, "along with producing an exceptional *Proyect*, is the same Sara Hirsch who succeeded in bringing the missing child, our very own *eim ha-bayit*, Geveret Katz into the arms of her anguished mother and family." Everyone applauds approvingly, but the greatest applause comes from within me for having—with Hashem's help, of course—accomplished something so great and heroic!

And then, if that was not enough to chase away any feeling of despair, I pictured myself at Chavie's wedding—the two of us dancing together fervently with everyone surrounding us, clapping and rejoicing along with the two best friends, knowing that, of course, it was Sara Hirsch that the *kallah* chose to dance with first. I could almost hear the beat of the music and found myself humming happily along, just thinking about it.

I let my movie projector of a mind continue playing its imaginary film even further.

I heard the telephone in my home ringing nonstop with offers for teaching jobs. I would select the one best suited for my growth as a teacher, the one that would help me to realize my dream of eventually becoming the well-known educator I was meant to be. I could visualize the headlines of The Rolland County Jewish News: "Sara Hirsch or Mrs. Sara (whatever-my-name-will-be by then), the famous educational consultant, is arriving tomorrow to present a workshop in—"

"He-llo? Sara," Shaindy Applegrat was waving a fork in front of my face, "the other tables don't have *any* forks and you've been putting *three* forks at each of these settings—"

"Oh, sorry, Shaindy." I felt my face turning red as my eyes quickly scanned the three tables I had just helped set. "I don't know what happened. Here," I started collecting the extra forks, "I'll finish up the rest of the tables. If you want, you can go."

"Thanks. You're sure you don't mind?" she asked while backing away. "It's almost time for the *seudah* and I didn't finish *davening* yet."

"No...no problem." She reached the doorway and I had to raise my voice so she could hear me, "It's my fault anyway."

I looked back down at the tables and sighed. *How silly of me! Three forks per person?*

"Hey, let me help you, Sara."

I swung around at the sound of Mimi's voice, my heart beginning to pound. "No thank you. I'm managing just fine."

"Of course you're managing fine," she laughed. "I can't imagine you not managing fine. I just figured—"

"I said *no thank you*," I muttered through clenched teeth as I abruptly turned back to setting the table.

"I just figured," Mimi hovered in back of me while I walked from one setting to the next, "that I'll help you, and then you'll be free and maybe we can take a walk together."

I did not look up, but continued placing the forks in their correct position, my heart beating harder. "I don't want your help and I don't want to go for a walk with you either."

"There's still enough time before the *seudah*, Sara. And it's such a gorgeous day. What a pity—"

"You can take your pity, Mimi Rosenberg, and give it to someone else."

"Pity? Sara, what's with you?" Mimi placed her hand on my shoulder. "Ever since we came back after Purim you've been so…so—"

I twirled around suddenly, pushing her hand off of me. "Maybe you should have thought about that before you left. Now…now just leave me alone," I managed to mumble before dropping the rest of the forks on the table and tearfully running out of the room.

Until this day, when my mind returns to that time and I replay those few passing seconds, a couple of blurry images gyrate in front of me in rapid succession and I feel my cheeks burning just from the memory.

The first thing I see is Mimi, her eyes and mouth open wide in shock. The next image is of the pile of forks falling onto the white table cloth, followed by the two or three girls I passed as I rushed out of the room and the stunned expressions on their faces.

I ran unthinkingly into the hallway; my only sane thought was that I had to get myself someplace private and quickly—my own room being too far away. Instinctively, I headed down the steps to the basement. I must have realized that no one else would need to go down there on Shabbos.

It was dark in the windowless, underground hallway, and my hands groped along the walls, searching for the door to the storage room.

When I found it, I turned the doorknob slowly, grateful to find the door unlocked. Shakily, I let myself into the storage room and I could hear the creaking sounds of the rusted hinges echoing down the long hallway. I was not sure, though, which was louder—the squeaking hinges or the thumping of my heart.

Fortunately, sunlight streamed in through the uncovered windows, enabling me to see where I was going in the cluttered room. I impatiently climbed over some broken pieces of furniture and then, finding an old, torn couch in the corner of the room, sank down into its bumpy cushions. The pent-up emotions of the last few days were free to rise to the surface now, and placing my hands over my face, I held back nothing. I was all alone. I began to sob hard.

Why was life being so unfair to me? How could Mimi and Adina do this? I thought, really thought, we were such great friends...so open...sharing such important private things with each other, and then they suddenly leave and forget all about me? What am I going to do now? How will I ever go back into that dining room? How many girls saw me run out like that and what will everyone think of me after such a scene? Oh, if only I was at home!

Thinking about my family, I cried harder. I missed them so much and I still had three and a half months to go until I would return to them!

Then, unexpectedly, the jolly wrinkled face of Michael Benshalom appeared in my mind and I felt overcome with guilt about exposing the truth. But right after that, the sorry image of Mazal's grandmother took its place. And poor Geveret Katz, all those lost years away from her true family. Everything was just so awful! And then I pictured Rochel Leah and her sad face, and even that caused more tears.

What's with me? So many people have things worse than I do—and still, I can't stop feeling miserable. And Chavie, how could she get engaged without me? I'm supposed to be happy for her—so why am I feeling so—

"Sara!"

I looked up. Mimi was standing at the door.

"Sara, could you please tell me what's going on with you?"

"Go away," I sniffed.

"No...I'm not going away." She closed the door and made her way over to the corner of the room where I was and sat down on an overturned crate opposite me. "Something's obviously bothering you and until it's straightened out, I'm not leaving."

"Whatever's bothering me is *my* business," I cried. "Go find someone else to make your *chesed* case."

"*That's* what you think?" she asked incredulously. "That I'm your friend out of pity? That you're some sort of *chesed* case?"

I did not say anything.

"Sara, that's ridiculous. For someone so practical you sure have a wild imagination."

"Imagination? Did I imagine that you and Adina went off to B'nei Brak and forgot all about me?"

"Oh...so *that's* it."

"Yes, that's it. Now you know and now you can finally stop pretending."

"Pretending?"

I nodded.

"You think I'm pretending that I'm your friend and that really you're some sort of *chesed* case?" She shook her head, "That's nuts, absolutely nuts."

For a few seconds neither of us said anything. And then Mimi began to speak. "Sara, you think Adina and I went off to B'nei Brak and forgot all about you—and that shows I'm really not a real friend. Right?"

"Right," I said faintly.

"So that's why…you haven't said a word to me since then. Because…you think I'm not a real friend. Right?"

"R-right."

"Sara, maybe you're the one who isn't the real friend."

"*Me?*"

"Yes, you! Because instead of trusting a friend…you right away jumped to conclusions, deciding that I didn't care about you…and that this…this friendship of ours isn't the real thing."

"I wasn't the one who ran off for a few days, forgetting all about you."

"I didn't forget about you. And believe me, if you could've come, I would've loved it. But…but this was different, and it had nothing to do with you."

"What do you mean?"

"I—I can't say."

"Why?"

"Because it has to do with Adina."

"So it wasn't true about the Mintz family…about their small apartment and how you couldn't ask them to bring one more friend with you?"

"They really do have a small apartment, Sara, and…and it would've been uncomfortable asking them."

"But you could've."

She nodded slowly. "I guess so."

"And you didn't."

"No...I really couldn't."

"And you call yourself a real friend? You *could've* but you *couldn't*? I don't know," I shook my head, "maybe I'm not very bright—"

"You're bright, Sara, very bright."

"So...so what was the problem?"

She shook her head and then lifted her shoulders helplessly. "The problem was...the problem is...Adina."

"Adina?"

"Yes," Mimi looked miserable. "Adina."

"And...and you can't say?" I stared at her through swollen eyes. "You can't tell me why you couldn't include me...be-because of Adina?"

She nodded and I could see one large tear roll down her cheek. "I want to...but I can't. Maybe some day. But for now, Sara, I'm asking you not to be upset, and...and to be a real friend. Trust me."

Trust.

If only I could truly grasp its meaning.

40

"OUI, JE L'ACH 'teyal. De quoi encore as tu besoin? Quelle sorte? Bon...Je serai à Jérusalem dans deux jours...oui je t'aime bien aussi et je ne peux guère attendre de voir." Ruti Katzenstein hung up the phone and turned to me, a wide smile on her face. "I am sorry, Sara, for you vait very long. My mother gives me long list of vhat to bring for ze trip home. She cannot vait to see me."

"I don't blame her. When are you leaving?" I tried to keep my voice buoyant as I lifted the receiver off the hook to make my telephone call.

"I leave to ze cousin near Tel Aviv today and fly to Paris on Sunday. You, Sara? Vhere do you go for Pesach?"

"Not home, of course. None of the American girls are going home for Pesach, except for Chani Frankel whose sister is getting married next week."

"Oh, *oui, oui,* of course. So where do you go?"

"I think...I think I'm going to Mazal Cohen or maybe...I'll go to Yerushalayim to someone Adina Stern knows..."

It was *Erev Rosh Chodesh* Nisan. Time to make my collect call home and time to confirm my plans for Pesach.

I did make the call home, and although there were only three months left until I would return to Rolland Heights, I hung up the telephone with a sudden wave of homesickness. It could be that if I had been feeling a bit more enthusiastic about my Pesach plans, I would not have been overwhelmed with such longing for my own home. But, as usual, my sensitive nature was getting the best of me.

I wanted to go with Mimi and Adina, I really did. *But how could I?*

Mimi had assured me that Adina wanted me to come with them to Hinda Klein. And Adina had also said that she expected me to join them.

If only I really felt wanted! I knew that Pesach in Yerushalayim and especially at Hinda Klein's would be uplifting. She was sure to have many different interesting guests for the *seudos*, her spare bedroom was comfortable, her food was delicious. *Davening* would be in the yeshivah, and from what I understood, we would participate with Savta Hinda for the first *Seder* at the *Rosh Yeshivah*'s home. The second *Seder*, Mimi eagerly informed me, would be with the Saperstein family in the Old City. They were a well-known English family who often came to Yerushalayim for Yamim Tovim and opened their home up to girls from *chutz la'aretz* who needed a place to celebrate the second day of Yom Tov. And who would not seize the opportunity to go there for a meal?

Yet, how could I go along if Adina did not really want me?

It was not as though I did not have another choice.

A few days after Purim was over, Mazal had called me and invited me for Pesach. She insisted that her family wanted me in Kiryat Yosef. Of course we both realized that there would be a problem with me eating by them—their Sephardic *minhagim* conflicted with mine. But Mazal assured me that they had successfully accommodated other Ashkenazim over Pesach in the past with food graciously provided by their close neighbors, the Gold family. I *really* could go to her.

Mimi urged me to come with them. She claimed that Pesach would be so much nicer if I was with her. According to Mimi, she had never had a friend like me.

"Come on," I exclaimed, "ever since I met you, you're practically never alone! You're always surrounded by everyone...always in the center of things. Mimi, you're probably the most popular girl in M.B.L.L. So, p-lea-ease!"

She went on to say that until she met me, it was true, she never had a shortage of friends and there was always someone to chat with, to have a great time with. "But with you, Sara, I have something much deeper. You've helped open up for me worlds that I never even dreamed of entering! You know me in a way that no one else does."

Really? No one else?

"How about Adina?" I suddenly heard myself ask.

"Adina?" Mimi's eyes met mine. "No…I never had a friend like Adina either."

And so, even though Mimi managed to convince me that she really felt our friendship was special (although admittedly I could not fathom why), I still knew that my going along with them to Hinda Klein would be an intrusion.

"I'm going to Mazal," I declared adamantly, "and that's that!"

Mimi was stubborn. "Sara, you have to come with us. I need you *and* Adina needs you."

"Adina doesn't need me. She has you."

"Sara, somehow you know how to get Adina to listen, to do the right thing."

"Me?"

"Have you forgotten how many times I tried to get her to take the part of the mother in *Metamorphosis*? And all you did was try one time and—"

"That was just…just…luck. Hashem caused me to say the right thing in the right way."

"Well, Sara, we're going to need some of that luck on Pesach too."

"What do you mean?"

"I need your help…we've got to get Adina to go to shul to say *Yizkor*."

"Oh, so that's why you really want me. Not because of me, but because of Adina."

"No, Sara, that's not true!"

"Forget it, Mimi. I'm going to Mazal for Pesach."

And I really planned to. There was no way I would go where I was not wanted—especially where it concerned Adina Stern.

I suppose it had to do with the fact that deep down I still was desperate to have Adina like me. And I was not going to do anything that might hinder whatever closeness we did share.

And so that *Rosh Chodesh* day—when I hung up the telephone, I had really been planning on spending Pesach with Mazal and her family. Yet, I felt myself wavering. In the back of my mind were those daily conversations Mimi had with me, trying to convince me to go with them.

Why did Mimi want me so badly? Was it really because she wanted to spend Pesach with me, as she claimed, or was there another reason? It really did not make sense that she hoped I would go along with them just so I could help her convince Adina to go to shul for *Yizkor*.

As I climbed the steps to the third floor and made my way to my room, I once again puzzled about my relationship with Mimi.

What in the world does she see in me?

I opened the door to my room.

"Hi, Sara!" Mimi sauntered in through the wash-up closet. "I heard you come in."

"Oh. Hello, Mimi."

"What's wrong, Sara?" she looked at me thoughtfully. "Oh, I see—you have that 'I-just-called-home' look on your face."

I walked over to the mirror and peered at my reflection, then forcibly spread my lips into a wide smile. "Now do I have that look?" I turned around to face Mimi.

"No…now you have the 'I'm-forcing-myself-to-smile-so-that-Mimi-will-leave-me-alone' look."

Despite my mood, I burst out laughing. "Oh, Mimi!"

"So, you'll come with us to Hinda Klein for Pesach. Right?"

I sank down onto my mattress. "You know the answer to that, Mimi."

She plunked herself down next to me. "But why not? Adina wants you, *I* want you and Mazal's not exactly going to be lonely without you, but I—"

"Right. Mimi Rosenberg is going to be lonely without me."

"I will, Sara," she insisted.

"Y-you don't need me. First of all, you have Adina and second—"

"Sara, *Adina* is not *you*."

"And why in the world do you want me?" The words slipped out of my mouth before I could stop them.

"And why in the world wouldn't I?"

"Because…I'm-I'm just…me."

"And what's wrong with you?"

"Mimi, I'm not…I'm not…" *How do I come out and say it?* I stood up and, with my back facing Mimi, slowly walked toward the window and stared longingly at the desert mountains. "You know, Mimi, I'm not like you."

"So what?"

I heard the creak of my mattress as she stood up, and the sound of her footsteps approaching me. My back remained facing her while I continued gazing out of the window.

She whispered conspiratorially in my ear, "By the way, Sara, it's a good thing you aren't like me."

"Ha, ha, Mimi."

"No really, Sara," she continued, this time in a normal tone. "If you were like me, we probably couldn't be such great friends."

"Why not?"

"Because that's the way it is. It's like a puzzle. Where one piece is missing something, the other piece has it sticking out. And that's what makes it fit together perfectly."

"So which one of us is missing something and which one is supplying the part that isn't there?"

"Sara, don't tell me you never played with puzzles."

I turned to face her. "Funny, Mimi. Of course I did."

"So, you know how a puzzle works. There are a bunch of pieces and each piece has parts that go in and parts that go out."

"Well, Mimi…you certainly have things that I don't have—"

"And you, Sara, also have things that I don't have."

Okay, so I have something Mimi's lacking, I turned away from her and stared contemplatively out of the window. *All these years, I had academic success, whereas Mimi suffered nonstop from her learning problem. But if only I could have a little bit of her…* "Mimi, I wish I wasn't so shy. I wish I had *your* personality."

"That's silly, Sara, because whatever personality I have came together with, you know…the other stuff," Mimi said matter-of-factly.

Staring at the mountainous scene, I suddenly felt so small and ashamed. *How can I complain when I have so much to be thankful for?*

And yet, could I deny my insecure feelings, my need to be something much greater than I was…my need to stand out?

Could I admit all this to Mimi?

She had seen me cry more than once—and make an utter fool of myself. She had read my poem and she still seemed to want to be my friend.

"Maybe you're right, Mimi, maybe it's silly, but I can't help the way I feel."

"What do you mean? Oh...like what you told me that time? That you feel like a plain, ordinary prop?"

I winced. *She really is a mind reader!* "I didn't exactly *tell* you that."

"Okay, I read it. Sorry. But anyway, like I told you then—we all come with our own combinations. Sara," she eased her way between me and the window, compelling me to look at her, "if you wouldn't be that way...what you call a prop...a quiet observer in the background, then you would never be able to observe things the way you do. You'd never be as perceptive as you are."

"Me? Perceptive?" My eyebrows lifted. "Mimi, you're the perceptive one, like when it came to getting through to Riki...to Ronit."

She shook her head. "Not true. *You* were the one who figured out how to get to Ronit, Sara. And you were the one who wrote the theme song for *Metamorphosis*. And don't forget, you were the one who managed to finally get Adina to open up...more than once. And you got *me* to open up too." Her eyes twinkled. "No one ever did that before."

"But...but...those things just happened."

"They didn't just happen, Sara. You have this special way of thinking about things, thinking about people...and...and you don't let go. You care and you really try to help. It's a special sensitivity. I wouldn't exactly call someone like that a plain, ordinary prop."

I sighed. "I don't know. That's how I feel...I've felt like that for so long."

"Well, maybe it's time to stop thinking like that. You're really a very special person, Sara."

"I don't know if I should believe you, maybe you're really..." I stopped talking mid-sentence, letting my words hang in the air.

"Maybe I'm really...what?" she crossed her arms over her chest, waiting. When I did not answer, she continued, "Don't you trust me, Sara? Don't you realize that without trust you can't have a friendship?

You...you're just like Adina."

I turned to her with a start. "What do you mean?"

"Obviously she has a major problem with trusting. She doesn't trust Hashem or anybody else for that matter, and *you* have a problem with trust too. You know," Mimi cocked her head to the side thoughtfully, her red hair shifting in that direction, "I'm not so sure that the two—trust in friends and trust in Hashem aren't connected."

"I don't have a problem in trusting Hashem. I don't know what you're—"

"You do too, Sara," Mimi said quietly. "You don't accept yourself. You have so many wonderful qualities, and yet, *you* want the *other* person's qualities. If you accepted Hashem's will—"

"I do accept Hashem's will," I protested.

"No you don't. Because if you really did, you wouldn't look at what others have. You'd feel so much better about yourself and you wouldn't think that you need to stand out to be something special. You'd realize that to Hashem everyone is special."

"Easy for you to say. No one would ever pass by you and not notice Mimi Rosenberg. Wherever you go, whatever you do, you'll always stand out."

"So what? Remember what we spoke about that time when I told you I'd trade in my brains for yours anytime, and you told me about the negatives and positives? So—"

"So now you're telling it to me."

"That's right. You taught me something very important, Sara...that it's a package deal. Maybe Hashem gave me extra ways of coping because I have this...this school problem...and maybe I had to be pushier to get by. Whatever—"

"Mimi, stop. I...I think I hear what you're trying to say."

"Remember when you told me about the blind person and—"

"And then you became kind of upset with me."

"But, I think you were right, Sara. If you are given a weakness in one area, Hashem provides you with special strength in another."

I looked at her, surprised. "You...you seem so accepting now, Mimi."

"I—I'm trying. And, well...you helped me, Sara. You told me the right things…in the right way."

I felt a lone tear unexpectedly escape down my cheek. I quickly brushed my finger over it and then found myself staring at the wet finger pensively, thinking, *really* thinking about what Mimi had said.

Then Mimi said something funny—I do not remember what—and we both burst into hysterical giggles and could not stop laughing.

Suddenly, Malkie, Devorah, and Adina came in through the wash-up closet, asking us what was so hilarious, and when we finally stopped laughing and could talk in a normal, conversational manner, we told them we had absolutely no idea. We could not remember what Mimi said that had gotten us started.

"Really?" Devorah asked.

"Really," Adina said. "You don't know Mimi."

"See?" Mimi whispered to me when the other three were out of ear shot. "With you, Sara, I can have the most serious, soul-searching talk and then minutes later we can be doubled over in laughter."

Then Chani popped her head into the room, reminding all of us that it was time for supper, and that it was the last supper that she would be having with us for a while, and that we had better hurry up if we wanted to participate in her goodbye party.

I walked downstairs alongside the others, trying to partake in their banter, but my mind clung to the conversation I had just had with Mimi.

Mimi really, really cared for me. Our friendship was indeed like two puzzle pieces that fit together, with each of us supplying what the other lacked.

Lacked?

Is Mimi right, I wondered uneasily. *Have I also been lacking in something I never before thought was missing?*

Impossible!

It can't be that I'm having trouble trusting Hashem, I told myself insistently. *Me? Sara Hirsch? A bitachon problem?*

Yet, the more I thought about what Mimi said, the clearer the truth became. *But would it really be possible for me to change?*

One thing, I knew for sure would *not* change.

With a heavy heart, I was still planning on going to Mazal for

Pesach and, with an even heavier heart, I still wondered what this big secret concerning Adina and B'nei Brak was.

Perhaps I would never know. I guess I really would just have to learn how to trust...

And I knew it would not be easy.

We ate our special *Rosh Chodesh* supper, then made a mini goodbye party for Chani and all the girls who were leaving over the next few days. Then, very soon, those "next few days" passed and the girls were gone.

Although almost all the girls from Beit Yaakov HaNegbah and most of the European M.B.L.L.ers departed for home during those first few days of Nisan, our dormitory surprisingly remained quite lively. And, despite the absence of a set schedule to our day, the atmosphere was anything but languid. In fact, to the contrary, there was an energy in the air and we were caught up in the frenetic activity surrounding us.

Most of our hours were filled with helping families prepare for Yom Tov. Girls were constantly coming or going, running back and forth to Kfar Amsdorf and other local neighborhoods, cleaning, babysitting, and even helping with the cooking. And, in whatever spare time would possibly remain during those hectic pre-Pesach days, M.B.L.L.ers could be seen avidly working on their *Proyect*.

The casualness and smallness of our group contributed to a feeling of closeness and familiarity between us. And thankfully, that helped alleviate any feelings of homesickness—at least for me.

Unbelievably, more than once, I actually felt disappointed when I realized that there were only two and a half more months until my return trip to Rolland Heights. Suddenly, our seminary year seemed to be flying and I found myself wanting to stop the hands of the clock from moving so rapidly.

"So-o-o, Sara, I hear you're going to Mazal for Pesach," Rochel Leah said to me one evening during supper, as she slipped into the seat directly opposite me. "Isn't that a problem—that is—don't Sephardim eat *kitniyos*?"

"Yes, they do," I said, while pulling off the top of my strawberry leben. "But when Mazal called me right after Purim, she explained that her family and her neighbors have an arrangement each Pesach to accommodate a guest's *minhagim*, so it isn't a problem."

"I'd love to invite you to come with me and Zehava to Kiryat Sanz," Rochel Leah said, "but the people we're staying with are already having tons of company."

"Th-that's okay. I-I'm really happy," I stammered, "that I-I'm going to Mazal."

"And I'm still trying to get her to come with me and Adina to Yerushalayim. Right, Adina?" Mimi said.

"Right," Adina mumbled, not looking up from the lachmaniah she was buttering.

Mimi winked at me and then shrugged. "But lo and behold, she nevertheless chooses to abandon us."

"Mimi…" I sent her a warning glance.

"Well, if you do decide to go with them," Rochel Leah was still looking at me, "we could all get together sometime over Yom Tov. It'd be so-o-o much fun."

"How about us?" Yehudis suddenly perked up from the middle of the table. "Hadassah and I are going to be at a relative of mine in Geulah. We could also get together with you."

"And me and Ahuvah," Chaya said, while pouring some tea into her cup. "We're going to be in Ezras Torah."

"Oh, that's great," Zehava said. "Then we're not going to be that far from you. For sure—"

"Where are you having the second *Seder*, Zehava?" Ahuvah interrupted. "Do you know yet?"

"I forgot the name," Zehava turned toward Rochel Leah. "Do you remember?"

"My mother's friend is arranging for us to eat with this wealthy family from England in the Old City, the Sapersteins—"

"The Sapersteins?" Mimi repeated excitedly. "Adina and I are also eating there."

"Really?" Rochel Leah's hazel eyes opened wide as she looked from Mimi to Adina. "That's great. We can pick you up on the way there and go together."

"Ahuvah, do you know what you're going to do for the second *Seder*?" Zehava asked concernedly.

We all looked at Ahuvah. She looked at Chaya. They both lifted their shoulders. "We—we're not exactly sure."

"You could come with us," Mimi said. "The Sapersteins have an open house. Anyone can come."

"Really?" Ahuvah and Chaya asked together.

"Yep. That's what I heard."

"So great," Zehava said. "Rochel Leah, don't we pass by Ezras Torah on the way?"

"Um…sure," Rochel Leah said.

"Good," Zehava smiled. "We'll pick you two up on the way there."

"Did you all forget about us?" Yehudis asked. "Hadassah, do you want to go with them to the Sapersteins?"

Hadassah nodded. "I heard all about them. That should be a very nice experience."

"Then it's settled," Zehava said. "We pass through Geulah too. We'll make up to meet you and Hadassah."

"It sounds like you're all going to have such a great time," Rivky said. "You're almost making me jealous…"

"So come join us," Mimi generously said.

Rivky smiled. "No thanks, Mimi. You know I'm going to the Shlomitzkys for Yom Tov. And I really love it there. I've gone with Chani so many times, I feel right at home."

"I guess you won't be able to walk to the Old City all the way from B'nei Brak."

"You guessed right, Mimi."

"I still have no idea where Tova, Devorah, and I are going to have the second day meals," Malkie put down her fork. "Everyone says there are tons of places and I shouldn't worry."

"You shouldn't, Malkie. The Zichermans said that they'll make an arrangement for all of us."

"But, Devorah, what happens if it doesn't work out, what happens if those other people don't have room, what'll we do then?"

"Malkie, I'm sure the Sapersteins won't mind a few more visitors," Mimi said. "I heard they own this huge house in the Old City with a gigantic roof that they use and—"

"But we're *three* people," Tova emphasized, while waving the three middle fingers of her right hand in the air.

"That's true. We can't just invade." Malkie anxiously said. "What happens if we come and they *don't* have room?"

"They're known to have a roof that stretches," Mimi said.

"Really?" Tova's eyes opened wide.

"Well not exactly, but sort of," Mimi grinned.

"Don't the Zichermans live in Arzei HaBirah?" Zehava asked.

"Yes."

"So we'll make up to meet you too on the way."

"I'm so excited," Ahuvah said. "It sounds like we're all going to have an absolute blast!"

"It sure does," Malkie enthused.

"I'm glad we'll get to see all of you," Devorah said aloud, but her eyes were focused on Adina.

"Hey," Mimi suddenly turned to me, "we almost forgot about you, Sara. Now you've really got to change your mind. You have to come with me and Adina."

"Um…It does sound like a lot of fun. I…I don't know…" *Maybe, if Adina shows she wants me…*

My gaze fell on Adina. Her eyes met mine and then she deliberately turned away. My heart sank. I turned to Mimi. "I…I'm going to Mazal," I told her determinedly. "And I'm not changing my mind."

The next morning I called Mazal to confirm my plans. *So what if Adina doesn't want me…at least Mazal does!*

When we finished talking, I did not return the receiver to its hook. There was another number I had to try…Gila's. Mazal's grandmother's condition was worsening and I wanted to know if Gila's husband was able to find out any new information since the last time we had spoken.

She assured me that, of course, he had not forgotten about our "investigation." He was, in fact, expanding his search about the Yitzchaki family to include a special file on adoptions that took place during that period, which he only recently found out existed.

Naturally, I became very excited when she told me that. A new development in our investigation was sure to bring us closer to our goal!

But then she was quick to inform me that she was uncertain when her husband would be returning to work. Unfortunately, he had been out of work this past week because he had come down with an especially bad case of chicken pox that he caught from their children. It was possible that he would be unable to return before the Pesach recess would begin.

I tried to hide my disappointment and to continue our conversation in a friendly manner. There were, however, numerous interruptions while we spoke, with her children continuously vying for her attention. She sounded unusually harried and finally admitted that with Pesach only one week away, her children's babysitter unavailable to give her extra hours, and her husband unwell, between work and preparations for the holiday, life was abnormally chaotic.

Apparently, Gila could use some help.

I immediately rushed off to Mimi and Adina's room, and with my eyes focused on Mimi, told them about the sorry state in Gila's household, making sure to occasionally glance in Adina's direction too. Mimi and I decided to go to Be'er Sheva to help out, and after a few minutes of Mimi's convincing, Adina acquiesced to come along.

All the way there, Adina continued to be polite and conversational with me, but ever since Purim, *I* was the one who was finding it difficult to converse with her. I could not help wondering what happened in B'nei Brak and why she did not want me to join her and Mimi. I felt resentful and hurt that she did not want me to go with them to Hinda Klein, either.

Well, I'll be polite and conversational back, I thought stoically. *But nothing more than that. No, I won't go where I'm not wanted.*

When we entered Gila's apartment, we realized that one day of help would just be a drop in the bucket. We would have to return the next day…and the next.

We helped scrub her stove, wash the floors, clean the toys, dust the shelves, and each day we came, we took the children to the park as well. Gila was beside herself with gratitude. "Sara," she said, "it was the best thing when Hashem put you in the seat next to me on the airplane."

I smiled contentedly. The more time we spent with her, the more she spoke about Hashem. Gila and her husband came from a traditional background, where customs were practiced mechanically, albeit with an almost complete absence of religiosity. Now, I could see that she was gravitating toward a more spiritual lifestyle and I felt rather pleased about it. I knew Adina and Mimi were too.

Well, when holiness permeates the air…when people spend hours together traveling back and forth to do *chesed* for others, it is bound to draw them closer together too. And that is what happened to us. Since Mimi and I had already been so close before, we were drawn together even closer now. The real surprise was the change that took place between Adina and me. I guess…*no*…I *know*, when people give to others unconditionally, it helps remove those barriers that imprison them within themselves. How could I remain resentful toward Adina when working altruistically beside her?

And Adina. She was learning to give in a way she never had before. She had to change diapers, wipe noses, and get down on her hands and knees and scrub…for someone else. And the three of us joked, laughed, sang, and had a wonderful time while doing it.

And that is what happened to our friendship. The giving became contagious. The more the three of us gave to Gila and her family, the more we found ourselves wanting to give to each other.

That is why I was feeling kind of down the morning of *bedikas chametz*, when I heard the two of them packing in the next room. I really wanted to go with them and I was no longer convinced that Adina did not want me.

Perhaps I was beginning to trust her…or maybe she was beginning to trust me.

Well…it was too late.

I could not just cancel out on Mazal. *Could I?*

And then the telephone call came from Mazal. She was sorry, *really, really, terribly sorry*. But her grandmother was going back into the hospital and the family was going to be spending Yom Tov in an apartment near the hospital. Of course, I was welcome to stay by the Gold family in Kiryat Yosef, if I would feel comfortable there.

If I would feel comfortable.

It was with a bittersweet feeling that I told Mimi and Adina the news. I would be going with them to Hinda Klein, after all.

41

IT WAS THE night before *Yizkor*, when we were almost finished washing the dishes from the Yom Tov *seudah*, that Mimi told me what had happened in B'nei Brak with Adina. And surprisingly, it did not turn out to be as earth shattering or shocking as I had anticipated.

We were alone in the apartment. Savta Hinda and Adina were still outside on their walk and all that remained for Mimi and me to do was to finish up with the cutlery. It seemed only a short time had passed since we convinced them to take a break and go outside for a stroll.

Although we tried to help Savta Hinda as much as possible with the baking, cleaning, peeling, chopping, and slicing, she insisted on doing all the cooking herself. She had been cooped up inside the apartment for many hours that afternoon, turning out one gourmet dish after another. After six days of a Pesach full of company and entertaining, and the prospect of facing a muggy kitchen that still needed cleaning up, a relaxing stroll outdoors with a pleasant Jerusalem breeze blowing against her face was certainly in order.

At first Savta Hinda protested. "No, girls, I cannot leave all this work to you."

"We only have the dishes left," Mimi told her. "Everyone helped with everything else."

"And you've been working so hard," I added. "Please, Savta Hinda, you need a break."

"Yes," Adina said, "you go and enjoy yourself a little. We'll take care of everything here."

"Oh…you girls are too good," she put her arm around Adina's shoulder. "You know what? I will go, if you come along with me, Adinaleh."

Yes, Hinda Klein was the only one who could get away with calling Adina…Adinaleh. That was what Adina was called when she was a baby and she did not bat an eyelash—even once—when Savta Hinda referred to her by that name.

"But the dishes," Adina pointed dismally at the towering pile overflowing in the sink.

"I'll do them," I said, stepping forward. "You did all the dishes this afternoon, Adina, before Yom Tov began. Now, it's my turn."

"And I'm here to help Sara," Mimi took a step next to me and saluted. "Right, captain."

"Right," I saluted back.

"So go, Adina." Mimi continued persuasively, "Savta Hinda could use some fresh air."

"Well, I am kind of hot too," Adina said to Savta Hinda and then turned to me. "You're sure you don't mind, Sara? There were so many guests here tonight."

"I'm sure I don't mind." I took the apron from the hook where it hung and slipped it over my head. "And if I do start minding, then Mimi will take over for me."

We walked them to the door and then returned to the kitchen. I looked at the sink—rather, its contents (the sink was not visible) and let out a long, slow breath.

"It's a lot of dishes," Mimi rolled her eyes.

"It sure is," I sighed. "Okay, Mimi, I think we had better take out three quarters of the stuff, otherwise we won't have a sink to work in."

"I think you're right."

We got to work. Mimi placed a few of the dirty large bowls on the counter; we put the cutlery inside them, and then filled them with hot soapy water. Then I began tackling one pile of dishes after the other.

I scrubbed with the special "Shabbos/Yom Tov brush," Mimi rinsed, and we both sang. Before we realized it, we had reached the bottom of the third pile. It was time to do the cutlery.

"Okay, Sara, it's my turn now," Mimi said, while heaving the heavy bowl filled with water and cutlery into the sink.

I switched places with her. Now it was her turn to wear the apron. I untied the back strings and slipped it over my head. Mimi took it, pushed her head and neck through the top, and then turned her back to me, allowing me to tie it.

"It would be great," I said when I finished twisting the two loops into a bow, "if we could set the table for tomorrow, tonight."

"There goes my practical friend," Mimi sang out as she turned the hot water on and began running the sudsy cutlery under it. "But you're right, Sara. Then, when we get up in the morning, we could just go straight to shul."

"Exactly." I reached for a dry towel. "That's what I figured."

"As they say…great minds think alike."

"So," I smiled while taking the first clean batch of cutlery from her and drying each piece, "we're really not that different after all."

"Sara," she grinned, "we're an absolutely perfect match."

"You mean—a perfect puzzle."

"Sara," Mimi's voice took on a sudden serious tone, "I really hope Adina does it tomorrow."

"Does what? The dishes?"

"No silly, not the dishes. I was referring to something a lot more serious than dishes."

"What in the world do you hope?…Oh!" my voice dropped. "Do you mean saying *Yizkor*?"

"Uh huh," she nodded. "I have a feeling that Savta Hinda is going to talk to her about it now."

"I'm sure glad you didn't ask me to, Mimi."

"I still might," Mimi threw me a warning glance.

"You'd better not. I don't want to do anything that could make Adina angry at me."

"Hopefully, I won't need to and Savta Hinda will be successful." Mimi continued rinsing the soapy suds off the cutlery and placed a new pile on the towel next to me. "But, then again…"

"Yes?"

"If Rabbanit Lerman couldn't convince her—"

"Rabbanit Lerman?"

"Yes, Rabbanit Lerman from B'nei Brak. She tried, but Adina wouldn't listen."

"What are you talking about, Mimi? Adina went to speak to Rabbanit Lerman? The woman who took in the thirteen children?"

Mimi nodded and then grimaced. "I really shouldn't have said anything."

"But you did. So please finish."

"Well, I…I'm not sure…" Mimi hesitated at first, then came to a decision and seemed relieved to continue. "Oh…all right. I don't really think Adina will mind anymore…not after a whole Yom Tov of being together. Not after all those talks with Savta Hinda and Rabbanit Gartenhaus." She took a deep breath and went on. "When I got that telephone call from Geveret Mintz inviting Mazal and me to join them for Purim—Adina sort of invited herself to come along. She knew Mazal couldn't come and she'd wanted to go back to B'nei Brak for a while."

"Really?" I looked into Mimi's green eyes. "Why?"

"Ever since she met Rabbanit Lerman she'd been…what's the word, Sara…when you want to know more about someone?"

"Um…curious?"

She shook her head. "No, more than just curious…stronger than that…"

"Intrigued?"

"Yes," Mimi's eyes lit up. "That's it. *Intrigued*. She'd been intrigued by a woman who could take in thirteen sick children, nurture them, become attached to them, and then…watch many of them die."

"She's an absolute *tzaddekes*."

"That's not the part that got to Adina. You see, Rabbanit Lerman has been living with death and loss for a long time. She survived the concentration camps, but lost her whole family there." Mimi sighed. "Then she took in children that she knew she would get attached to and might lose. Well, Adina's been dealing with loss too, ever since she was little."

"I know," I said softly. "And not just the loss of her mother, but also the loss of her father's ability to be a good father."

"So," Mimi went on, "she felt this need to go talk to Rabbanit Lerman."

"I can understand that."

"But she couldn't bring herself to go there on her own," Mimi shook her head. "So when she heard about my invitation from the Mintz family, she jumped at the chance to go with me."

"And she didn't want me around."

"Trust me, Sara, I would have loved to invite you—"

"But the Mintz's have a tiny apartment."

"They do. But I would've been willing to sleep on a mattress on the floor so you could also come—"

"But Adina didn't want me."

"It's not that she didn't want you, Sara, and it's not that she doesn't like you. I—I think she's just plain embarrassed."

"Embarrassed? Of what?"

"Of her vulnerabilities."

"Vulnerabilities?" I repeated incredulously. "But it's not her fault her mother died or that her father—"

"It doesn't matter if it's her fault or not. I mean, it's the same thing with you, Sara. You also get embarrassed about your feelings—"

I felt myself blushing. "But that's different, Mimi."

"Why's it so different? You walk around thinking of yourself as a prop and—"

"Mimi...stop. It's not the same."

"Why not?"

"Because she didn't cause her mother to die or her father to—"

"And *you* caused yourself to be the way you are—and not the way you wish you were?"

"No, but I could change my thoughts. She can't change all that happened to her."

"You could change the way you handle things, Sara, but you can't change the...the ingredients you were born with. And it's the same with Adina. She can't change her ingredients either, but she can change the way she handles things."

"Like you, Mimi."

"Like me?"

"Yes." I looked down at the cutlery I was still holding and then back at Mimi. "Over these past few months, Mimi, you went from someone who was so used to putting all her energy into camouflaging her problem to someone who now—instead of hiding it and dancing around it—seems to really be tackling it."

"No, you're wrong," Mimi shook her head. "I'm not tackling it. I'm trying to take it—— and use it to step on and help me climb higher. Remember what you told me the night before Chanukah?"

I nodded, but did not say anything.

"Well, I don't think *I'll* ever forget. Sara, that's when you said something that changed my life forever. First you spoke about our muscles getting stronger with exercise and that struggling with our challenges are the muscle builders of our lives. And then you said that instead of using my energy to drag that piece of baggage and hide it, I should instead use it to climb on to reach higher heights."

I stared at Mimi, my eyes filling. "Mimi, you're so special."

"But, Sara, you're the one who taught me all this."

"And now," I looked down embarrassed, "I need to teach it to myself."

"I think…" Mimi's head tilted to the side, contemplating, "I think that first you have to recognize your strengths. *Your* strengths, Sara, not someone else's…not the ones you wish you had. You need to realize you've already got whatever Hashem feels you need."

I bit my lip. "Like the right prescription eye glasses?"

She nodded. "Like the right prescription eye glasses…"

I did not get to hear that evening what exactly transpired in Rabbanit Lerman's home in B'nei Brak, when Adina and Mimi went to visit her on Purim, or what was said to Adina about *Yizkor*, either. Our conversation came to an abrupt halt less than a minute later, when we heard Savta Hinda and Adina at the door and the sounds of their entry into the apartment.

We did manage, though, to set the table that night before going to sleep and we did get to go to shul early the next morning.

Shul was in the same yeshivah that Adina's father had learned in many years ago, when he had been a budding *talmid chacham*. His *Rosh Yeshivah*, HaRav Gartenhaus was no longer living, but the Rebbitzen was. Her son-in-law, HaRav Schpitzman, was now the *Rosh Yeshivah*. He had been learning elsewhere during the time that Mr. Stern had been a student in the yeshivah, and did not know him, but the rest of the family remembered Adina's father and mother quite well.

Throughout the long Yom Tov, we had visited Rabbanit Gartenhaus and her family several times, and were treated to lovely stories about Adina's parents.

We had gone to shul whenever the opportunity arose. The *tefillos* there were inspiring, with the blend of *Chassidish* and *Litvish* intonations threaded together through rousing melodies. And I found myself praying there in a way that I never had before. Each day, the congregants were treated to an uplifting *dvar Torah* from the *Rosh Yeshivah*. He spoke in an uncomplicated *Ivrit* that was not too difficult to follow, probably because "*Devarim ha-yotzim min ha-lev nichnasim el ha-ev*—when someone speaks from the heart, the words enter the heart." *Davening* there truly was an exceptionally stirring experience.

Each time after *davening*, Rabbanit Gartenhaus would insist that her good friend, Hinda Klein, and her charges (us) come up to her apartment for Kiddush—which we often did. When we had to decline because other guests were expected, she would invite us to return in the afternoon for a visit.

For Adina, it was like discovering a long lost relative. But more importantly, it was like finding the mother she never had a chance to know—the mother her grandparents and father were too afraid to talk about. Rabbanit Gartenhaus spoke of Aviva Stern with such warmth and pride. It was exactly as we pictured her from the diary and letters. But a diary and letters are just written words. Here were live human beings who remembered, filled in all kinds of details, and sometimes cried, everything in a normal, healthy, wholesome way.

Before our eyes, we watched Adina's cold, reserved exterior melt like the frozen surface of a lake in the spring, revealing its watery depth. True, a lot had happened to Adina during the past seminary year—she had opened up in ways she never had before. She had also seen how others lived and yearned for that kind of life for herself. Adina had taken advantage of this year to discover and to grow. But now, Mimi and I saw—as clear as the blue sky that draped itself over Yerushalayim—that Adina was beginning to heal.

Sitting in shul that *Shevi'i shel Pesach* morning, I found myself frequently flipping the pages of my *machzor* to where the *Yizkor* prayer was. We were getting closer and closer to it. Would Adina stay? Would she get over that deep-seated fear from her childhood? Would she stop being so angry at her mother for leaving her and at Hashem for taking her mother away?

I was sitting next to Mimi and Mimi was next to Adina. My eyes shifted to the front row where Savta Hinda sat next to Rabbanit Gartenhaus and Rabbanit Schpitzman.

The *leining* was over and a hush fell over the *beis midrash*. The *Rosh Yeshivah* was about to speak.

I listened closely. In a tear-choked voice, he spoke about the souls of the deceased for whom some would soon being saying *Yizkor*. When physical life ends, he explained, only the body dies. The soul, however, is eternal and can ascend to higher levels. Yet, the performance of good deeds is the exclusive domain of living human beings, who must struggle to make the right choices every day.

"How, then, can our departed love ones ascend to higher spiritual realms if they can no longer perform good deeds?" the *Rosh Yeshivah* asked.

I quickly glanced at Adina. The top of her *machzor* was pressed against her forehead, completely covering her face.

"If we, the living, carry on in their righteous ways or give *tzedakah* and do mitzvos in the merit of our departed loved ones, then we enable their souls to benefit and ascend higher."

For a moment or two, the room was wrapped in complete silence. Then slowly, we heard the sounds of chairs scraping against the stone floor and the shuffling of footsteps, as those leaving headed quietly out of the room.

Simultaneously, Mimi and I stood up to leave. And without turning to look at Adina, the two of us made our way outside…

When we returned to the *Ezras Nashim* about fifteen minutes later, I tried not to look at Adina. But, it was impossible for me not to. She was not at her seat, and when I searched around the room to find her, I saw that she was standing in between Savta Hinda and Rabbanit Gartenhaus. They each had an arm around her shoulders and I could see that her eyes were red.

I turned to Mimi and Mimi, as though feeling my eyes on her, turned to me. A soft, faint smile spread across her lips, and instantly, I smiled back at her.

Later that afternoon Rochel Leah and Zehava dropped by for a visit. Despite our protests that we were not hungry and she need not bother, Savta Hinda brought out some fruit, petel with soda water, and cake. She sat with us around the dining room table schmoozing for a while, enjoying the sounds of our youthful banter and laughter echoing through her apartment.

Savta Hinda, despite her age, always managed to be part of the group. Her warmth and delight in helping others, her friendliness and affection for her fellow human beings, broke down any age or language barriers.

She could have become embittered by the adversities in her life, but instead she chose to give and give and give. She took her situation, her quiet apartment, and turned it into a retreat for girls coming from *chutz l'aretz*, so that they could have a quiet place to study or find the warmth of a home away from home.

I could see that Rochel Leah was clearly fascinated with her. At one point Savta Hinda stood up. "I'll leave you girls now on your own. Time for me to go lie down a bit." I peered across the table at Rochel Leah. She looked disappointed that Savta Hinda was leaving us.

As soon as Savta Hinda left the room, Adina stood up, saying that she too was tired and that she was going to our room to take a nap. Mimi and I looked at each other surprised. *What's with Adina? She never took an afternoon nap before!*

I guess tiredness can sometimes be catching. Suddenly, I was yawning, and then Mimi had her hand over her mouth, trying to stifle a yawn too.

Now it was Zehava who stood up. "I think, Rochel Leah, it's time to go."

Rochel Leah laughed. "I think you're right. We'll see you guys tomorrow at the Sapersteins for the last meal."

After walking them to the front door, Mimi and I headed for our bedroom. We took off our shoes before opening the door, so that we would not wake up Adina, and then carrying them in our hands, turned the knob slowly and tiptoed inside.

Our precautions were entirely unnecessary.

Adina was sitting up on her bed, her back against the wall, reading something. She seemed to be completely engrossed by it.

"Uh hum…" Mimi grunted to announce our presence.

Adina looked up for a moment. "Oh, hi, you two." Her head went back down and she continued reading.

I sat down on my bed and Mimi sat down on hers. "That's a good idea. Maybe I'll read something too. This way I can rest without sleeping," I said, "because if I fall asleep now, I might not be able to sleep tonight."

Not surprisingly, Mimi did not seem interested in reading. She would rather talk. "What are you reading, Adina?"

Adina looked up with a start. "Reading? My mother's diary and the letters she wrote to me when I was a baby."

"You brought them with you?"

"Yes, I read them over every so often," she admitted, "but today I especially felt drawn to reread them."

"You feel closer now to your mother?" Mimi asked softly.

Adina's eyes watered and she nodded. "I think…I think after hearing so much about her over Yom Tov, I was beginning to feel something. And then today…"

"When you said *Yizkor*?" I offered.

"Yes…today when I said *Yizkor*, I felt a connection…a real connection," Adina looked straight into my eyes and my heart fluttered. "You were right, Sara. Remember what you told me that time in the woods?"

Slowly, I nodded.

"I think it happened…this connection…maybe because I felt like I was doing something…for her."

"So that's why you decided to read the letters again, now?" Mimi crossed her legs and leaned forward. "Because you felt the connection?"

Adina nodded slowly. "Yes. I wanted to read over everything I had. I already know her voice from the tape recording. I know her different facial expressions from Savta Hinda's pictures of her, and now, after we came back from *davening*, I wanted to again read what she wanted to tell me."

"Did it...seem different this time, I mean...you know...when you read it?" I asked hesitantly.

"I think so," Adina said. "I think I noticed things now that I hadn't really taken such strong notice of before."

"Like what?" Mimi bluntly asked.

"Adina, you don't have to say if it's private or—"

"It's all right, Sara," Adina smiled at me kindly. "I—I want to share it with you...both of you. You've both been there for me this year in a way no one else has ever been. You've been...closer to me than any friends I've ever had before."

My eyes filled and my heart warmed.

"You see," Adina continued, "I guess I never really paid attention to this part of the letter before." She looked down at the top sheet in the pile of papers in her hand. "In this letter, my mother wrote of the time she spent in Machon Beit Leah LeMorot." She looked up from the letter. "I always knew that my mother went there. Even from the little my father spoke about her, I knew that much and I knew that she loved teaching preschoolers. That was one of the reasons I chose to go to M.B.L.L.—because I figured that it would make my father happy if I did what my mother had done."

"You did it to make your *father* happy?" Mimi asked, the incredulity in her voice clearly evident.

Adina nodded. "Well, I had to go away to seminary anyway. There was no way I'd stay in Ballington."

"But you chose M.B.L.L. because that's where your mother went," I said.

"Adina did it to make her *father* happy," Mimi said emphatically. "Adina, you didn't need—"

"Yes, I did," Adina's voice rose an octave. "I wanted to make him happy. I wanted to please him. He missed my mother; his life was ruined. I wanted to make it up to him."

"But there's no way you could ever do that, Adina," Mimi insisted. "And it's not your responsibility to—"

"Stop it, Mimi," Adina was visibly upset. "You don't understand. Just like you want to make up to your parents for what you couldn't give them all these years…I…I… also have that need."

I sat there watching them, wishing in those moments that I could suddenly become invisible. There they were…wanting so badly to make up to their loved ones for what was missing in their lives. And I…I felt so spoiled, so embarrassingly pampered compared to the two of them.

"Okay, I'm sorry, Adina. You're entitled to feel the way you want," Mimi apologized. "I just think you're burdening yourself unnecessarily."

"It's not really a burden," Adina said, "Look, it brought me here. If I wouldn't have come to M.B.L.L., then I wouldn't have met you two and I wouldn't have met Hinda Klein or Rabbanit Gartenhaus, either."

"And…and you wouldn't have had the opportunity to know your mother better," I added gently.

Adina nodded. "And now that I'm getting to know her…"

"Yes?" Mimi and I both looked at Adina expectantly.

"And I read over that letter where she wrote…here, listen," Adina lifted the letter and read aloud. *"I was just thinking, Adinaleh. Wouldn't it be cute if, when you get older and you want to teach, you end up at Machon Beit Leah LeMorot? Maybe, you'll be the winner of the Goldstone Award and I'll be the proud mother shepping nachas."*

Adina looked up from what she was reading, and for the second time ever since I met her, I saw huge tears rolling down her cheeks. Yet, surprisingly, her face did not display a sad expression. No. There was no sadness at all.

"You see, I want to give her *nachas*…to fulfill her dream and make my father happy," she stared ahead pensively, her blue eyes open wide, the tears making them shine even more. "So that's why I'm going to do whatever I can to win the Goldstone Award," she went on, her voice vibrant and strong, "That's right…I'll do whatever I can!"

42

I WILL NEVER forget the wonderfully warm feeling that enveloped me when we returned to the dormitory that Sunday afternoon after Yom Tov. And I will also never forget how quickly those feelings dissipated, turning abruptly into feelings of trepidation.

When Adina, Mimi, and I arrived at the dorm, we were not surprised to find the majority of the Israeli girls already settled in. *Isru Chag* for them had been Thursday and that gave them plenty of time to help out at home, pack, and return to the dormitory by early Sunday afternoon.

Our eighth day of Pesach finished Thursday night. As soon as Yom Tov was over, we put on our weekday clothes, rolled up our sleeves, and got to work. We washed and put away Savta Hinda's Pesach dishes and helped get her apartment back in order. It took us from *Motzaei Yom Tov* through Friday morning. By early afternoon we were able to go to Geulah and Mea Shearim for grocery supplies, managing to amply restock Savta Hinda's refrigerator and pantry, with just enough time to shower and dress for Shabbos.

We ate with Savta Hinda at the *Rosh Yeshivah*'s house—a home that was really becoming a second home for all of us. By now we were no longer strangers to the various family members, as well as frequent guests at the Schpitzmans' table, and we delighted in the delicious food and friendly atmosphere, along with the spiritually uplifting *divrei Torah*. But the greatest pleasure of all was watching Adina come out of her shell and flourish under the shielding, compassionate arm of the elderly Rabbanit Gartenhaus.

When the *Rosh Yeshivah* sliced through the warm and tasty *shlissel* challah and gave everyone a piece, he prayed aloud that the *schlissel*, the Yiddish word for 'key,' should help unlock the gates of sustenance for us, just as Hashem had provided for *B'nei Yisrael* after their first Pesach in Eretz Yisrael. Until then, he explained, the Jewish Nation had been dependent on the *mann*—the open miracle that Hashem had rained down upon them to provide them with their daily nourishment. But then, not long after entering Eretz Yisrael, each person had to toil and work the land in order to have food. "This too," he told us, "needs the blessing of a daily miracle.

"Sometimes," he continued, "when people work hard for something and then eventually see success, it can *chalilah* blind them into thinking that it was their own hard work that brought it. We must always remember that, yes, we must work hard to reach our goals, but ultimately, the key to success in all our achievements comes from the *Ribbono Shel Olam*'s blessings."

The children were very excited when his knife scraped against the metal of the key and he then triumphantly lifted it high up in the air for everyone to see. As I looked at that metal key encrusted with challah, I suddenly remembered a different key. That was when Geveret Spitz's words that I had read aloud to Mimi so many months before, vividly came back to me…

Every educator must continuously strive to create tactics and strategies to pierce the soul of each student. How can I open the door to this child's soul is a question that every teacher must ask herself. One may never give up. No door is impenetrable, no problem is unsolvable, and no one is a lost cause. Every closed door has a key… you just have to find the right one.

I looked at Mimi and then at Adina and felt my eyes filling. *Every closed door has a key…you just have to find the right one…*

And for a fleeting second, I wondered about my own door. *Has it also been closed all this time and will I ever find my own key?*

On Sunday morning, we decided to return to Meah Shearim. Mimi wanted to order some gifts for her family and friends in Barclay and I decided that it would be a good idea to order rings for my sisters with

Chapter 42

their names on them as well. We did not get to leave Yerushalayim until after we finished the sumptuous lunch that Savta Hinda prepared for us, which turned out to be at a fairly late hour. We were not worried, though. There was no need to rush back early, since classes were not resuming until Monday morning and we knew that our arrival late Sunday afternoon would give us plenty of time to unpack and resettle ourselves back into dorm life.

So as I mentioned earlier, it was not surprising for us to find the Israeli girls sitting around in the lounge—and not in their rooms unpacking. What was surprising, though, was *how* they were sitting around.

We had been dragging our suitcases from the lobby toward the main staircase, completely oblivious to what was taking place right then in the nearby lounge. Other groups of girls were arriving at the same time as us and we all greeted each other warmly, recapping our Yom Tov experiences, in no hurry to go upstairs. Everyone seemed to be in a jovial mood, laughing and giddy, while hauling luggage that was too heavy, resulting in our playfully bumping and falling over each other. I remember feeling grateful about how happy I was coming back this time to the dormitory, compared to the way it had been for me way back in September.

Passing by the opened lounge doors, I glanced nonchalantly inside, expecting to see the usual scene of girls relaxing, reading, and schmoozing. Instead, what I saw gripped me with a sudden sense of foreboding.

The girls were sitting on the edge of their seats, grasping *sifrei Tehillim*, and swaying back and forth fervently.

My eyes first met Mimi's and then Adina's. All at once, we dropped our suitcases on the stone floor and rushed inside.

"*Mah karah?*" Mimi whispered to Carmella Sinai, who was sitting nearest the door.

"*Lo shamaten?*" She looked deliberately from Mimi, to Adina, to me. Her eyes rested on me. "*Sara, at lo debart im Mazal?*"

"No," I shook my head, my heart sinking. "I just got back. What happened?"

In hushed tones, she told us that a short while earlier Mazal called the dorm and said that her grandmother's condition had taken a turn for the worse—a drastic turn making the situation critical. She begged everyone to gather together and say *Tehillim* for Margalit *bat* Miryam.

Ignoring our luggage standing in middle of the hallway, we removed several *sifrei Tehillim* from the shelves, pulled over a few chairs, and joined the group of Israeli girls. As the minutes passed and more girls arrived in the dorm, they too joined our circle of girls wrapped together in prayer. At one point our *eim ha-bayit* came into the room and joined us. A tremor ran through me. Does she realize *who* she is saying *Tehillim* for?

I glanced at Mimi and Adina. They were looking into their *sefarim*, their lips moving along with the others. Guiltily, I looked back into my *Tehillim*.

We continued saying various chapters together, with one girl reciting each *pasuk* aloud and the others repeating after her. Then, after around an hour passed, Geveret Katz stood up and solemnly told us how wonderful and caring we all were, but that now we should go on with whatever we were doing and that in the merit of everyone's prayers may Mazal's grandmother have a complete recovery.

Mazal's grandmother? I felt like running over to her and shouting, *your mother, you mean! Your mother!*

But of course I could not say anything…yet.

Slowly, we mounted the stairs, lugging our suitcases with us. Gone was the cheerful bantering of an hour earlier.

All at once, I froze in my place. *Gila's husband must have returned to work on Friday or maybe even on Thursday! Surely by now he has an answer for me.* I had not yet checked if there were any messages waiting for me. Well now, there was no time to lose! I had to confirm what happened all those years ago to the missing Yitzchaki baby. And I had to do it now! *Now, before it would be too late!*

"Sara, why are you just standing there?" Adina asked.

"I'll be up soon," I managed to say, before I rushed back down the steps I had just climbed.

I hurried into the *eim ha-bayit*'s office, and after being given permission to make my call, dialed Gila's telephone number. There was no answer. I tried again. *I'm so nervous, I probably dialed the wrong number.*

Chapter 42

The telephone kept on ringing. I glanced at my watch. *Of course, there's no answer. The kids aren't sick anymore and are probably at the babysitter, and Gila must still be at work,* I thought disappointedly.

I trudged back up the steps to where I had left my suitcase and bags. They were not there.

I went all the way upstairs to the room next to mine, knocked and entered, and noticed that Mimi had just finished undoing the buckles of her suitcase.

"Did any of you see my suitcase and bags?" I asked.

Mimi flipped open the top of her suitcase. "Adina, did you see Sara's suitcase?"

"I certainly saw it on the staircase. Why, what's the problem?" She placed a neatly folded blouse on top of her perfectly piled stack of blouses. "Is it missing by any chance?"

"I left it on the steps. I ran to call Gila to ask her if she had any news for me—"

"Well, did she?"

"No, Adina—I mean, I don't know, maybe she did. I tried calling her, but she's not home."

"She's probably at work." Mimi took her slippers out of her suitcase, dropped them onto the floor, and then slipped her feet inside them. "Why don't you take it easy and wait until—"

"I *can't* take it easy, Mimi! Mazal's grandmother is dying and Geveret Katz has no idea that she's the missing—"

"And you have no idea, either, Sara." Adina lifted a dress from her suitcase and began shaking it vigorously to remove its creases. "It's just a theory."

"It's not *just* a theory!" I walked over to Adina's bed and plunked myself down beside her suitcase. "It makes perfect sense. I know it. I feel it inside me...Geveret Katz *is* the missing Hodaya."

"Come on, Sara. You can't just go by a feeling."

"I'm not, Adina. That's why I need Gila's husband to get me the proof—to show us in writing what happened to the missing Yitzchaki child. And now that he's going to check the adoption files—"

"But who says that she's even in them, Sara?" Mimi took her sleeping sweatshirt from her suitcase and stuffed it under her pillow. "I think you're setting yourself up for a major disappointment."

"Not true, Mimi. And especially after I met Geveret Katz's father—I mean—her *supposed* father. Remember what I told you? He looks exactly the way Geveret Cohen described the *shomer*."

"Sara," Adina said, "I'm really surprised at you regarding this whole thing. Usually you're so sensible…"

"She's sensible and practical and even very factual," Mimi sang out and then added, grinning, "but she also has a great imagination."

I stood up indignantly. "Now you're making fun of me!"

"I'm *not* making fun of you," Mimi protested. "I just think you're getting carried away."

"Sara, Mimi's just trying to protect you from getting hurt. What happens if you're mistaken?" Adina asked. "It's true that your theory makes sense, lots of sense. But imagine how disappointed you'll be if you're wrong. And then what?"

"Well, I'm sure I'm right about this, Adina. And besides…lots of times people hope things will turn out a certain way and then, if they don't," I argued, "life just goes on."

"Sara," Mimi interrupted, apparently trying to change the subject, "I think you'd better *just go on* and unpack already. But first you've got to find your missing suitcase."

"Wait and see, you two. Eventually when the truth comes out, you'll be claiming you were part of it all along. You'll see," I entered the tiny wash-up closet and mumbled, "But now I better go and find out what happened to all my stuff…"

I pushed open the door that led into my room, and there were my bags and suitcase sitting on the floor between the two beds, awaiting my return. A warm feeling enveloped me. Mimi and Adina had lugged everything the rest of the way upstairs!

They really are great friends— even if they won't go along with my Geveret Katz/Hodaya Yitzchaki theory. And as disappointing as it felt, I had to admit, I really could not blame them for trying to keep me grounded.

I lifted my suitcase off the floor and heaved it onto my bed.

"Sara, are you coming?" I heard Mimi's voice before I saw her. "Oh, good, you found your suitcase."

"Yes, Mimi, and…thanks."

"It wasn't just me. Believe me, after carrying mine up the all these stairs, I couldn't lift another one by myself. Adina helped me drag it."

"It's almost *shkiyah!*" we heard Adina calling through the doorway. "Are you two coming to the library?"

"Yes…we're coming." Mimi led the way out of the room with me following quickly behind, and then, stepping over the threshold, she announced with a flourish, "And now, ta ta da dum! We're here!"

Adina and I chuckled. *Boy, am I going to miss Mimi when I return to Rolland Heights!*

My eyes met Adina's and I smiled. "Thanks for lugging up my suitcase for me."

"No prob," she looked at Mimi and then at me, grinning. "After all, what are friends for?"

And suddenly my heart broke out into the widest, most amazingly fantabulous smile ever after.

But this time I would not allow my happiness to depend on the satisfaction of a growing and fulfilling friendship, as I had over a month ago, at the conclusion of *Metamorphosis*. No, as special and as meaningful as this friendship was, it was not enough. Because even though I was certain that nothing could ever again pull us apart, there was still something else I wanted.

It was not just my friends' approval that I craved. I needed my own approval of me. And I was planning to get that through the Goldstone Award.

Oh, I knew the competition was stiff—M.B.L.L. was full of hardworking, brilliant girls. But I also knew that no one ever before had a *Proyect* that was based on helping an elderly Yemenite mother reunite with her long lost kidnapped daughter. And the way I planned on tying it together with the work I was doing with Ronit blended beautifully with my *pasuk*. My idea really was quite clever and unique, and I was sure—absolutely, positively sure—it would work!

But, in order to reach that goal, I would have to act fast.

As soon as I finished *Minchah*, I went to the *eim ha-bayit*'s office to call Gila and found the office door locked. *How could I have forgotten?* Of course Geveret Katz had already returned to her cottage for the night.

Now, I would have to use the public telephone. I went all the way up to my third floor room to find some *asimonim*, and then remembered that I had used them all up before Pesach and had not yet replenished my supply.

When I reached the dining room, the usual clattering of cutlery touching dishes and lively chatter of girls eating together was completely absent. Instead, one voice echoed throughout the room and into the hallway.

Rabbanit Abrams was giving a "welcome back" speech. Feeling my cheeks growing hot, I slipped into the room, edging my way along the wall until I came to the table where Mimi and Adina sat. I slid into the first empty seat I found.

I could not concentrate on what Rabbanit Abrams was saying. I kept thinking of Mazal, her grandmother, and Geveret Katz, and how I must make that call to Gila immediately—before it was too late.

Well, Hashem is in charge, I tried telling myself over and over again. *If it's meant to be, it'll be. Look how Hashem arranged for me to be with Mimi and Adina over Yom Tov—even though that wasn't the original plan, and how He took the three of us and put us together, enabling our friendship to deepen and grow in a way like none of us ever experienced before.*

So, if Hashem wants this reunion to happen, it'll happen. I'm doing my part by trying to prove that Geveret Katz is the missing Yitzchaki child. All right, so I can't deny that I'm dreaming of being this major heroine and hoping that in the long run it'll also help me with the Goldstone Award—but, well…what's wrong with that?

If I end up helping someone else and I also help myself at the same time, what harm does that do? As long as I'm doing the right thing…

I stood up, applauding along with everyone else, as Rabbanit Abrams finished her speech and made her way out of the door.

"Do any of you have any spare *asimonim*?" I asked at my table once supper commenced and conversation resumed.

"No way," Mimi answered. "I used them all up before Pesach."

"I have some, Sara," Tova said, "but not here. They're in my room."

"Are you sure the telephone is working?" Devorah asked. "Last I heard, it was broken."

"That was before Pesach, Devorah," Naomi told her. "By now, for sure it was fixed."

"I wouldn't be so sure," Devorah replied. "How would they get a repairman in over Pesach?"

"Pesach was over Wednesday night."

"But the dorm was closed."

"That's true…"

"So does anyone have any *asimonim* down here?" I tried again.

"What good are *asimonim* if the telephone doesn't work?" Tova asked.

"*Mah at omeret?*" Odelya suddenly jumped in. "*Hatelephone b'seder.*"

"Odelya, *at betuchah?*" I asked hopefully.

"*Betach ani betuchah, Sara. Tziltzalti ha-baytah lifnei sha'ah.*"

"So, does anyone have any *asimonim* down here to lend Sara?" Adina asked.

I looked at her gratefully.

"Sorry."

"No."

"So do you mind, Tova, if we go upstairs to get them?" I looked at her anxiously. "I have this really important phone call I need to make."

"I'm starving. I hardly ate a thing all day. But I could tell you where to find them. Go to my room and…"

Once again I ran upstairs, but this time I only had to go to the second floor. As per Tova's instructions, I breathlessly made my way into her room. There they were, stuffed into her sock—which was sitting in her shoe in the corner of her closet, just as she had said.

Finally, I let out a deep sigh, *I'll be able to call Gila.*

I went back to the first floor and into the lounge where the public telephone was and, following the directions for how to use the *asimonim*, inserted them through the slot and dialed the number.

I heard ringing.

Please answer, I implored.

The telephone continued to ring. *Why isn't she home? Doesn't she have to give her kids supper…put them to sleep? What's going on?* The ringing stopped.

I tried again and the same thing happened. I slammed the telephone down onto the receiver.

What should I do now?

Return to the dining room? I had no appetite. Try again? What for? *Oh, I know what. I'll try Mazal. Maybe she'll be home.*

When I called her, she was indeed home, despite the terrible situation with her grandmother. As she explained to me, someone needs to run the house, and the biggest help she could be to her mother was to keep the home ship sailing and say *Tehillim* the rest of the time.

I told her that we were all concerned, and that everyone had gathered together in the lounge to say *Tehillim*, and that we even made a *mishebeirach* for her grandmother.

She expressed her gratitude and her hope that it would indeed help her grandmother have a *refuah sheleimah*.

"But I do not think it will happen, Sara."

"What?" I clutched the receiver more tightly than necessary. "Hashem can send a *refuah* in a second, Mazal. After all, with all the *Tehillim* being said and—"

"I very thankful, Sara, and I too believe Hashem can do *nissim*. But Savta now is—"

"Yes?"

"She understand everything now. She like different person from person you meet. The same Savta like I remember before. No…not exactly the same."

"What do you mean?" I asked, trying to understand.

Mazal's voice came through the receiver firmly. "She not the same—she seem sharper, her mind stronger than I can remember from before."

"Oh."

"That is why, Sara, I think it near end," her voice caught. "All the time I know her she never this *tzlulah*. Ima say it is like she remember Savta, how Savta was when Ima was a little girl. This is how Savta was before, in Yemen. The way she talk with Ima now. She so…"

"Normal?"

"*Kain.*" Mazal stopped talking for a few moments. I heard her quiet sobs. "*Ani mefachedet shehasof higiah.*"

Chapter 42

Tears were dripping down my cheeks too. "Mazal, don't cry. Please. It's never too late."

"*Hayta la kol kach harbei tzarot b'chayeha,*" Mazal's voice came out muffled, "*kol kach harbei tzarot.*"

"Mazal…listen." I wiped my tears with the edge of my sleeve. "I've been trying to find your mother's missing sister. And I think—"

"*Mah?*"

"I said I've been trying to find Hodaya. You know…your mother's missing little sister."

"I not hearing very good." I had to pull the receiver away from my ear because she began speaking very loudly. "What did you say?"

"I said," some girls began entering the lounge and I was forced to lower my voice, "I said I have been searching for your mother's missing sister."

There was silence on the other end of the line.

"Hello…hello, Mazal. Are you there?"

"Yes, I here. How? How can this be possible?"

"It doesn't matter, Mazal. I just wanted you to know that we are working on it. I'm hoping to have an answer very, very soon."

When I hung up from Mazal and dialed Gila's telephone number, I knew—I just knew the answer *would* come soon. *Very* soon.

And this time I was compelled to do something about it—immediately.

43

"MIMI, ADINA! IT's him! It's her! It's him!"

"What?"

"I said it's him, Mimi, it's him and now we know for sure it's her!"

"Sara, pardon. But, what are you making such a—"

"You heard me, Adina," I was practically jumping, I was so excited. "We've got to go now. I just found out, it's him!"

"Who's *him*?" Mimi leaned forward at the edge of her seat.

I glanced quickly around the dining room and saw that there were still a few girls left sitting around talking, some *bentching*. I lowered my voice, but it was steely with determination. "I'll tell you later. Just come with me now, fast...both of you!"

"Sara, would you take it easy?" Mimi pointed to the salad in the middle of the table. "Have something to eat."

"Eat?" I looked at her incredulously. "How can I even *think* of food at a time like this?"

"Time like what?" Adina's eyebrows lifted.

"Please!" I pulled on Mimi's arm while looking beseechingly at Adina. "Just come!"

Mimi doubtfully began to rise. "All right, Sara, but I wish you'd explain what's going on."

"Listen to me, Mimi...Adina." My heart was pounding hard against my chest as I looked from one to the other. "Please! I'm sorry, but there's no time to explain anything right now. Just come with me."

"Where are we going?" Adina asked as she and Mimi followed me out of the dining room and into the hallway.

"Right. What's all this mystery about?"

I put my finger over my lips and threw Mimi a guarded look. "Soon," I mouthed, while leading them to the front door.

I pushed the door open and we were greeted by a soft breeze carrying the fragrant scent of lilacs toward us.

"Now will you tell us what's going on?" Mimi asked as soon as we stepped outside.

I nodded while letting out a deep breath. "We're going to see Geveret Katz now."

It was one of those beautiful, mid-April Upper Negev evenings, with perfect air—not too hot and not too cool. The crickets were buzzing softly in the background and the sky was a clear velvety black, with twinkling stars scattered about. That is the picture the camera of my mind snapped just then, and when I dig down into those invisible albums of the unconscious and recall that night's atmosphere, that is what I remember. But at the time, I am sure I did not notice anything around me and neither did Mimi or Adina.

Who could pay attention to our surroundings at a time like this?

"Now?" Adina asked. "You want to go to Geveret Katz now?"

"Why?" Mimi moaned. "Come on, Sara. Did Gila just tell you that Geveret Katz is the missing Hodaya Yitzchaki?"

"Yes!" I sang out happily.

"What?"

"Well, not exactly. She said…she said that they found the name Yitzchaki among the adoption records." I kept walking as I spoke. "And guess who was in charge of the adoptions listed in the same folder as the Yitzchaki baby?"

Mimi shrugged. "I don't know. What difference—"

"Who was it, Sara?" Adina's eyes narrowed. "Was it her father? Geveret Katz's father?"

"Adina…Adina…" I grabbed her hand and started singing and skipping along the graveled path, pulling her along with me. "Yes, yes, yes! The name on the top of that folder was…Michael Benshalom."

"I don't believe it," Mimi shook her head, then quickened her steps to keep pace with us. "I absolutely don't believe it!"

"Well, Gila wouldn't lie. And besides, I never told her that Geveret Katz's father's name is Michael Benshalom," I said impatiently, but with a smug smile. "And so you see, he handled her adoption. He wanted a child so badly, and Geveret Cohen reminded him of his murdered daughter. But she was too old. He knew he'd never get away with kidnapping her. She was too mature to suddenly be told that she had a new father. So—"

"So he took the baby?"

"Right."

"Come on-n!" Mimi said mockingly.

"Why? We know that the *shomer* kept hanging around near the Yitzchaki's barrack. Geveret Cohen told us all about it."

"But who says that Michael Benshalom was the *shomer*?"

"He handled the adoptions—"

"So maybe he handled the adoptions. That doesn't mean he was the *shomer* and it doesn't mean—"

"Mimi, even *you* heard Geveret Katz telling us that her father was a *shomer* in a camp for Yemenite refugees. And her parents are from Warsaw and I even—"

"Mimi, think about it," Adina interrupted. "There are too many coincidences."

"Thanks, Adina," I said, gratitude showing in my eyes. "Come on, Mimi, we're here already. Let's go in…I can't exactly break the news to Geveret Katz by myself, and who knows how little time Mazal's grandmother has left."

Mimi was still hesitant. "But what if we're wrong?"

"We're not wrong, Mimi. Come on, trust me. Let's go."

"Sara, it's not right to just barge into Geveret Katz's cottage."

"So what should we do? Wait till tomorrow? By then it might be too—"

"Hello girls," we unexpectedly heard a voice through the opened kitchen window. A light went on over the small porch leading into the cottage, the door opened, and Geveret Katz stepped onto the porch. "I thought I heard voices out here. Is everything all right? Did you girls need something?"

I can still picture how we must have appeared to Geveret Katz just then. Three pale-faced girls standing dumbstruck, one next to the other on the gravel path leading up to her cottage—like deer caught in a car's headlights. Then Mimi and Adina slowly turned and looked at me, waiting for me to speak.

Me?

I looked helplessly at Mimi, but Mimi just shrugged and looked right back at me, waiting. I turned to Adina, but she just waited patiently for me to begin.

My gaze fell on our *eim ha-bayit*. Her dark eyes stared back into mine, puzzled. "Are you sure everything is all right?" she asked.

"Sara wanted to tell you something," Mimi said. Mimi, of course, would not allow a situation to remain indefinitely tense.

Yet, what I had to say was fraught with tension. *How does one begin something like this?* I opened my mouth and then closed it.

Geveret Katz took a step forward. "Yes, Sara?"

"I...you know...Mazal's grandmother..."

Her eyes flashed alarmingly. "You've heard something? Did anything happen?"

I shook my head. "*Baruch Hashem*, she's...she's still all right. I spoke to Mazal before...right after *Minchah*."

"And?"

"And her grandmother...she's more lucid now than she's been in a long while...at least that's what Mazal's mother told her."

"You mean, more lucid than before she fell ill?"

"Um...no...more lucid than she's been...since...since her baby was stolen from her."

"Stolen from her?"

"Yes," I nodded. "When she came from Yemen..."

"Ah...in the *ma'abarot*? I had no idea," she shook her head sadly and repeated, "I had no idea. I had heard such stories...but until now I never actually knew of anyone involved..."

I glanced first at Mimi, then at Adina. Their eyes were focused on Geveret Katz. I was hoping that one of them would say something to help me out, but they just stood there watching her and waiting for me to continue.

I took a deep breath, "So...um...when Geveret Cohen told us what happened and we understood the seriousness of Mazal's grandmother's condition we...we decided—"

"*Sara* decided," Mimi mumbled.

"*We* decided," I repeated, hoping Geveret Katz had not heard her, "to...to try...and find the missing daughter."

"You what?"

"Um...we decided to try and find the missing daughter."

"That's what I thought you said." She had a bemused expression on her face. "So...how did you go about this—ahem—search?"

"Well," I began hesitantly and then the words began to flow as my confidence grew, "we...we found out that there are records...documents regarding some of the adopted children from that particular camp stored in the basement of the Be'er Institute and—"

"You girls received permission to go to the Be'er Institute?"

"No," I shook my head, "in one of the families that we do *chesed* for...we...*Mimi, Adina* and I," I glared at each of them deliberately (and beseechingly) while emphasizing their names, "the husband works there and he has access to the archives."

"That's interesting. He works in the archives department?"

I shook my head and corrected myself. "He got permission to access the archives."

"I see. And was he helpful?"

"Until tonight we...he wasn't really getting anywhere. B-but tonight..."

"Yes, Sara. What happened tonight?"

"Geveret Katz," I suddenly blurted out, "it must be *min HaShamayim*. Tonight, Gila's husband—Gila is the woman we do *chesed* for—discovered the name of the missing child, Hodaya Yitzchaki, on a list of children that were adopted."

"And it gives the name of the family who adopted her?"

I shook my head, "No...of course not. But it says the name of the man who handled her adoption. And it's obvious to us—"

"Obvious to Sara," Mimi inserted.

"It's *obvious* that this man is the same man who took this child and adopted her."

"How is it obvious, Sara? These things are usually kept top secret.

Chapter 43

Most adoptive families and even the biological families don't necessarily care to have this information publicly accessible. I can't imagine that in this case it says on the paper that the man who handled the adoptions adopted one particular child."

"That's true, but the whole time they were in that camp, the *shomer* in charge kept looking longingly at Mazal's mother. He had lost a young daughter during the war and seemed to desperately want another child, but his wife had become mentally ill and had to be institutionalized. So—"

"So you think that this *shomer* took the baby for himself, since he was also in charge of the adoptions?"

"Yes," I nodded, "yes."

"And now you found out the name of the *shomer*?"

I nodded again, this time my eyes filling.

"And you think that all these years the baby was with him, growing up in his home and thinking that *he* was her real father?"

"It...it could be she knew she was a-adopted, but had no idea that it...it was done illegally and...and that really she'd been k-kidnapped," I stammered. "And that she has another family...her *real* family."

"Am I to understand, Sara, that you would like to approach her now...and reunite her with her dying mother?"

I could not answer her. For so many months I had been dreaming of this moment. I had not realized, though, that while bringing joy, it might also cause much pain to the daughter who would be forced to face her father's betrayal. So instead, I did the only thing I could do.

I slowly nodded.

"How do you know where she lives and how do you know if she's even alive?"

"Be...be...because..."

"Because Sara found out," Adina continued for me softly, "that the name of the man who was in charge of the adoption was Michael Benshalom."

"Michael Benshalom? My father?"

Again I nodded.

"And...and you think I'm the missing daughter?"

The tears were rolling down my cheeks. I do not know how I did it, but somehow I managed a faint yes."

"And now you've come here to tell me...so that I, the supposed missing daughter, can run to the arms of Mazal's grandmother and—"

"And let her see you once again before she dies," I finally cried out.

If this had been a play, at that point the music would have reached a crescendo. Tears would be running down the cheeks of everyone in the audience. And indeed, all the actresses on stage would be weeping and falling gratefully into each other's arms.

But it was not a play. It was real life.

And in real life, there is a real Director Whose script is not necessarily what the audience hopes for or the actors demand.

All at once Geveret Katz started laughing.

And laughing.

I looked at Adina, Adina looked at Mimi, Mimi looked at me, and we all looked at Geveret Katz. But none of *us* were laughing.

I know *I* was about to cry. Hard.

"I'm sorry," Geveret Katz finally sobered and said. "Sara, it was really very commendable of you. But you are mistaken. *Completely* mistaken."

I will not go into detail of what happened next. I will not specify all the various proofs Geveret Katz gave me, demonstrating clearly that although she was adopted as a child, she was not nor ever would be Hodaya Yitzchaki. I will not attempt to describe what it was like sitting in her kitchen when she called her father and had him describe his job as *shomer* of the Tel Tzion Refugee Camp, where he not only ran the camp (and *only* that camp), but also handled numerous legal adoptions (and *only* legal adoptions) for many refugee orphans during that time.

Included in his list of accomplishments was the legal adoption of his and his late wife's third child, the orphaned baby Esther, whose parents both died shortly after they reached Israel, from an illness they contracted in the Yemeni desert. She even showed me copies of her biological parents' death certificates and old photographs and documents attesting to her adoptive father's *aliyah* to Eretz Yisrael before the outbreak of World War II, when Israel was still called Palestine.

I will not describe how Mimi and Adina escorted an utterly stunned, heartbroken, and completely mortified Sara Hirsch back to her room, and gently helped her into her bed and under the shelter of her covers, only leaving the room when they were sure she was fast asleep.

No, I will not go into detail about any of this. Even today, so many years later, I am absolutely and completely humiliated just thinking of the embarrassing blunder I made, its memory etched permanently in my mind.

And the next morning when my alarm clock rang, I absolutely did not want to get out of bed, even though it was the first day of school after the long Pesach break. Groggily, I fumbled for the "off" button, pressed it down, and retreated under my covers. My head was aching, my heart was breaking, and I was sure that I would never again leave the safety of my room.

Oh, Hashem—how could You do this to me?

There was no way I would ever be able to face Geveret Katz. *What a fool she must think I am!* And Mazal. I failed her and her grandmother too. *And just last night I was making all these promises to her. Some heroine I turned out to be!*

I closed my eyes tightly, wishing I could sleep for the next two months until I could escape into the safety of the airplane that would bring me back home to Rolland Heights. There, I would never again have to look into the eyes of Geveret Katz, Adina, Mimi, and Mazal.

Sara, how could you have been so foolish?

True, it said Yitzchaki on that paper. But it never actually said "Hodaya Yitzchaki." And Mr. Benshalom said that the name Yitzchaki was not uncommon among the Yemenite families—and during those years he must have arranged for the adoption of more than one Yitzchaki child. But, he reiterated, he only dealt with children whose parents were both dead. As he regretfully noted in reference to the missing Hodaya Yitzchaki, if it was indeed true that Yemenite children had been stolen and given to other people in a dishonest and criminal manner, then certainly such illegal activity would have been committed without leaving a paper trail that could eventually lead to the guilty parties' exposure.

Didn't Mimi keep telling me that I didn't have adequate proof? Why didn't I listen to her? How could I have been so unreasonable? And now, what do Mimi and Adina think of me? No friendship, not even the best, could withstand something like this!

Ugh! I just can't take this anymore! I pulled the covers over my face. *I ruined everything...everything! My friendships with Mimi and Adina and even Mazal; my Proyect—I was counting on this. My whole theme revolved around the story with Mazal's grandmother; my reputation—what Geveret Katz and her father must think of me now. I'm ruined, totally ruined...Oh, I am an utter failure! I'll never ever trust myself again!*

If only I could fall asleep...escape to those tranquil turquoise waters and let myself drift off into the sea's peaceful depths—

"Sa-ra!" a voice called to me from a distance.

I'm not here!

"He-llo, Sara!" the voice sang as it drew closer. "Time to get up. Rise and shine!"

Go away! I stuck my head under my pillow.

"Come on, Sara. You've got to get up already. You don't want to be late the first day back after such a long vacation."

I don't care if I'm late...I don't care if I never go to school again...I don't care about anything! I tried burying myself deeper into my mattress.

"Hey, maybe she *is* still sleeping," I heard the voice mumble to itself. Then I felt hands shaking me. "Are you still sleeping by any chance?"

I did not move, pretending to be.

"Um...Sara, do you hear me? I need a blouse. I forgot to wash my uniform blouses before Pesach, so I don't have any clean ones now."

Sure!

Then, another voice came through the wash-up closet. "Mimi, what's going on? She's still sleeping?"

"I've been trying to wake her, Adina. I really think she's up, but she's probably ignoring me."

Determined, quick footsteps approached my bed. "Sara, enough of this. Out of bed," Adina's voice commanded, "now!"

"No," I mumbled from under my pillow.

"All right," Adina said in a clipped manner. "So stay in bed the rest of your life. After all, you made a mistake, so now you're ruined forever."

I sat up abruptly, my pillow falling onto the floor.

From the corner of my eyes, I saw Mimi throw an admiring "how-

Chapter 43

in-the-world-did-you-do-that?" look at Adina, except Adina did not seem to notice. She was looking directly at me.

I looked back at her helplessly, but Adina, her blue eyes penetrating, demanded that I speak.

"I—I feel so foolish," I finally managed to say.

"Everyone can make a mistake," Mimi announced cheerfully. "But we love you anyway."

Adina ignored her. "You don't just feel foolish, Sara. I think you're really angry."

I sat up straighter. "Huh?"

"Yes. You're angry at yourself—angry that you made such a big mistake."

"Anyone can make a mistake, Adina," Mimi repeated, this time more determinedly than before, a bewildered expression on her face.

Adina waved her hand dismissively at Mimi, her eyes still focused on me. "You're angry at yourself and—"

"Could you... just leave me alone?" I was close to tears.

"Of course you want me to leave you alone, Sara, so you can continue to lie here and wallow in self-pity." She took a step closer to me. "But I won't...because I care. And maybe it's time for *you* to start hearing what you've been telling me."

My eyelids blinked. *No, I will not cry!* I lifted my chin. "I...I don't know what you're talking about."

"Adina, like I said before," Mimi interjected, "anyone can make a mistake."

"Will you stay out of this, Mimi?"

Mimi's face paled and her lips clamped shut.

Adina brusquely turned back to me. "You're also angry at Hashem, Sara."

What? The nerve! She's just trying to get back at me for all those times...And she says she cares? Angrily, I threw my covers to the side and swung my legs over my bed, stamping them onto the floor. "I don't know why you're saying all this, Adina Stern! Could you just—"

"Leave? I should leave?"

"Yes—both of you!"

"Why? So that you can slam your door on us?"

"Adina!" Mimi stepped forward.

"Mimi, I told you to stay out of it!"

"No, Adina," Mimi's green eyes flashed, "we came in here to comfort her, to get her to get up and ready for school, not to—"

"You're wrong, Mimi," Adina's blue eyes glared back. "She doesn't need some sweet little cream to salve her poor little disappointed nerves. I know what kind of comforting she needs."

"She needs us to be friends, Adina, not—"

"I *am* being her friend and right now she needs a little taste of her own medicine. Just because something didn't work out the way she wanted it to, she falls apart!"

"She's upset, Adina. She made a big mistake and she's—"

"That's right, Mimi, she's upset, because Hashem didn't follow her script and now she's feeling so helpless and—"

"I'm *not* helpless!" I protested. "And I'm *not* falling apart!"

They both turned to me.

"So why won't you get out of bed?" Adina looked me steadily in the eye.

"Because I…" I looked down at my hands on my lap.

"Because you what?" Adina's voice softened.

"Because…because…I can't. I'm so ashamed and angry at myself. I thought…I really thought…it made so much sense. Mimi," I lifted my eyes and turned toward her, "I can't believe how I kept on insisting. You kept telling me—"

"It's all right, Sara. Like I said before, everyone makes mistakes."

"But I was so sure and," I looked at Adina, "and maybe you're right. I am angry. Angry at myself for believing in something that turned out to be so wrong…and…and for dragging you both down there with me, and for everything else that happened with this…with Mr. Benshalom, with Geveret Katz, for disappointing Mazal. But…"

"But what?" Adina prodded.

"I don't know…I didn't think…how could it be that I'm angry at Hashem? It's not His fault that I made such a fool of myself."

"But it didn't turn out the way you wanted," Adina insisted, "so you—"

"So she was *disappointed*, Adina," Mimi stressed. "That doesn't

Chapter 43

mean she was angry—"

"Disappointment," Adina said, "is a quiet kind of anger...isn't it? And weren't you the one, Sara, who told me that whatever Hashem does is perfect? So if you're disappointed, then that means you're angry at the way things turned out and you're not finding Hashem so perfect now, right?"

"No," I shook my head forcefully, horrified at such a thought, "of course not. I just thought...it made so much sense. I just thought..." I looked away.

"What did you think, Sara?" Mimi asked.

"I—I thought things would turn out differently. I thought Hashem would..."

"Would what, Sara?" Adina crossed her arms, waiting. "Make everything turn out 'happily ever after'?"

"Well, not exactly, but—"

"But that's pretty much what you thought, Sara. I remember that day when we had just left the library in Devorah. You said Hashem would help and I told you that if He had wanted to help, He wouldn't have permitted the kidnapping or whatever it was that happened in the first place. And you thought I was some kind of *apikores*."

"I did not!"

"You did—and now it didn't work out the way you hoped and so—"

"So she's disappointed, Adina, *disappointed*, not—"

"Right, I'm *just* disappointed," I looked gratefully at Mimi. "I thought...I hoped..."

"Yes?" Adina's arms were still crossed in front of her chest.

I looked at her. "Okay, Adina, so I'm a little more than just disappointed."

She nodded knowingly.

"Of course, I wanted to help Mazal's grandmother and family and Geveret Katz. It's true, I thought there would be this wonderful reunion," I swallowed hard, mentally adding, *and I thought I'd become this wonderful heroine for all of you to look up to and admire.*

"Right," Adina was tapping her arm with her finger, "and it didn't happen that way."

"Right," my voice broke, "it sure didn't."

If anything, it turned out the opposite for me. I looked away ashamed and bit down hard on my bottom lip. Any respect I thought I had earned from them in the past, any flowering of friendship I thought had taken root between us, was surely gone by now.

"Sara," Mimi said. "At least you tried."

"Right...and look how it all turned out," I mumbled.

"That's just my point," Adina told Mimi. "She tried and it didn't work out, so she falls apart."

"I did not fall a—"

"Sara," Mimi interrupted, "maybe this is your kind of challenge. Remember what we spoke about?"

"Challenge?" Adina's rough laugh stabbed me. "She tries to solve a mystery, is convinced she has all the answers, and finds out she made a mistake. That's a challenge?"

"There are all different kinds of challenges, Adina," Mimi quietly told her.

"I certainly wouldn't mind *that* kind of challenge, Mimi. It sure beats our kind."

"Well, no one asked us Adina. No one gave us a choice…"

No one gave us a choice.

Mimi was right. No one asked her if she preferred to have her learning disability, even though it came together with an outstanding personality, over my feelings of inferiority and my desperate need to be some kind of heroine; no one asked Adina if she would rather her mother and father had not had their brief but wonderful marriage and instead of her mother dying so young lived a life like Rochel Leah's mother, separated from her husband—but a living mother nonetheless. And no one consulted with Mazal's grandmother either. No…no one gave us a choice—at least not in this world, as Geveret Abrams had explained to me.

But is Adina also right? Am I guilty of "falling apart"? Am I really angry at Hashem because things didn't work out the way I wanted and instead went according to His plans?

And is that a challenge? Are these relatively small tests really challenges or are they complaints about nothing? And are complaints about nothing really challenges that one must work on to grow from?

"Adina," I suddenly found myself saying, as the tears I had somehow kept in check until now slowly began trickling down my cheeks, "you're right. I'm extremely grateful to Hashem for giving me two healthy parents all these years…wonderful parents. So…so maybe you feel like laughing at me…at my foolishness, at my making a big deal out of what you think is nothing. But you should know, as much as you think *I* have things easy…you should know…it's…it's still not as easy as you think."

I brushed my finger tips against my cheeks, trying to wipe away my tears, wishing once again that they did not flow so easily. Feeling completely foolish, I looked down, studying my nails.

"You know, Adina," Mimi wedged herself in between me and my nightstand, "it's true. None of us can judge the next person's challenges." She placed her arm comfortingly around my shoulder and then added, "After all, it's not like these…these challenges come in One Size Fits All."

And then the most remarkable thing happened!

Adina sat down on the other side of me. "I—I'm sorry, Sara. I didn't mean it to sound that way. Stop crying…please."

I did not look up. I wanted her to continue. There is something especially satisfying about having the person you so desperately want to like you sit next to you and try to get you to stop crying.

"I…I was just trying to help," she explained.

"Some help," I murmured.

"Really, Sara," Adina's tone sounded startlingly anxious, compelling me to shift my gaze to her. I could not believe it! Her eyes glistened. "Our…friendship really means a lot to me. I wasn't trying to hurt you, Sara."

I looked into her blue eyes. Incredibly, they were tinged with a kind of urgency. "Then…why, Adina, why?"

"Because, Sara, it's…it's the way I feel. I always thought you had everything. You know…your wonderful family, the way you're able to give so freely of yourself to others. I…I wanted to be like you."

"Like *me*?"

"Yes. You have…what I always wanted. And then…and then you

helped me. You pointed out certain things to me...that I myself was not aware of. I thought that now maybe I would do the same for you. I said what I said because...believe it or not, I really, really care."

"And...and you were just trying to help me?"

"Yes, she was," Mimi was emphatic.

"It's strange," Adina continued tentatively, "it never was like this with me before. I...I don't understand it myself, but for the first time in my life, the two of you have gotten me to really care about you. And now I don't want anything to come between us."

"But I made such a fool of myself," I sniffed, while reaching for a tissue on my nightstand. "How will either of you ever trust me again?"

"Anyone can make a mistake," the sides of Adina's mouth turned upward and once again her smile reminded me of the sun breaking through the clouds on a rainy day. She winked at Mimi. "Right, Mimi?"

"Right," Mimi grinned back, while handing me the box of tissues. "And the main thing is to realize that the three of us have something incredibly strong between us. Each of our own situations, challenges—whatever you want to call them—the negative parts mixed with the positive parts, have brought us together, connecting us to each other."

"If...one of us does something," Adina said, "that the others don't understand...it's all right. We have to be there for each other, no matter what."

I looked at Adina through teary eyes. "No matter what?"

"Yes, Sara, even...even if I sometimes think you're making a big deal about nothing."

I started.

She held up her hand. "I mean...I have to try to be more understanding...like Mimi. Challenges? I guess everyone has different challenges."

I relaxed.

"And, Sara, you should know," her gaze held mine, "if it wasn't for you, I wouldn't have opened up so quickly to Mimi, and if it wasn't for Mimi, there's no way I would have shared so much with Savta Hinda and Rabbanit Gartenhaus. I would have just gone on...never having ever experienced this closeness, this openness with others. I wouldn't have found anything out about my mother. All these questions I've been carrying around with me...all these doubts. You...you have to try to understand me."

"I do, Adina."

"She does, Adina," Mimi insisted, "she really does."

And if I thought this morning's conversation was evolving into something I could never have foreseen, Adina's next comment *really* caught me entirely by surprise. "You're both the best friends a girl could ever ask for..."

I felt a new rush of tears, but this time they were tears of happiness.

If only my other dream could also become a reality!

And it was just about then that the next surprise took place...

"So that's what friends are for," Mimi said pragmatically. "Even if one friend doesn't understand why something's so important to the other, or if one friend flops at something—"

I winced.

"You've still got to stick together," she continued, "through thick and thin."

Thick and thin, I swallowed hard. *The good times as well as the hard times...*

All at once, a sudden surge of adrenaline rushed through me as a new thought entered my mind. *The good times and the hard times. YES! It'll work!* I thought excitedly, *it really will work!*

Until that moment, I had thought that my chances of winning the Goldstone Award were gone forever.

Ever since Purim, I had planned on tying it all together—the search for the missing Yitzchaki daughter and the theme for my *Proyect*, and I had worked diligently along that line of thought. It had blended flawlessly with my *pasuk*, run smoothly with the work I was doing with Ronit, and threaded seamlessly around all my different experiences that year. With characteristic attentiveness, I had been working on it during all my free time and was sure that, along with the success of finding Mazal's aunt, the theme of my *Proyect* would flow in perfect precision, leading me to become the recipient of the Goldstone Award.

And then the previous night, when my colossal mistake was discovered, I thought it was all over. All my dreams…gone!

When Mimi said those words about sticking together through thick and thin, she had no idea that she had given me the solution that would save my *Proyect*. Although I knew my original plan was not going to work, I now had an even better idea.

And with this new plan, I was certain I could be…I *would* be the winner of the Goldstone Award.

Yes…the Director above did not forget about me.

There was, though, one niggling thought in the back of my mind. If I won, then Adina and Mimi would not. These two girls, who were so close to me and who each held a significant part of my heart in a way no one else ever had before, and who each wanted so much to be the winner of the Goldstone Award—could not be the winner if I was.

I tried to comfort myself.

Mimi, I knew, could never win. *No…no way.* Yes, she was creative, she was perceptive, and she made incredible strides throughout the year. Even the teachers had periodically complimented her on her enormous progress during the previous months. But, putting her *Proyect* down on paper—constructing it properly, this was not something that was feasible for Mimi, even with my help. *And yet, who knows,* I thought with a glimmer of hope. *Maybe Mimi will find some way to succeed. Maybe she'll become one of the honorable mention winners.*

I thought of Adina. Until that seventh day of Pesach, after Adina said *Yizkor*, after she finally felt that deep connection with her mother, she had never aspired to be the winner of the Goldstone Award. And then, all at once, it became her greatest wish! No, Adina did not have a need to be noticed as I did. Adina always stood out, whether she wanted to or not. Yet, Adina had a different need. She wanted to fulfill her mother's dream and she wanted to please her father in a way that no one but she could grasp. This is what would make Adina happy. But did I want her to find happiness at the risk of not attaining my own?

Three friends. Three friends whose ties ran deep, whose souls were intertwined. All wanting the same thing.

The painful feeling I experienced with this thought cut deeper than I could ever have imagined. And yet, it did not prevent me from still wanting to be the winner, especially after this latest fiasco. I now had to be the winner...*needed* to be the winner to prove myself more than I ever had before.

If only it were feasible for there to be three winners!

Well, if this were a fairy tale, then everything would turn out happily ever after. Mimi and Adina could be the two honorable mention winners and I could be the main recipient of the award. Mimi would be quite content with that and Adina, who had only harbored her dream for a short while, surely would not be disappointed with that either. And of course, they would both be happy for me.

If this were a fairy tale.

A great big *if*.

44

LIKE ALL FAIRY tales with happy endings, we made it into Rabbanit Greenstein's class just in the nick of time, right before she entered the room. I do not know how we did it, but we did.

Breathlessly, we slipped into our seats as Rabbanit Greenstein took hers, Adina and I sharing with each other brief, but relieved, smiles.

Those smiles, though, did not stay on our faces very long.

Life, after all, is not a fairy tale.

As soon as *Chumash* class was over, Rabbanit Greenstein informed me that I was wanted, along with Adina and Mimi, in the *eim ha-bayit*'s office.

In Geveret Katz's office? *Oh no! There's absolutely no way I can face her after last night.*

We left the school building together, making our way through the weaving flowered paths that led to the dormitory, wondering all the way why she wanted to see us. Mimi and Adina tried dismissing my fears that she must have informed Rabbi Grossman about what happened—and that he now wanted to have a word with us. They also attempted to allay my other worry—that her father, Mr. Benshalom, was sitting in her office wanting to discuss my unfounded suspicions. Mimi and Adina both claimed that it was impossible, that Geveret Katz was not the type to dwell on things, and that what happened the night before was over and done with.

I hoped they were right. I could not imagine anything more

embarrassing or uncomfortable than facing Mr. Benshalom and/or Rabbi Grossman.

I was wrong.

When we reached Geveret Katz's office, she was sitting at her desk, the telephone receiver wedged between her left ear and shoulder, while she was jotting something down on a piece of paper. She saw us and gestured with her free hand in front of the desk, indicating that we should pull over a few chairs.

Gingerly, we sat down and waited for her to complete her phone call.

When she hung up, she looked at us and let out a deep sigh. "About forty minutes ago I received a telephone call and sent a message to your classroom for you to come here as soon as your class was finished."

"Rabbanit Greenstein told us," Mimi said, "and we rushed right over."

She studied each of our faces for a moment and then allowed her gaze to rest on me before continuing. "I know how close you all are with Mazal Cohen. You must know who her other good friends at M.B.L.L. are too. I'd like you to make a list of all those girls who are close to her and…and would want to go to…to her grandmother's *levayah*."

"*Levayah?*" And then, to make sure I had heard correctly, I repeated the word again, this time in English. "Funeral?"

"Yes," she nodded sadly, "she passed away early this morning. The *levayah* will take place in a couple of hours. They're just waiting for all the relatives living in Israel to reach Kiryat Yosef."

I shook my head slowly, trying to grasp what she was saying.

"Sara, I know that you were Mazal's roommate and that you two, Adina, Mimi," she nodded to each of them respectively, "were in the room next door. But I'll need you to put a list together of the rest of the M.B.L.L. girls who'd want to attend. Tehilla Friedlander was already informed, and she will be in charge of arranging the Beit Yaakov HaNegbah contingent."

"Um…will there be a bus?" Adina asked.

"Yes, it'll be leaving in less than an hour from the gates in back of the courtyard, so you need to work quickly. I don't want to cause any unnecessary disruptions and that's why I want you to take care of this as soon and as discreetly as you can. Later in the day an assembly will be arranged. But in the meantime…"

We went to the funeral that day in Kiryat Yosef, and around ten days later Mazal rejoined us at M.B.L.L. There was no "welcome back" party for her, but she was greeted warmly by everyone. I wondered if her return would now affect my relationship with Adina and Mimi next door—and if so, how.

At the beginning I hardly felt Mazal's presence. She spent most of the time with Tehilla, catching up on the work she had missed. Mimi and I continued studying together and reviewing our schoolwork on a daily basis, and we still went to the resource room and worked diligently with the students there. Adina and I shared talks and thoughts between classes, consulted one another when either of us had a question on a school assignment, and enjoyed taking long walks together in the nearby woods. At night, the three of us talked and talked—philosophizing, analyzing, schmoozing, and giggling.

We spoke of our families, the future, our fears, our hopes and dreams. But there was one thing I never mentioned to either of them…my wish to become the winner of the Goldstone Award and the goals I hoped to achieve through it.

Although Mimi, having discovered my poem so many months back, was aware of my "prop complex," she had no idea that I fervently believed that the award was the antidote I needed to cure me of such feelings. Adina, of course, knew nothing of these deeply hidden thoughts.

At least that is what I thought.

At certain times of the afternoon and evening, we would each go our own ways—to the library, lounge, our individual rooms, and sometimes to a secluded spot in the garden or onto the new patio outside the library to work on our *Proyect*. Graduation was approaching and the momentum was building. Even those girls who had no aspirations to win the Goldstone Award still had much work to do, for their *Proyect* had to be completed properly in order for them to graduate and receive the coveted Machon Beit Leah LeMorot diploma.

My heart would fill with a mingling of pity and guilt every time I saw Mimi walk off with her files and notebooks. She was taking it all so much more seriously than I could ever have imagined and I blamed myself for having put such an unrealistic goal in her head. And then, to assuage my guilt, I would offer to help her, but she would smile and firmly turn me down.

"No thanks, Sara," she would shake her head, her green eyes twinkling, "You've got your own *Proyect* to do, and besides, if I win, I want it to be because I was able to do it on my own."

"But, Mimi…" I protested, knowing she could really use the help.

And then that mischievous gleam would enter her eyes, making them sparkle even more than they usually did. "Don't worry, Sara," she let out her deep, throaty laugh, "I've got my ways of doing things…"

After a while I gave up volunteering my assistance, but those guilty, pitying feelings did not give up on me.

With Adina it was different. I could not deny Adina's brilliance or her perfection in anything she did and everything she accomplished. I had to admit that I often felt threatened by the realization and resulting fear that one of my closest friends was also one of my strongest competitors. But then, I would remind myself, Adina did not become serious about the Goldstone Award until the end of Pesach, and although she was certainly capable of putting together a more superior *Proyect* than most people, I had been working on this from the beginning. *Besides*, I thought hopefully, *there really could be three winners…*

Even with our preoccupation with our schoolwork, student teaching, and *Proyect* research, the bonds of our friendship did not weaken. The opposite occurred. With each passing day we drew closer to one another, our friendship becoming stronger than ever before. The worries I had about Mazal's reentry into our lives and the changes that might result from it, proved unfounded. Adina, Mimi, and I really were a trio. We had shared things with each other that we had never before shared with anyone else, and nothing could uproot that.

I hoped.

The special closeness I had with Mazal, despite the language barrier and cultural differences was still there, but it took time after her long absence for us to readjust to one another. Mimi, Adina, and I tried to include her in our nightly talks as well. And it became clearer to me than ever before—when true friendships are shared—the flame that ignites one, combined with the others, becomes greater, not smaller.

She spoke to us about her grandmother; we discussed death, old age, loneliness, marriage, teaching, *shidduchim* and so much more, into the early morning hours.

Occasionally Rochel Leah, Zehava, Chani, Rivky, Devorah, Malkie and some others would join us, mostly in one of our rooms and sometimes in theirs. Often, Mimi would take out her guitar, enthralling us with her music. We would all sing together, sometimes fast-paced, lively, cheerful tunes and sometimes the slow, soul-searching ones—our bodies swaying in unison and our voices lifting jointly in harmony.

And as the weeks began rolling by faster than I could ever have imagined and the time to confirm our reservations for our return trip drew near, a new kind of sadness engulfed me. What would happen when we all returned to our homes? Would these friendships continue or would they eventually become distant memories?

Mimi would be returning to Barclay, a two-and-a-half-hour plane ride from Rolland Heights. We could speak on the telephone, but we knew that it would never be the same as it was in the dorm, when we saw and spoke to each other on a daily basis. And despite Mimi's cheerful and optimistic façade, I knew she was quite fearful of life back in the "real world." How I wished I could go with her and give her the support she so badly needed!

It was Adina, though, who had important decisions to make. London or Ballington? The familiarity of her grandparents' home, with its quiet formality and inevitable loneliness, or entry into her father's new family life, amid the natural chaos of young children, where she was uncertain she would ever find her place and truly belong.

Ballington was only twenty minutes from Rolland Heights by car. I knew what I wished Adina's choice would be.

And then one day—it was late afternoon—I unexpectedly found out about a new, troubling situation facing Adina.

Mimi and I had completed the homework due for the next day and had even managed to review all the material for our *Chumash* final. We still had a good two and a half hours left until supper. Mimi went into her room to work on her *Proyect* and I sat down at my desk to work on mine.

I had just finished arranging my material and opening up the *sefer* I

Chapter 44

was going to be using, when Mimi sauntered in to tell me that she was going someplace else to work on her *Proyect*, and that if anyone came looking for her (she didn't know where Adina was), to tell them that she would be back by suppertime. Until then, she would be working and did not want any distractions.

I recall shaking my head and smiling as I watched her walk out of my room, carrying her *Proyect* material in one hand and her tape recorder in the other, and thinking, *that's Mimi!* Even if she tries to be studious, she still abhors the quiet of working alone and needs to listen to lively music.

Around a half-hour went by. I had been sitting in my room by myself, completely absorbed in my *Proyect*, when I heard Adina's quick knock as she glided inside.

I twisted around in my seat and all at once I saw that her eyes were red and puffy.

I stood up. "Adina, what's wrong? What happened?"

"Do you know where Mimi is?"

I shook my head. "No. Why? What happened?"

"Where could she have gone?"

"She went somewhere to work on her *Proyect*." I swallowed hard. "I guess I'm not good enough."

"Not good enough?"

"Yes, to tell me what's bothering you. You prefer Mimi."

"Oh, I'm sorry, Sara," she sat down on Mazal's bed. "No, it's just that I once discussed this with Mimi and…and now it's come up again."

"What's come up, Adina?"

She hesitated for only a moment. "He wrote me, Sara. He wants me to stay longer."

"Who wrote you and who wants you to stay longer?"

"My father. He wants me to stay here at least until the Tuesday after graduation…because…because my mother's *yahrtzeit* is on *gimmel Tammuz*."

"So what's the problem?" I asked, looking at her red-rimmed eyes. "You didn't confirm your reservations yet, did you?"

"You don't understand, Sara. My father wants me to stay so that I'll go to the cemetery where she's buried."

"Oh!" I gulped and sat down next to her. "I'm sorry, Adina, I didn't realize what you were trying to say. He wants you to go on her *yahrtzeit*."

"Yes...on her *yahrtzeit*."

"And...and you don't want to."

"No, Sara...I don't," she shook her head, her eyes filling. "First he convinces me to go to *Yizkor*...and now this."

"Adina, why don't you want to go? Was it so terrible...when you stayed for *Yizkor*?"

She shook her head again. "But this is different."

"Why?"

"Because...because it just is. I wrote to him already that I'm not going."

"Why don't you think about it first?"

"There's nothing to think about. He's been writing to me about this for a while—telling me about my mother's *yahrtzeit*. He keeps saying that now that I'm in Eretz Yisrael it would be a good opportunity for me...but I already wrote to him a few weeks ago that it's out of the question. I'm not going."

"And now he wrote again?"

"Yes. He sent me this big envelope. He wrote about how important it is that I go...and that he expects me...at age eighteen to make the right decision and go. There were some letters from his wife's children—colorful drawings, a card saying, 'We love you, Adina' and—"

"Adina, that's so nice!"

"Really? So nice? They hardly know me...but write 'we love you.' Come on, Sara."

"I mean that they sound so warm and friendly. Adina...come to Ballington. We'll be near each other and maybe you'll end up liking Bina and her children. And if you don't feel so comfortable there, I'm only a twenty-minute car ride away." I rushed on, "You could always come to my house and spend time with us. You'll meet my mother, Shuli, Chevy—"

"I told you already...my grandparents told me their home is always open." She stared ahead and then added tersely, "I still have to decide."

"Well...I just want you to know, Adina, how happy it would make me if you would be close by."

"Anyway, my father's wife also wrote to me."

"Bina Scheinerman?"

Her eyebrows lifted. "Bina *Stern*, Sara, *Stern*. I don't even know what *I'm* going to call her."

I bit my nail. "So what did she write?"

"She wrote about the first time she went to her husband's *kever*, you know—the husband who died."

"Um...I figured that's what you meant."

"You know, Sara, all this time I never thought of Bina as someone who also suffered a major loss."

"Well...it's understandable, Adina. You were surrounded by so much of your own suffering."

"So, she wrote about how difficult it was for her to go to her husband's *kever*...like by going...it was almost admitting that it really happened. She said that until she went, it was as though she was in denial that the accident had really happened. And by going...she was finally able to face the facts and begin...begin to heal."

"Adina...maybe this is what you really need. Maybe deep down...you feel like your mother left, but will come back..."

"You know, Sara, sometimes I do feel that way."

"But meanwhile, Adina, you...you're kind of angry at her for leaving. Maybe by going to the *kever*..."

"I'll get rid of this anger?"

I held my breath. This was the first time Adina ever admitted to being angry at her mother for leaving. It was also the first time she did not react angrily toward me for suggesting it. "I don't know, Adina, but it can't be bad for you to go...especially on her *yahrtzeit*."

"I really don't want to go...it's so hard for me."

"Adina...if I go with you...if I stand right next to you, then would you agree to go?"

It took a long time. I cajoled her by speaking about the wonderful opportunity of healing this could turn out to be. I warned her that she wouldn't have another chance to go there, specifically on the day of her mother's *yahrtzeit*, for a long time. I reminded her of the feeling of contentment that came over her when she said *Yizkor* and I condemned her for trying to punish her father by not going. Then I went through the whole cycle again and again until Mazal came in to get something and warned us that we had better hurry down or we would miss supper.

As soon as Mazal left the room, Adina let out a deep breath and said, "All right, Sara, if you'll go there with me, then I'll go."

We tearfully hugged each other.

And then to my utter amazement, Adina looked me straight in the eye and said, "Sara, you know…I don't have to tell you…how much our friendship means to me."

"It…it means a lot to me too, Adina," I replied hoarsely.

A shadow passed over her. "It's different for you, though, Sara, than it is for me."

"W-why?" I stammered defensively. "I-I knew I wanted to become friends with you r-right away—"

"That's not what I mean."

I felt my cheeks growing hot. "Huh?"

"For you, Sara, this thing, friendship…it's not new. But, until you and Mimi, I never opened up to anybody."

"You were afraid to."

She nodded. "Yes, I was afraid. My mother left me…I was so young. Then…then my father—"

"Adina," I placed my hand tenderly on her shoulder, "you don't have to explain."

"But I want to. Sara, I was afraid to trust my feelings to others. I remember…" her voice suddenly broke, "I was only three and a half years old, but still I remember that feeling of loving…of loving my mother and being loved by her and by my father. And then…"

"I know, Adina, I know," the tears were sliding slowly down my cheeks.

"So, I locked those feelings away. And somehow, you and Mimi found the key—and opened things up for me."

I watched Adina pull a few tissues from the box on my nightstand. She handed several to me and then blew her nose. A moment or two passed and the only sounds in the room were of Adina and me sniffling.

"Sara...," she began.

I lifted my face. "Yes, Adina?"

She was looking me steadily in the eyes. "Sara, can I tell you something...something that's been buried deep in my heart and I never shared with anyone ever?"

I held my breath. "Of course, Adina."

"I use to think...I use to think that I'll never want to get married. I didn't think I had it in me to trust someone else...to love someone else. Not my husband...not my babies..."

"But now you see you really could. Right?"

"I think so," she nodded slowly. "I'm telling you all this, Sara, because I think you're right....about the *kever*. I think that by going to my mother's *kever* on her *yahrtzeit* with you...with the one person I can really trust...I'll be able to finally start to live..."

"Oh, Adina, you will! We'll go and you'll see things will really turn around for the better."

"You know, Sara, when I was the mother in *Metamorphosis*, something inside me began to—"

"Open up?"

"Yes," Adina smiled and then chuckled lightly. "I think you're beginning to know what I'm thinking, Sara."

"I think that's because I think a lot about you." I grinned back.

"So thanks, Sara. Thanks for thinking about me and thanks for letting me lean on you." And, as we made our way down the steps a few minutes later, she added, "You know, Sara, I owe you one."

"Owe me?"

"Remember that day when you stayed back with me to go to the dentist and missed going to the *kevarim* with everyone else?"

"I remember," I replied. "I can't believe that I've been here for almost a whole year and haven't yet gone to Kever Rochel and Me'aras HaMachpelah."

"So, Sara, since we'll be in Yerushalayim that day, let's arrange to go to the other *kevarim* too. That's the least I can do...for such a loyal friend who's always there for me whenever I need her."

Yes, as the weeks slipped past, our friendship deepened and grew beyond any expectations, and I found myself wishing more than ever that Adina would choose to return with me to Ballington, rather than live in England.

I was in middle of talking over Adina's dilemma with Mimi one afternoon during our walk back to the Beit Yaakov HaNegbah campus. We had stayed a little later than usual to help Geveret Spitz finish up some work in the resource room, and decided to first detour to "town" to check if there was any mail at the post office before returning to the dorm.

"I wish that was my situation, Sara," Mimi said as we turned onto Rechov Amsdorf.

"Excuse me, Mimi," I stopped short, "but aren't you the one who told me not to be jealous of other people's situations? Besides, how could you want to be in Adina's position?"

"That's not what I meant, Sara. I was just trying to say that I wish you and I could be twenty minutes away from each other." A shadow fell across her face. "Sara, how will I ever get a job in Barclay? How will I ever teach there?"

"Mimi, don't worry," I said as we continued walking, "You've been an unbelievable success in the resource room here. I'm sure Geveret Spitz will give you a terrific letter of recommendation."

"But Barclay doesn't have any resource rooms. There's no way I'll ever get a job teaching in a regular classroom, Sara. You know that."

"Mimi, you're really very good."

"Thanks a lot," Mimi kicked the ground sharply, "but be realistic, Sara. Who would hire me?"

I looked at the earnest expression on her face. "Mimi...maybe the school needs someone to direct the plays, maybe..."

"Come on, Sara, I don't want to direct plays for the rest of my life. I want to teach. You know that!"

"You're right, Mimi, I'm sorry."

"I want to work with children." We reached the front door of the post office. Mimi stopped walking and so did I. "I—I want to help them. Figure out what makes each child tick, what are their problems, find the keys..."

"You're very good at that, Mimi."

"And...if...if I could be one of the winners of the Goldstone

Award…I know it's a dream, Sara, but it's so important to me."

"I know."

"You see, Sara, if I could win…not only would it make my parents very proud of me…it would also open up doors of opportunity for me. It would help change the way people've viewed me all these years, it would give me the fresh start I've been desperate for…"

The door swung open and the two girls emerging from the post office nearly bumped into us. "Oh, Mimi…Sara! Yikes!"

"Hi, Malkie. Hi, Devorah," I stepped aside. "Sorry, we were blocking the door. We were just about to go in."

Mimi did not say anything. She stood trancelike, her mind elsewhere.

"It's a good thing it was only you two," Malkie went on. "I would have been so embarrassed bumping into strangers. You never know what could happen…what if it would've been an elderly person or someone from the yeshivah—"

"Well, *baruch Hashem*, it was only us."

"Anyway, I'm glad we did bump into you," Devorah said. "You've got a couple of letters, Sara."

"Oh good!" I replied eagerly.

"How about me?" Mimi was with us once again. "No mail for me?"

"Sorry, Mimi," Devorah began checking through the pile. "Nothing for you…but here, this letter's for Adina. If you're going straight back to the dorm, you could bring it to her."

"Devorah and I are stopping off first at Pinat HaGlidah," Malkie said.

"Well, if *I* don't get mail, at least my roommate does." Mimi was back to her cheerful self.

"Here, Sara, these are for you," Devorah handed me two envelopes, "we'll see you both later."

"Thanks," I said, fingering my mail as they walked off. One letter was enclosed in airmail stationery, with my home's return address written in Shuli's handwriting, and the other envelope was made from thick cream-colored paper. I turned it over "Oh wow, Mimi! Look, Chavie's invitation finally came."

Chavie had been too busy to write to me since her engagement, and so a few weeks earlier I splurged and called her. In the three minutes we had, she told me that the wedding would be on a Monday night in the last week of June. She spoke about the problems she was having with her gown. (She was planning on wearing Mindy's and the seamstress was having a hard time making the adjustments to Chavie's liking.) Then there was her apartment in Lakewood (which her *chasan* and his parents chose and she had not yet seen, but was hoping she would love) and whatever else could be discussed in a timed, three-minute unplanned telephone conversation.

At the start of those three minutes, there were a few seconds of uncomfortable silence—then we were both talking at once. Suddenly the operator was telling me that my time was up.

As Mimi and I made our way toward the end of the street in the direction of the Kfar Amsdorf woods, I tore open the envelope and took out the invitation.

"Mimi, look here," I pointed to the monogram on the invitation cover, "isn't this cute?"

"Um…I guess," she skeptically eyed the intertwined letters designed into the shape of a *shofar*. "What's it suppose to be?"

"You see, the *chasan*'s name is Yitzchak, so they made the initials into the shape of a *shofar*." I traced each letter with my finger as I pointed them out to Mimi, "*ches, alef* for Chava Esther and *yud, alef* for Yitzchak Aryeh, with a big *gimmel* because his last name is Goldberg. Isn't it cute?" I repeated while opening it up to the center.

"It is," Mimi said and then looked at me dreamily. "I wonder, Sara, what initials will come next to my two *mems* on *my* monogram."

"Me too," I giggled. "I also wonder. But, I'm glad in a way that I don't have to think much about that now. I've got Shuli ahead of me."

"And what will you do if she doesn't get engaged so soon—and you want to?"

"That's impossible, Mimi."

"Why? It's happened plenty of times when there's an older sister who is close in age to a younger one."

"Well, that's not going to happen with us. Shuli is so much more…so…whatever. It's just not going to happen."

We came to the end of the street and saw a group of Beit Yaakov HaNegbah girls heading toward the path leading into the woods. We hurried along, preferring to walk behind them rather than walking through the woods alone.

I still had the invitation open and was reading aloud as we walked. "*Rabbi and Mrs. Yisrael Hershkowitz*, they're Chavie's parents," I enthusiastically filled Mimi in and then continued, "and *Rabbi and Mrs. Mendel Goldberg*. I still can't believe she's getting married, Mimi," I commented before continuing, "*would be honored by your presence at the marriage of their children Chava Esther and Yitzchak Aryeh, Monday the twenty-second of June, Nineteen hundred—*"

"Sara, did you say the twenty-second of June?"

I blinked and, bringing the invitation closer to my eyes, read again, "*Monday the twenty-second of June.*" I felt my heart sinking. "You're right, Mimi, that's what it says."

"But I thought—"

"I know. So did I. She said the wedding is in the last week of June and that it's on a Monday night. So when I checked the calendar I assumed—she meant the next Monday, the twenty-ninth." I turned to Mimi hopefully, "Maybe she made a mistake?"

"Who? Your friend, Chavie?"

"Yes. Maybe she—or rather the invitation people wrote the wrong date. Maybe there was a misprint. Maybe they really meant to write Monday the twenty-ninth."

"It's not likely, Sara. These things get checked over and over again." Mimi paused. "So, what'll you do?"

"I—I don't know," I said numbly. "I guess I could change my ticket."

"There'll be a charge, but it's probably not a big deal considering the circumstances."

"The circumstances?"

"Yes, your friend's wedding."

I stopped walking. "Mimi, what in the world will I do about Adina?"

"Adina? What's the question, Sara? You can't miss your friend's wedding for your other friend's mother's *yahrtzeit*."

"I can't? You're right...I can't. I guess, I-I'll have to change my ticket."

We continued walking silently. By the time we were once again on our way, the group we were following was way ahead of us, their voices hardly audible. We could hear the crunching sounds of our feet walking on the forest floor and the chirping sounds of the birds hopping from one branch to the next. Otherwise, it was completely silent—that is—with the exception of the loud pounding of my heart beating against my chest.

"I wonder, though, what Adina's going to do now," Mimi broke the silence.

"Huh?"

"I said, I wonder what Adina will do now—if you go."

"I was just thinking about that too."

"I wish I could stay, Sara, but, I really—"

"Can't. We've discussed that before, Mimi. You've got to leave on the eighteenth, the day after graduation, and that's that."

"I know...I wish...but if I don't go then, I won't be able to make it to camp by Monday."

"There's nothing to talk about, Mimi. You're one of the head counselors and, as it is, you'll be arriving in camp only a few days before the campers. It's impossible for you to push off your trip even one day, let alone five."

"But what about Adina?"

"Adina won't be upset with you, Mimi, that's for sure. She knew right off that you wouldn't be able to go with her."

"I wasn't worried about that. I was wondering what she's going to do. She agreed to go because of you, Sara. What do you think will happen now?"

"I don't know...I'm trying to think." A couple of seconds passed. "Mimi, is there any chance that she would go with Savta Hinda or Rabbanit Gartenhaus?"

"Rabbanit Gartenhaus is out of the question. She's way too elderly and weak. She barely makes it to her own husband's *kever*."

"How about her daughter? Do you think she would do it?"

"Adina for sure wouldn't agree to go with her," Mimi replied. "She doesn't feel that close to Rabbanit Schpitzman. She didn't have the same relationship with Adina's mother like Rabbanit Gartenhaus did. She was just a young girl when Adina's parents were a newlywed couple." Mimi shook her head again. "No, Adina wouldn't agree to go with her, and I really can't blame her."

"You're right. It's not the kind of thing you can do with someone you're not especially close to." I sighed. "I don't know why I asked."

"You asked," Mimi said, "because you feel bad that Adina agreed to go to her mother's *kever* for the first time ever *and* on her *Yahrtzeit*—only because she thought you'd go with her."

"Now you're making me feel even more guilty."

"Sorry," Mimi said, "but I guess I'm just worried that now she might refuse to go at all."

We continued on, each lost in her own thoughts.

If only Savta Hinda could do it. Adina certainly feels close to her. But will she be upset with me for backing out? She was relying on me and now she'll feel like I let her down.

"I can't believe I got the days mixed up. I really wanted to go with her."

"It has nothing to do with you, Sara. Your friend didn't consult you about her wedding date and it's not your fault that Adina's mother's *yahrtzeit* falls out on the same day."

"But I feel so horrible."

"Sara, like I just said, it's not your fault. Look, I would have liked to be there for Adina too."

"But you told her right away that you'd be leaving the day after graduation. You didn't try to convince her to go to her mother's *kever* the way I did. We spent more than two hours talking, *two* hours! I kept telling her that I'd be there with her, Mimi, I kept telling her...and she trusted me..."

As we continued walking along silently, each of us immersed in our own thoughts, the memories of that afternoon came back to me vividly...hauntingly...and I remembered how Adina said that I was always there for her whenever she needed me.

Always there for her?

"So, now Mimi, what am I going to do?" I sighed heavily, my mind returning to the present. "Adina and I spent more than two hours talking and I kept telling her that I'd be there for her, that I'd go along. If…if I don't go with her, she might not go at all. And it's so important that she goes."

"Your friend's wedding is also important, Sara. And you can't be in two places at one time." She bit her bottom lip pensively. "I know what. This Shabbos, when we go to Savta Hinda, one of us will keep Adina busy in one room and the other one will speak to Savta Hinda about the situation in the other room. If she feels able to handle it—I'm sure she'll volunteer to go with Adina."

"Mimi, you're right. If Savta Hinda can go…Adina hopefully will forgive me." I let out a deep breath.

We exited the woods in a better frame of mind than the one we had been in when we first entered it.

Yes, Hinda Klein would be our key!

Relieved of my worries, I inhaled the air happily as we stepped foot onto the graveled path that wound its way from the wooded area we just left through the garden that led to the dormitory. The aroma of fried eggplant and onions, mingled with the fragrant scent of coralberry and elder, wafted toward us. And as my eyes feasted on the multi-hued assortment of exotic plants and flowers, olive trees, and date palms dotting the surrounding landscape, a feeling of expectation filled the atmosphere and I felt my insides smiling along with it. *Yes, there's a wonderful Shabbos to look forward to!*

We had not been to Yerushalayim since Pesach, more than four weeks ago. The three of us would once again be going to Savta Hinda Klein, and a Shabbos with her was one that we anticipated with enthusiasm. Yerushalayim! The Kosel, visits with Rabbanit Gartenhaus and the *Rosh Yeshivah*'s family, *davening* within the holy walls of the yeshivah's *beis midrash*…all the guests, the great food, the comfortable quarters. It was all so special!

We would ask Savta Hinda to help us out with Adina and to go along with her to her mother's *kever* on the *yahrtzeit*. I was sure she would do it. Adina would be all right and I would get to dance up a storm at Chavie's wedding after all.

Hopefully everything would work out just perfectly.

Chapter 44

As we climbed the steps to our third floor rooms, bantering lightly, I squeezed Shuli's letter that I had stuffed into my pocket while reading Chavie's invitation. I yearned for its contents to be upbeat this time. Lately, Shuli's letters were missing the optimism that had always been so much a part of her character. Maybe things were finally turning around for the better.

The room was empty. *Mazal must've gone down already.*

I flung my book bag onto the floor, placed Chavie's invitation on my nightstand, and then sank down into my mattress while ripping open Shuli's letter.

I was just about to begin reading it when Mimi burst into my room through the wash-up closet.

I looked up.

"You're not going to believe this, Sara," Mimi breathlessly said. "Adina just told me that while we were out, she got a call from Rabbanit Schpitzman."

"Yes?" my pulse quickened.

"She told her—she said that this morning Savta Hinda slipped. They think she broke her hip!"

"How awful, Mimi!" I cried out. "That must be so painful!"

"Well, believe it or not, Savta Hinda was worried about *us*, since we're supposed to go to her for Shabbos. She wanted to make sure that Rabbanit Schpitzman called us and invited us to go to them, since she'll still be in the hospital."

"She was thinking about us?" I was incredulous. I shook my head worriedly. "That poor woman, bedridden and…all alone."

"That was my reaction too, but Adina said that Rabbanit Schpitzman told her that the girls in the different seminaries in Yerushalayim are organizing time slots, so that someone is always with her."

"Oh good! Savta Hinda always does so much for everyone else, it's about time we all do something for her." I paused for a moment. "Mimi, for sure you, Adina, and I have to make a trip to Yerushalayim to visit her."

"Of course we do. Adina said the same thing. Maybe we could get permission to go on Sunday."

"Unless we go to the Schpitzmans for Shabbos."

"Right…unless we go for Shabbos." Mimi led out a deep sigh. "Sara, you realize what else this means?"

All I could think about was poor Savta Hinda with no husband, no children…in so much pain! And what kept her going all those years? How did she survive her loneliness? How did she move on with that smile of hers that never left her face despite her lot in life?

Her *chesed*, her constant giving to others…that was her lifeline…that was what kept her pulse beating, her face radiant and shining.

And what would this do to her now…being bedridden? Would it hinder her ability to give and thus remove that beautiful light from her eyes?

"Sara, did you hear me?'

"What, Mimi…what did you say?"

"I said, do you realize what this means? If Savta Hinda broke her hip, you should know…she's going to be incapacitated for a while."

"That means—"

"That means," Mimi voice was thick, "there's no way she'll be going with Adina to her mother's *kever*."

45

"SARA, ARE YOU ready yet?"

"Yes, Adina." I glanced quickly at my reflection in the mirror while smoothing out my hair with my fingertips. "I'm coming!"

"Sara, you look gorgeous," Mimi sang out while poking her head through the door between our rooms before entering. "Adina's already in the hallway waiting."

"I know, Mimi, I'm ready. Let's go!"

We exited through my door into the hallway and the three of us dashed down the steps together and out into the late morning sunshine.

It was close to noon, and we had to hurry in order that we not keep Geveret Spitz and her family waiting. She had informed us that they usually began their *seudah* at around twelve o'clock. Despite waking up much earlier than usual and dressing and *davening* right away, we suddenly found ourselves rushing at the last minute.

We had *davened* in the lounge, then went into the dining room to make *Kiddush* and get something to eat, since we knew it would be quite a while until we would be eating our Shabbos *seudah*. We found ourselves sitting around a table in the corner of the room, contentedly schmoozing over *kakosh* cake and milk with a few other girls. I guess we must have been having such a good time chatting that we had not realized how quickly the time had flown by. Suddenly, Adina glanced at her watch and announced in a panicked voice that it was eleven-forty.

We were still wearing our slippers, so we ran upstairs, changed into shoes, and were now breathlessly hurrying along the graveled path to the Spitzs' cottage.

We did not end up going to the Schpitzman family in Yerushalayim for Shabbos, after all. We knew that they had an open home with steady Shabbos guests who slept over every Shabbos, and that to accommodate us, the children would have to give up their own beds. So although they warmly insisted that we come, we chose instead to remain in the dormitory and planned a trip to Yerushalayim on Sunday to visit Savta Hinda.

Our dorm was pretty empty, since it was not a Shabbat *chovah*, and many girls chose that Shabbos to visit families they had become attached to throughout the year. We would be returning home soon and wanted to make the most of the time we had left by spending it with those with whom we had formed close ties. Most of the Israeli girls went home too, including Mazal. Of course she invited us to join her in Kiryat Yosef. We declined her invitation, though, feeling that it would be somewhat of an intrusion for the Cohens.

The thirteen of us who chose to stay for Shabbos ate our Friday night *seudah* in the dorm's dining room. It was an evening I shall always remember…an evening where a special warmth wrapped itself around us, a reminder of the unique bonding that had taken place over the past nine months of living and learning together. We sat clustered around one table in the middle of that large room, with the flames of the Shabbos candles casting their glow on our faces and reflecting another kind of radiance mirrored in each other's eyes—the radiance of mutual love and friendship. We sang and sang until late at night, wishing we could cling to that feeling forever.

For the Shabbos afternoon *seudah*, however, we were divided into groups of two and three and placed with the various staff members at their homes on the Beit Yaakov HaNegbah campus.

The familiar and enticing aroma of cholent bubbling on the *blech* floated toward us, even before we reached the gravel path leading to the Spitzs' cottage. When we turned the bend, we could see that their door was opened welcomingly and a small toddler was standing with her slightly older sister at the threshold, anxiously awaiting our arrival.

Not surprisingly, there was not much left for us to do. The table was set, a fruit cup next to each setting and a large bowl of salad in the center of the table. Geveret Spitz, the organized person that she was, had the meal completely prepared before we came. Everything, except for the *cholent*, was already laid out on plates and platters in the refrigerator, waiting for the time they would be served.

Watching Geveret Spitz go swiftly and cheerfully from one task to the next, I told myself that when I got married and had a home of my own, I would do the exact same thing before each Shabbos and Yom Tov *seudah*. I would be fully prepared and organized just like Geveret Spitz.

The food was delicious, the *divrei Torah* inspiring, and the conversation stimulating. It was a beautiful *seudah*, and once again, as I watched her move about, I marveled at Geveret Spitz's competence and easy warmth. She had the unique combination of being super-efficient while still maintaining an easygoing manner. How I wished I too could be that way!

When the *seudah* was over, we offered to take the children to the nearby playground so that Geveret Spitz and her husband could take a Shabbos rest. We were in no rush to return to the dormitory. The Shabbos day was much longer now that we were nearing the summer months, and besides, we were glad to do something that could be of assistance to Geveret Spitz. After filling two bottles with water and juice, and packing some biscuitim into small bags, we strapped the children into their strollers and waved goodbye to Geveret Spitz, all of us thanking each other at once.

We had a pleasant afternoon at the playground. Tova and Naomi were there too. They had eaten their *seudah* with Geveret Katz and were taking her children to the playground, as well. We sat around schmoozing, alternating with one another between sitting and chatting on the benches and pushing the children on the swings. Their gleeful cries combined with our cheerful bantering caused the time to pass quickly.

When Mimi, Adina, and I returned to the Spitz cottage, the younger of the two, Breindy, was already fast asleep in her stroller and Goldie's eyes were fighting to stay open. Geveret Spitz came down the porch steps, greeting us all warmly. She kissed the cheeks of her two little children and then waved goodbye to her husband, who was just leaving to meet his *chavrusa* at the yeshivah.

Watching him walk off, she mentioned that his *chavrusa* was her nephew from Chicago, who had just come to Yeshivat Kfar Amsdorf after Pesach and that they had recently begun having these Shabbos afternoon study sessions together.

"I didn't know Beit Midrash Kfar Amsdorf had Americans learning there," Mimi commented as she and Adina lifted the stroller with the sleeping toddler and carried it up the porch steps.

I unstrapped Goldie and followed right behind them, holding the happy toddler who was no longer looking sleepy. Geveret Spitz held the door open for all of us and then took Goldie from me as soon as we were all inside.

"Thank you, girls. Let's just wheel the carriage further in. Breindy will sleep better if I don't switch her to her crib. She must be exhausted." She turned to Mimi, "Oh, you asked about the yeshivah. The *bachurim* are mostly Israelis, but they do have some Americans and other foreigners learning there, too. The kollel, on the other hand, is really a more balanced mixture."

"It didn't bother your nephew that he's from the minority of boys, that he's a foreigner?" I asked. I knew I certainly would mind being one of the only Americans, there.

"No, not really, Sara," she smiled and shook her head while kissing the top of Goldie's and slipping her into her high chair. "Firstly, I guess he wanted a change from the yeshivah he was in, and he's the type to fit in no matter whether he's familiar with the social situation or not, and secondly, I suppose the fact that his uncle is learning there helps."

"But isn't Geveret Spitz's family leaving after this year?" Adina asked.

"Actually, Rabbi Grossman and the parents in Kfar Amsdorf have asked me to stay on…and my husband is really benefiting so much from the yeshivah. Girls, could you please keep an eye on Goldie for a minute?" She began wheeling Breindy toward the back of the cottage. "I just want to put Breindy in the back bedroom. She'll sleep better there. I left some *oneg Shabbos* on the dining room table for you. I'll be right back."

We glanced at the table, then at each other, shrugged our shoulders and sat down. There were potato chips, cakes, cookies, and candies spread out before us, as well as a bottle of *mitz tapuzim*, soda water, and *petel*. I pulled Goldie's highchair toward us and broke a cookie into little pieces. By the time I placed them down on the highchair's tray, Geveret Spitz was back in the room.

"Thanks again for taking the children out." She pointed to the assortment of food on the table. "Girls, please help yourselves."

"Geveret Spitz didn't have to bother."

"Oh, it was no bother, Adina, it was my pleasure." She walked into the kitchen area that adjoined the small dining room, opened the refrigerator, and took out a hard-boiled egg, placing it on a small ceramic plate. Then, opening a drawer, she removed a sharp knife and sliced the egg into a few wedges.

She came around the peninsula that separated the kitchenette from the dining room, sat down next to us, and began feeding the egg slices to Goldie. "So, as I was saying, we had a wonderful year here, and now my husband has been asked to give a *shiur* in the *yeshivah gedolah*." She smiled at us. "We're seriously considering staying."

"That's wonderful," I said. "It would be a pity to have started this resource room program and then let it die down."

"Oh, it wouldn't die down even if I didn't stay, Sara. Like I've told you girls in the past, we've established this program in various other places in the United States. And once the seeds are sown, with *siyyata de'Shemaya*, we hope they will grow and flourish."

"Well, I hope it doesn't die down in me," Mimi's voice was uncharacteristically gloomy.

We all looked at her in surprise.

"Why should it?" Geveret Spitz asked rhetorically. "You're an extremely talented girl, Mimi—and you've proven it beautifully throughout the year. You have so much potential to be a wonderful teacher."

"In the resource room, maybe, but in Barclay they don't have any resource rooms."

"*Yet*, Mimi," Geveret Spitz emphasized, "*yet*."

"Huh?" Mimi and I both asked together.

"Maybe you'll be one of the people to help start one there."

"Me?"

"Yes, Mimi. *You.*" Geveret Spitz stood up, went around the peninsula, and brought out a platter of cut melon from the refrigerator. "I almost forgot about the fruit," she said while putting it down on the table. "Please girls, have some."

"We're so full," I said. "I don't think we can eat anything else."

Geveret Spitz laughed. "The *seudah* was finished a while ago, Sara, and I'm sure the afternoon air helped build up your appetites. Please, girls," she began assembling an assortment of fruits onto some small glass plates and placed one before each of us. "The fruits of Eretz Yisrael have a special flavor." Then, as she positioned one of the plates in front of Mimi, she unexpectedly said, "You know, Mimi, it's almost funny that *I* ended up in the education field."

"What?"

"You heard correctly. I was," she chuckled, "not exactly the world's best student."

I stopped chewing the piece of watermelon I had just put into my mouth.

"Without getting into details," Geveret Spitz went on smoothly, "my home environment was not especially conducive toward academic success. My brains certainly could have used some polishing. I had a terrible memory, poor reading and writing skills, and to top it off, the small school I went to was staffed by teachers who were poorly qualified to teach, but unfortunately were quite good at dispensing punishments."

Her home environment? School? Punishments?

"So how…how did Geveret Spitz do it?" Mimi's eyes opened wide.

"It's a long, long and very painful story, but *baruch* Hashem I did. Anyway, Mimi, the point is—as I've said many times before—there's always a solution for everything. We can't give up so easily; we've just got to find the key."

The three of us sat there shocked. Life had not always been perfect for this perfect teacher sitting before us? *How could that be?* We could not say anything—we were so stunned. Goldie, however, did not seem aware of our discomfort. She was banging impatiently on her highchair with her little plastic spoon, demanding another wedge of egg.

Suddenly, Adina spoke up. "Um…may I ask Geveret Spitz a question?"

"Of course," Geveret Spitz smiled pleasantly, while putting a piece of the egg on the highchair tray.

Goldie cooed. Geveret Spitz tickled her under her chin, causing her to giggle.

"Um…how did Geveret Spitz deal with that…er…pain?"

"What do you mean, Adina?" she seemed genuinely surprised. "As I began to experience one success after another, the pain became a distant memory. *Baruch Hashem*, I have what I have now…I don't dwell on painful memories."

"But don't you resent those teachers who hurt you? Aren't you angry at…at whomever was responsible for not giving you the home environment you needed to thrive?"

"Resentful? Angry?" she looked puzzled. "Why?"

"Because…because if those teachers would have helped you instead of punishing you and…and if your home environment would've been proper, then things wouldn't have been so hurtful. You wouldn't have had to suffer."

"Who says?"

Adina's forehead furrowed. "But…I thought Geveret Spitz said that the teachers, the home weren't—"

"I did, Adina, but who says that I wouldn't have gone through whatever suffering I went through anyway."

"I don't understand…didn't they cause it? Aren't they to blame?"

"Adina, do you remember learning in *Navi* about when Dovid HaMelech was fleeing from his son, Avshalom? Shimi ben Gerah threw stones at Dovid and cursed him."

Adina nodded. "Yes, of course."

"And what happened?"

"One of Dovid's men wanted to kill Shimi for rebelling against Dovid HaMelech, because rebelling against the king was punishable by death," Adina responded correctly and concisely, as though she had been asked the question in class.

"And, Adina, how did Dovid react?"

"He…he said that they shouldn't harm Shimi because…because…it was really coming from Hashem."

"Exactly," Geveret Spitz smiled. "A person must realize that whatever happens to him is actually coming from Hashem. Those people who do us wrong or don't do the right thing are only Hashem's messengers. So, to answer your question, Adina, no, I am not resentful or angry at anyone."

I remember looking into her light brown eyes as she spoke and thinking that she must be one of the most beautiful people I had ever met. I suppose that is what happens to someone who is so full of love and forgiveness—that there is no room left for any negativity. Her eyes retained a special sparkle and her face a unique glow…

When we made our way back to the dormitory, both Adina and Mimi were pensive and reticent. I did not have to be a genius to guess what either of them must have been thinking.

The next morning we left bright and early to Yerushalayim, in a far more talkative mood than we had all been in the day before. We had been granted special permission to miss that day's classes and we were looking forward to visiting Hinda Klein.

The three of us were sitting next to each other on the back seat of the bus, chatting pleasantly while planning out the day. Our primary destination, of course, was Shaarei Tzedek Hospital, where Savta Hinda was recuperating. However, before we went there, we wanted to find a florist stand and bring a beautiful, fresh bouquet to her. We also decided to stop off in Geulah to get something to eat. We had risen early and davened, but the dorm's kitchen was still not open when it was time to leave and catch the bus. By the time we were nearing Yerushalayim, we were feeling quite hungry.

"Do you think it'll be a problem if we go to the El Al office before we leave Yerushalayim?" Adina unexpectedly asked. "Is it necessary for me to call Geveret Katz to ask permission?"

"Oh, Adina…does this mean you've decided where you're going to live?"

"Yes, Sara, I…I suppose it's only right if I go first to my father and see how things work out with him. Later on, I could—"

"I'm so glad!" I exclaimed eagerly. "You'll be so near me!"

"Right, that's one of the reasons," she smiled at me and I thought my heart would burst.

"Hey, are you two forgetting about me already?" Mimi complained with an exaggerated frown.

"No way," I said, "we'd never do that, Mimi. You'll come to me whenever you have off from work and we'll all get together and then—"

Adina laughed. "Sara, before we make any plans, I really think I should make reservations. I figured I'd fly together with you, since we're leaving the same time and going to the same place." Her eyebrows lifted. "Do you remember your flight number?"

Silence.

"Sara? Did you hear me?"

"The flight number?" I repeated.

"Yes…you told me that you're planning on flying Wednesday, the twenty-fourth, right? Two days after my mother's *yahrtzeit*. So, it's perfect. We'll fly together."

"Together," I said dully.

"Sara, what's with you?" Adina asked.

But I was not looking at her.

I was looking at Mimi and Mimi was staring back at me.

Mimi had asked me a few times in the last few days if I had broken the news concerning the change of plans to Adina yet. Each time I shook my head, telling her that I still had not found the right opportunity, and that she should not worry, I would soon get around to it.

Soon.

Well, "soon" came and went and Mimi was staring at me with a what-are-you-going-to-do-now expression. I just looked back at her helplessly, wondering, *what AM I going to do now?*

Fortunately, right then someone (obviously an American tourist glad to find other English speaking visitors traveling in the same bus) came over to us and asked for directions to some place in Yerushalayim. Although none of us were experts on getting around there, Mimi and I tried to be as helpful as possible. We kept talking, asking. I even got up and went to some other people to find out if they knew the exact, best route to the address this woman was seeking. Right then I would to anything…anything to steer myself away from conversing with Adina about the topic of my return ticket to America.

And luckily, by the time the woman was helped—her directions written and mapped out in clear detail, our bus pulled into the main bus station and we gladly disembarked.

We unkinked our arms and legs, our joints stiff from the long ride on the bus, relieved to finally be free. My mind, though, was not free at all. It was still stuck in my latest dilemma: how to tell Adina—and would she...could she ever forgive me?

Mimi seemed to think that there was no question of what my priorities should be. Chavie's wedding took precedence over Adina's mother's *yahrtzeit*. And Adina would just have to understand.

I was not as certain.

Adina will feel that I—her good, loyal friend who she supposedly could lean on—had let her down.

I kept thinking about the slow, tentative steps taken to build our friendship. Trust was not something that came easily to Adina—life had betrayed her too many times. And then she opened up to me. She trusted me. She said that it was only because of me that she would go to her mother's *kever*. She revealed to me her deepest secret because she thought I would be there for her.

And now, how could I betray that trust?

No, Adina did not trust easily. And if I let her down, she probably would not end up going to the *kever*. She would lose the opportunity to come to terms with her mother's death, to deal with the anger, to begin to heal. She would give up on her future. And worst of all—she might never trust again.

And it would be my fault.

Because I let her down.

That's it...I'm staying and flying back with her. Mimi's wrong—I can't take an earlier flight. I'll have to miss Chavie's wedding.

Chavie's wedding? My best friend all these years...

Suddenly, before my mind's eye, I saw myself dancing vigorously with her in the center of the lively circle at her wedding. We would embrace in one of those long emotional hugs that summed up our many years of devotion to one another. Everyone would be clapping happily, looking on admiringly, and perhaps even a trifle enviously. *Oh that's the kallah's best friend, Sara Hirsch. Yes, I heard she just got back from Machon Beit Yaakov LeMorot. They've been the closest of friends forever...*

How could I give that up?

Then I saw Adina's blue eyes looking straight into mine. *Sara, you know, I don't have to tell you how much our friendship means to me.*

And then another flashback...

I think that by going to my mother's kever on her yahrtzeit with you...with the one person I can really trust...I'll be able to finally start to live...

How could I abandon Adina now?

But Chavie!

How about Adina?

Sara, what do you want to do?

What do *I* want to do?

Where would it be more beneficial, more fun, more gratifying for *me* to be? At Chavie's wedding, of course. But which choice would make me feel better...more heroic...(*Look, I'm giving up something really important to me. I'm making a real sacrifice for someone else!*) Being there for Adina, naturally.

Chavie, my dear friend, Chavie will understand...

"Sara, what's with you? In the bus, you were tuning out and now I've just asked you a question three times about which—"

"Oh, sorry, Adina," I turned to her calmly. "Everything's all right. I had...I had something on my mind," I glanced quickly at Mimi and her eyes met mine, "but it's okay right now. I've already decided."

"You've decided what, Sara?" Adina asked.

"That...that...nothing," my gaze shifted away from Adina to Mimi, "that I'm not going to do anything."

"Not going to do anything?" Adina shrugged. "Sara, you really are acting kind of strange..."

"Sara," Mimi's eyebrows lifted, "you—you're not going to—"

"No!" I gave her a sharp look to silence her, and then, anxious to change the subject, turned to Adina and cheerfully asked, "Adina, which bus do you think we should take to Geulah?"

She glanced at me curiously. "I'm not sure. That's what I was trying to ask you. It says over here on the sign that the number..."

Within fifteen minutes we were standing in one of the better-known bakery shops ordering hot potato *borekas* with sesame seeds sprinkled on top and three bottles of *mitz tapuzim*. There was one small round table in the rear of the store. We sat down, ate, drank, said a *berachah acharonah*, and were on our way to the hospital.

It was only a half-hour walk to the hospital. It took us a little longer, though, because we stopped at a flower stand to buy a bouquet of red roses and fill out the card we attached to it.

The hospital was older and seemed slightly rundown compared to the modern one in Rolland Heights, but the care and the warmth of the nurses and medical staff there more than made up for anything lacking in its décor. Or perhaps Savta Hinda's concern and tenderness inspired the various hospital employees to be so assiduous in their care of her.

She greeted us from the confines of her bed with her cheery smile. "Ah, my girls...I cannot believe it," her eyes sparkled affectionately. "You come to me all the way from Kfar Amsdorf and on a school day, when you are so busy."

"How are you?" we gathered around her and handed her the bouquet.

Her smile widened. "And such beautiful roses." She closed her eyes and inhaled, "How lovely they smell! How did you know, *shoshanim*—they are my favorite flowers. Oh, girls, you are just too wonderful to me!"

She introduced us to the various medical personnel going in and out of the room throughout the morning as her surrogate grandchildren.

They laughed, telling us that was how she introduced all her visitors.

At around one o'clock in the afternoon, when a few girls from B.R.J. and B.Y.E. showed up, we left to get some lunch. We had falafel and soda and then returned to the hospital. Mimi knew two of the girls from B.Y.E. and they spoke excitedly about camp plans until it was time for them to go.

When they left, we shared many of the events of the past few weeks with Savta Hinda—how we spent the different Shabboses, some of the *divrei Torah* we heard, and other interesting thoughts.

She really did seem proud of us...*just like a grandmother.*

Then, at one point, Rabbanit Schpitzman and her oldest daughter,

Dini, showed up.

"What are you doing here?" Savta Hinda looked uncharacteristically upset as they entered the room. "You're supposed to be at the Levi bar mitzvah."

"The rest of the family went," Rabbanit Schpitzman explained. "We wanted to be here with you."

"No, absolutely not. You belong at the *simchah*."

Rabbanit Schpitzman was visibly shaken. "But we wanted to be here."

"No," Savta Hinda was adamant, "right now there is a bar mitzvah going on and Geveret Levi will notice that the *Rosh Yeshivah*'s wife is missing."

"But I want to be here with you during your…difficulty. There are many others there. The Levis have a large family from both sides."

"No," Savta Hinda shook her head again, this time even more insistently, "there is only one you. Who says it is a greater mitzvah to help out in a difficult situation than to give encouragement to someone by participating in their *simchah*?"

Huh?

I contemplated Savta Hinda's words as we left the hospital and I thought about them as we stopped off at the El Al office to arrange Adina's return ticket. And I did not stop thinking about them on the bus ride all the way home.

They would not leave my mind.

Suddenly I was not so sure if I was doing the right thing by not returning earlier for Chavie's wedding just so that I could be by Adina's side for her first visit to her mother's *kever*.

"There is only one you,"` Savta Hinda had told Rabbanit Schpitzman.

And there is only one me, I reminded myself.

Where was the right place for me to be, with Chavie or with Adina?

46

"SARA...COULD I ASK you something?" The question was asked in a soft undertone in order that no one else would hear.

I shifted my eyes away from the *historia* notes I had been reviewing, surprised. Adina never talked during a study period. "Sure, Adina, what's up?" I whispered back.

"Are you...are you upset at me about something?"

"What? Upset at you?"

"Uh huh," she murmured, "you've seemed kind of distant...ever since last Sunday, when we went to visit Savta Hinda."

"I—I don't know what you mean."

"Maybe I'm imagining it, but it's almost...almost like you're trying to avoid me."

"Avoid you, Adina? No...no way. I—I just have a lot on my mind lately...the *Proyect* and everything."

"Oh, I guess that must be it," she smiled shyly. "Okay, forget that we had this conversation." She turned back to her notebook and I turned back to mine.

But I did not see my *historia* notes in front of me.

Instead, I saw the faces of my two friends...Adina and Chavie. Two faces that persisted in flashing stubbornly before my eyes without respite; when I did my schoolwork, when I sat in class, and when I tried to fall asleep.

I still had not gone to change my ticket reservations to an earlier date and I still had not told Adina about Chavie's wedding coinciding with her mother's *yahrtzeit*.

I did not want to miss Chavie's wedding, but I could not abandon Adina, either.

And then, of course, there was that little voice inside my head. That sly whisper that snaked its way in, slithering here and there, worming its way into my heart, telling me—commanding me in its self-righteous tone—*Sara, give up what you want to help someone else. You want to be a heroine, you really do…*

Stop! another small voice cried out. *If you did this, would you really be a heroine? Are you genuinely thinking of Adina? Are your intentions pure or is this like all your wasted attempts to turn Geveret Katz into the missing Hodaya Yitzchaki?*

And are you once again trying to lift yourself up under the guise of sacrificing for others?

And then *my* voice turned to the other voices, pleading.

But if I don't go with Adina, she won't go at all. She'll stop trusting her friends, won't she? And yet if I go with Adina and miss Chavie's wedding—I might always regret it, not knowing if that was really the right thing to do. Didn't Savta Hinda say it's not necessarily a greater mitzvah to help out in a difficult situation than to give encouragement to someone by participating in their simchah? On the other hand, I remember learning in school that it's better to go to a house of—

All at once, I stood up with a groan.

"Sara, are you all right?"

"Um…yes. I—I'll see you later, Adina." I dashed out of the room and into the hallway, leaving my books and book bag at my desk and Adina staring at me with a shocked expression on her face.

I walked down the long corridor quickly and determinedly until I found myself standing in front of the ninth grade classroom's closed door. Frantically, I paced back and forth in front of the door, waiting impatiently for the bell to ring and ignoring the stares of the passers-by. My head was aching, my stomach churning, and my heart was pounding.

When the bell finally rang, I stood off to the side while all the ninth graders streamed out of their classroom, heading off to the dining room for lunch. I remained there until the classroom was completely empty of students.

Then I knocked on the open door.

"Yes?" Rabbanit Abrams looked up from the notes she was perusing, surprised. "Oh, Sara, I didn't know anyone was here and waiting to speak to me."

"I'm sorry. I know the Rabbanit just dismissed her class and deserves a break—"

"It's not a problem, Sara. Please, come sit down."

I slipped into the seat closest to her desk.

She smiled warmly. "What's on your mind, Sara?"

"I…I have a problem." I took a deep breath. "It might seem minor to the Rabbanit compared to—"

"No problem is minor, Sara, when it interferes with a person's happy functioning in their *avodas Hashem*. So please," she turned her palm to me expectantly, "go ahead."

"Okay," I swallowed hard. "I have a friend, a very good friend—my best friend from all my growing-up years—getting married in the States at the end of June *im yirtzeh Hashem*."

"*Mazal tov*, Sara."

"The thing is—a very close friend from over here in seminary needs me on that same day for something extremely important."

"And you don't know where you should be."

"Right," I let out a deep sigh. The burden I was carrying was already feeling lighter.

"Where would you rather be?"

"At the wedding, of course."

"So why is that a problem?"

"Well, because…because this friend over here is in a…um…critical situation. Without trying to sound overly dramatic, if…if I don't go with her to her mother's *kever*—oops!" my hand quickly slammed over my mouth.

"It's all right, Sara. You didn't reveal anything private. The bottom line is you would rather go to the wedding in the States, but something quite compelling, something involving Adina's tragic past, is causing you to waver."

I nodded. "Yes, and I really don't know what to do."

Rabbanit Abrams sighed. "Sara, no one can make that decision for you. If you don't go to the wedding, your friend in the States might be upset with you. It could take away from her *simchah* and you yourself might lose out. You might never forgive yourself for missing such a beautiful *simchah*. And yet, on the other hand, Adina needs you to go with her to her mother's *kever* and—"

"And, I'm sorry to interrupt, but I remember learning in *Sefer Koheles* that it is better to go to a house of mourning than to a house of feasting."

"True," Rabbanit Abrams smiled. "But when Shlomo HaMelech says *beis mishteh*…a house of feasting, he's talking about a house of drinking, where the participants imbibe in alcohol and escape the responsibilities and realities of this world. He's not talking about a *chasunah*, which should be a beautiful and holy experience for all those in attendance."

"So are you…I mean, is Rabbanit Abrams saying that I *should* go to the wedding?"

"No, I didn't say that, Sara. I'm just saying that in this situation, the choice of where to go—the *chasunah* or the *kever*—has nothing to do with that *pasuk* in *Koheles*."

"Oh."

"Sara, let's say your friend in the United States understands and fully forgives you and you give up going to the *chasunah* to stay here a little longer. How would you feel then?"

"I…I guess…I mean I *know* I would still feel kind of bad about missing the wedding—but I would also feel good."

"Good?"

"Yes, for having given up something important to me for the sake of someone else."

"You would almost feel like a martyr?"

"Yes," I nodded, my heart skipping a beat. I was already beginning to feel like the heroine I wanted so badly to be.

"Sara, I just want to make one thing clear. When you give up something for someone else, you've got to do it because you really think it's the right thing to do—that it's what you feel Hashem wants from you and that it's not just you trying to feel heroic by pleasing another person. Sacrifices," she said firmly, "can only be offered to Hashem and no one else. If you choose to be self-sacrificing for the wrong reasons—you might not end up getting the payback you expected…"

We spoke a while longer, but as I made my way back to my classroom, my mind kept returning to what Rebbetzin Abrams had said. If a person is willing to give up something, thus causing him to feel like a hero, it might not really be true heroics after all. What happens if it does not work out as planned or if your efforts go unnoticed or unappreciated?

I reflected back to the embarrassment I felt when my Geveret Katz/Hodaya Yitzchaki theory proved false. If I was to learn anything from that fiasco, it would be that had my intentions really been altruistic, my disappointment at being wrong would not have been so devastating. I also would not have allowed myself to become so blind to the weakness of my assumptions, problems with my reasoning that were staring me in the face.

And isn't that the way it is with everything?

Like Rabbanit Abrams said, a *korban* can only be given to Hashem. And yet, I shivered, *wasn't I in the habit of doing just the opposite—sacrificing—to ingratiate myself with others?*

It would not be easy to rid myself of old habits. If I decided to stay with Adina and not go to the wedding, it would have to be because I truly wanted to help Adina and not because I wanted to come out feeling like some heroine!

Arriving at my classroom, I discovered that the girls were no longer there. Of course, it was lunchtime! My books were put away neatly in my desk. My book bag, however, was nowhere to be found. *Adina must have taken it back to the dormitory along with her own*, I thought to myself. *Well, I had better hurry up if I want any lunch. And, during today's long break between classes,* I told myself firmly, *there's a long letter waiting to be written.*

When that long break between classes arrived, I opened my notebook to a fresh page, mumbled some quick explanation to Adina, hunched over my desk, and began to write.

Dear Me, Myself, and I,

I looked up, staring pensively into space. *Isn't this really a weird thing to do: write myself a letter? No,* I shook my head. *It's really not so different from writing in a diary or keeping a written cheshbon hanefesh. Isn't this what I did when I had to decide whether to help Mimi or to let things run their course until her slot opened for Chavie way back in December?* Indeed it had helped—writing down the cold facts and viewing the situation less subjectively.

> I have an extremely important decision to make: Chavie's wedding or Adina's mother's *yahrtzeit*. And only I can decide.
>
> If I go to Chavie's wedding, I'm sure I'll have a great time and it would be extremely wonderful for Chavie to have me there. If I don't go and I explain the situation to her, I know she'll be disappointed, but she won't be insulted. She'll still have the wedding without me, and she'll still experience all the joy of being a *kallah* at her own *chasunah*. Sure, she'll miss me—but there is so much else there for her. She has a huge extended family, loads of friends, and she'll be surrounded with tons and tons of happiness that my not being there won't erase.
>
> On the other hand, if I go home early for the wedding, where does that leave Adina?
>
> She'll have no one else to go with to her mother's kever and she'll possibly end up not going at all, yet she stands to gain so much from the experience. She'll also feel betrayed by me because I had been the one to convince her to go in the first place. Sure, she'll understand. She'll tell me that I belong at my friend's wedding and she probably won't even be upset with me for very long. But, she'll lose something she was just beginning to gain. She'll lose that willingness to open up freely to others and she'll lose what going to the kever potentially could do for her.
>
> Is there really a choice?
>
> Rabbanit Abrams said that when it comes to making decisions, we must keep asking ourselves—what does Hashem want us to do? We must keep davening to Him for *siyyata de'Shemaya* to help us make the right decision to do His will. And we must try as best as we can to remove ourselves from the picture. She emphasized that it doesn't mean our own feelings don't count. She said that they certainly do and that, if in this situation, I

definitely would feel horribly disappointed by not going to the wedding, then that's where I belong.

Yes, I would feel disappointed missing the wedding, but I would also feel disappointed missing the experience with Adina and missing the opportunity to give her a chance to reconnect with her mother after all these years. I really, really wish I could be in two places at one time!

Well, I can't. So now I have to choose.

There'll be other weddings. True, there's only one Chavie, but hopefully I'll join her for her *Sheva Berachos* and she'll understand. But when will I ever have an opportunity to help Adina this way again?

And I'm not doing this to feel like some heroine. Yes, I'll feel good—good to have sacrificed one important thing for another important thing that could never really be rectified without my presence. I truly feel that this is what Hashem wants me to do, since He put me in this situation where Adina needs me more than ever and there's no one else who could take my place. Adina must never know about the choice I had to make. (That's my way of proving to myself that I have no ulterior motive.)

Well, believe it or not, I already feel better. I know it's still going to hurt and I've got a lot of explaining to do to Chavie and my parents, but in my heart of hearts I feel Hashem is pleased with my decision.

Do you sign off on a letter to yourself? I have no idea, since I never really did this before. So, I guess I'll just sign…

Love,
Sara

That night was *Rosh Chodesh* Sivan and I dialed the telephone with shaky fingers. I know my parents were shocked when I told them about the mix-up regarding the dates of Chavie's wedding and the commitment I had already made to another friend, and my resolution to abide by it. They kept telling me that I should not worry, that they would cover the cost of changing my reservation. But then, when I repeatedly insisted that it was not the money I was concerned about, I think they finally understood. I suppose they must have heard something compelling in my voice—a brief phone call was not enough for detailed explanations—because by the time our conversation ended, they told me that this sounded extremely important and that they trusted me to make the right decision.

Before I hung up, I got to speak to Chevy, who apologized profusely for not writing to me in a long time. She was so busy with everything—school performances, new friendships, studying, and everything else, that she barely had a chance to pick up a pen to write a letter.

And then she said, "Sara, really it's your fault."

"*My* fault?"

"Yep. If it wasn't for all your wonderful advice to me throughout the year, I never would have gotten so busy with making new friends. I'd still be moping around about being separated from Shoshana. But then I tried your body language idea—"

"I guess it worked, Chev."

"It sure did. Like you told me to do, I kept smiling, even if I didn't feel like it. First I made friends with the more quiet girls, and then more girls joined us, and now even the popular girls want to hang around with us. You know what?" she bubbled. "The phone doesn't stop ringing!"

"Great! I'm so glad it helped you, Chevy."

"And so did your tutoring advice. Did I tell you what I got on the math final? I got a…"

If my father had not finally taken the telephone away from Chevy, we would have continued talking endlessly. My heart lifted joyfully when I returned the receiver in Geveret Katz's office to its hook. Chevy sounded so happy and I was gratified that I had been able to help her, despite the many miles separating us.

As I climbed the stairs and headed back to my room, I found myself reviewing the telephone conversation. The first person I had spoken to was Shuli, who had answered the call on the first ring. Remembering our disturbing talk, I was suddenly not as cheerful as I had been only a few seconds earlier.

I knew from her last letter that she had begun the *shidduch* process, but just could not put her finger on what was bothering her about it…what it was she expected and what was causing such disillusionment.

Her friends from school and camp were beginning to get married, and yet, she did not feel ready to jump on the bandwagon along with them. And then, while we discussed all this, she suddenly said something that I found rather troubling.

"You know, Sara, soon you'll be coming home—"

"Right, Shuli, in just a little over a month…"

"And maybe you'll want to begin *shidduchim*. You know, after all, Chavie's getting married soon. All your friends are going to start—"

"Come on, Shuli, don't be silly. You know what a scaredy cat I am. I'm definitely not starting before you clear the path for me."

"You might not feel that way when you come home, Sara."

"Don't worry—I've got plenty to do to readjust to the real world before I can even *think* about *shidduchim*."

"You'll see, Sara, you'll see how you'll feel then…"

As I made my way into my room, I considered the many changes Shuli had encountered during her first year in the "real world," and how things were not flowing in the same easy manner that they always had for her in the past. I knew that despite her volunteering in Beis Yaakov, she must have felt like somewhat of a failure for quitting her teaching career before it even had much of a chance to get started. And *shidduchim* were also not running the course we thought they would for her. Not because people were not coming up with great suggestions for Shuli, but because *she* was so unsure of what to do with these suggestions.

Once again I thought about challenges and the "muscles" they built, enabling one to deal with all the inevitable obstacles that were bound to obstruct one's path.

I reached under my bed for my *Proyect* notebook, glanced inside it for a moment, and then tossed it onto my bed.

Something was gnawing at me.

Was it the fact that I had not yet spoken or written to Chavie? I shook my head. *No, that's not it. I'll write to her soon and when I'm sure she received the letter, I'll call her. She'll understand.* Did it have anything to do with these troubling thoughts regarding Shuli? *No. For sure that's bothering me, but I'll be seeing her in five weeks.* I shook my head again and looked at my *Proyect* notebook.

That's it! That's what's bothering me!

All these months when I had been working on my *Proyect*, I had followed a certain course according to my theme. And now, so much of what I had recently gone through was coming together and suddenly something seemed wrong. Something was missing. I was using the *pasuk*, but I was not sure that I understood it the right way, and I now realized that there was a blatant inconsistency in what I had been writing—the examples I had been giving, the experiences I had been presenting.

True, we submitted sections of our *Proyect* periodically throughout the year and much of what I had written really was excellent. But when I thought of my experiences of late, I knew there were important changes waiting to be made and a lot of rewriting for me to do.

Now when I should be practically finished, I sighed heavily, *I've still got so much work ahead of me*. Graduation was only four weeks away and the *Proyect* had to be presented one week earlier.

I just hoped I was not too late.

I got to work immediately and worked at a feverish pace. The next few days passed by in what seemed like the blink of an eye and all at once it was Shavuos.

Once again we experienced another inspiring Yom Tov, however this time most of the girls remained on campus. The year was winding down and so we preferred to stay near "home." Besides, for us non-Israelis, an additional day of the holiday would be celebrated, and since the dormitory was open, providing us *chutznickiot* with the extra *seudos*, Mimi, Adina, and I remained, along with most of the others.

And then Shavuos was over. There were two weeks left until the *Proyect* report had to be presented.

There was tension in the air as everyone frantically did their best to finish their reports, while simultaneously studying for finals. The one respite was that there were no longer daily classes to attend, enabling us to utilize every minute for studying for our tests and working on our *Proyect* reports.

Sometimes I chose to do my work out in the garden under the shade of the date palms, inhaling the scent of lilacs and freshly cut grass, and sometimes I preferred the privacy of my room with its limited distractions. Adina usually worked in the library, where she enjoyed access to the many *sefarim* lining the walls, or sometimes she worked in her room—just as Mazal and I often did. Mimi, though... Mimi worked, well, none of us were quite sure where Mimi worked. She would simply walk off with her *Proyect* paraphernalia in one hand and her tape recorder in the other, a secretive look on her face.

One day, a week after Shavuos had passed—I think it was around three or four o'clock in the afternoon—something entirely unexpected happened. Something that would affect me in ways I could never have anticipated.

I was completely engrossed in my work. I could hardly allow myself to pay attention to the time. I know that I was cuddled up on my bed, my back against the wall for support, my *Proyect* notebook leaning against my knees. I was busily rereading and correcting the pages all the way from the beginning of my *Proyect*. Much to my chagrin, I was only one third of the way through!

Mazal was sitting at the desk, fully absorbed in the pages of her *Proyect* as well. We were both working diligently, hardly stopping to talk. Even if I had wanted to, I would not have dared suggest taking a break. I knew that although she had no ambition to be the winner of the Goldstone Award, Mazal fervently wanted to earn the M.B.L.L. diploma in order to realize her dream of becoming a teacher in Kiryat Yosef. Due to her long absence, she could ill afford to waste a moment. She too had a deadline to meet.

We each worked quietly and alone at our individual spots, in companionable silence.

Suddenly, something broke that silence.

Mimi burst into our room through the hallway door, panting, "Sara, Mazal, listen!" She then ran over to the wash-up closet and called out loudly, "Adina! Come here quickly, I'm in Sara and Mazal's room! I have news to tell all of you!"

"What is the news, Mimi?" Mazal twisted around in her chair at the desk. "You make such noise. Are you *kallah*?"

I sat up rigidly. "Is everything all right, Mimi?"

"It sure is," Mimi looked at me, her eyes twinkling. Then she turned back toward the wash-up closet. "Are you coming already, Adina?"

"Yes," Adina said, "that is, if you'll let me through, Mimi. You're blocking—"

"Oh, sorry." Mimi stepped aside and, waving her hand with a dramatic flourish, beckoned Adina into the room.

"*Nu*, Mimi, *ma karah?*"

"You'll never believe it," Mimi faced all three of us with shining eyes.

"We'll never believe what?" I asked.

"You'll never believe—guess!"

"Oh no, not again," I leaned back against the wall, then sighed. "Let's see, it's going to be your birthday in…um…" I started counting on my fingers.

"Seven months," Mimi grinned. "But nope, Sara, that's not it. You're never going to guess."

Adina sunk down onto my bed next to me. "So, instead of keeping us in suspense, Mimi, tell us. I've got to get back to my *Proyect* already."

"When you hear what I have to say, you're not going to be able to concentrate on anything…"

"*When* we hear what you have to say," Adina said dryly.

"It's like this…" Mimi began excitedly. She literally looked as though she would burst. And then suddenly, she stopped. "You're really never going to believe it!"

"Mimi," I was trying not to sound impatient, "the *Proyect* is due in seven days, *seven days*! Don't you also have work to do?"

"Yes, but when you hear my news…listen," Mimi voice dropped conspiratorially. "I just spoke with Geveret Spitz. She told me that she's staying on next year at M.B.L.L. and running the resource room again."

"*That's* your news?" Adina began to rise.

"We knew that Geveret Spitz was thinking about it, Mimi." I picked up my notebook to resume working. "For *that* you interrupted us when time is of the essence?"

Mazal just grunted and turned back to her desk.

For a second or two Mimi stood in the middle of the room, a stunned expression on her face as she looked from Mazal, to me, then to Adina, who was about to return to her room through the wash-up closet. If I had not been so concerned about finishing my *Proyect*, I might have found more empathy for Mimi's somber expression and the disappointment in her eyes. But, I had a lot of work to do! I was about to turn away from Mimi, when all at once her green eyes sparkled with a fresh burst of life.

"Wait, Adina, don't go yet. I didn't finish," Mimi announced. "Here comes the main part."

"All right," Adina replied, slightly annoyed, "but really, I've got to get back to my work."

"I told you Geveret Spitz is staying next year to teach methods at M.B.L.L. like she did this past year," Mimi continued with a lilt in her voice. "And she'll continue running the resource room in Kfar Amsdorf. But for next year, she requested to have an assistant to run the resource room along with her. And guess who was offered that position?"

Adina stood stock-still. "Who?"

I sat up straight. "Who?"

Mazal's jaw dropped open.

"Who?" Mimi let out her deep throaty laugh. "Who do you think?" She stepped forward and pointed to herself. "Me. That's who!"

47

ON JUNE TENTH, one week before graduation, we handed in our *Proyect* reports. Finals were over, classes were no longer in session, and the only academic requirements awaiting completion were the oral presentation and question session regarding our *Proyect* that was scheduled over the next few days.

Each of us was to meet individually with Rabbi Grossman and a group of faculty members during our allotted time slot, where we would speak about the theme on which we had based our *Proyect*. After concluding our presentations (the written reports would already have been thoroughly examined by each member of the judging committee by the time they met with with us), we would be questioned extensively on what we wrote.

Naturally, everyone was nervous.

Everyone, that is, but Mimi.

She was the only one who walked around seemingly relaxed.

Now, had this been the beginning of the school year—it would have been completely in character. But this was June!

For months Mimi had worked on squeezing through the barriers that had for all these past years prevented her from achieving success. And she had done well—beyond any of our wildest dreams. Just like the rest of us, Mimi had thrown herself into making her *Proyect* as perfect as possible and handing it in on time—diligently working on it every spare minute for the last month.

She would go off by herself—her *Proyect* material and her "trusty tape recorder," as she called it, for company—and would disappear for hours at a time. I would swallow hard, knowing she still desperately wanted to be one of the Goldstone awardees and feeling sad because of the unlikelihood of it happening.

Then, it was time for us to submit our written reports. I asked Mimi if she wanted me to look over her hers, proofread or edit it—after all, I had seen the earlier segments of it—but Mimi shook her head no.

I was definitely hurt by her refusal. Did she think I would copy something from her *Proyect*? Or worse, did she feel too embarrassed to share it with me?

Mimi immediately put an end to those thoughts. She said that although she would be forever grateful to me for everything I had done for her until then, it would mean a lot to her if she could complete the rest of it independently.

And now, lurking in front of us were our scheduled individual meetings with the faculty committee. No, our apprehension did not simply fade away with the submission of our written reports, as it seemed to with Mimi. I know she still wanted her *Proyect* to be a success. But now that the work was done, the research completed, the report handed in—she must have felt that she could afford to sit back and relax. The hard part for her was over. Performing and public speaking had always been her forte, so naturally she would not be experiencing the same tension as the rest of us.

It could be, I reflected, *that now that she has the job offer from Geveret Spitz, she no longer has that same desperate need to be the winner of the Goldstone Award.* Her parents would already be proud of her and she no longer needed the award to open doors for her to be offered teaching positions. Her work experience next year would do that. *Maybe that's why she's suddenly so nonchalant.*

I, for one, felt better knowing Mimi had that job offer.

As much as I wanted to be the winner, it truly hurt me that my two closest friends were competing against me for the same thing. I knew that my happiness could not be complete if I won and the other two did not, but now that Mimi had something so wonderful to look forward to next year, I felt I did not have to worry about her.

I still worried about Adina, though.

Adina had lost so much over the years and felt that winning could somehow fill that void by realizing her mother's wishes. *Sara, how then could you justify walking away with the main prize over Adina*, my conscience questioned me.

And yet I could not relinquish my dream. I still wanted to win…desperately.

When my turn came and I was called into Rabbi Grossman's office, I sternly commanded my voice not to shake and my heart to stop pounding so rapidly. But neither my voice nor my heart paid attention to what my brain was telling them. My voice continued shaking and my heart beat even harder, and it got worse! My throat felt dry, my stomach was full of butterflies, and my hands were clammy. *How in the world will I make it through this?*

Well…somehow I spoke.

I was not going to abandon my dream because of a small bout of anxiety. After all, I wanted to teach—to get up in front of a full classroom of children. And here I was, petrified when there were just a few people sitting across the table from me?

People! I told myself, *they're just people!*

And then, as I continued speaking and the minutes went by, I began to relax. The staff members facing me smiled encouragingly, asking me the necessary questions in tones that were more like colleagues than judges, making them appear less intimidating and helping me to be more forthcoming. My *pasuk* took over and the words and the experiences I had gone through during the course of the year began to pour forth. The theme spoke for itself. I explained how it affected me and the effect it had on Ronit, the student I had worked with. I detailed my progress with her, showed samples, presented various *meforshim*, and exhibited the reports and charts I had created.

I could not be mistaken!

There was a perceptible charge in the room. Rabbi Grossman and the other faculty members were overtly impressed. When I exited the room, I knew I had made an excellent impression.

I let out a huge sigh of relief. It was over! There was nothing left for me to do anymore but pray and wait.

The days passed, leaving an overwhelming mixture of emotions in the air—some expressed aloud to one another and some left unsaid, but powerfully felt. Those who had not yet presented their *Proyect* were still nervous and those who had felt a measure of relief, but could not help obsessing over every word they said and the impression they had made or not made.

Like a whirling color wheel flashing its hues of red, green, yellow, and blue, a wide range of emotions spun around us, reflecting off our faces. There was excitement—we would soon be returning to our families and friends, and there was longing for those we would soon be leaving behind forever. There was that feeling of eagerness—we had our whole lives in front of us—but there was also fear for our unknown futures. Of course, there was that desire to hold onto that with which we were familiar, to remain where we were and not take that next step, coupled with an irresistible urge to plunge ahead into that daunting adult world.

Some of the girls like Mimi would be leaving the day after graduation, and therefore they spent these last days packing and saying their goodbyes to friends and family in Eretz Yisrael.

Walking around the dorm, one could see suitcases lying open on beds and dotting the floors, with clothing and various items—reminders of the past year—strewn about. How I would miss everybody and everything, and how much I longed for the continuance of these beautiful and wonderful friendships! Was it only ten months ago that all this had seemed so strange and overwhelming?

Mimi and a large group left bright and early to Yerushalayim on Tuesday morning, the day before graduation, to make their farewells to their friends and relatives there, culminating in their leave-taking of the Kosel HaMa'aravi. Mimi, I knew, would most likely be returning next year.

But...me?

I wondered how I would be able to say goodbye to the Kosel next week.

Adina and I planned on going to the Kosel after we visited her mother's *kever* next Monday, the same day as Chavie's wedding. That day, I had promised Chavie, I would *daven* fervently for her and her future husband when I visited the *mekomos ha-kedoshim*. I felt that was the least I could do!

I think that pleased her—reconciling any doubts that I had about what I was doing. Chavie, for her part, had been unbelievably understanding and forgiving. *Just make sure that you keep davening for us,* she insisted.

When Mimi returned late Tuesday night, a whole bunch of us gathered in her room, which was a hodgepodge of suitcases and cluttered paraphernalia. Although such disorderliness was completely contradictory to Adina's temperament, Adina did not seem to mind in the least. She did not even seem to notice. She just looked contemplatively at Mimi—and I knew what she was thinking. I also wondered how I would go on without Mimi's daily dosage of cheerfulness and warmth, and how much I would miss the true depth of her character and sharp, perceptive abilities.

We sang, harmonizing and swaying together as one. Mimi played the guitar, singing from the heart, her words a plea for the future, a cry from the spirit, melding all of our souls together, leading us from one song to the next. Many tears were unashamedly shed that night as we let songs and their melodies be the "quill of the soul," our hearts lifted up in prayer, our fingers intertwined around the hands or shoulders of our friends sitting next to us.

We kept on singing. More girls entered the room, somehow finding a place to sit, and joined in.

No one left.

The darkness of the night transformed before us, as the sun rose into the velvety black sky, cascading rays of dawn's golden shades before us and the moon bade the night goodbye.

No one wanted to move. No one really wanted tomorrow to arrive just yet.

But the inevitable happened. And tomorrow came.

Tomorrow.

Graduation day.

My heart pounded. This was it. This was what I had been waiting for. This was what prompted me to come to M.B.L.L. in the first place.

And it was only a few short hours away.

I *davened* carefully, but I do not remember if I ate anything that morning. I cannot imagine that I did or that I even *could*.

As the hour drew near, I returned to my room, grabbed my stuff, made my way down the hallway, and showered. I wrapped myself in my white terry robe and blow-dried my hair more slowly than usual. *Was it really only ten months ago that I stood in my bedroom at home, wrapped in my mother's terry cloth robe, and slammed down the top flap of my suitcase as Chavie rang the doorbell? Is it really true that I almost didn't come?*

I dressed and then looked in the mirror, studying my reflection carefully. I had to make sure every hair was in place, that my white blouse and navy blue skirt were perfectly smoothe, that I was completely presentable. *If I win and I'm called up to the stage…*

Steadily, I made my way with Mazal, Mimi, and Adina down the dormitory steps and out into the early afternoon sunshine. We were joined by other groups of girls. Some were giggling and bantering lightly and others (like me) were more subdued as we followed the paved path that led to the Beit Yaakov HaNegbah building. The entire high school student body, as well as all faculty members, would be in attendance in the main auditorium. After the speeches ended and the awards were given, each girl (hopefully) would receive her diploma. This was to be followed by a gala banquet prepared by Geveret Mendlowitz and a group of grade twelve Beit Yaakov HaNegbah helpers.

A banquet?

How in the world will I be able to eat if I win and how will I ever eat again if I don't?

We slid into our seats. First Adina, then me, then Mimi, and then Mazal.

Rabbi Grossman was getting up to speak. What was he saying? *Concentrate, Sara, concentrate,* I commanded myself.

He was telling us something about this year's seminary students being especially successful (*Doesn't he say that every year?*) and how pleased the entire faculty was with each and every student's accomplishments. He continued on about how proud the Goldstones would have been with this new crop of young women entering the field of education.

Please do it already! Say who the winner is…

I wished he would get it over with and make the announcement—*no, don't do it, don't say it yet! What if it's not me…what if…*

"Sara, take it easy," Mimi whispered to me.

I had not realized how tightly I was squeezing her hand. I glanced sideways at Adina. We were also clasping each other's hands, but I do not think Adina was aware that we were. She was staring ahead, following Rabbi Grossman's every word.

Rabbi Grossman recapped for the audience the history of the Zev Goldstone Outstanding Student Teacher Award, repeating what he had told us at the beginning of the year.

Why can't he get to the winners already? We all know the story!

I swallowed hard. "Mimi," I whispered, "I'm so nervous."

"I know," she squeezed my hand reassuringly. "But don't worry, Sara. Whatever will be will be."

"And so girls, I don't want to keep you in suspense any longer. Without further ado, it's my honor to call up the winner of the Zev Goldstone Outstanding Student Teacher Award." He cleared his throat. "I would like to ask Batsheva Perlowitz to come up to the stage."

Batsheva Perlowitz?

Not me? Not Sara Hirsch?

I looked over at Adina. *Not Adina Stern either?*

I applauded politely along with everyone else and watched Batsheva make her way to the stage. *I didn't win. I'm not the main winner.* I stared ahead incredulously as Batsheva took the envelope Rabbi Grossman handed her. What was even more surprising to me than my not winning was my reaction. *Why am I not feeling as utterly grief-stricken as I thought I would?*

I could barely pay attention to Batsheva's speech. She was summing up her *Proyect* and her theme—but I was still trying to figure out why I was not experiencing total despondency. *What's going on?*

Perhaps deep down I never really thought I would be the main winner. After all, even Shuli did not achieve that. But there were still the two honorable mention winners…

I glanced at Mimi. She was listening intently to what Batsheva was saying. *Mimi will be all right. She's got that job offer. But, Adina…* I turned to Adina and saw the outline of her perfect profile, her blue eyes glued to the stage. *Oh, Hashem…there are only two honorable mention winners. Make them Adina and me…please!*

I took a deep breath and swallowed hard. Batsheva was returning to her seat and Rabbi Grossman was once again at the microphone.

"And now for the two honorable mention winners…"

I was at the edge of my seat.

"The first one is Michal Weinman."

Applause.

Michal went up to the stage and began her speech. *So it wasn't Adina or me. How could that be?* I knew Michal was one of the smartest girls at M.B.L.L. and quite studious. I had gone to her many times to ask questions when I did not understand something. *But still…*

Then, as she left the stage, Rabbi Grossman once again took the microphone.

Sara, it's not you, my heart pounded. *So you didn't do it. You didn't do what Shuli did. Maybe her year was easier. It doesn't mean anything.* I bit down hard on my bottom lip. *Now smile; try not to be disappointed. It's going to have to be Adina—make sure you show her how happy you are for her. Just keep smiling, Sara. Take those lips and spread them out wider…wider…*

"And now, last but certainly not least, we are very proud to call to the stage the second honorable mention awardee…"

I held my breath.

"…Mimi Rosenberg."

"WHAT!"

As Mimi stood up and made her way to the stage, I sunk down in my chair, wishing I could sidle my way out of the room. *Had I actually screamed that "what" aloud or had I screamed it silently in my heart?*

Mimi Rosenberg…how could that be? Mimi…had learning problems…Mimi could barely write a normal sentence…How could Mimi have won?

I felt something tugging at my left hand. Adina. I dragged my eyes away from the floor and looked up—at Adina's face. She was smiling…a genuinely happy smile. She was truly pleased for our friend Mimi.

How could that be? How could Mimi have won over us?

I followed her gaze to the front of the room…to the stage. Mimi was whispering something to Rabbi Grossman and he was nodding encouragingly, a smile on his face.

And then Mimi...Mimi, who had no fear of public speaking, began...

"Hi," she said, smiling, "I can't believe it's me...Miriam Mina Rosenberg standing up here."

She paused while the audience chuckled accommodatingly.

"I hope you don't mind, but I'm so much more comfortable speaking in English; it'll be much easier for me to express myself. So, with Rabbi Grossman's and the honored faculty's permission, I'll continue in English and I ask that Mazal Cohen please come up to the stage to translate what I say, so that everyone can understand."

An enthusiastic murmur rippled through the audience as Mazal made her way to the front of the room. *With Mimi, nothing would be typical.*

"Anyway...I'm still in a bit of shock about being one of the winners...so please bear with me while I gather my thoughts together."

She swallowed. So did I. I felt Adina squeezing my hand tighter as Mimi actually began to speak, and I found myself tightening my grip on her hand as well.

Mimi cleared her throat. "I came to M.B.L.L. with expectations that were probably different than most of yours. You see, I came with baggage...and I'm not talking about the same suitcases that the rest of you came with."

Mimi's green eyes stared straight into mine.

"Ever since I can remember, I had a learning problem—I couldn't read like the normal kids. Letters would swim in front of me in all different strange ways and so, of course, I couldn't learn the way everyone else did.

"I tried to get by. Sometimes I succeeded in faking it and sometimes I became the class clown, since I figured if everyone was going to laugh at me—they might as well laugh because I did something funny and not at my wrong answers to the teacher's questions. Anyway," Mimi paused for a moment reflectively, "the bottom line is that I grew up feeling like an academic failure...someone who could never learn, let alone teach. Feel like an academic failure? Let me rephrase that...I was an academic failure."

She tucked a loose strand of red hair behind her ear. "And then I came to M.B.L.L., and thanks to a wonderful and encouraging faculty and a very good friend of mine, I found out that this baggage that I'd been lugging around could actually help me grow in ways I never dreamed of.

"The *pasuk* I chose for my *Proyect* is from *sefer Tehillim*. It's in *perek lamed* and, I think, *pasuk beis*, and it goes like this: '*Aromimcha Hashem ki dilisani*...' which means, 'I will exalt You, Hashem, for You have drawn me up.' Once, when I went with another good friend to Rabbanit Lerman in Bnei Brak..." Mimi said and paused. I saw she was looking at Adina—and Adina was staring straight back at her. Mimi continued, "...she explained to us that the word *dilisani* is from the root word *d'li*. The Sfas Emes tells us that in this *pasuk*, *d'li* means a bucket. Just as a bucket must be lowered down into the depths of the well to bring up its life-giving waters, so too sometimes Hashem must lower us to the bottom before raising us up—for often the descent is the beginning of our rising."

She took a deep breath. "Because of what I've gone through, the difficulties I had with learning, I was often forced to find other ways to get to where I had to go. It's like the detours someone sometimes has to take when there's an obstacle on the road blocking its path.

"That's why, for the first time in my life, I found academic success here. In the resource room, Geveret Spitz showed us that different people learn in different ways. Who's to say what's the right way and what's the wrong way? There are different keys to unlock different doors of learning and the main thing is to find the specific key that will open each individual door.

"*Dilisani* also has the word *deles* in it. A door. By finding the key and opening up the door, we can try to find out what steps we need to take to raise us from the depths and free ourselves from those obstacles that hold us back.

"I guess my experience with detours has helped me recognize, or rather, makes me more aware of those keys. Just like an eye doctor doesn't prescribe the same glasses for all his patients, the approach that helps one person won't necessarily help the next."

Mimi again looked directly at me and I found myself nodding encouragingly.

"And on a broader scale, that's the way it is with anything and everything in life. As a result of all the different experiences I went through this year, I learned that Hashem has given us all our own individual prescriptions for what we need in order to grow, and one person's eye glasses doesn't necessarily help the next person to see better.

"Sometimes we go through situations that seem frustrating and unfair. But if we look closely—it's those specific challenges that help us reach greater heights. It's like what Rabbanit Abrams explained to us about a bird's wings. They could seem like a burden, but in reality they're there to help us fly. And it's like what we saw in the play *Metamorphosis*. In order for the butterfly to strengthen its wings and free itself from the walls of the cocoon, it first needed to beat its wings against those walls. Otherwise it wouldn't develop properly from a caterpillar into a strong butterfly.

"I know this might sound confusing," Mimi delivered one of her infectious laughs, "but the way I understand it—very often we have to go through what we have to go through—in order to become all that we are capable of becoming.

"So, just as the *d'li*, the bucket, is suspended over the well's depths, we've got to remember that if something was drawn up from somewhere below, it must have had its support coming from Somewhere above.

"I've felt that support throughout the year. Hashem sent me here at the last minute in a way that was a clear example of *siyyata de'Shemaya*. And along the way, He sent me special messengers—*shlichim*—who've been there for me throughout the year.

"I could never have achieved any of this," Mimi looked at me again and I could see her eyes glistening, "if it wasn't for my dear friend, Sara Hirsch. This award belongs to Sara just as much as it does to me…"

I was staring at the stage, but I could not hear what she was saying, nor could I see her clearly. The applause drowned out her words and my tears blurred her face

I did not care that everyone was looking at me right then—I cared only about Mimi and what she would say next. Through teary eyes I continued gazing at her, waiting expectantly for her to continue.

"Anyway, before I finish my speech, I want to add something I just remembered and didn't include in my *Proyect*."

I sat up straight.

"I was around six years old and in first grade at the time. It was during recess and I remember it was a rainy, dreary day—and that's why we spent our recess time indoors that afternoon in our classroom. We were each given one piece of white paper and told to take out our crayons and draw a picture, and that at the end of recess all the pictures would be hung on the hallway bulletin board. But we were warned, we would be given only one paper. I guess our teacher didn't want us to keep coming back for more.

"Anyway, I quickly drew my picture. It had a small house on it with a large scruffy tree at the side. I was pretty pleased with the way my picture came out. Well, the girl sitting next to me told me that my tree was really very ugly and then she proceeded to add a few apples to my tree. That might have been fine, only the crayon she used was black.

"She ruined my tree!

"I looked at that damaged picture and knew it wouldn't hang proudly on the bulletin board in the hallway—no, not the way it was. But I didn't want to be the only one in the classroom without a picture hanging on the bulletin board either.

"So I took that picture with the black apples on the tree and turned those apples into birds. Now my picture looked even better than before. My tree was beautiful. It had birds flying from branch to branch. The whole picture was alive!

"And during that week, whenever I passed the bulletin board outside my classroom and saw that picture, I remember proudly thinking that the picture was really beautiful. I even overheard older girls from higher classes admiring 'that first grader's picture.'

"And here's another true story that emphasizes this point. It happened to my friend's brother."

She took a deep breath before continuing. "He was making a wooden pen at a woodworking course, and when his pen was almost completely finished, he mistakenly sanded down the upper part of it too much, causing it to have a lopsided look. He looked around at everyone else's pens, ashamed that his was so ugly. Then, figuring that he had nothing to lose, he began sanding down the other side of the pen, forming an intricate wave along the upper half.

"To make a long story short, his pen turned out to be the nicest one by far.

"You see," Mimi paused, "sometimes things that are damaged come out looking better than the original, because if you work on the damaged part – it really can be beautiful—even more beautiful than it would have been had it not been damaged in the first place.

"So instead of our baggage, our problems, being a hindrance, let's take that suitcase, put it on the floor and step right on top of it. That way it will help us go higher and reach greater heights."

Mimi flashed a wide grin indicating that her speech was over. There was loud applause and a standing ovation.

And I was feeling…

Confused?

On one hand I kept thinking…it should have been me. I should have been the winner. And on the other hand I felt immensely satisfied that if it could not be me, at least it was Mimi.

No. I was not jealous of her.

Could a parent envy her child? Could a teacher resent her student? Could a friend who gave freely be jealous of the friend who received?

As Mimi and I tearfully hugged each other, I tried not thinking, *Why did she win and not me? Was Mimi's theme really so different from mine?*

Observing Adina's happiness for Mimi made me feel ashamed. *Wasn't Adina's need to win even greater than mine?*

Not really, something inside me whispered.

Stop thinking, I warned myself. *Smile. The banquet is about to begin.*

And I kept smiling throughout the banquet, with a smile pasted on my face while the hour hand moved slowly around the clock until it reached the number eleven the next morning and it was suddenly time to say goodbye to Mimi.

Adina, Mazal, and I helped her bring her luggage and guitar case to the front of the dormitory building, where the rest of the girls' suitcases were already gathered. A minibus would be transporting everyone who was leaving that day to the airport in less than a quarter of an hour.

It was a gorgeous, sunny day. The cloudless sky was bluer than blue. The air was warm, but not stuffy. The birds were chirping nearby, cheerfully hopping from branch to branch. It was a perfect day for flying...

But for saying goodbye to a dear friend? Is there such a thing as a perfect day to say that kind of goodbye?

Cameras were flashing. A picture of Mimi sitting on top of her suitcases... a picture of Mimi with Mazal... then with Adina... and then with me. A picture of all of us together. Mimi's camera, my camera... then Adina's camera flashed. Geveret Katz was standing outside with us, saying her goodbyes and offering her farewell wishes to all the girls who were leaving. She handed out "care packages" loaded with drinks, crackers, pretzels, and fresh fruits. I slipped a bag of caramels into Mimi's bag and Mazal put in a small box of chocolate sandwich cookies.

Everyone was hugging—some giddily, some tearfully, no one unemotionally.

Rivky was telling Mimi that she wasn't really saying goodbye to her since she'd be seeing her next week in camp. Chani proclaimed her unequivocal envy—wishing that she too could go to camp, but instead her parents wanted her home so she could begin, as she put it, "you know what." Everyone who heard her laughed. Zehava complained that life was getting too serious, Tova in her straightforward way said, "That's life!", Rochel Leah commented that growing up was scary, and Mimi joked that it sure beat the alternative!

And of course, everyone laughed again.

Rochel Leah and I embraced. She was also leaving that day and would be on the same flight with Mimi. She would be going first to New York and then flying from there to Miami.

"Sara, I visit Woodlake a lot to be with my father—and I spend time there with Zehava's family. Rolland Heights isn't so far, maybe we could get together?"

"I'd love that, Rochel Leah."

"I'm really glad I got to know you, Sara."

"Me too, Rochel Leah."

Chapter 47

We embraced once more.

"Hey, Sara, did you forget about me?'

I turned around. Mimi was standing under a tree…waiting.

I went to her, forgetting about Rochel Leah and everyone else, forgetting about all the noise and hustle surrounding us, forgetting about the gorgeous weather and chirping birds.

I saw only one thing.

A redheaded girl with a pointy chin standing against the bark of a tall palm tree. Alone. Waiting to say goodbye to me.

I swallowed hard. There was this huge lump in my throat that refused to budge.

We stood facing each other.

"Mimi…"

She looked at me. Her green eyes were glistening and looking deep into mine. "Sara, I can't."

"I can't either, Mimi."

"So we won't."

I shook my head, the lump in my throat getting bigger. "Mimi…"

"Sara—I owe you everything."

"No, Mimi," I shook my head again, "I'm the one who owes *you* everything."

She tried wiping away the tears that were rolling down her cheeks. "Sara, do you think we'll ever see each other again?"

"Of course. You'll come to Rolland Heights…"

"I'm…I'm coming back to Eretz Yisrael after the summer."

"So you decided?"

She nodded. "Yes. My parents agreed. Especially after…yesterday."

"You mean…the Goldstone Award?"

She nodded again. "Uh huh."

"They…they must've been so proud of you, Mimi."

"Um…sure they were."

I looked away, averting her gaze.

"Sara?"

"Huh?" I was staring at a pebble on the ground.

"Sara?" she repeated.

"What?" I looked up.

"Were you terribly disappointed?"

"Dis-a....no," my eyes blinked involuntarily. "Why should I be?"

"Come on, Sara...I thought for sure *you* would be the winner. You were working so hard and you—"

"Obviously, not everyone thought that way."

"So...so you were hurt."

A brief moment passed with neither of us saying anything.

"Sorry, Sara. That was kind of tactless of me. Of course you're upset."

"Mimi...I'm really happy for you," I said sincerely.

"I believe you, Sara. And...and I don't know if this helps, but I really feel for you too."

"I know you do."

"And what I said publicly yesterday, Sara, wasn't just so I could make a pretty speech...my award really, really is also yours. Maybe you're not going to walk around with it or take it back with you to Rolland Heights, but you really, truly have earned it just as much as I."

"I'm...I'm not so sure about that, Mimi." I looked her directly in the eye. "You did three quarters of your *Proyect* on your own."

"True," she paused, "but it was only because you got me started on the first quarter."

"Come on," I murmured, managing a low chuckle.

"No, really. Without your help in the beginning, I couldn't have done the rest of it."

"Mimi, how did you do it?" My head tilted to the side, puzzled. "I mean...all that writing...on your own?"

"What writing? Oh..." she let out one of her delicious giggles, "good question, Sara. You know my trusty tape recorder?"

"You mean—"

"Yep," she grinned, that mischievous sparkle returning to her eyes, "I didn't hand in a written *Proyect*. I took the detour—I did it all on tape."

"Mimi," I laughed, shaking my head, "you're incredible. You'll always get where you've got to go and you'll never let anything stand in your way."

"I hope that's a compliment, Sara."

"It sure is."

"Mimi!" A voice unexpectedly interrupted us.

We both turned at once to see who was calling her.

"Everyone is on the bus," the *eim ha-bayit* was saying. "They're waiting for you."

Suddenly we grasped each other's hands, desperately wishing we could also hold back the hands of the clock from moving on.

Mimi's eyes stared intently into mine. "Sara…I can't."

"I know, Mimi," I trembled, my voice cracking. "I can't either."

"So we won't," a sob escaped her. "We won't say goodbye."

I was clinging to her and crying, "Right, for us it'll always be hello."

She loosened herself from my grip. "All right, Sara…hello!"

She turned around and went onto the bus.

I went as close to the bus as I could, standing directly next to one of the windows so I could watch her until the bus pulled away.

I saw her make her way sorrowfully down the bus aisle, and in my mind, contrasted it with the first time I met her. I pictured a petite red-headed girl jauntily walking down the airplane aisle, with a disproportionately large guitar case in hand. And as Mimi took her seat near the window facing me and pressed her nose against the glass so that she could see me better, I stood rooted to where I was, the tears streaming uncontrollably down my cheeks, unable to wrench my eyes away from her.

The bus began moving.

Mimi was waving to me, her hand moving up and down vigorously, the vapor from her heavy breathing fogging up the window, but it did not hide her swollen eyes and wet, glistening cheeks.

I ran alongside the slowly moving bus calling, "Mimi…Mimi…keep in touch! Mimi," I lifted my hand, "goodbye…"

I could see Mimi shaking her head forcefully. "No, Sara," she mouthed as the tears dripped down her cheeks and onto the glass window. "Not goodbye…hello!"

48

MONDAY, THE THIRD day of Tammuz.

Another day of goodbyes.

When the girls heard that Adina and I planned on going to Yerushalayim, Me'aras HaMachpelah, and Kever Rochel, it was decided that since so many others besides us wanted to go to the *kevarim* before they left, we would all chip in and hire a van to take us around. It was a practical and convenient solution, economically feasible, and Adina and I were not disappointed with the change of plans. Really, it did not alter things for us that much anyway. It just reversed the order of our trip. Instead of first going to Yerushalayim, we would leave from the dorm and go straight to Chevron, from there to Beis Lechem, and then on to Yerushalayim.

Sharing a van with the others would in no way compromise Adina's privacy when we went to her mother's *kever*. Once we reached Yerushalayim, everyone would split up and go about their rounds of visits, goodbyes, shopping, and doing whatever else they wanted to do there. Then, at nine o'clock that evening, we would all meet at the Kosel for our ride home.

Adina and I packed sandwiches, some fruit, and biscuitim to take along with us. Drinks, we knew, we could purchase when needed. So, when our alarm clocks rang early Monday morning, we dressed and *davened* without delay in order to meet the others in the courtyard at seven-thirty as scheduled.

Surprisingly, I managed to catch a few winks of sleep as the van wiggled its way along the windy and bumpy roads to Chevron. Actually, it really was not so surprising. I had hardly slept the night before.

Adina and I had spent Shabbos with the Cohens in Kiryat Yosef and returned on Sunday afternoon. We had been busy packing, schmoozing with the others, preparing the food, and planning out the next day's schedule—and suddenly the clock said it was half past midnight.

I cannot say that I was disappointed at the lateness of the hour. By then, I hoped that the silence in the dorm would not seem so…so deafening… the way it felt during the daytime.

Ever since Thursday morning when Mimi left, something inside me also departed, leaving a gaping emptiness within me. The dorm became intolerably quiet and it was not just because many of the girls left with her.

No…it was because Mimi was no longer there. And I felt myself missing her more than I could have ever imagined.

Mimi.

Was it really possible that one year earlier I had not even known her? *How could that be? How could it be that we hadn't always been friends?*

Then, on Friday morning Adina and I went with Mazal to Kiryat Yosef. I must say I felt relieved to leave the dormitory. Mimi's absence kept screaming out at me. *How I missed her!*

Naturally, we had a wonderful Shabbos at the Cohens, but it was tinged with sadness. Mazal was not coming back with us on Sunday. That morning we said goodbye to Mazal and her family, and thanked them for all those wonderful "Shabbatot" throughout the year. I invited them to come to Rolland Heights if they ever came to America. They laughed, saying that they probably never would. We all agreed that hopefully *Mashiach* would come very soon and bring us all to Yerushalayim, where all of *Am Yisrael* would be gathered together.

Later that afternoon, we arrived back at the quiet dorm. It really was ridiculously silent there. The Israelis had all returned to their homes over the weekend and many of the non-Israelis, who had not gone to the airport on Thursday, left earlier that morning.

Only ten of us still remained.

Adina and I decided to use my room for our luggage and her room for our sleeping quarters. She helped me carry my sheet, pillow, and quilt into her room and we spread my linen on Mimi's bed.

Where would Mimi sleep next year when she returned and assisted Geveret Spitz? I wondered as I lay on my back with my palms cushioning my head, staring into the darkness. *Would she become one of the faculty members or would she still be the life of the dorm...one of the girls?*

I could not imagine Mimi as a faculty member.

Perhaps she would arrange another Chanukah performance? Or would she organize another production like *Metamorphosis*? I still could not believe that *I* had been involved in writing that script, that *I* had been the one to write the theme song. *Little old me...Sara Hirsch. Who would've believed it?*

If it had not been for Mimi's encouragement, I never would have done it.

I do not know what time it was when I finally managed to fall asleep that night, but like I said, I was not really surprised to have dozed off in the van taking us to Chevron. I was surprised, though, at how quickly we arrived at Me'aras HaMachpelah. Suddenly, we were climbing the steps and making our way inside.

Leah Imeinu.

I stood before the *kevarim* praying that all our *tefillos* would be accepted in the merit of our forefathers and matriarchs buried there, but my mind kept returning to Leah.

How could it have felt to be the "less" loved wife? Each of the names she gave her first three sons were an expression of appreciation to Hashem for trying to comfort her by giving her those sons, those future *shevatim*, yet they also reflected the pain of being number two and not number one. Still, she expressed her thanks to Hashem anyway, and when Yehudah, her fourth son, was born, she articulated that gratitude completely.

I know she was a great tzaddekes and I—none of us—come anywhere near that kind of greatness. But isn't that why the Torah tells us about her and all the other Imahos...why we read the parshiyos over and over again? So that we can learn from them and try to emulate them?

I stared at the velvet curtain embroidered with her name.

So, she hadn't been given the main part—but she wasn't just a prop either. And the Torah tells us so much about her, so much that we can learn from her. Instead of complaining and being unhappy with her lot, she rose to meet the challenge Hashem sent her. *And didn't Hashem reward her by making her the mother of Levi, the shevet of the Kohanim, and the mother of Yehudah, the shevet of royalty?*

Shouldn't I learn from her? So what if Hashem didn't make me as pretty or as lively as Shuli. So what if I didn't win the Goldstone Honorable Mention Award like she did. Shouldn't I try harder to appreciate everything Hashem did give me...that Hashem gives me every single day of my life...instead of comparing myself to her and complaining about what I don't have and wish I could be?

I *davened* then like I never had before—begging Hashem to help me serve Him on His terms, just like our mother, Leah, and to set me free from the obstacles that narrow my ability to really know Him and feel His love.

And when we entered Kever Rochel, I thought about Rochel Imeinu and her sacrifice...how she gave up her *chuppah* to Leah, something that was so important to her. *Important?* It was everything to her, and yet, to spare her sister from humiliation, she was willing to forego it all.

I remembered that time, all those months before, on the day of Rochel Imeinu's *yahrtzeit*, when I was originally supposed to go on this trip and I had wondered if I too could give up something for someone I loved. *Did I have it in me?*

I had wanted so much to be able to be a heroine, and then recently Rabbanit Abrams pointed out to me what a true heroine is...and how sacrifices can be offered only to Hashem by doing what Hashem wants us to do.

Davening there at the *kever* of Rochel Imeinu, I thought about that. I thought about all those heroes and heroines...the ones I used to dream about in bed and wish I could emulate. I remembered my frustration, contemplating the unfairness of it all. Had I been born around the time of the Holocaust, then surely I would have had the opportunity to prove myself—to give of myself in a way that would have shown true sacrifice. But I was not born then. So instead I dreamed about other heroic acts—about reuniting a lost daughter with her dying mother, about winning an award that would grant me an express trip to the top of the education hierarchy.

But sacrifices could be offered only to Hashem by doing what Hashem wants us to do.

No, I did not get to choose my situation or my challenge. And perhaps realizing that and accepting it—would be my first step toward true heroism.

The time in Beis Lechem passed quickly, and then we were off and climbing the hills to Yerushalayim. We parted from the other girls in Geulah, and then made our way over to the Schpitzmans to visit Savta Hinda. We ended up eating lunch there, the sandwiches which we had packed the night before together with a delicious Israeli vegetable salad prepared by Dini Schpitzman, and some fresh melon salad that her grandmother, Rabbanit Gartenhaus, insisted we have.

And then sadly, it was time to make our farewells. My heart went out to Adina. She had finally established a close relationship with people who had known her mother well and now she would be leaving them. It was really difficult—all this parting.

Rabbanit Gartenhaus arranged for a driver to take us to Adina's mother's *kever*. We waved goodbye to her, Savta Hinda, Rabbanit Schpitzman, and Dini as the car drove off.

All the way there I felt overcome with tension. *How will Adina react? Will it do for her what we'd been hoping? It had better! Isn't this why I stayed, isn't this the reason I'm missing Chavie's wedding?*

And then finally we arrived at the cemetery.

Adina did not fall weeping upon her mother's grave as I had envisioned. It was…well…more subdued.

Adina quietly swayed to and fro, saying some special *tefillos* one says at a mother's gravesite. I watched as she stopped for a few minutes to study the writing on the monument, her blue eyes deciphering the engraved letters with her mother's name, and then she opened her *sefer Tehillim*, her lips whispering Dovid HaMelech's comforting words.

Standing a little further back, off to the side and sweating profusely under the blazing afternoon sun, I was also saying certain chapters of *Tehillim* and praying fervently for my parents' health and well-being. In the back of my mind, though, I was all the while wondering. When would the skies open and the thunder roar…when would Adina's

Chapter 48

emotions finally be unleashed?

And then, after around a half-hour had passed, Adina turned to me and told me that she was finished and ready to go.

That's it?

For this I missed Chavie's wedding?

Sara, a voice warned me, *haven't you learned by now that you're not the one in charge? The script is not necessarily going to go according to your plan...*

"Are you sure, Adina?"

"Am I sure about what?"

I took a deep breath. "Are you sure that you're finished here?" I deliberately made a show of looking at my watch. "We've still got plenty of time."

"I'm finished...for now."

"For...now?"

"Yes, for now. I suppose I'll be back again sometime in the near future." She looked at me impassively. "I think we're supposed to go and wash our hands now. I noticed some faucets—up there—at the front gate not far from where the car's waiting." She pointed in the direction that we had come from and then began the uphill trek while speaking over her shoulder. "If it's all right with you, I want to go to Meah Shearim. I still have some gifts that I'd like to buy."

"All right," I said as I trailed behind her. "That's fine with me. But..."

"But what?" She turned around to face me.

I shaded my squinting eyes with my hand so I could see her better. "But...are you sure you're finished...here?"

"Yes," she said briskly, "that's what I said."

"Oh...okay," I murmured. "Sorry...I...I just didn't want you to feel that you needed to rush because of me."

"I didn't rush, Sara. I took all the time I needed."

"Oh...all right."

She climbed over the rocks and onto the stony path with me following, panting and clumsy behind her. *The least she could do is wait for me!* My eyes burning, I blinked away angry tears that rose to the surface. *If only she knew about the sacrifice I made by staying for her and missing Chavie's wedding, maybe she'd slow down a bit or at least show a little appreciation.*

But Adina knew nothing about the sacrifice. That was the way I had wanted it...*hadn't I?* That was the way I was going to prove to myself that I was doing this for Adina—for Hashem and not for me.

So why was I feeling so bitterly disappointed?

Was it because I thought I would witness something...that did not happen?

Was it because I thought I would be given the opportunity to tangibly prove what a perfect friend I am—by being the net that would catch my falling friend? But nothing happened. She did not fall.

Yes, Adina, *perfect* Adina had not fallen apart at her mother's grave and now her long legs took her swiftly to the top of the hill, where she washed her hands before I even got there. She left the cup for me upside down on the ground and I took it while she entered the waiting car. I reached the car a few minutes after her, sweating and breathless, and once again feeling awkward beside her.

Looking cool and relaxed, she was sipping from a water bottle and handed one to me. "Here, Sara, you sure look like you could use a drink."

"Thanks." I took it from her. "I'm glad we listened to Rabbanit Gartenhaus and brought these water bottles along," I said while twisting off the cap and placing a straw inside. "I didn't realize how thirsty I'd be."

"Sure. Oh, and thanks for coming with me."

I gulped. "No problem."

No problem? I just missed my best friend's wedding because of you...and all I get is an "oh, and thanks for coming with me."

I leaned back against the vinyl seat and squeezed my eyes shut.

Sara, stop it, stop it right now! You wanted to be a heroine. Do you think that's the way Rochel Imeinu reacted when she gave her place to Leah? Do you think she was dripping with resentment the way you are? How about all those Holocaust heroines? Do you think they were bitter when they gave up their time, mone,y and strength to save lives and those people they rescued didn't express proper gratitude to them?

You wanted to be a heroine. So start behaving like one!

I let out a heavy sigh while opening my eyes and forced myself to smile. "So, Adina, where are we off to?"

"I figured that we'll ask the driver to drop us off in Meah Shearim. We could do some shopping there, get something to eat, and then it'll be time to go to the Kosel. We'll have at least an hour there before our van leaves back to the dorm."

Adina conducted herself normally, conversing, eating, and shopping. She even chose a present for her father and Bina—for their new house. Then, she picked out gifts for Bina's children, telling me their ages and asking me for my opinion regarding her choices.

I was the one who was not behaving normally. I could not stop thinking about the wedding and weighing the trade-off I had made by staying. I kept asking myself… *was it worth it?*

I guess if Adina would have reacted more dramatically at her mother's *kever*, the way I had imagined she would—if I had felt like a true rescuer, like my being there was absolutely essential, I am certain I would not have entertained such ambivalent feelings about what I gave up. I would have relished my time alone with Adina. But I had not felt very needed, after all. And now, I was not feeling very happy either.

At around six o'clock, we decided to head to the Kosel by foot. The sun was no longer burning with the same intensity as it had been earlier in the day and we had plenty of time on our hands. Everything we had wanted to do was done. We each carried a shopping bag with gifts, but they were mostly lightweight and our pocketbooks did not contain much, just our wallets, *siddurim*, and a water bottle. We were not hungry, as we had just finished a very satisfying falafel washed down with a tall glass of delicious, freshly squeezed orange juice.

In just forty-eight hours, we knew we would be on the airplane heading to the United States, flying over Europe and hovering above the Atlantic. We would no longer be in Yerushalayim *ir ha-kodesh*.

And so, feeling refreshed and energized from our break in the falafel shop and filled with a longing to hold on to Yerushalayim's holy air while we still could, we decided to take the twisted route to the Kosel and walk through the Old City.

It was sometime during that leisurely and enjoyable walk that—Adina dropped the bombshell.

We made our way through Sha'ar Yaffo, passed by the Tourist Information Center, went through the Armenian Quarter, and then at last reached the Jewish Quarter. As I looked around and observed the Old City's unique architecture, with its structures built from grayish peachy stone and its entranceways arched as they had been for centuries, a powerful yearning engulfed me. We admired the contrast between contemporary Yerushalmi children playing among the ancient ruins.

I remember mentioning something about it being quite different from Rolland Heights and Adina made a comment that it certainly had no resemblance to Hendon or Ballington either.

That powerful longing and love for Eretz Yisrael kept growing stronger with the realization that my time here was running out, and I suppose Adina was feeling the same as me. *Who knew when I'd be coming back?* With Adina, though, it was different. I did not think financial constraints would prevent her from returning. Other concerns might hold her back. I was wondering about that right then, when I heard her voice cutting into my thoughts.

"So, Sara, Mimi's really lucky to be coming back here next year...don't you think?"

"She sure is. I wonder if her parents would have agreed to let her come back if she hadn't won the award."

"Not likely."

I turned to face her. "Do you really think so, Adina? You really think they wouldn't have?"

She continued walking. "Well, remember that day when Mimi broke the news to us about Geveret Spitz's job offer?"

"Of course, it was a real shocker and we were all so busy trying to finish our reports."

"Right. Well, after Mimi made her announcement, she went to call her parents."

"And they weren't impressed?"

"It's not that they weren't proud of her." Adina sighed. "It's really strange. Here they are such brilliant and accomplished people—I think they just never grasped the magnitude of Mimi's problem."

"Still...what does that have to do with their not allowing her to come back next year?"

"I didn't say they said no. They told Mimi that they needed to think about it."

"And what did Mimi think they'd say? She didn't seem nervous about the *Proyect* like the rest of us."

"Well, you know Mimi." Adina smiled. "She's always been so optimistic about everything."

"So she figured that she'd go home and get her parents to understand that Geveret Spitz's offer was really something special, and then they'd grant her permission?" I asked the question rhetorically.

"Not exactly," Adina replied. "She *hoped* she'd be able to convince them."

"And we both know how persuasive Mimi can be." I grinned.

"It wasn't so simple," Adina said. "Mimi felt that her parents really didn't have such a keen understanding of what a resource room was and couldn't appreciate the significance of a job in that field."

"Even though Mimi was so successful with the children there?"

"Yes, Sara," Adina shook her head sadly. "You have to understand where Mimi's parents are coming from."

I thought about the way Mimi had described her parents. *Sometimes brilliance can just make you...so out of touch.* "I guess they view the education field in a much more conventional manner, Adina, and aren't open to this more individualistic approach."

"You guess right," Adina sighed. "So, Mimi knew it wasn't going to be easy getting them to agree to allow her to take the job. If this is really a specialized field then—"

"Then they'd want her to specialize in it?" I asked. "Like—continue her schooling?"

"Yes, Sara, they'd want her to do it right, further her education, get the proper degree."

"But Mimi would never do that," I protested. "She can't!"

Adina shrugged. "Her parents weren't here with us this year, Sara. They didn't get to see what she did with Riki, the impact she made with *Metamorphosis*, the way she discovered the keys to all those kids in the resource room." Adina shifted her shopping bag to her left hand and switched the strap of her pocketbook to her other shoulder. "I suppose they view another year here as a waste of time, as though Mimi would just be some nursery assistant or tutor, not the educator she really could be."

"But now that she won the Goldstone Award—"

"Yes," Adina said, "I'm sure that made a huge difference to them. I'm awfully glad that I told them how we felt."

"Told whom how who felt?"

"Rabbi Grossman and the faculty members about us."

"Us?"

"Yes. You and me."

"Huh?"

Adina gave me a strange look, as though to say *why are you being so obtuse and acting as though you don't know what I'm talking about?* "I'm glad," she said slowly and distinctly, "that I told Rabbi Grossman and the teachers how you and I felt about the Goldstone Award."

Something inside me began to tremble. "Adina, what in the world are you talking about?"

"I knew that you felt the same way as I did, Sara," she said simply. "So, when I was called into the room to make my presentation and I saw that they loved it, I told them."

"You told them *what*?" I stood stock still, unable to take another step. "What exactly did you tell them, Adina?"

"I told them that I hoped it wasn't disrespectful of me—but that if they were deciding between you, Mimi, and me, it would be completely all right with you and me—if they chose Mimi—"

"You WHAT?"

"Shush, Sara, everyone is looking at us."

Reflexively, I glanced around and saw those same Yerushalmi children, who we had so recently been admiring, gaping at us curiously. *So what! Let them stare! Let them look at us strangely, as though there was something wrong with us. I don't care!*

There was only one thing I cared about right then. There was only one thing I saw. A stage…a stage with Mimi graciously speaking at the microphone…with Mimi smilingly receiving the coveted award and then suddenly…that image of Mimi was being replaced with…a picture of someone else—*me*.

And Adina had changed that.

My heart was pounding wildly and my knees felt weak. I could barely breathe.

"Are you okay, Sara? What's wrong?"

"No, I'm not okay," I hissed, "and everything's wrong, everything!"

"Sara, please…stop. Let's sit down."

Dazed, I allowed myself be led to a nearby metal bench. If I had been thinking rationally, I almost certainly would have ignored her and walked away furious, never to speak to her again. But I must have been in a state of shock. I was not thinking.

I sat down, staring straight ahead, the tears close to the surface. But I was stunned…too stunned to cry.

How could this be happening?

All my hard work…my dream had been destroyed…and who was responsible? The same person for whom I had just made an inconceivable sacrifice.

I won't ever forget, I can't ever forgive!

"Sara, could you please tell me what's wrong? Why do you look so upset?"

I swallowed hard. But I did not say anything. *I will not lower myself and allow her to know how much I sacrificed for her.*

"Sara, please… talk to me." Large tears were spilling out of her eyes. "You're…you're frightening me!"

"How could you," I finally managed to utter through gritted teeth, "how could you do that?"

"What?"

"*What?*" I repeated imitating her British accent mockingly. "*What?* You have the nerve to ask that!"

"You're mad at what I did…you're mad that I told them it would be all right with us if we didn't win—"

"You had no right to do such a thing—"

"*I* didn't decide anything, Sara. *They* decided. I just let them know that if it was down to the three of us, that it—"

"You had no right!"

"I'm sorry, Sara. I didn't realize how important it was to you."

"Maybe it wasn't important to you, but to me it—"

"You're wrong about that, *very* wrong. It was extremely important to me. Ever since I realized it had been my mother's wish, it was—"

"So then...*why?*" I glared at her.

"Because of you, Sara."

"*What are you talking about?*"

"I wanted very much to be like you...to be able to give something that was important to me to someone else. Ever since I met you, I wanted to be like you. I saw you in the airplane—how lonely you were—"

"Right," my voice was heavy with sarcasm, "but you didn't even bother to—"

"Wait, let me finish. I saw that you were lonely, yet you were busy helping Gila—only I didn't know it was Gila right then. She was just a stranger. Then you tried being friendly to me even though I...even though I couldn't be friendly back. Then, throughout the year, I saw how you were always there for Mimi, helping her—"

"Rabbi Grossman asked me to," I said frostily.

"It doesn't matter why. You were there for her and I know it wasn't always easy. And then I used to watch you writing all those letters—"

"And you'd react so nastily." *No more sugar-coating from me!*

"I know...but I didn't mean it. Please...believe me. It was only because I longed for what you had...all those people...all that caring."

I bit my bottom lip, but did not say anything.

"Then," she continued, "there was that time that you missed going with everyone else to the *kevarim* in order to accompany me to the dentist—even though I was behaving horrendously to you."

"You already thanked me."

"I wanted to be like that, Sara...I kept hoping I would get the opportunity to give like you gave. But it never happened."

"You took the part of the mother in *Metamorphosis*," I said more coldly than I had meant to, "and you certainly didn't want to do that."

Adina winced. "Sara, you know that doesn't count. It was so...so public, so full of accolades. Not like what you did."

I crossed my arms over my chest. "So?"

"So, I waited...waited for something to happen. Waited to have the opportunity to *think about someone else for the first time in my life.*"

This time *I* winced.

Adina continued, "And then Mimi came to us with the news about *Geveret* Spitz's job offer. I knew Mimi was working hard on her *Proyect*…I knew about the tape recorder."

My stomach took a dip. "She told you about it?"

"Not exactly," Adina said. "It was supposed to be her big secret. But, we're roommates and I caught her speaking into the tape recorder, and well…I put two and two together and confronted her. She admitted it to me. I knew how badly she wanted to win…and she let me listen to part of the recording. I saw that her *Proyect* had real potential. It…it was an excellent theme and she was able to back it up beautifully with stories and proofs."

"So you decided to give the judging committee the green light."

"No, Sara, it didn't happen that way. First of all, they don't need my green light."

I swallowed hard. "That's true…but you helped them decide."

"No way," she shook her head adamantly. "I just told them—"

"That if they have to decide between the three of us, *it's okay with you and Sara—*"

"I—I really, truly thought you felt the same way. If I had even the slightest doubt, I never would've spoken in your name. But, after Mimi told me about your friend's wedding—"

"My friend's wedding?"

Her hand closed over her mouth. "I wasn't supposed to let you know that I knew."

"Mimi told you about that too?"

She nodded. "Mimi knew how much you were sacrificing to be here with me. I think she was trying to sound me out about just how important it was for you to stay. She really didn't tell me about it intentionally. She was kind of testing the waters, to figure out whether I would go to the *kever* without you, and then it kind of came out."

"I see."

"So, you understand—it never entered my mind that you would object. I promise you that if I would've had even an inkling of an idea of how important it was to you, I wouldn't—"

"You wouldn't have been so free to use my name."

"Right.

"And you did this—"

"Because I wanted to be like you, Sara."

Again I bit my bottom lip, this time harder. *Sara, don't cry,* I warned myself, *don't!*

"You remember, Sara, that time in the Kfar Amsdorf woods, when you tried to convince me to take the part of the mother in *Metamorphosis*?"

"How could I forget?" my voice was thick. "You just—"

"Yes," she nodded her head vigorously, "I just repeated to you what you…what you told me. That I should think about someone else for once in my life, and that maybe then I'd stop being so angry at myself. And…Sara…when you said that, you…you managed to break through that prison of anger that kept me so locked up."

My eyes welled.

"And then…and then you explained that by doing something for someone else, helping them when they're desperate for help, it'd make me feel so—"

"So much…happier?" I whispered.

"Right. So I tried it," she said hoarsely. "I gave up something that was very important to me. Maybe Mimi would've won anyway—or maybe this helped push their decision in that direction. I don't know, Sara. I don't think we'll ever know. But there was one thing I was sure of—"

"Yes?"

"That you and I would leave here still feeling accomplished, that we'd get teaching jobs. *We'd* manage. But Mimi—she wouldn't be able to teach in a regular classroom, and even if she could—"

"She'd accomplish so much more by helping children in a resource room," I said softly.

"Right, and this was an opportunity she couldn't afford to miss."

I swallowed hard. "So you gave up something important to you…"

"But I'm not feeling good about it," her voice cracked, "not if I've hurt you. Not if I've ruined our friendship."

"You…you didn't ruin our friendship, Adina. I guess…I guess what really bothers me…is that you did this behind my back."

"But I explained—"

"I know." I looked down at my nails and then shifted my gaze back to her. "I understand now why you did it and why you thought it would be all right with me."

"So you're not so upset anymore about…about losing the opportunity…about not winning the award?"

Slowly, I shook my head. "You know, Adina? You said something to me just now…about that time in the Kfar Amsdorf woods…about helping you get out of that prison of anger. Remember?"

She grinned shyly. "How could I forget?"

I returned a faint smile. "I…I think I'm beginning to realize that in a way…in a way I've also been locked up all this time in a prison."

"*You?*"

I nodded and stood up slowly, ready to resume our walk to the Kosel. *I needed the Kosel!*

"For so long, Adina—all I could think of was winning. The Goldstone Award…that was going to be the solution to everything."

We picked up our bags and steadily made our way down a wide alley, our footsteps echoing softly on the stone pavement. Adina listened closely while I opened up my heart and poured out my secret dream.

"And then surprisingly, when I didn't win, I wasn't as upset as I thought I'd be. I still don't understand why." I shook my head. "You see, I always wanted to be this great big heroine—"

"Really?"

"Yes…I wanted to do something great…you know, save people, save lives—"

"Well, you have, Sara. You helped Mimi—you gave her something she never could have achieved without that start. All those years it was as if she was also in a prison and, Sara, you helped her get out of it. You helped her with that suitcase idea."

I shook my head. "Mimi helped herself."

"But you pushed her, you encouraged her. You told her to take all of her energy and you gave her the goal to aim for…"

"The Goldstone Award?"

"Yes. And because of you, she took that suitcase, turned it over, and climbed right out of the window of her prison to…to freedom. And me too, Sara," Adina's voice broke. She quickly wiped away an escaped tear that rolled down her cheek. "If it weren't for you—there's no way I would have ever opened up and…and, yes…come out of the prison I'd been locked in all these years."

"But I was also in a prison, Adina," I said quietly. "Not just you and Mimi."

"Come on, Sara—"

"No really, Adina. Remember what Mimi said about challenges not coming in One Size Fits All?"

"Yes, but you come from this great, loving family with two wonderful, supportive parents. You've got brains and a great—"

"Stop it." I held up my hand. "Just because I don't have *your* problems or Mimi's, doesn't mean I don't have my own struggles."

"Like?"

I looked around. Mothers were standing at the top of steps, calling their little ones inside. We saw two boys running into a narrow alley and two little girls swinging a jump rope in circles above the cobble stone pavement, with a third friend ready to jump. I turned back to Adina. "Like comparing myself all the time to other people…like thinking that I'm nothing special and assuming that, had I been born in different circumstances, I'd be able to prove myself…reach greater heights."

"But look, Sara…look at what you've done with what you have. Look at how you've helped others with your desire to give…"

"That's the point I'm trying to make. Our challenges, our tests, our problems come in all kinds of packages. They're gifts with all kinds of wrapping paper—and sometimes instead of the stepping stones they're meant to be, they turn into prison walls, and instead of thanking Hashem, we complain to Him. You know," I let out a deep breath, "it's really kind of strange. This whole year I was working on my *Proyect*. At one point—I found the *pasuk* I wanted to use and I kept steering my report toward that theme. But I don't think I was really paying attention to what I wrote…at least not regarding myself."

We passed under an arch. "What was your *pasuk*, Sara?"

I looked into her deep blue eyes. "Promise not to laugh, Adina?"

"I promise."

We reached the steps overlooking the Kosel and stopped. I took a deep breath. "The *pasuk* I based my *Proyect* on was *Hotziah mimasger nafshi, lehodos es shemecha*—Release my soul from its prison, to acknowledge Your Name."

"That's...that's unbelievable! That's what we were just talking about."

I looked out into the distance and saw the surrounding hills—hills that had witnessed centuries of change—wars, construction, sin, imprisonment, growth, rebuilding, freedom. "Adina," I said aloud, but I was really talking to myself, "those words I chose for my *Proyect*...I think they're really a *tefillah*."

"Well, that makes sense. Dovid HaMelech wrote them."

"I think maybe he wrote them...for me."

"Isn't that what we learned? Isn't that the way we're all supposed to look at *Tehillim*—like it was written especially for each one of us?"

"I think so." I nodded thoughtfully. "If only..."

"If only...what?"

"If only I really could..."

"Really could what?"

"Learn how to accept that whatever Hashem has given *me*—is the best thing for *me*."

"Sara...stop being so hard on yourself. Changes don't just happen over night."

"I know...I know..." I looked ahead bleakly.

"*Sometimes, when it seems life is a long, struggling night,*" Adina's voice was soft, but steely with determination, "*when problems are overwhelming, when things don't feel right—*"

"Yes, Adina." I turned to her, my face breaking out into a broad grin. "That sounds kind of familiar."

"*When we feel trapped and imprisoned, surrounded by an impenetrable wall,*" she continued, her eyes twinkling, her lips curving into a playful smile. "*When we yearn to break free and our weeping becomes a call...*"

"*Crying out—set me free,*" I went on with a lilt in my voice, "*and—open the doors of this prison...*"

"*I must remember,*" Adina and I said together, smilingly looking into each others' eyes, "*I was put down here to fulfill a certain mission.*"

הַכֹּל יוֹדוּךָ וְהַכֹּל יְשַׁבְּחוּךָ, וְהַכֹּל יֹאמְרוּ
אֵין קָדוֹשׁ כַּה'... הָאֵל הַפּוֹתֵחַ בְּכָל יוֹם...

"All will thank You, and all will praise You, and all will declare, nothing is as holy as Hashem…the G-d Who opens doors each day…"

(BIRCHOS KERIAS SHEMA)

Part Five

Epilogue

"AND THEY LIVED happily ever after..."

No. That is not the way my story ends. Because this is life...*real life*. And in real life nobody ever lives happily ever after.

Adina and I returned to Rolland County—Adina to Ballington and I to Rolland Heights. Adina had plenty of adjusting to do coming into her father's home, into his new life. No, it could never really be "home" to her, despite Bina Stern's warm and welcoming manner, but I was there for her throughout. She spent a lot of time with us—she loved talking to my wise mother and enjoyed the friendly "dormitory" atmosphere of our third floor bedroom.

Mimi went back to Eretz Yisrael a week after camp was over. It was during that week between camp and Eretz Yisrael that I finally got to speak to her. I tried calling her a number of times when she was in camp, but it was impossible to reach, her and then finally when she arrived home I left a message with her mother. She returned my call the next day. When I heard her voice, tears rushed to my eyes. I guess I had not realized until then how much I missed her.

We spoke and promised to keep in touch. Like Mimi said before we hung up, "Remember, Sara, for us it's never goodbye—so...hello."

It took a while for me to rid myself of that empty feeling I was left with when I replaced the receiver on the hook.

Keeping in touch with Mimi turned out to be difficult. *Difficult?* Almost impossible.

I was a great letter writer, but often I felt as though I was writing to myself. Mimi just did not seem to have the time to write. Then again, writing had never been her forte. I knew it had nothing to do with me.

It was not that she did not value our friendship, she barely managed to write to Adina either. And tapes? Mimi did not seem to have the time for that, either.

And then Mimi became even busier.

Around Chanukah time, she shocked us all with the unbelievable news that she had become a *kallah*. Mimi…engaged? Incredible!

Her *chasan*, and this is where the news became even more amazing, turned out to be Geveret Spitz's nephew…the one who had come to learn in Beit Midrash Kfar Amsdorf. Naturally, Geveret Spitz and her husband had been the *shadchanim* and, from the way things sounded, all of Kfar Amsdorf, the M.B.L.L. seminary, and the Beit Yaakov HaNegbah campus were enveloped in the *simchah* and bursting with joy!

Not surprisingly, Mimi had already left a huge imprint on the resource room and on everyone else who crossed her path. She was organizing productions for the seminary and high school students, working with the M.B.L.L.ers on helping them find the "keys" to their students' problems, and she was also busy assisting the teachers in the Bnot Yisrael Elementary School.

She returned to America for around two weeks to celebrate her wedding and first few *sheva berachos*. Adina and I managed to make it to Barclay despite a heavy snowstorm. The three of us danced and danced together. I am sure anyone observing us would not have needed to be especially perceptive to realize how special our friendship was.

As Mimi had said—our friendship was like a puzzle. Each of us had something which the other lacked, and together we were a perfect fit.

But would the three of us ever get together again?

Mimi and her husband returned to Eretz Yisrael. He to the kollel in Kfar Amsdorf and she to Geveret Spitz's resource room.

Mimi was thriving. She had picked up those wings by her sides, flapped them, and soared!

I wish I could say the same for myself.

I had filled out teaching applications for every Beis Yaakov, day school, private nursery, and high school in all of Rolland County. Of course I made sure to include a copy of my Machon Beit Leah LeMorot teaching certificate and letters of recommendation from Geveret Spitz, as well as other teachers. The only problem was that there were only two openings. One job was to be an assistant teacher in a private nursery, and the other one was to assist the second grade teacher in Beis Yaakov of Rolland Heights during reading time.

I took the job in Beis Yaakov of Rolland Heights.

I tried. I gave it all I had.

It was often boring, definitely not what I wanted, but I did not quit—and then around Purim time, I was informed by our principal that she was thinking of starting a resource room in our school that coming September. She remembered Geveret Spitz's recommendation letter and offered me the position of assisting the new teacher who would be coming to Rolland Heights to set up the program.

I was thrilled! My dream was coming true. I would excel…I would prove myself beyond anyone's wildest expectations and eventually I would take over, becoming the main teacher. I would be asked to give worldwide conferences on teaching in resource rooms…someone like Geveret Spitz. *Oh… my dreams!*

Adina took a job working in a private nursery in Ballington. She had wanted to do what her mother had done, and with her natural appeal, she was hired on the spot. Having someone like Adina as an employee could only be a plus. Besides…she was Oscar Scheinerman's relative. That alone opened up doors of opportunities.

But Adina did not really enjoy working with preschoolers. She had only chosen that profession because of her mother, or perhaps it was because of the reasons Mimi had perceived—she was trying to recapture her lost childhood.

Anyway, Adina quit her job, but not before she had another one lined up. The high school in Walnut Lake was looking for someone like Adina…someone charismatic, smart, and with a proper Beis Yaakov outlook, to come into the school and fill in as a substitute when necessary and help girls who were having trouble academically or even socially. When Bina heard about the job, she mentioned it to her father, who, as a member of the school's board, recommended Adina.

At first Adina was hesitant to take the job. She confessed that if it were not for Mr. Scheinerman's involvement, they probably would not have considered her—a newcomer, fresh out of seminary—for the position.

But I managed to convince her to take the job anyway. "After all," I told her, "why shouldn't you take advantage of an opportunity that comes your way? You're certainly as good as anyone else…probably better…"

Well, in the end Adina took the "post," as she called it, and could not stop thanking me for convincing her to do it.

It worked out well for her. She loved helping the girls with their different problems and I think that helping them deal with their various issues was therapeutic for her too. It also had the flexibility (I guess that was the compensation for the mediocre salary) of allowing her to take longer "holidays." She was able to get away more often than another job would have allowed and she visited her grandparents frequently.

She often visited Eretz Yisrael during her trips to Europe, and would see Mimi from time to time. Sometimes, she would bring back a lengthy cassette tape that Mimi managed to record for me and sometimes she would bring back photographs.

I will never forget the tears that came to my eyes when I saw that first photograph of Mimi's baby daughter. Rochel was her name. She had an adorable pointy chin and a full head of red hair!

Time was flying…

Chavie would return to Rolland Heights for the Yamim Tovim and I got to play with her adorable babies. And then she would start pressuring me to look into different *shidduchim*. She always had another suggestion for me…a friend of her husband's, a relative of Mindy's.

And I always responded…*not yet*.

Shuli was still not married. The offers from matchmakers continued coming in for her, but definitely not with the same frequency as they had when I first returned from Eretz Yisrael. Shuli could not make up her mind! Sometimes the meetings would progress. Excitement would fill the air, hinting of an impending celebration, as if it were finally going to happen.

And then…nothing.

Shuli would say, "He's not for me." And then she would do what she had been doing ever since I came home from seminary. She would insist that I begin the *shidduch* process already. And I would counter that I was unwilling to and that I was waiting for her.

I felt quite heroic about what I was doing...and at the same time a trifle guilty. I would observe the sad worry lines around my parents' eyes. I knew how much they wanted to see *nachas*.

And then my brother Yisrael became a *chasan*. I watched him and his *kallah*, a wonderful girl from the neighborhood who had been two classes below me in high school, and I started to think that maybe it was time for me to begin.

But...Shuli.

Could I give up something important to me for someone I loved?

I was not sure if this fell under the category of giving up something for someone I loved, something Hashem would want me to do...or giving up something to make myself feel better...causing me to feel like some kind of heroine. And so meanwhile, I continued to say "not yet."

And when our little sister Chevy was packing her bags to go to seminary in Eretz Yisrael...yes, she too was going to M.B.L.L., we were both there—Shuli and I—in our room helping her pack. We were not as Chevy had wistfully predicted all those years back "a bunch of old married ladies."

Adina was thriving at her job, and although I did not become this great lecturer in the field of Special Education, I was doing well as a teacher in the resource room in B.Y.R.H. I was quite content. I had a good job that I enjoyed, I had my sister who had become a close friend (most of her friends were already married), and I had my close friend, Adina, who had become almost like a sister.

And then around a year after Chevy came back from seminary, Adina went off to England to spend the Yamim Tovim with her grandparents. Only this time she did not come back.

That is—not as Adina Stern. She became a *kallah* over there and her father, Bina, and all the children flew to England for the wedding, where her elderly grandparents could attend and participate in the *simchah*. I also went along, and it was a good thing I did. Bina had a newborn infant and two toddlers—all three under the age of three and a half, and that was in addition to her older children. I was glad that I was there to help.

When we returned from England, I finally gave in to my parents' and Shuli's insistence that I begin the *shidduch* process. And in a short time, I too became a *kallah*.

And it was at my wedding that my *chasan*'s brother's mother-in-law saw Shuli and thought of her for her nephew. Well, you guessed it…Shuli finally did get engaged. It did not happen immediately after my wedding, though. Months passed and then, when Chevy was about to meet her first *shidduch* prospect, Shuli was at last able to say yes.

I still do not know, I guess I will never know for sure—but I am pretty certain that had Shuli met him earlier on, she would have ended her meetings with him the way she had ended all the previous ones. That is not to say that he was not the right one for her. What I am trying to stress is that in this case the timing had to be right. My vivacious sister, the one who had never experienced challenges throughout all her growing-up years, could not deal with difficulties or complicated decisions as an adult. But once she saw me settling down, and her little sister about to take the big step, she thankfully did too…

And life moved on.

Our parents' home finally began to fill with the little voices of grandsons and granddaughters running about. Seeing them reap the rewards of all these past struggling years and enjoying their *nachas* was extremely gratifying. This had been their dream and they relished every minute of it!

Dreams.

I too was living the "dream" life. I had adorable children, a wonderful marriage, a pretty house—life was perfect. Well, *almost* perfect.

Sometimes, in the back of my mind, I would think about those other dreams I had…of wanting to be something special…someone who would stand out.

Sara, I would scold myself. *Dreams? Ambitions? Be happy that you manage to get a hot meal on the dinner table, your little ones into bed on time, and the older ones' homework done in a warm and cheerful manner.*

Life. Life had taken over.

I was no longer working in the resource room, as I had many years earlier. I just could not do it. I had missed too much time in the classroom when each of my children was born, and after my husband left *kollel* and began bringing in a paycheck, I could not justify leaving my children with a babysitter for so many hours a day. I still continued tutoring at home and occasionally I went in to B.Y.R.H. to do remedial work with the students there, but my job never developed into anything impressive or high profile. I did not become the prominent principal or the world-renowned, inspirational lecturer I had once dreamed of becoming.

Instead, I lovingly cooked, baked, sewed, doted on my darling children, and did the myriad tasks necessary to keep a lively house thriving and happy. And no, except for perhaps our first Shabbos home alone, I never did quite succeed in having all my platters prepared and waiting in the refrigerator before the *seudah* began, as I had seen Geveret Spitz do.

Most of the time I contentedly floated along with life's inevitable waves—the ups as well as the downs. Sometimes, though, I would look at others and think that they had it so much easier than I did. Or I'd wonder, *how come she's able to do it and I can't?* And other times, I would feel guilty for having been granted more than the usual share of blessings, and then I would feel even more guilty for my wrongful display of ingratitude.

Whenever that happened—whenever the pendulum swung in that misguided direction—a little voice would rise to the surface, reminding me about prescription eyeglasses and warning me that I would never see better through someone else's lenses. Then I would smile sheepishly, uplifted by a renewed sense of hope, remembering my idealistic seminary days.

Seminary...where was everybody?

Chani was living in Lakewood, her husband a well-known *maggid shiur*, Mazal was teaching high school in Kiryat Yosef—we occasionally wrote to one another, and Zehava was still waiting for the blessing of children. I had not been in touch with her, but Rochel Leah told me that Zehava was instrumental in establishing the first support group in her community for religious couples who had not yet had children. Rochel Leah, with her now much shorter but still beautiful chestnut hair, unfortunately was still not married and was often a guest at our Shabbos table. She kept herself very busy though, teaching, arranging *shiurim*, and had recently emulated her friend, Zehava, by setting up a program to help people who were having difficulties with *shidduchim*. Speaking of *shidduchim*, Rivky Weiss became the well-known, much sought after *shadchanta* Rebbitzen Rivka Rothman in New York. I know she was constantly trying to help Rochel Leah.

Adina moved to England soon after her marriage and began to raise her family there. They all regularly returned to Ballington for Yamim Tovim and it was then that we would get together and often reminisce about the "old days." By now Adina and her father's wife had developed a special, unique relationship. Once Adina was married, she was a great deal more receptive to Bina's overtures and they became much closer than either of us could ever have imagined.

When we visited each other and our children played together, I often noticed one of Adina's children cuddling next to her. Then I would remember that conversation we had that afternoon in my room way back in Sem, when Adina confessed that she used to think she would never want to get married…

"I use to think…I use to think that I'll never want to get married. I didn't think I had it in me to trust someone else…to love someone else. Not my husband…not my babies…"

"But now you see you really could. Right?"

"I think so," she nodded slowly. *"I'm telling you all this, Sara, because I think you're right….about the kever. I think that by going to my mother's kever on her yahrtzeit with you…with the one person I can really trust…I'll be able to finally start to live…"*

I gazed at her and her children, and my eyes filled. I knew I could never regret that I had stayed on with her. I remembered the overwhelming feeling of disappointment that had enveloped me when she did not react in some earth-shattering way at her mother's graveside and felt utterly foolish for having even thought what I did.

When Adina was not visiting, we wrote to each other and, occasionally, we would speak on the telephone as well.

It was during one of those conversations that she told me about Mimi.

"You know, Sara, Mimi has now become the principal of Bnot Yisrael."

"What? I don't believe it! Mimi…Mimi Rosenberg?"

Epilogue

"No, Sara, not Mimi Rosenberg…Mimi Rabinowitz."

"Okay, Adina…Mimi Rabinowitz, same thing. I still can't believe it!" I exclaimed incredulously.

"Why's it so difficult to believe, Sara? You know, Mimi's been running the resource room for years, and she's been totally involved with the teachers and students at Bnot Yisrael all this time. The resource room is not like it was in our days. It practically runs the school now."

"Wow! I still can't believe it…"

It had been years since I had spoken to Mimi, let alone written a letter. If it had not been for Adina, I would have known nothing about her at all. Obviously, letter writing with Mimi never took off and—telephone calls?

I did call Mimi occasionally at the beginning…but she was always so busy, and well, life just took over. Our telephone calls eventually dwindled down to once a year before Rosh Hashanah, and then even that ultimately decreased to one call every couple of years.

I must call her and congratulate her on her new job, I told myself as soon as I hung up with Adina. *It'll be strange at first, I'm sure. We haven't spoken in ages…*

Determinedly, I turned the pages of my telephone book and punched in the numbers of the international call before I could change my mind, or before my baby would climb out of his crib, demanding my attention.

It was strange. My heart pounded heavily along with the rhythmically beeping sound coming through my end of the receiver, while I waited for Mimi to answer her telephone on the other side of the world. And when a voice did come through on the other end, it was an unfamiliar one, speaking in Hebrew. *Oh, that must be her daughter.* In my broken Hebrew I asked to speak to her mother.

And then I heard her. "Sara, is that really you?"

Mimi!

It was still her…principal…successful educator…but it was still her.

I heard her deep throaty laugh and the delicious lilt of her voice, and the years just melted away.

"Sara, I'm absolutely thrilled that you called!"

We talked and talked and I tried very hard to ignore the digital clock's numbers that kept changing on my microwave oven, warning me of the escalating cost of this telephone call.

When Mimi apologized for the fifth time for having put me on hold, "I'm really sorry, Sara—parents and teachers keep calling. And the last call was from one of my students—she had a major problem...There I go again, Sara, keeping you waiting..."

I brushed off her apologies. I knew I should hang up. Mimi really had to go—she had all these crises that demanded her attention and my telephone bill was mounting with each passing second...but something kept me cleaving to the call. It was so hard to say goodbye to Mimi.

And I told her that.

"Well, this time, Sara, we can't let so much time pass before we speak to each other again. Our friendship is just too important."

"I feel the same, Mimi. I've learned so much from you—"

"No, Sara, I've learned so much from you."

And then we both started laughing.

"I really wish I could go to Eretz Yisrael," I said. "Then maybe we could get together. I know you're so busy—"

"Not too busy to get together with you, Sara. You'll be our guest and—"

"It's wishful thinking, Mimi. Well...you're getting another call-waiting 'click.' I'm going to let you go."

"Okay, Sara...but we've got to speak again soon."

"Goodbye...Mimi..."

"No, Sara...I haven't forgotten. With us, it'll never be goodbye...so hello."

"Hello, Mimi."

And with that I placed the receiver on the hook.

I stared at the telephone for a while, unable to move.

My mind suddenly started churning. *Oh, Adina's so lucky! She gets to go to Eretz Yisrael all the time.* She made her annual trip there on her mother's *yahrtzeit*, and that was besides the other times she and her husband went with their children. Money had never really been an issue with her, and besides, the close proximity of Israel to England definitely made traveling there easier. *And every time Adina goes, she manages to visit Mimi.*

Of course, I really was glad for Adina. If anyone deserved happiness, it was she. But I too wanted to visit Eretz Yisrael, to one day return to the Kosel. I had not been back there since Seminary. I would have loved to visit the *mekomos ha-kedoshim*, old friends, and especially to see Mimi. And my husband also wanted to go. If only we could manage to somehow put it together…

It became our dream.

Our eldest child, Shlomo, would be bar mitzvah in two years. Tragically, when he was nine years old, he had been hit by a car and needed a series of surgical procedures. *Baruch Hashem*, they were not life threatening, but they were nevertheless painful and serious. He had missed months of school, which resulted in his falling behind both academically and socially. We were working hard to help him catch up in his schoolwork and spent time doing whatever was necessary to encourage him to cultivate his friendships. He had been a real trooper through it all. But it was difficult. I had given birth prematurely in the interim and there were his many younger siblings also vying for our attention.

We would put the money aside. We would save. It would be a special experience…for him and for us. We would only go for one week. I was concerned, however; it would be the first time I ever left my children. But Shuli and Chevy reassured me, alleviating any feelings of anxiety. They would gladly watch our other children, guaranteeing repeatedly that my little ones would be in good hands. Slowly but surely…our dream of a visit to Eretz Yisrael was coming to fruition.

And when Shlomo turned twelve and a half—we knew it would happen. We were going!

Whoever said "half the fun is in the planning" spoke the truth. Our excitement over the next sixth months was palpable. Our parents, my husband's and mine, also planned on coming with us. It was a first grandson for all of them, and they were absolutely overjoyed by the prospect of coming to Eretz Yisrael with us and sharing this special time with Shlomo.

I was busy with all the exciting travel plans and, of course, with the actual *simchah* as well. We arranged for a small *seudah* to take place in

Yerushalayim the night Shlomo turned thirteen—to mark his transformation from childhood to adulthood in a concrete way. My husband and Shlomo also planned on making a *siyyum* that evening, and we thought it would be appropriate to celebrate this special occasion with whichever friends and family in Eretz Yisrael could be with us. Along with all the arrangements this entailed, we also planned on having a small *Kiddush* in our shul after Shlomo *lained* his *parashah* the Shabbos after we returned, and we were looking forward to having all our relatives and friends from Rolland Heights join us there. So, besides everything else, I was busy baking, cooking, and freezing everything I possibly could prepare ahead of time—in order to be amply organized for that Shabbos—and not have to do it all when jet-lagged and exhausted from our return trip. Then, as the time drew nearer, there was the packing for us travelers, and the individual suitcases for each child I was leaving behind, with their schedules, personal wants, and needs.

It was an overwhelmingly busy time, but my excitement knew no bounds and my adrenaline kept me going. And then finally it was here. At long last we were on the way!

The whirlwind visit was turning into everything I had hoped. We went to the Kosel, we toured, we visited relatives, and we spent valuable, spiritually uplifting time together. It was absolutely wonderful and I felt happiness coursing through every single part of me!

We had been so busy, in fact, that I had not had the chance to call or visit Mimi, Mazal, or any other old friends, but I comforted myself with the thought that I would hopefully be seeing them all at the bar mitzvah.

I heaved a sigh of relief when I saw Adina entering the small *simchah* hall the night of the *seudah*. I had hoped she would make it on time. I knew she was traveling in from England that afternoon for a four-day visit to Eretz Yisrael, and I was afraid that she would be delayed.

She was wearing a smart, stylish suit and looked as stunning as ever. We embraced warmly.

"I wonder if Mimi will show up," I commented offhandedly. "It would be great if we could have a reunion, Adina. You know, Mazal's also coming."

Adina looked at me strangely, but did not say anything.

I shrugged. "Oh well…" I had sent Mimi an invitation along with the others, but had not received a reply, and with the hectic turn my life had taken in the last few months, I had been remiss in following it up with a telephone call. Actually, that was not really true. I had called once or twice and did not get through, and with the different time zones and our busy schedules, I could not properly coordinate the right time to finally reach her. *It wasn't my fault,* I told myself, *she could've also called—even if she is busy being a principal and everything…*

Anyway, I was too busy enjoying the *simchah* to think about who was there and who was not. I welcomed relatives and cousins who were studying in yeshivos and seminaries. Hinda Klein, now in her nineties, also showed up. I wanted to make sure she had a comfortable seat and was well taken care of. My husband had two aunts there with large families. I was meeting that side of his family for the very first time and was trying to remember everyone's names. I proudly pointed out my son to many of my guests and reminisced with a few old seminary friends during a lull in between speeches.

It was wonderful seeing all those new and old faces, and I felt gratified that they had taken the time to participate in our *simchah*!

I passed Adina and again I told her, "It's really a pity that Mimi didn't come."

And again she did not say anything.

Mimi…it was really strange. Even though I had not spoken to her in ages, there was still something strong that neither time nor space could take away. I felt it that last time we talked. There had been something almost tangible…so real. And I knew that the second we would see each other…the moment we would begin speaking to each other…all the years would disappear.

I just knew it!

But Mimi had not shown up and I was too happy right then to be disappointed.

The next morning there was a knock at the door to the apartment we were renting.

It was Adina.

Her face was pale and her eyes puffy, their blueness veiled by…something.

And that was when she told me the news. The news that, incredibly, she and everyone else had refrained from telling me the night before.

She said she didn't want to say anything to me yesterday during my *simchah*, "But, Sara, yesterday...yesterday was...was—"

"Yesterday was what?"

"Yesterday...Sara, yesterday was...it was..."

"What?" cold fingers grabbed my heart. "Adina...tell me!"

"Sara," she took a step toward me, "Sara...yesterday was Mimi's...Mimi's..." she looked down at her pocketbook, biting her lower lip.

My heart was pounding hard. "Mimi's what, Adina? Mimi's *what*?"

"Mimi's...Mimi's...Sara..." She looked up slowly and I saw the tears streaming down her cheeks. "Sara, yesterday was Mimi's *levayah*."

"*Levayah?*" I repeated dumbly. "Funeral?"

She nodded, her pain-filled eyes looking into mine. "Come, Sara," she led me gently by the hand, "we need to pay her family a *shivah* call."

Numbly, I told my husband what had happened and then left the apartment with Adina. She whipped out her cell phone, punched in some numbers, and within seconds a *monit* drove up to the curb where we stood.

Did I say that I left the apartment with Adina? To be more accurate, I was propelled out of the apartment by Adina.

It was not just that I was shocked...stunned. It was not just that my knees were shaky, that I was too numb to cry. I was filled with...a certain fear.

We hardly spoke as the driver skillfully wound his way down the modern highway, away from Yerushalayim to the upper Negev hills and to the newly paved roads leading into Kfar Amsdorf.

But I did not see any of that, at least not consciously. All I saw was Mimi...with her dancing green eyes, her bouncy, wavy red hair, and her smile that could light up a dark room. *Mimi! Why didn't I keep calling her...why didn't I try harder to reach her?*

And then suddenly, we were there. Walking up the steps of her building to her second floor apartment. Standing before the door. Entering the *shivah* home...Mimi's home.

And that was when I saw her daughter, her daughter who looked so much like her, but seemed so different…and the memories of that incredible year came flooding back to me, when long-suppressed feelings surfaced, and I began to once again experience the storms of the past.

My loneliness and insecurities…

Mimi and Adina. Our dreams…the disappointments…the challenges… our hopes.

My reverie was interrupted by a small group of girls, who must have been Mimi's students.

Stooped somberly, they rose from their seats at the front of the room, their eyes downcast and heavy with grief. They stood wavering awkwardly before the *aveilim*, as they murmured the customary words that are said when departing from the mourner during *shivah*. Then two women, one sobbing and the other one leading her out of the room, made their exit and a few others up front changed seats.

After everyone resettled in their seats, except for some soft sniffling sounds in the back, the room suddenly seemed too quiet. Mimi's mother, her chin cupped in her hand, elbow resting on her knee, sat with her head bent downward. Her eyes were closed. Perhaps she was lost in her memories. Or maybe exhaustion overcame her and she had fallen into a light sleep.

All eyes focused on Mimi's oldest daughter…*Rochel, that's her name.* Shoulders hunched over, she squirmed uneasily. I could only imagine how unbearable the silence must have felt to her, especially with the realization that we were all waiting for her to speak.

She was pulling dispassionately at some loose threads of her dark brown sweater. The silence continued. My heart went out to her.

It was never comfortable in a house of mourning. No one knew what to say…if they should say anything at all.

If Mimi were here, she would know how to break this unbearable silence. *If Mimi were here…*

I looked around. Someone had draped a covering over the mirror, but the room still radiated a certain glow…a glow that said "Mimi." There were photographs, children's paintings, and arts and crafts projects displayed on the wooden shelves. An attractive, lovingly embroidered sampler in a simple wooden frame hung on the wall. I strained my eyes to see what it said, and I "heard" Mimi's voice as I read, "Often we have to go through what we go through to become all that we are capable of becoming." I saw that from that last "g" was stitched a colorful butterfly in flight.

Mimi! The signs of her were everywhere, and when we eventually moved to the front of the room, we did our best to comfort the mourners—sharing with them a little of our own feelings about Mimi. I wanted so much to tell them that someone so special like her...although leaving this world, had thankfully left so much of herself behind. I tried to express it and I hope I succeeded.

And yet...there was still so much left unsaid—so many memories I would have loved to share. But it was hard for me to talk...the wound was still so raw...so deep. *Maybe when I get home, I'll write it all down...I'll send them a long letter...*

"Adina, did...did you know anything...about her being sick, I mean?" I asked her as we left Mimi's building.

She shook her head. "No, yesterday at the *levayah* I was told that she had been ill for the last few months, and except for family and some of the people she worked with, no one knew a thing. She wanted it that way. You know Mimi. She always walked around smiling—"

"Yes...smile and the world smiles with you, cry and you cry alone," I mumbled.

"What?"

"Oh...nothing," I murmured, looking around.

A few silent moments passed.

"I was packing for my trip two nights ago when...when I got the telephone call. Luckily, I made it onto an earlier flight."

"And you still managed to come to the bar mitzvah."

"Of course I came, Sara. And so did all the rest of—"

"How were you able...and the others...I had no idea, I didn't realize a thing."

"Good. I didn't want your *simchah* to be disturbed."

"But—"

"Sara, I never would've imagined that...something so sad and so happy, happening to two of my very good friends, would happen on the same day. But at least...I...I was able to do what had to be done...I didn't have to choose..."

"Like..."

"Like a very good friend of mine did so many years back," she said and slowly smiled, her blue eyes looking deeply into mine.

My own eyes filled. I shifted my gaze away from her, staring in the direction of the Kfar Amsdorf woods.

"Let's take a walk," Adina kindly suggested.

She was trying to help me get over the initial shock. I suppose she must have absorbed what had happened—to some extent—over the past two days, while I, on the other hand, was still in a state of numbness. *Maybe it isn't such a bad idea to look around, see the dorm.* "I...I haven't been back since Seminary, and as long as I'm here, I guess—"

"Listen, Sara, I've got the rest of the day free. The walk will do you good. You know Geveret Katz is still there, and so is Rabbanit Abrams and, of course, Rabbi Grossman," she said as we began to make our way.

"I don't know about the rest—"

"I'm...I'm not really in the mood to visit anyone, Adina, and I do have to get back to Yerushalayim to prepare for our return trip tomorrow. I just thought...you're right...a small walk. I'd like to look around M.B.L.L. a bit."

"That's fine with me. Remember," she said when we reached a large iron gate, "this is the way through the Kfar Amsdorf woods."

"Oh my goodness, Adina—- I never would have recognized it. It's like a park now."

"You should see what town looks like now. There's a mini-mall, a *real* post office, a huge, modern supermarket, and Pinat HaGlidah is a large dairy restaurant —"

"I don't believe it!"

We began walking on the paved path through what once was the Kfar Amsdorf woods. The path was lined with stone benches every few yards. So much was different, and yet there was that old, familiar woodsy scent of bark and greenery blended with the sweet aroma of the fruit trees that wafted pleasantly through the air. Tall palm trees lined the path we walked on, but off to the side were the same woods we had walked through, the same trees we had stood under.

And the picture came back to me vividly.

A brown-haired girl and her shorter red-headed friend walking beside her, weighted down with their book bags hanging over their shoulders…talking…dreaming…

I remembered *that* walk with Mimi. How we had tried to keep up with the Israeli girls walking ahead of us, but could not…we had stopped, troubled, caught in the dilemma of what to do about my friend Chavie's wedding coinciding with the day of Adina's mother's *yahrtzeit*.

I recalled our other walks…other talks. The first time we met the resource room kids we would be working with—how enthusiastic I was as we walked through these same woods and how unusually subdued Mimi was. There was that Sunday on the way back from the resource room, when Mimi offered advice on how best to handle Ronit and I had felt insulted when she told me to concentrate more on Ronit and stop looking at her and Riki…Mimi and her caramels…Mimi and her guitar… Mimi preparing the resource room kids for their parts in *Metamorphosis*…Mimi being kind to a lonely, shy girl who came without any friends. And then there were those talks, when Mimi confided that she did not want to be directing plays for the rest of her life. *The rest of her life…*

The tears were flowing freely down my cheeks.

"It's not easy," Adina's voice broke through my thoughts.

I shook my head, wiping away my tears with a tissue. "But at least she carried out her dream."

"Yes…I'll never forget the speech she made. Mimi really did know how to take something damaged and turn it into something beautiful."

"And so did you, Adina," I managed a faint smile through my tears, "so did you."

"Me?" she paused for a moment as she flicked a leaf off her blazer. "Make something out of what I went through? I guess, you're right, Sara. Building a family of my own was my greatest wish, and *baruch Hashem* I've been blessed," she said quietly. "You know that bucket that Mimi talked about in her speech? How it has to get lowered in order to fill up with water?"

"Yes…I remember."

"It was true. I still don't understand why my mother had to die so young…why I was left alone so much. And, I'll probably never know, but—"

"Lots of times we don't know why we have to go through what we have to go through—"

"To become all that we are capable of becoming? A quote from Mimi?"

I nodded. "Yes…a quote from Mimi."

We reached the end of the woods a lot quicker than I recalled and emerged onto the Beit Yaakov HaNegbah campus. A soft breeze carrying the fragrant scent of coralberry and elder greeted us. The luxuriant garden still stretched out before us and exotic plants, nut and fruit trees, olive and date palms, along with red, yellow, and white honeysuckles and flowers of all colors still vibrantly dotted the landscape, just as they had all those years earlier.

We could see high school and seminary students milling about, some sitting with opened schoolbooks on blankets spread out on the lush grass and some grouped together around picnic tables. And they all looked so young. *Were we ever so young?*

"But, Sara," Adina tucked a strand of her dark wig behind her ear, "I have to say, that because of what I went through, you know, growing up without my mother, my father often away on business, it was always my goal to be the best mother I possibly could be to my children."

"And you are Adina."

"Well—I certainly try."

We passed the dormitory building and that recognizable smell of *schnitzel* and fried *chatzilim* drifted toward us.

"They're lucky, your kids."

"That's nice of you to say, Sara."

"I mean it…I—I wish I could be that way."

She stopped walking. "What do you mean?"

"Adina," I bit my bottom lip, "I don't think you could understand."

"Why?"

"Because someone like you—"

All at once we both burst out laughing.

"Sara, isn't that supposed to be my line? Didn't I always say that to you?"

"Yes…and sometimes Mimi also said that. And the truth is," I let out a deep sigh, "I don't think even *I* understand."

"Huh?" Adina lifted her eyebrows and we both laughed again.

"Adina, now *you're* starting to sound like me. But, well, the truth is, I know it up here," I pointed to my head. "Mimi accomplished what she needed to do. She became this highly esteemed educator, and you, Adina, you're so content with motherhood and building your family. And even though I'm also thoroughly content…sometimes…in my heart," I pointed to my chest, "I start to think about those dreams I once had and…"

"And you start to feel inadequate?"

I nodded.

"Everyone feels that way sometimes. But, Sara, you've got to remember, you *are* doing something great—"

"I know…believe me, I really know it and I *am* extremely grateful that I've been able to be home all these years with my children—and I truly *wouldn't* want to have it any other way, but there's still that need to reach higher—"

"That's wonderful, Sara. We're supposed to keep climbing, but you've got to stop reaching in the wrong direction."

I stiffened. *Hadn't Mimi said that to me once? You're working hard, Sara, but maybe…in the wrong direction. It's like you want to go North but you're traveling South.* "The wrong direction?"

"Look, you were handed a gift in beautiful wrapping paper. You're the one who once pointed that out to me. But your wrapping paper isn't the same as Mimi's and neither is the gift that's inside. And it's not the same as mine either." She took a deep breath. "Sara, when I think of how you handled Shlomo's accident four years ago—I don't know what *I* would've done in such a situation, and the way your house is always open for guests like your parents' home, and I could never sew or bake the way—"

"Stop, Adina."

"I'm just trying to say that you *are* constantly climbing. Heroines come in all different packages."

"And *we're* not the ones who choose our package."

"No." She shook her head thoughtfully. "I've come to realize it's not some kind of grab bag."

"I guess you're right." We began making our way back toward Kfar Amsdorf. "I mean, I *know* you're right. I just wish I could *always* keep that feeling inside me, that feeling of being content with my own lot and not let those *other* thoughts, the ones that—"

"Come on, Sara, stop being so hard on yourself."

"Adina, I'm not a young seminary girl anymore. By now I should be—"

"Perfect? No, Sara, we don't finish working on ourselves just because we're older. You keep thinking everything has to end 'happily ever after.' But like you just said, inside all of us there's always that need to reach higher."

The walk back seemed even shorter than the walk there. Once again, we were standing in front of Mimi's building.

"That must be her porch," I said, pointing toward a large balcony jutting out of a wide doorway on the second floor. It was the one that was crowded with inflated lounge chairs that had large "smiley" pictures on them. A guitar case leaned against the side wall where an awning hung overhead.

"Yes, that's it," Adina nodded her eyes filling. "I've sat there with her in past visits. She loved the beautiful view of the desert mountains that can be seen from up there."

I could not tear my eyes away from the large balcony. "It's such a pity after all this time, I've finally come and...now...."

"I know how you feel, Sara."

I felt the wetness of my tears against my cheeks as I murmured half to myself, half aloud, "Why does it always have to be too late?"

"You did what you could do," Adina's voice was just above a whisper, "you had no way of knowing. None of us did."

I did not respond. My hand groped for my tissue.

"Um...Sara," Adina said softly, "there's a car service located right around the bend. I'll go order a car and we'll come...get you. Stay here meanwhile...if you need the time..."

My eyes remained focused on Mimi's porch. "Thanks, Adina," I said without looking at her. "I'd appreciate that."

I heard her footsteps receding, but I continued staring at the guitar on Mimi's terrace. *If only I would've come to visit her a few days ago...If only I would've reached her by telephone...If only...*

And had I come? And had we spoken?

And when I would have seen Mimi—who took her challenges and used them as stepping stones to realize her dreams, would I have been overcome by those feelings of inadequacy that sometimes managed to snake there way in because I was unsure if I had reached mine?

What would Mimi have told me if I would have admitted to occasionally feeling incomplete and unaccomplished?

Sara, don't you realize that by comparing yourself to others you're viewing Hashem's handiwork as damaged?

I heard a car honk and I turned around to see a *monit* pull up behind me. Adina was in the back seat. I motioned to her that I needed one more minute.

I turned back to Mimi's porch.

And don't you see, I could almost hear Mimi's voice whispering in my ear, *on Hashem's stage, each and every actor, each scene, each prop, each act is special? It's just not possible for everyone to have the same exact part.*

I took a deep breath. *You know, you're right, Mimi. And of course, by now I know it...and most of the time I really feel it. But sometimes, I could use a little reminding. After all, like Adina just said, our job isn't over yet. So, when I need it...somehow keep reminding me.* I smiled faintly through my tears, my heart lifting, *Like you would say, Mimi, "Hey, Sara, we're a perfect puzzle."*

I turned around and opened up the door to the *monit* and tossed my pocketbook inside, beside Adina.

And then before entering the car, I swung around for one last glance.

So, we won't say goodbye, Mimi, I whispered, my lips spreading further, *because for us...it'll always be hello.*

Sources

Chapter 8, p. 92

Geveret Spitz's analogy of an educator to a diamond cutter was adapted from *Nesivos Shalom: Nesivei Chinuch* by HaRav Sholom Noach Berezovsky zt"l (Feldheim Publishers, p. 64).

Chapter 16, p. 215

The girls removed the *cholent* pot from the *platah* or *blech* "without thinking," as noted by Sara. Therefore, since they did not have the proper intention when they placed the *cholent* pot on the counter, were no longer holding onto the pot, and had not met other necessary conditions, they were not allowed to return it to the *blech*. See *Shemirath Shabbath* by Rav Yehoshua Y. Neuwirth (Feldheim Publishers, vol. I, pp. 7-8).

Chapter 29, p. 380

Moshe Rabbeinu asked Hashem (*Shemos* 33:18), "*Haraini na es Kevodecha*—Show me now Your glory" and Hashem answered Moshe (*Shemos* 33:20), "*Lo suchal liros es panai ki lo yirani ha-adam va'chai*—You will not be able to see My face, for no human can see My face and live." The commentaries explain *panai*—My face—as a simile referring to a complete and unadulterated perception of Hashem and why He does what He does.

"*Simchaso b'chol inyan she'yatikahu*—he rejoices in every situation in which he is placed." See *Chovos HaLevavos, Duties of the Heart* by R. Bachya ben Joseph ibn Paquda (Feldheim Publishers, vol. I, pp. 292-293).

Chapter 35, p. 452, p. 454

Sara's reference to Adina about covering one's eyes when saying *Shema Yisrael*, demonstrating our acceptance of Hashem's will, is based on explanations on *Kerias Shema*, as found in *Rav Schwab on Prayer* by Rabbi Shimon Schwab (Mesorah Publications, Ltd., p. 315).

The conversation with Geveret Abrams regarding the materialistic circumstances of our lives before we enter this world is based on Rabbeinu Bachya's *perush* to *Devarim* 22:8, which talks about the mitzvah of *ma'akeh*. "*Ki yipol ha-nofel*," which means "if a fallen one falls from it." The person is referred to as a *nofel*, a "fallen one" even before he has fallen. The *midrash* explains that this is because the person was "destined to fall ever since the Six Days of Creation." Rabbeinu Bachya explains that a person's circumstances in life are shown to him before creation and that everything was done with his will and consent.

Chapter 37, p. 480

The script *Metamorphosis* is an embellished adaptation of a popular story by an unknown author.

Chapter 45, p. 603

The conversation between Geveret Spitz and her students regarding the importance of not taking revenge or holding a grudge, because everything that happens is from Hashem, is emphasized by the example of Dovid HaMelech when he (was fleeing from his son Avshalom, who had usurped his throne and) was pelted by stones and cursed by Shimi ben Gerah (*Shmuel II* 16:5-13).

Chapter 46, p. 613

Sara's conversation with Rabbanit Abrams regarding whether it is preferable to go to a house of mourning or a house of feasting is based on what Shlomo HaMelech says in *Koheles* 7:2: "*Tov laleches el beis aivel mi'leches el beis mishteh*—It is better to go to a house of mourning than to a house of drinking." This is because a house of mourning will remind a person of his true purpose in this world and hopefully arouse him to repent and mend his ways. Rabbanit Abrams points out to Sara that not always is the choice straightforward, and that according to some *meforshim*, "a house of feasting" is referring not to a *se'udas mitzvah* but to a place that is literally a *beis mishteh*—a house of drinking, and that sometimes one is compelled to join a *se'udas mitzvah* rather than attend "the house of mourners." It is important to note that there are special circumstances that dictate choosing one over the other and one should always consult *daas Torah* when confronted with a conflict of this nature.

And in general:

Although the girls' dialogues in various parts of the book might sometimes involve speaking about others, a competent halachic authority should always be consulted when imparting information about others.

A Special Note to
Camps, Schools, and Organizations...

A script for performances of *Set Me Free* can be obtained through the publisher or directly from the author by writing to:

E. Florans
PO Box 113, Parkville Station
Brooklyn, New York 11204

Please note that without **written permission** from the **author,** no part of this book, the subject, or anything relating to it may be used for performances of any kind.